The Second
Inspector Morse Omnibus

The Second Inspector Morse Omnibus

The Secret of Annexe 3
The Riddle of the Third Mile
Last Seen Wearing

Colin Dexter

BCA
LONDON · NEW YORK · SYDNEY · TORONTO

This edition published in 1991 by BCA
by arrangement with
MACMILLAN LONDON LIMITED
Cavaye Place London SW10 9PG
and Basingstoke

CN 2217

Typeset by Macmillan Production Limited
Printed by Mackays of Chatham plc, Chatham, Kent

CONTENTS

The Secret of Annexe 3

for

Elizabeth, Anna, and Eve

Acknowledgements

The author and publishers wish to thank the following who have kindly given permission for the use of copyright material:

George Allen & Unwin (Publishers) Ltd, for a quotation by Bertrand Russell.

Curtis Brown Group Ltd, London, on behalf of the Estate of Ogden Nash for a quotation by him.

Peter Champkin for an extract from his book *The Waking Life of Aspern Williams*.

Faber and Faber Ltd, for an extract from 'La Figlia Che Piange' in *Collected Poems* by T. S. Eliot.

A. M. Heath & Company Ltd, on behalf of the Estate of the late Sonia Brownell Orwell for an extract from *Shooting an Elephant* by George Orwell, published by Secker & Warburg Ltd.

Henry Holt & Company Inc, for a quotation by Robert Frost.

A. D. Peters & Company and Jonathan Cape Ltd, on behalf of the Executors of the Estate of C. Day Lewis, for an extract from 'Departure in the Dark' in *Collected Poems*, 1954, published by the Hogarth Press.

The Society of Authors on behalf of the Bernard Shaw Estate for a quotation by Bernard Shaw.

A. P. Watt Ltd, on behalf of The National Trust for Places of Historic Interest or Natural Beauty, for an extract by Rudyard Kipling from *The Thousandth Man*.

Every effort has been made to trace all the copyright holders but if any have been inadvertently overlooked the publishers will be pleased to make the necessary arrangement at the first opportunity.

Chapter One

November

The pomp of funerals has more regard to the vanity of the living than to the honour of the dead.

La Rochefoucauld, *Maxims*

When the old man died, there was probably no great joy in heaven; and quite certainly little if any real grief in Charlbury Drive, the pleasantly unpretentious cul-de-sac of semi-detached houses to which he had retired. Yet a few of the neighbours, especially the womenfolk, had struck up some sort of distanced acquaintance with him as they pushed prams or shopping trolleys past his neatly kept front lawn; and two of these women (on learning that things were fixed for a Saturday) had decided to be present at the statutory obsequies. Margaret Bowman was one of them.

'Do I look all right?' she asked.

'Fine!' His eyes had not left the racing page of the tabloid newspaper, but he knew well enough that his wife would always be an odds-on favourite for looking all right: a tall, smart woman upon whom clothes invariably hung well, whether for dances, weddings, dinners – or even funerals.

'Well? Have a *look* then! Yes?'

So he looked up at her and nodded vaguely as he surveyed the black ensemble. She *did* look fine. What else was there to say? 'You look fine,' he said.

With a gaiety wholly inappropriate she twirled round on the points of her newly purchased black-leather court shoes, fully aware, just as he was, that she did look rather attractive. Her hips had filled out somewhat alarmingly since that disappointing day when as a willowy lass of twenty (a year before marrying Tom Bowman) her application to become an air hostess had proved unsuccessful; and now, sixteen years later, she would have more than a little trouble

5

(she knew it!) in negotiating the central aisle of a Boeing 737. Yet her calves and ankles were almost as slender as when she had slipped her nightgowned body between the stiff white sheets of their honeymoon bed in a Torquay hotel; it was only her feet, with a line of whitish nodules across the middle joints of her slightly ugly toes, that now presaged the gradual approach of middle age. Well, no. It wasn't *only* that – if she were being really honest with herself. There was that hebdomadal visit to the expensive clinic in Oxford . . . But she cast that particular thought from her mind. ('Hebdomadal' was a word she'd become rather proud of, having come across it so often in her job in Oxford with the University Examining Board.)

'Yes?' she repeated.

He looked at her again, more carefully this time. 'You're going to change your shoes, aren't you?'

'What?' Her hazel eyes, with their markedly flecked irises, took on a puzzled, appealingly vulnerable aspect. Involuntarily her left hand went up to the back of her freshly brushed and recently dyed blonde hair, whilst the fingers of her right hand began to pluck fecklessly at some non-existent speck that threatened to jeopardise her immaculate, expensive nigritude.

'It's bucketing down – hadn't you noticed?' he said.

Little rivulets were trickling down the outside of the lounge window, and even as he spoke a few slanted splashes of rain re-emphasised the ugly temper of the windswept sky.

She looked down at the specially purchased black-leather shoes – so classy-looking, so beautifully comfortable. But before she could reply he was reinforcing his line of argument.

'They're going to inter the poor sod, didn't you say?'

For a few moments the word 'inter' failed to register adequately in her brain, sounding like one of those strangely unfamiliar words that had to be sought out in a dictionary. But then she remembered: it meant they wouldn't be cremating the body; they would be digging a deep, vertically sided hole in the orange-coloured earth and lowering the body down on straps. She'd seen the sort of thing on TV and at the cinema; and usually it had been raining then, too.

She looked out of the window, frowning and disappointed.

'You'll get your feet drenched – that's all I'm trying to say.' He turned to the centre pages of his newspaper and began reading about the extraordinary sexual prowess of a world-famous snooker player.

For a couple of minutes or so at that point the course of events in the Bowman household could perhaps have continued to drift along in its normal, unremarkable neutral gear. But it was not to be.

The last thing Margaret wanted to do was ruin the lovely shoes she'd bought. All right. She'd bought them *for* the funeral; but it was ridiculous to go and waste more than £50. It wasn't necessary to go and trample all over the muddy churchyard of course; but even going out in them in this weather was pretty foolish. She looked down again at her expensively sheathed feet, and then at the clock on the mantelpiece. Not much time. But she *would* change them, she decided. Most things went reasonably well with black, and that pair of grey shoes with the cushioned soles would be a sensible choice. But if she was going to be all in black apart from just her shoes, wouldn't it be nicely fashionable to change her handbag as well? Yes! There was that grey leather handbag that would match the shoes almost perfectly.

She tripped up the stairs hurriedly.

And fatefully.

It was no more than a minute or so after this decision – not a decision that would strike anyone as being particularly momentous – that Thomas Bowman put down his newspaper and answered the confidently repeated stridencies at the front door, where in friendly fashion he nodded to a drably clad young woman standing at the porch in the pouring rain under a garishly multicoloured golf umbrella, and wearing knee-length boots of bright yellow plastic that took his thoughts back to the Technicolor broadcasts of the first manned landing on the moon. Some of the women on the estate, quite clearly, were considerably less fashion-conscious than his wife.

'She's nearly ready,' he said. 'Just putting on her ballet shoes for your conducted tour across the ploughed fields.'

'Sorry I'm a bit late.'

'You coming in?'

'Better not. We're a bit pushed for time. Hello Margaret!'

The chicly clad feet which moments ago had flitted lightly up the stairs were now descending more sombrely in a pair of grey, thickish-soled walking shoes. A grey-gloved hand hurriedly pushed a white handkerchief into the grey handbag – and Margaret Bowman was ready, at last, for a funeral.

Chapter Two

November

'Nobody ever notices postmen, somehow,' said he thoughtfully; 'yet they have passions like other men.'
G. K. Chesterton, *The Invisible Man*

It was a little while after the front door had closed behind the
two women that he allowed himself an oblique glance across the
soggy lawn that stretched between the wide lounge-window and
the road. He had told Margaret that she could have the car if she
wanted it, since he had no plans for going anywhere himself. But
clearly they had gone off in the other woman's, since the maroon
Metro still stood there on the steepish slope that led down to the
garage. Charlbury Drive might just as well have been uninhabited,
and the rain poured steadily down.

He walked upstairs and went into the spare bedroom, where
he opened the right-hand leaf of the cumbrous, dark-mahogany
wardrobe that served to store the overflow of his wife's and his own
clothing. Behind this leaf, stacked up against the right-hand side of
the wardrobe, stood eight white shoe-boxes, one atop the other; and
from this stack he carefully withdrew the third box from the bottom.
Inside lay a bottle of malt whisky about two-thirds empty – or about
one-third full, as a man who is thirsting for a drink would probably
have described it. The box was an old one, and had been the secret
little hiding-place for two things since his marriage to Margaret. For
a week, in the days when he was still playing football, it had hidden
a set of crudely pornographic photographs which had circulated from
the veteran goalkeeper to the fourteen-year-old outside-left. And
now (and with increasing frequency) it had become the storage
space for the whisky of which he was getting, as he knew, rather
dangerously over-fond. Guilty secrets both, assuredly; yet hardly sins
of cosmic proportions. In fact, he had slowly grown towards the view
that the lovely if somewhat overweight Margaret would perhaps have
forgiven him readily for the photographs; though not for the whisky,
perhaps. Or *would* she have forgiven him the whisky? He had sensed
fairly early on in their married life together that she would probably
always have preferred unfaithful sobriety to intoxicated fidelity. But
had she changed? Changed recently? She must have smelled the

stuff on his breath more than once, although their intimacy over the past few months had been unromantic, intermittent, and wholly unremarkable. Not that any such considerations were bothering his mind very much, if at all, at this particular juncture. He took out the bottle, put the box back, and was just pushing two of his old suits back into place along the rail when he caught sight of it – standing on the floor immediately behind the left-hand leaf of the wardrobe, a leaf which in his own experience was virtually never opened: it was the black handbag which his wife had at the very last minute decided to leave behind.

At first this purely chance discovery failed to register in his mind as an incident that should occasion any interest or surprise; but after a few moments he frowned a little – and then he frowned a lot. Why had she put the handbag behind the door of the wardrobe? He had never noticed any of her accessories there before. Normally she would keep her handbag on the table beside the twin bed that stood nearer the window – her bed. So why . . .? Still frowning, he walked across the landing into their bedroom and looked down at the two black-leather shoes, one toppled on to its side, which had been so hurriedly taken off and carelessly left at the foot of her bed.

Back in the spare bedroom he picked up the handbag. An incurious man who had seldom felt any fascination for prying into others' affairs, he would never have thought of opening one of his wife's letters – or opening one of her handbags. Not in normal circumstances. But why had she tried to conceal her handbag? And the answer to that question now seemed very obvious indeed. There was something, perhaps more than one thing, *inside* the handbag that she didn't want him to see; and in her rush she hadn't had the time to transfer all its contents to the other one. The catch opened easily and he found the letter, four pages of it, almost immediately.

You are a selfish thankless bitch and if you think you can just back out of things when you like you'd better realise that you've got another big thick headaching think coming because it could be that I've got some ideas about what I like. You'd better understand what I'm saying. If you can act like a bitch you'd better know I can be a bit of a sod too. You were glad enough to get what you wanted from me and just because I wanted to give it to you you think that we can just drop everything and go back to square one. Well this letter is to tell you we can't and like I say you'd better understand what I'm telling you. You can be sure I'll get my own back on you . . .

His throat was dry as he rapidly skimmed the rest of the letter: it had no salutation on page one, no subscription on page four. But there was no doubt about the message of the letter – a message that screamed so loudly at him that even some under-achieving idiot would require no prompting about its import: *his wife was being unfaithful to him* – probably had been for a period of several months.

A sharp pain throbbed in the centre of his forehead, the blood was pounding in his ears, and for several minutes his thought processes were utterly incapable of any sharp tuning. Yet curiously enough he appeared to be adequately in control of the rest of his body, for his hands trembled not the merest millimetre as he filled the shabby little cylindrical glass he always used for the whisky. Sometimes he added a little cold tap-water; sometimes not. Now he sipped the whisky neat: first just a small sip; then a larger sip; then two large gulps of the burning liquor, and the glass was empty. He refilled his glass and soon had drained that, too. The last drops from the bottle just filled the third glass to the brim and this he sipped more slowly, feeling as he did so the familiar surge of warmth that slowly suffused his brain. And now it happened, paradoxically and totally unexpectedly, that instead of the vicious jealousy which a few minutes ago had threatened to swamp his foundering senses he was gradually becoming ever more conscious of the love he felt for his wife. This renewed consciousness reminded him vividly of the day when, under-prepared and over-confident, she had failed her first driving test; and when, as she sadly and quietly explained to him where she thought she had gone wrong, he had felt an overwhelming surge of sympathy for her. Indeed such had been his awareness of her vulnerability that day, so fierce his determination to protect her whenever possible from future disappointment, that he would willingly have shot the examiner who had been allotted the unavoidable task of reporting adversely on his wife's incompetence.

The glass was empty – the bottle was empty; and Thomas Bowman walked slowly but steadily down the stairs, the empty bottle in his left hand, the letter in his right. The car keys were on the kitchen table, and he picked them up and put on his mackintosh. Before getting into the Metro, he inserted the bottle beneath the four or five bundles of kitchen refuse which almost filled the larger of the two dustbins standing beside the garden shed. Then he drove off: there was one very simple little job he would do immediately.

It was only a mile or so to his place of work in Chipping

Norton, and as he drove he was conscious of the surprisingly clear-cut logicality of what he was proposing to do. It was only when he'd returned some fifteen minutes later to Charlbury Drive and replaced the letter in the handbag, that he became fully aware of the blazing hatred he was feeling against the man, whoever he was, who had robbed him of his wife's affection and fidelity; a man who hadn't even got the guts to sign his name.

The woman with the grey handbag stood at the graveside, the purplish-yellow clay sucking and clinging to her sensible shoes. The rain had now almost stopped, and the fresh-faced young vicar intoned the interment rites with unrushed and edifying dignity. From the snatches of conversation she had heard, Margaret Bowman learned that the old fellow had been with the Allied spearhead on the Normandy beaches and that he had fought right through to VE day. And when one of his old colleagues from the British Legion had thrown a Remembrance Day poppy down on to the top of the coffin lid, she had felt the tears welling up at the back of her eyes; and before she could turn her head away (though no one noticed it) a great blobby tear had splashed down on her gloves.

'That's it, then!' said the woman in the yellow boots. 'No port and ham sandwiches today, I'm afraid.'

'Do they usually have that after funerals?'

'Well, you need something to cheer you up. Specially on a day like this.'

Margaret was silent, and remained so until she got into the car.

'Would you like to nip along to the pub?' asked her companion.

'No. I'd better not. I'd better get home I think.'

'You're not going to cook him a meal, are you?'

'I said I'd get us a snack when I got in,' she said, rather weakly.

The yellow-booted driver made no further attempt to influence the course of events: it would be sensible, she knew, to get her nervous-looking passenger home as quickly as possible and then go and join some of the others at the local.

Margaret Bowman wiped her shoes on the front-door mat and slid her latchkey into the Yale lock.

'I'm ho-ome,' she called.

But she received no reply. She looked quickly into the kitchen, the lounge, the bedroom – and then the spare room: but he wasn't there, and she was glad. The Metro hadn't been in the drive when she had come in; but he might of course have driven it into the garage out of the rain. More likely though he'd driven down to the local for a drink – and if he had, she was glad about that, too. In the spare room she opened the door of the wardrobe, picked up her handbag, and looked inside it: obviously she needn't have worried at all, and she began to wish she'd agreed to join her fellow mourners for a consolatory gin at the Black Horse. But that didn't really matter. The pile of shoe-boxes on the right looked rather precariously askew and she squared them into a neater stack. In all, it was a great relief, and she promised herself that she would be far more careful in the future.

She reheated the left-overs from the chicken risotto she'd cooked the previous evening, but the few mouthfuls she managed to swallow tasted like the Dead Sea apples. What a mess she was in! What an unholy, desperate mess she'd landed herself in! She sat in the lounge and listened to the one-o'clock news, and learned that the pound had perked up a little overnight on the Tokyo Stock Exchange. Unlike her heart. She turned on the television and watched the first two races from Newbury without having any recollection whatsoever of which horses had been first past the post. It was only after the third race had similarly bypassed her consciousness that she heard the squeak of the Metro's brakes on the drive. He kissed her lightly on the cheek, and his voice sounded surprisingly sober as he asked a few perfunctory questions about the funeral. But he had been drinking heavily, she could tell that; and she was not one whit surprised when he declared that he would have a lie-down for the remainder of the afternoon.

But Thomas Bowman rested little that Saturday afternoon, for a plan of action had already begun to form in his mind. The room at the post office housing the Xerox machine had been empty; and after copying the letter he had stood there looking out at the fleet of postal vans in the rear park. A small post-office van (he had never quite seen things this way before) was as anonymous as any vehicle could be: no passer-by was interested in the identity of its driver, hemmed in as the latter was (from all but a directly frontal encounter) by the closed side of the secretive little red van that could creep along unobtrusively from one parking point to the next, immune from the tickets of the predatory traffic wardens who prowled the busier streets of Oxford. In the letter, the man who was making such a misery of Margaret's life had begged her to meet him at ten minutes to one on Monday outside the Summertown

Library in South Parade – and yes! he, Tom Bowman, would be there too. There would be no real problem about borrowing one of the vans; he could fix that. Furthermore, he had often picked up Margaret, before she had passed her test, along exactly that same road, and he remembered perfectly clearly that there was a little post office right on the corner of South Parade and Middle Way, with a post-box just outside. There could hardly have been a more suitable spot . . .

Suddenly the thought struck him: how long had the letter been in her bag? There was no date on the letter – no way at all of telling which particular Monday was meant. Had it been *last* Monday? There was no way he could be certain about things; and yet he had the strong conviction that the letter, presumably addressed to her at work, had been received only a day or so previously. Equally, he felt almost certain that Margaret was going to do exactly what the man had asked her. On both counts, Thomas Bowman was correct.

In the wing-mirror at ten minutes to one the following Monday he could see Margaret walking towards him and he leaned backwards as she passed, no more than two or three yards away. A minute later a Maestro stopped very briefly just ahead of him, outside the Summertown Library, the driver leaning over to open the passenger door, and then to accelerate away with Margaret Bowman seated beside him.

The post-office van was three cars behind when the Maestro came to the T-junction at the Woodstock Road, and at that moment a train of events was set in motion which would result in murder – a murder planned with slow subtlety and executed with swift ferocity.

Chapter Three

December

'I have finished another year,' said God,
'In grey, green, white, and brown;
I have strewn the leaf upon the sod,
Sealed up the worm within the clod,
And let the last sun down.'

Thomas Hardy, *'New Year's Eve'*

The tree-lined boulevard of St Giles' is marked at three or four
points by heavy cast-iron street-plaques (the latter painted white on
a black background) that were wrought at Lucy's foundry in nearby
Jericho. And Oxford being reckoned a scholarly city, the proper
apostrophe appears after the final 's': indeed, if a majority vote
were to be taken in the English Faculty, future signwriters would
be exhorted to go for an extra 's', and print 'St Giles's'. But few
of the leading characters who figure in the following chronicle were
familiar with Fowler's advice over the difficulties surrounding the
possessive case, for they were people who, in the crude distinction
so often drawn in the city, would be immediately – and correctly –
designated as 'Town' rather than 'Gown'.

At the northern end of St Giles', where in a triangle of grass
a stone memorial pays tribute to the dead of two world wars, the
way divides into the Woodstock Road, to the left, and the Banbury
Road, to the right. Taking the second of these two roads (the road,
incidentally, in which Chief Inspector Morse has lived these many
years) the present-day visitor will find, after he has walked a few
hundred yards, that he is viewing a fairly homogeneous stretch of
buildings – buildings which may properly be called 'Venetian Gothic'
in style: the houses have pointed arches over their doorways, and
pointed arches over their clustered windows, which are themselves
vertically bisected or trisected by small columns of marble. It is as
though Ruskin had been looking over the shoulders of the architects
as they ruled and compassed their designs in the 1870s. Most of
these houses (with their yellowish-beige bricks and the purple-blue
slates of their roofs) may perhaps appear to the modern eye as
rather severe and humourless. But such an assessment would be
misleading: attractive bands of orange brick serve to soften the

ecclesiastical discipline of many of these great houses, and over the arches the pointed contours are re-emphasised by patterns of orange and purple, as though the old harlot of the Mediterranean had painted on her eye-shadow a little too thickly.

This whole scene changes as the visitor walks further northwards past Park Town, for soon he finds houses built of a cheerful orange-red brick that gives an immediate impression of warmth and good fellowship after the slightly forbidding façades of the Venetian wedge. Now the roofs are of red tile, and the paintwork around the stone-plinthed windows of an almost uniform white. The architects, some fifteen years older now, and no longer haunted by the ghost of Ruskin, drew the tops of their windows, sensibly and simply, in a straight horizontal. And thus it is that the housing for about half a mile or so north of St Giles' exhibits the influences of its times – times in which the first batches of College Fellows left the cloisters and the quads to marry and multiply, and to employ cohorts of maids and under-maids and tweeny maids in the spacious suburban properties that slowly spread northward along the Banbury and Woodstock Roads in the last decades of the nineteenth century – their annual progress leaving its record no less surely than the annular tracings of a sawn-through tree of mighty girth.

Betwixt the two rings sketched briefly above, and partaking something of each, stands the Haworth Hotel. It will not be necessary to describe this building – or, rather, these buildings – in any great detail at this point, but a few things should be mentioned immediately. When (ten years since) the house had been put on the market, the successful purchaser had been one John Binyon, an erstwhile factory-hand from Leeds who had one day invested a £1 Treble-Chance stake on the Pools, and who (to the incredulity of the rest of the nation) had thought fit to presume, in an early round of the FA Cup, that the current leaders of the First Division would be unable to defeat a lowly bunch of non-league part-time no-hopers from the Potteries – Binyon's reward for such effrontery being a jackpot prize of £450,000 from Littlewoods. The large detached residence (first named the Three Swans Guest House and then the Haworth Hotel) had been his initial purchase – a building that paid tribute both to the staid Venetian planner of the 1880s and to his gayer rosy-fingered colleague of the 1890s. Yellow-bricked, red-roofed, the tops of doors and windows now compromised to gentle curves, the house openly proclaimed its divided loyalties in a quietly genteel manner, standing back from the road some ten yards or so with a slightly apologetic air, as if

awaiting with only partial confidence the advent of social accepta-
bility. After a few disappointing months, trade began to pick up for
Binyon, and then to prosper most satisfactorily; after two years of
a glorified B & B provision, the establishment was promoted to the
hotel league, boasting now a fully licensed restaurant, colour-TV'd
and showered or bathroomed accommodation, and a small exercise
room for fitness fanatics; and four years after this, the proprietor
had been able to stand under his own front porch and to look
up with pride at the yellow sign which proclaimed that the AA
had deemed it appropriate to award the Haworth Hotel one of
its stars. Thereafter such was mine host's continued success that
he was soon deciding to expand his operations – in two separate
directions. First, he was able to purchase the premises immediately
adjacent on the south side, in order to provide (in due course and
after considerable renovation) a readily accessible annexe for the
increasingly large number of tourists during the spring and summer
seasons. Second, he began to implement his growing conviction that
much of the comparatively slack period (especially weekends and
holidays) from October to March could be revitalised by a series of
tastefully organised special-rate functions. And it was for this reason
that a half-page advertisement for the Haworth Hotel appeared (now
for the third year running) in the 'Winter Breaks with Christmas and
New Year Bonanzas' brochures which were to be seen on the racks
of many a travel agent in the autumn of the year in which our story
begins. And in order that the reader may get the flavour of the
special features which attracted those men and women we are to
meet in the following pages we reproduce below the prospectus in
which the hotel was willing to offer 'at prices decidedly too difficult
to resist' for a three-day break over the New Year.

TUESDAY

NEW YEAR'S EVE

12.30 p.m.   Sherry reception! John and Catherine Binyon extend a
happy welcome to as many of their guests as can make
this early get-together.

1.00 p.m.   Buffet lunch: a good time for more introductions –
or reunions.

The afternoon will give you the opportunity for strolling
down – only ten minutes' walk to Carfax! – into the centre
of our beautiful University City. For those who prefer a

little lively competition to keep them busy and amused, tournaments are arranged for anyone fancying his (her!) skills at darts, snooker, table-tennis, Scrabble, and video games. Prizes!

5.00 p.m.   Tea and biscuits: nothing – but nothing! – else will be available. Please keep a keen edge on your appetite for . . .

7.30 p.m.   OUR GRAND FANCY-DRESS DINNER PARTY
It will be huge fun if everyone – yes, everyone! – comes to the dinner in fancy dress. But *please* don't think that we shall be any less liberal with the pre-prandial cocktails if you can't. This year's theme is 'The Mystery of the East', and for those who prefer to improvise their costumes our own Rag Bag will be available in the games room throughout the afternoon.

10.00 p.m.   Fancy-Dress Judging: Prizes!! – continuing with live Cabaret and Dancing to keep you in wonderful spirits until . . .

Midnight –   Champagne! Auld Lang Syne! Bed!!!
1.00 a.m.

WEDNESDAY

NEW YEAR'S DAY

8.30 –   Continental Breakfast (quietly please, for the benefit
10.30 a.m.   of any of us – all of us! – with a mild hangover).

10.45 a.m.   CAR TREASURE-HUNT, with clues scattered round a care-free, car-free (as we hope) Oxford. There are plenty of simple instructions, so you'll never get lost. Be adventurous! And get out for a breath of fresh air! (Approximately one and a half hours to complete.) Prizes!!

1.00 p.m.   English Roast-Beef Luncheon.

2.00 p.m.   TOURNAMENTS once more for those who have the stamina; and the chance of an afternoon nap for those who haven't.

4.30 p.m.   Devonshire Cream Tea.

6.30 p.m.   Your pantomime coach awaits to take you to *Aladdin* at the Apollo Theatre.

There will be a full buffet awaiting you on your return, and you can dance away the rest of the evening at the DISCO (live music from Paper Lemon) until the energy (though not the bar!) runs out.

THURSDAY

9.00 a.m.   Full English Breakfast – available until 10.30 a.m. The last chance to say your farewells to your old friends and your new ones, and to promise to repeat the whole enjoyable process again next year!

Of course (it is agreed) such a prospectus would not automatically appeal to every sort and condition of humankind. Indeed, the idea of spending New Year's Eve being semi-forcibly cajoled into participating in a darts match, or dressing up as one of the Samurai, or even of being expected *de rigueur* to wallow in the company of their fellow men, would drive some solid citizens into a state of semi-panic. And yet, for the past two years, many a couple had been pleasingly surprised to discover how much, after the gentlest nudge of persuasion, they had enjoyed the group activities that the Binyons so brashly presented. Several couples were now repeating the visit for a second time; and one couple for a third – although it is only fair to add that neither member of this unattractive duo would ever have dreamed of donning a single item of fancy dress, delighting themselves only, as they had done, in witnessing what they saw as the rather juvenile imbecilities of their fellow guests. For the simple truth was that almost all the guests required surprisingly little, if any, persuasion to dress up for the New Year's Eve party – not a few of them with brilliant, if bizarre effect. And such (as we shall see) was to be the case this year, with several of the guests so subtly disguised, so cleverly bedecked in alien clothing, that even long-standing acquaintances would have recognised them only with the greatest difficulty.

Especially the man who was to win the first prize that evening.

Yes, especially him.

Chapter Four

December 30th/31st

The feeling of sleepiness when you are not in bed, and can't get there, is the meanest feeling in the word.

E. W. Howe, *Country Town Sayings*

Whenever she felt tired – and that was usually in the early hours of the evening – the almost comically large spherical spectacles which framed the roundly luminous eyes of Miss Sarah Jonstone would slowly slip further and further down her small and neatly geometrical nose. At such times her voice would (in truth) sound only perfunctorily polite as she spoke into whichever of the two ultra-modern phones happened to be purring for her expert attention; at such times, too, some of the lated travellers who stood waiting to sign the register at the Haworth Hotel would perhaps find her expression of welcome a thing of somewhat mechanical formality. But in the eyes of John Binyon, this same slightly fading woman of some forty summers could do little, if anything, wrong. He had appointed her five years previously: first purely as a glorified receptionist; subsequently (knowing a real treasure when he spotted one) as his unofficial 'manageress' – although his wife Catherine (an awkward, graceless woman) had still insisted upon her own name appearing in that senior-sounding capacity on the hotel's general literature, as well as in the brochures announcing bargain breaks for special occasions.

Like Easter, for example.

Or Whitsun.

Or Christmas.

Or, as we have seen, like New Year.

With Christmas now over, Sarah Jonstone was looking forward to her official week's holiday – a whole week off from everything, and especially from the New Year festivities – the latter, for some reason, never having enthused her with rapture unconfined.

The Christmas venture was again likely to be over-subscribed, and this fact had been the main reason – though not quite the only reason – why John Binyon had strained every nerve to bring part of the recently purchased, if only partially developed, annexe into premature use. He had originally applied for planning permission for a single-storey linking corridor between the Haworth Hotel and this adjoining freehold property. But although the physical distance in question was only some twenty yards, so bewilderingly complex had proved the concomitant problems of potential subsidence, ground levels, drains, fire exits, goods access and gas mains, that he had abandoned his earlier notions of a formal merger and had settled for a self-standing addendum physically separated from the parent hotel. Yet even such a limited ambition was proving (as Binyon saw it) grotesquely expensive; and a long-term token of such expenditure was the towering yellow crane which stood like some enormous capital Greek Gamma in what had earlier been the chrysanthemumed and fox-gloved garden at the rear of the newly acquired property. From late August, the dust ever filtering down from the planked scaffolding had vied, in degrees of irritation, with the daytime continuum of a revolving cement-mixer and the clanks and hammerings which punctuated all the waking and working hours. But as winter had drawn on – and especially during the record rainfall of November – such inconveniences had begun to appear, in retrospect, as little more than the mildest irritancies. For now the area in which the builders worked day by day was becoming a morass of thick-clinging, darkish-orange mud, reminiscent of pictures of Passchendaele. The mud was getting everywhere: it caked the tyres of the workmen's wheelbarrows; it plastered the surfaces of the planks and the duck-boards which lined the site and linked its drier spots; and (perhaps most annoying of all) it left the main entrance to the hotel, as well as the subsidiary entrance to the embryo annexe, resembling the approaches to a milking parlour in the Vale of the Great Dairies. A compromise was clearly called for over the hotel tariffs, and Binyon promptly amended the Christmas and New Year brochures to advertise the never-to-be-repeated bargain of 15 per cent off rates for the rooms in the main hotel, and 25 per cent (no less!) off the rates for the three double rooms and the one single room now available on the ground floor of the semi-completed annexe. And indeed it *was* a bargain: no workmen; no noise; no real inconvenience whatsoever over these holiday periods – except for that omnipresent mud . . .

The net result of these difficulties, and of further foul weather in early December, had been that, in spite of daily hooverings and daily scrapings, many rugs and carpets and stretches of linoleum were so sadly in need of a more general shampoo after the departure of the Christmas guests that it was decided to put

into operation a full-scale clean-up on the 30th in readiness for
the arrival of the New Year contingent – or the majority of it –
at lunchtime on the 31st. But there were problems. It was difficult enough at the best of times to hire waitresses and bedders
and charladies. But when, as now, extra help was most urgently
required; and when, as now, two of the regular cleaning women
were stricken with influenza, there was only one thing for it: Binyon
himself, his reluctant spouse Catherine, Sarah Jonstone, and Sarah's
young assistant-receptionist, Caroline, had been called to the colours
early on the 30th; and (armed with their dusters, brushes, squeegees,
and Hoovers) had mounted their attack upon the blighted premises
to such good effect that by the mid-evening of the same day all
the rooms and the corridors in both the main body of the hotel
and in the annexe were completely cleansed of the quaggy, mire-
caked traces left behind by the Christmas revellers, and indeed
by their predecessors. When all was done, Sarah herself had seldom
felt so tired, although such unwonted physical labour had not –
far from it! – been wholly unpleasant for her. True, she ached in
a great many areas of her body which she had forgotten were still
potentially operative, especially the spaces below her ribs and the
muscles just behind her knees. But such physical activity served
to enhance the delightful prospect of her imminent holiday; and
to show the world that she could live it up with the rest and the
best of them, she had wallowed in a long 'Fab-Foam' bath before
ringing her only genuine friend, Jenny, to say that she had changed
her mind, was feeling fine and raring to go, and would after all be
delighted to come to the party that same evening at Jenny's North
Oxford flat (only a stone's throw, as it happened, from Morse's own
small bachelor property). Jenny's acquaintances, dubiously moral
though they were, were also (almost invariably) quite undoubtedly
interesting; and it was at 1.20 a.m. precisely the following morning
that a paunchy, middle-aged German with a tediously repeated
passion for the works of Thomas Mann had suddenly asked a
semi-intoxicated Sarah (yes, just like that!) if she would like to
go to bed with him. And in spite of her very brief acquaintance
with the man, it had been only semi-unwillingly that she had been
dragged off to Jenny's spare room where she had made equally brief
love with the hirsute lawyer from Bergisch Gladbach. She could not
remember too clearly how she had finally reached her own flat in
Middle Way – a road (as the careful reader will remember) which
stretches down into South Parade, and at the bottom of which stands
a post office.

At nine o'clock the same morning, the morning of the 31st, she was awakened by the insistent ringing of her doorbell; and drawing her dressing-gown round her hips, she opened the door to find John Binyon on the doorstep: Caroline's mother (Sarah learned) had just rung to say that her daughter had the flu, and would certainly not be getting out of bed that day – let alone getting out of the house; the Haworth Hotel was in one almighty fix; could Sarah? would Sarah? it would be well worth it – very much so – if Sarah could put in a couple of extra days, please! And stay the night, of course – as Caroline had arranged to do, in the nice little spare room at the side, the one overlooking the annexe.

Yes. If she could help out, of course she would! The only thing she *couldn't* definitely promise was to stay awake. Her eyelids threatened every second to close down permanently over the tired eyes, and she was only half aware, amidst his profuse thanks, of the palms of his hands on her bottom as he leaned forward and kissed her gently on the cheek. He was, she knew, an inveterate womaniser; but curiously enough she found herself unable positively to dislike him; and on the few occasions he had tested the temperature of the water with her he had accepted without rancour or bitterness her fairly firm assurance that for the moment it was little if anything above freezing point. As she closed the door behind Binyon and went back to her bedroom, she felt a growing sense of guilt about her early morning escapade. It had been those wretched (beautiful!) gins-and-Campari that had temporarily loosened the girdle round her robe of honour. But her sense of guilt was, she knew, not occasioned just by the lapse itself, but by the anonymous, mechanical nature of that lapse. Jenny had been utterly delighted, if wholly flabbergasted, by the unprecedented incident; but Sarah herself had felt immediately saddened and diminished in her own self-estimation. And when finally she had returned to her flat, her sleep had been fitful and unrefreshing, the eiderdown perpetually slipping off her single bed as she had tossed and turned and tried to tell herself it didn't matter.

Now she took two Disprin, in the hope of dispelling her persistent headache, washed and dressed, drank two cups of piping-hot black coffee, packed her toilet bag and night-clothes, and left the flat. It was only some twelve minutes' walk down to the hotel, and she decided that the walk would do her nothing but good. The weather was perceptibly colder than the previous

day: heavy clouds (the forecasters said) were moving down over
the country from the north, and some moderate falls of snow were
expected to reach the Midlands by the early afternoon. During the
previous week the bookmakers had made a great deal of money after
the tenth consecutive non-white Christmas; but they must surely
have stopped taking any more bets on a white New Year, since
such an eventuality was now beginning to look like a gilt-edged
certainty.

Not that Sarah Jonstone had ever thought of laying a bet with
any bookmaker, in spite of the proximity of the Ladbrokes office
in Summertown which she passed almost daily on her way to work.
Passed it, indeed, again now, and stared (surely, far too obviously!)
at the man who had just emerged, eyes downcast, from one of the
swing-doors folding a pink, oblong betting slip into his wallet. How
extraordinarily strange life could become on occasions! It was just
like meeting a word in the English language for the very first time,
and then – lo and behold! – meeting exactly the same word for the
second time almost immediately thereafter. She had seen this same
man, for the first time, the previous evening as she had walked up
to Jenny's flat at about 9.30 p.m.: middle-aged; greyish headed;
balding; a man who once might have been slim, but who was now
apparently running to the sort of fat which strained the buttons on
his shabby-looking beige raincoat. *Why* had she looked at him so
hard on that former occasion? *Why* had she recorded certain details
about him so carefully in her mind? She couldn't tell. But she did
know that this man, in his turn, had looked at *her*, however briefly,
with a look of intensity which had been slightly (if pleasurably)
disturbing.

Yet the man's cursory glance had been little more than a
gesture of approbation for the high cheekbones that had thrown
the rest of her face into a slightly mysterious shadow under the
orange glare of the street lamp which illuminated the stretch of
road immediately outside his bachelor flat. And after only a few
yards, he had virtually forgotten the woman as he stepped out
with a purpose in his stride towards his nightly assignation at
the Friar.

Chapter Five

Tuesday, December 31st

Serious sport has nothing to do with fair play. It is bound
up with hatred, jealousy, boastfulness, and disregard of all
the rules.

George Orwell, *Shooting an Elephant*

In view of the events described in the previous chapter, it is not
surprising that from the start of subsequent police investigations
Sarah Jonstone's memories should have resembled a disorderly
card-index, with times and people and sequences sometimes hopelessly confused. Interview with one interrogator had been followed
by interview with another, and the truth was that her recollection of
some periods of December 31st had grown as unreliable as a false
and faithless lover.

Until about 11.30 a.m. she spent some time in the games room:
brushing down the green baize on the snooker table; putting up the
ping-pong net; repolishing the push-penny board; checking up on
the Monopoly, Scrabble and Cluedo sets; and putting into their
appropriate niches such items as cues, dice, bats, balls, chalk,
darts, cards and scoring pads. She spent some time, too, in the
restaurant; and was in fact helping to set up the trestles and spread
the tablecloths for the buffet lunch when the first two guests arrived
– guests signed in, as it happened, by a rather poorly and high-
temperatured Mrs Binyon herself in order to allow Sarah to nip
upstairs to her temporary bedroom and change into regulation long-
sleeved cream-coloured blouse, close-buttoned to the chin, and
regulation mid-calf, tightly fitting black skirt which (Sarah would
have been the first to admit) considerably flattered waist, hips,
thighs and calves alike.

From about noon onwards, guests began to arrive regularly, and
there was little time, and little inclination, for needless pleasantries.
The short-handed staff may have been a little short-tempered here
and there – particularly with each other; but the frenetic to-ings
and fro-ings were strangely satisfying to Sarah Jonstone that day.
Mrs Binyon kept out of the way for the most part, confining
her questionable skills to restaurant and kitchen before finally
retiring to bed; whilst Mr Binyon, in between lugging suitcases

along corridors and up stairs, had already repaired one squirting radiator, one flickering TV and one noisily dripping bath-tap, before discovering in early afternoon that some of the disco equipment was malfunctioning, and spending the next hour seeking to beg, cajole and bribe anyone with the slightest knowledge of circuits and switches to save his hotel from imminent disaster. Such (not uncommon) crises meant that Sarah was called upon to divide her attention mainly between Reception – a few guests had rung to say that the bad weather might delay their arrival – and the games room.

Oh dear – the games room!

The darts (Sarah soon saw) was not going to be one of the afternoon's greater successes. An ex-publican from East Croydon, a large man with the facility of lobbing his darts into the treble-twenty with a sort of languid regularity, had only two potential challengers for the championship title; and one of these could hardly be said to pose a major threat – a small, ageing charlady from some-where in the Chilterns who shrieked with juvenile delight whenever one of her darts actually managed to stick in the board instead of the wooden surround. On the other hand, the Cluedo players appeared to be settling down quite nicely – until one of the four children booked in for the festivities reported a 'Colonel Mustard' so badly dog-eared and a 'Conservatory' so sadly creased that each of the two cards was just as easily recognisable from the back as from the front. Fortunately the knock-out Scrabble competition, which was being keenly and cleanly played by a good many of the guests, had reached the final before any real dissension arose, and that over both the spelling and the admissibility of 'Caribbean'. (What an unpropitious omen *that* had been!) But these minor worries could hardly compare with the consternation caused on the Monopoly front by a swift-fingered checker-out from a Bedford supermarket whose palm was so extraordinarily speedy in the recovery of the two dice thrown from the cylindrical cup that her opponents had little option but to accept, without ever seeing the slightest evidence, her instantaneously enunciated score, and then to watch helplessly as this sharp-faced woman moved her little counter along the board to whichever square seemed of the greatest potential profit to her entrepreneurial designs. No complaint was openly voiced at the time; but the speed with which she bankrupted her real-estate rivals was later a matter of some general dissatis-faction – if also of considerable amusement. Her prize, though, was to be only a bottle of cheap, medium-sweet sherry; and since she did not look the sort of woman who would ever own a real-life hotel in Park Lane or Mayfair, Sarah had said nothing, and done nothing, about it. The snooker and the table-tennis tournaments were happily free from any major controversy; and a friendly cheer in mid-afternoon proclaimed that the ageing charlady from the Chilterns (who appeared to be getting on very nicely thank-you with the ex-publican from East Croydon) had at last managed to hit the dartboard with three consecutive throws.

Arbiter, consultant, referee, umpire – Sarah Jonstone was acquitting herself well, she thought, as she emulated the impartiality of Solomon that raw but not unhappy afternoon. Especially so since she had been performing, indeed was still performing, a contemporaneous rôle at the reception desk.

In its main building, the Haworth Hotel boasted sixteen bedrooms for guests – two family rooms, ten double rooms and four single rooms – with the now partially opened annexe offering a further three double rooms and one single room. The guest-list for the New Year festivities amounted to thirty-nine, including four children; and by latish afternoon all but two couples and one single person had registered at the desk, just to the right of the main entrance, where Sarah's large spectacles had been slowly slipping further and further down her nose. She'd had one glass of dry sherry, she remembered that; and one sausage roll and one glass of red wine – between half-past one and two o'clock, that had been. But thereafter she'd begun to lose track of time almost completely (or so it appeared to those who questioned her so closely afterwards). Snow had been falling in soft, fat flakes since just before midday, and by dusk the ground was thickly covered, with the white crystalline symbols of the TV weatherman portending further heavy falls over the whole of central and southern England. And this was probably the reason why very few of the guests – none, so far as Sarah was aware – had ventured out into Oxford that afternoon, although (as she later told her interrogators) it would have been perfectly possible for any of the guests to have gone out (or for others to have come in) without her noticing the fact, engaged as she would have been for a fair proportion of the time with form-filling, hotel documentation, directions to bedrooms, general queries, and the rest. Two new plumbing faults had further exercised the DIY skills of the proprietor himself that afternoon; yet when he came to stand beside her for a while after the penultimate couple had signed in, he looked reasonably satisfied.

'Not a bad start, eh, Sarah?'

'Not bad, Mr Binyon,' she replied quietly.

She had never taken kindly to *too* much familiarity over Christian names, and 'John' would never have fallen easily from those lips of hers – lips which were slightly fuller than any strict physiognomical proportion would allow; but lips which to John Binyon always looked softly warm and eminently kissable.

The phone rang as he stood there, and she was a little surprised to note how quickly he pounced upon the receiver.

'Mr Binyon?' It was a distanced female voice, but Sarah could hear no more: the proprietor clamped the receiver tight against his ear, turning away from Sarah as he did so.

'But you're not as sorry as I am!' he'd said . . .

'No – no chance,' he'd said . . .

'Look, can I ring you back?' he'd said. 'We're a bit busy here at the minute and I could, er, I could look it up and let you know . . .'

Sarah thought little about the incident.

It was mostly the *names* of the people, and the association of those names with the *faces*, that she couldn't really get fixed in her mind with any certitude. Some had been easy to remember: Miss Fisher, for example – the embryo property tycoon from Bedford; Mr Dods, too ('Ornly t'one "d" in t'middle, lass!') – she remembered *his* face very clearly; Fred Andrews – the mournful-visaged snooker king from Swindon; Mr and Mrs J. Smith from Gloucester – a marital appellation not unfamiliar to anyone who has sat at a hotel reception desk for more than a few hours. But the others? It really was very difficult for her to match the names with the faces. The Ballards from Chipping Norton? *Could* she remember the Ballards from Chipping Norton? They must, judging from the register, have been the very last couple to sign in, and Sarah *thought* she could remember Mrs Ballard, shivering and stamping her snow-caked boots in front of Reception, looking not unlike an Eskimo determined to ward off frostbite. Names and faces . . . faces and names . . . names which were to echo again and again in her ears as first Sergeant Phillips, then Sergeant Lewis, and finally a distinctly brusque and hostile Chief Inspector Morse, had sought to reactivate a memory torpid with shock and far-spent with weariness. Arkwright, Ballard, Palmer, Smith . . . Smith, Palmer, Ballard, Arkwright.

It was funny about names, thought Sarah. You could often tell what a person was like from a name. Take the Arkwright woman, for instance, who had cancelled her room, Annexe 4 – the drifting snow south of Solihull making motoring a perilous folly, it appeared. Doris Arkwright! With a name like that, she just had to be a suspicious, carefully calculating old crab-crumpet! And she wasn't coming – Binyon had just brought the message to her.

Minus one: and the number of guests was down to thirty-eight.

Oddly enough, one of the things very much on Sarah Jonstone's mind early that evening was the decision she had made (so authoritatively!) to allow 'Caribbean' in the Scrabble final. And she could hardly forget the matter, in view of a most strange coincidence. Later on in the evening, the judge for the fancy-dress competition would be asking whether another 'Caribbean' should be allowed, since one of the male entrants had gaily bedecked himself in a finely authentic Rastafarian outfit. 'The Mystery of the East' (the judge suggested) could hardly accommodate such an obviously West Indian interpretation? Yet (as one of the guests quietly pointed out) it wasn't really 'West Indian' at all – it was 'Ethiopian'; and Ethiopia had to be East in anyone's atlas – well, Middle East, anyway. Didn't it all depend, too (as another of the guests argued with some force), on exactly what this 'East' business meant, anyway: didn't it depend on exactly whereabouts on the globe one happened to be standing at any particular time? The upshot of this difference of opinion was that 'Caribbean' was accepted for a second time in the Haworth Hotel that New Year's Eve.

It would be a good many hours into New Year's Day itself before anyone discovered that the number of guests was down to thirty-seven.

Chapter Six

December 31st/January 1st

Beware of all enterprises that require fancy clothes.

Thoreau

During the times in which these events are set, there occurred a quite spectacular renaissance in fancy-dress occasions of all types. In pubs, in clubs, in ballrooms, at discos, at dinner parties – it was

as if a collective mania would settle upon men and women wherever they congregated, demanding that at fairly regular intervals
each of them should be given an opportunity to bedeck the body
in borrowed plumes and for a few hours to assume an entirely
alien personality. Two years previously (the Haworth's first such
venture) the New Year's party had taken 'What we were wearing
when the ship went down' as its theme, with the emphasis very
much upon the degree of imagination, humour and improvisation
that could be achieved with a very minimum of props. The theme
for the following New Year's Eve had been 'This Sporting Life';
and since that theme had been announced in the brochure, some of
the guests had taken the challenge most seriously, had turned their
backs on improvisation, and had brought appropriate costumes
with them. This year, in accord with the temper of the times,
participants had been given even wider scope than before, with
ample time and opportunity to hire their chosen outfits and to
acquire suitable make-up and accessories – in short, to take the
whole thing far too seriously. The hotel's 'Rag Bag' still stood
in the games room, but only one or two had rummaged through
its contents that afternoon. After all, the current theme had been
likewise pre-announced, and all the guests knew exactly what was
coming; and, to be fair, in many cases the fancy-dress evening was
one of the chief reasons for them choosing the Haworth Hotel in
the first place. On such occasions, the greatest triumph would be
registered when a person went through the first part of the evening
– sometimes a good deal longer – totally unrecognised even by
close acquaintances: a feat which Binyon himself had accomplished
the previous year when only by a process of elimination had even
his hotel colleagues finally recognised the face of their proprietor
behind the bushy beard and beneath the Gloucestershire cricket-
cap of Dr W. G. Grace.

This year the enthusiasm of the guests was such – all but six
had presented themselves in various guises – that even Sarah, not
by nature one of the world's obvious have-a-go extroverts, found
herself wishing that she were one of the happy band drinking red or
blue cocktails in the restaurant-cum-ballroom on the ground floor at
the back of the hotel, where everything was now almost ready. The
whole of the area was surprisingly warm, the radiators round the
walls turned up to their maximum readings, and a log fire burning
brightly in a large old grate that was simultaneously the delight of
guests and the despair of management. But tonight the fire was
dancing smokelessly and merrily, and the older folk there spoke of

the times when their shadows had passed gigantic round the walls of their childhood, and when in the late hours of the night the logs had collapsed of a sudden in a firework of sparks. Abetting this fire, in a double illumination, were tall red candles, two on each of the tables, and all already lit, with the haloes that formed around them creating little pools of warm light amid the darkling, twinkling dining room, and reflecting their elongated yellow flames in the gleaming cutlery.

It would have been easiest to divide the original guest-list into three tables of thirteen; but in deference to inevitable superstition Binyon had settled for two tables of fourteen and one of eleven, with each place set only for two courses. At each place, a small white card denoted the seating arrangements for these first two courses, spouse duly positioned next to spouse; but each of these cards also had two numbers printed on it, denoting a different table for the third and fourth courses, and a different table again for the fifth and sixth. This system had been tried out the previous year; and although on that occasion one or two of the couples had failed to follow instructions too carefully, the social mix effected thereby had proved a huge success. The only real problem attendant upon such a system was the awkwardness of transferring side plates from one seat to another, but this had been solved by the supremely simple expedient of dispensing with rolls and butter altogether.

It was at about a quarter to eight (eating would begin at eight o'clock) when the nasty little episode occurred: Sarah could vouch for the time with reasonable confidence. One of the women guests from the annexe, one dressed in the black garb of a female adherent of the Ayatollah, informed Sarah in a voice muffled by the double veil of her yashmak that there was something rather unpleasant written on the wall of the Ladies' lavatory, and Sarah had accompanied this woman to inspect the offending graffito. And, yes, she agreed with the voice behind the veils that it was not really very nice at all: 'I'm nuts' had been daubed on the wall over one of the wash-basins in a black-felt pen; and underneath had been added 'So are Binyon's B—'. Oh dear! But it had taken only a few minutes with sponge and detergent to expunge these most distressing words – certainly to the point of illegibility.

The cocktails turned out to be a huge success, for even the most weirdly bedizened strangers were already beginning to mix together happily. Binyon himself, gaudily garbed as the Lord High Executioner, was making no attempt this year to cloak his identity, and in a kindly way (so Sarah thought, as she looked in briefly) was making a successful fuss of one of the children, a small-boned nervous little girl dressed up prettily in Japanese costume. The mystical lure of the Orient had clearly provoked a colourful response, and there were one or two immediate hits – the most stunning being a woman with a lissomely sinuous figure, whose Turkish belly-dancer's outfit (what little there was of it) was causing several pairs of eyes (besides Binyon's) to sparkle widely with fornicatory intent. There was, as far as Sarah could see, only one real embarrassment amongst the whole lot, and that in the form of the gaunt-faced snooker king from Swindon, who had turned up as a rather too convincing version of Gandhi – a Gandhi, moreover, clearly in the latter stages of one of his emaciating fasts. But even he appeared happy enough, holding a cocktail in one hand, and ever hitching up his loin-cloth with the other.

It would not be long now before the guests began to drift to their places, to start on the Fresh Grapefruit Cerisette – already laid out (to be followed by the Consommé au Riz); and Sarah picked up a Tequila Sunrise and walked back through to Reception, where she locked the front door of the hotel. Her head was aching slightly, and the last thing she wanted was a six-course meal. An early night was all she really craved for; and that (she told herself) was what she *would* have, after giving a hand (as she'd promised) with the Grilled Trout with Almonds and then with the Pork Chop Normandy. (The Strawberry Gâteau, the cheese and biscuits and the coffee, Binyon had assured her, would be no problem.) She had never herself been a big eater, and for this reason she was always a little vexed that she could put on weight so easily; and unlike the Mahatma, perhaps, she most certainly did not wish to face the new year with a little extra poundage.

The cocktail tasted good; and with ten or fifteen minutes to spare before the grapefruit plates would need to be cleared Sarah lit one of the half dozen cigarettes she allowed herself each day, enjoying the sensation as she sat back in her chair and inhaled deeply.

Ten minutes to eight.

It could have been only some two or three minutes later that she heard the noise, fairly near her. And suddenly, illogically – with the stillness of the half-lit, empty entrance hall somehow emphasised by the happy voices heard from the dining room – she experienced a sense of fear that prickled the roots of her honey-coloured hair. And then, equally suddenly, everything was normal once again. From the door of the Gents' lavatory there emerged a gaily accoutred person-age who on any normal evening might justifiably have been the cause

of some misgiving on her part; but upon whom she now bestowed
a knowingly appreciative smile. It must have taken the man some
considerable time to effect such a convincing transformation into a
coffee-coloured, dreadlocked Rastafarian; and perhaps he hadn't
quite finished yet, for even as he walked across to the dining room he
was still dabbing his brown-stained hands with a white handkerchief
that was now more chocolate than vanilla.

Sarah drank some more of the liberally poured cocktail – and
began to feel good. She looked down at the only letter that had
found its way into her tray that morning: it was from a Cheltenham
lady thanking the hotel for the fact that her booking of a room had
been answered with 'laudable expedition' ('very quickly', translated
Sarah), but at the same time deploring the etiquette of these degenerate days that could allow the 'Dear Madam' of the salutation
to be complemented by the 'Yours sincerely' of the valediction.
Again, Sarah smiled to herself – the lady would probably turn out
to be a wonderful old girl – and looked up to find the Lord High
Executioner smiling down, in turn, at her.

'Another?' he suggested, nodding to the cocktail.

'Mm – that would be nice,' she heard herself say.

What had she remembered then? She could recall, quite certainly,
clearing away after the soup course; picking up the supernumerary
spoons and forks that marked the place of that pusillanimous spirit
from Solihull, Doris Arkwright; standing by in the kitchen as a Pork
Chop Normandy had slithered off its plate to the floor, to be replaced
thither after a perfunctory wipe; drinking a third cocktail; dancing
with the Lord High Executioner; eating two helpings of the gâteau
in the kitchen; dancing, in the dim light of the ballroom, a sort of
chiaroscuro cha-cha-cha with the mysterious 'Rastafarian' – the latter
having been adjudged the winner of the men's fancy-dress prize;
telling Binyon not to be so silly when he'd broached the proposition
of a brief dive beneath the duvet in her temporary quarters; drinking
a fourth cocktail, the colour of which she could no longer recall;
feeling slightly sick; walking up the stairs to her bedroom before
the singing of 'Auld Lang Syne'; feeling *very* sick; and finally finding
herself in bed. Those were the pretty definite events of a crowded
evening. ('But there must have been so many other little things, Miss
Jonstone?') And there *were* other things, yes. She remembered, for
example, the banging of so many doors once the music and the singing had finally ended – half-past midnight, it must have been – when
standing by her window (alone!) she had seen the guests from the

annexe walking back to their rooms: two of the women, their light-coloured raincoats wrapped around them, with the prize-winning Rastafarian between them, a hand on either shoulder; and behind that trio, another trio – the yashmak-ed, graffito-conscious woman, with a Samurai on one side and Lawrence of Arabia on the other; and bringing up the rear the Lord High Executioner, with a heavy, dark coat over his eastern robes. Yes! And she remembered quite clearly seeing all of them, including Binyon, go *into* the annexe, and then Binyon, fairly shortly afterwards, coming *out*, and fiddling for a moment or two with the Yale lock on the side door of the annexe – presumably to secure the inmates against any potential intruders.

It was just before 7 a.m. when Sarah woke, for a few seconds finding some difficulty in recalling exactly where she was. Then, it had been with a wholly childlike delight that on opening her curtains she saw the canopy of snow that enveloped everything – four or five inches of it on the ledge outside her window, and lodging heavily along the branches of the trees. The world outside looked so bitterly chill. But she was happily conscious of the square little radiator, now boiling hot, that made her room under the eaves so snugly warm; and through the frost-whorled window-panes she looked out once more at the deep carpet of snow: it was as if the Almighty had taken his brush, after the last few hours of the death-struck year, and painted the earth in a dazzling Dulux Super-White. Sarah wondered about slipping back into bed for a brief while, but decided against it. Her head was beginning to ache a little, and she knew there were some Aspirin in the kitchen. In any case she'd promised to help with the breakfasts. Much better to get up – even to go out and walk profanely across the virgin snow. As far as could be seen, there were no footprints, no indentations whatsoever, in the smooth surface of snow that surrounded the strangely still hotel, and a line from a poem she'd always loved came suddenly to mind: 'All bloodless lay the untrodden snow . . .'
  The water in the wall-basin became very hot indeed after only ten or fifteen seconds, and she was taking her flannel from her washing bag when she noticed a creosote-looking stain on the palm of her right hand; and then noticed the same sort of stain on one of the fluffy white towels she must have used before going to bed. And, of course, she knew immediately where *that* had come from. Had that wretched Rastafarian stained her blouse as well, when his left hand had circled her waist (perhaps a fraction too intimately) above her black tight-fitting skirt? Yes! He had! Blast

it! For a few minutes as her headache became gradually worse she moistened the offending patch on her cream blouse and cleaned off the stain as best she could. No one would notice it, anyway.

It was seven forty-five when she walked into the kitchen. Seemingly, she was the only person stirring in the whole hotel. And, had Sarah Jonstone known it at that time, there was a person in the same hotel who never would be seen to stir again. For in the room designated, on the key-hook board behind Reception, as 'Annexe 3', a man lay stiffly dead – the window of his ground-floor room thrust open, the radiator switched completely off, and the temperature around the body as icily frigid as an igloo's.

The end of the year had fallen cold; and the body that lay across the top of the coverlet on one of the twin beds in Annexe 3 was very, very cold indeed.

Chapter Seven

Wednesday, January 1st: p.m.

But if he finds you and you find him,
The rest of the world don't matter;
For the Thousandth Man will sink or swim
With you in any water.
            Rudyard Kipling, *'The Thousandth Man'*

For the Chief Constable of Oxfordshire, a man internationally renowned for his handling of terrorist sieges, the new year dawned upon fewer problems than had been anticipated. With the much-publicised CND march from Carfax to Greenham Common badly hit by the weather, and with the First Division game between Oxford United and Everton inevitably postponed, many of the extra police drafted in for special duties in both the city and the county had not been required. There had been, it was true, a whole string of minor accidents along the A40, but no serious injuries and no serious hold-ups. Indeed, it had been a very gentle New Year's Day; and at 6.30 p.m. the Chief Constable was just about to leave his office on the second floor of the Kidlington Police HQ when Superintendent

Bell rang from the City Police HQ in St Aldate's to ask whether among extra personnel available that day there happened to be any spare inspectors from the CID division.

The phone had been ringing for a good while before the sole occupant of the bachelor flat at the top of the Banbury Road in North Oxford turned down the mighty volume of the finale of *Die Walküre* and answered it.

'Morse!' he said curtly.

'Ah, Morse!' (The Chief Constable expected his voice to be instantly recognised, and it almost always was.) 'I suppose you've just staggered out of bed all ready for another night of debauchery?'

'A Happy New Year to you, too, sir!'

'Looks like being a pretty good new year for the crime rate, Morse: we've got a murder down at the bottom of your road. I'm assuming you had nothing to do with it, of course.'

'I'm on furlough, sir.'

'Well, never mind! You can make up the days later in January.'

'Or February,' mumbled Morse.

'Or February!' admitted the Chief Constable.

'Not tonight, I'm afraid, sir. I'm taking part in the final of the pub quiz round at the Friar.'

'I'm glad to hear others have got such confidence in your brains.'

'I'm quite good, really – apart from Sport and Pop Music.'

'Oh, I know that, Morse!' The Chief Constable was speaking very slowly now. 'And *I* have every confidence in your brains, as well.'

Morse sighed audibly into the phone and held his peace as the Chief Constable continued: 'We've got dozens of men here if you need 'em.'

'Is Sergeant Lewis on duty?' asked a Morse now fully resigned.

'Lewis? Ah yes! As a matter of fact he's on his way to pick you up now. I thought, you know, that er . . .'

'You're very kind, sir.'

Morse put down the phone and walked to the window where he looked down on the strangely quiet, muffled road. The Corporation lorries had gritted for a second time late that afternoon, but only a few carefully driven cars were intermittently crawling past along the icy surfaces. Lewis wouldn't mind coming out, though. In fact, thought Morse, he'd probably be only too glad to escape the first night of the new year television.

And what of Morse himself? There was perhaps just a hint of

grim delight to be observed on his features as he saw the police car pull into the gutter in a spurt of deep slush, and waved to the man who got out of it – a thick-set, slightly awkward-looking man, for whom the only blemishes on a life of unexciting virtuousness were a gluttonous partiality for egg and chips, and a passion for fast driving.

Sergeant Lewis looked up to the window of the flat, and acknowledged Morse's gesture of recognition. And had Lewis been able to observe more closely at that moment he might have seen that in the deep shadows of Morse's rather cold blue eyes there floated some reminiscences of an almost joyful satisfaction.

Chapter Eight

Wednesday, January 1st: p.m.

I therefore come before you armed with the delusions of adequacy with which so many of us equip ourselves.

Air Vice-Marshal A. D. Button

Lewis pulled in behind the two other police cars outside the Haworth Hotel, where a uniformed constable in a black-and-white chequered hat stood outside the main entrance, with one of his colleagues, similarly attired, guarding the front door of the adjacent property further down the Banbury Road.

'Who's in charge?' asked Morse, of the first constable, as he passed through into the foyer, stamping the snow from his shoes on the doormat.

'Inspector Morse, sir.'

'Know where he is?' asked Morse.

'Not sure, sir. I've only just got here.'

'Know him by sight, do you?'

'I don't know him at all.'

Morse went on in, but Lewis tapped the constable on the shoulder and whispered in his ear: 'When you meet this Morse fellow, he's a *chief* inspector – all right? – and a nasty one at that! So watch your step, lad!'

'Famous pair, we are!' murmured Morse as the two of them stood at Reception, where in a small room at the back of the desk Sergeant Phillips of the City CID (Morse recognised him) stood talking to a pale-faced, worried-looking man who was introduced as Mr John Binyon, the hotel proprietor. And very soon Morse and Lewis knew as much – or as little – as anyone about the tragedy so recently discovered in his own hotel by the proprietor himself.

The two Anderson children had been putting the finishing touches to their snowman just as it was getting dark that afternoon when they were joined by their father, Mr Gerald Anderson. And it had been he who had observed that one of the rear windows on the ground floor of the annexe was open; and who had been vaguely uneasy about this observation, since the weather was raw, with a cutting wind sweeping down from the north. He had finally walked closer and seen the half-drawn curtains flapping in the icy draught – although he had not gone all the way up to the window, under which (as he'd noticed) the snow was still completely undisturbed. He had mentioned this fact to his wife once he was back in the hotel, and it was at her instigation that he reported his disquiet to the proprietor himself – at about 5 p.m., that was; with the result that the pair of them, Anderson and Binyon, had walked across to the annexe and along the newly carpeted corridor to the second bedroom on the right, where over the doorknob was hooked a notice, written in English, French and German, instructing potential intruders that the incumbent was not to be disturbed. After repeated knockings, Binyon had opened the door with his master-key, and had immediately discovered why the man they found there had been incapable (for some considerable time, it seemed) of responding to any knocking from within or to any icy blast from without.

For the man on the bed was dead and the room was cold as the grave.

The news of the murder was known almost immediately to everyone in the hotel; and despite Binyon's frenetic protestations, some few of the guests (including, it appeared, *everyone* from the annexe) had taken the law into their own hands, packed their belongings, strapped up their cases (and in one case not paid any part of the bill), and disappeared from the Haworth Hotel before Sergeant Phillips from St Aldate's had arrived at about 5.40 p.m.

'You *what*?' bellowed Morse as Phillips explained how he'd allowed four more of the guests to leave the hotel when full names and addresses had been checked.

'Well, it was a very difficult situation, sir, and I thought—'

'Christ, man! Didn't someone ever tell you that if you've got a few suspicious circumstances you're expected to hold on to a few of the *suspects*? And what do *you* do, Sergeant? You tell 'em all to bugger off!'

'I got all the details—'

'Bloody marvellous!' snapped Morse.

Binyon, who had been standing by in some embarrassment as Morse (not, it must be admitted, without just cause) lashed the luckless Phillips, decided to come to the rescue.

'It really was a very difficult situation, Inspector, and we thought—'

'*Thought?*' Morse's instantaneous repetition of the monosyllable sounded like a whiplashed retaliation for such impertinence, and it was becoming abundantly clear that he had taken an instant dislike to the hotel proprietor. 'Mr Binyon! They don't pay you, do they, for having any thoughts about this case? No? But they *do* pay *me*! They even pay Sergeant Phillips here; and if I was angry with him just now it was only because I basically respect what *he* thought and what he tried to do. But I shall be obliged if *you* will kindly keep your thoughts out of things until I ask for them – all right?'

In the latter part of this little homily, Morse's voice was as cool and as level as the snow upon which Sarah Jonstone had looked out early that same morning; and she herself as she sat silently at Reception was more than a little alarmed by this new arrival; more than a little upset by his harsh words. But gossip had it that the corpse found in the room called Annexe 3 had been horridly mutilated about the face; and she was relieved that the police seemed at least to have matched the gravity of the crime by sending a man from the higher echelons of its detective branch. But he was disturbingly strange, this man with the hard-staring, startling eyes – eyes that had at first reminded her of the more fanatical politicians, like Benn or Joseph or Powell, as she'd watched them on TV; eyes that seemed uncommunicative and unseeing, eyes fixed, it seemed, upon some distanced, spiritual shore. And yet that wasn't true, and she knew it; for after his initial ill-temper he had looked so directly and so daringly into her eyes that for a second or two she could have sworn that he was about to wink at her.

A man she'd seen three times now in three days!

Another man had come in – the humped-back man she'd seen earlier – and he, too, was in Sarah's eyes one of the more unusual specimens of humankind. With a cigarette hanging down at forty-five degrees from a thin-lipped, mournful mouth, and with the few remaining strands of his lank, black hair plastered in parallels across a yellowish dome of a skull, anyone could perhaps be forgiven for supposing his profession to be that of a moderately unsuccessful undertaker. (Oddly, enough, over the fifteen years they had known – and respected – each other, Morse had invariably addressed this police surgeon by his Christian name, whilst the surgeon had never addressed Morse by anything other than his surname.)

'I was here an hour ago,' began the surgeon.

'You want me to give you a medal or something?' said Morse.

'You in charge?'

'Yes.'

'Well, go and have a look at things. I'll be ready when you want me.'

Following closely behind Binyon and Phillips and Lewis, Morse was walking over to the annexe when he stopped halfway and gazed up at the giant crane, its arm outstretched some 120 feet above the ground as if in benediction, or perhaps in bane, upon one or other of the two blocks of buildings between which it was positioned.

'Not a job they'd get me on, Lewis,' he said, as his eyes went up towards the precarious-looking box at the top of the structure, in which, presumably, some operator would normally sit.

'No need, sir. You can operate those things from the bottom.' Lewis pointed to a platform, only some six feet above the ground, on which a series of knobbed levers stuck up at various angles through the iron floor. Morse nodded; and averted his eyes from the crane's nest atop the criss-crossed iron girders that stood out black against the heavy, darkened sky.

Through the side door of the annexe they proceeded, where Morse looked along the newly carpeted passage that stretched some ten to twelve yards in front of him, its terminus marked by pieces of boarding, nailed (not too professionally) across an aperture which would, in due course, lead through to the front entrance hall of the annexe. Morse strode to the far end of the corridor and looked through the temporary slats to the foyer beyond, where rickety-looking planks, resting on pairs of red bricks, were set across the recently cemented floor. Dust from such activities had filtered through, and was now lying, albeit lightly, on the surfaces just a few feet inside the completed section of the ground-floor annexe, and it seemed clear that there had been no recent entrance, and no recent exit, from that particular point. Morse turned, and for a few seconds looked back up the short corridor down which they had walked; looked at the marks of many muddy shoes (including their own) on the purple carpeting – the latter seeming to Morse almost as distasteful as the reproduction of the late Renoir, 'Les nues dans l'herbe', which hung on the wall to his right.

As he stood there, still looking back up to the side entrance, he noted the simple geography of the annexe. Four doors led off the corridor: to his right were those numbered 2 and 1; immediately opposite 1 was 4; and then, set back behind a narrow, uncarpeted flight of stairs (temporarily blocked off but doubtless leading to the hitherto undeveloped first floor) a door numbered 3. From what he had already learned, Morse could see little hope of lifting any incriminatory fingerprints from the doorknob of this last room which had been twisted quite certainly by Binyon and probably by others. Yet he looked at the knob with some care, and at the trilingual notice that was still hooked over it.

'There should be an umlaut over the "o" in "Stören",' said Morse.

'Ja! Das sagen mir alle,' replied Binyon.

Morse, whose only knowledge of German stemmed from his addiction to the works of Richard Wagner and Richard Strauss, and who was therefore supremely unfitted to converse in the language, decided that it would be sensible to say no more on the point; decided, too, that Binyon was not perhaps quite the nonentity that his weak-chinned appearance might seem to signify.

Inside Annexe 3, a door immediately to the right gave access to a small, rather cramped toilet area, with a wash-basin, a WC, and a small bath with shower attachment. In the bedroom itself, the main items of furniture were twin beds, pulled close together, with matching white coverlets; a dressing table opposite them, a TV set in the corner; and just to the left of the main door a built-in wardrobe. Yet it was not the furniture which riveted the attention of Morse and Lewis as they stood momentarily in the doorway. Across the further of the two beds, the one that stood only some three or four feet from the opened window, lay the body of the dead man. Morse, as he invariably did, recoiled from an immediate inspection of the corpse; yet he knew that he had to look. And an extraordinary oddity it was upon which he looked: a man dressed in Rastafarian clothes lay on his side, his face towards them, his head lying in a great, coldly clotted pool of blood, like red wine poured across the snow. The dead man's left hand was trapped beneath the body; but the right hand was clearly visible below the long sleeve of a light-blue shirt; and it was – without any doubt – the hand of a white man.

Morse, now averting his eyes from this scene of gory mutilation, looked long and hard at the window, then at the TV set, and finally put his head inside the small washroom.

'You've got a good fingerprint man coming?' he asked Phillips.

'He's on his way, sir.'

'Tell him to have a go at the radiator, the TV, and the lever on the WC.'

'Anything else, sir?'

Morse shrugged. 'Leave it to him. I've never had much faith in fingerprints myself.'

'Oh, I don't know, sir—' began Phillips.

But Morse lifted his hand like a priest about to pronounce a benediction, and cut off whatever Phillips had intended to say. 'I'm not here to argue, lad!' He looked around again, and seemed just on the point of leaving Annexe 3 when he stepped back inside the room and opened the one drawer, and then the other, of the chest below the TV set, peering carefully into the corners of each.

'Were you expecting to find something?' asked Lewis quietly as he and Morse walked back across to the Haworth Hotel.

Morse shook his head. 'Just habit, Lewis. I once found a ten-pound note in a hotel in Tenby, that's all.'

Chapter Nine

Wednesday, January 1st: p.m.

The great advantage of a hotel is that it's a refuge from home life.

G. B. Shaw

On their return to the main building, Morse himself addressed the assembled guests in the ballroom area (not, as Lewis saw things, particularly impressively), telling everyone what had happened (they knew anyway), and asking everyone to be sure to tell the police if they had any information which might be of use (as if they wouldn't!).

None of those still remaining in the hotel appeared at all anxious to return home prematurely. Indeed, it soon became apparent to Lewis that the 'Annexe Murder' was, by several kilometres, the most exciting event of most lives hitherto; and that far from wishing to distance themselves physically from the scene of the crime, the majority of the folk left in the hotel were more than happy to stay where they were, flattered as they had been to be told that their own recollections of the previous evening's events might possibly furnish a key clue in solving the murder which had been committed. None of these guests appeared worried about the possibility of an indiscriminate killer being abroad in Oxford's semi-civilised acres – a worry which would, in fact, have been totally unfounded.

Whilst Lewis began the documentation of the hotel guests, Morse was to be seen sitting at the receipt of custom, with Sarah Jonstone to his right, looking through the correspondence concerned with those annexe guests whom (the duly chastened) Sergeant Phillips had earlier blessed or semi-blessed upon their homeward ways.

A pale Sarah Jonstone, a nerve visibly twitching at her left nostril, lit a cigarette, drew upon it deeply, and then exhaled the rarefied smoke. Morse, who the previous day (for the thousandth time) had rid himself of the odious habit, turned to her with distaste.

'Your breath must smell like an old ash-tray,' he said.

'Yes?'

'Yes!'

'Who to?'

' "To whom?", do you mean?'

'Do you want me to help you or not?' said Sarah Jonstone, the skin around her cheekbones burning.

'Room 1?' asked Morse.

Sarah handed over the two sheets of paper, stapled together, the lower sheet reading as follows:

> 29A Chiswick Reach
> London, W4
> 20 Dec.

Dear Sir(s)

My wife and I would like to book a double room – preferably with double bed – for the New Year Offer your hotel is advertising. If a suitable room is available, we look forward to hearing from you.

> Yours faithfully,
> F. Palmer

On top of this originating handwritten letter was the typewritten reply (ref JB-SJ) to which Morse now briefly turned his attention:

Dear Mr Palmer,
    Thank you for your letter of 20 Dec. Our New Year programme has been extremely popular, and we are now fully booked as far as the main hotel is concerned. But you may be interested in the Special Offer (please see last page of current brochure) of accommodation in one of the rooms of our newly equipped annexe at three-quarters of the normal tariff. In spite of a few minor inconveniences, these rooms are, we believe, wonderfully good value, and we very much hope that you and your wife will be able to take advantage of this offer.
    Please be sure to let us know immediately – preferably by phone. The Christmas post is not likely to be 100% reliable.
                                                        Yours sincerely,

There was no further correspondence; but across the top letter was a large tick in blue biro, with 'Accepted 23rd Dec' written beneath it.

'You remember them?' asked Morse.

'Not very well, I'm afraid.' She recalled (she thought) a darkly attractive woman of about thirty or so, and a smartly dressed, prosperous-looking man about ten years her senior, perhaps. But little else. And soon she found herself wondering whether the people she was thinking of were, in fact, the Palmer pair at all.

'Room 2?'

Here the documentary evidence Sarah produced was at an irreducible minimum: one sheet of hotel paper recorded the bare facts that a Mr Smith – a 'Mr J. Smith' – had rung on December 23rd and been told that there had been a late cancellation in the annexe, that a double room would now be available, and that written confirmation should be put in the post immediately.

'There's no confirmation here,' complained Morse.

'No. It was probably held up in the Christmas post.'

'But they came?'

'Yes.' Again, Sarah thought she remembered them – certainly *him*, a rather distinguished-looking man, hair prematurely grey, perhaps, with a good-humoured, twinkling sort of look about him.

'You get quite a few "John Smiths"?'

'Quite a few.'

'The management's not worried?'

'No! Nor me. Or would you prefer "Nor I"?'

'That'd be a little bit pedantic, wouldn't it, miss?'

Sarah felt the keen glance of his eyes upon her face, and again (maddeningly) she knew that her cheeks were a burning red.

'Room 3?'

Sarah, fully aware that Morse already knew far more about the situation in Room 3 than she did, handed over the correspondence without comment – this time a typewritten originating letter, stapled below a typewritten reply.

84 West Street
Chipping Norton
Oxon
30th Nov

Dear Proprietor,

Please book in my husband and myself for the Haworth Hotel's New Year Package as advertised. We would particularly wish to take advantage of the rates offered for the 'annexe rooms'. As I read your brochure, it seems that each of these rooms is on the ground floor and this is essential for our booking since my husband suffers from vertigo and is unable to climb stairs. We would prefer twin beds if possible but this is not essential. Please answer as a matter of urgency by return (s.a.e. enclosed) since we are most anxious to fix things up immediately and shall not be at our present address (see above) after 7th December, since we shall be moving to Cheltenham.

Yours sincerely,
Ann Ballard (Mrs)

The prompt reply (dated 2nd December) was as follows:

Dear Mrs Ballard,

Thank you for your letter of 30th November. We are glad to be able to offer you a double room on the ground-floor annexe, with twin beds, for our New Year Package.

We look forward to your confirmation, either by letter or by phone.

We very much look forward to meeting you and your husband, and we are confident that you will both greatly enjoy your stay with us.

Yours sincerely,

In biro across this letter, too, the word 'Accepted' was written, with the date '3rd Dec'.

Morse looked down again at the letter from Mrs Ballard, and seemed (at least to Sarah Jonstone) to spend an inexplicably long time re-reading its meagre content. Finally he nodded very slowly to himself, put the two sheets of paper down, and looked up at her.

'What do you remember about that pair?'

It was the question Sarah had been afraid of, for her recollections were not so much vague as confused. She thought it had been *Mrs* Ballard who had collected the key from Reception; Mrs Ballard who had been nodded in the direction of the annexe at about 4 p.m. that New Year's afternoon; Mrs Ballard who had appeared in her Iranian outfit just before the evening festivities were due to begin and pointed out the distasteful graffito in the Ladies' loo. And it had been *Mr* Ballard, dressed in his distinctively Rastafarian outfit of light-blue shirt, white trousers, baggy checked cap, and maroon knee-boots, who had emerged from the Gents' loo just before everyone was due to eat; Mr Ballard who in fact had eaten very little at all that evening (indeed Sarah herself had cleared away his first two courses virtually untouched); Mr Ballard who had kept very close to his wife throughout the evening, as if they were still in some lovey-dovey idyll of a recent infatuation; Mr Ballard who had asked her – Sarah! – to dance in the latter part of an evening which was becoming less and less of a distinct sequence of events the more she tried to call it back to mind . . .

All these things Sarah told a Morse intensely interested (it seemed) in the vaguest facts she was able to dredge up from the chaotic jumble of her memory.

'Was he drunk?'

'No. I don't think he drank much at all.'

'Did he try to kiss you?'

'No!' Sarah's face, she knew, was blushing again, and she cursed herself for such sensitivity, aware that Morse appeared amused by her discomfiture.

'No need to blush! Nobody'd blame a fellow for wanting to kiss someone like you after one of your boozy midnight parties, my love!'

'I'm not your "love"!' Her upper lip was trembling and she felt the tears beginning to brim behind her eyes.

But Morse was looking at her no more: he picked up the phone and dialled Directory Enquiries on 192.

'There's no Ballard at 84 West Street,' interrupted Sarah. 'Sergeant Phillips—'

'No, I know that,' said Morse quietly, 'but you don't mind if I just check up, do you?'

Sarah was silent as Morse spent a few minutes speaking to some supervisor somewhere, asking several questions about street names and street numbers. And whatever he'd learned, he registered no surprise, certainly no disappointment, as he put down the phone and grinned boyishly at her. 'Sergeant Phillips was right, Miss Jonstone. There isn't a Mr Ballard of 84 West Street, Chipping Norton. There isn't even a number 84! Which makes you think, doesn't it?' he asked, tapping the letter that Sarah herself had written to precisely that non-existent address.

'I'm past thinking!' said Sarah quietly.

'What about Room 4?'

Here, the initiating letter, addressed from 114 Worcester Road, Kidderminster, and dated 4th December, was a model of supremely economical, no-nonsense English, and written in a small, neat hand:

Dear Sir,
    Single – cheapest available – room for your New Year Package. Confirm, please.

Yours,
Doris Arkwright.

Such confirmation had been duly forthcoming in the form of an almost equally brief reply, this time signed by the proprietor himself, and dated 6th December. But across this letter was now pencilled 'Cancelled 31st Dec – snow.'

'Did she ring up?' asked Morse.

'Yes, she must have rung Mr Binyon, I think.'

'You don't ask for a deposit?'

She shook her head. 'Mr Binyon doesn't think it's good business practice.'

'You don't get many cancellations?'

'Very few.'

'Really? But you've had two out of the four rooms in the annexe!'

Yes, he was right. And he looked like the wretched sort of man who would *always* be right.

'Have you ever had this old biddy staying with you before?' continued Morse.

'What makes you think she's an "old biddy", Inspector?'

'With a name like Doris Arkwright? Straight out of the Lancashire mills, isn't it? Pushing a sprightly ninety, I shouldn't wonder, and drives an ancient Austin.'

Sarah opened her mouth, but closed it again. Morse (as she watched him) had perched a pair of NHS half-lenses on his Jewish-looking nose and looked again at the short letter from Doris Arkwright.

'Do you think she's got anything to do with the case?' asked Sarah.

'Do I think so?' He waited for a few pregnant seconds before taking off his spectacles and looking at her quizzically. 'No, I don't think she's got anything at all to do with the murder. Do *you*, Miss Jonstone?'

Chapter Ten

Wednesday, January 1st: p.m.

He was once a doctor but is now an undertaker; and what he does as an undertaker he used to do as a doctor.

Martial

For Lewis, the next two hours of the evening of New Year's Day were hardly memorable. A good deal of the earlier excitement had dissipated, with even the novelty of murder worn thin; and the Haworth Hotel now looked an uninviting place, its high-ceilinged rooms harshly lit by neon strips, its guests standing or sitting in small groups, quiet and unsmiling – and waiting. Morse had asked him to check (factually) with Phillips all the names and addresses of those staying in the hotel, and briefly himself to interview as many vital witnesses as he could find – with Phillips to take on the rest; to try to form a picture (synoptically) of the scene at the hotel on the previous evening; and to keep his antennae attuned (almost metaphysically, it appeared) for any signals from an unsuspected psychopath or any posthumous transmissions from the newly dead. Festivities – all of them, including the pantomime – had been cancelled, and the hotel was now grimly still, with not even the quiet click of snooker balls from the games room to suggest that murder was anything but a deadly serious matter.

Lewis himself had never spent a Christmas or a New Year away from home since his marriage; and although he knew that family life was hardly prize-winning roses all along the way, he had never felt the urge to get away from his own modest semi-detached house up in Headington over such holiday periods. Yet now – most oddly, considering the circumstances – he began to see for the first

time some of the potential attractions: no frenetic last-minute pur-
chases from supermarkets; no pre-feastday preparations of stuffings
and sauces; no sticky saucepans to scour; no washing-up of plates
and cutlery. Yes! Perhaps Lewis would mention the idea to the
missus, for it seemed perfectly clear to him as he spoke to guest
after guest that a wondrously good time was being had by all –
until a man had been found murdered.

Exactly where Morse had been during the whole of this period,
Lewis had little idea, although (Lewis had heard part of it) the
chief inspector had interviewed the woman on Reception at some
considerable length – a woman (as Lewis saw her) most pleasingly
attractive, with a quiet, rather upper-class manner of speaking
that contrasted favourably with the somewhat abrasive questioning
she was being subjected to – with Morse obviously still in a tetchy
frame of mind after his altercations with the luckless Phillips,
and apparently quite unconcerned about venting his temporary ill-
humour on anyone and everyone, including Sarah Jonstone.

It was just after 10 p.m. that the police surgeon came back
into the main building again, the inevitable long-ashed cigarette
drooping from his lips, his black bag in one hand, two sheets of
A4 in the other.

'My god, you do pick 'em, Morse!' began the surgeon as the
three of them, Max, Morse and Lewis, sat down together in the
deserted games room.

'Get on with it, Max!' said Morse.

The surgeon looked quickly at his notes – then began.

'One – he's a wasp, Morse.'

'He's a *what*?'

'He's a WASP – a White Anglo-Saxon Protestant – though he
could well be a Catholic, of course.'

'Of course.'

'Two – his age is about thirty to forty, though he could be
twenty-nine or forty-one, for that matter.'

'Or forty-two,' said Morse.

The surgeon nodded. 'Or twenty-eight.'

'Get on with it!'

'Three – his height's five foot seven and a half inches. You
want that in metres, Morse?'

'Not so long as it's accurate in inches.'

'Can't promise that.'

'Christ!'

'Four – he's dressed up as a Rastafarian.'

'Very perceptive!'

'Five – he's got a wig on: black, curlyish.'

'Something several of us could do with!'

'Six – he's got dreadlocks.'

'Which are?'

'Long, thin bits of hair, plaited into strands, with cylindrical beads at the end.'

'I saw them! It's just that I didn't know—'

'Seven – these strands of hair are stapled to the inside of the hat he's wearing.'

Morse nodded.

'Eight – this hat is a sort of baggy, felt "cap", with a big peak, a black-grey-white check pattern, filled out with folded toilet paper. You want to know which brand?'

'No!'

'Nine – his face is darkened all over with what's known in theatrical circles as "stage-black".'

Again Morse nodded.

'Ten – this stage-black stretches down to the top of the shirt-level, just round his neck; the backs of the hands are similarly bedaubed, Morse, but not the palms.'

'Is that important?'

'Eleven' – the surgeon ignored the question – 'his light-blue shirt has got six buttons down the front, all but the top one done up, long-sleeved, obviously very new and probably being worn for the first time.'

No comment from Morse.

'Twelve – his white trousers are made of some cheap summer-wear material, a bit worn here and there.'

'And nothing in the pockets,' said Morse; but it wasn't a question.

'Thirteen – he's got three longish chains round his neck: junk stuff that you'd find in a cheap second-hand shop.'

Morse was beginning to show the first signs of restlessness.

'Fourteen – there was a pair of sunglasses on the floor just between the two beds, the ear-hooks quite shallowly slanted.'

'As if they'd fall off his ears, you mean?'

'They *did* fall off his ears.'

'I see.'

'Fifteen – a false moustache, affixed with strong adhesive, still exactly in position across the upper lip.'

'Why do you say "affixed", instead of just plain "fixed"?'

'Sixteen – a pair of high-heeled, knee-level boots: highly polished, light maroon plastic.'

'You sure it's not a *woman* we've got there on the bed, Max?'

'Seventeen – time of death: difficult to judge.'

'As well we might have known!'

'About sixteen to twenty-four hours before the body was found – at a guess. But the room temperature is only just above freezing point – which could upset calculations either way.'

'So?'

For the first time, the surgeon seemed slightly less than happy with himself: 'As I say, Morse, it's very difficult.'

'But you *never* come up with a plain statement of when—'

'They pay me to report facts.'

'And they pay me to find out who killed the poor sod, Max.' But Morse, it seemed, was making little impression upon the mournful man who lit another cigarette before continuing.

'Eighteen – cause of death? A mighty whack, probably only one, across the front of the skull, with the bone smashed in from the top of the right eye across the nasal bridge to the left cheekbone.'

Morse was silent.

'Nineteen – he wasn't a navvie, judging from his fingernails.'

'Now you're getting down to things.'

'No I'm not, Morse. I've nearly finished.'

'You're going to tell me who he is, you mean?'

'Twenty – he had flat feet.'

'You mean he *has* flat feet?'

The surgeon permitted himself a bleak smile. 'Yes, Morse. When he was alive he had flat feet, and in death those feet were not unflattened.'

'What does that suggest, Max?'

'Perhaps he's a policeman, Morse.' The surgeon stood up, the cigarette ash dropping on to his black waistcoat. 'I'll let you have the written report as soon as I can. Not tonight though.' He looked at his watch. 'We've got half an hour if you want to nip up to the Gardener's? I've got a car.'

For a moment or two, Lewis almost thought that Morse was going to resist the temptation.

Chapter Eleven

Wednesday, January 1st: p.m.

When I drink, I think; and when I think, I drink.
                                                    Rabelais

'Gin-and-Campari for me, Morse, and buy yourself one as well.
My GP keeps on telling me it's sensible to keep off the spirits.'

Soon the two old friends were seated facing each other in the
lounge bar, the surgeon resting his heavy-looking dolichocephalic
skull upon his left hand.

'Time of death!' said Morse. 'Come on!'

'Nice drink this, Morse.'

'The science of thanatology hasn't advanced a millimetre in
your time, has it?'

'Ah! Now you're taking advantage of my classical education.'

'But nowadays, Max, you can look down from one of those
space-satellite things and see a house-fly rubbing its hands over a
slice of black pudding in a Harlem delicatessen – you know that?
And yet *you* can't—'

'The room was as cold as a church, Morse. How do you
expect—'

'You don't know anything about churches!'

'True enough.'

They sat silently for a while, Morse looking at the open fire
where a log suddenly shifted on its foundations and sent a shower
of red-glowing sparks against the back of the old grate, beside
which was a stack of wood, chopped into quartered segments.

'Did you notice they'd chopped down a couple of trees at the
back of the annexe, Max?'

'No.'

Morse sipped his gin. 'I could develop quite a taste for this.'

'You think it might have been the branch of a tree or something . . . ? Could have been, I suppose. About two feet long, nice
easy grip, couple of inches in diameter.'

'You didn't see any wood splinters?'

'No.'

'What about a bottle?'

'No broken glass on his face, either, as far as I could see.'

'Tough things, though. Some of these people who launch battleships have a hell of a job breaking champagne bottles.'

'We may find something, Morse.'

'When can you let me have a report?'

'Not tonight.'

'Much blood, would there have been?'

'Enough. No spurting though.'

'No good asking the guests if they saw a fellow walking around with blood all over his best shirt?'

'What about a *woman*, Morse? With blood all over her liberty bodice?'

'Perhaps, I suppose.'

The surgeon nodded non-committally and looked into the fire: 'Poor sod . . . Do *you* ever think of death? *Mors, mortis*, feminine – remember that?'

'Not likely to forget a word like that, am I? Just add on "e" to the end and . . .'

The surgeon smiled a sour acknowledgement of the point and drained his glass. 'We'll just have the other half. Then we'll get back, and show you round the scene of the crime again.'

'When the body's out of the way?'

'You don't like the sight of blood much, do you?'

'No. I should never have been a policeman.'

'Always turned me on, blood did – even as a boy.'

'Unnatural!'

'Same again?'

'Why not?'

'What turns *you* on?' asked the surgeon as he picked up the two glasses.

'Somebody from the *Oxford Times* asked me that last week, Max. Difficult, you know – just being asked out of the blue like that.'

'What did you say?'

'I said I was always turned on by the word "unbuttoning".'

'Clever!'

'Not really. It comes in one of Larkin's poems somewhere. It's just that you know nothing about the finer things in life . . .'

But the surgeon, apparently unhearing, was already standing at the bar and rattling an empty glass imperiously on the counter.

Chapter Twelve

Wednesday, January 1st: p.m.

Close up the casement, draw the blind,
Shut out that stealing moon.

Thomas Hardy

Under the surgeon's supervision, the frozen-footed ambulance-men had finally stretchered away the white-sheeted corpse to the morgue at the Old Radcliffe at 11.30 p.m., and Lewis was glad that the preliminaries of the case were now almost over. The two fingerprint-men had departed just after eleven, followed ten minutes later by the spiky-haired young photographer, clutching the neck of his flash-bulb camera as if it were some poisonous serpent. The surgeon himself had driven off in his old black Ford at a quarter to midnight, and the hotel seemed strangely still as Lewis followed Morse across the slush and blackened snow to the room called Annexe 3, where the two men stood for the second time that evening, and where, each in his own way, they now took a more detailed mental inventory of what they saw.

Immediately to the left in the spacious room (about twenty feet by fourteen feet) stood a built-in wardrobe of white wood, in which nine plastic coat-hangers hung from the cross-rail; beyond it stood a dressing table, its drawers (as we have seen) quite empty, with a brochure of the hotel lying on its top, next to a card with the handwritten message: 'Welcome – your room has been personally prepared by Mandy'; a colour TV set stood in the corner; and, between it and the dressing table, a ledge some four feet from the floor held a kettle, a small teapot, two cups and two saucers, and a rectangular plastic tray, on which, in separate compartments, were small cellophaned packets of biscuits, sachets of Nescafé, sachets of sugar, teabags, and little squat tubs of Eden Vale milk.

Along the far wall was a long low radiator, and just above its top the sill of an equally long window, the latter a triptych of panes, the centre one fixed, but the left and right panes still opened outwards to the elements at an angle of forty-five degrees, and the darkish-green curtains drawn only half across. Liberally sprinkled fingerprint powder was observable all round the window, where a few daubs of unpromising-looking blotches had been circled with a black-felt pen.

'Perhaps,' said Morse, a shiver running down his vertebrae, 'we should take our first positive moves in this case, Lewis, eh? Let's close those bloody windows! And turn on the radiator!'

'You're not worried about the prints, sir?'

'It's not going to help us to arrest anybody if we land up in some intensive-care unit with bronchial pneumonia.'

(Lewis, at that moment, felt quite unconscionably happy.)

The twin beds occupied most of the area in the rest of the room, their tops close against the wall to the right, beneath a long headboard panel of beige plastic, set into which were the controls for TV and radio, loudspeakers, various light switches, and an early-morning-alarm unit with what seemed to Lewis instructions that were completely incomprehensible. On a small table between the beds was a white digital telephone; and on a shelf beneath that, the Holy Bible, as placed by the ever-persevering Gideons. The walls and ceiling were painted in a very pale shade of apple green, and the floor was carpeted wall to wall in a grey-green chequered pattern.

All very neat, very clean, and very tidy – apart from the obscene blotch of dried blood across the further bed.

Completing the circuit of this accommodation, the two men came to the tiny bathroom, only some seven feet by five feet, whose door stood a few feet inside and to the right of the main entrance to Annexe 3. Immediately facing was the WC, a unit of the usual white enamel, the bowl a sparkling tribute to the ministrations of the conscientious Mandy; on the left was a wash-basin by which stood two tumblers and a diminutive bar of soap (unopened) in a pink-paper wrapping bearing the name 'Haworth'; to the right was a bath, fairly small, with shower attachment, and a ledge let into the wall containing a second bar of soap (also unopened); finally, on the wall opposite, to the left of the WC, were racks for a whole assortment of fluffy white towels (all seemingly unused), and fixtures for toilet paper and Kleenex tissues. The walls were tiled in a light olive-green, with the Vinyl flooring of a slightly darker, matching green.

'They don't look, whoever they were, as if they made much use of the facilities, sir.'

'No-o.' Morse walked back into the main part of the room and stood there nodding to himself. 'Good point! I wonder if . . .' He fiddled with some of the buttons and switches which appeared to determine the reception of a TV programme; but with no effect.

'Shall I plug it in, sir?'

'You mean . . . ?' Again Morse appeared deep in thought as an
indeterminate blur dramatically developed into a clearly delineated
picture, and a late-night newsreader announced that in Beirut the
Shi-ite and the Christian Militias had begun the new year with
exactly the same implacable hatred as they had finished the old one.

'Funny, you know, Lewis – turn that thing off! – you'd have
thought they would have made *some* use of the facilities, wouldn't
you?' Morse carefully drew back the coverings on the bed nearer
the window; but the sheets appeared quite virgin, apart from the
indentations caused by the superimposition of a corpse. With the
other bed, too, the evidence seemed very much the same: someone might well have sat on the side, perhaps, but it seemed reasonably clear that neither bed had been the scene of any frolicsome
coition.

It was Lewis, emerging from the bathroom, who had found the
only tangible trace of the room's most recent tenants: a screwed-up
brown-stained Kleenex tissue, which had been the only item in the
waste-bin.

'Looks like this is the only thing they left behind, sir.'

'Not blood is it?'

'It's the stage-black for the make-up, I think.'

'Well, at least we've got *one* clue, Lewis!'

Before leaving, Morse once more slid open the door of the
wardrobe along its smooth runners and took another look inside.

'Doesn't look as if your fingerprint lads did much dusting here.'

Lewis looked at the powder marks that covered several points
on the white outer-door: 'I wouldn't say that, sir. It looks as if—'

'I meant *inside*,' said Morse quietly.

It was midnight before Sarah Jonstone got to bed that night,
and way into the early hours before she finally dropped off
into a restless slumber. Her mind was reverting continually to
the strangely disturbing chief inspector – a man she was growing
to dislike intensely – and to what he had asked, and asked, and
asked her. Occasionally, as he had listened to her answers, he
had seemed to promote a simple, honest confession of ignorance
or forgetfulness on her part to the status of an almost unforgivable
sin. And above all her mind reverted to his repeated insistence that
she must try to recall anything unusual: anything *unusual*; *anything
unusual* . . . The words had re-echoed round the walls of her brain
– being all the more disturbing precisely because there *had*,
she thought, been something unusual . . . Yet this 'something'

continued to elude her: almost, on several occasions, she had it
in her grasp – and then it had slithered away like a slippery bar
of soap along the bottom of the bath.

Chapter Thirteen

Thursday, January 2nd: a.m.

Snow is all right while it is snowing: it is like inebriation,
because it is very pleasing when it is coming, but very
unpleasing when it is going.

Ogden Nash

Morse had decided that it was needful, at least for a couple of
days, to set up a temporary Murder HQ *in situ*; and from the
comparatively early hours of the next morning, the room at the
rear of the annexe building, a broad-windowed area that looked as
if it would make an excellent classroom, was taken over by Lewis
and Morse as an official 'Operations Room'.

An innocently deep night's sleep, an early-morning shower and a
fried breakfast of high cholesterol risk had launched a zestful Lewis
on his way to the Haworth Hotel at 6.30 a.m., where an ill-rested,
unshowered, unbreakfasted Morse had joined him twenty minutes
later.

At half-past seven it was John Binyon, the hotel proprietor, who
was the first of many that day to sit opposite the two detectives at
a rickety trestle table.

'It's a terrible thing,' said Binyon. 'Terrible! Just when we'd
started getting things going nicely, too.'

'Never mind, sir,' said Morse, calling upon all his powers of
self-control to force the last of these three words through the
barrier of his teeth. 'Perhaps you'll have a long queue of people
waiting to sleep in the famous room.'

'Would you queue for it, Inspector?'

'Certainly not!' said Morse.

The talk turned to the subject of guests in general, and Binyon
admitted that things had changed a good deal, even during his own

limited experience. 'They don't even pretend these days, some of
them – don't even put a ring on, some of the women. Mind you, we
turn one or two away – well, you know, make out we're full up.'

'Do you think you could always spot them – if they weren't
married?'

Binyon gave the question serious thought. 'No! No – I wouldn't
say that. But I think I'd know if they were staying together for the
first time.'

'How so?'

'Lots of things. The way they act, I suppose – and they always
pay by cash – and they often get addresses wrong. For example,
we had a fellow last month who came with his girlfriend, and he
put down his address as Slough, *Berks*!'

'What did you do?' asked Morse, frowning.

'Nothing. I wasn't on the desk when he signed in; but I
was when he booked out, and I told him straight that the next
hotel he went to it might be valuable to know that Slough was in
Bucks.'

'What did *he* say?' asked Morse, frowning more than ever.

'He just grinned – as if he hadn't heard me.'

'But Slough *is* in Berks!' said Morse.

The proprietor's general grasp of hotel procedures was clearly
considerably in advance of his knowledge of geography, and Morse
found himself not unfavourably impressed by his succinct account
of current practice at the Haworth Hotel. Normally, between 80 per
cent and 90 per cent of the guests contacted the hotel, in the first
instance, by phone. Often, there would be insufficient time to seek or
to obtain confirmation by letter. Most usually, a credit-card number
was sufficient warranty from the hotel's point of view to establish a
bona fides; but for something so specifically pre-planned and widely
advertised as a Christmas or a New Year function, obviously the
great majority of guests had *some* correspondence with the hotel.
As far as actual registration was concerned, the pattern was (the two
detectives learned) exactly what any seasoned traveller would expect
at any established hostelry: 'Name?' would be the first question;
and, when this was checked against the booking list, a card would
be handed over which asked for surname, forename(s), company,
company address, home address, method of settling account, nationality, car registration, passport number, and finally signature. Such
a fairly straightforward task completed, the guest (or guests) would
be given a card showing details of room number, tariff, type of
breakfast, type of room, and the like. With a room key handed

over from one of the hooks behind Reception, 'registration' was now appropriately effected, with only a final negotiation remaining about the choice of a morning newspaper. And that was that. In such a comparatively small hotel, no porter was employed to carry cases, although the management was of course always on the lookout to ensure suitable assistance for any ageing couples who appeared at risk from cardiac arrest at the prospect of lugging their belongings to the first-floor landing.

At eight fifteen, confirmation was received from Chipping Norton that none of the five Ballard couples on the local Electoral Register had a wifely component answering to the name Ann; and that the town's official archivist, after delving as far back towards Domesday as local records allowed, was prepared to state quite categorically that there was not, nor ever had been, a number 84 along the thoroughfare now known, and always known, as West Street, Chipping Norton.

At eight forty-five, Superintendent Bell rang through from St Aldate's to ask if Morse required any further men to help him. But Morse declined the offer; for the moment he could think of nothing he could profitably effect with a posse of policemen, except perhaps to conduct some inevitably futile house-to-house enquiries in and around Chipping Norton to ascertain whether anyone had knowledge of a man of indeterminate age, partner to a pseudonymous Ann Ballard, with neither a club-foot, nor a withered arm, nor a swastika tattooed on his forehead to assist any possible identification. Further, it became quite clear from the guests interviewed later that morning that none of them would with any certitude be able to recognise Mr Ballard again. Such diffidence (as Morse saw things) was hardly surprising: the only time the other guests had met Ballard was during that one evening; up until then he had been a complete stranger to them; and he had spent most of the evening closely shielded and chaperoned by what others had taken to be a jealously possessive wife. Indeed the only reason that many could recall him at all was the extremely obvious one: he had won first prize in the men's fancy-dress competition, dressed in the consummately skilful disguise of a West Indian reggae musician. The only new fact of any substance to emerge was that he had, certainly in the later part of the evening, drunk more than one glass of whisky – Bell's, according to Mandy, the stand-in barmaid. But there was also general agreement, fully corroborating Sarah Jonstone's earlier evidence, that Ballard had eaten very little indeed. Several witnesses had a clear recollection of him dancing with his yashmak-ed companion (lover? mistress? wife?), and only with her, for most of the evening; but Mr Dods ('With t'one "d" ') was almost prepared to swear on Geoffrey Boycott's batting average that Ballard had also danced, towards midnight, with an animated youngish woman named Mrs Palmer – 'Philippa' or 'Pippa' Palmer, as he recalled – as well as with the hotel receptionist ('a little tipsy, Inspector, if ah mair sair sor!'). And that was about that. And towards the end of the morning it was becoming increasingly obvious to both Morse and Lewis that the only firm and valuable testimony they were going to get was that given the previous evening by Sarah (tipsy or not!) Jonstone, who had claimed in her statement to Lewis that she had peeped out of her window at about 1 a.m. and seen at that late, flake-falling, whitely covered hour, the prize-winning Rastafarian walking back across to the annexe with an arm around each of the women on either side of him. It seemed good to Morse, therefore, to summon the fair Miss Jonstone once again.

She sat there, her legs crossed, looking tired, every few moments pushing her spectacles up to the top of her nose with the middle finger of her ringless left hand – and thereby irritating Morse to a quite disproportionate extent – as he himself hooked his half-lenses behind his ears and trusted that he projected an appropriate degree of investigative acumen.

'After the annexe lot left the party, the others finished too – is that right?'

'I think so.'

'You don't *know* so?'

'No.'

'You say Ballard had his arms round these two women?'

'No, he had one arm round one woman and one—'

'Which two women?'

'Mrs Palmer was one – I'm fairly sure of that.'

'And the other one?'

'I think it was . . . Mrs Smith.'

'You'd had quite a lot to drink, hadn't you!'

Sarah Jonstone's pale face coloured deeply; and yet perhaps it was, that morning, more from anger than from shame. 'Oh yes!' she said, in a firm, quiet voice. 'I don't think you'll find a single person in the hotel who would disagree with that.'

'But you saw the women fairly clearly?' (Morse was beginning to appreciate Miss Jonstone more and more.)

'I saw them clearly from the back, yes.'

'It was snowing, wasn't it?'

'Yes.'

'So they had their coats on?'

'Yes. Both of them had light-coloured winter macs on.'

'And you say' – Morse referred to her statement – 'that the other three members of the annexe sextet were just behind them?'

Sarah nodded.

'So, if you're right about the first three, that leaves us with Mrs Ballard, Mr Palmer and Mr . . . Smith – yes?'

Sarah hesitated – and then said 'Yes!' – then pushed her spectacles up once more towards her luminous eyes.

'And behind them all came Mr Binyon?'

'Yes – I think he was going to make sure that the side door to the annexe was locked up after them.'

'That's what *he* says, too.'

'So it might be true, Inspector.'

But Morse appeared not to have heard her. 'After Mr Binyon had locked up the annexe, no one else could have got *in* there?'

'Not unless he had a key.'

'Or *she* had a key!'

'Or she had a key, yes.'

'But anyone could have got *out* of the annexe later on?'

Again Sarah hesitated before answering. 'Yes, I suppose so. I hadn't really thought of it, but – yes. The lock's an ordinary Yale one, and any of the guests could have got out, if they'd wanted to.'

It was Lewis who, at this point, made an unexpected intervention.

'Are you absolutely *sure* it was snowing then, Miss Jonstone?'

Sarah turned towards the sergeant, feeling relieved to look into a pair of friendly eyes and to hear a friendly voice. And she *wasn't* quite sure, now she came to think of it. The wind had been blowing and lifting up the settled snow in a drifting whirl around her window; and whether it *had* been snowing, at that particular moment, she wasn't really prepared to assert with any dogmatism.

'No,' she said simply. 'I'm *not* absolutely sure.'

'It's just,' continued Lewis, 'that according to the weatherman on Radio Oxford the snow in this area had virtually stopped falling just about midnight. There may have been the odd flurry or two; but it had pretty well finished by then – so they say.'

'What are you trying to get at, Sergeant? I'm not . . . quite sure . . .'

'It's just that if it *had* stopped snowing, and if someone had left the annexe that night, there would have been some footprints, wouldn't there? Wouldn't such a person have to make his way across to the main road?'

Sarah was thinking back, thinking back so very hard. There had been *no* prints the next morning leading from the annexe across to the Banbury Road. None! She could almost swear to that. But *had* it been snowing when she looked out that fateful evening? Yes, it had!

Thus it was that she answered Lewis simply and quietly. 'No, there were no footprints from the annexe to be seen that morning – yesterday morning. But yes, it *was* snowing when I looked out – I'm sure of it.'

'You mean that the weatherman at Radio Oxford has got things all wrong, miss?'

'Yes, I do, Sergeant.'

Lewis felt a little taken aback by such strong and such conflicting evidence, and he turned to Morse for some kind of arbitration. But as he did so, he noticed (as he had so often in the past) that the chief inspector's eyes were growing brighter and brighter by the second, in some sort of slow incandescence, as though a low-powered filament had been switched on somewhere at the back of his brain. But Morse said nothing for the moment, and Lewis tried to rediscover his bearings.

'So from what you say, you think that Mr Ballard must have been murdered by one of those five other people there?'

'Well, yes! Don't you? I think he was murdered by Mr or Mrs Palmer, or by Mr or Mrs Smith, or by Mrs Ballard – whoever *she* is!'

'I see.'

During these exchanges, Morse himself had been watching the unshadowed, unrouged, unlipsticked blonde with considerable interest; but no longer. He stood up and thanked her, and then seemed relieved that she had left them.

'Some shrewd questioning there, Lewis!'

'You really think so, sir?'

But Morse made no direct answer. 'It's time we had some refreshment,' he said.

Lewis, who was well aware that Morse invariably took his lunchtime calories in liquid form, was himself perfectly ready for a pint and a sandwich; but he was a little displeased about Morse's apparently total lack of interest in the weather conditions at the time of the murder.

'About the snow, sir—' he began.

'The snow? The snow, my old friend, is a complete white herring,' said Morse, already pulling on his greatcoat.

In the back bar of the Eagle and Child in St Giles', the two men sat and drank their beer, and Lewis found himself reading and reading again the writing on the wooden plaque fixed to the wall behind Morse's head:

C. S. LEWIS, his brother, W. H. Lewis, J. R. R. Tolkien, Charles Williams, and other friends met every Tuesday morning, between the years 1939–1962 in the back room of this their favourite pub. These men, popularly known as the 'Inklings', met here to drink beer and to discuss, among other things, the books they were writing.

And strangely enough it was Sergeant Lewis's mind, after (for him) a rather liberal intake of alcohol, which was waxing the more imaginative as he pictured a series of fundamental emendations to this received text: 'CHIEF INSPECTOR MORSE, with his friend and colleague Sergeant Lewis, sat in this back room one Thursday, in order to solve . . .'

Chapter Fourteen

Thursday, January 2nd: p.m.

'Is there anybody there?' he said.
Walter de la Mare, *'The Listeners'*

If, as now seemed probable, the Haworth Hotel murderer was to be sought amongst the fellow guests who had been housed in the annexe on New Year's Eve, it was high time to look more carefully into the details of the Palmers and the Smiths, the guests (now vanished) who had been staying in Annexe 1 and Annexe 2 respectively; and Lewis looked at the registration forms he had in front of him, each of them fully filled in; each of them, on the face of it, innocent enough.

The Palmers' address, the same on the registration form as on the earlier correspondence, was given as 29A Chiswick Reach; and the telephone operator confirmed that there was indeed such a property, and that it did indeed have a subscriber by the name of Palmer, P. (sex not stated) listed in the London Telephone Directory. Lewis saw Morse's eyebrows lift a little, as if he were more than a fraction surprised at this intelligence; but for his own part he refused to assume that everyone who had congregated quite fortuitously in the Haworth annexe was therefore an automatic criminal. He dialled the number and waited, letting the phone at the other end ring for about a minute before putting down the receiver.

'We could get someone round there, perhaps?'

'Not yet, Lewis. Give it a go every half hour or so.'

Lewis nodded, and looked down at the Smiths' card.

'What's their address?' asked Morse.

'Posh sort of place, by the look of it, "*Aldbrickham*, 22 Spring Street, Gloucester".'

This time Lewis saw Morse's eyebrows lift a lot. 'Here! Let me look at that!' said Morse.

And as he did so, Lewis saw him shake his head slowly, a smile forming at the corners of his mouth.

'I'm prepared to bet you my bank-balance that there's no such address as that!'

'I'm not betting anything!'

'I know the place, Lewis. And so should you! It's the street where Jude and Sue Fawley lived!'

'Should I know them?'

'In *Jude the Obscure*, Lewis! And "Aldbrickham" is Hardy's name for Reading, as you'll remember.'

'Yes, I'd forgotten for the moment,' said Lewis.

'Clever!' Morse nodded again as though in approbation of the literary tastes of Mr and Mrs John Smith. 'There's no real point in trying but . . .' Lewis heard an audible sigh from the girl on 192 as she heard that Lewis wanted Smith, J.; and it took her a little while to discover there was no subscriber of that name with a Spring Street address in Gloucester. A further call to the Gloucester Police established, too, that there was not a Spring Street in the city.

Lewis tried Chiswick again: no reply.

'Do you reckon we ought to try old Doris – Doris Arkwright?' asked Morse. 'Perhaps she's another crook.'

* * *

But before any such attempt could be made, a messenger from the pathology lab came in with the police surgeon's preliminary findings. The amateurishly typewritten report added little to what had already been known, or assumed, from the previous evening's examination: age thirty-five to forty-five; height five foot eight and a half ('He's grown an inch overnight!' said Morse); no fragments of wood or glass or steel in the considerable facial injury, caused likely enough by a single powerful blow; teeth – in exceptionally good condition for a male in the age-group, with only three minor fillings in the left-hand side of the jaw, one of them very recent; stomach – a few mixed vegetables, but little recent intake by the look of things.

That, in essence, was all the report said. No further information about such key issues as the time of death; an array of medical terms, though, such as 'supra-orbital foramen' and 'infra-orbital fissure', which Morse was perfectly happy to ignore. But there was a personal note from the surgeon written in a spidery scrawl at the foot of this report. 'Morse: A major drawback to any immediate identification is going to be the very extensive laceration and contusion across the inferior nasal concha – this doesn't give us any easily recognisable lineaments for a photograph – and it makes the look of the face harrowing for relatives. In any case, people always look different when they're dead. As for the time of death, I've nothing to add to my definitive statement of yesterday. In short, your guess is as good as mine, although it would come as a profound shock to me if it was any better. Max.'

Morse glanced through the report as rapidly as he could, which was, to be truthful, not very rapidly at all. He had always been a slow reader, ever envying those of his colleagues whose eyes appeared to have the facility to descend swiftly through the centre of a page of writing, taking in as they went the landscape both to the left and to the right. But two points – two simple, major points – were firmly and disappointingly apparent: and Morse put them into words.

'They don't know who he is, Lewis; and they don't know when he died. Bloody typical!'

Lewis grinned: 'He's not a bad old boy, though.'

'He should be pensioned off! He's too old! He drinks too much! No – he's not a bad old boy, as you say; but he's on the downward slope, I'm afraid.'

'You once told me *you* were on the downward slope, sir!'

'We're *all* on the downward slope!'

'Shall we go and have a look at the other bedrooms?' Lewis

spoke briskly, and stood up as if anxious to prod a lethargic-looking Morse into some more purposive line of enquiry.

'You mean they may have left their Barclaycards behind?'

'You never know, sir.' Lewis fingered the great bunch of keys that Binyon had given him, but Morse appeared reluctant to get moving.

'Shall I do it myself, sir?'

Morse got up at last. 'No! Let's go and have a look round the rooms – you're quite right. You take the Palmers' room.'

In the Smiths' room, Annexe 2, Morse looked around him with little enthusiasm (wouldn't the maid have tidied Annexe 1 and Annexe 2 during the day?) finally turning back the sheets on each of the twin beds, then opening the drawers of the dressing table, then looking inside the wardrobe. Nothing. In the bathroom, it was clear that one or both of the Smiths had taken a shower or a bath fairly recently, for the two large white towels were still slightly damp and the soap in the wall-niche had been used – as had the two squat tumblers that stood on the surface behind the wash-basin. But there was nothing to learn here, Morse felt sure of that. No items left behind; no torn letters thrown into the waste-paper basket; only a few marks over the carpet, mostly just inside the door, left by shoes and boots that had tramped across the slush and snow. In any case, Morse felt fairly sure that the Smiths, whoever they were, had nothing at all to do with the crime, because he thought he knew just how and why the pair of them had come to the Haworth Hotel, booking *in* at the last possible moment, and getting *out* at the earliest possible moment after the murder of Ballard had been dis-covered. 'Smith, J' (there was little doubt in Morse's mind) was an ageing rogue in middle management, drooling with lust over a new young secretary, who'd told his long-suffering spouse that he had to go to a business conference in the Midlands over the New Year. Such conduct was commonplace. Morse knew that; and perhaps there was little point in pursuing the matter further. Yet he would like to meet her, for she was, according to the other guests, a pleasingly attractive woman. He sat on one of the beds, and picked up the phone.

'Can I help you?' It was Sarah Jonstone

'Do you know what's the first thing they tell you if you go on a course for receptionists?'

'Oh! It's you.'

'They tell you never to say "Can I help you?" '

'Can I hinder you, Inspector?'

'Did the Smiths make any telephone calls while they were here?'
'Not from the bedroom.'

'You'd have a record of it – on their bill, I mean – if they'd phoned anyone?'

'Ye-es. Yes we would.' Her voice sounded oddly hesitant, and Morse waited for her to continue. 'Any phone call gets recorded automatically.'

'That's it then.'

'Er – Inspector! We've – we've just been going through accounts and we shall have to check again but – we're almost sure that Mr and Mrs Smith didn't square up their account before they left.'

'Why the hell didn't you tell me before?' snapped Morse.

'Because – I – didn't – know,' Sarah replied, spacing the four words deliberately and quietly and only just resisting the impulse to slam the receiver down on him.

'How much did they owe?'

Again, there was a marked hesitation at the end of the line. 'They had some champagne taken to their room – expensive stuff—'

'Nobody's ever had a *cheap* bottle of champagne – in a hotel – have they?'

'And they had four bottles—'

'*Four?*' Morse whistled softly to himself. 'What exactly was this irresistible vintage?'

'It was Veuve Clicquot Ponsardin 1972.'

'Is it good stuff?'

'As I say, it's expensive.'

'How expensive?'

'£29.75 a bottle.'

'It's *what?*' Again Morse whistled to himself, and his interest in the Smiths was obviously renascent. 'Four twenty-nines are . . . Phew!'

'Do you think it's important?' she asked.

'Who'd pick up the empties?'

'Mandy would – the girl who did the rooms.'

'And where would she put them?'

'We've got some crates at the back of the kitchen.'

'Did anyone else raid the champagne cellar?'

'I don't think so.'

'So you ought to have four empty bottles of '72 whatever-it-is out there?'

'Yes, I suppose so.'

'No "suppose" about it, is there?'

'No.'

'Well, check up – straight away, will you?'

'All right.'

Morse walked back into the bathroom, and without picking up the tumblers leaned over and sniffed them one by one. But he wasn't at all sure if either smelled of champagne, though one pretty certainly smelled of some peppermint-flavoured toothpaste. Back in the bedroom, he sat down once more on the bed, wondering if there was something *in* the room, or something *about* the room, that he had missed. Yet he could find nothing – not even the vaguest reason for his suspicions; and he was about to go when there was a soft knocking on the door and Sarah Jonstone came in.

'Inspector, I—' Her upper lip was shaking and it was immediately clear that she was on the verge of tears.

'I'm sorry I was a bit short with you—' began Morse.

'It's not that. It's just . . .'

He stood up and put his arm lightly round her shoulders. 'No need to tell me. It's that penny-pinching Binyon, isn't it? He's not only lost the Smiths' New Year contributions, he's an extra one hundred and nineteen pounds short – yes?'

She nodded, and as the eyes behind the large round lenses brimmed with glistening tears Morse lightly lifted off her spectacles and she leaned against his shoulder, the tears coursing freely down her cheeks. And finally, when she lifted her head and smiled feebly, and rubbed the backs of her hands against her tear-stained face, he took out his only handkerchief, originally white and now a dirty grey, and pushed it into her grateful hands. She was about to say something, but Morse spoke first.

'Now don't you worry, my girl, about Binyon, all right? Or about these Smiths, either! I'll make sure we catch up with 'em sooner or later.'

Sarah nodded. 'I'm sorry I was so silly.'

'Forget it!'

'You know the champagne bottles? Well, there are only *three* of them in the crate. They must have taken one away with them – it's not here.'

'Perhaps they didn't quite finish it.'

'It's not very easy to carry a half-full bottle of bubbly around.'

'No. You can't get the cork back in, can you?'

She smiled, feeling very much happier now, and found herself looking at Morse and wondering if he had a wife or a series of women-friends or whether he just wasn't interested: it was difficult to tell. She was conscious, too, that his mind hadn't seemed to be on her at all for the last few minutes. And indeed this was true.

'You feeling better?' she heard him say; but he appeared no longer to have any interest in her well-being, and he said no more as she turned and left him in the bedroom.

A few minutes later he poked his head round the door of Annexe 1 and found Lewis on his hands and knees beside the dressing table.

'Found anything?' he asked.

'Not yet, sir.'

Back in the temporary Operations Room, Morse rang the pathology lab and found the police surgeon there.

'Could it have been a bottle, Max?'

'Perhaps,' admitted that morose man. 'But if it was it didn't break.'

'You mean even you would have found a few lumps of glass sticking in the fellow's face?'

'Even me!'

'Do you think with a blow like that a bottle *would* have smashed?'

'*If* it was a bottle, you mean?'

'Yes, *if* it was a bottle.'

'Don't know.'

'Well, bloody *guess*, then!'

'Depends on the bottle.'

'A champagne bottle?'

'Many a day since I saw one, Morse!'

'Do you think whoever murdered Ballard was left-handed or right-handed?'

'If he was a right-handed tennis player it must have been a sort of back-hand shot: if he was left-handed, it must have been a sort of smash.'

'You're not very often as forthcoming as that!'

'I try to help.'

'Do you think our tennis player was right-handed or left-handed?'

'Don't know,' said the surgeon.

Lewis came in a quarter of an hour later to report to his rather sour-looking superior that his exhaustive search of the Palmer suite had yielded absolutely nothing.

'Never mind, Lewis! Let's try the Palmer number again.'

But Morse could hear the repeated 'Brr-brrs' from where he

sat, and sensed somehow that for the moment at least there would be no answer to the call. 'We're not having a great afternoon, one way or another, are we?' he said.

'Plenty of time yet, sir.'

'What about old Doris? Shall we give her a ring? We know *she's* at home – warming her corns on the radiator, like as not.'

'You want me to try?'

'Yes, I do!'

But there was no Arkwright of any initial listed in the Kidderminster area at 114 Worcester Road. But there *was* a subscriber at that address; and after some reassurance from Lewis about the nature of the enquiry the supervisor gave him the telephone number. Which he rang.

'Could I speak to Miss Doris Arkwright, please?'

'I think you've got the wrong number.'

'That *is* 114 Worcester Road?'

'Yes.'

'And you haven't got a Miss or a Mrs Arkwright there?'

'We've got a butcher's shop 'ere, mate.'

'Oh, I see. Sorry to have troubled you.'

'You're welcome.'

'I just don't believe it!' said Morse quietly.

Chapter Fifteen

Thursday, January 2nd: p.m.

Even in civilized mankind, faint traces of a monogamic instinct can sometimes be perceived.

Bertrand Russell

Helen Smith's husband, John, had told her he would be back at about one o'clock, and Helen had the ingredients for a mushroom omelette all ready. Nothing for herself, though. She would have found it very difficult to swallow anything that lunchtime, for she was sick with worry.

The headlines on 'The World at One' had just finished when she heard the crunch of the BMW's wheels on the gravel outside – the same BMW which had spent the New Year anonymously enough in the large multi-storey car park in the Westgate shopping centre at Oxford. She didn't turn as she felt his light kiss on the back of her hair, busying herself with excessive fussiness over the bowl as she whisked the eggs, and looking down at the nails of her broad, rather stumpy fingers, now so beautifully manicured . . . and so very different from the time, five years ago, when she had first met John, and when he had mildly criticised her irritating habit of biting them down to the quicks . . . Yes, he had smartened her up in more than one way in their years of marriage together. That was certain.

'Helen! I've got to go up to London this afternoon. I may be back later tonight; but if I'm not, don't worry. I've got a key.'

'Um!' For the moment, she hardly dared risk a more fully articulated utterance.

'Is the water hot?'

'Mm!'

'Will you leave the omelette till I've had a quick bath?'

She waited until he had gone into the bathroom; waited until she heard the splash of water; even then gave things a couple of minutes more, just in case . . . before stepping out lightly and quietly across the drive and trying the front passenger door of the dark-blue BMW – almost whimpering with anticipation.

It was open.

Two hours after Mr John Smith had stretched himself out in his bath at Reading, Philippa Palmer lay looking up at the ceiling of her own bedroom in her tastefully furnished, recently redecorated, first-floor flat in Chiswick. The man who lay beside her she had spotted at 12.30 p.m. in the Cocktail Lounge of the Executive Hotel just off Park Lane – a tall, dark-suited, prematurely balding man, perhaps in his early forties. To Philippa, he looked like a man not short of a few pounds, although it was always difficult to be certain. The exorbitant tariffs at the Executive (her favourite hunting-ground) were almost invariably settled on business expense accounts, and bore no necessary correlation with the apparent affluence of the hotel's (largely male) clientèle. She'd been sitting at the bar, nylon-stockinged legs crossed, split skirt falling above the knee; he'd said 'Hullo', pleasantly; she'd accepted his offer of a drink – gin and tonic; she'd asked him, wasting no time at all, whether he wanted to be 'naughty' – an epithet which, in her wide experience, was wonderfully efficacious in beguiling the vast majority of men;

he had demurred, slightly; she had moved a little closer and shot a sensual thrill throughout his body as momentarily she splayed a carmine-fingered hand along his thigh. The 'How-much?' and the 'When?' and the 'Where?' had been settled with a speed unknown in any other professional negotiating body; and now here she lay – a familiar occurrence! – in her own room, in her own bed, waiting with ineffable boredom for the two-hour contract (at £60 per hour) to run its seemingly interminable course. She'd gauged him pretty well correctly from the start: a man of rather passive, voyeuristic tendencies rather than one of the more thrusting operatives in the fornication field. Indeed, the aggregate time of his two (hitherto) perfunctory penetrations could hardly have exceeded a couple of minutes; and of that Philippa had been duly glad. He might, of course, 'after a few minutes' rest' as the man had put it, rise to more sustained feats of copulatory stamina; but blessedly (from Philippa's point of view) the few minutes' rest had extended itself to a prolonged period of stertorous slumber.

The phone had first rung at about 2.30 p.m., the importunate burring making the man quite disproportionately nervous as he'd undressed. But she had told him that it would only be her sister; and he had appeared to believe her, and to relax. And as she herself had begun unzipping her skirt, he had asked if she would wear a pair of pyjamas while they were in bed together – a request with which she was not unfamiliar, knowing as she did that more than a few of her clients were less obsessed with nudity than with *semi*-nudity, and that the slow unbuttoning of a blouse-type top, with its tantalising lateral revelations, was a far more erotic experience for almost all men than the vertically functional hitch of a nightdress up and over the thighs.

It was 3.15 p.m. when the phone rang again, and Phillipa felt the man's eyes feasting on her body as she leaned forward and picked up the receiver.

'Mrs Palmer? Mrs Philippa Palmer?' The voice was loud and clear, and she knew that the man at her side would be able to hear every word.

'Ye-es?'

'This is Sergeant Lewis here, Thames Valley Police. I'd like to have a word with you about—'

'Look, Sergeant. Can you ring me back in ten minutes? I'm just having a shower and—'

'All right. You'll make sure you're there, Mrs Palmer?'

'Of course! Why shouldn't I be?'

The man had been sitting on the edge of the bed pulling on his socks with precipitate haste from the words 'Sergeant Lewis' onwards, and Philippa was relieved that (as always) pecuniary matters had been fully settled before the start of the performance. Seldom had Philippa seen a man dress himself so quickly; and his hurried goodbye and immediate departure were a relief to her, although she knew he was probably quite a nice sort of man, really. She admitted to herself that his underclothes had been the cleanest she had seen in weeks; and he hadn't mentioned his wife, if he had one, once.

It was a different voice at the end of the line when the telephone rang again ten minutes later: an interesting, educated sort of voice that she told herself she rather liked the sound of, announcing itself as Chief Inspector Morse.

Morse insisted that it would be far more sensible for himself (not Lewis) to go to interview the woman finally found at the other end of a telephone line in Chiswick. He fully appreciated Lewis's offer to go, but he also emphasised the importance of someone (Lewis) staying at the hotel and continuing to 'sniff around'. Lewis, who had heard this sort of stuff many times, was smiling to himself as he drove Morse down to Oxford station to catch the 4.34 train to Paddington that afternoon.

Chapter Sixteen

Thursday, January 2nd: p.m.

And he that seeketh findeth.
St Matthew 7:8

On his return from Oxford railway station, Lewis was tempted to call it a day and get off home. He had been up since 5 a.m., and it was now just after 5 p.m. A long enough stretch for anybody. But he didn't call it a day; and in retrospect his decision was to prove a crucial one in solving the mystery surrounding Annexe 3.

He decided to have a last look round the rooms in the annexe before he went home, and for this purpose he left the Operations

Room by the front door (the partition between the main annexe entrance and the four rooms in use had not been dismantled) and walked round the front of the building to the familiar side-entrance, where a uniformed constable still stood on duty.

'It's open, Sarge,' Lewis heard as he fumbled with his embarrassment of keys.

'Give it till seven, I reckon. Then you can get off,' said Lewis. 'I'll just have a last look round.'

First, Lewis had a quick look round the one room that no one had as yet bothered about, Annexe 4; and here he made one small find – alas, completely insignificant. On the top shelf of the built-in wardrobe he found a glossy magazine illustrated with lewdly pornographic photographs, and filled out with a minimum of text which (judging from a prevalence of ø-looking letters) Lewis took to be written in some Scandinavian tongue. If Morse had been there (Lewis knew it so well) he would have sat down on the bed forthwith and given the magazine his undivided attention; and it often puzzled Lewis a little to understand how an otherwise reasonably sensitive person such as Morse could simultaneously behave in so unworthily crude a fashion. Yet he knew that nothing was ever likely to change the melancholy, uncommitted Morse; and he put the magazine back on the shelf, deciding that his superior should know nothing of it.

In Annexe 3 itself, there were so many chalked marks, so many biro-ed circles, so many dusted surfaces, so much shifted furniture, that it was impossible to believe any clue would now be found there that had not been found already; and Lewis turned off the light and closed the door, making sure it was locked behind him.

In Annexe 1, the Palmers' room, Lewis could find nothing that he had missed in his earlier examination, and he paused only for a moment before the window, seeing his own shadow in the oblong of yellow light that was thrown across the snow, before turning the light off there too, and closing the door behind him. He would have a quick look at the last room, the Smiths' room, and then he really would call an end to his long, long day.

In this room, Annexe 2, he could find nothing of any import; and Morse (Lewis knew) would have looked over it with adequate, if less than exhaustive, care. In any case, Morse had a creative imagination that he himself could never hope to match, and often in the past there had been things – those oddly intangible things – which the careful Lewis himself had missed and which Morse had almost carelessly discovered. Yet it would do no harm to have one final eleventh-hour check before permission was given to Binyon (as soon it must be) for the rooms to be freed for hotel use once more.

It was five minutes later that Lewis made his exciting discovery.

Sarah Jonstone saw Lewis leave just before 6 p.m., his car headlights, as he turned in front of the annexe, sending revolving patches of yellow light across the walls and ceiling of her unlit room. Then the winter darkness was complete once more. She had never minded the dark, even as a little girl, when she'd always preferred the door of her bedroom shut and the light on the landing switched off; and now as she looked out she was again content to leave the light turned off. She was developing a slight headache and she had dropped two soluble Disprin into a glass of water and was slowly swishing the disintegrating tablets round. Mr Binyon had asked her to stay on another night, and in the circumstances it would have been unkind for her to refuse. But it was an oddly unsatisfactory, anti-climactic sort of time: the night was now still after so many comings and goings; the lights in the annexe all switched off, including the light in the large back room which Morse and Lewis had been using; the press, the police, the public – almost everyone seemed to have gone; gone, too, were all the New Year revellers, all of them gone back home again – all except one, of course, the one who would never see his home again. The only signs left of all the excitement were the beribboned ropes that still cordoned off the annexe area, and the single policeman in the flat, black-and-white checked hat who still stood at the side entrance of the annexe, his breath steaming in the cold air, stamping his feet occasionally, and pulling his greatcoat ever more closely around him. She was wondering if she ought to offer him something – when she heard Mandy, from just below her window, call across and ask him if he wanted a cup of tea.

She herself drank the cloudy, bitter-tasting mixture from the glass, switched on the light, washed the glass, smoothed the wrinkled coverlet on which she had earlier been lying, turned on the TV, and listened to the main items of the six-o'clock news. The world that day, that second day of the brand-new year, was familiarly full of crashes, hi-jackings, riots and terrorism; yet somehow such cataclysmic, collective disasters seemed far less disturbing to her than the murder of that one man, only some twenty-odd yards from where she stood. She turned off the TV, and went over to the window to pull the curtains across; she would smarten herself up a bit before going down to have her evening meal with the Binyons.

Odd!

A light was on again in the annexe, and she wondered who it could be. Probably the constable, for he was no longer standing by the side door. It was almost certainly in Annexe 2 that the light was on, she thought, judging from the yellow square of snow in front of the building. Then the light was switched off; and standing there at her window, arms outspread, Sarah was just about to pull the curtains across when she saw a figure, just inside the annexe doorway, pressed against the left-hand wall. Her heart seemed to miss a beat, and she felt a constriction somewhere at the back of her throat as she stood there for a few seconds completely motionless, mesmerised by what she had seen. Then she acted. She threw open the door, scampered down the stairs, rushed through to the main entrance and then along to the side door of the main building, where the constable stood talking with Mandy over a cup of steaming tea.

'There's someone across there!' Sarah whispered hoarsely as she pointed over to the annexe block.

'Pardon, miss?'

'I just saw someone in the doorway!'

The man hurried across to the annexe, with Sarah and Mandy walking nervously a few steps behind. They saw him open the side door (it hadn't been locked, that much was clear) and then watched as the light flicked on in the corridor, and then flicked off.

'There's no one there now,' said the worried-looking constable, clearly conscious of some potentially disastrous dereliction of duty.

'There *was* someone,' persisted Sarah quietly. 'It was in Annexe 2 – I'm sure of it. I saw the light on the snow.'

'But the rooms are all locked up, miss.'

Sarah said nothing. There were only two sets of master-keys, and Binyon (Sarah knew) had given one of those sets to Sergeant Lewis. But Sergeant Lewis had gone. Had Binyon used the other set *himself*? Had the slim figure she had seen in the doorway been Binyon's? And if so, what on earth—?

It was Binyon himself, wearing a raincoat but no hat, who had startlingly materialised from somewhere, and who now stood behind them, insisting (once he had asked about the nature of the incident) that they should check up on the situation forthwith.

Sarah followed him and the constable into the annexe corridor, and it was immediately apparent that someone *had* stood – and that within the last few minutes or so – in front of the door to Annexe 2. The carpet just below the handle was muddied with the marks of slushy footwear, and little slivers of yet unmelted snow winked under the neon lighting of the corridor.

Back in her room, Sarah thought hard about what had just happened. The constable had refused to let the door of Annexe 2 be touched or opened, and had immediately tried to contact Lewis at the number he had been instructed to ring should anything untoward occur. But Lewis had not yet arrived home; and this fact tended to bolster the belief, expressed by both Binyon and the constable, that it had probably been Lewis who had called back for some unexpected though probably quite simple reason. But Sarah had kept her counsel. She knew quite certainly that the figure she had glimpsed in the annexe doorway could never have been the heavily built Sergeant Lewis. *Could* it have been Mr Binyon, though? Whilst not impossible, that too, thought Sarah, was wildly improbable. And, as it happened, her view of the matter was of considerably greater value than anyone else's. Not only was she the sole witness to the furtive figure seen in the doorway; she was also the only person, at least for the present, who knew a most significant fact: the fact that although there were only two sets of master-keys to the annexe rooms, it was perfectly possible for *someone else* to have entered the room that evening without forcing a door or breaking a window. *Two other people*, in fact. On the key-board behind Reception, the hook was still empty on which should have been hanging the black-plastic oblong tab, with 'Haworth' printed over it in white, and the room key to Annexe 2 attached to it. For Mr and Mrs John Smith had left behind their unsettled account, but their room key they had taken with them.

Chapter Seventeen

Thursday, January 2nd: p.m.

Aspern Williams wanted to touch the skin of the daughter,
thinking her beautiful, by which I mean separate and to be
joined.
                Peter Champkin, *The Waking Life of Aspern Williams*

Morse walked through the carpeted lounge of the Great Western
Hotel where several couples, seemingly with little any longer to say
to each other, were desultorily engaged in reading paperbacks, consulting timetables or turning over the pages of the *London Standard*.
Time, apparently, was the chief item of importance here, where
a video-screen gave travellers up-to-the-minute information about
arrivals and departures, and where frequent glances were thrown
towards the large clock above the Porters' Desk, at which stood two
slightly supercilious-looking men in gold-braided green uniforms. It
was 5.45 p.m.
    Immediately in front of him, through the revolving door that
gave access to Praed Street, Morse could see the white lettering
of PADDINGTON on the blue Underground sign as he turned
right and made his way towards the Brunel Bar. At its entrance,
a board announced that 5.30 p.m. to 6.30 p.m. encompassed 'The
Happy Hour', with any drink available at half-price – a prospect
doubtless accounting for the throng of dark-suited black-briefcased
businessmen who stood around the bar, anxious to get in as
many drinks as possible before departing homewards to Slough
or Reading or Didcot or Swindon or Oxford. Wall-seats, all in
a deep maroon shade of velveteen nylon, lined the rectangular
bar; but after finally managing to purchase his half-priced pint of
beer, Morse sat down near the main entrance behind one of the
free-standing, mahogany-veneered tables. The tripartite glass dish
in front of him offered nuts, crisps and cheese biscuits, into which
he found himself dipping more and more nervously as the hands
of the clock crept towards 6 p.m. Almost (he knew it!) he felt
as excited as if he were a callow youth once more. It was exactly
6 p.m. when Philippa Palmer walked into the bar. For purposes of
recognition, it had been agreed that she should carry her handbag
in her left hand and a copy of the *London Standard* in her right.

But the fact that she had got things the wrong way round was of little consequence to Morse; he himself was quite incapable of any instant instinctive knowledge of east and west, and he would have spotted her immediately. Or so he told himself.

He stood up, and she walked over to him.

'Chief Inspector Morse?' Her face betrayed no emotion whatsoever: no signs of nervousness, embarrassment, co-operation, affability, humour – nothing.

'Let me get you a drink,' said Morse.

She took off her raincoat, and as Morse waited his turn again at the crowded bar he watched her from the corner of his eye: five foot five or six, or thereabouts, wearing a roll-necked turquoise-blue woollen dress which gently emphasised the rounded contours of her bottom but hardly did the rest of her figure much justice, perhaps. When he set the glass of red wine in front of her, she had crossed her nyloned legs, her slim-style high-heeled shoes accentuating the slightly excessive muscularity of her calves; and across the back of her right ankle Morse noticed a piece of Elastoplast, as though her expensive shoes probably combined the ultimate in elegance with a sorry degree of discomfort.

'I tried to run a half-marathon – for charity,' she said, following his eyes, and his thoughts.

'For the Police Welfare Fund, I trust!' said Morse lightly.

Her eyes were on the brink of the faintest smile, and Morse looked closely at her face. It was undeniably an attractive face, framed by a head of luxuriant dark-brown hair glinting overall with hints of auburn; but it was the eyes above the high cheekbones – eyes of a deep brown – that were undoubtedly the woman's most striking feature. When she had spoken (with a slight Cockney accent) she had shown rather small regular teeth behind a mouth coated with only the thinnest smear of dark-red lipstick, and a great many men (Morse knew it) would find her a very attractive woman; and more than a few would find her necessary, too.

She had quite a lot to tell, but it took no great time to tell it. She was (she admitted) a high-class call-girl, who regularly encountered her clients in the cocktail bars of the expensive hotels along Park Lane and Mayfair. Occasionally, especially in recent years with wealthy Arabian gentlemen, she would dispense her favours on the site, as it were, in the luxury apartments and penthouse suites on the higher floors of the hotels themselves. But with the majority, the more usual routine was a trip back to Chiswick in a taxi, where her own discreet flat, on the eighth (and top) floor of a private, modern block, was ideal, served as it was by a very superior lift, and where no children, pets or hawkers (in that order) were allowed. This flat she shared with a happy-souled, feckless, mightily bosomed, blonde dancer who performed in the Striporama Revue Club off Great Windmill Street; but the two of them had agreed from the start that no men visitors should ever be invited to stay overnight, and the agreement had as yet remained unbreached. So that was her CV – not much else to say, really. 'Mr Palmer', a stockbroker from Gerrards Cross, she had met several times previously; and when the prospect cropped up of a New Year conference in Oxford – well, that's how this business had all started. They needed an address for correspondence, and she, Philippa, had written and booked the room from her Chiswick flat – perfectly above board. (An address *was* needed, she insisted; and Morse refrained from arguing the dubious point.) She herself had completed the documentation for both of them at lunchtime on the 31st, though not filling in the registration number of the Porsche which they had left in the British Rail car park. He'd had a good time, her client – she was quite sure of that until . . . And then, of course, there was every chance of him being found out – 'Just like being caught by the police in a raid on a Soho sex-joint!' – and he'd asked her to settle up immediately in cash, and then he'd got the pair of them out of there in double quick time, taking her with him to the station in a taxi and leaving her on the platform. From what he'd told her, he was going to book in at the Moat Hotel (at the top of the Woodstock Road) for the rest of the conference, and keep as big a distance as he possibly could between himself and the ill-fated annexe at the Haworth. Did the inspector *really* have to know his name? And in any case she hadn't the faintest idea of his address in Gerrards Cross. Quite certainly, in her view, he could have had nothing whatsoever to do with the killing of Ballard, because when she'd gone back to her room after the party she'd actually walked across to the annexe *with Ballard*, and then gone immediately into her own room with her, well, her sleeping companion, and she could vouch for the fact that he hadn't left the room that night – or left the bed for that matter! Assuredly not!

Morse nodded, a little enviously, perhaps. 'He was a pretty rich man, then?'

'Rich enough.'

'But not rich enough to afford a room in the main hotel?'

'There weren't any rooms left. We had to take what was going.'

'I know, yes. I'm glad you're telling me the truth, Miss Palmer. I've seen your correspondence with the hotel.'

For a few seconds her dark eyes held his – eyes that seemed momentarily to have grown hard and calculating – before she continued in a somewhat casual tone: 'He gave me the cash – in £20 notes. He was happy for me to make all the arrangements.'

'You made a bit on the side, then?'

'Christ!' It seemed as if she were about to explode at such a banal accusation, and her eyes flashed darkly with anger. 'You think that I have to rely on fiddling a few quid like that to make a living?'

But Morse couldn't answer. He was furious with himself for his stupid, naïve, condescending question; and he was relieved when she agreed to a second glass of red wine.

The Happy Hour was over.

The New Year party itself? It had been good fun, really – and the food had been surprisingly good. She herself had dressed up – maybe the inspector preferred 'dressed down'? – as a Turkish belly-dancer; with her companion, to her surprise, entering into the party spirit with considerable zest and ingenuity, and fashioning for himself from the rag-bag provided by the hotel an outfit not unworthy of an Arabian sheik. Quite a success, too! Not half as good as Ballard's, of course; but then some people took these things too seriously, as *he* had done – coming along all prepared with the necessary gear and grease and everything. As far as Philippa could remember, the Ballards had come in a few minutes later than all the rest; but she wasn't really very clear about the point, or about a lot of other things that went on during that evening. There had been eating and drinking and dancing and no doubt a little bit of semi-licit smooching (yes! on her part, too – just a little) in the candle-lit ballroom, and perhaps later on still a bit of . . . Philippa appeared to have difficulty in finding the right words for what Morse took to be some incidence of *sub mensa* gropings. Ballard, she thought, hadn't really come to life until after the judging of the fancy dress, spending much of the earlier part of the evening looking into the eyes (about the only feature he could look into!) of his yashmak-ed wife – or whatever was another word for 'wife'. For it had seemed pretty clear to Philippa that she was not the only one involved that evening in extra-conjugal infidelity.

Anything else? She didn't think so. She'd already mentioned that Ballard had walked back to the annexe with her? Yes, of course she had. One arm round her, and one arm round Helen

Smith: yes, she remembered Helen Smith; *and* liked her. Liked her husband, John, too, if he *was* her – augh! What was the point? She didn't know what their relationship was, and she wasn't in the slightest degree concerned! The next day? New Year's Day? She'd had a terrible head – which only served her right; had nothing but coffee at breakfast; had missed the Treasure Hunt; had spent the hour pre-lunch in bed; had enjoyed the roast beef; had spent the hour post-lunch in bed; and had only begun to take any interest in hotel activities during the late afternoon when she'd played ping-pong with one of the young lads. Oddly enough, she had been looking forward a good deal to going to the pantomime until . . . No, she hadn't seen anything at all of Mrs Ballard all that day, not so far as she could remember; and, of course, quite certainly nothing of Mr Ballard, either . . .

Morse got another drink for each of them, conscious that he was beginning to make up questions just for the sake of things. But why not? She couldn't tell him anything of importance, he was *almost* sure of that; but she was a lovely girl to be with – he was *absolutely* sure of that! They were sitting close together now, and gently she moved her left leg against the roughish tweed of his trousers. And, just as gently, he responded, saying nothing and yet saying everything.

'Would you like to treat me to a night in the Great Western Hotel?' She asked the question confidently; and yet there had been (had Morse but known it) a vibrancy and gentleness in her voice that had seldom been heard by any other man. Morse semi-shook his head, but she knew from the slow, sad smile that played about his lips that such an immediate reaction was more the mark of sad bewilderment than of considered refusal.

'I don't snore!' said Philippa softly against his ear.

'I don't know whether I do or not,' replied Morse. He was suddenly desperately aware that the time for a decision had come; but he was conscious, too, of the need (he had drunk four pints of beer already) to relieve himself, and he left her for a while.

On his return from the ground-floor Gents', he walked over to Reception and asked the girl there whether there was a room available for the night.

'Just for yourself, is it, sir?'

'Er, no. A double room – for myself and my wife.'

'Just a second . . . No, I'm awfully sorry, sir, we've no rooms left at all this evening. But we may get a cancellation – we often get one or two about this time. Will you be in the hotel for a while, sir?'

'Yes – just for a while. I'll be in the bar.'

'Well, I'll let you know if I hear of anything. Your name, sir?'

'Er, Palmer. Mr Palmer.'

'All right, Mr Palmer.'

It was ten minutes later that the Muzak was switched off and a pleasantly clear female voice made the announcement to everyone in the Great Western Hotel, in the lounge, in the restaurant, and in the bar: 'Would Chief Inspector Morse please come to Reception immediately. Chief Inspector Morse, to Reception, please.'

He helped her on with her mackintosh, an off-white expensive creation that would have made almost any woman look adequately glamorous; and he watched her as she pulled the belt tight and evened out the folds around her slim waist.

'Been nice meeting you, Inspector.'

Morse nodded. 'We shall probably need some sort of statement.'

'I'd rather not – if you can arrange it.'

'I'll see.'

As she turned to leave, Morse noticed the grubby brown stain on the left shoulder of her otherwise immaculate raincoat: 'Were you wearing that when you left the party?' he asked.

'Yes.' She squinted down at the offending mark. 'You can't walk around semi-nude in the snow, can you?'

'I suppose not.'

'Pity, though. Cost a fiver at least to get it cleaned, that will. You'd 'a'thought, wouldn't you, if you dress up as a black guy you might keep your 'ands off . . .'

The voice had slipped, and the mask had slipped; and Morse felt a saddened man. She could have been a lovely girl, but somehow, somewhere, she was flawed. A man had been savagely murdered – a man (who knows? with maybe just a little gentleness in his heart) who after a party one night had put his left hand, sweatily stained with dark-brown stage make-up, on to a woman's shoulder; and she was angry because it would possibly cost a few pounds to get rid of a stain that might detract from her appearance. They said farewell, and Morse sought to hide his two-fold disappointment behind the mask that he, too, invariably wore for most occasions before his fellow men. Perhaps – the thought suddenly struck him – it was the masks that were the reality, and the faces beneath them that were the pretence. So many of the people in the Haworth that fatal evening had been wearing some sort of disguise – a change of dress, a change of make-up, a change of attitude, a change of partner, a change of life almost; and the man who had died had been the most consummate artist of them all.

After she had left, Morse walked back through the lounge to Reception (it *must* be Lewis who had rung for him – Lewis was the only person who had any idea where he was) and prayed that it would be a different young girl on duty. But it wasn't. Furthermore she was a girl who obviously possessed a fairly retentive memory.

'I'm afraid we haven't had any cancellations yet, Mr Palmer.'

'Oh, Christ!' muttered Morse under his breath.

Chapter Eighteen

Thursday, January 2nd: p.m.

> Men seldom make passes
> At girls who wear glasses.
> Dorothy Parker

Mr John Smith returned home that evening, unexpectedly early, to find his wife Helen in a state of tear-stained distraction; and once he had persuaded her to start talking, it was impossible to stop her . . .

Helen had caught the 3.45 train from Reading that afternoon, and arrived in Oxford at 4.20. Apart from the key to Annexe 2 which she clasped tight in the pocket of her duffel coat, she carried little else: no handbag, no wallet, no umbrella – only the return ticket to Reading, two pound coins, and a few shillings in smaller change. A taxi from Oxford station might have been sensible, but it certainly wasn't necessary; and in any case she knew that the twenty-minute walk would do her no harm. As she began to make her way to the Haworth Hotel her heart was beating as nervously as when she had opened the front passenger door of the BMW, and had frantically felt all over the floor of the car, splayed her hands across and under and down and round the sides of seats and everywhere – *everywhere*! And found nothing: nothing except a two-pence piece, a white indigestion tablet, a button from a lady's coat (not one of her own) . . .

She walked quickly past the vast glass-fronted Blackwell's building in Hythe Bridge Street, through Gloucester Green, and then along Beaumont Street into St Giles', where at the Martyrs' Memorial she crossed over to the right-hand side of the thoroughfare and, now more slowly, made her way northwards along the Banbury Road.

Opposite the Haworth Hotel she could see the two front windows of the annexe clearly – and so very near! There seemed to be some sort of light on at the back of the building somewhere; but each of the two rooms facing the street – and especially one of them, the one on the left as she watched and waited – was dark and almost certainly empty. A glass-sided bus shelter almost directly opposite the annexe protected her from the drizzle, if not from the wind, and gave her an ideal vantage point from which to keep watch without arousing suspicion. A bus came and picked up the two people waiting there, a very fat West Indian woman and a wiry little English woman, both about sixty, both (as Helen gathered) cleaners in a nearby hospice, who chatted together on such easy and intimate terms that it was tempting to be optimistic about future prospects for racial harmony. Helen stood aside – and continued to watch. Soon another bus was coming towards her, its headlights illuminating the silvery sleet; but she stood back inside the shelter, and the bus passed on without stopping. Then she saw something – something which seemed to make her heart lurch towards her mouth. A light had been turned on in the room on the right, Annexe 1: the window, its curtains undrawn, glared brightly in the darkness, and a figure was moving around inside. Then the light was switched off, and the light in the next room – *her* room – was switched on. A bus had stopped, the doors, folding inwards, inviting her to climb aboard; and she found herself apologising and seeing the look on the driver's face as he tossed his head in contempt before leaning forward over the great steering-wheel and driving away. The light was still on in Annexe 2, and she saw a figure silhouetted against the window for a few seconds; and then that light too was switched off. A man came out of the side door, walked round to the front of the annexe, immediately opposite to her, and disappeared inside; and the two rooms facing the street were dark and empty once more. *But the policeman was still there at the side entrance.* He had been there all along, his black-and-white checkered cap conspicuous under the light that illuminated the path between the Haworth Hotel and the

cordoned area of the annexe – the red, yellow and white tabs on
the ropes tilting back and forth in the keen wind.

If Helen Smith had ever been likely to despair, she would have
done so at this point. And yet somehow she knew that she would
not despair. It may have been the cold, the hopelessness, the futility
of it all; it may have been her awareness that there could be nothing
more for her to lose. She didn't know. She didn't want to know.
But she sensed within herself a feeling of wild determination that
she had never known before. Her whole being seemed polarised
between the black-and-white hat across the road and the key still
clutched so tightly and warmly in her right hand. There had to be
some way of diverting the man's attention, so that she would have
the chance to slip swiftly and silently through the side door. But it
had been so much easier than that! He had just walked across to
the main hotel, where he now stood drinking a cup of something
from a white plastic beaker, and happily engrossed in conversation
with a young woman from the hotel.

Helen was in the corridor almost before her courage had been
called upon.

No problem! With shaking hand she inserted the key in the lock
of Annexe 2, closed the door behind her, and stood stock-still for a
moment or two in the dark. Then she felt her way across to the bed
nearer the window, and ran her hands along the smooth sheets, and
beneath and around the pillow, and along the headboard, and finally
over the floor. They *had* been there: they *had* been underneath her
pillow – she *knew* it. And an embryo sob escaped her lips as again
her hands frantically, but fruitlessly, searched around. There were
two switches on the headboard, and she turned on the one above
the bed she had slept in: she *had* to make sure! For half a minute
she searched again desperately in the lighted room; but to no avail.
And now, for the first time, it was fear that clutched her heart as she
switched off the light, left the room and edged her way noiselessly
through the side door. Then she froze where she stood against the
wall. Immediately opposite, at one of the windows on the first floor
of the main hotel, a woman stood watching her – and then was gone.
Helen felt quite certain that the woman had seen her, and an icy
panic seized her. She could remember little of how she left the hotel;
but fear had given its own winged sandals to her feet.

The next thing she knew, she was walking along the Banbury
Road, a good way down from the Haworth Hotel, her heart thumping like a trip-hammer in an ironmaster's yard. She walked without looking back for a single second; she walked and walked like

some revenant Zombie, oblivious to her surroundings, still panic-stricken and trembling – yet safe, blessedly safe! At the railway station, with only ten minutes to wait, she bought herself a Scotch, and felt fractionally better. But as she sat in a deserted compartment in the slow train back to Reading, she knew that each of the wearisome stops, like the stations of the cross, was bringing her nearer and nearer to a final reckoning.

Morse had made no secret of the fact that he would be meeting Philippa Palmer at the Great Western Hotel, and had agreed that should Lewis think it necessary he might be reached there. The news *could* wait until the morning of course – Lewis knew that; and it probably wasn't crucially important in any case. Yet everyone is anxious to parade a success, and for Lewis it had been a successful evening. In Annexe 2, the room in which Mr and Mrs John Smith had spent the night of December 31st, he had found, beneath the pillow of the bed nearer the window, in a brown imitation-leather case, a pair of spectacles: small, feminine, rather fussy little things. At first he had been disappointed, since the case bore no optician's name, no address, no signification of town or county – nothing. But inside the case, squashed down at the very bottom, he had found a small oblong of yellow material for use (as Lewis knew) in the cleaning of lenses; and printed on this material were the words 'G. W. Lloyd, Opticians, High Street, Reading'. Fortunately Mr Lloyd, a garrulous Welshman hailing from Mountain Ash, had still been on the premises when Lewis rang him, and had willingly agreed to remain so until Lewis arrived. If it had taken Lewis only forty minutes to reach Reading, it had taken Lloyd only four or five to discover the owner of the lost spectacles. In his neat records the resourceful Lloyd kept full information about all his clients: this defect, that defect; long sight, short sight; degrees of astigmatism; type of spectacle frames; private or NHS. And tracing the spectacles had been almost childishly easy. Quite an able fellow, Lewis decided, this little Welshman who had opted for ophthalmology.

'I found them under the pillow, sir,' said Lewis when he finally got through to Morse at Paddington.
    'Did you?'
    'I thought it wouldn't perhaps do any harm just to check up on things a bit.'
    'Check up on me, you mean!'
    'Well, we can all miss things.'

'You mean to say they were there when I looked over that room? Come off it, Lewis! You don't honestly think I'd have missed something like that, do you?'

The thought that the spectacles had been planted in Annexe 2 by some person or other *after* Morse had searched the room had not previously occurred to Lewis, and he was beginning to wonder about the implications of such a strange notion when Morse spoke again.

'I'm sorry.'

'Pardon, sir?'

'I said I'm sorry, that's all. I must have missed the bloody things! And there's something else I want to say. Well done! No wonder I sometimes find it useful having you around, my old friend.'

Lewis was looking very happy when, after giving Morse the Smiths' address, he put down the phone, thanked the optician, and drove straight back to Oxford. He and Morse had agreed not to try to see either of the mysterious Smith couple until the following day. And Lewis was glad of that since he was feeling very tired indeed.

Mrs Lewis could see that her husband was happy when he finally returned home just before 9 p.m. She cooked him egg and chips and once again marvelled at the way in which Chief Inspector Morse could, on occasions, have such a beneficent effect upon the man she'd married. But she was very happy herself, too; she was always happy when he was.

Deciding, after he had finished his telephone conversation with Lewis, that he might just as well stay on in London and then stop off at Reading the following morning on his return to Oxford, Morse approached the receptionist (the same one) for the third time, and asked her sweetly whether she could offer him a single room for the night. Which she could, for there had been a cancellation. The card which she gave him Morse completed in the name of Mr Philip Palmer, of Irish nationality, and handed it back to her. As she gave him his room key, the girl looked at him with puzzlement in her eyes, and Morse leaned over and spoke quietly to her. 'Just one little t'ing, miss. If Chief Inspector Morse happens to call, please send him up to see me immediately, will you?'

The receptionist, now utterly bewildered, looked at him with eyes that suggested that either he was quite mad, or she was. And when he walked off towards the main staircase, she wondered whether she should ring the duty manager and acquaint him with her growing suspicion that she might have just booked an IRA terrorist into the hotel. But she decided against it. If he had a bomb with him, it was quite certainly not in his suitcase, for he had no suitcase; had no luggage at all, in fact – not even a toothbrush by the look of things.

Chapter Nineteen

January 2nd/3rd

Love is strong as death; jealousy is cruel as the grave.
                                        Song of Solomon 8:6

The whole desperate business had acquired a gathering momentum born of its own progress. It was, for Margaret Bowman, like driving a car whose brakes had failed down an ever more steeply inclined gradient – where the only thing to do was to try to steer the accelerating vehicle with the split-second reactions of a racing driver and to pray that it would reach the bottom without a fatal collision. To stop was utterly impossible.

It had been about a year ago when she had first become aware that her husband was showing unmistakable signs of becoming a semi-drunkard. There would be days when he would not touch a drop of alcohol; but there were other periods when two or three times a week she would return from work to find him in a sort of slow-thinking half-daze after what must clearly have been fairly pro-longed bouts of drinking, about which her own occasional criticism had served merely to trigger off an underlying crude and cruel streak in his nature which had greatly frightened her. Had it been because of his drinking that (for the first time in their marriage) she had been unfaithful to him? She wasn't sure. Possibly – probably, even – she might in any case have drifted into some sort of illicit liaison with one or two of the men she had recently got to know at work. Everyone changed as the years went by, she knew that. But Tom, her husband, seemed to have undergone a fundamental change of character, and she had become increasingly terrified of him finding out about her affair, and deeply worried about what dreadful things he would do to her; and to *him*, and perhaps to himself, if he ever

did find out. Her infidelity had spanned the late summer and most
of the autumn before she began to realise that any affair was just
as fraught with risk as marriage was. For the first few weeks, a
single afternoon a week had sufficed: he, by regulating his varied
weekend workings, was able to take a day off every week, and this
was easily synchronised with her own afternoon off (on Thursdays)
when the pair of them made love in the bedroom of an erstwhile
council house in North Oxford which he now owned himself. That
had been the early pattern; and for the first two or three months
he had been interesting to be with, considerate, anxious to please.
But as time went on, he too (just like her husband) had appeared
to change: he became somewhat crude in one or two respects,
more demanding, less talkative, with (quite clearly to Margaret
Bowman) his own craving for sexual gratification dominating their
post-meridian copulations. Progressively he'd wished to see her
more often, ever badgering her to fabricate for her employers a
series of visits to dentists, doctors and terminally ill relatives; or to
take home to her husband tales of overtime working necessitated
by imaginary backlogs. And while she despised the man to some
degree for so obviously allowing all his professed love for her to
degenerate into an undisguised lust, yet there was a physical side to
her own nature, at once as crude and selfish and demanding as his,
which welded them into an almost perfect partnership between the
sheets. The simple truth was that the more he used and abused her,
the more sexual satisfaction he managed to wring from her, the
more she was conscious of her pride in being the physical object of
his apparently insatiable appetite for her body. Indeed, as the year
moved into its last quarter, she began to suspect that she needed
him almost as much as he needed her, although for a long time
she refused to countenance, even to herself, the full implications
of such a suspicion. But then she was forced to face them. He was
soon making *too* many demands upon her, begging her to be with
him even for an odd half hour at lunchtimes when (truth to tell) she
would more often than not have preferred a glass of red wine and
a ham sandwich with her friend and colleague Gladys Taylor in the
Dew Drop. And then had come the show-down, as perhaps she'd
known would be inevitable. He'd asked her to leave her husband
and come to live with him: it was about time, surely, that she left
the man she didn't love and moved in with the one she did. And
although coming within an ace of saying 'yes', she'd finally said 'no'.

Why Margaret Bowman had thus refused, she would herself have
found difficult to explain. Perhaps it was because (for the present

at least) it was all far too much *bother*. The rather dull, the slightly overweight, the only semi-successful man who was her husband, was the man with whom she had shared so much for so many years now. And there were far too many other shared things to think of packing everything up just like that: payments on the car, life insurances, the house mortgage, family friends and relations, neighbours – even the disappointments and the quarrels and the boredoms, which all seemed to form a strangely binding sort of tie between them. Yet there was perhaps, too, one quite specific reason why she had refused. Gladys (Margaret had come to work in the same section as Gladys in the spring) had become a genuine friend; and one day in the Dew Drop she had told Margaret how she had been temporarily jilted by her husband, and how for many months after that she had felt so hurt and so belittled that she'd wondered whether she would ever be able to lift up her head in life again. 'Having had it done to me' (she'd confided) 'I couldn't ever think of doing it to anyone else.' It had been a simple little thing to say, and it had not been said with any great moral fervour; yet it had made its point with memorable effect . . .

That particular Thursday afternoon when she had finally said 'no' they'd had their first blazing row, and she had been alarmed by the look of potential violence in his eyes. Although he had finally calmed down, she found herself making excuses for the whole of the next week, including the hitherto sacrosanct p.m. period on Thursday. It had been a sad mistake, though, since the following fortnight had been a nightmare. He had rung her at work, where she had taken the message in front of all the other women in the section, their eyes glued on her as (nonchalantly, she hoped) she promised to get in touch. Which she *had* done, asking him sensibly, soberly, just to let things ride for a few weeks and see if they would sort themselves out. Then there had been the first letter, addressed to her at work – pleasantly, lovingly, imploring her to go back to the old pattern of their former meetings. And then, when she did not reply to the first letter, a second one, which was addressed to her home and which she'd picked up from the front-hall mat at eight o'clock on a wet and miserable November morning *when she was going to a funeral*. Tom was still in bed, and she'd hurriedly torn the envelope open and looked through the letter – the cruel, vindictive, frightening letter which she'd quickly stuck into the bottom of her handbag as she heard the creak at the top of the stairs.

When, that same morning, her husband sat opposite her at the kitchen table, she seemed engrossed in the half dozen brochures she had picked up the previous lunchtime in Summertown Travel, giving details of trips ranging from gentle strolls round the hill-forts of Western England to lung-racking rambles in the Himalayan foothills. *Yet how fervently at that moment did she wish her lover dead!*

Tom Bowman had not told his wife about his discovery of the letter until the following Wednesday evening. It had been a harrowing occasion for her, but Tom had not flown into a rage or threatened her with physical violence. In retrospect, she almost wished he had done so; for far more frightening, and something that sent the four guardians scurrying from the portals of her sanity, was the change that seemed to have come over him: there was a hardness in his voice and in his eyes; an unsuspected deviousness about his thinking; a firmness of purpose about his frightening suggestions; and, underlying all (she suspected), a terrifyingly vicious and unforgiving jealousy against the man who had tried to rob him of his wife. What he said that evening was so fatuous really, so fanciful, so silly, that his words had not registered with her as forming any plausible or practicable plan of revenge. Yet slowly and inexorably the ideas which he had outlined to her that evening had set in motion a self-accelerating series of events which had culminated in murder.

Even now, right at the end of things, she was aware of the ambivalence of all her thoughts, her motives, her hopes – and her mind would give her no rest. After watching the late-night news on BBC 2 she took four Aspirin tablets and went to bed, where (wonderfully!) she fell easily enough into sleep. But by a quarter past one she was awake once more, and for the next four hours her darting eyes could not remain still for a second in their burning sockets as the whirligig of her brain sped round and round without any hint of slowing down, as if the fairground operator had pushed the lever forward on to 'Fast' and then fallen into an insensate stupor over the controls.

That same night, the night of January 2nd, Morse himself had a pleasantly refreshing sleep, with a mildly erotic dream (about a woman with a large Elastoplast over one ankle) thrown in for good measure. He told himself, on waking at 6.30 a.m., that if only there had been a double room available the night before . . . But he had never been a man to be unduly perturbed by the 'if onlys' of life, and he possessed a wholly enviable capacity for discounting most disappointments. Remembering a programme he had heard the previous week on cholesterol (a programme which the Lewis family had obviously missed), Morse decided to forgo the huge and rare treat of a fried breakfast in the restaurant, and caught the 9.10

train to Reading from platform 2. In the second-class compartment in which he made the journey were two other persons: in one corner, an (equally unshaven) Irishman who said nothing whatsoever after a polite 'Good morning, sorr!' but who thereafter smiled perpetually as though the day had dawned exceedingly bright; and in the other corner, a pretty young girl wearing (as Morse recognised it) a Lady Margaret Hall scarf, who scowled unceasingly as she studied a thick volume of anthropological essays, as though the world had soured and worsened overnight.

It seemed, to Morse, a metaphor.

Chapter Twenty

Friday, January 3rd: a.m.

There's a kind of release
And a kind of torment in every goodbye for every man.

C. Day Lewis

For many hours before Morse had woken, Helen Smith had been lying wide-awake in bed, anticipating the worries that would doubtless beset her during the coming day. After her dreadful ordeal of the previous day, it had been wonderfully supportive of John to show such understanding and forgiveness; indeed, he had almost persuaded her that, even if she *had* left anything potentially incriminating behind, police resources were so overstretched in coping with major felonies that it was very doubtful whether anyone would find the time to pursue their own comparatively minor misdemeanours. And at that point, she had felt all the old love for him which she had known five years previously when they had met in Yugoslavia, her native country; and when after only two weeks' courtship she had agreed to marry him and go to live in England. He had given her the impression then – very much so! – of being a reasonably affluent businessman; and in any case she was more than glad to get away from a country in which her family lived under the shadow of a curiously equivocal incident from the past, in which her paternal grandfather, for some mysterious reason, had been shot by the Titoists outside Trieste. But from the earliest days in England she had become aware of her husband's strange lifestyle, of his dubious background, of his shady present, and of his far from glittering prospects for the future. Yet in her own quiet, gentle way, she had learned to love him, and to perform (without overmuch reluctance) the rôle that she was called upon to play.

At 7.30 a.m. they sat opposite each other over the pine-wood table in the small kitchen of their rented property, having a breakfast of grapefruit juice, toast and marmalade, and coffee. When they had finished, John Smith looked across at his wife and put his hand over hers. In his eyes she was still a most attractive woman – that at least was a point on which he had no need to lie. Her legs, for the purist, were perhaps a little too slim; and likewise her bust was considerably less bulging than the amply bosomed models who unfailingly featured on one of the earlier pages of their daily newspaper; her face had a pale, Slavonic cast, with a slightly pitted, rather muddy-looking skin; but the same face, albeit somewhat sullen in repose, was ever irradiated when she smiled, the intense, greenish eyes flashing into life, and the lips curling back over her regular teeth. She was smiling, though a little sadly, even now.

'Thank you!' she said.

At 8 a.m. John Smith told his wife that he wanted her to go up to the January sales in Oxford Street and buy herself a new winter coat. He gave her five £20 notes, and would countenance no refusal. He took her down to the station in the car, and waited on the platform with her until the 8.40 '125' pulled in to carry her off to the West End.

As her train drew into Paddington's platform 5 at 9.10 a.m., another '125' was just pulling out of platform 2 and soon gliding along the rails at a high, smooth speed towards Reading. In a second-class compartment (as we have already seen), rather towards the rear of this train, and with only two wholly uncommunicative fellow-passengers for company, sat Morse, reading the *Sun*. At home he invariably took *The Times*, though not because he much enjoyed it, or even read it (apart from the letters page and the crossword); much more because the lady local councillor who ran the newsagent's shop down in Summertown was fully aware of Morse's status, and had (to Morse's knowledge) more than once referred to him as 'a really civilised gentleman'; and he had no wish prematurely to destroy such a flattering illusion.

If the serious-minded undergraduette from Lady Margaret Hall had bothered to lift her eyes from her reading, she would have seen a man of medium height who had filled out into a somewhat barrel-shaped figure, with his waist and stomach measurements little altered from his earlier days and yet with his shirt now stretching tight around his chest. His unshaven jowls (the young student might have thought) suggested an age of nearer sixty than fifty (in fact, the man was fifty-four), and his face seemed cast in a slightly melancholy mould, not at all brightened that morning by the insistence of the young ticket-collector that he was obliged to pay a surcharge on the day-return ticket he had paid for the previous evening.

The taxi carrying its fare from Reading railway station to the Smiths' newly discovered address was told to pull up fifty yards into Eddleston Road, where Morse told the driver to wait as he walked across the road and rang the bell on the door of number 45.

When John Smith turned into the street, he immediately saw the taxi opposite his house, and stopped dead in his tracks at the corner shop where he appeared to take an inordinate interest in the hundred-and-one rectangular white notices which announced a multitude of wonderful bargains, from a pair of training shoes (hardly ever worn) to a collection of Elvis Presley records (hardly ever played). The taxi's exhaust was still running, sending a horizontal stream of vapour across the lean, cold air; and reflected in the corner-shop window Smith could see a man in an expensive-looking dark-grey overcoat seemingly reluctant to believe that neither of the occupants of the house could be at home. Finally, slowly, the importunate caller walked away from the house, stood back to take a last look at the property, and then got back into the taxi, which was off immediately in a spurt of dirty slush.

John Smith entered the shop, purchased a packet of twenty Silk Cut, and stood for three or four minutes at the magazine rack leafing through *Wireless Weekly*, *Amateur Photographer* and the *Angling Times*. But apparently he had decided that none of these periodicals was exactly indispensable, and he walked out empty-handed into the street. He had always prided himself on being able to sniff out danger a mile away. But he sensed there was none now; and he strolled down the street with exaggerated unconcern, and let himself into number 45.

He had a fastidiously tidy mind, and even now was tempted to wash up the few breakfast things that stood in the kitchen sink, particularly the two knives that looked almost obscenely sticky from the polyunsaturated Flora and Cooper's Thick-cut Oxford Marmalade. But the walls were closing in, he knew it. The BMW would have been the riskiest thing; and half an hour ago he had sold the three-year-old beauty at Reading Motors for a ridiculously low-pitched £6,000 in cash. Then he had gone along to the town-centre branch of Lloyds Bank, where he had withdrawn (again in cash) the £1,200 which stood in the joint account of John and Helen Smith.

Helen had spent a brief but successful time in Selfridges (she had bought herself a new white mackintosh) and was back in the house just after noon, when she immediately saw the note beside the telephone.

Helen, my love!
They are on to us, and there's little option for me but to get away. I never told you quite everything about myself but please believe that if they catch up with me now I shall be sent to prison for a few years – I can't face that. I thought they might perhaps confiscate the little savings we managed to put together, and so I cashed the lot and you'll find thirty £20 notes in your favourite little hiding place – that's a precaution just in case the police get here before you find this! If I ever loved anyone in the world, I loved you. Remember that! I'm sorry it's got to be like this.

Ever yours,
John

She read the brief letter without any sense of shock – almost with a sense of resigned relief. It couldn't have gone on for ever, that strange life she'd led with the oddly maverick confidence-man who had married her, and who had almost persuaded her at times that he loved her. Yes, that was the only really deep regret: if he had *stayed* – stayed with her and faced the music whatever tune they played – then life would indeed have been an undoubted triumph for the dark young lady from Yugoslavia.

She was upstairs in the front bedroom, changing her clothes, when she heard the front-door bell.

Chapter Twenty-one

Friday, January 3rd: mostly a.m.

As when heaved anew
Old ocean rolls a lengthened wave to shore
Down whose green back the short-lived foam, all hoar
Bursts gradual, with a wayward indolence.

John Keats

Morse had felt tempted to ring Lewis and tell him not to bother with their original plan of meeting in Eddleston Road at 11 a.m. But he didn't so do. The prospect of more trains and more taxis was an intolerable one; and in any case he was now almost completely out of ready cash. At 10.50 he was again knocking on the door of the Smiths' house; once again without getting any reply. The road was part of a reasonably elegant residential quarter. But leading off from it, on the southern side, were smaller, meaner streets of Victorian two-storey red-brick terraced houses; and as Morse strolled through this area he began to feel pleasantly satisfied with life, a state of mind that may not have been unconnected with the fact that he was in unfamiliar circumstances, with nothing immediately or profitably to be performed, with a small public house on the next corner facing him and with his wrist-watch showing only a minute or so short of opening time.

The Peep of Dawn (as engagingly named a pub as Morse could remember) boasted only one bar, with wooden wall-seats, and after finding out from the landlord which bitter the locals drank he sat with his pint in the window alcove and supped contentedly. He wasn't quite sure whether his own oft-repeated insistence that he could always think more lucidly after an extra ration of alcohol was wholly true. He certainly *believed* it to be true, though; and quite certainly many a breakthrough in previous investigations had been made under such attendant circumstances. It was only in recent months that he had found himself querying his earlier assumption about such a *post hoc, ergo propter hoc* proposition; and it had occasionally occurred to him that fallacious logic was not infrequently the offspring of wishful thinking. Yet for Morse (and he quite simply accepted the fact) the world *did* invariably seem a much warmer, more manageable place after a few pints of beer; and quite certainly he knew that (for himself, at any rate) it was on such occasions that the imaginative processes usually *started*. It may have been something to do with the very *liquidity* of alcohol, for he had often seen these processes in terms of just such a metaphor. It was as if he were lulled and sitting idly on the sea-front, and watching, almost entranced, as some great Master of the Tides drew in the foam-fringed curtains of the waters towards his feet and then pulled them back in slow retreat to the creative sea.

But whatever the truth of the matter, he knew he would have to do some serious thinking very soon, and for the moment the problem that was uppermost in his mind was how a letter which had been written from a non-existent address had also been received at the very same non-existent address. It was easy of course to write any-thing *from* anywhere in the world – say from 'Buckingham Palace, Kidlington'; but how on earth, in turn, was it possible for a letter to be delivered *to* such improbably registered premises? Yet that is what *had* happened, or so it seemed. The man who had been murdered was, on the face of things, the husband of a woman who had booked a room from an address which did not exist; had booked the room by letter; and had received confirmation of the booking, also by letter – with the pair of them duly arriving on December 31st, taking part in the evening's festivities (incidentally, with outstanding success), and finally, after joining their fellow guests in wishing themselves, one and all, a happily prosperous new year, walking back to their room in the annexe. And then . . .

'You'd not forgotten me, had you?' said a voice above him.

'Lewis! You're a bit late aren't you?'

'We agreed to meet at the house, if you remember, sir!'

'I went there. There's no one at home.'

'I *know* that. Where do you think *I've* been?'

'What's the time now?'

'Twenty past eleven.'

'Oh dear! I am sorry! Get yourself a drink, Lewis – and a refill for me, please. I'm a bit short of cash, I'm afraid.'

'Bitter, was it?'

Morse nodded. 'How did you find me?'

'I'm a detective. Had you forgotten that, too?'

But it would have taken more than Morse's meanness with money, and more than Morse's cavalier notions of punctuality, to have dashed Lewis's good spirits that morning. He told Morse all about his encounter with the Welsh optician; and Morse, in turn, told Lewis (almost) all about his encounter with the fair Philippa at

Paddington. At a quarter to twelve Lewis made another fruitless visit to Eddleston Road. But half an hour later, this time with Morse, it was immediately clear that someone had returned to number 45. It was the only house in the row whose occupants had dispensed with the need for keeping its front garden in any neat trim by the simple (albeit fairly drastic) expedient of covering the whole area with small beige pebbles, which crunched noisily as the two men walked up the sinking shingle to the door.

Chapter Twenty-two

Friday, January 3rd: p.m.

You can fool too many of the people too much of the time.
             James Thurber

Throughout the whole of the last five years (admitted Helen Smith) the two of them had successfully contrived to defraud dozens of honourable institutions of their legitimate income. But neither her husband John nor herself had the means whereby to make any reparation even fractionally commensurate with such deceit. She, Helen, fully understood why society at large should expect some expiation for her sins; but (she stressed the point) if such compensation were to be index-linked to its £. s. d. equivalents, there was no prospect whatsoever of any settlement of the overdue account. She showed Lewis the note she had found on her return from London; and would be happy to show him, too, the little hidey-hole beneath the second floorboard from the left in the spare bedroom where she had duly found the £600 referred to – that is if Lewis wanted to see it. (Lewis didn't.) Unshakeably, however, she refused to hazard any information about where her husband might have made for; and indeed her refusal was genuinely founded in total ignorance, both of his present whereabouts and of his future plans.

  The pattern had seldom varied: ringing round half a dozen hotels at holiday periods; taking advantage of late cancellations (an almost inevitable occurrence); there and then accepting, by phone, any vacancy which so lately had arisen; promising a.s.a.p. a confirmatory

letter (with both parties appreciating the unreliability of holiday-
time postal services); staying only two nights where 'The Businessman's Break' was scheduled for three; or staying just the one night
where it was scheduled for two. And that was about it. Easy enough.
There were of course always a few little secrets about such professional deception: for example, it was advisable *always* to carry
as little baggage as was consistent with reasonably civilised standards
of hygiene; again, it was advisable *never* to park a car on the
hotel premises, or to fill in the section on the registration form
asking for car-licence numbers. Yet there was one principle above
all that had to be understood, namely, that the more demands you
made upon the establishment, the more enhanced would be your
status vis-à-vis the management and staff of all hotels. Thus it was
that the Smiths had learned *always* to select their meals from the
higher echelons of the *à la carte* specialities of the chef, and wines
and liqueurs from any over-valued vintage; to demand room-service
facilities at the most improbable periods of day or night; and, finally,
never to exchange too many friendly words with anyone in sight –
from the manager down, through receptionist to waitress, porter or
cleaner. Such (Helen testified) were the basic principles she and her
husband had observed in their remarkably successful bid to extract
courtesy and respect from some of the finest hotels across the length
and breadth of the United Kingdom. The only thing then left to be
staged was their disappearance, which was best effected during that
period when no one normally booked out of hotels – mid-afternoon.
And that had usually been the time when the Smiths had decided
to take leave of their erstwhile benefactors – sans warning, sans
farewell, sans payment, sans everything.

When Helen Smith came to court (inevitably so, as Lewis saw
things) it seemed wholly probable that this darkly attractive,
innocent-looking defendant would plead guilty to the charges
brought against her, and would pretty certainly ask, too, for one-
hundred-and-one other offences to be taken into consideration. But
she hardly looked or sounded like a criminal, and her account of
the time she had spent at the Haworth Hotel appeared honest and
clear. Four (yes!) bottles of champagne had been ordered – they
both liked the lovely stuff! – two on New Year's Eve and two on
New Year's Day, with the last of the four still in the larder if
Lewis wanted to see it. (Lewis did.) Yes, she remembered a few
things about the Ballards, *and* about the Palmers; but her recollections of specific times and specific details were even hazier than

Philippa Palmer's had been the previous evening. Like Philippa, though, she thought that the evening had been well organised – and great fun; and that the food and drink had been very good indeed. The Smiths, both of them, enjoyed fancy-dress parties; and that New Year's Eve they had appeared – an oddly uncomplementary pair! – as a seductive Cleopatra and as a swordless Samurai. Would Lewis like to see the costumes? (Lewis would.) Whether Ballard had eaten much or drunk much that evening, she couldn't remember with any certainty. But she did remember, most clearly, Ballard walking back with her through the snow (Oh yes! it had been snowing heavily then) to the hotel annexe, and ruining the right shoulder-lapel of her mackintosh, where his right hand had left a dirty dark-brown stain – which of course Lewis could see if he so desired. (As Lewis did.)

During the last part of this interview Morse had seemed only minimally interested in Lewis's interrogation, and had been leafing through an outsize volume entitled *The Landscape of Thomas Hardy*. But now, suddenly, he asked a question.

'Would you recognise *Mrs* Ballard if you saw her again?'

'I – I don't really know. She was in fancy dress and—'

'In a yashmak, wasn't she?'

Helen nodded, somewhat abashed by the brusqueness of his questions.

'Didn't she *eat* anything?'

'Of course, yes.'

'But you can't eat anything in a yashmak!'

'No.'

'You must have *seen* her face, then?'

Helen knew that he was right; and suddenly, out of the blue, she *did* remember something. 'Yes,' she began slowly. 'Yes, I did see her face. Her top lip was a bit red, and there were red sort of pin-pricks – you know, sort of little red spots . . .'

But even as Helen spoke these words, her own upper lip was trembling uncontrollably, and it was clear that the hour of questioning had left her spirits very low indeed. The tears were suddenly springing copiously and she turned her head sharply away from the two policemen in total discomfiture.

In the car, Lewis ventured to ask whether it might not have been wiser to take Helen Smith back to Oxford there and then for further questioning. But Morse appeared unenthusiastic about any such immediate move, asserting that, compared with the likes of Marcinkus & Co. in the Vatican Bank, John and Helen Smith were sainted folk in white array.

It was just after they had turned on to the A34 that Morse mentioned the strange affair of the yashmak-ed lady's upper lip.

'How did you guess, Lewis?' he asked.

'It's being married, sir – so I don't suppose you ought to blame yourself too much for missing it. You see, most women like to look their best when they go away, let's say for a holiday or a trip abroad or something similar; and the missus has a bit of trouble like that – you know, a few unsightly hairs growing just under the chin or a little fringe of hairs on the top lip. A lot of women have the same trouble especially if they've got darkish sort of hair—'

'But your missus has got *fair* hair!'

'All right; but it happens to everybody a bit as they get older. You get rather self-conscious and embarrassed about it if you're a woman, so you often go to one of the hair clinics like the *Tao* or something and they give you electrolysis and they put a needle sort of thing into the roots of the hairs and – well, sort of get rid of them. Costs a bit though, sir!'

'But being a rich man you can just about afford to let the missus go along to one of these beauty parlours?'

'Just about!'

Lewis suddenly put down his foot with a joyous thrust, turned on his right-hand flasher, took the police car up to 95 m.p.h., veered in a great swoop across the outside lane, and netted a dozen lorries and cars which had thoughtfully decelerated to the statutory speed limit as they'd noticed the white car looming up in their rear mirrors.

'The treatment they give you,' continued Lewis, 'makes the skin go a bit pinkish all over and they say if it's on the top lip it's very sensitive and you often get a histamine reaction – and a sort of tingling sensation . . .'

But Morse was no longer listening. His own body was tingling too; and there crossed his face a beatific smile as Lewis accelerated the police car faster still towards the City of Oxford.

Back in Kidlington HQ, Morse decided that they had spent quite long enough in the miserably cold and badly equipped room at the back of the Haworth annexe, and that they should now transfer things back home, as it were.

'Shall I go and get a few new box-files from the stores?' asked Lewis. Morse picked up two files which were heavily bulging with excess paper, and looked cursorily through their contents.

'These'll be OK. They're both OBE.'

'OBE, sir?'

Morse nodded: 'Overtaken By Events.'

The phone rang half an hour later and Morse heard Sarah Jonstone's voice at the other end. She'd remembered a little detail about Mrs Ballard; it might be silly of her to bother Morse with it, but she could almost swear that there had been a little red circular sticker – an RSPCA badge, she thought – on Mrs Ballard's coat when she had booked in at registration on New Year's Eve.

'Well,' said Morse, 'we've not done a bad job between us, Lewis. We've managed to find two of the three women we were after – and it's beginning to look as if it's not going to be very difficult to find the last one! Not tonight, though. I'm tired out – and I could do with a bath, and a good night's sleep.'

'*And* a shave, sir!'

Chapter Twenty-three

Saturday, January 4th

Arithmetic is where the answer is right and everything is nice and you can look out of the window and see the blue sky – or the answer is wrong and you have to start all over and try again and see how it comes out this time.

Carl Sandburg, *Complete Poems*

The thaw continued overnight, and lawns that had been totally subniveal the day before were now resurfacing in patches of irregular green under a blue sky. The bad weather was breaking; the case, it seemed, was breaking too.

At Kidlington HQ Morse was going to be occupied (he'd said) with other matters for most of the morning; and Lewis, left to his own devices, was getting progressively more and more bogged down in a problem which at the outset had looked comparatively simple. The Yellow Pages had been his starting point, and under 'Beauty Salons and Consultants' he found seven or eight addresses in Oxford which advertised specialist treatment in what was variously called Waxing, Facials, or Electrolysis; with another five in Banbury; three more (a gloomier Lewis noticed) in Bicester; and a good many other establishments in individual places that could be reached without too much travelling by a woman living in Chipping Norton – if (and in Lewis's mind it was a biggish 'if') 'Mrs Ballard' *was* in fact a citizen of Chipping Norton.

But there were *two* quadratic equations, as it were, from which to work out the unknown 'x': and it was the second of these – the cross-check with the charity flag-days – to which Lewis now directed his thinking. In recent years, the most usual sort of badge received from shakers of collection tins had come in the form of a little circular sticker that was pressed on to the lapel of the contributor's coat; and Lewis's experience was that such a sticker often fell off after a few minutes rather than stuck on for several days. And so Morse's view, Lewis agreed, was probably right: if Mrs Ballard was still wearing a sticker on New Year's Eve, she'd probably bought it the same day, or the day before at the very outside. But Lewis had considerable doubts about Morse's further confidently stated conviction that there must have been an RSPCA flag day in Oxford on the 30th or 31st, and that Mrs Ballard had bought a flag as she went into a beauty salon in the city centre. 'Beautifully simple!' Morse had said. 'We've got the time, we've got the place – and we've almost got the woman, agreed? Just a little phoning around and . . .'

But Lewis had got off to a bad start. His first call elicited the disappointing information that the last street-collection in Oxford for the RSPCA had been the previous July; and he had no option but to start making another list, and a very long list at that. First came the well-known medical charities, those dealing with multiple sclerosis, rheumatoid arthritis, heart diseases, cancer research, blindness, deafness, *et cetera*; then the major social charities, ranging from Christian Aid and Oxfam to War on Want and the Save the Children Fund, *et cetera*; next came specific societies that looked after ambulancemen, lifeboatmen and ex-servicemen, *et cetera*; finally were listed the local charities which funded hospices for the terminally ill, hostels for the criminally sick or the mentally unbalanced, *et cetera*. Lewis could have added scores of others – and he knew he was getting into an awful mess. He could even have added the National Association for the Care and Resettlement of Criminal Offenders. But he didn't.

Clearly some sort of selection was required, and he would

have been more than glad to have Morse at his side at that moment. It was like being faced with a difficult maths problem at school: if you weren't careful, you got more and more ensnared in some increasingly complex equations – until the master showed you a beautifully economic short-cut that reduced the problem to a few simple little sums and produced a glittering (and correct) solution at the foot of the page. But his present master, Morse, was still apparently otherwise engaged, and so he decided to begin in earnest: on the second of the two equations.

Yet an hour later he had advanced his knowledge of charity collections in Oxford not one whit; and he was becoming increasingly irritated with telephone numbers which didn't answer when called, or which (if they did answer) appeared manned by voluntary envelope-lickers, decorators, caretakers or idiots – or (worst of all!) by intimidating answering machines telling Lewis to start speaking 'now'. And after a further hour of telephoning, he hadn't found a single charitable organisation which had held a flag day in Oxford – or anywhere else in the vicinity, for that matter – in the last few days of December.

He was getting, ridiculously, nowhere; and he said as much when Morse finally put in another appearance at 11 a.m. with a cup of coffee and a digestive biscuit, both of which (mistakenly) Lewis thought his superior officer had brought in for him.

'We need some of those men we've been promised, sir.'

'No, no, Lewis! We don't want to start explaining everything to a load of squaddies. Just have a go at the clinic angle if the other's no good. I'll come and give you a hand when I get the chance.'

So Lewis made another start – this time on those Oxford hair-clinics which had bothered to take a few centimetres of advertising space in the Yellow Pages: only four of them, thank goodness! But once again the problem soon began to take on unexpectedly formidable dimensions as he began to consider the sort of questions he could ask a clinic manageress – *if* she was on the premises. For what *could* he ask? He wanted to find out if a woman whose name he didn't know, whose appearance he could only very imperfectly describe, and of whose address he hadn't the faintest notion, except perhaps that it might just be in Chipping Norton – whether such a woman had been in for some unspecified treatment, but probably upper-lip depilation, at some unspecified time, though most probably on the morning of, let him say, any of the last few days of December. What a farce, thought Lewis; and what a fruitless farce it did in fact become. The first of the clinics firmly refused to answer questions, even to the police, about such 'strictly confidential' matters; the second was quite happy to inform him that it had no customers whatsoever on its books with an address in Chipping Norton; a recorded message informed him that the third would re-open after the New Year break on January 6th; and the fourth suggested, politely enough, that he must have misread the advertisement: that whilst it cut, trimmed, singed and dyed, the actual *removal* of hair was not included amongst its splendid services.

Lewis put down the phone – and capitulated. He went over to the canteen and found Morse – the only one there – drinking another cup of coffee and just completing *The Times* crossword puzzle.

'Ah, Lewis. Get yourself a coffee! Any luck yet?'

'No, I bloody haven't,' snapped Lewis – a man who swore, at the very outside, about once a fortnight. 'As I said, sir, I need some help: half a dozen DCs – that's what I need.'

'I don't think it's necessary, you know.'

'Well, I *do*!' said Lewis, looking as angry as Morse had ever seen him, and about to use up a whole month's ration of blasphemies. 'We're not even sure the bloody woman *does* come from Chipping Norton. She might just as well come from Chiswick – like the tart you met in Paddington!'

'Lew-is! Lew-is! Take it *easy*! I'm sure that neither the "Palmers" nor the Smiths had anything at all to do with the murder. And when I said just now it wasn't necessary to bring any more people in on the case, I didn't mean that you couldn't have as many as you like – if you really need them. But not for this particular job, Lewis, I don't think. I didn't want to disturb you, so I've been doing a bit of phoning from here; and I'm waiting for a call that ought to come through any minute. And if it tells me what I think it will, I reckon we know exactly who this "Mrs Ballard" is, and exactly where we should be able to find her. Her name's Mrs Bowman – Mrs Margaret Bowman. And do you know where she lives?'

'Chipping Norton?' suggested Lewis, in a rather wearily defeated tone.

Chapter Twenty-four

Sunday, January 5th

A man is in general better pleased when he has a good dinner upon his table than when his wife talks Greek.

Samuel Johnson

Morse had been glad to accept Mrs Lewis's invitation to her traditional Sunday lunch of slightly undercooked beef, horseradish sauce, velvety-flat Yorkshire pudding, and roast potatoes; and the meal had been a success. In deference to the great man's presence, Lewis had bought a bottle of Beaujolais Nouveau; and as Morse leaned back in a deep-cushioned armchair and drank his coffee, he felt very much at his ease.

'I sometimes wish I'd taken a gentle little job in the Egyptian Civil Service, Lewis.'

'Fancy a drop of brandy, sir?'

'Why not?'

From the rattle and clatter coming from the kitchen, it was clear that Mrs Lewis had launched herself into the washing-up, but Morse kept his voice down as he spoke again. 'I know that a dirty weekend away with some wonderful woman sounds just like the thing for some jaded fellow getting on in age a bit – like you, Lewis – but you'd be an idiot to leave that lovely cook you married—'

'I've never given it a thought, sir.'

'There are one or two people in this case, though, aren't there, who seem to have been doing a bit of double-dealing one way or another?'

Lewis nodded as he, too, leaned back in his armchair sipping his coffee, and letting his mind go back to the previous day's startling new development, and to Morse's explanation of how it had occurred . . .

'. . . If you ever decide to kick over the traces' (Morse had said) 'you've *got* to have an accommodation address – that's the vital point to bear in mind. All right, there are a few people, like the Smiths, who can get away without one; but don't forget they're professional swindlers and they know all the rules of the game backwards. In the normal course of events, though, you've got to get involved in some sort of correspondence. Now, if the princess you're going away with isn't married or if she's a divorcee or if she is just living on her own anyway, then there's no problem, is there? She can be your mistress *and* your missus for the weekend and *she* can deal with all the booking – just like Philippa Palmer did. She can use – she *must* use – her own address and, as I say, there are no problems. Now let's just recap for a minute about where we are with the third woman in this case, the woman who wrote to the hotel as "Mrs Ann Ballard" and who booked in as "Mrs Ann Ballard" from an address in Chipping Norton. Obviously, if we can find her, and find out from her what went on in Annexe 3 on New Year's Eve – or New Year's morning – well, we shall be home and dry, shan't we? And in fact we know a good deal about her. The key thing – or what I *thought* was the key thing – was that she'd probably gone to a hair clinic a day or so before turning up at the Haworth Hotel. I'm sorry, Lewis, that you've had such a disappointing time with that side of things. But there was this *other* side which I kept thinking about – the address she wrote *from* and the address the hotel wrote *to*. Now you can't exchange correspondence with a phoney address – obviously you can't! And yet, you know, you *can*! You *must* be able to – because it *happened*, Lewis! And when you think about it you can do it pretty easily if you've got one particular advantage in life – just the one. And you know what that advantage is? *It's being a postman.* Now let's just take an example. Let's take the Banbury Road. The house numbers go up a long, long way, don't they? I'm not sure, but certainly to about four hundred and eighty or so. Now if the last house is, say, number 478, what exactly happens to a letter addressed to a non-existent 480? The sorters in the main post office are not going to be much concerned, are they? It's only *just* above the last house-number; and as likely as not – even if someone did spot it – he'd probably think a new house was being built there. But if it were addressed, say, to 580, then obviously a sorter is going to think that something's gone askew, and he probably won't put that letter into the appropriate pigeon-hole. In cases like that, Lewis, there's a tray for problem letters, and one of the higher-echelon post-office staff will try to sort them all out later. But whichever way things go, whether the letter would get into the postman's bag, or whether it would get put into the problem tray – it wouldn't matter! You see, the postman himself would be there on the premises while all this sorting was taking place! I *know*! I've had a long talk on the phone with the Chief Postmaster from Chipping Norton – splendid fellow! – and he said that the letter we saw from the Haworth Hotel, the one addressed to 84 West Street, would pretty certainly have gone straight into the West Street pigeon hole, because it's only a couple over the last street-number; and even if it had been put in the problem tray, the postman waiting to get his sack over his shoulder would have every opportunity of seeing it, and taking it. And there were only two postmen who delivered to West Street in December: one was a youngish fellow who's spending the New Year with his girlfriend in the Canary Islands; and the other is this fellow called Tom Bowman, who lives at Charlbury Drive in Chipping Norton. But there's nobody there – neither him nor his wife – and none of the neighbours knows where they've gone, although Margaret Bowman was at her work in Summertown on Thursday and Friday last week: I've checked that. Anyway there's not much more we can do this weekend. Max says he'll have the body all sewn up and presentable again by Monday, and so we ought to know who he is pretty soon.'

It had been after Morse had finished that Lewis ventured the most important question of all: 'Do you think the murdered man is Tom Bowman, sir?' And Morse had hesitated before replying. 'Do you know, Lewis, I've got a strange sort of feeling that *it isn't* . . .'

Morse had nodded off in his chair, and Lewis quietly left the room to help with the drying-up.

That same Sunday afternoon Sarah Jonstone at last got back to her flat. She knew that she would almost certainly never have such an amazing experience again in her life, and she had been reluctant to leave the hotel whilst police activity was continuously centred upon it. But even the ropes that had cordoned off the area were gone, and no policeman now stood by the side door of the annexe block. Mrs Binyon (who had not originally intended to stay at the Haworth for the New Year anyway, but who had been pressed into reluctant service because of the illnesses of so many staff) had at last, that morning, set off on her trip north to visit her parents in Leeds. Only half a dozen people were booked into the hotel that Sunday evening, although (perversely!) the staff who had been so ill were now almost fully recovered. Sarah was putting on her coat at 3.30 p.m. when the phone went in Reception and a young woman's voice, a quietly attractive one, asked if she could please speak to Mr Binyon if he was there.

But when Sarah asked for the woman's name, the line went suddenly dead.

Sarah found herself recalling this little incident later in the evening as she sat watching TV. But it wasn't important, she told herself; probably just a line cut off by some technical trouble or other. *Could* it be important though? Chief Inspector Morse had begged her to dredge her memory to salvage *anything* that she could recall; and there *had* been that business about the sticker on Mrs Ballard's coat . . . But there was something else, she knew, if only her mind could get hold of it.

But, for the moment, it couldn't.

Chapter Twenty-five

Monday, January 6th: a.m.

By working faithfully eight hours a day, you may eventually get to be a boss and work twelve hours a day.

Robert Frost

Gladys Taylor would be very sorry to leave 'The University of Oxford Delegacy of Local Examinations'. It was all a bit of a mouthful when people asked her where she worked; but the Examination Board's premises, a large, beige-bricked, flat-roofed building in Summertown, had been her happy second home for nineteen and a half years now – and some neat streak within her wished it could have been the full twenty. But the 'Locals', as the Board was affectionately known, insisted that those women like herself – 'supernumeraries', they were called – had their contracts terminated in the session following their sixtieth birthday. These 'sessions', four or five of them every academic year, varied in duration from three or four weeks to nine or ten weeks; and the work involved in each session was almost as varied as its duration. For example, the current short session (and Gladys's last – for she had been sixty the previous November) involved three weeks of concentrated arithmetical checking of scripts – additions, scalings, transfers of marks – from the autumn GCE retake examinations. The entry was very much smaller than the massive summer one, comprising those candidates who had failed adequately to impress the examiners on the earlier occasion. But such young men and women (the 'returned empties', as some called them) were rather nearer Gladys Taylor's heart than many of the precious summer thoroughbreds (she knew a few of them!) who seemed to romp around the academic racecourses with almost arrogant facility. For, in her own eyes, Gladys had been a bit of a failure herself, leaving her secondary-modern school at the beginning of the war, at the age of fifteen, with nothing to show any prospective employer except a luke-warm testimonial to her perseverance and punctuality. Then, at the age of forty-one, following the premature death of a lorry-driver husband who, besides faltering in fidelity, had failed to father any offspring, she had applied to work at the Locals – and she had been accepted. During those first few months she had brought to her duties a care over detail that was almost pathological in its intensity, and she had often found herself waking up in the early hours and wondering if she had perpetrated some unforgivable error. But she had settled down; and thoroughly enjoyed the work. Her conscientiousness had been recognised by her supervisors and acknowledged by her fellow 'Supers'; and finally, over the last few years, she had been rewarded by a belated promotion to a post of some small responsibility, part of which involved working with inexperienced women who came to join the various teams; and for the past six months Gladys had been training a very much younger woman in the mysteries of the whole complex apparatus. This younger woman's name was Margaret Bowman.

For the past three sessions, the two of them had worked together, becoming firm friends in the process, and learning (as women sometimes do) a good many things about each other. At the start, Margaret had seemed almost as diffident and insecure as she herself, Gladys, had been; and it was – what was the word? – yes, such vulnerability that had endeared the younger woman to Gladys, and very soon made the older woman come to look upon Margaret more as a daughter than a colleague. Not that Margaret was ever *too* forthcoming about the more intimate details of her life with Tom, her husband; or (during the autumn) about the clandestine affair she was so obviously having with someone else (Gladys never learned his name). How could anyone *not* have guessed? For the affair was engendering the sort of bloom on the cheek which (unbeknown to Gladys) Aristotle himself had once used in seeking to define his notion of pure happiness.

Then, in the weeks of late autumn, there had occurred a change
in Margaret: there were now moments of (hitherto) unsuspected
irritability, of (hitherto) uncharacteristic carelessness, and (perhaps
most disturbing of all) a sort of coarseness and selfishness. Yet the
strangely close relationship between them had survived, and on two
occasions Gladys had tried to ask, tried to help, tried to offer more
than just a natural friendliness; but nothing had resulted from these
overtures. And when on a Friday in mid-December the last session
of the calendar year had finally come to its close, that was the last
Gladys had seen of her colleague until the new-year resumption –
on January 2nd, a day on which it hardly required the talents of a
clairvoyant to see that there was something quite desperately wrong.

Smoking was banned from the room in which the Supers
worked; but several of the women were moderately addicted to
the weed, and each day they greatly looked forward to the morning
coffee-breaks and afternoon tea-breaks, both taken in the Delegacy
canteen, in which smoking *was* allowed. Hitherto – and invariably –
during the time Gladys had known her, Margaret would sit patiently
puffing her way through a single cigarette a.m.; a single cigarette
p.m. But on that January 2nd, and again on the 3rd, Margaret had
been getting through three cigarettes in each of the twenty-minute
breaks, inhaling deeply and dramatically on each one.

Margaret's work, too, during the whole of her first day back,
had been quite unprecedentedly slack: ten marks missed at one
point in a simple addition; a wrong scaling, and a very obvious
one at that, not spotted; and then (an error which would have made
Gladys herself blanch with shame and mortification) an addition of
104 and 111 entered as 115 – a total which, but for Glady's own
rechecking, would probably have given some luckless candidate an
'E' grade instead of an 'A' grade.

At lunchtime on Friday, January 3rd, Gladys had invited
Margaret for a meal at the Chinese restaurant just across the
Banbury Road from the Delegacy; and over the sweet-and-sour pork
and the Lotus House Special chop-suey, Margaret had confided to
Gladys that her husband was away on a course over the New Year
and that she herself had been feeling a bit low. And how enormously
it had pleased Gladys when Margaret had accepted the invitation to
spend the weekend with her – in Gladys's home on the Cutteslowe
housing estate in North Oxford.

Mrs Mary Webster, the senior administrative assistant who kept a
very firm (if not unfriendly) eye upon the forty or so women who

sat each day in the large first-storey room overlooking the playing
fields of Summerfields Preparatory School, had not returned to her
accustomed chair after the coffee-break on the morning of January
6th. Most unusual! But it was the intelligence gleaned by Mrs
Bannister (a woman somewhat handicapped in life by a bladder of
minimal capacity, but whose regular trips to the downstairs toilet
afforded, by way of compensation, a fascinating window on the
world) that set the whole room a-buzzing.

'A police car!' she whispered (audibly) to half the assembled
ladies.

'Two men! They're in the Secretary's room!'

'You mean the police are down there talking to *Mrs Webster*?'
asked one of Mrs Bannister's incredulous colleagues.

But further commentary and interpretation was immediately
forestalled by Mrs Webster herself, who now suddenly entered the
door at the top of the long room, and who began to walk down the
central gangway between the desks and tables. The whole room was
immediately still, and silent as a Trappist's cell. It was not until she
reached Gladys's table, almost at the very bottom of the room, that
she stopped.

'Mrs Bowman, can you come with me for a few minutes, please?'

Margaret Bowman said nothing as she walked down the wooden
stairs, one step behind Mrs Webster, and then into the main corridor
downstairs and directly to the room whose door of Swedish oak bore
the formidable nameplate of 'The Secretary'.

Chapter Twenty-six

Monday, January 6th: a.m.

The cruellest lies are often told in silence.
                                    Robert Louis Stevenson

'The Secretary' was one of those endearingly archaic titles in
which the University of Oxford abounded. On the face of it, such
a title seemed to point to a personage with Supreme (upper-case,
as it were) Stenographic Skills. In fact, however, the Secretary of

the Locals, Miss Gibson, was a poor typist, her distinction arising from her outstanding academic and administrative abilities which had led, ten years previously, to her appointment as the boss of the whole outfit. Grey-haired, tight-lipped, pale-faced, Miss Gibson sat behind her desk, in an upright red-leather chair, awaiting the arrival of Mrs Margaret Bowman. Arranged in front of her desk were three further red-leather chairs, of the same design: in the one to the Secretary's left sat a man of somewhat melancholy mien, the well-manicured fingers of his left hand occasionally stroking his thinning hair and who was at that moment (although Miss Gibson would never have guessed the fact) thinking what a very attractive woman the Secretary must have been in her earlier years; in the middle sat a slightly younger man – another policeman, and one also in plain clothes – but a man both thicker set, and kindlier faced. Miss Gibson introduced the two police officers after Margaret Bowman had knocked and entered and been bidden to the empty chair.

'You live in Chipping Norton?' asked Lewis.

'Yes.'

'At 6 Charlbury Drive, I think?'

'Yes.' Even with the two monosyllabic answers, Margaret knew that her tremulous upper lip was betraying signs of her nervousness, and she felt uncomfortably aware of the fierce blue-grey eyes of the other man upon her.

'And you work here?' continued Lewis.

'I've been here seven months.'

'You had quite a bit of time off over Christmas, I understand?'

'We had from Christmas Eve to last Thursday.'

'Last Thursday, let's see – that was January the second?'

'Yes.'

'The day after New Year's Day.'

Margaret Bowman said nothing, although clearly the man had expected – hoped? – that she would make some comment.

'You had plenty of things to occupy you, I suppose,' continued Lewis. 'Christmas shopping, cooking the mince pies, all that sort of thing?'

'Plenty of shopping, yes.'

'Summertown's getting a very good shopping centre, I hear.'

'Very good, yes.'

'And the Westgate down in the centre – they say that's very good, too.'

'Yes, it is.'

'Did you shop in Summertown here – or down in Oxford?'

'I did all my shopping at home.'

'You didn't come into Oxford at all, then?'

Why was she hesitating? Was she lying? Or was she just thinking back over things to make sure?

'No – I didn't.'

'You didn't go to the hairdressers'?'

Margaret Bowman's right hand went up to the top of her head, gently lifting a few strands of her not-so-recently-dyed-blonde hair, and she permitted herself a vague and tired-looking smile: 'Does it look like it?'

No, it doesn't, thought Lewis. 'Do you go to any beauty salons, beauty clinics, you know the sort of thing I mean?'

'No. Do you think I ought to?' Miraculously almost, she was feeling very much more at ease now, and she took a paper handkerchief from her black leather handbag and held it under her nose as she snuffled away some of the residual phlegm from a recent cold.

For his own part, Lewis was conscious that his questioning was not yet making much progress. 'Does your husband work in Oxford?'

'Look! Can you please give me some idea of why you're asking me all these things? Am I supposed to have done something wrong?'

'We'll explain later, Mrs Bowman. We're trying to make all sorts of important enquiries all over the place, and we're very glad of your co-operation. So, please, if you don't mind, just answer the questions for the minute, will you?'

'He works in Chipping Norton.'

'What work does he do?'

'He's a postman.'

'Did he have the same time off as you over Christmas?'

'No. He was back at work on Boxing Day.'

'You spent Christmas Day together?'

'Yes.'

'And you celebrated the New Year together?'

The question had been put, and there was silence in the Secretary's office. Even Morse who had been watching a spider up in the far corner of the ceiling stopped tapping his lower teeth with a yellow pencil he had picked up, its point needle-sharp. *How long was the well-nigh unbearable silence going to last?*

It was the Secretary herself who suddenly spoke, in a quiet but firm voice: 'You must tell the police the truth, Margaret – it's far

better that way. You didn't tell the truth just now – about being in
Oxford, did you? We saw each other in the Westgate Car Park on
New Year's Eve, you'll remember. We wished each other a Happy
New Year.'

Margaret Bowman nodded. 'Oh yes! Yes, I do remember now.'
She turned to Lewis. 'I'm sorry, I'd forgotten. I did come in that
Tuesday – I went to Sainsbury's.'

'And then you went back and you spent the New Year at
home with your husband?'

'No!'

Morse, whose eyes had still been following the little spider as it
seemed to practise its eight-finger exercises, suddenly shifted in his
chair and turned round fully to face the woman.

'Where is your husband, Mrs Bowman?' They were the first six
words he had spoken to her, and (as events were to work themselves
out) they were to be the last six. But Margaret Bowman made no
direct answer. Instead, she unfastened her bag, drew out a folded
sheet of paper and handed it over to Lewis. It read as follows:

31st December

Dear Maggie

You've gone into Oxford and I'm here sitting at home. You will
be upset and disappointed I know but please try and understand. I
met another woman two months ago and I knew straightaway that
I liked her a lot. I've just got to work things out that's all. Please
give me that chance and don't think badly of me. I've decided that
if we can go away for a few days or so we can sort things out. You
are going to want to know if I love this woman and I don't know yet
and she doesn't know either. She is not married and she is thirty one.
We are going in her car up to Scotland if the roads are alright. Nobody
else need know anything. I got a week off work quite officially though
I didn't tell you. I know what you will feel like but it will be better for
me to sort things out.

Tom

Lewis read through the letter quickly – and then looked at Mrs
Bowman. Was there – did he notice – just a brief flash of triumph
in her eyes? Or could it have been a glint of fear? He couldn't be
sure, but the interview had obviously taken a totally unexpected
turn, and he would have welcomed at that point a guiding hand
from Morse. But the latter still appeared to be perusing the letter
with inordinate interest.

'You found this note when you got back home?' asked Lewis. She nodded. 'On the kitchen table.'

'Do you know this woman he mentions?'

'No.'

'You've not heard from your husband?'

'No.'

'He's taking a long time to, er "sort things out".'

'Has – has my husband had an accident – a car accident? Is that why—'

'Not so far as we know, Mrs Bowman.'

'Is that – is that all you want me for?'

'For the minute, perhaps. We shall have to keep the letter – I'm sure you'll understand why.'

'No, I *don't* understand why!'

'Well, it might not be from your husband at all – have you thought of that?' asked Lewis slowly.

' 'Course it's from him!' As she spoke these few words, she sounded suddenly sharp and almost crude after her earlier quietly civilised manner, and Lewis found himself wondering several things about her.

'Can you be sure about that, Mrs Bowman?'

'I'd know his writing anywhere.'

'Have you got any more of his writing with you?'

'I've got the very first letter he wrote me – years ago.'

'Can you show it to us, please?'

From her handbag she brought out an envelope, much soiled, drew from it a letter, much creased, and handed it to Lewis, who cursorily compared the two samples of handwriting, and pushed them along the desk to Morse – the latter nodding slowly after a few moments: it seemed to him that by amateur and professional experts alike, the writing would pretty certainly be adjudged identical.

'Can I please go now?'

Lewis wasn't at all sure whether or not this oddly unsatisfactory interview should be temporarily terminated, and he turned to Morse – receiving only a non-committal shrug.

So it was that Margaret Bowman left the office, exhorted in a kindly way by the Secretary to get herself another cup of coffee from the canteen, and to be ready to come down again if the police needed her for further questioning.

'We're sorry to have taken so much of your time, Miss Gibson,' said Morse after Mrs Bowman had left. 'And if we could have a room for an hour or so we'd be most grateful.'

'You can stay here if you like, Inspector. There are a good many things I've got to see to round the office.'

'What do you make of all that, sir?' asked Lewis when they were alone.

'We haven't got a thing to charge her with, have we? We can't take her in just for forgetting she bought a pound of sausages from Sainsbury's.'

'We're not getting far, are we, sir? It's all a bit disappointing.'

'What? Disappointing? Far from it! We've just been looking at things from the wrong end, Lewis, that's all.'

'Really?'

'Oh yes. And we owe a lot to Mrs Bowman – it was about time somebody put me on the right track!'

'You think she was telling the truth?'

'Truth?' Morse shook his head. 'I didn't believe a word of her story, did you?'

'I don't know, sir. I feel very confused.'

'Confused? Surely not!' He turned to Lewis and put the yellow pencil down on the Secretary's desk. 'Do you want to know what happened in Annexe 3 on New Year's Eve?'

Chapter Twenty-seven

Monday, January 6th: a.m.

It is a bad plan that admits of no modification.
                                        Publilius Syrus

'Let me explain one thing from the start. I just said we've been looking at things from the wrong end and I mean just that. Max gave us a big enough margin for the time of death, and instead of listening to him I kept trying to pin him down. Even now it's taken a woman's pack of lies to put me on the right track, because the most important thing about Mrs Bowman is that she was forced to show us the letter, supposedly from her husband, to give herself a reasonable alibi. It was the last shot in her locker; and she had no option but to use it, because we were getting – we *are* getting! – dangerously close to the truth. And I just said "supposedly from her husband" – but that's not the case: it *was* from her husband, you can be certain of that. Everything fits, you see, *once you turn the pattern upside down.* The man in Annexe 3 wasn't murdered after the party: he was murdered *before the party.* Let's just assume that Margaret Bowman has been unfaithful, and let's assume that she gets deeply involved with this lover of hers, and that he threatens to blackmail her in some way if she doesn't agree to see him again – threatens to tell her husband – to cut his own throat – to cut *her* throat – anything you like. Let's say, too, that the husband, Tom Bowman, deliverer of Her Majesty's mail at Chipping Norton, finds out about all this – let's say that he intercepts a letter; or, more likely, I think, she's desperate enough to tell him all about it – because there must have been some sort of reconciliation between them. Together, they decide that something has got to be done to get rid of the threat that now affects *both* of them; and at that point, as I see it, the plot was hatched. They book a double room for a New Year break at a hotel, using a non-existent accommodation address so that later on no one will be able to trace them; and Tom Bowman is exactly the person to cope with that problem – none better. So things really start moving. Margaret Bowman tells this dangerous and persistent lover of hers – let's call him Mr X – that *she can spend the New Year with him.* He's a single man; he's head over heels about her; and now he's over the moon, too! He thought she'd ditched him. But here she is offering to spend a couple of whole days with him. *She's* taken the initiative; *she's* fixed it all up; *she's* booked the hotel; *she* wants *him!* She's even told him – and she must have expected he'd agree – that *she'll* provide the fancy-dress costumes they're going to wear at the New Year party. She tells him to be ready, let's say, from four o'clock on the 31st. She herself probably books in under her false name and a false address an hour or so earlier, but a bit later than most of the other guests. She wants to be seen by as few of the others as possible, but she's still got to give herself plenty of time. She finds herself alone at the reception desk, she turns up her coat and pulls her scarf around her face, she signs the form, she takes the room key, she takes her suitcase over to Annexe 3 – and all is ready. She rings up X from the public phone-box just outside the hotel, tells him what their room number is, and he's on his way like a shot. And while the rest of the guests are playing Cluedo, he's spending the rest of that late afternoon and early evening with his bottom on the top sheet, as they say. Then, when most of the passion's spent itself, she tells him that they'd better start dressing up for the party; she shows him what she's brought for the pair of them to wear; and about 7 p.m. the pair of them are ready: she rubs a final bit of stage-black on his hands – makes some excuse about leaving her purse or her umbrella at Reception – says she'll be back in a minute – takes the key with her – pulls her mackintosh over her costume – and goes out bang on the stroke of seven. Tom Bowman, *himself dressed in exactly the same sort of outfit as X*, has been waiting for her, somewhere in the immediate vicinity of the hotel; and while Margaret Bowman spends the most nerve-racking few minutes of her life, probably in the bus shelter just across from the hotel, *Tom Bowman lets himself into Annexe 3.*

'Exactly what happened then, we don't know – and we may never know. But very soon the Bowmans are playing out the rest of the evening as best they can – pretending to eat, pretending to be lovey-dovey with each other, pretending to enjoy the festivities. There's little enough chance of them being recognised, anyway: she's hiding behind her yashmak, and he's hiding behind a coat of dark grease-paint. But they both want to be seen going into the annexe after the party's over, and in fact Tom Bowman performs his rôle with a bit of panache. He waits for the two other women he knows are lodged in the annexe, throws an arm across their shoulders – incidentally ruining their coats with his greasy hands – and gives the impression to all and sundry that he's about to hit the hay. As it happens, Binyon was bringing up the rear – pretty close behind them. But the lock on the side door is only a Yale; and after Binyon had made sure all was well, the Bowmans slipped out quietly into the winter's night. They went down and got their car from the Westgate – or wherever it was parked – and Tom Bowman dropped Margaret back to Charlbury Drive, where she'd left the lights on anyway so that the neighbours would assume she was celebrating the New Year. And then Bowman himself took off into the night somewhere so that if ever the need arose he could establish an alibi for himself up in Inverness or wherever he found himself the next morning, leaving Margaret the pre-planned note about his fictitious girlfriend. And that's about it, Lewis! That's about what happened, as far as I can make out.'

Lewis himself had listened with great interest, and without interruption, to what Morse had said. And although, apart from the *time* of the murder, it wasn't a particularly startling analysis, it was just the sort of self-consistent hypothesis that Lewis had come to expect from the chief inspector, bringing together, as it did, into one coherent scheme all the apparently inconsistent clues and puzzling testimony. But there were one or two weaknesses in Morse's argument: at least as Lewis saw things.

'You said they spent the afternoon in bed, sir. But we didn't, to be honest, find much sign of anything like that, did we?'

'Perhaps they performed on the floor – I don't know. I was just telling you what probably happened.'

'What about the maid, sir – Mandy, wasn't it? Doesn't someone usually come along about seven o'clock or so and turn down the counterpane—'

'Counterpane? Lewis! You're still living in the nineteenth century. And this wasn't the Waldorf Astoria, you know.'

'Bit of a risk, though, sir – somebody coming in and finding—'

'They were short-staffed, Lewis – you know that!'

'But the *Bowmans* didn't know that!'

Morse nodded. 'No-o. But they could have hung one of those "Do Not Disturb" signs on the door. In fact, they *did*.'

'Bit risky, though, hanging out a sign like that if you're supposed to be at a party.'

'Lewis! Don't you understand? They were taking risks the whole bloody time.'

As always when Morse blustered on in such fashion, Lewis knew that it was best not to push things overmuch. Obviously, what Morse had said was true; but Lewis felt that some of the explanations he was receiving were far from satisfactory.

'If, as you say, sir, Bowman was dressed up, all ready to go, in exactly the same sort of clothes as the other fellow, where was he—?'

'*Where?* I dunno. But I'm sure all he had to do was put a few finishing touches to things.'

'Do you think he did that in Annexe 3?'

'Possibly. Or he could have used the Gents just off Reception.'

'Wouldn't Miss Jonstone have seen him?'

'How am I supposed to know? Shall we *ask* her, Lewis? Shall *I* ask her? Or what about *you* asking her – you're asking *me* enough bloody questions.'

'It's only because I can't quite understand things, that's all, sir,'

'You think I've got it all wrong, don't you?' said Morse quietly.

'No! I'm pretty sure you're on the right lines, sir, but it doesn't all *quite* hang together, does it?'

Chapter Twenty-eight

Monday, January 6th: a.m.

What is the use of running when we are not on the right road?
German proverb

There was a knock on the door and Judith, the slimly attractive personal assistant to the Secretary, entered with a tray of coffee and biscuits.

'Miss Gibson thought you might like some refreshment.' She put the tray on the desk. 'If you want her, she's with the Deputy – the internal number's 208.'

'We don't get such VIP treatment up at HQ,' commented Lewis after she'd left.

'Well, they're a more civilised lot here, aren't they? Nice sort of people. Wouldn't harm a fly, most of them.'

'Perhaps *one* of them would!'

'I see what you mean,' said Morse, munching a ginger biscuit.

'Don't you think,' said Lewis, as they drank their coffee, 'that we're getting a bit too complex, sir?'

'Complex? Life *is* complex, Lewis. Not for *you*, perhaps. But for most of us it's a struggle to get through from breakfast to coffee-time, and then from coffee-time—'

There was a knock on the door and Miss Gibson herself re-entered. 'I saw Mrs Webster just now and she said that Mrs Bowman hadn't got back to her work yet. I thought perhaps she might be back here . . .'

The two detectives looked at each other.

'She's not in the canteen?' asked Morse.

'No.'

'She's not in the Ladies?'

'No.'

'How many exits are there here, Miss Gibson?'

'Just the one. We've all been so worried about security recently—'

But Morse was already pulling on his greatcoat. He thanked the Secretary and with Lewis in his wake walked quickly along the wooden-floored corridor towards the exit. At the reception desk sat the Security Officer, Mr Prior, a thick-set, former prison officer, whose broad, intelligent face looked up from the Court Circular of the *Daily Telegraph* as Morse fired a salvo of questions at him.

'You know Mrs Bowman?'

'Yessir.'

'How long ago did she leave?'

'Three – four minutes.'

'By car?'

'Yessir. Maroon Metro – 1300 – A reg.'

'You don't know the number?'

'Not offhand.'

'Did she turn left or right at the Banbury Road?'

'Can't see from here.'

'She was wearing a coat?'

'Yessir. Black, fur-collared coat. But she hadn't changed her shoes.'

'What do you mean?'

'Most of 'em come in boots this weather – and then change into something lighter when they're here. She still had a pair of high heels on – black; black leather, I should think.'

Morse was impressed by Prior's powers of observation, said as much, and asked if he'd noticed anything else that was at all odd.

'Don't think so. Except perhaps when she said "Goodbye!" '

'Don't most people say "Goodbye" when they leave?'

Prior thought for a second before replying: 'No, they don't! They usually say "See you!" or "Cheers!" or something like that.'

Morse walked from the Locals, his eyes downcast, a deep frown on his forehead. The snow had been brushed away from the shallow steps that led down to the car park, and a watery-looking sun had almost dried the concrete. The forecast was for continued improvement in the weather, although in places there were still patches of hazardous ice.

'Where to?' asked Lewis as Morse got into the passenger seat of the police car.

'I'm – not – quite – sure,' replied Morse as they drove up to the black-and-yellow striped barrier that regulated the progress of unauthorised vehicles into Ewert Place, the narrow street that led down to the Delegacy's private car park. Bob King, the courteous, blue-uniformed attendant, touched his peaked cap to them as he pressed the button to raise the barrier; but before going through, Morse beckoned him round to his window and asked him if he remembered a maroon Metro leaving a few minutes earlier; and if so whether it had turned left or right into the Banbury Road. But whilst the answer to the first question had been 'yes', the answer to the second question had been 'no'. And for the minute Morse asked Lewis to stop the car where it was: the Straw Hat Bakery ('Everything baked on the Premises') on the left; and, to the right (its immediate neighbour across the narrow road), the giant Allied Carpets shop, whose vast areas of glass frontage were perpetually plastered over with notices informing the inhabitants of Summertown that the current sale must undoubtedly rank as the biggest bargain in the annals of carpetry. Betwixt and between – there the car stood: left, down into Oxford; right, up and out of the city and, if need be, thence to Chipping Norton.

'Chipping Norton,' said Morse suddenly – 'quick as you can!'

Blue rooflight flashing, siren wailing, the white Ford raced up to the Banbury Road roundabout then across to the Woodstock Road roundabout, and was soon out on the A34, a happy-looking Lewis behind the wheel.

'Think she'll go back home straight away?'

'My God, I hope so!' said Morse with unwonted vehemence.

It was when the car had passed the Black Prince and was climbing the hill out of Woodstock that Morse spoke again. 'Going back to what you were saying about Annexe 3, Lewis, you *did* have a look at the bed-linen, didn't you?'

'Yes, sir. In both beds.'

'You don't think you missed anything?'

'Don't think so. Wouldn't matter much if I did, though. We've still got all the bedclothes – I sent everything along to the path lab.'

'You did?'

Lewis nodded. 'But if you want my opinion, nobody'd been sleeping in either of those two beds, sir.'

'Well, you couldn't tell with the one, could you? It was all soaked in blood.'

'No, it wasn't, sir. The blood had seeped through the counterpane or whatever you call it, and a bit through the blankets; but the sheets weren't marked at all.'

'And you don't think that they'd been having sex that afternoon or evening – in either of the beds.'

Lewis was an old hand in murder investigations, and some of the things he'd found in rooms, in cupboards, in wardrobes, in beds, under beds – he'd have been more than happy to be able to forget. But he knew what Morse was referring to, and he was more than confident of his answer. 'No. There were no marks of sexual emissions or anything like that.'

'You have an admirably delicate turn of phrase,' said Morse, as Lewis sped past an obligingly docile convoy of Long Vehicles. 'But it's a good point you made earlier, you know. If the old charpoy *wasn't* creaking all that afternoon . . .'

'As you said, though, sir – they might have made love on the carpet.'

'Have you ever made love on the carpet in mid-winter?'

'Well, no. But—'

'Central heating's one thing. But you get things like draughts under doors, don't you?'

'I haven't got much experience of that sort of thing myself.'

The car turned off left at the Chipping Norton/Moreton-in-Marsh/Evesham sign; and a few minutes later Lewis brought it to a gentle stop outside 6 Charlbury Drive. He noticed the twitch of a lace curtain in the front window of number 5; but no one seemed to be about at all, and the little road lay quiet and still. No maroon Metro stood outside number 6, or in the steep drive that led down to the white-painted doors of the single garage.

'Go and have a look!' said Morse.

But there was no car in the garage, either; and the front-door bell seemed to Lewis to re-echo through a house that sounded ominously empty.

Chapter Twenty-nine

Monday, January 6th: a.m.

The last pleasure in life is the sense of discharging our duty.
                                                    William Hazlitt

Where Morse decided to turn right past Allied Carpets, Margaret Bowman, some five minutes earlier, had decided to turn left past the Straw Hat, and had thence proceeded south towards the centre of the city. In St Giles', the stiff penalty recently introduced for any motorists outstaying their two-hour maximum (even by a minute or so) had resulted in the unprecedented sight of a few free rectangles of parking space almost invariably being available at any one time;

and Margaret pulled into the one she spotted just in front of the
Eagle and Child, and walked slowly across to the ticket machine,
some twenty-odd yards away. For the whole of the time from when
she had sat down in the Secretary's office until now, her mind
had been numbed to the reality of her underlying situation, and
far-distanced, in some strange way, from what (she knew) would be
the disastrous inevitability of her fate. Her voice and her manner, as
she had answered the policemen, had been much more controlled
than she could have dared to hope. Not *quite* all the time; but
anyone, even someone who was wholly innocent, would always
be nervous in those circumstances. Had they believed her? But
she knew now that the answer even to such a crucial question
was perhaps no longer of any great importance. (She prodded her
fingers into the corner of her handbag for the necessary change.)
But to say that at that very moment Margaret Bowman had finally
come to any conclusion about ending her life would be untrue. Such
a possibility had certainly occurred to her – oh, so many times! –
over the past few days of despair and the past few nights of hell.
Academically, she had not been a successful pupil at the Chipping
Norton Comprehensive School, and in O-level *Greek Literature in
Translation* (Margaret had not been considered for the high fliers'
Latin course) she had been 'Unclassified'. Yet she remembered
something (in one of the books they were supposed to read) about
Socrates, just before he took the hemlock: when he'd said that he
would positively welcome death if it turned out to be just one long
and dreamless sleep. And that's what Margaret longed for now – a
long, a wakeless and a dreamless sleep. (She could not find the exact
number of coins which the notice on the ticket machine so inexorably
demanded.) And then she remembered her mother, dying of cancer
in her early forties, when Margaret was only fourteen: and before
dying saying how desperately tired she was and how she just wanted
to be free from pain and never wake again . . .
    Margaret had found five 10p coins – still one short – and she
looked around her with a childlike pleading in her eyes, as though
she almost expected her very helplessness to work its own deliver-
ance. A hundred or so yards away, just passing the Taylorian, and
coming towards her, she saw a yellow-banded traffic warden, and
suddenly a completely new and quite extraordinary thought came
to her mind. Would it matter if she *were* caught? Didn't she *want* to
be caught? Wasn't there, after all hope had been cruelly cancelled,
a point when even total despair could hold no further terrors? A
notice ('No Change Given') outside the Eagle and Child informed

Margaret that she could expect little help from that establishment; but she walked in and ordered a glass of orange juice.

'Ice?'

'Pardon?'

'You want ice in it?'

'Oh – yes. Er – no. I'm sorry, I didn't quite hear . . .'

She felt the hard eyes of the well-coiffeured bar-lady on her as she handed over a £1 coin and received 60p in exchange: one 50p piece, and one 10p. Somehow she felt almost childishly pleased as she put her six 10p pieces together and held the little stack of coins in her left hand. She had no idea how long she stayed there, seated at a table just in front of the window. But when she noticed that the glass in front of her was empty, and when she felt the coins so warmly snug inside her palm, she walked out slowly into St Giles'. It occurred to her – so suddenly! – that there she was, in St Giles'; that she had just come down the Banbury Road; that she must have passed directly in front of the Haworth Hotel; and that *she hadn't even noticed it.* Was she beginning to lose control of her mind? Or had she got *two* minds now? The one which had pushed itself into auto-pilot in the driving seat of the Metro; and the other, logical and sober, which even now, as she walked towards the ticket machine, was seeking to keep her shoes (the ones she had bought for the funeral) out of the worst of crunching slush. She saw the celluloid-covered document under the near-side windscreen-wiper; and caught sight of the traffic warden, two cars further up, leaning back slightly to read a number plate before completing another incriminating ticket.

Margaret walked up to her, pointing to the maroon Metro.

'Have I committed an offence?'

'Is that your car?'

'Yes.'

'You were parked without a ticket.'

'Yes, I know. I've just been to get the right change.' Almost pathetically she opened her left palm and held the six warm coins to view as if they might just serve as some propitiatory offering.

'I'm sorry, madam. It tells you on the sign, doesn't it? If you haven't got the right change, you shouldn't park.'

For a moment or two the two women, so little different in age, eyed each other in potential hostility. But when Margaret Bowman spoke, her voice sounded flat, indifferent almost.

'Do you enjoy your work?'

'Not the point, is it?' replied the other. 'There's nothing *personal* in it. It's a job that's got to be done.'

Margaret Bowman turned and the traffic warden looked after her with a marked expression of puzzlement on her face. It was her experience that on finding a parking ticket virtually all of them got into their cars and drove angrily away. But not this tall, good-looking woman who was now walking away from her car, down past the Martyrs' Memorial; and then, almost out of sight now, but with the warden's last words still echoing in her mind, across into Cornmarket and up towards Carfax.

Chapter Thirty

Monday, January 6th: noon

Then the devil taketh him up into the holy city, and setteth him on a pinnacle of the temple.

St Matthew 4:5

Margaret Bowman stood beneath Carfax Tower, a great, solid pile of pale-yellowish stone that stands on the corner of Queen Street and Cornmarket, and which looks down, at its east side, on to the High. White lettering on a background of Oxford blue told her that a splendid view of the city and the surrounding district was available from the top of the tower: admission 50p, Mondays to Saturdays, 10 a.m. to 6 p.m.; and her heart pounded as she stood there, her eyes ascending to the crenellated balustrade built four-square around the top. Not a high balustrade either; and often in the past she'd noticed people standing there, almost half their bodies visible as they gazed out over Oxford or waved to friends who stood a hundred feet below. She was not one of those acrophobes (as, for example, Morse was) who burst into a clammy sweat of vertiginous panic when forced to stand on the third or the fourth rung of a household ladder. But she was always terrified of being *pushed* – had been ever since one of the boys on a school party to Snowdon had *pretended* to push her, and when for a split second she had experienced a sense of imminent terror of falling over the precipitous drop that yawned almost immediately below her feet. People said you always thought of your childhood before you died, and she was conscious that twice already – no, three times – her mind had reverted to early memories. And now she was conscious of a fourth – of the words her father had so often used when she tried to put off writing a letter, or starting her homework: 'The longer you put things off, the harder they become, my girl!' Should she put things off now? Defer any fateful decision? No! She pushed the door to the tower. But it was clear that the tower was shut; and it was with a sense of despairing disappointment that she noticed the bottom line of the notice: '20th March – 31st October'.

The spire of St Mary the Virgin pointed promisingly skywards in front of her as she walked down the High, and into the Mitre.

'Large Scotch – Bell's, please – if you have it.' (How often had she heard her husband use those self-same words!)

A young barmaid pushed a tumbler up against the bottom of an inverted bottle, and then pushed again.

'Ice?'

'Pardon?'

'Do you want ice?'

'Er – no. Er – yes – yes please! I'm sorry. I didn't quite hear . . .'

As she sipped the whisky, a hitherto dormant nerve throbbing insistently along her left temple, the world seemed to her perhaps fractionally more bearable than it had done when she'd left the Delegacy. Like some half-remembered medicine – foul-tasting yet efficacious – the whisky seemed to do her good; and she bought another.

A few minutes later she was standing in Radcliffe Square; and as she looked up at the north side of St Mary's Church, a strange and fatal fascination seemed to grip her soul. Halfway up the soaring edifice, his head and shoulders visible over the tricuspid ornamentation that marked the intersection of tower and spire, Margaret could see a duffel-coated young man, binoculars to his eyes, gazing out across the northern parts of Oxford. The tower must be open, surely! She walked down the steps towards the main porch of the church and then, for a moment, turned round and gazed up at the dome of the Radcliffe Camera behind her; and noticed the inscription on the top step: *Dominus custodiat introitum tuum et exitum tuum*. But since she had no Latin, the potential irony of the words escaped her. TOWER OPEN was printed in large capitals on a noticeboard beside the entrance; and just inside, seated behind a table covered with postcards, guidebooks and assorted Christian literature, was a middle-aged woman who had already assumed that Margaret Bowman wished to ascend, for she held out a maroon-coloured ticket and asked for 60p. A few flights of wide wooden stairs led up to the first main landing, where a notice on a locked door to the left advised visitors that here was the Old Library – the very first one belonging to the University – where the few books amassed by the earliest scholars were so precious that they were chained to the walls. Margaret had seldom been interested in old churches, or old anythings for that matter; but she now found herself looking down at the leaflet the woman below had given her:

> when Mary became Queen and England reverted to Roman Catholicism, Archbishop Cranmer and two of his fellow bishops, Latimer and Ridley, were tried in St Mary's for heresy. Latimer and Ridley were burned at the stake. Cranmer himself, after officially recanting, was brought back to St Mary's and condemned to death. He was burned at the stake in the town ditch, outside Balliol College, holding his right hand (which had written his recantation) steadily in the flames . . .

Margaret looked at her own right hand – a couple of blue biro marks across the bottom of the thumb – and thought of the tortured atonement that Cranmer had sought, and welcomed, for his earlier weaknesses. A tear ran hurriedly down her cheek, and she took from her handbag a white paper handkerchief to dry her eyes.

The stairs – iron now, and no longer enclosed for the next two flights – led up and over the roof of the Lady Chapel, and she felt a sense of exhilaration in the cold air as she climbed higher still to the Bell Tower, where the man with the binoculars, his hair windswept, had just descended the stone spiral staircase that led to the top.

'Not much further!' he volunteered. 'Bit blowy up there, though. Bit slippery, too. Be careful!'

For several seconds as she emerged at the top of the tower, Margaret was conscious of a terrifying giddiness as her eyes glimpsed, just below her feet, the black iron ring that circled the golden-painted Roman numerals of the great clock adorning the north wall of the church. But the panic was soon gone, and she looked out across at the Radcliffe Camera; and then to the left of the Camera at the colleges along Broad Street; then the buildings of Balliol where Cranmer had redeemed his soul amid the burning brushwood; then she could see the leafless trees along St Giles', and the roads that led off from there into North Oxford; and then the giant yellow crane that stood at the Haworth Hotel in the

Banbury Road. She took a few steps along the high-walk towards the north-western corner of the tower, and she suddenly felt a sense of elation, and the tears welled up again in her eyes as the wind blew back her hair, and as she held her head up to the elements with the same joyous carelessness she had shown as a young girl when the rain had showered down on her tip-tilted face . . .

At a point on the corner, her wholly inadequate and unsuitable shoes had slipped along the walkway, and a man standing below watched the black handbag as it plummeted to the earth and landed, neatly erect, in a drift of snow beneath the north-west angle of the tower.

Chapter Thirty-one

Monday, January 6th: p.m.

Everything comes to him who waits – among other things, death.

F. H. Bradley

Morse was dissatisfied and restless – that much was obvious as they sat outside the Bowmans' house in Charlbury Drive. Ten minutes they waited, Morse just sitting there in the passenger seat, his safety-belt still on, staring out of the window. Then another ten minutes, with Morse occasionally clicking his tongue and taking sharp audible breaths of impatient frustration.

'Think she's coming back?' said Lewis.

'I dunno.'

'How long are we going to wait?'

'How do *I* know!'

'Just asked.'

'I tell you one thing, Lewis. I'm making one bloody marvellous mess of this case!'

'I don't know about that, sir.'

'Well you *should* know! We should never have let her out of our sight.'

Lewis nodded, but said nothing; and for a further ten minutes the pair of them sat in silence.

But there was no sign of Margaret Bowman.

'What do you suggest we do, Lewis?' asked Morse finally.

'I think we ought to go to the post office: see if we can find some of Bowman's handwriting – there must be something there; see if any of his mates know anything about where he is or where he's gone; that sort of thing.'

'And you'd like to get somebody from there to go and look at the body, wouldn't you? You think it *is* Bowman!'

'I'd just like to check, that's all. Check it *isn't* Bowman, if you like. But we haven't done anything at all yet, sir, about identification.'

'And you're telling me it's about bloody time we did!'

'Yessir.'

'All right. Let's do it your way. Waste of time but—' His voice was almost a snarl.

'Are you feeling all right, sir?'

' 'Course I'm not feeling all right! Can't you see I'm dying for a bloody cigarette, man?'

The visit to the post office produced little information that was not already known. Tom Bowman had worked on the Thursday, Friday and Saturday following Christmas Day, and then had taken a week's holiday. He should have been back at work that very day, the 6th; but as yet no one had seen or heard anything of him. It seemed he was a quiet, punctual, methodical sort of fellow, who had been working there for six years now. No one knew his wife Margaret very well, though it was common knowledge that she had a job in Oxford and took quite a bit of trouble over her clothes and her personal appearance. There were two handwritten letters from Bowman in the personnel file: one dating back to his first application to join the PO; the second concerning itself with his options under the PO pension provisions. Clearly there had been little or no calligraphic variance in Bowman's penmanship over the years, and here seemed further evidence – if any were required – that the letter Margaret Bowman had produced from her handbag that morning was genuinely in her husband's hand. Mr Jeacock, the co-operative and neatly competent postmaster, could tell them little more; but, yes, he was perfectly happy for one of Bowman's colleagues to follow the police officers down into Oxford to look at the unidentified body.

'Let's hope to God it's *not* Tom!' he said as Morse and Lewis got up and left his small office.

'I honestly don't think you need to worry about that, sir,' said
Morse.

As always, the cars coming up in the immediate rear had all
decelerated to the statutory speed limit; and by the time the
police car reached the dual carriageway just after Blenheim Palace,
with Mr Frederick Norris, sorter of Her Majesty's mail in Chipping
Norton, immediately behind, there was an enormous tailback of
vehicles. Morse, who had told Lewis to take things quietly, sat silent
throughout the return journey, and Lewis too held his peace. At the
bottom of the Woodstock Road he turned right into a narrow road
at the Radcliffe Infirmary and stopped on an 'Ambulances Only'
parking lot outside the mortuary, to which the body found in the
Haworth annexe had now been transferred. Norris got out of the
car that pulled up behind them.
    'You coming, sir?' asked Lewis.
    But Morse shook his head.

Fred Norris stood stock-still for a few seconds, and then –
somewhat to Lewis's bewilderment – nodded slowly, his own
pallor only a degree less ghastly than the skin that backed the livid
bruising of the murdered man's features. No words were spoken;
but as the mortuary attendant replaced the white sheet, Lewis put
a kindly, understanding hand on Norris's shoulder, and then gently
urged him out of the grim building into the bright January air.
    An ambulance had pulled in just ahead of the police car, and
Lewis, as he stood fixing a time with Norris for an official statement, saw the ambulance driver unhurriedly get out and speak to
one of the porters at the Accident entrance. From the general lack
of urgency, Lewis gathered that the man was probably delivering
some fussy octogenarian for her weekly dose of physiotherapy. But
the back doors were suddenly opened to reveal the body of a
woman covered in a red blanket, with only the shoeless stockinged
feet protruding. Lewis's throat was dry as he walked past the
police car, and saw Morse (the latter still unaware of the dramatic
news that Lewis was about to impart) point to the back of the
ambulance.
    'Who is she?' asked Lewis as the two ambulance men prepared
to fix the runners for the stretcher.
    'Are you . . . ?' The driver jerked his thumb towards the
police car.
    'Chief Inspector Morse – him! Not me!'

'Accident. They found her—'

'How old?'

The man shrugged. 'Forty?'

'You know who she is?'

The man shook his head. 'No one knows yet. No purse. No handbag.'

Lewis drew back the blanket and looked at the woman's face, his heart pounding in anticipatory dread – for such an eventuality, as he well knew, was exactly what Morse had feared.

But the ambulance driver was right in suggesting that no one knew who she was: Lewis didn't know, either. For the dead woman in the back of the ambulance was certainly not Mrs Margaret Bowman.

That same lunch-hour, some fifty minutes before Norris had positively identified the man murdered at the Haworth Hotel as Mr Thomas Bowman, Ronald Armitage, an idle, dirty, feckless, cold, hungry, semi-drunken 63-year-old layabout – unemployed and unemployable – experienced a remarkable piece of good fortune. He had spent the previous night huddled up on a bench in the passage that leads from Radcliffe Square to the High, and had spent most of the morning on the same bench, with an empty flagon of Bulmer's Cider at his numbed feet, and one dirty five-pound note and a few 10p coins in the pocket of the ankle-length greatcoat that for many years had been his most treasured possession. When he had first seen the black handbag as it plummeted to the ground, and came to rest in a cushion of deep snow at the corner of the church, his instinctive reaction was to look sharply and suspiciously around him. But for the moment the square was empty; and he quickly grabbed the handbag, putting it beneath the front of his coat, and walked hurriedly off over the snow-covered cobbles outside Brasenose into the lane on the left that led through to the Turl. Here, with none of his cronies in sight – like a wolf which grabs a great gobbet of meat from the kill and takes it away from the envious eyes of the rest of the pack – he examined his exciting discovery. Inside the handbag he found a lipstick, a powder compact, a comb, a cheap cigarette-lighter, a packet of white paper handkerchiefs, a leaflet about St Mary the Virgin, a small pair of nail scissors, a bunch of car keys, two other keys – and a brown-leather purse-cum-wallet. The plastic cards – Visa, Access, Lloyds – he ignored, but he quickly pocketed the two beautifully crisp ten-pound notes and the three one-pound coins he found therein.

In mid-afternoon, he wandered slowly up the High to Carfax, and then turned left down past Christ Church and into St Aldate's Police Station where he handed the bag over to Lost Property.

'Where did you find it?' asked the sergeant on duty.

'Someone must have dropped it—'

'You better leave your name—'

'Nah! Don't fink so.'

'Might be a reward!'

'Cheers, mate!'

Chapter Thirty-two

Monday, 6th January: p.m.

Wordsworth recalls in 'The Prelude' how he was soothed by the sound of the Derwent winding among grassy holms.
Literary Landscapes of the British Isles

It was seldom that Morse ever asked for more personnel. Indeed, it was his private view that the sight (as so often witnessed on TV) of a hundred or so uniformed policemen crawling in echelon across a tract of heathland often brought the force into something approaching derision. He himself had once taken part in such a massive sweep across a field in North Staffordshire, ending up, as he had done, with one empty packet of Featherlite Durex, one empty can of alcohol-free lager – and (the next morning) a troublesome bout of lumbago.

But he *did* ask for more personnel on the afternoon of January 6th; and Lewis, for one, was glad that much needed help (in the shape of Sergeant Phillips and two detective constables) had been summoned to follow up all enquiries regarding Margaret Bowman.

Oddly enough (yet almost everything about him was odd, as Lewis knew) Morse had shown no great surprise on hearing the news that the murdered man was Thomas Bowman; indeed, the only emotion he showed – and that of immense relief – was after learning that the other corpse on view that lunchtime was *not* Margaret Bowman's. In fact, Morse suddenly seemed much more at peace with himself as he sat with Lewis in the Royal Oak, just opposite the hospital – a circumstance (as Lewis rightly guessed) not wholly unconnected with the fact that after his Herculean efforts over Christmas and the New Year he had finally surrendered and bought himself a packet of cigarettes. At two thirty, they were once more on the A34 to Chipping Norton, this time with a much firmer mission – to investigate the property at 6 Charlbury Drive, which had now quite definitely become the focus of the murder enquiry.

'Shall we break one of the front windows or one of the back ones?' Morse asked as they stood in front of the property, faces at a good many windows in the quiet cul-de-sac now watching the activity with avid curiosity. But such forcible ingress proved unnecessary. Lewis it was who suggested that most people ('Well, the missus does') leave a key with the neighbours: and so it proved in this case, with the elderly woman in number 5 promptly producing both a back-door and a front-door key. Mrs Bowman, it appeared, had gone out on Friday evening, saying she wouldn't be back until Monday after work; hadn't been back, either – as far as the woman knew.

Finding nothing of immediate interest in the downstairs rooms, Lewis went upstairs where he found Morse in one of the two spare bedrooms looking into a cumbrous dark-mahogany wardrobe which (apart from an old-fashioned armchair) was the only item of furniture there.

'Found anything, sir?'

Morse shook his head. 'Lots of shoes he had.'

'Not much help.'

'No help at all.'

'Can you smell anything, sir?'

'Such as?'

'Whisky?' suggested Lewis.

Morse's eyes lit up as he sniffed, and sniffed again.

'I reckon you're right, you know.'

There was a stack of white shoe-boxes, and they found the half-full bottle of Bell's in the third box from the bottom.

'You think he was a secret drinker, sir?'

'What if he was? *I'm* a secret drinker – aren't you?'

'No, sir. And I wouldn't have got away with this. The missus cleans all my shoes.'

The other spare room upstairs (little more than a small boxroom) was similarly short on furniture, with three sheets of newspaper spread out across the bare floorboards on which ranks of large, green cooking-apples were neatly arranged. 'They take the *Sun*,' observed Lewis, as his eye fell on a young lady leaning forward to maximise the measurements of a mighty bosom. 'You think he was a secret sex-maniac?'

'*I'm* a secret—' But Morse broke off as he saw the broad grin across his sergeant's face, and he found himself smiling in return.

The main bedroom, though furnished fully (even tastefully, as Morse saw it), seemed at first glance to offer little more of interest than the rest of the house. Twin beds, only a few inches apart, were neatly made, each covered with an olive-green quilt, each with a small bedside table – the feminine accoutrements on the one nearer the window clearly signifying 'hers'. On the right as one entered the room was a large white-wood wardrobe, again 'hers', and on the left a tallboy obviously 'his'. A composite piece of modern furniture, mirror in the middle, three shelves above (two of them full of books), with drawers below, stood just beyond the tallboy – at the bottom of Margaret Bowman's bed. Since there seemed about three times as much of her clothing as of his, Morse agreed that Lewis should concentrate on the former, he on the latter. But neither of them was able to come up with anything of value, and Morse soon found himself far more interested in the two shelves of books. The thick spines of four white paperbacks announced a sequence of the latest international best-sellers by Jackie Collins, and beside these stood two apparently unopened Penguins, *Brideshead Revisited* and *A Passage to India*. Then two large, lavishly illustrated books on the life and times of Marilyn Monroe; an ancient impression of the *Concise Oxford Dictionary*; and, a very recent purchase by the look of things, a book in the 'Hollywood Greats Series' covering the career of Robert Redford (a star – unlike Miss Monroe – who had yet to swim into Morse's ken). On the wall beside this top shelf of books were two colour photographs cut from sporting periodicals: one of Steve Cram, the great middle-distance runner; the other of Ian Terence Botham, his blond locks almost reaching the top of his England cricket sweater. The title *Sex Parties*, on the lower shelf, caught Morse's eye and he took it out and opened a page at random:

> Her hand slid across the gear-lever and touched his leg below the tennis shorts. 'Let's go to my place – quick!' she murmured in his ear.

'I shan't argue with that, my love!' he replied huskily as the powerful Maserati swerved across the street . . .

As they lay there together the next morning –

Such anti-climactic pianissimo porn had no attraction whatever for Morse and he was putting the book back in its slot when he noticed that there was something stuck in the middle of the large volume next to it, a work entitled *The Complete Crochet Manual*. It was a holiday postcard from Derwentwater, addressed to Mrs M. Bowman, the date stamp showing July 29th, the brief message reading:

> Greetings from Paradise
> Regained — I wish
> you were there
>   Edwina

Morse turned the card over and looked lovingly at the pale-green sweep of the hills before putting the card back in its place. An odd place, perhaps, his brain suggested gently? And not the sort of book, surely, that Tom Bowman would often dip into for amusement or instruction? Edwina was doubtless one of Margaret's friends – either a local woman or one of her colleagues at Oxford. For the moment, he thought no more about it.

Downstairs once more, Lewis collected up the pile of documents he'd already selected from the mass of letters and bills that appeared to have been stuffed haphazardly into the two drawers of the corner cabinet in the lounge – water, electricity, mortgage, HP, bank statements, car insurance. Morse, for his part, sat down in one of the two armchairs and lit a cigarette.

'They kept their accounts and things in one hell of a mess, sir!'

Morse nodded. 'Mm!'

'Looks almost as if someone has been looking through all this stuff pretty recently.'

Morse shot up in the armchair as if a silken-smooth car driver had suddenly, without warning, decided to practise an emergency stop. 'Lewis! You're a genius, my son! The paper! There's a pile of newspapers in the kitchen, and I glanced at them while you were in here. Do you know something? *I think today's copy's there!*'

Lewis felt the blood tingling in his own veins as he followed Morse into the kitchen once more, where beneath a copy of the previous week's *Oxford Times* was the *Sun*, dated January 6th.

'She must have been here some time today, sir.'

Morse nodded. 'I think she came back here *after we saw her this morning*. She must have picked up the paper automatically from the doormat—'

'But surely somebody would have seen her?'

'Go and see if you can find out, Lewis.'

Two minutes later, whilst Morse had progressed no further than page three of the Bowmans' daily, Lewis came back: the woman still peeping at events from the window immediately opposite had seen Margaret Bowman get out of a taxi.

'A *taxi*?'

'That's what she said – and go into the house, about half-past one.'

'When we were on the way back to Oxford . . .'

'I wonder what she wanted, sir?'

'She probably wanted her building-society book or something – get a bit of ready cash. I should think that's why those drawers are in such a mess.'

'We can check easily enough – at the building societies.'

'Like the beauty clinics, you mean?' Morse smiled. 'No! Let Phillips and his lads do that – tedious business, Lewis! I'm really more interested to know why she came in a taxi.'

'Shall we get Sergeant Phillips to check on the taxis, too?' grinned Lewis, as for the present the two men left 6 Charlbury Drive. The house had been icily cold, and they were glad to get away.

Margaret Bowman's Metro was located, parking ticket and all, in St Giles' at 4.45 p.m. that same day, and the news was immediately rung through to Kidlington. But a folding umbrella, a can of de-icing spray, and eight 'Scrabble' tokens from Esso garages did not appear to Morse to be of the slightest help in the murder enquiry.

It was not until ten thirty the following morning that Sergeant Vickers rang Kidlington from St Aldate's with the quite extraordinary news that Margaret Bowman's handbag had been found. Morse himself, Vickers learnt (not without a steady sinking of his heart), would be coming down immediately to view the prize exhibit.

Chapter Thirty-three

Tuesday, 7th January: a.m.

JACK (gravely): In a handbag,
LADY BRACKNELL: A handbag?
Oscar Wilde

'Whaa—?'

Morse's inarticulate utterance sounded like the death agonies of a wounded banshee, and Lewis felt his sympathy going out to whichever of the officers in St Aldate's had been responsible the previous day for the Lost Property inventory.

'We get a whole lot of lost property in every day, sir—'

'—and not all of it' (Morse completed the sentence with withering scorn) 'I would humbly suggest, Sergeant, a prime item of evidence in a murder enquiry – and if I may say so, *not* an enquiry of which this particular station is wholly ignorant. In fact, only yesterday afternoon your colleague Sergeant Phillips and two of your own detective constables were specifically seconded from their duties here to assist in that very enquiry. Remember? And do you know who asked for them – me! And do you know why I'm so anxious to show some interest in this enquiry? Because this bloody station *asked* me to!'

Palely, Sergeant Vickers nodded, and Morse continued.

'You! – and you'll do it straight away, Sergeant – you'll get hold of the bloody nincompoop who sat in that chair of yours yesterday and you'll tell him I want to see him immediately. Christ! I've never known anything like it. There are rules in this profession of ours, Sergeant – didn't you know that? – and they tell us to get names and addresses and occupations and times and details and all the rest of it – and here we are without a bloody clue who brought it in, where it was found, when it was found – nothing!'

A constable had come through in the midst of this shrill tirade, waiting until the peroration before quietly informing Morse there was a telephone call for him.

After Morse had gone, Lewis looked across at his old pal, Sergeant Vickers.

'Was it you, Sam?'

Vickers nodded.

'Don't worry! He's always flying off the handle.'

'He's right, though. I tell everybody else to fill in the forms and follow the rules but . . .'

'Do you remember who brought it in?'

'Vaguely. One of the winos. We've probably got him on the books for pinching a bottle of cider from a supermarket or something. Poor sod! But the last thing we can cope with is having the likes of him here! I suppose he nicked the money when he "found" the bag and then just brought it in to square his conscience. I didn't discover where he found it, though – or when – or what his name was. I just thought – well, never mind!'

'He can't shoot you, Sam.'

'It's not as if there's much in it to help, I don't think.'

Lewis opened the expensive-looking handbag and looked through its contents: as Vickers had said, there seemed little enough of obvious interest. He pulled out the small sheaf of cards from the front compartment of the wallet: the usual bank and credit cards, two library tickets, two creased first-class stamps, a small rectangular card advertising the merits of an Indian restaurant in Walton Street, Oxford, and an identity pass-card for the Locals, with a coloured photograph of Margaret Bowman on the left. One by one, Lewis picked them up and examined them, and was putting them back into the wallet when he noticed the few words written in red biro on the back of the white restaurant card:

```
M. I love you
darling. T.
```

Obviously, thought Lewis, a memory from happier days, probably their first meal together, when Tom and Margaret Bowman had sat looking dreamily at each other over a Bombay curry, holding hands and crunching popadums.

A brighter-looking Morse returned.

An intelligent and resourceful Phillips, it appeared, had discovered that Margaret Bowman had gone back – not in her own car, of course – to Chipping Norton the previous lunchtime, and had withdrawn £920 of her savings in the Oxfordshire Building Society there – leaving only a nominal £10 in the account.

'It's all beginning to fit together, Lewis,' said Morse. 'She was obviously looking for her pay-in book when she got a taxi back there. And this clinches things of course' – he gestured to the handbag. 'Car keys there, I'd like to bet? But she must have had an extra house key on her . . . Yes! Cheque card, I see, but I'd be surprised if she kept that *and* her chequebook together. Most people have more sense these days.'

Lewis, not overjoyed by the high praise bestowed upon his fellow sergeant, ventured his own comments on the one item in the hand-bag which had puzzled him – the (obviously very recently acquired) leaflet on St Mary the Virgin. 'I remember when I was a lad, sir, somebody jumped from the tower there, and I was wondering—'

'Nonsense, Lewis! You don't do that sort of thing these days. You take a couple of boxes of pills, don't you, Sergeant Vickers?'

The latter, so unexpectedly appealed to, decided to take this opportunity of putting the record straight. 'Er, about the handbag, sir. I wasn't exactly telling you the whole truth earlier—'

But Morse was not listening. His eyes were staring at the small oblong card which Lewis had just examined and which lay on top of the little pile of contents, the handwritten message uppermost.

'What's that?' he asked with such quietly massive authority in his voice that Vickers found the hairs rising up on his brawny forearms.

But neither of the two sergeants could answer, for neither knew what it was that the chief inspector had asked, nor why it was that his eyes were gleaming with such triumphant intensity.

Morse looked cursorily through the other items from the handbag, quickly deciding that nothing merited further attention. His face was still beaming as he clapped a hand on Lewis's shoulder. 'You are – not for the first time in your life – a bloody genius, Lewis! As for you, Vickers, we thank you for your help, my friend. Forget what I said about that idiot colleague of yours! Please, excuse us! We have work to do, have we not, Lewis?'

'The Indian restaurant, is it?' asked Lewis as they got into the car.

'You hungry, or something?'

'No, sir, but—'

'I wouldn't say no to a curry myself, but not just for the time being. Put your foot down, my son!'

'Er – where to, sir?'

'Chipping Norton! Where else?'

* * *

Lewis saw that the fascia clock showed a quarter past twelve as the car passed through Woodstock.

'Fancy a pint?' asked a cheerful Lewis.

Morse looked at him curiously. 'What's the matter with you this morning? I hope you're not becoming an alcoholic.'

Lewis shook his head lightly.

'You want to be like me, Lewis. I'm a dipsomaniac.'

'What's the difference?'

Morse pondered for a while. 'I think an alcoholic is always trying to *give up* drink.'

'Whereas such a thought has never crossed your mind, sir?'

'Well put!' said Morse, thereafter lapsing into the silence he habitually observed when being driven in a car.

As they neared the Chipping Norton turning off the A34, a woman driving a very ancient Ford Anglia passed them on her way down from Birmingham to spend a night at the Haworth Hotel.

Chapter Thirty-four

Tuesday, January 7th: p.m.

A certain document of the last importance has been purloined.

Edgar Allan Poe

'Well, I'll be buggered!' Morse shook his head in bewildered disappointment as he stood, once again, in Margaret Bowman's bedroom – *The Complete Crochet Manual* in his hands. 'It's gone, Lewis!'

'*What's* gone?'

'The card I showed you – the card from the Lake District – the one signed "Edwina".'

'You never showed it to me,' protested Lewis.

'Of course I— Perhaps I didn't. But the handwriting on that postcard was the same as the handwriting on the back of your whatsitsname Indian place in Walton Street. *Exactly the same!* I can swear to it! The postcard was from Ullswater or some place like that and' (Morse sought to bully his brain into a clearer remembrance) 'it said something like "It's Paradise Regained – I wish you were here". But, you know, it's a bit odd, on a postcard, to say "*I* wish you were here". Nineteen times out of twenty, people just say "*Wish* you were here", don't they? Do you see what I mean? That postcard *didn't* say "It's Paradise Regained" – then a dash – "I wish you were here"; it said "It's Paradise Regained *minus one*. Wish you were here". That card was from Margaret Bowman's lover, telling her there was only one thing missing from his Paradise – *her*!'

'Not much use if it's gone,' said Lewis dubiously.

'It *is* though! Don't you see? The very fact that Margaret Bowman came back a second time shows exactly *how* important it is. And I *think* I remember the postmark – it was August. All we've got to do is to find out who spent his holidays up in the Lake District last August!'

'It might have been the August before.'

'Don't be so pessimistic, man!' snapped Morse.

'But we *ought* to be pessimistic,' persisted Lewis, remembering his recent experience with the beauty clinics. 'Millions of people go up to the Lakes every summer. And who's this "Edwina"?'

'He's the lover-boy. Tom Bowman would have been very suspicious, wanting to know who the fellow was if he'd signed his own name. But the man we're dealing with, Lewis – *the man who almost certainly murdered Bowman* – is pretty clever: he changed his name – but he didn't change it too much! And that gives us a whacking great clue. The fellow signs himself "T" on the Indian thing – and then signs himself "Edwina" on the postcard. *So we've already got his Christian name, Lewis!* The "T" doesn't stand for Tom – it stands for Ted. And "Ted" is an abbreviation of "Edward"; and he signs himself in the feminine form of it – "Edwina"! QE bloody D Lewis – as we used to say in the Lower Fourth! All right! You say there are a few millions every year who look forward to hearing the rain drumming on their caravan roofs in Grasmere. But not all that many of them were christened "Edward", and about half of *them* would be too old – or too young – to woo our fair Margaret. And, what's more, he'll pretty certainly live in Oxford, this fellow we're looking for – or not too far outside. And if he can afford to spend a holiday in the Lake District, he's probably in work, rather than on the dole, agreed?'

'But—'

'*And* – just let me finish! – not everybody's all that familiar with

Paradise Regained. Mr Milton's not everybody's cup of tea in these degenerate days, and I'm going to hazard a guess that our man was a grammar-school boy!'

'But they're all comprehensives now, sir.'

'You know what I mean! He's in the top 25 per cent of the IQ range.'

'The case seems to be closed, then, sir!'

'Don't be so bloody sarcastic, Lewis!'

'I'm sorry, sir, but—'

'I've not finished! What was the colour of Bowman's hair?'

'Well – blondish, sort of.'

'Correct! And what have Robert Redford, Steve Cram and Ian Botham got in common?'

'All the girls go for them.'

'No! Physical appearance, Lewis.'

'You mean, they've all got blond hair?'

'Yes! And if Margaret Bowman's running to form, this new beau of hers has got fair hair, too! And if only about a quarter of Englishmen have got fair hair—'

'He could be a Swede, sir.'

'What? A Swede who's read *Paradise Regained*?'

For Lewis, the whole thing was becoming progressively more improbable; yet he found himself following Morse's deductive logic with reluctant admiration. If Morse were right there couldn't be all that many employed, fair-haired people christened Edward, in the twenty-five to forty-five age range, living in or just outside Oxford, who had spent their most recent summer holidays in the Lake District, could there? And Lewis appreciated the force of one point Morse had just made: Margaret Bowman had been willing to make *two* extraordinarily risky visits to her house in Charlbury Drive over the last twenty-four hours. If the *first* had been to fetch her building society book (or whatever) and to get some ready cash out, it couldn't really be seen as all that incriminating. But if the overriding purpose of the *second*, as Morse was now suggesting, had been to remove from the house any pieces of vital evidence that might have been hidden in the most improbable places . . .

Lewis was conscious, as he sat there in the Bowmans' bedroom that afternoon, that he had not yet even dared to mention to Morse the thought that had so obstinately lodged itself at the back of his mind. At the time, he had dismissed the idea as utterly fanciful – and yet it would not wholly go away.

'I know it's ridiculous, sir, but – but I can't help worrying about that crane at the back of the hotel.'

'Go on!' said Morse, not without a hint of interest in his voice.

'Those cranes can land the end of a girder on a sixpence: they *have* to – to match up with the bolts and everything. So if you wanted to, you could pick up a box, let's say, and you could move it wherever you wanted – *outside a window, perhaps?* It's only a thought, sir, but could it just be that Bowman was murdered *in the main part of the hotel*? If the murderer wraps up the body, say, and hooks it on to the crane, he can pinpoint it to just outside Annexe 3, where he can get an accomplice in the room to pull the box gently in. The murderer himself wouldn't be under any suspicion at all, because he's never been *near* the annexe. And if it had been snowing – like the forecast said – there wouldn't be any footprints *going in*, would there? There's so much mess and mud outside the back of the hotel, though, that nobody's going to notice anything out of the ordinary there; and nobody's going to hear anything, either – not with all the racket of a disco going on. I know it may be a lot of nonsense, but it does bring all those people staying in the hotel back into the reckoning, doesn't it? And I think you'll agree, sir, we *are* getting a bit short of suspects.'

Morse, who had been listening with quiet attention, now shook his head with perplexed amusement. 'What you're suggesting, Lewis, is that *the murderer's a crane-driver*, is that it?'

'It was only a thought, sir.'

'Narrows things down, though. A fair-haired crane-driver called Ted who spent a week in Windermere or somewhere . . .' Morse laughed. 'You're getting worse than I am, Lewis!'

Morse rang HQ from the Bowmans' house, and two men, Lewis learned, would immediately be on their way to help him undertake an exhaustive search of the whole premises at 6 Charlbury Drive.

Morse himself took the car keys and drove back thoughtfully into Oxford.

Chapter Thirty-five

Tuesday, January 7th: p.m.

No words beyond a murmured 'Good-evening' ever passed
between Hardy and Louisa Harding.
The Early Life of Thomas Hardy

Instead of going straight back to Kidlington HQ, Morse drove
down once more into Summertown and turned into Ewert Place
where he drove up to the front steps and parked the police car.
The Secretary, he learned, was in and would be able to see him
almost immediately.

As he sat waiting on the long wall-seat in the foyer, Morse
was favourably struck (as he had been on his previous visit) by the
design and the furnishings of the Delegacy. The building was surely
one of the (few) high spots of post-1950 architecture in Oxford, and
he found himself trying to give it a date: 1960? 1970? But before he
reached a verdict, he learned that the Secretary awaited him.

Morse leaned back in the red leather armchair once again.

'Lovely building, this!'

'We're very lucky, I agree.'

'When was it built?'

'Finished in 1965.'

'I was just comparing it to some of the hideous structures
they've put up in Oxford since the war.'

'You mustn't think we don't have a few problems, though.'

'Really?'

'Oh, yes. We get floods in the basement fairly regularly. And
then, of course, there's the flat roof: anyone who designs a building
as big as this with a flat roof – in England! – hardly deserves the
Queen's medal for architecture. Not in my book, anyway.'

The Secretary had spoken forcefully, and Morse found himself
interested in her reaction. 'You've had trouble?'

'*Had?* Yes, we've had trouble, and we've got trouble now, and
it'll be a great surprise if we don't have more trouble in the future.
We've only just finished paying for a complete re-roofing repair –
the *third* we've had!'

Morse nodded in half-hearted sympathy as she elaborated the
point; but his interest in the Delegacy's roofing problems soon

dissipated, and he moved to the reason for his visit. He told the Secretary, in the strictest confidence, almost everything he had discovered about the Bowmans, and he hinted at his deep concern for Margaret Bowman's life. He asked whether Margaret had any particular women friends in the Delegacy; whether she had any *men* friends; whether there might have been any gossip about her; whether there was anything at all that might be learned from interviewing any of Margaret's colleagues.

The result of this request was the summoning to the Secretary's office of Mrs Gladys Taylor, who disclaimed all knowledge of Margaret Bowman's married life, of any possible extramarital infidelity, and of her present whereabouts. After only a few minutes Morse realised he was getting nowhere with the woman; and he dismissed her. He was not at all surprised that she knew so little; and he was aware that his own abrupt interlocutory style had made the poor woman hopelessly nervous. What Morse was not aware of – and what, with a little less conceit, he might perhaps have divined – was that Gladys Taylor's nervousness had very little at all to do with the tone of Morse's questioning, but everything to do with the fact that, after spending the weekend at Gladys's council house on the Cutteslowe Estate in North Oxford, Margaret Bowman had turned up *again* – dramatically! – late the previous evening, begging Gladys to take her in and making her promise to say nothing to anyone about her whereabouts.

The former prison officer at Reception deferred his daily perusal of the Court Circular and saluted the Chief Inspector as Morse handed in the temporary badge he had been given – a plastic folder, with a metal clip, containing a buff-coloured card on which was printed VISITOR, in black capitals, and under which, in black felt-tip pen, was written 'Insp. Morse'. A row of mailbags stood beside the front door, waiting for the post office van, and Morse was on the point of leaving the building when he turned back – struck by the appropriate juxtaposition of things – and spoke to the Security Officer.

'You must feel almost at home with all these mailbags around!'

'Yes! You don't forget things like that, sir. And I could still tell you where most of 'em were made – from the marks, I mean.'

'You can?' Morse fingered one of the grey bags and the Security Officer walked round to inspect it.

'From the Scrubs, that one.'

'Full of criminals, they tell me, the Scrubs.'

'Used to be – in my day.'

'You don't get many criminals here, though?'

'There's a lot of things here they'd *like* to get their hands on – especially all the question papers, of course.'

'And that's why you're here.'

'Can't be too careful, these days. We get so many people coming in – I'm not talking about the permanent staff – I'm talking about the tradesmen, builders, electricians, caterers—'

'And you give them all a pass – like the one you gave me?'

'Unless they're pretty regular. Then we give 'em a semi-permanent pass with a photograph and all that. Saves a lot of time and trouble.'

'I see,' said Morse.

A letter was awaiting Morse at Kidlington: a white envelope, with a London postmark, addressed to Chief Inspector Morse (in as neat a piece of typewriting as one could wish to find) and marked 'Strictly Private and Personal'. Even before he opened the envelope, Morse was convinced that he was about to be apprised of some vital intelligence concerning the Bowman case. But he was wrong. The letter read as follows:

This is a love letter but please don't feel too embarassed about it because it doesn't really matter. You are now engaged on a murder enquiry and it was in connection with this that we met briefly. I don't know why but I think I've fallen genuinely and easily and happily in love with you. So there!

I wouldn't have written this silly letter but for the fact that I've been reading a biography of Thomas Hardy and he (so he said) could never forget the face of a girl who once smiled at him as she rode by on a horse. He knew the girl by name and in fact the pair of them lived quite close, but their relationship never progressed even to the point of speaking to each other. At least I've done that!

Tear this up now. I've told you what I feel about you. I almost wish I was the chief suspect in the case. Perhaps I *am* the murderer! Will you come and arrest me? Please!

The letter lacked both salutation and signature, and Morse's expression, as he read it, seemed to combine a dash of distaste with a curiously pleasurable fascination. But as the girl herself (whoever she was!) had said – it didn't really matter. Yet it would have been quite extraordinary for any man not to have pondered on the identity of such a correspondent. And, for several minutes, Morse did so ponder as he sat silently at his desk that winter's afternoon. She sounded a nice girl – and she'd only made the one spelling error . . .

The call from Lewis – a jubilant Lewis! – came in at 5.10 p.m. that day.

Chapter Thirty-six

Tuesday, January 7th: p.m.

If you once understand an author's character, the comprehension of his writing becomes easy.

Longfellow

It had been in the inside breast pocket of a rather ancient sports jacket that Lewis had finally found the copied letter. And such a discovery was so obviously what Morse had been hoping for that he was unable to conceal the high note of triumph in his voice as he reported his find. Equally, for his part, Morse had been unable to conceal his own delight; and when (only some half an hour later) Lewis delivered the four closely handwritten sheets, Morse handled them with the loving care of a biblical scholar privileged to view the *Codex Vaticanus*.

You are a selfish thankless bitch and if you think you can just back out of things when you like you'd better realise that you've got another big thick headaching think coming because it could be that I've got some ideas about what I like. You'd better understand what I'm saying. If you can act like a bitch you'd better know I can be a bit of a sod too. You were glad enough to get what you wanted from me and just because I wanted to give it to you you think that we can just drop everything and go back to square one. Well this letter is to tell you we can't and like I say you'd better understand what I'm telling you. You can be sure I'll get my own back on you. You always say you can't really talk on the phone much but you didn't have much trouble on Monday did you. Not much doubt about where you stood then. Not free this week, and perhaps not next week either, and the week after that is a bit busy too!! I know I've not been round quite as long as you but I'm not a fool and I think you know I'm not. You say you're not going to sign on next term for night classes and that was the one really long time we did have together. Well I don't want any Dear John letter thank you very much. But I do want one thing and I'm quite serious about saying that I'm going to get it. I must see you again – at least once again. If you've got any sense of fairness to me you'll agree to that. And if you've got just any plain <u>sense</u> – and forget any fairness – you'll still agree to see me because if you don't I shall get my own back. Don't drive me to anything like that. Nobody knows about us and I want to leave things like that like they were. You remember how careful I was always and how none of your colleagues ever knew. Not that it matters much to me, not a quarter of what it matters to you. Don't forget that. So do as I say and meet me next Monday. Tell them you've got a dental appointment and I'll pick you up as usual outside the Summertown Library at ten to one. Please make sure you're there for your sake as much as mine. Perhaps I ought to have suspected you were cooling off a bit. When I was at school I read a thing about there's always one who kisses and one who turns the cheek. Well I don't mind it that way but I must see you again. There were lots of times when you wanted me badly enough – lots of times when you nearly set a world record for getting your clothes off, and that wasn't just because we only had forty minutes. So be there for sure on Monday or you'll have to face the consequences. I've just thought that last sentence sounds like a threat but I don't really want to be nasty about all this. I suppose I've never said too much about what I really feel but I think I was in love with you the very first time I saw the top of your golden head in the summer sunshine. Monday – ten to one – or else!

Morse read the letter through twice – each time slowly, and (much to Lewis's delight) appeared to be highly satisfied.

'What do you make of it, sir?'

Morse put the letter down and leaned back in the old black-leather chair, his elbows resting on the arms, the tips of his middle fingers tapping each other lightly in front of a well-pleased mouth. 'What would *you* say about that letter, Lewis, eh? What do *you* learn from it?'

Lewis usually hated moments such as this. But he had been asking himself exactly the same question since he'd first read the letter through, and he launched into what he hoped Morse would accept as an intelligent analysis.

'It's quite clear, sir, that Margaret Bowman was unfaithful to her husband over quite a while. He talks in the letter about night classes and I think they were probably held in the autumn term – say, for about three or four months – after he first saw her, like he says, in the summer. I'd say from about July onwards. That's the first thing.' (Lewis was feeling not displeased with himself.) 'Second thing, sir, is this man's age. He says he's not been around quite as long as she has, and he's underlined the word "quite". He probably teased her a bit

– like most people would – if she was a little bit older than he was: let's say, six months or a year, perhaps. Now, Margaret Bowman – I've found out, sir – was thirty-six last September. So let's put our prime suspect in the thirty-five age-bracket then, all right?' (Lewis could recall few occasions on which he had seemed to be speaking with such fluent authority.) 'Then there's a third point, sir. He asks her to meet him outside the library at ten minutes to one – so he must know it takes about five minutes for her to get there *from* the Locals – and five minutes to get back. That leaves us with fifty minutes from the hour they're given at the Locals for a lunch-break. But he mentions *"forty* minutes": so, as I see things' (how happy Lewis felt!) 'he must live only about five minutes' drive away from the library in South Parade. I don't think they just went to a pub and held hands, sir. I think, too, that this fellow probably lives on the *west* side of Oxford – let's say off the Woodstock Road somewhere – because Summertown Library would be a bit of a roundabout place to pick her up if he lived on the *east* side, especially with such a little time they've got together.'

Morse had nodded in agreement at several points during this exposition; and had been on the point of congratulating his sergeant when Lewis resumed – still in full spate.

'Now if we add these new facts to what we've already discovered, sir, I reckon we're not all that far off from knowing exactly who he is. We can be far more precise about where he lives – within five minutes' drive, at the outside, from Summertown; and we can be far more precise about his age – pretty certainly thirty-four or thirty-five. So if we had a computerised file on everybody, I think we could spot our man straight away. But there's something else – something perhaps much more helpful than a computer, sir: that night-school class! It won't be difficult to trace the people in Mrs Bowman's class; and I'd like to bet we shall find somebody who had a vague sort of inkling about what Margaret Bowman was up to. Seems to me a good line of enquiry; and I can get on with it straight away if you agree.'

Morse was silent for a little while before replying. 'Yes, I think I *do* agree.'

Yet Lewis was conscious of a deeper undercurrent in Morse's tone: something was worrying the chief, pretty surely so.

'What's the matter, sir?'

'Matter? Nothing's the matter. It's just that – well, tell me what you make of that letter *as a whole*, Lewis. What *sort* of man is he, do you think?'

'Bit of a mixture, I'd say. Sounds as if he's genuinely fond of the woman, doesn't it? At the same time it sounds as if he's got quite a cruel streak in him – bit of a coarse streak, too. As if he loved her – but always in a selfish sort of way: as if perhaps he might be prepared to do anything just to keep her.'

Morse nodded. 'I'm sure you're right. I think he *was* prepared to do almost anything to keep her.'

'Have you got any idea of what really happened?' asked Lewis quietly.

'Yes! – for what it's worth, I have. Clearly Bowman found this letter somewhere, and he realised that his wife was going with another fellow. I suspect he told her what he knew and gave her an ultimatum. Most men perhaps would have accepted the facts and called it a day – however much it hurt. But Bowman didn't! He loved his wife more than she could ever have known, and his first instinctive reactions mustered themselves – not against his wife – *but against her lover*. He probably told her all this, in his own vague way; and I think he decided that the best way to help Margaret and, at the same time, to save his own deeply injured pride, was *to get rid of her lover!* We've been on a lot of cases together, Lewis – with lots of people involved; but I don't reckon the motives are ever all *that* different – love, hate, jealousy, revenge . . . Anyway, I think that Bowman got his wife to agree to collaborate with him in a plot to get rid of the man who – at least for the moment – was a threat to both of them. What *exactly* that plan involved, we may never know – unless Margaret Bowman decides to tell us. The only firm thing we know about it so far is that Bowman himself wrote a wholly genuine letter which would rather cleverly serve two purposes when lover-boy was found murdered – that is, if any suspicion were ever likely to fall on either of the Bowmans: first, it would put Margaret Bowman in a wholly sympathetic light; second, it would appear to put Tom Bowman some few hundreds of miles away from the scene of the immediate crime.'

'Didn't we know most of that already—'

'Let me finish, Lewis! At some particular point – I don't know when – *the plan was switched*, and it was switched by the only person who could switch it – by Margaret Bowman, who decided that if she had to take a profoundly important decision about life (as she did!) she would rather throw in her lot with her illicit lover than with her licit husband. Is that clear? Forget the details for the minute, Lewis! The key thing to bear in mind is this: instead of having a plot involving the death of a troublesome lover, we have a plot involving the death of an interfering husband!'

'You don't think the letter helps much at all, then?' Lewis's initial euphoria slipped a notch or two towards his wonted diffidence.

'My goodness, yes! And your own reading of that letter was a model of logic and lucidity! But . . .'

Lewis's heart sank. He knew what Morse was going to say, and he said it for him. 'But you mean I missed some vital clue in it – is that right?'

Morse waited awhile, and then smiled with what he trusted was sympathetic understanding: 'No, Lewis. You didn't miss one vital clue, at all. You missed two.'

Chapter Thirty-seven

Tuesday, January 7th: p.m.

Stand on the highest pavement of the stair –
Lean on a garden urn –
Weave, weave the sunlight in your hair

T. S. Eliot

'Apart from your own admirable deductions, Lewis, there are, as I say, a couple of other things you could have noticed, perhaps. First' (Morse turned to the letter and found the appropriate reference) 'he says, "You remember how careful I always was and how none of your colleagues ever knew". Now that statement's very revealing. It suggests that this fellow *could* have been very careless about meeting Margaret Bowman; careless in the sense that, if he'd wanted to, he could easily have made Margaret's colleagues aware of what was going on between them – pretty certainly by others actually *seeing* the evidence. It means, I think, that the pair of them were very often *near* each other, and that he very sensibly agreed to avoid all contact with her *in the place where they found themselves*. And you don't need me to tell you where that might have been – *must* have been – do you? It was on the Locals site itself, where twenty-odd workmen were employed on various jobs – but mostly on the roof – between May and September last year.'

'Phew!' Lewis looked down at the letter again. If what Morse was saying were true . . .

'But there's a second thing,' continued Morse, 'that's more specific still. There's a rather nice little bit of English at the end of the letter – "but I think I was in love with you the very first time I saw the top of your golden head in the summer sunshine". Now you were right in saying that this tells us roughly when he first met her. But it also tells us something else, and something even more important. Don't you see? It tells us from which *angle* he first saw her, doesn't it, Lewis? *He saw her from above!*'

Lewis was weighing up what Morse had just said: 'You mean this fellow might have been *on the roof*, sir?'

'Could be!' Morse looked extremely pleased with himself. 'Yes, he could have been on the roof. Or he could have been – *higher*, perhaps? The flat roof at the Locals has been causing a lot of trouble, and last summer they had a complete new go at the whole thing.'

'So?'

'So they had quite a few workmen there, and they'd need something to lift all that stuff . . .'

'A crane!' The words were out of Lewis's excited lips in a flash.

'It makes sense, doesn't it?'

'Did they have a crane on the site?'

'Don't know, do I.'

'Do you remember,' said Lewis slowly, 'that it was *me* who suggested he might be a crane-driver?'

'Nonsense!' said Morse happily.

'But I—'

'You may have got the right answer, Lewis, but you got it for the wrong reasons, and you can't claim much credit for that.'

Lewis's smile was as happy as Morse's. 'Shall I give the Secretary a ring, sir?'

'Think she's still there? It's gone half-past five.'

'Some people stay on after office hours. Like I do!'

The Secretary was still at her desk. Yes, there had been a crane on the site – a big yellow thing – from May to October! And no, the Secretary had no objection at all to the police coming to look at the security passes kept all together in a filing cabinet in Reception.

Morse got up from his chair and pulled on his greatcoat. 'And there's something else, you know, Lewis. Something to crown the whole lot, really. They keep all their records carefully at the Locals – well, the chap on the desk does. All passes have to be shown and I'd like to bet that those workmen were given semi-permanent passes so that they could make use of the facilities there without having to get a badge every time they went to the lavatory or whatever. Just think of it! We sit here and rack our brains – and all the time the fellow we're looking for is sitting there on a little card – in a little drawer at the Locals – with a photograph of himself on it! By Jove, this is the simplest case we've ever handled, my old friend. Come on. On your feet!'

But for a while, Lewis sat where he was, a wistful expression across his square, honest face. 'You know, it's a pity in a way, isn't it? Like you say, we've done all this thinking – we've even given the fellow a name! The only thing we never got round to was deciding where he lives, that's all. And if we'd been able to work that out – well, we wouldn't need any photograph or anything, would we? We'd have, sort of, *thought* it all out.'

Morse sat on the edge of his desk nodding his balding head. 'Ye-es. 'Tis a pity, I agree. Amazing, you know, what feats of logic the human brain is capable of. But sometimes life eludes logic – and sometimes when you build a great big wonderful theory you find there's a fault in the foundations and the whole thing collapses round your ears at the slightest earth tremor.'

Morse's voice had sounded strangely earnest, and Lewis noticed how tired his chief looked. 'You don't think we're in for an earth-quake, do you?'

'Hope not! Above all I hope we get a chance to save Margaret Bowman – save her from herself as much as anything. Nice looker, you know, that woman. Lovely head of hair!'

'Especially when viewed from the top of a crane,' said Lewis, as he finally rose to his feet and pulled on his coat.

As they were leaving the office, Morse paused to look at a large white map of Oxford City that was fastened on the wall to the left of the door. 'What do you think, Lewis? Here we are: South Parade – that's where he picked her up. Now we want somewhere no more than five minutes away, so you say. Well, one thing's certain – he either turned left or he turned right at the Woodstock Road, agreed?' Morse's finger slowly traced a route that led off to the south: it seemed most unlikely that the man would be living in any of the large villa-type residences that lined the road for most of the way down to St Giles', and Morse found himself looking at the map just below St John's College playing fields, and especially at the maze of little streets that criss-crossed the heart of Jericho. For his part, Lewis's eyes considered the putative route that might have been taken if the man had turned right and towards the north; and soon he spotted a small cluster of streets, between the Woodstock Road itself and, to the west of it, the canal and the railway. The writing on the map was very small but Lewis could just about read the names: St Peter's Road; Ulfgar Road; Pixey Place; Diamond Close . . . All council property, if Lewis recalled correctly – or used to be until, in the 1980s, the Tories remembered Anthony Eden's promises of a property-owning democracy.

Chapter Thirty-eight

Tuesday, January 7th: p.m.

I keep six honest serving-men
(They taught me all I knew):
Their names are What and Why and When
And How and Where and Who.

Rudyard Kipling

The most obvious improvements effected by those who had bought their own red-brick houses had been to the doors and the windows: several of the old doors were replaced completely by stout oaken affairs – or at the very least painted some colour other than the former regulation light-blue: and most of the old windows, with their former small oblong panes, were now replaced by large horizontal sheets of glass set in stainless-steel frames. In general, it seemed fairly clear, the tone of the neighbourhood was on the 'up'; and number 17 Diamond Close was no exception to this pattern of improved properties. A storm door (behind which no light was visible) had been built across the small front porch; and the front fence and garden had been redesigned to accommodate a medium-sized car – like the light-green Maestro which stood there now. Under the orange glare of the street-lamps, the close was strangely still.

The two police cars had moved slowly along St Peter's Road
and then stopped at the junction with Diamond Close. Morse,
Lewis and Phillips were in the first car; two uniformed constables
and a plain-clothes detective in the second. Both Phillips and the
plain-clothes man had been issued with regulation revolvers; and
these two (as prearranged) got out of their cars and without slamming the doors behind them walked silently along the thirty or so
yards to the front of number 17, where, with the plain-clothes man
rather melodramatically pointing his revolver to the stars, Sergeant
Phillips pushed the white button of the front-door bell. After a few
seconds, a dull light appeared from somewhere at the back of the
house, and then a fuller light and the silhouette of a figure seen
through the glass of the outer door. At that moment the watching
faces of Morse and Lewis betrayed a high degree of tension: yet,
in retrospect, there had been nothing whatsoever to occasion such
emotion.

From the outset the man in the thick green sweater had
proved surprisingly co-operative. He had requested to be allowed
to finish his baked beans (refused), to collect a packet of cigarettes
(granted), to drive to Police HQ in his own car (refused), and to take
his scarf and duffel coat (granted). At no stage had he mentioned
writs, warrants, lawyers, solicitors, civil rights, unlawful arrest or
Lord Longford, and Morse himself was beginning to feel a little
shamed-faced about the death-or-glory scenario of the arrest. But
one never knew.

In the interview room it was Lewis who began the questioning.
'Your full name is Edward Wilkins?'
'Edward James Wilkins.'
'Your date of birth?'
'Twentieth September, 1951.'
'Place of birth?'
'17 Diamond Close.'
'The house you live in now?'
'Yes. My mother lived there.'
'Which school did you go to?'
'Hobson Road Primary – for a start.'
'And after that?'
'Oxford Boys' School.'
'You passed the eleven-plus to go there?'
'Yes.'
'When did you leave?'

'In 1967.'

'You took your O-levels?'

'Yes. I passed in Maths, Physics and Engineering Drawing.'

'You didn't take English Literature?'

'Yes, I did. But I failed.'

'Did you read any Milton?' interrupted Morse.

'Yes, we read *Comus*.'

'What did you do after you left school?' (Lewis had taken up the questioning once more.)

'I got an apprenticeship at Lucy's Ironworks in Jericho.'

'And then?'

'I didn't finish it. I stuck it for eighteen months and then I got offered a much better job with Mackenzie Construction.'

'You still work for them?'

'Yes.'

'What's your job, exactly?'

'I'm a crane-driver.'

'You mean you sit up in the cabin and swing all the loads round the site?'

'That's one way of putting it.'

'This company – Mackenzie Construction – they did some re-roofing last year at the Oxford Delegacy – Oxford Locals, I think you call it. Is that right?'

'Yes. About April to September.'

'You worked there all that time?'

'Yes.'

'Not *all* that time, surely?'

'Pardon?'

'Didn't you have any summer holiday?'

'Oh yes, I'm sorry. I was off a fortnight.'

'When was that?'

'Late July.'

'Where did you go?'

'Up to the north of England.'

'Whereabouts exactly?'

'The Lake District.'

'And where in the Lake District?'

'Derwentwater.'

'Did you send any postcards from there?'

'A few. Yes.'

'To some of your friends here – in Oxford?'

'Who else?'

'Oh, I don't know, Mr Wilkins. If I'd known I wouldn't have asked, would I?'

It was the first moment of tension in the interview, and Lewis (as Morse had instructed him) left things there for a while, saying nothing; and for a little while the silence hung heavily over the bare, rather chilly room at the rear of Police HQ in Kidlington.

From the doorway Sergeant Phillips, who had never previously been present at such an interrogation, watched events with a touch of embarrassment. The prolonged period of silence seemed (as Phillips saw things) particularly to affect Wilkins, whose hands twice twitched at his hip pocket as if seeking the solace of a cigarette, but whose will-power appeared for the minute in adequate control. He was a large-boned, fairish-haired, pleasantly spoken man who seemed to Phillips about the last person in the world who would suddenly display any symptoms of homicidal ferocity. Yet Phillips was also aware that the two men in charge of the case, Morse and Lewis, had great experience in these affairs, and he listened to Lewis's further questions with absorbed fascination.

'When did you first meet Mrs Margaret Bowman?'

'You know all about that?'

'Yes.'

'I met her when I was working at the Locals. We had the use of the canteen and some of us used to have a meal there and that's when I met her.'

'When did you first meet her outside working hours?'

'She had a night-school class, and I used to meet her for a drink afterwards.'

'Quite regularly, you did this?'

'Yes.'

'And you invited her back to your house?'

'Yes.'

'And you made love to each other?'

'Yes.'

'And then she got a bit fed up with you and wanted the affair to stop – is that right, Mr Wilkins?'

'That's not true.'

'You were in love with her?'

'Yes.'

'You still in love with her?'

'Yes.'

'Is she in love with you?' (Morse was delighted with such a beautifully modulated question.)

'I didn't force her along, did I?' (For the first time a little hesitancy – and a little coarseness – had crept into Wilkins' manner.)

'Did you write this?' Lewis handed over a Xeroxed copy of the letter found in Bowman's jacket.

'I wrote it, yes,' said Wilkins.

'And you still say you weren't forcing her along a bit?'

'I just wanted to see her again, that's all.'

'To make love to her again, you mean?'

'Not just that, no.'

'Did you actually see her that day – in South Parade?'

'Yes.'

'And you took her to your house?'

'Yes.'

'Was anyone following you – in a car?'

'What do you mean?'

'Mr Bowman knew all about you – we found that copy of the letter in one of his jackets.'

Wilkins shook his head, as if with regret. 'I didn't know that – honestly, I didn't. I always said to Margaret that whatever happened I never wanted to – well, to *hurt* anybody else.'

'You didn't know that Mr Bowman knew all about you?'

'No.'

'She didn't tell you?'

'No. I stopped seeing her after that day I met her in South Parade. She said she couldn't cope with the strain and everything, and that she'd decided to stay with him. It was a bit hard to take, but I tried to accept it. I hadn't got much option, had I?'

'When did you last see her?'

For the first time in the interview, Wilkins allowed himself a ghost of a smile, showing regular though nicotine-stained teeth. 'I saw her,' he looked at his wrist-watch, 'just over an hour ago. She was in the house when you called to bring me here.'

Morse closed his eyes momentarily in what looked like a twinge of intolerable pain; and Lewis began 'You mean . . . ?'

'She came about a quarter to six. She just said she didn't know what to do – she wanted help.'

'Did she want money?'

'No. Well, she didn't mention it. Not much good asking *me* for money, in any case – and she knew that.'

'Did she say where she was going?'

'Not really, but I think she'd been in touch with her sister.'

'She lives where?'

'Near Newcastle, I think.'

'You didn't tell her she could stay with you?'

'That would have been a mad thing to do, wouldn't it?'

'Do you think she's still in your house?'

'She'd be out of there like a bat out of hell immediately we'd gone.'

(Morse gestured to Sergeant Phillips, spoke a few words in his ear and dismissed him.)

'So you think she's off north somewhere?' continued Lewis.

'I don't know. I honestly don't know. I advised her to get on a boat or something and sail off to the Continent – away from everything.'

'But she didn't take your advice?'

'No. She couldn't. She hadn't got a passport, and she was frightened of applying for one because she knew everybody was trying to find her.'

'Did she know that everybody was trying to find *you*, as well?'

'Of course she didn't! I don't know what you mean.'

'I'm sure you know why we've brought you here,' said Lewis, looking directly across into Wilkins' eyes.

'Really? I'm afraid you're wrong there.'

'Well, she *did* know that everybody was looking for you. You see, Mr Wilkins, she went back to her own house in Chipping Norton, at considerable risk to herself, to remove any incriminating evidence that she thought might be lying around. For example, she took the postcard you wrote to her from the Lake District.'

There was a sudden dramatic silence in the interview room, as though everybody there had taken a sharp intake of breath – and was holding it.

'It's my duty as a police officer,' continued Lewis, 'to tell you formally that you are under arrest for the murder of Thomas Bowman.'

Wilkins slumped back in his chair, his face ashen-pale and his upper lip trembling. 'You're making the most terrible mistake,' he said very quietly.

Chapter Thirty-nine

Tuesday, January 7th: p.m.

When angry, count four; when very angry, swear.
Mark Twain

'Am I doing all right?' asked a slightly subdued Lewis as, five minutes after this preliminary interview, he sat in the canteen drinking coffee with Morse.

'Very good – *very* good,' said Morse. 'But we've got to tread a bit carefully from now on because we're getting to the point where we're not *quite* sure of the ground – by which I mean it's going to be difficult to *prove* one or two things. So let's just recap a minute. Let's go back to the beginning of things – Plan One, let's call it. Bowman follows his wife up to Diamond Close that day, and later he confronts her with the evidence. She's getting desperate anyway, and she goes along with the quite extraordinary plan he's concocted. As we've seen he fixes up the phoney address and books a New-Year-Package-for-Two at the Haworth Hotel. She tells Wilkins that her husband's gone off on a course and that they can spend all that time together; and he jumps at the chance. Once she's safely in her room, she rings Wilkins – we still haven't checked on that, Lewis – to give him the room number and soon she's giving him the happy hour between the sheets. Then they both get ready for the fancy dress – which she's already told Wilkins about, and which he's already agreed to. If he *hadn't*, Lewis, the plan couldn't have worked. At about seven o'clock she makes some excuse to go out, when she gives the key to Bowman himself, who's waiting some-where near the annexe, and who's dressed up in exactly the same sort of garb as Wilkins. Now Wilkins is a stronger man, I suspect, than Bowman ever was, and I should think that Bowman wouldn't have taken any chance about letting the whole thing develop into a brawl – he's probably got a knife or a revolver or something. Then the deed is done, and the next part of the deception begins. They could disappear from the scene straight away, but they agree that's far too risky. Somebody's going to find the body immediately if they do, because the "Ballards" as they called themselves won't be there for the party. There's virtually no risk in their being recognised, anyway: they're both in fancy dress for the rest of the evening –

he's got his face blacked, she's wearing a veil; and the only time a busy receptionist had seen Margaret Bowman was when she'd been muffled up in a scarf and hood – with a pair of dark ski-ing glasses on, for all we know.'

Lewis nodded.

'That was the original plan – and it must have been very much as I've described it, Lewis; otherwise it's impossible to account for several facts in the case – for instance, the fact that Bowman wrote a letter to his wife that would give them both a reasonable alibi – if the worse came to the worst. It wasn't a bad plan, either – except in one vital respect. Bowman was beginning to know quite a bit about Wilkins, but he never quite knew *enough*. Above all, he didn't know that Wilkins was beginning to dominate his wife in an ever increasing way, and that she'd become so sexually and emotionally dependent on him that she came to realise, at some point, that it was her husband, Tom Bowman, she wanted out of her life for good – not her lover. Maybe Bowman had become so obsessed with this revenge idea of his that she saw, perhaps for the first time, what a crudely devious man he really was. But for whatever reason, we can know one thing for certain: *she told Wilkins what they were planning*. Now you don't need to be a genius – and I don't think Wilkins *is* a genius – to spot an almost incredible opportunity here: the plan can go ahead as Bowman had devised it – exactly so! – but only up to the point when Bowman would let himself into the room. This time it would be *Wilkins* who's waiting behind the door *for Bowman* with a bottle of whatever it was to smash down on the back of his head.'

'Front, sir,' murmured Lewis if only, for conscience's sake, to put the unofficial record straight.

'So that's what happened, Lewis; and it's Plan Two that's now in operation. After murdering Bowman, Wilkins is all ready to go along to the party in exactly the same outlandish clothes as the murdered man would be found in. The two men were roughly the same height and everybody is going to assume that the man in the Rastafarian rig-out at the party is the same as the man in the Rastafarian rig-out later found dead on the bed in Annexe 3. Almost certainly – and this is in fact what happened – the corpse isn't going to be found until pretty late the next day; and if the heating is turned off – as it was – and if the window's left half-open – as it was – then any cautious clown like Max is going to be even cagier than usual about giving any categorical ruling on the time of death, because of the unusual room temperature. I'm not sure, myself, that it wouldn't have been far more sensible to turn the radiator on full and close all the windows. But, be that as it may, Wilkins clearly wanted to give the impression that the murder had taken place *as late as possible.* Agreed?'

'I can't quite see *why* though, sir.'

'You will do, in due course. Have faith!'

Lewis, however, looked rather less than full of faith. 'It's getting a bit too complicated for my brain, sir. I keep forgetting who's dressed up for what and who's planning to kill who—'

' "Whom", Lewis. Your grammar's as bad as Miss Jonstone's.'

'You're sure he *is* the murderer? – Wilkins?'

'My son, the case is over! There are bound to be one or two details—'

'Do you mind if we just go over one or two things again?'

'I can't spell things out *much* more simply, you know.'

'You say Wilkins wanted the murder to look as if it took place as late as possible. But I don't see the point of that. It doesn't give him an alibi, does it? I mean, whether Bowman's murdered at seven o'clock or after midnight – what does it matter? Wilkins and Margaret Bowman were there *all the time*, weren't they?'

'Yes! But who said they'd got an alibi? *I* didn't mention an alibi. All I'm saying is that Wilkins had a reason for wanting to mislead everyone into believing that the murder was committed after the party was over. That's obvious enough, isn't it?'

'But going back a minute, don't you think that in Bowman's original plan – Plan One, as you call it – it would have been far more sensible to have committed the murder – murder Wilkins, that is – and then to get out of the place double quick? With any luck, no one's going to suspect a married couple from Chipping Norton – even if the body's found very soon afterwards.'

Morse nodded, but with obvious frustration.

'I *agree* with you. But somehow or other we've got to explain how it came about that Bowman was found dressed up in identically the same sort of outfit as Wilkins was wearing at the party. Don't you *see* that, Lewis? We've got to explain the facts! And I refuse to believe that anyone could have dressed up Bowman in all that stuff *after* he'd been murdered.'

'There's one other thing, sir. You know from Max's report it says that Bowman could have been eating some of the things they had at the party?'

'What about it?'

'Well – was it just coincidence he'd been eating the same sort of meal?'

'No. Margaret Bowman must have known – she must have found out – what the menu was and then cooked her husband some of it. Then all Wilkins had to do was just eat a bit of the same stuff—'

'But how did Margaret Bowman know?'

'How the hell do I know, Lewis? But it *happened*, didn't it? I'm not making up this bloody corpse, you know! I'm not making up all these people in their fancy dress! You do realise that, don't you?'

'No need to get cross, sir!'

'I'm *not* bloody cross! If somebody decides to make some elaborate plan to rub out one side of the semi-eternal triangle – we've got to have some equally elaborate explanation! Surely you can see that?'

Lewis nodded. 'I agree. But just let me make my main point once again, sir – and then we'll forget it. It's this business of *staying on after the murder* that worries me: it must have been a dreadfully nerve-racking time for the two of them; it was very complicated; and it was a bit chancy. And all I say is that I can't *really* see the point of it. It just keeps the pair of them on the hotel premises the whole of the evening, and whatever time the murder was committed they haven't got any chance of an alibi—'

'There you go again, Lewis! For Christ's sake, come off it! *Nobody's got a bloody alibi.*'

The two men were silent for several minutes.

'Cup more coffee, sir?' asked Lewis.

'Augh! I'm sorry, Lewis. You just take the wind out of my sails, that's all.'

'We've got him, sir. That's the only thing that matters.'

Morse nodded.

'And you're absolutely sure that we've got the right man?'

'It's a big word – "absolutely" – isn't it?' said Morse.

Chapter Forty

Tuesday, January 7th: p.m.

Alibi (*n.*) – the plea in a criminal charge of having been elsewhere at the material time.

Chambers 20th Century Dictionary

It was, in all, to be an hour or so before the interrogation of Wilkins was resumed. Morse had telephoned Max, but had learned only that if he, Morse, continued to supply the lab with corpses about twenty-four hours old, he, Max, was not going to make too many fanciful speculations: he was a forensic scientist, not a fortune-teller. Lewis had contacted the Haworth Hotel to discover that one local call had in fact been made – untraceable, though – from Annexe 3 on New Year's Eve. Phillips, who had returned from Diamond Close with the not unexpected news that Margaret Bowman (if she *had* been there) had flown, now resumed his duties in the interview room, standing by the door, his feet aching a good deal, his eyes idly scanning the bare room once again: the wooden trestle-table, on which stood two white polystyrene cups (empty now) and an ashtray (rapidly filling); and behind the table, the fairish-haired, fresh-complexioned man accused of a terrible murder, who seemed to Phillips to look perhaps rather less dramatically perturbed than should have been expected.

'What time did you get to the Haworth Hotel on New Year's Eve?'

'Say that again?'

'What time did you get to the hotel?'

'I didn't go to any hotel that night—'

'You were at the Haworth Hotel and you got there at—'

'I've never played there.'

'Never played what?'

'Never *played* there!'

'I'm not quite with you, Mr Wilkins.'

'We go round the pubs – the group – we don't often go to hotels.'

'You play in a pop group?'

'A jazz group – I play tenor sax.'

'So what?'

'Look, Sergeant. You say you're not with *me*: I'm not with *you*, either.'

'You were at the Haworth Hotel on New Year's Eve. What time
did you get there?'

'I was at the Friar up in North Oxford on New Year's Eve!'

'Really?'

'Yes, really!'

'Can you prove it?'

'Not offhand, I suppose, but—'

'Would the landlord there remember you?'

' 'Course he would! He paid us, didn't he?'

'The group you're in – was playing there?'

'Yes.'

'And you were there *all the evening*?'

'Till about two o'clock the next morning.'

'How many others in the group?'

'Four.'

'And how many people were there at the Friar that night?'

'Sixty? – seventy? – on and off.'

'Which bar were you in?'

'Lounge bar.'

'And you didn't leave the bar all night?'

'Well, we had steak and chips in the back room at about –
half-past nine, I suppose it was.'

'With the rest of the group?'

'*And* the landlord – *and* the landlady.'

'This is New Year's Eve you're talking about?'

'Look, Sergeant, I've been here a long time already tonight,
haven't I? Can you please ring up the Friar and get someone here
straightaway? Or ring up any of the group? I'm getting awfully tired
– and it's been one hell of an evening for me – you can understand
that, can't you?'

There was a silence in the room – a silence that seemed to
Phillips to take on an almost palpable tautness, as the import of
Wilkins' claim slowly sank into the minds of the detectives there.

'What does your group call itself, Mr Wilkins?' It was Morse
himself who quietly asked the final question.

'The "Oxford Blues",' said Wilkins, his face hard and unamused.

Charlie Freeman ('Fingers' Freeman to his musical colleagues) was
surprised to find a uniformed constable standing on his Kidlington
doorstep that evening. Yes, the 'Oxford Blues' had played the Friar
on New Year's Eve; yes, *he'd* played there that night, with Ted
Wilkins, for about five or six hours; yes, he'd be more than willing

to go along to Police HQ immediately and make a statement to that effect. No great hardship for him, was it? After all, it was only a couple of minutes' walk away.

By 9.30 p.m. Mr Edward Wilkins had been driven back to his home in Diamond Close; Phillips, at long last, had been given permission to call it a day; and Lewis, tired and dejected, sat in Morse's office, wondering where they had all gone so sadly wrong. Perhaps he might have suspected – and he'd actually *said* so – that Morse's ideas had all been a bit too bizarre: a man murdered in a fancy-dress outfit; and then another man spending the night of the party pretending he *was* the murdered man and dressed in a virtually identical outfit. Surely, surely, the simple truth was that *Thomas Bowman* had been the man at the party, as well as the man who'd been murdered! There would be (as Lewis knew) lots of difficulties in substantiating such a view; but none of them was anywhere near as insurmountable as trying to break Wilkins' alibi – an alibi which could be vouched for by sixty or seventy wholly disinterested witnesses. Gently, quietly, Lewis mentioned his thoughts to Morse – the latter sitting silent and morose in the old black-leather armchair. 'You could be right, Lewis.' Morse rubbed his left hand across his eyes. 'Anyway, it's no good worrying about it tonight. My judgement's gone! I need a drink. You coming?'

'No. I'll get straight home, if you don't mind, sir. It's been a long day, and I should think the missus'll have something cooking for me.'

'I should be surprised if she hasn't.'

'You're looking tired, sir. Do you want me to give you a lift?'

Morse nodded wearily. 'Just drop me at the Friar, if you will.'

As he walked up to the entrance, Morse stopped. Red, blue, green and orange lights were flashing through the lounge windows, and the place was athrob with the live music of what sounded like some Caribbean delirium at the Oval greeting a test century from Vivian Richards. Morse checked his step and walked round to the public bar, where in comparative peace he sat and drank two pints of Morrell's bitter and watched a couple of incompetent pool-players pretending to be Steve Davises. On the wall beside the dartboard he saw the notice:

7th January
LIVE MUSIC 7–11 p.m.
Admission Free!!
The fabulous
CALYPSO QUARTET

Morse pondered a quick third pint; but it wanted only a couple
of minutes to eleven, and he decided to get home – just a few
minutes' walk away, along Carlton Road and thence just a little
way down the Banbury Road to his bachelor flat. But something
thwarted this decision, and he ordered another pint, a large Bell's
Scotch and a packet of plain crisps.

At twenty minutes past eleven he was the last one in the public
bar, and the young barman wiping the table-tops suggested that
he should finish his drink and leave: it was not unknown (Morse
learned) for the police to check up on over-liquored loiterers after
a live-music evening.

As he left, Morse saw the Calypso Quartet packing away its collection of steel drums and sundry other Caribbean instruments into the
back of an old, oft-dented Dormobile. And suddenly Morse stopped.
He stopped dead. He stopped as if petrified, staring at the man who
had just closed the back door of the vehicle and who was languidly
lolling round to the driving seat. Even in the bitter late-night air
this man wore only a blood-red, open-necked shirt on the upper part
of his loose-limbed body; whilst on his head he had a baggy black-
and-white checked cap that covered all his hair apart from the beaded
dreadlocks which dangled on either side of his face like the snakes
that once wreathed the head of the stone-eyed Gorgon.

'You all right, man?' enquired the coloured musician, holding
both hands up in a mock gesture of concern about a fellow mortal
who seemed to have imbibed too freely perhaps and too well. And
Morse noticed the hands – hands that were almost like the hands
of a white man, as though the Almighty had just about run out of
pigment when he came to the palms.

'You all right man?' repeated the musician.

Morse nodded, and there appeared on his face a stupidly beatific
smile such as was seldom seen there – save when he listened to the
love duet from Act One of *Die Walküre*.

Morse should (he knew it!) not have left things where they were
that night. But his eyelids drooped heavily over his prickly-tired
eyes as he walked back to his flat; and in spite of his elation, he

had little enough strength left, little appetite for anything more
that day. But before throwing himself on the longed-for bed, he
did ring Lewis; and prevailed upon Mrs Lewis (still up) to rouse
her husband (an hour abed) for a few quick words before January
7th drew to its seemingly interminable close. And when, after only a
brief monologue from Morse, a weary-brained Lewis put his receiver
down, he, too, knew the identity of the man who on New Year's Eve
had walked back to the annexe of the Haworth Hotel with Helen
Smith on the one side and Philippa Palmer on the other.

Chapter Forty-one

Wednesday, January 8th: a.m.

Matrimony is a bargain, and somebody has to get the worst
of the bargain.

Helen Rowland

At the desk of the Haworth Hotel the following morning, Sarah
Jonstone greeted Sergeant Lewis as if she were glad to see him;
which indeed she was, since she had at last remembered the little
thing that had been troubling her. So early in the day (it was only
eight-thirty), her excessively circumferenced spectacles were still
riding high upon her pretty little nose, and it could hardly be claimed,
at least for the present, that she was being hectically overworked; in
fact Lewis had already observed her none-too-convincing attempt to
conceal beneath a pile of correspondence the book she had been
reading when he had so unexpectedly walked in – on Morse's
instruction – to interview her once again.

It was just a little corroboration (Lewis had pointed out) that was
needed; and Sarah found herself once again seeking to stress the few
unequivocally certain points she had made in her earlier statement.
Yes, she *did* remember, and very clearly, the man coming out of the
Gentlemen's lavatory just before the New Year's Eve party was due
to begin; yes (now that Lewis mentioned it) perhaps his hands *hadn't*
been blackened-over as convincingly as the rest of him; yes, the two

of them, 'Mr and Mrs Ballard', *had* kept themselves very much to themselves for the greater part of the evening – certainly until that hour or so before midnight when a series of eightsome reels, general excuse-me's and old-time barn-dances had severed the last ties of self-consciousness and timidity; and when 'Mr Ballard' had danced with her, his sweaty fingers leaving some of their dark stain on her own hands, *and* on her blouse; yes, without a shadow of a doubt that last fact *was* true, because she remembered with a sweet clarity how she had washed her hands in the bedroom wall-basin before going to bed that night, and how she had tried to sponge the stain off her blouse the following morning.

A middle-aged couple stood waiting to pay their bill; and while Sarah fetched the account from the small room at the back of Reception, Lewis turned his head to one side and was thus able to make out the title on the white spine of the book she had been reading: MILLGATE: *Thomas Hardy – A Biography*. O.U.P.

The bill settled, Sarah resumed her seat and told Lewis what she had remembered. It had been odd, though it didn't really seem all that important now. What had happened was that someone – a woman – had rung up and asked what the New Year's Eve menu was: that was all. As far as she could recall, the little incident had taken place on the Monday before – that would be December 30th.

Knowing how pleased Morse would be to have one of his hunches confirmed, Lewis was on the point of taking down some firm statement from Sarah Jonstone when he became aware of an extraordinarily attractive brunette standing beside him, shifting the weight of her beautifully moulded figure from one black-stockinged leg to the other.

'Can I have my bill, please?' she asked. Although the marked Birmingham accent was not, as he heard it, exactly the music of the spheres, Lewis found himself staring at the woman with an almost riveted fascination.

The whispered voice in his ear was totally unexpected: 'Take your lecherous eyes off her, Lewis!'

'Thank you very much, Miss Arkwright!' said Sarah Jonstone, as the woman turned and left, flashing a brief, but almost interested, glance at the man who had just come in.

'Good morning, Miss Jonstone!' said Morse.

'Oh, hello!' There was nothing about her greeting that could be construed as even wanly welcoming.

'Is she the same one?' asked Morse, gesturing after the departed beauty. 'The one who was due for the New Year?'

'Yes!'

'Well, well!' said Morse, looking quite extraordinarily pleased with himself and with life in general; and quite clearly pleased with the sight of Miss Doris Arkwright in particular. 'Could you please ask *Mrs* Binyon to come along to Reception, Miss Jonstone? There's something rather important—'

'She's not here, I'm afraid. She's gone up to Leeds. She *was* going there for the New Year, but—'

'Really? How *very* interesting! Well thank you very much, Miss Jonstone. Come on, Lewis! We've a busy morning ahead.'

'Miss Jonstone remembered something—' started Lewis.

'Forget it for the minute! Bigger things to worry about just now! Goodbye, Miss Jonstone!'

Morse was still smirking to himself with infinite self-satisfaction as, for the last time, the two men walked from the Haworth Hotel.

An hour later, a man was arrested at his home in south-east Oxford. This time, there were no revolvers on view; and the man in question, promptly cautioned by Sergeant Lewis of the Oxfordshire CID, made no show of resistance whatsoever.

Chapter Forty-two

Wednesday, January 8th: noon

Lovers of air travel find it exhilarating to hang poised between the illusion of immortality and the fact of death.
                                                        Alexander Chase

The Boeing 737 scheduled to take off from Gatwick at 12.05 hours was almost fully booked, with only four or five empty seats visible as the air hostesses went through their dumb-shows with the oxygen masks and the inflatable life-jackets. It was noticeable that almost all the passengers were paying the most careful attention to the advice being offered: several tragic air crashes during the previous months had engendered a sort of collective pterophobia, and airport lounges throughout the world were reporting a dramatic rise in the sales of tranquillising pills and alcoholic spirits. But quite certainly there were two persons on the aircraft (and there may have been others) who listened only perfunctorily to the safety instructions being rehearsed that lunchtime. For one of these two persons, the transit through the terminal had been a nightmare: and yet, as it now seemed, there had been no real cause for anxiety. Documentation, baggage, passport – none had brought any problem at all. For the second of these two persons, worries had sprung from a slightly different source; yet he, too, was now beginning to feel more relaxed. As he looked down from his window-seat on to the wet tarmac, his left hand quietly slid the half-bottle of brandy from his anorak pocket, allowing his right hand to unscrew the cap. The attention of those passengers sitting immediately around him was still focused on the slim-waisted stewardesses, and he was able to pour himself a couple of tots without his imbibings being too obvious. And already he felt slightly better! It had been a damnably close-run thing – but he'd made it! A sign came on just above him, bidding all passengers to fasten their seatbelts and to refrain from smoking until further notice; the engines vibrated anew along the fuselage; and the stewardesses took their seats, facing the passengers, and smiling (perhaps with slightly spurious confidence) upon their latest charges. Gradually the giant plane moved forward in a quarter-turn, took up its proper station, and stood there for a minute or two preparing, like a long-jump finalist in the Olympic Games, to accelerate along the runway. The man seated by the window knew that any second now he would be able to relax – almost completely. Like so many fellow criminals, he was under the happy delusion that there was no extradition treaty between Spain and the United Kingdom, and he had read of so many criminals – bank robbers, embezzlers, drug-pedlars and pederasts – who were even now lounging lazily at various resorts along the Costa del Sol. Suddenly the aircraft's throttles were opened completely and the mighty power seemed almost a tangible entity.

Then the engines seemed to die a little.

And then they seemed to die completely.

And two members of Gatwick Security Police boarded the aircraft.

For the man in the window-seat, beside whom these men stopped, there appeared little point in even thinking of escape. Where was there to escape to?

The Boeing was only very slightly delayed; and five minutes behind schedule it was shooting off the earth at an angle of forty-five degrees

and heading for its appointed destination. Very soon, passengers
were told that they could unfasten their seatbelts: everything was
fine. And six rows behind the now empty window-seat, a woman
lit a cigarette and inhaled very deeply.

Chapter Forty-three

Wednesday, January 8th: p.m.

No mask like open truth to cover lies,
As to go naked is the best disguise.
William Congreve

Morse sat in Superintendent Bell's office in St Aldate's, awaiting
Lewis – the latter having been deputed the task of taking down in
his rather laborious long-hand the statement from the man arrested
earlier that day at his home in south-east Oxford.

'Damned clever, you know!' reiterated Bell.

Morse nodded: he liked Bell well enough perhaps – though not
overmuch – and he found himself wishing that Lewis would get a
move on.

'Well done, anyway!' said Bell. 'The Chief Constable'll be
pleased.'

'Perhaps he'll let me have a day or two's holiday before the end
of the decade.'

'We're *very* grateful, though – you know that, don't you?'

'Yes,' said Morse, honestly enough.

It was a highly euphoric Lewis who came in at a quarter past one,
thrusting a statement – four pages of it – on the desk in front of
Morse. 'Maybe a few little errors in English usage here and there,
sir; but on the whole a splendid piece of prose, I think you'll find.'

Morse took the statement and scanned the last page:

in the normal way, but we were hard up and I lost my job in November
and there was only playing in the group left with a wife and my four
little children to feed and look after. We'd got the Social Security but

the HP was getting bad, and then this came along. All I had to do was what he told me and that wasn't very difficult. I didn't really have any choice because I needed the money bad and it wasn't because I wanted to do anything that was wrong. I know what happened because I saw it in the *Oxford Mail* but when I agreed I just did what I was told and I never knew what things were all about at the time. I'm very sorry about it. Please remember I said that, because I love my wife and my little children.

As dictated to Sergeant Lewis, Kidlington CID, by Mr Winston Grant, labourer (unemployed), of 29 Rose Hill Gardens, Rose Hill, Oxford. 8 Jan.

'The adverb from "bad" is "badly",' mumbled Morse.

'Shall we keep him here?' asked Bell.

'He's your man,' said Morse.

'And the charge – officially?'

' "Accessory to murder", I suppose – but I'm not a legal man.'

' "*Party* to murder", perhaps?' suggested Lewis, who had seldom looked so happy since his elder daughter announced her first pregnancy.

Back at Kidlington HQ, Morse sat back in the old black-leather armchair, looking (for the while) imperturbably expansive. The man arrested at Gatwick, almost two hours earlier, was well on his way to Oxfordshire, expected (Morse learned) within the next fifteen minutes. It was a time to savour.

Lewis himself now knew exactly what had happened on New Year's Eve in Annexe 3; knew, too, that the murderer of Thomas Bowman had neither set foot inside the main hotel building, nor bedecked himself in a single item of fancy dress. And yet, as to how Morse had arrived at the truth, he felt as puzzled as a small boy witnessing his first conjuring performance. 'What really put you on to it, sir?'

'The *key* point was, as I told you, that the murderer tried desperately hard to persuade us that the crime was committed *as late as possible*: after midnight. But as you yourself rightly observed, Lewis, there would seem to be little point in such a deception if the murderer stayed on the scene the whole time from about eight that night to one o'clock the next morning. But there was every point if he *wasn't* on the scene in the latter part of the evening – a time for which he had an *alibi*!'

'But, sir—'

'There were three clues in this case which should have put us on to the truth much earlier than they did. Each of these three clues, in itself, looks like a pedestrian little piece of information; but taken together – well . . . The *first* vital clue came largely from Sarah Jonstone – the only really valuable and coherent witness in the whole case – and it was this: that the man posing as "Mr Ballard" ate virtually nothing that evening! The *second* vital clue – also brought to our notice, among others, by Miss Jonstone – was the fact that the man posing as "Mr Ballard" was still staining whatever he touched late that evening! Then there was the *third* vital clue – the simplest clue of the lot, and one which was staring all of us in the face from the very beginning. So obvious a clue that none of us – none of us! – paid the slightest attention to it: the fact that the man posing as "Mr Ballard" won the fancy-dress competition!

'You see, Lewis, there are two ways of looking at each of these clues – the complex way, and the simple way. And we'd been looking at them the wrong way – we've been looking at them the *complex* way.'

'I see,' said Lewis, unseeing.

'Take the food business,' continued Morse. 'We almost got in some hopelessly complex muddle about it, didn't we? I read carefully what dear old Max said in his report about what had been floating up and down in the ascending and descending colons. You, Lewis, were bemused enough to listen to what Miss Jonstone said about someone ringing up to ask what the menu was. Why the hell *shouldn't* someone ring up and ask if they're in for another few slices of the virtually inevitable turkey? And do you know what we didn't do amid all this cerebration, Lewis? We didn't ask ourselves a very simple question: if our man had eaten nothing of the first two courses, shouldn't we assume he might be getting a little *hungry*? And even if he's been told he'd better go through the evening secretly sticking all the goodies into a doggie-bag, you might have thought he'd be tempted when he came to the next two courses on the menu – especially a couple of succulent pork chops. So why, Lewis – just think simply! – why didn't he have a mouthful or two?'

'Like you say, sir, he was told not to, because it was vital—'

'No! You're still getting too *complicated*, Lewis. There's a very *simple* answer, you see! Rastafarians aren't allowed to eat pork!

'Now let's come to this business of the stains this man was leaving behind on whatever he touched – even after midnight! We took down all the evidence, didn't we – we got statements

from Miss Palmer, and Mrs Smith, and Sarah Jonstone – about
how the wretched fellow went round ruining their coats and their
blouses. And we almost came to the point – well, *I* did, Lewis –
of getting them all analysed and seeing if the stains were the same,
and trying to find out where the original theatre-black came from
and – well, we were getting too *complex* again! The simple truth
is that any make-up *dries* after a few hours; it comes off at first,
of course, on anything that's touched – but after a while it's no
problem at all. Yet in this case it *remained* a problem. And the
simple answer to this particular mystery is that our man *wanted*
to leave his marks late that evening; he deliberately put *more* stain
on his hands; and he deliberately put his hands where they *would*
leave marks. All right, Lewis? He had a stick of theatre-black in
his pocket and he smeared it all over the palms of his hands in the
final hour or so of the New Year party.

'And then there's the last point. The man won a prize, and
we made all sorts of complex assumptions about it; he'd been the
most painstaking and imaginative competitor of the lot; he'd been
so successful with his make-up that no one could recognise him;
he'd been anxious for some reason to carry off the first prize in
the fancy-dress competition. And all a load of *complex* nonsense,
Lewis. The fact is that the very last thing he wanted was to draw
any attention to himself by winning the first prize that evening.
And the almost childishly *simple* fact of the matter is that if you
want to dress up and win first prize *as*, let's say, Prince Charles,
well, the best way to do it is to *be* Prince Charles. And we all
ought to have suspected, perhaps, that the man who dressed up
in that Rastafarian rig-out and who put on such a convincing and
successful performance that night *as* a Rastafarian, might perhaps
have owed his success to the simple fact that he *was* a Rastafarian!'

'Mr Winston Grant.'

'Yes, Mr Winston Grant! A man, in fact, I met outside the
Friar only last night! And if anyone ever tells you, Lewis, that
there isn't a quite extraordinary degree of coincidence in this world
of ours – then you tell him to come to see me, and I'll tell him
different!'

'Should you perhaps say "differently"?' asked Lewis.

'This man had been a builder's labourer; he'd worked on
several sites in Oxford – including the Locals; he'd lost his job
because of cutbacks in the building industry; he was getting short
of money for himself and his family; he was made an extraordinarily
generous offer – we still don't know *how* generous; and he agreed

to accept that offer in return for playing – as he saw things – a minor rôle for a few hours at a New Year's party in an Oxford hotel. I doubt we shall ever know all the ins and outs of the matter but—'

Sergeant Phillips knocked and announced that the prisoner was now in the interview room.

And Morse smiled.

And Lewis smiled.

'Just finish off what you were saying, will you, sir?'

'Nothing more to say, really. Winston Grant must have been pretty carefully briefed, that's for sure. In the first place he'd be coming into the hotel directly from the street, and it was absolutely essential that he should wait his time, to the second almost, until Margaret Bowman had created the clever little distraction of taking Sarah Jonstone away from the reception desk to inspect the graffito in the Ladies' – a graffito which she, Margaret Bowman, had herself just scrawled across the wall. Then, I'm sure he must have been told to say as little as possible to anyone else all the evening and to stick close to Margaret Bowman, as if they were far more interested in each other than in the goings-on around them. *But there was no chance of him opting out of the fancy-dress competition!* I suspect, too, that he was told not to eat anything – if he could manage not to, without drawing too much attention to himself; and remember, he was helped in this by the way Binyon had scheduled the various courses at different tables. But it may well be, Lewis, that we're over-estimating the extent to which the plan was completely thought out. Above all, though, he had to carry through that final, extraordinarily clever, little deception: he was to make every effort to *pretend* that he was a black man – even though he *was* a black man. And there was one wonderfully simple way in which such a pretence could be sustained, and that was by rubbing dark-stain on to his hands – *hands that were already black* – so that everyone who came into physical contact with him should believe that he was *not* a black man – but a white man. And that, Lewis, in the later stages of that New Year's party is what he did, making sure he left a few indelible marks on the most obvious places – like the shoulders of the light-coloured winter mackintoshes worn by both Miss Palmer and Mrs Smith—'

'—and the white blouse of Sarah Jonstone.'

'Cream-coloured actually,' said Morse.

* * *

For Sergeant Phillips it was all somewhat *déjà vu* as he resumed his vigil at the door of the interview room, his feet still aching, his eyes scanning the bare room once again: the wooden trestle-table on which stood a white polystyrene coffee cup (full) and an ash-tray (as yet empty); and behind the table, the same fairish-haired, fresh-complexioned man who had sat there the previous evening – Mr Edward Wilkins.

Chapter Forty-four

Wednesday, January 8th: p.m.

Felix qui potuit rerum cognoscere causas.

Virgil, *Georgics*

At 5 p.m., Mr James Prior, Security Officer at the Locals, put on his bicycle clips and prepared to leave. Before he did so he had a final look round Reception to make sure that everything that should be locked up *was* locked up. It was odd though, really, to think that the only thing the police had been interested in was the one drawer that *wasn't* locked up – the drawer in which he kept all the out-of-date security passes, elastic-banded into their various bundles. Like the bundle for the last lot of building workers from which the police had already taken two passes away: that of Winston Grant, a Rastafarian fellow whom Prior remembered very well; and that of a man called Wilkins, who'd operated the giant yellow crane that had towered over the Delegacy building throughout the summer months. After Morse's call early that morning, Prior had looked briefly through the rest of that particular bundle, and had wondered whether there were any other criminals lurking among those very ordinary-looking faces. But the truth was that one could never tell: he, far more than most people, was fully aware of that.

That afternoon, Wilkins had been resignedly co-operative about every detail of the whole case – with the exception of the act of murder itself, which he stubbornly and categorically refused to discuss in any respect whatsoever: it was as if that single, swift despatch (to which he now confessed) had paralysed his capacity to accept it as in any way a piece of voluntary, responsible behaviour. But for the rest, he spoke fully and freely; and there was nothing surprising, nothing new, that emerged from his statement. Naturally enough, perhaps, he expressed the hope that Winston Grant should be treated with appropriate leniency, although it seemed to others (certainly to Lewis) that such an accomplice must have been rather more aware of the nature of his assignment than either Grant or Wilkins was prepared to admit.

About Margaret Bowman, the only piece of new information Wilkins was able to give was that he had more than once picked her up from a beauty clinic in Oxford, and Lewis shook his head ruefully as he learned that this clinic was the very first one he had rung – the one refusing to divulge any confidential details. About Margaret's present fate Wilkins appeared strangely indifferent. He hadn't (he said) the faintest idea where she'd finally drifted off to; but presumably the police would be concentrating on her various relatives up around Alnwick or Berwick or Newcastle or wherever they were. For his part, he was perhaps glad to get shot of the woman. She'd brought him nothing but trouble, although he fully accepted that it had been far more his fault than hers that things had finally . . . But that was all over now. And in an odd sort of way (he'd said) he felt relieved.

It was just after 6.30 p.m. when Sergeant Phillips escorted Wilkins down to St Aldate's where temporarily, together with Grant, he would be held, awaiting (in the short term) the provision of alternative custodial arrangements and (in the long term) the pleasure of Her Majesty.

Morse insisted that both he himself and Lewis should call it a day; and Lewis was just closing the box-file on the Haworth Hotel case when he noticed a letter which he had never been shown: one beginning 'This is a love letter . . .' He read the first few lines with some mystification – until he came to the quite extraordinary statement that the anonymous correspondent had been 'reading a biography of Thomas Hardy . . .'!

Should he tell Morse? He read the letter through again with the greatest interest.

Well, well, well!

At 7 p.m. Morse (Lewis thought he had gone) came back into his office once more. 'Listen, Lewis! This Wilkins is one of the cleverest buggers we've ever had! You realise that? He's pulled the wool over

my eyes about the most central, central, central issue of the lot!
And you know what that is? That he, Wilkins, was – is! – hopelessly
in love with this woman, Margaret Bowman; and that he'd do anything – *did* do anything – to keep her. In fact, he murdered her
husband to keep her! And likewise, Lewis, the fact that he'd do anything to protect her *now*! You remember what he said last night? Just
get the transcript, Lewis – the bit about the passport!'

Lewis found the document and read aloud:

'I advised her to get on a boat or something and sail off to the
Continent – away from everything.'
  'But she didn't take your advice?'
  'No, she couldn't. She hadn't got a passport and she was frightened
of applying for one because she knew everybody was trying to find
her . . .'

'God, I'm a fool, Lewis! I wonder how many lies he *has* told us?
That she was at his house last night? That she was up with her sister
in Newcastle? Has she *got* a sister, Lewis? Oh dear! She hasn't got
a passport, he says? And we believe him! So we don't watch all the
boats—'
  'Or the planes,' added Lewis quietly.
  'I don't believe it!' said Morse softly, after a pause.
  'What's worrying you, sir?'
  'Get a telex off to Gatwick straight away! Get the passenger
list of flight number whatever-it-was!'
  'You don't think—?'
  '*Think?* I'm almost *sure*, Lewis!'

When Lewis returned from the telex office, Morse already had
his greatcoat on and was ready to leave.
  'You know that letter you had from one of your admirers, sir?'
  'How do you know about that?'
  'You left it in the box.'
  'Oh!'
  'Did you notice the postmark on the original letter?'
  'London. So what?'
  'London? Really?' (Lewis sounded like a man who knows all
the answers.) 'You get a lot of people going up to the London
sales from all over the country, don't you? I mean anyone from
anywhere – from Oxford, say – could go up to the January sales
and drop a letter in a postbox outside Paddington.'

Morse was frowning. 'What exactly are you trying to tell me, Lewis?'

'I just wondered if you had any idea of who'd written that letter to you, that's all.'

Morse's hand was on the doorknob. 'Look, Lewis! You know the difference between you and me, don't you? You don't use your *eyes* enough! If you *had* done – and very recently, too! – you'd know perfectly well who wrote that letter.'

'Yes?'

'Yes! And it so happens – since you're suddenly so very interested in my private affairs, Lewis – that I'm going to take the particular lady who wrote that particular letter out for a particularly fine meal tonight – that's if you've no objections?'

'Where are you taking her, sir?'

'If you must know, we're going out to Springs Hotel near Wallingford.'

'Pretty expensive, so they say, sir.'

'We shall go halves – you realise that, of course?' Morse winked happily at Lewis – and was gone.

Lewis, too, was smiling happily as he rang his wife and told her that he wouldn't be long.

At 7.50 p.m. the telex reply came through from Gatwick: on the scheduled 12.05 flight that had left that morning for Barcelona, the passenger list had included, apart from a Mr Edward Wilkins, a Mrs Margaret Bowman, the latter giving an address in Chipping Norton, Oxfordshire.

At 8.00 p.m., Lewis pulled on his overcoat and left Kidlington HQ. He wasn't at all sure whether Morse would be pleased, or displeased, with the news he had just received. But the last thing he was going to do was to ring Springs Hotel. He just hoped – very much he hoped – that Morse would have an enjoyable evening, and an enjoyable meal. As for himself, the missus would have the egg and chips ready; and he felt very happy with life.

The Riddle of the
Third Mile

For

My Daughter, Sally

And whosoever shall compel thee to go a mile,
go with him twain.

St Matthew 5, 41

THE FIRST MILE

Chapter One

Monday, 7th July

In which a veteran of the El Alamein offensive finds cause
to recall the most tragic day of his life.

There had been the three of them – the three Gilbert brothers:
the twins, Alfred and Albert; and the younger boy, John, who
had been killed one day in North Africa. And it was upon his
dead brother that the thoughts of Albert Gilbert were concentrated
as he sat alone in a North London pub just before closing-time:
John, who had always been less sturdy, more vulnerable, than the
formidable, inseparable, and virtually indistinguishable pair known
to their schoolmates as 'Alf 'n Bert'; John, whom his elder brothers
had always sought to protect; the same John whom they had not
been able to protect that terrible day in 1942.

It was in the early morning of 2nd November that 'Operation
Supercharge' had been launched against the Rahman Track to
the west of El Alamein. To Gilbert, it had always seemed strange
that this campaign was considered by war historians to be such a
miraculous triumph of strategic planning, since from his brief but
not unheroic participation in that battle he could remember only
the blinding confusions around him during that pre-dawn attack.
'The tanks must go through' had been the previous evening's orders,
filtered down from the red-tabbed hierarchy of Armoured Brigade to
the field-officers and the NCOs of the Royal Wiltshires, into which
regiment Alf and Bert had enlisted in October 1939, soon to find
themselves grinding over Salisbury Plain in the drivers' seats of
antique tanks – both duly promoted to full corporals, and both

shipped off to Cairo at the end of 1941. And it had been a happy day for the two of them when brother John had joined them in mid-1942, as each side built up reinforcements for the imminent show-down.

On that morning of 2nd November, at 0105 hours, Alf and Bert moved their tanks forward along the north side of Kidney Ridge, where they came under heavy fire from the German 88s and the Panzers dug in at Tel Aqqaqir. The guns of the Wiltshires' tanks had spat and belched their shells into the enemy lines, and the battle raged furiously. But it was an uneven fight, for the advancing British tanks were open targets for the anti-tank weapons and, as they nosed forward, they were picked off piecemeal from the German emplacements.

It was a hard and bitter memory, even now; but Gilbert allowed his thoughts full rein. He could do so now. Yes, and it was important that he *should* do so.

About fifty yards ahead of him, one of the leading tanks was burning, the commander's body sprawled across the hatch, the left arm dangling down towards the main turret, the tin-helmeted head spattered with blood. Another tank, to his left, lurched to a crazy standstill as a German shell shattered its left-side track, four men jumping down and sprinting back towards the comparative safety of the boundless, anonymous sands behind them.

The noise of battle was deafening as shrapnel soared and whistled and plunged and dealt its death amidst the desert in that semi-dawn. Men shouted and pleaded and ran – and died; some blessedly swiftly in an instantaneous annihilation, others lingeringly as they lay mortally wounded on the bloody sand. Yet others burned to death inside their tanks as the twisted metal of the hatches jammed, or shot-up limbs could find no final, desperate leverage.

Then it was the turn of the tank immediately to Gilbert's right – an officer leaping down, clutching a hand that spurted blood, and just managing to race clear before the tank exploded into blinding flame.

Gilbert's turret-gunner was shouting down to him.

'Christ! See that, Bert? No wonder they christened these fuckin' things "Tommycookers"!'

'You just keep giving it to the bastards, Wilf!' Gilbert had shouted back.

But he received no reply, for Wilfred Barnes, Private in the Royal Wiltshire Yeomanry, had spoken his last words.

The next thing Gilbert saw was the face of Private Phillips as the latter wrestled with the driver's hatch and helped him out.

'Run like hell, corporal! The other two have had it.'

They had struggled only some forty yards before flinging themselves down as another shell kicked up the sand just ahead of them, spewing its steel fragments in a shower of jagged metal. And when Gilbert finally looked up, he found that Private Phillips, too, was dead – a lump of twisted steel embedded in his lower back. For several minutes after that, Gilbert sat where he was, severely shocked but apparently uninjured. His eyes looked down at his legs, then at his arms; he felt his face and his chest; then he tried to wriggle his toes in his army boots. Just thirty seconds ago there had been four men. And now there was only one – *him*. His first conscious thought (which he could recall so vividly) was a feeling of ineffable anger; but almost immediately his heart rejoiced as he saw a fresh wave of 8th Armoured Brigade tanks moving up through the gaps between the broken or blazing hulks of the first assault formation. Only gradually did a sense of vast relief surge through him – relief that he had survived, and he said a brief prayer to his God in gratitude for coming through.

Then he heard the voice.

'For Christ's sake, get out of here, corporal!' It was the officer with the bleeding hand, a lieutenant in the Wiltshires – a man who was known as a stickler for discipline, and a bit pompous with it; but not an unpopular officer, and indeed the one who the night before had relayed to his men the Montgomery memorandum.

'You a'right, sir?' Gilbert asked.

'Not too bad.' He looked down at his hand, the right index finger hanging only by a tissue of flesh to the rest of his hand. 'What about you?'

'I'm fine, sir.'

'We'll get back to Kidney Ridge – that's about all we *can* do.' Even here, amid the horrifying scenes of carnage, the voice was that of a pre-war wireless announcer, clipped and precise – what they called an 'Oxford' accent.

The two men scrambled through the soft sand for a few hundred yards before Gilbert collapsed.

'Come *on*! What's the matter with you, man?'

'I dunno, sir. I just don't seem . . .' He looked down at his left trouser-leg, where he had felt the fire of some intense pain; and he saw that blood had oozed copiously through the rough khaki. Then he put his left hand to the back of his leg and felt the sticky morass of bleeding flesh where half his calf had been shot away. He grinned ruefully:

'You go on, sir. I'll bring up the rear.'

But already the focus had changed. A tank which had seemed to be bearing down upon them suddenly slewed round upon its tracks so that now it faced backwards, its top completely sheared away. Its engine, however, still throbbed and growled, the gears grinding like the gnashing of tortured teeth in hell. But Gilbert heard more than that. He heard the voice of a man crying out in the agony of some God-forsaken despair, and he found himself staggering towards the tank as it lurched round yet again in a spurting spray of sand. The man in the driver's seat was alive! Thereafter Gilbert forgot himself completely: forgot his leg-wound, forgot his fear, forgot his relief, forgot his anger. He thought only of Private Phillips from Devizes . . .

The hatch was a shattered weld of hot steel that just would not open – not yet. *Almost* it came; and the sweat showered down Gilbert's face as he swore and wrenched and whimpered at his task. The petrol-tank ignited with a soft, almost apologetic 'whush', and Gilbert knew it was a matter only of seconds before another man was doomed to death inside a Tommycooker.

'For Chrissake!' he yelled to the officer behind him. 'Help! Please! I've – nearly – ' He wrenched for the last time at the hatch, and the sweat poured again on to his bulging, vein-ridged forearms.

'Can't you fuckin' well see? Can't you . . .' His voice tailed off in desperation, and he fell to the sand, overwhelmed by failure and exhaustion.

'Leave it, corporal! Come away! That's an *order!*'

So Gilbert crawled away across the sand and wept in frenetic despair, his grimed face looking up to see through his tears the glaze in the officer's eyes . . . the glaze of frozen cowardice. But he remembered little else except the screaming of that burning fellow soldier. And it was only later that he thought he'd recognised the voice – for he hadn't seen the face.

He was picked up (so they told him) soon after this by an army truck, and the next thing he could remember was lying comfortably in very white sheets and red blankets in a military hospital. They didn't tell him until two weeks later that his brother John, tank-driver with the 8th Armoured Brigade, had been killed in the second-phase offensive.

Then Albert Gilbert had been almost sure; but even now, he

wasn't *quite* sure. He knew one thing, though, for nothing could erase from his cerebral cortex the name of the officer who, one morning in the desert, in the battle for the ridge at Tel Aqqaqir, been tried in the balance of courage – and been found wanting. Lieutenant Browne-Smith, that was the name. Funny name, really, with an 'e' in the middle. A name he'd never seen again, until recently.

Until very recently indeed.

Chapter Two

Wednesday, 9th July

We are in the University of Oxford, at the marks-meeting of the seven examiners appointed for 'Greats'.

'He would have walked a First otherwise,' said the Chairman. He looked down again at the six separate assessments, all of them liberally sprinkled with alphas and beta pluses except for the one opposite Greek History, where stood a feeble-looking beta double minus/delta. Not, this last, the category of the finest minds.

'Well, what do you think, gentlemen? Worth a viva, surely, isn't he?'

With minimal effort, five of the other six men, seated at a large table bestrewn with scripts and lists and mark-sheets, raised the palms of their hands in agreement.

'*You* don't think so?' The Chairman had turned towards the seventh member of the examining panel.

'No, Chairman. He's not worth it – not on this evidence.' He flicked the script in front of him. 'He's proved quite conclusively to me that he knows next to nothing outside fifth-century Athens. I'm sorry. If he wanted a First, he ought to have done a bit more work than *this*.' Again he flicked the script, an expression of disgust further disfiguring a face that had probably been sour from birth. Yet, as all those present knew, no one else in the University could award a delicate grading like B+/B+?+ with such confident aplomb, or justify it with such fierce conviction.

'We all know, though, don't we,' (it was one of the other members) 'that sometimes it's a bit hit-and-miss, the questions we set, I mean – especially in Greek History.'

'*I* set the questions,' interrupted the dissident, with some heat. 'There's never been a fairer spread.'

The Chairman looked very tired. 'Gentlemen. We've had a long, hard day, and we're almost at the finishing-post. Let's just—'

'Of course he's worth a viva,' said one of the others with a quiet, clinching authority. 'I marked his Logic paper – it's brilliant in places.'

'I'm sure you're right,' said the Chairman. 'We fully take your point about the history paper, Dr Browne-Smith, but . . .'

'So be it – you're the Chairman.'

'Yes, you're quite right. I *am* the Chairman and this man's going to get his viva!'

It was a nasty little exchange, and the Logic examiner immediately stepped in with a peace proposal. 'Perhaps, Dr Browne-Smith, you might agree to viva him yourself?'

But Browne-Smith shook his aching head. 'No! I'm biased against the fellow, and all this marking – it's been quite enough for me. I'm doing nothing else.'

The Chairman, too, was anxious to end the meeting on a happier note: 'What about asking Andrews? Would *he* be prepared to take it on?'

Browne-Smith shrugged. 'He's quite a good young man.'

So the Chairman wrote his final note: 'To be viva-ed by Mr Andrews (Lonsdale), 18th July'; and the others began to collect their papers together.

'Well, thank you all very much, gentlemen. Before we finish, though, can we just think about our final meeting? Almost certainly it's got to be Wednesday 23rd or Thursday 24th.'

Browne-Smith was the only one of the panel who hadn't taken out his diary; and when the meeting was finally fixed for 10 a.m. on Wednesday the 23rd, he appeared to take no notice whatsoever.

The Chairman had observed this. 'All right with you, Dr Browne-Smith?'

'I was just about to say, Chairman, that I'm afraid I probably shan't be with you for the final meeting. I should very much like to be, of course, but I – I've got to be . . . Well, I probably shan't be in Oxford.'

The Chairman nodded a vague, uneasy understanding. 'Well, we'll try to do our best without you. Thank you, anyway, for all the help

you've been – as ever.' He closed the thick, black volume in front
of him, and looked at his wrist-watch: 8.35 p.m. Yes, it had been
a long, hard day. No wonder, perhaps, that he'd become a little
snappy at the end.

Six members of the panel agreed to repair to the King's Arms in
Broad Street; but the seventh member, Dr Browne-Smith, begged
leave to be excused. Instead, he left the Examination Schools,
walked slowly along the High, and let himself through the back-door
('Senior Fellows Only') into Lonsdale College. Once in his rooms,
he swallowed six Paracetamol tablets, and lay down fully-clothed
upon his bed, where for the next hour his brain blundered around
uncontrollably in his head. Then he fell asleep.

On the morning of the next day, Thursday, 10th July, he
received a letter. A very strange and rather exciting letter.

Chapter Three

Friday, 11th July

In which we learn of an Oxford don's invitation to view the vice
and viciousness of life in a notorious area of the metropolis.

Never throughout his life – almost sixty-seven years of it now –
had Oliver Maximilian Alexander Browne-Smith (with an 'e' and
with hyphenation) MC, MA, D.Phil., really come to terms with
his inordinately ponderous names. Predictably, in his prep-school
days he had been nicknamed 'Omar'; and now, with only one year
before his University appointment was due to be statutorily terminated, he knew that amongst the undergraduates he had acquired
the opprobrious sobriquet of 'Malaria', which was not so predictable
and very much nastier.

It was some small surprise to him, therefore, to find how quickly
he had managed to bring himself to terms, in a period of only a
few weeks, with the fact that he would quite certainly be dead well
within a twelvemonth ('At the very outside, since you insist on the
truth, Dr Browne-Smith'). What he did not realise, however, as he
walked on to Platform One at Oxford Station, was that he would

be dead within a shorter period than that so confidently predicted by his distinguished and expensive consultant.

A very much shorter period.

As he made his way to the rear end of the platform, he kept his eyes lowered, and looked with distaste at the empty beer-cans and litter that bestrewed the 'up' line. A few of his University colleagues, some from Lonsdale, were fairly frequent passengers on the 9.12 a.m. train from Oxford to Paddington, and the truth was that he felt no wish to converse with any of them. Under his left arm he held a copy of *The Times*, just purchased from the station bookstall; and in his right hand he held a brown leather briefcase. For a fine, bright morning in mid-July, it was surprisingly chilly.

The yellow-fronted diesel snaked its slow way punctually through the points just north of the station, and two minutes later he was seated opposite a young couple in a non-smoking compartment. Although an inveterate and incurable smoker himself, one who had dragged his wheezing lungs through cigarettes at the rate of forty-plus a day for fifty years, he had decided to impose upon himself some token abstinence during the hour-long journey that lay ahead of him. It seemed, somehow, appropriate. When the train moved out, he folded *The Times* over and started on the crossword, his mind registering nothing at all on the first three of the clues across. But on the fourth, a hint of a grin formed around his slightly lopsided mouth as he looked down again at the extraordinarily apposite words: 'First thing in Soho tourist's after? (8).' He quickly wrote in 'stripper'; and with more and more letters thenceforth making their horizontal and vertical inroads into the diagram-grid, the puzzle was finished well before Reading. Then, hoping that the couple opposite had duly noted his cruciverbalistic competence – if not the ugly stump of his right index finger, chopped off at the first joint – he leaned back in his seat as far as his longish legs would allow, closed his eyes, and concentrated his thoughts on the very strange reason that was drawing him to London that day.

At Paddington he was almost the last person to leave the train and, as he walked to the ticket-barrier, he saw that it was still only 10.15 a.m. Plenty of time. He collected a Paddington–Reading–Oxford timetable from the Information Bureau, bought a cup of coffee at the buffet, where he lit a cigarette, and looked up the possible trains for his return journey. Curiously enough, he felt relaxed as he lit a second cigarette from the first, and wondered vaguely what times the pubs – and clubs – would be open in London. 11 a.m. perhaps? But that was a matter of no great moment.

It was 10.40 a.m. when he left the station buffet and walked briskly to the Bakerloo line, where, as he queued for his ticket, he realised that he must have left his timetable in the buffet. But that was of no great moment, either. There were plenty of trains to choose from, and he'd made a mental note of some of the times.

He could not have known, of course, that he would not be travelling back to Oxford that night.

On the tube he opened his briefcase and took out two sheets of paper: the first was a letter addressed to himself, amateurishly typed but perfectly literate – a letter that still seemed very strange to him; the second was a more professionally typed sheet (indeed, typed by Browne-Smith himself) comprising a list of students from Oxford University, with the names of their colleges appended in brackets, and the words 'Class One, *Literae Humaniores*' printed across the top in bold, red capitals. But Browne-Smith glanced only cursorily at the two sheets through his bifocal lenses. It appeared that he was merely reassuring himself that both were still in existence. Nothing more.

At Edgware Road he looked up above the carriage-windows, noting that there were only two more stops, and for almost the first time he felt a flutter of excitement somewhere in his diaphragm. It was that letter . . . *Very* odd! Even the address had been odd, with the full details carefully stated: Room 4, Staircase T, Second Quad, Lonsdale College, Oxford. Such specificity was rare, and seemed to suggest that whoever had sent the letter was more than usually anxious for it not to go astray – more than a little knowledge-able, too, about the college's geography . . . Staircase T, Second Quad . . . In his mind's eye, Browne-Smith saw himself climbing those few stairs once more; climbing them, as he had done for the past thirty years, up to the first landing, where his own name, hand-printed in white, Gothic lettering, still stood above the door. And immediately opposite him, Room 3 – where George Westerby, the Geography don, had lived for almost exactly the same time: just one term longer than himself, in fact. Their mutual hatred was intense, the whole college knew that, though it might just have been different if Westerby had ever been prepared to make the feeblest gesture towards some reconciliation. But he had never done so.

Via the ziggurat of steep escalators, Browne-Smith emerged at 11.05 a.m. into the bright sunlight of Piccadilly Circus, crossed over into Shaftesbury Avenue, and immediately plunged into the maze of roads and alley-ways that criss-cross the area off Great Windmill Street. Here abounded small cinemas that featured films of hard, uncompromising porn, with stills outside of nudes and semi-nudes, vast-breasted and voluptuous; clubs that promised passers-by the prospects of erotic, non-stop nudity; bookshops that boasted the glossiest, grossest magazines for paedophiles and buffs of bestiality. And it was along these gaudy streets, beneath the orange and the yellow signs, past the inviting doors, that Browne-Smith walked slowly, savouring the uncensored atmosphere, and feeling himself inexorably sucked into the cesspool that is known as Soho.

It was in a narrow lane just off Brewer Street that he spotted it – as he'd known he would: 'The Flamenco Topless Bar: No Membership Fee: Please Walk Straight Down.' The wide, shallow steps that led from the foyer down to the subterranean premises had once been carpeted in heavy crimson, but now the middle of the tread resembled more the trampled sward of a National Trust beauty-spot at the height of a glorious summer. He was walking past, but there must have been some tell-tale hesitation in his step, for the acne-faced youth who lounged just inside the doorway had spotted him already.

'Lovely girls in here, sir. Just walk straight down. No membership fee.'

'The bar is open, is it? I only want a drink.'

'Bar's always open here, sir. Just walk straight down.' The young man stepped aside, and Browne-Smith took his fateful step across the entrance and slowly descended to The Flamenco Topless Bar. *Facilis descensus Averno.*

At the foot of the stairs further progress was barred by a velvet drape, and he was wondering what he should do when a seemingly disembodied head poked through a gap in the middle of the curtain – the head of an attractive young girl of no more than nineteen or twenty years, the hazel eyes luridly blued and blackened by harsh mascaras, but the sensuous mouth devoid of any lipstick. A pink tongue completed a slow circuit round the soft-looking mouth, and a pleasant voice asked simply and sweetly for only £1.

'There's no membership fee; it says so outside. And the man on the door said so.'

The face smiled, as it always smiled at the gullible men who'd trodden those broad and easy stairs.

'It's not a membership fee – just admission. You know what I mean?' The eyes held his with simmering sexuality, and the note passed quickly through the crimson curtain.

The Flamenco Bar was a low-ceilinged affair with the seats grouped in *alcôves à deux*, towards one of which the young girl escorted him. She was, herself, fully clothed; and, after handing her client a buff-coloured drinks-list, she departed without a further word to her wonted seat behind a poor imitation of a drinking-man's bar, whereat she was soon deeply engrossed in her zodiacal predictions as reported in the *Daily Mirror*.

It seemed to Browne-Smith, as he struggled to interpret the long bill of fare, that the minimum charge for any semi-alcoholic beverage was £3. And he was beginning to suspect that the best value for such an exorbitant charge was probably two (separate) half-glasses of lager – when he heard her voice.

'Can I take your order?'

Over the top of his glasses he looked up at the young woman who stood in front of him. She was leaning forward, completely naked from the waist upwards, her long, pink skirt split widely to the top of her thigh.

'The lager, I think, please.'

She made a note on the pad she held. 'Would you like me to sit with you?'

'Yes, I would.'

'You'd have to buy me a drink.'

'All right.'

She pointed to the very bottom of the card:

Flamenco Revenge – a marriage of green-eyed Chartreuse with aphrodisiac Cointreau.
Soho Wallbanger – a dramatic confrontation of voluptuous Vodka with a tantalising taste of Tia Maria.
Eastern Ecstasy – an irresistible alchemy of rejuvenating Gin and pulse-quickening Campari.
Price: £6.00

£6.00!

'I'm sorry,' said Browne-Smith, 'but I just can't afford—'

'I can't sit with you if you won't buy me a drink.'

'It's so terribly expensive, though, isn't it? I just can't aff—'

'All right!' The words were clipped and final, and she left his table, to return a few minutes later with his first small glass of lager, setting the meagre measure before him with studied indifference and departing immediately.

From the alcove behind him, Browne-Smith could hear the conversation distinctly:

'Where you from?'

'Ostrighlia.'

'Nice there?'

'Sure is!'

'You'd like me to sit with you?'

'Sure would!'

'You'd have to buy me a drink.'

'Just you nime it, bighby!'

Browne-Smith swallowed a mouthful of his flat and tepid lager and took stock of the situation. Apart from the proximate Australian, he could see only one other customer, a man of indeterminate age (forty? fifty? sixty?) who sat at the bar reading a book. In contrast to his balding pate and the grey-white patches at his temples, the neatly-trimmed and black-brown beard was quite devoid of grizzled hairs; and for a few seconds the fanciful notion occurred to Browne-Smith that the man might be in disguise, this notion being somewhat reinforced by the fact that he was wearing a pair of incongruous sun-glasses which masked the eyes whilst not, apparently, blurring the print of the page upon which he appeared so totally engrossed.

From where Browne-Smith sat, the décor looked universally cheap. The carpet, a continuation of the stairway crimson, was dirty and stained, with threadbare patches beneath most of the plastic tables; the chairs were flimsy, rickety, wickerwork structures which seemed barely capable of supporting the weight of any over-fleshed client; the walls and ceiling had clearly once been painted white, but were now grubby and stained with the incessant smoke of cigarettes. But there was one touch of culture – a most surprising one: the soberly-volumed background music was the slow movement of Mozart's 'Elvira Madigan' piano concerto (played by Barenboim – Browne-Smith could have sworn it), and this seemed to him almost as incongruous as listening to Shakin' Stevens in St Paul's Cathedral.

Another man was admitted through the curtain and was duly visited by the same white-breasted beauty who had brought his own lager; the man at the bar turned over another page of his book; the Australian, clearly audible still, was none too subtly prodding his hostess into revealing what exactly it was she was selling, because she'd got what he wanted and his only concern was the price she might be asking for it; the girl behind the bar had obviously exhausted whatever the *Daily Mirror* could prognosticate; and Barenboim had landed lightly upon the final notes of that ethereal movement.

Browne-Smith's glass was now empty, and the only two hostesses on view were happily supping whatever the management had decided were today's ingredients for Soho Wallbangers, Flamenco Revenges, *et al*. So he got up, walked over to the bar and sat himself down on a stool.

'I've got another one paid for, I think.'

'I'll bring it to you.'

'No, don't bother. I'll sit here.'

'I said I'd bring it to you.'

'You don't mind me sitting here, do you?'

'You si' down where you were – you understand English?' All pretence at civility had vanished, and her voice sounded hard and mean.

'All right,' said Browne-Smith quietly. 'I don't want to cause any trouble.' He sat down at a table a few yards from the bar, and watched the girl, and waited.

'You still didn't 'ear wha' I *said*, did you?' The voice was now crudely menacing, but Browne-Smith decided that a few more rounds of small-arms fire could safely be expended; not *quite* time yet for the heavy artillery. He was enjoying himself.

'I *did* hear you, I assure you. But—'

'Look! I told you!' (Which she hadn't.) 'If you want a bloody rub-off there's a sauna right across the road. OK?'

'But I don't—'

'I shan't tell you again, mister.'

Browne-Smith stood up, and stepped slowly to the bar, where the man reading the book flicked over another page, disinterestedly neutral, it appeared, in the outcome of the escalating hostilities.

'I'd like a pint of decent beer, if you have one.' He spoke quietly.

'If you don't want tha' lager—'

Abruptly Browne-Smith crashed his glass on the counter, and fixed the girl with his eyes. 'Lager? Let me tell *you* something, miss! That's not lager – that's horse-piss!'

The battle odds had changed dramatically, and the girl had clearly lost her self-control as she pointed a shaking, carmined finger towards the crimson curtain: 'Get out!'

'Oh no! I've paid for my drinks.'

'You heard what the lady said.' It was the man sitting reading his book by the bar. Although he had neither lifted his eyes one centimetre from the text, nor lifted, it seemed, his flat (West Country?) voice one semitone above its customary pitch, the brief words sounded ominously final.

But Browne-Smith, completely ignoring the man who had just

spoken to him, continued to glare at the girl. 'Never speak to me like that again!'

The hissed authority of these words reduced the girl to speechlessness, but the seated man had slowly closed his book, and now at last he raised his eyes. The fingers of his right hand crept across to the upper muscles of his left arm and, although as he eased himself off the bar-stool he stood some two or three inches shorter than Browne-Smith, he looked a dangerous adversary. He said nothing more.

The velvet curtains by which Browne-Smith had entered were only some three yards to his left, and there were several seconds during which a quick, if inglorious, exit could easily have been effected. But no such decision was taken; and before he could consider the situation further he felt his left wrist grasped powerfully, and found himself propelled towards a door marked 'Private'.

Two things he was to remember as his escort knocked quietly upon this door. First, he saw the look on the face of the man from Australia, a look that was three parts puzzlement and one part panic; second, he observed the title of the book the bearded man was reading: *Know Your Köchel Numbers.*

The anonymous Australian, sitting no more than four or five yards from the door, was destined never to mention this episode to another living soul. And indeed, even had he reason to do so, it seems most improbable that he would have mentioned that enigmatic little moment, just before the door closed behind the two men, when the one of them who seemed to be causing the trouble, the one whose name he would never know, had suddenly looked at his wrist-watch, and said in a voice that sounded inexplicably calm: 'My goodness! I see it's exactly twelve noon.'

For a few seconds after he had crossed the threshold of the office, Browne-Smith experienced that dazzling, zigzag pain again that seemed to saw its way across his brain, momentarily cutting him off from any recollection of himself and of what he was doing. But then it stopped – as suddenly as it had started – and he thought he was in control of things once more.

Looking out over the lawn of Second Quad, George Westerby had watched the tallish figure (several inches taller than himself) striding out towards the Porters' Lodge at 8.15 a.m. that same morning. Uppermost in his mind at that moment – and he gloried in it – was the realisation that he would be seeing very little more of his detested colleague, Browne-Smith. He himself, George Westerby, having recently celebrated his sixty-eighth birthday, was retiring at last. Indeed, a removal firm had already been at work on his vast accumulation of books; and the treasured rows from more than half his shelves had been removed in blocks, stringed up, and stacked into the tea-chests that now occupied an uncomfortably large area of the floor space. And soon, of course, there would be the wooden crates, and the lumbering, muscled men who would transfer his precious possessions to the flat he had purchased in London. A smaller place, naturally, and one that might well pose a few storage problems. That could wait though, certainly until after his forthcoming holiday in the Aegean Isles . . . over to Asia across that azure sea . . .

But even as he stood there by the window, nodding slowly and contentedly to himself for a few moments, it was Browne-Smith who still dominated his thoughts. It had always been 'Browne-Smith' with him – not even 'Malaria' Browne-Smith, as though such familiarity might compromise his eternal antagonism. There would be only a few more nights now when he would have to dine in Hall with that odious man; just a few more lunches, occasionally standing awkwardly proximate over the cold buffets; only one more college meeting, at the beginning of next week – the very last one. For the Trinity Term was almost over now; his last term, and very soon his last day and his last hours; and then the moment (when it came) of looking down for the very last time on that immaculate lawn . . .

George Westerby was collectively conscious of all these things as he stood watching from his first-floor window on that chilly early morning of the 11th July. What he did not know at that time – what he could not have known – was that Lonsdale College was never again to welcome Browne-Smith within its quiet quads.

Chapter Four

Friday, 11th July

In which we have a tantalising glimpse of high-class harlotry.

The taxi-driver knew the street, and Browne-Smith settled himself in the back seat with a heightened sense of excitement. He would have wished to savour these moments longer, but in less than five minutes the taxi pulled up at the kerb of Number 29, a large four-storied balconied building in a fashionable terrace just behind Russell Square. In general, although the original brickwork on the lower reaches of the walls had been smutted by traffic-fumes and smoke, the house seemed to have maintained its elegant façade with comparative ease. The black door, with its polished brass knobs and letter-box, was framed by white pillars; and the woodwork of the windows was also painted white, with neatly-kept window-boxes adding their splash of greens and reds. Black railings, set in concrete, were stretched along the front; behind which, after a gap of about five feet, the wall of the house continued down to a basement. On these railings a board had been affixed:

> Luxury Apartments for Sale or to Let
> Please apply: Brooks and Gilbert
> (Sole Agents) Tel. 01-483 2307
> Viewing by appointment only

Browne-Smith walked up the three shallow steps, and pressed the single bell, apprehensively fingering the blue card that was now in his inside jacket-pocket. He waited. But he had heard no sound of ringing on the other side of the great door, and he could see no sign of life. At this moment, and for the first time, the idea filtered into his mind that he might have been cruelly duped for the silly fool – the silly *old* fool – that he was, in going along with the whole disreputable and dishonourable business. He turned to look at the busy street and saw an aristocratic female disembarking from a taxi only a few doors away. No, it wasn't too late even now! He could just forget it all, hail the taxi . . .

But the door had opened silently behind him.

'Can I help you?' (That West Country intonation again.)

'I'm a friend of Mr Sullivan's.' (Hardly the customary tone of his Mods tutorials – hesitant and slightly croaky.)

'You have an appointment?'

He took out the small, oblong card and handed it to her. The typewritten legend was exceedingly brief, but also (as Browne-Smith saw it) exceedingly significant: 'Please admit bearer' – nothing else, except for that little constellation of asterisks clustered in the top right-hand corner.

The woman stood aside and beckoned him over the threshold, closing the door (again noiselessly) behind them. 'You're an important client, sir, and we welcome you.' She smiled appropriately as they moved through the large entrance-hall, carpeted in a light-olive shade, with the same carpeting leading up the wide staircase which faced the front door. She turned to him as she walked on ahead up these stairs, and Browne-Smith noticed her inappropriately ugly teeth as she smiled again. 'All blue cards are on the first floor, sir. I'm afraid we haven't got our full complement of girls just for the moment – it's the evenings usually that we have our busiest time. But I'm sure you won't be disappointed in any way. No one's ever disappointed here.'

On the first landing, she turned to him again, her eyes assessing him shrewdly, like a tailor mentally measuring some wealthy customer. Then, after looking along the corridor to left and right, she appeared to decide where the most appropriate prospects lay, for she opened the door immediately across the landing with a brusqueness which seemed clearly to betoken her mistress-ship of the establishment.

At a table immediately inside the room on the left sat a woman of some forty summers, blonde and big-breasted, wearing a low-cut, full-length purple gown; and, as the lady of the house introduced her client, she stood up and slowly smiled.

'You're free, I think, this afternoon, Yvonne?'

'Thees eevening, also, madame, eef you weesh it.' The blonde smiled bewitchingly again, showing her beautifully even teeth. She was exquisitely made up, a moist lipstick marking the contours of her sensuous mouth, her hair piled immaculately on top of her finely-boned head.

'Is Paula free, too?'

'She weel be, madame. She 'ave a client for lernch, but she weel be free aftair.'

'Well' (madame spoke directly to Browne-Smith) 'if you're happy to stay here with Yvonne, sir?'

He swallowed and nodded his unequivocal assent.

'Good. I'll leave you, then. But you are to have everything you want, sir – I hope you understand that? Absolutely *everything*.'

'I'm most grateful.'

She turned to go. 'You must know Mr – er – Sullivan *very* well, sir?'

'I was just able to do him a little favour, that's all. You know how these things are.'

'Of course. And you promise to let me know if there's anything that Yvonne here can't—'

'I don't think you need worry.'

Then madame was gone, and the back of Browne-Smith's throat

felt parched as he fought to stem the flood of erotic imaginings that threatened to swamp him. He had little help from the woman who, briefly resuming her seat in order to make some entry in a red leather-bound diary on the table, leant forward as she did so and revealed even to the most casual glance that beneath her dress she was wearing little else – at least above her rather ample hips.

'I am weeth you now, sir.' She rose from her chair and walked round to him. 'Let me take you coat.'

Browne-Smith took off the light-brown summer raincoat he had worn continuously since leaving Oxford, and watched her as she folded it neatly over her left arm, slid her right hand under his elbow, and guided him over to a door at the far end of the room.

Compared with the somewhat austere and sparsely furnished room they had just left, this inner room was lavishly and (to Browne-Smith's tastes) rather luridly equipped. Two blood-red lamps, affixed to the inner wall, cast a subdued light around, and thick, yellow curtains, drawn fully across the single window, cut out all but the narrowest chink of natural light. The other furnishings were gaudily provocative with a cohort of multi-coloured cushions covering the long, low settee, and, behind that, bright yellow sheets and pillows on the widely welcoming bed, its coverlet already turned back. Opposite the settee was a tall, well-stocked, drinks-cabinet, its doors standing open; and beside it a film-projector, pointing a protruding snout towards the white expanse of wall to the left of the curtained casement. Pervading all was the heavy, heady smell of some sweet scent, and Browne-Smith felt a semi-permanent, priapic push between his loins.

'You'd like a dreenk?'

She went over to the cabinet and recited a comprehensive choice: whisky, gin, campari, vodka, rum, martini . . .

'Whisky, please.'

'Glenfeeddich?'

'My favourite.'

'And mine.'

There seemed to be two bottles of each drink, one of them as yet unopened, as though the liquid capacity of even the most dedicated toper had been nobly anticipated. And he watched her (why was he puzzled?) as she ripped the seal off a new bottle, poured out a half-tumbler of the pale malt-whisky, and brought it over to him.

'Aren't you going to have one, er . . .'

'Eevone. Please call me "Eevone". I call you "sir" – because, madame, she inseest on eet. But for me – Eevone!'

Even as she spoke, Browne-Smith found himself thinking, albeit vaguely, that her French accent was carefully cultivated and – yes, completely phoney. But why worry about that? More important, for his own fastidious tastes, was the fear that someone else might enter the room. So he took a large gulp of Scotch and voiced his anxiety.

'We shan't be interrupted, shall we?'

'Non, non! Madame, you raymember, she say you 'ave everything you want? So? Eef you want me to lock the door, I lock eet. Eef you want Paula, per'aps, you 'ave Paula, OK? But I 'ope you want me, non?'

Phew!

She went over to the door and turned the key, went over to the cabinet and poured herself a gin-and-dry-martini, and finally came to sit beside him on the settee, her thigh pressing closely against his own. She clinked their glasses: 'I'm sure we 'ave a good time together, eh? I always like it eef I dreenk.'

Browne-Smith took a further gulp of his Scotch, sensing even at this early stage that the alcohol was having an unwontedly powerful effect upon him.

'I feel you up a leetle?'

Momentarily he misunderstood her pronunciation of that second word; but when she took his glass he nodded in happy acquiescence, watching her in a wonderful anticipation as she walked away.

'You like my dress?' She was in front of him now, the replenished glass in her left hand. 'Eet show off my figure, non?'

'You have a lovely figure.'

'You theenk so? But eet ees so 'ot in 'ere. You take off your coat, per'aps?' She leaned over him, helping to remove his jacket, the dress soft against him, her body soft, the lighting soft; and he sat there passively as she slid her hands beneath the cuffs of his shirt, and deftly unfastened the cufflinks (Oxford University) before pushing the sleeves slowly up the arms. 'Just to see eef you 'ave a leetle, what you call eet, "tattoo"?'

'No, I haven't, actually.'

'Nor 'ave I. But soon you weel be able to see for yourself, non?' She sat closely beside him again, and Browne-Smith gulped back another large mouthful of his drink and willed himself to relax for a while. But she gave him little chance, taking his right hand and placing it on the shoulder of her dress.

'You like that?' she asked.

My God! His hand fumbled for a few seconds with the material of the dress, and then slipped tentatively beneath it, feeling the soft flesh around her neck.

'Can I—?'

'You can do anytheeng.' Even as she spoke those blissful words her eyes sparkled, and she jumped to her feet, pulling him up in turn with both hands. 'But we 'ave a leetle feelm first, OK?'

Reluctantly, Browne-Smith did as he was bidden, taking his seat in an upright chair in front of the projector, and seeking to prepare himself for the voyeuristic aperitif. Clearly the pattern of events she'd suggested was not an unusual one; she, doubtless, must occasionally feel the need for some erotic stimulus. It was rather sad, this last fact, but he was too intelligent a man to feel surprised.

The scenes now witnessed on the white patch of wall beside the yellow curtaining were wilder by a dozen leagues than the few X-certificated films that Browne-Smith had paid to see at the ABC cinema during the Oxford vacations. It was a pity that the woman wasn't seated close to him; but (as she'd explained) unless she continually made some slight adjustments to the focusing mechanism, the technicolour delineation tended to drift out of true.

It was all so strangely *déjà vu*.

A man, in a smartly-cut business suit; a beautiful blonde in a full-length, purple gown; a few intimate drinks on a multi-cushioned settee; the man's hand slipping slowly inside the low-cut bodice and hoisting therefrom a bronzed, globed breast; then a teasingly slow, provocative undress on the part of the blonde, followed by much mutual grasping and gasping – before a finale that was fully orchestrated by climactic groans and an energetic spurting of semen.

The whirring, clicking projector was now switched off, and he felt her hands on his shoulders from behind.

'You like eet again?' She came round and sat on his knees. 'Or would you rather 'ave *me*?'

He swallowed the first '*You!*', but managed the second.

'There ees a long zeep at the back of my dress – that's eet. Just pull down – pull! Yes, that's eet!'

Browne-Smith felt the sinuous movement of her hips pressing down on him as his fingers ventured across her naked back; and then she got up and walked over to the bed.

'Come and let me undress you.'

Her back was turned away from him as she shrugged the dress

off her shoulders, bent down to slip off her black, high-heeled shoes, stepped professionally out of her dress, and folded it neatly over the chair at the foot of the bed. Then she turned fully towards him, and he felt an enormously urgent need to take her immediately; but still she teetered on the brink of things, and he thought of the mercilessly tortured Tantalus and the illicit grapes that dangled just above his lips.

'One more leetle drink, per'aps?'

Browne-Smith, now almost in a delirium of anticipation, watched her as she walked over to the cabinet, watched her as she poured the two drinks, watched her as her beautifully-formed breasts bounced towards him once more.

'Just lie there a leetle meenite. You can 'ave me very soon.'

She had disappeared through the only other door in the room, doubtless (judging by the flushing of water) a bathroom. And he, for his part, lay there almost fully clothed upon the yellow sheets, wondering in a hazily distanced sort of way just what was going on. Although his mouth seemed dry as the Sahara, he put down his drink untasted on the bedside-table, and for a while his mind grew clearer. Why had she used the *other* bottle of Glenfiddich? Perhaps . . . perhaps it had been watered down a bit? Just as the Bursar always said at a Gaudy: 'Let them have the good stuff first.'

When, after what seemed an eternity, she returned, he watched her again, leaning half-upright on his right elbow. But his request was the oddest she had ever heard.

'Have you got any sort of *cream*, or something? My lips are awfully dry.'

She fetched her handbag from the settee, opened the flap, and delved around for a few seconds. Then, unscrewing a circular container, she leaned over him, her breasts suspended only inches from his eyes, and smoothly smeared some cream along his lips.

'That ees better, *non*? Dreenk up, darleeng!'

She unfastened his tie; then unfastened the front of his shirt, one button at a time, at each stage her fingers splaying across his chest.

For Browne-Smith these moments were almost unbearably erotic, and he knew that he had little hope of lasting out much longer. Yet he made one further quite extraordinary request. 'Can you open the curtains – just a little bit?'

When the woman returned she saw that the man's jacket, hitherto folded at the foot of the bed, was now lying beside him; and as she looked down at his motionless body, she saw the tell-tale stain that seeped around the front of his well-cut, dark-blue trousers. His eyes were closed and his breathing steady, the right hand hanging loosely over the side of the bed, the index finger missing below the proximal inter-phalangeal joint. His glass, on the table beside his head, was now empty. She gently took his right arm and lay it alongside his body. Almost, for a moment or so, she felt a pang of tenderness. Then she hurriedly re-dressed, unlocked the door of the room, went out, and spoke in whispers to a man standing outside – a man who was reading a book entitled *Know Your Köchel Numbers*.

Her duties were done.

Chapter Five

Friday, 11th July

A woman of somewhat dubious morals seeks to relax, although such is her nature that she recalls too clearly, and too often, the duties she has been paid so handsomely to perform.

In the latish evening of the day on which the events described in the previous chapter took place, a woman was seated alone in an upstairs flat, bedsitter-cum-bathroom-cum-kitchen, of a house situated in one of the many residential streets that lead south off the Richmond Road. Half an hour earlier she had walked from East Putney tube-station, and now she felt tired. Piccadilly to Earl's Court, change trains, across the Thames to Putney – how many times had she made that tiresome journey? It would have been so much easier to live in Soho, and there had been no lack of opportunity on that score! But she enjoyed her two lives – her two spheres of existence which intersected at (almost) no single point. Here, in soberly bourgeois suburbia, she was a middle-aged woman with a job in the city. Here, she kept herself very much to herself, quietly, pleasantly, comfortably, dealing with rent and rates and household bills, and furnishing her few rooms at lavish expense. Yet these rooms were for *her* enjoyment only, since she had never invited another person into them, except for the cleaning woman (two hours per week). Except, too, for the man who had come to see her only four days ago.

The woman we are describing looked to be about forty, but was in fact some ten years older. Yet one could readily be forgiven for such misjudgement. She was a large-breasted woman, with hips that had put on several inches over recent years, but her legs were finely graceful still, her ankles slim and firm. There were, certainly, a few tell-tale lines at the corners of her mouth, and again at the sides of her eyes; but the mouth itself was as delicately, deliciously sensitive as it had always been, and the eyes were normally as clear and bright as a summer's noon in the Swedish hills.

Tonight, however, those self-same eyes were dull and sombre. Seated in an armchair, she crossed her nyloned legs, rested her blonde head upon her left arm, and stared down for many minutes at the richly-patterned Wilton carpet. She still felt that residual sense of triumph and achievement; but she felt, too, a certain tension and concern which, over the last few hours, had been growing inexorably into a sense of guilt-ridden remorse.

It had all had its beginnings early on the previous Monday morning, almost immediately after the Sauna Select (just off Brewer Street) had opened its doors to the men who frequented that establishment. There was nothing common, nothing mean about it all; just a gentlemanly and a ladylike understanding that with little fuss and large finance the whole gamut of erotic refinements was readily available. Many of the steady if unspectacular clients were men of middle or late-middle age; some of them were undisguisedly and indisputably ancient. But all were wealthy, since that was the *sine qua non* of the business. How else could the management afford the princessly salaries of its four assorted hostesses? For (as the woman so often reminded herself) it *was* a big salary – far better than her former wages as a popular stripper in the Soho clubs, commuting with her bulky case of costumes from one cramped dais to another.

It had been 10.35 a.m. when the man had come in. He'd wanted a sauna, he said; he wanted nothing else. That's what they all said; but soon the moisture and the heat and the inhibitions slowly dissipating in a world of steam and relaxation would almost always lead to something else. And this man? He had assessed the four of them with an almost embarrassing thoroughness – their figures, their complexions, their eyes – and he had chosen *her*; thereafter being escorted to the steam-room, and thence to one of the private massage parlours (£20 extra) in which the expertly-fingered and minimally-clad girls would exercise their skills.

He was sweating profusely under the belted white towelling that reached down to mid-thigh. She, for her part, cool and elegant, was dressed in the regulation white-cotton housecoat, with only the thinly transparent bra and pants beneath.

'Would you like to lie down on the couch, sir? On your back, please.'

He had said nothing at that stage, obeying her suggestions mechanically and closing his eyes as she stood behind him, her fingers gently massaging the muscles round his neck.

'Nice?'

'Lovely!'

'Just relax!' She insinuated her hands beneath the towelling and massaged his shoulders with the tips of her strong and beautifully manicured fingers, working down from the neck towards the armpits – repeatedly, gently, sensually. And then, as she'd done a thousand times before, she walked round the couch and stood at his side, leaning over him, the top two buttons of her tunic already unfastened.

'Would you like me to undress while I massage you?' Wonderful question! And almost invariably an offer that couldn't be refused, even when the price of such an optional extra was clearly stated in advance.

It was a surprise to the woman, therefore, when her apparently pliable and co-operative client had slowly sat up, swung his legs off the couch, leaned forward to fasten the buttons of her tunic, pulled the white towelling back over his shoulders, and said 'No'.

But there followed an even bigger surprise.

'Look! I think I know you, and I certainly knew your father. Is it safe to talk here?'

Her father! Yes, she could still remember him. Those interminable rows she had heard so often from her lonely bedroom when the amiable drunkard had finally reached home from the local – rows apparently forgotten by the following dawns, when the household moved about its normal business. Then, in 1939, he had been called up in the army, when she had been only eight years old; and his death, three years later, had seemed to her little more than the indefinite prolongation of an already lengthy period of absence from her life. There had been many reminders of him, of course: photographs, letters, clothes, shoes. But, truth to tell, the death of her father had been an event that was less-than-tragic and only dimly comprehended. But it had been otherwise for her mother, who had wept so often through those first few weeks and months. And it was largely to try to compensate for such an uneven burden of things that the young girl had tried so very hard with her schoolwork, helped so regularly with the housework, and even (later on) kept in check those symptoms of teenage rebelliousness that had threatened to swamp all sense of filial piety. As the years went by, she had gradually taken over everything from an increasingly neurotic and feckless mother, who had sunk into premature senility by her early fifties, and into her grave before reaching her sixtieth year.

When the man had fastened up her buttons, she had felt belittled and cheap – on the wrong side of the habitual transaction. But she also felt deeply interested.

'Yes, it's safe,' she said, finally answering his question.

'No microphones? No two-way mirrors?'

She shook her head. 'About my father—'

'You don't remember me, do you?'

She looked at him: a man over sixty, perhaps; fairly well-preserved by the look of him; head balding, teeth nicotined, jowls blue, chin somewhat sagging, but the mouth still firm and not without some sensitivity. No, she couldn't remember him.

'I called at your house once, but that was a long time ago. You were, I don't know, fifteen or sixteen – still at school, anyway, because your mother asked you to go and do your homework in the kitchen. It was the year after the war was over, and I'd known your father – we were in the same mob together. In fact, I was with him when he died.'

'What do you want?' she asked abruptly.

'I want you to do something for me – something you'll be paid for doing – paid very well.'

'What—?'

But he held up his hand. 'Not now! You're living at 23A Colebourne Road – is that right?'

'Yes.'

'I'd like to come and see you, if I may.'

He had come the next evening, and talked whilst she listened. And, when she'd expressed her willingness to do what he asked, a deal was done, a partial payment made. And now, this very day, she had acted the role that he had asked of her, and the final payment had been made. A lot of easy money for a little easy work, and yet . . .

Yes, it was that little 'and yet' that caused her mind to fill with nagging doubts as she sat and sipped her China tea. She knew *enough*, of course – she'd insisted on that. But perhaps she should have insisted on knowing more, especially about the sequel to her own performance in the drama. They couldn't – they wouldn't, surely – have . . . *killed* him?

Her lips felt dry, and she reached for her handbag, opened the flap, and delved around for a few seconds before unscrewing a circular container – for the second time that day.

Chapter Six

Wednesday, 16th July

In which the Master of Lonsdale is somewhat indiscreet to a police inspector, and discusses his concern for one of his colleagues, and for the niceties of English grammar.

On the fifth morning after the events described in the preceding chapter, Detective Chief Inspector Morse, of the Thames Valley Constabulary, was seated in his office at Kidlington, Oxon. One half of him was semi-satisfied with the vagaries of his present existence; the other half was semi-depressed. Earlier that very morning he had sworn himself a solemn vow that the day ahead would be quite different. His recent consumption of food, tobacco, and alcohol had varied only within the higher degrees of addictive excess; and now, at the age of fifty-two, he had once again decided that a few days of virtually total abstinence was urgently demanded by stomach, lungs, and liver alike. He had arrived at his office, therefore, unbreakfasted, having already thrown away a half-full packet of cigarettes, and having left his half-empty wallet on the bedside-table. Get thou behind me, Satan! And, indeed, things had gone surprisingly well until about 11.30 a.m., when the Master of Lonsdale had rung through to HQ and invited Morse down to lunch with him.

'Half-past twelve – in my rooms – all right? We can have a couple of snifters first.'

'I'd like that,' Morse heard himself saying.

As he walked towards the Master's rooms in the first quad, Morse passed two young female students chattering to each other like a pair of monkeys.

'But surely *Rosemary's* expecting a First, isn't she? If she doesn't get one—'

'No. She told me that she'd made a *terrible* mess of the General Paper.'

'So did I.'

'And *me!*'

'She'll be awfully disappointed, though . . .'

Yes, life was full of disappointments, Morse knew that better than most; and, as he half-turned, he watched the two young, lovely ladies as they walked out through the Porters' Lodge. They must be members of the college – two outward and happily visible signs of the fundamental change of heart that had resulted in the admission of women to these erstwhile wholly-masculine precincts. Now when he himself had been up at St John's . . . But, abruptly, he switched off the memories of those dark, disastrous days.

'What'll it be, Morse? No beer, I'm afraid but – gin and tonic – gin and French?'

'Gin and French – lovely!' Morse reached over and took a cigarette from the well-stocked open box on the table.

The Master beamed in avuncular fashion as he poured his mixtures with a practised hand. He had changed little in the ten years or so that Morse had known him: going to fat a little, but as distinguished-looking a man now, in his late fifties, as he had been in his late forties; a tall man, with that luxuriant grey hair still framing the large head; the suits (famed throughout the University) as flamboyant as ever they were, and today eye-catchingly complemented by a waistcoat of green velvet. A successful man, and a proud man. A Head of a House.

'You've got women here now, I see,' said Morse.

'Yes, old boy. We were almost the last to give in – but, well, it's been a good thing on the whole. Very good, some of them.'

'Good-looking, you mean?'

The Master smiled. 'A few.'

'They sleep in?'

'Some of them. Still, some of them always did, didn't they?'

'I suppose so,' said Morse; and his mind drifted back to those distant days just after the war, when he had come up to Oxford with an exhibition in Classics from one of the Midland grammar schools.

'Couple of Firsts this year – among the girls, I mean. One in Greats, one in Geography. Not bad, eh? In fact the Classics girl, Jane—' Suddenly the Master stopped and leaned forward earnestly, awkwardly twiddling the large, onyx dress-ring on the little finger of his left hand. 'Look Morse! I shouldn't have said – what I just said. The class-lists won't be out for another week or ten days—'

Morse waved his right hand across the space between them, as though any mental recollection of the indiscretion had already been expunged. 'I didn't hear a word you said, Master. I know what you were going to tell me, though.'

'Oh?'

'She's got the top First in the University, and she'll soon get a summons for a congratulatory viva. Right?'

The Master nodded. 'Super girl – bit of a honey, too, Morse. You'd have liked her.'

'Still would, I shouldn't wonder.'

The Master's eyes were twinkling with merriment now. How he enjoyed Morse's company!

'She'll probably marry some lecherous sod,' continued Morse, 'and end up with half a dozen whining infants.'

'You're not exactly full of the joys of summer.'

'Just envious. Still there are more important things in life than getting a first in Greats.'

'Such as?'

Morse considered the question a few moments before shaking his head. 'I dunno.'

'I'll tell you one thing. There's not likely to be anything much more important for *her*. We shall probably offer her a junior fellowship here.'

'You mean you've already offered her one.'

'Please don't forget, will you, that I – er – I shouldn't have said anything about all this. I'm normally very discreet.'

'Must be the drink,' said Morse, looking down into his empty glass.

'Same again? Mixture about right?'

'Fraction more gin, perhaps?' Morse reached for another cigarette as the Master refilled the glasses. 'I suppose she could take her pick of all the undergrads?'

'*And* the dons!'

'You never married, did you, Master.'

'Nor did you.'

For some minutes the two of them sat silently sipping. Then Morse asked: 'Has she got a mother?'

'Jane Summers, you mean?'

'You didn't mention her surname before.'

'Odd question! I don't know. I expect so. She's only, what, twenty-two, twenty-three. Why do you ask?'

But Morse was hardly listening. In the quad outside it had been comparatively easy to pull the curtain across the painful memories. But now? Not so! His eyes seemed on the point of shedding a gin-soaked tear as he thought again of his own sad days at Oxford . . .

'You listening?'

'Pardon?' said Morse.

'You don't seem to be paying much attention to what I'm saying.'

'Sorry! Must be the booze.' His glass was empty again and the Master needed no prompting.

'Will you keep a gentle eye on things for me, then? You see, I'm probably off myself this weekend for a few days.'

'Few weeks, do you mean?'

'I'm not sure yet. But if you could just, as I say, keep an eye on things – you'd put my mind at rest.'

'Keep an eye on *what*?'

'Well, it's just – so *unlike* Browne-Smith, that's all. He's the most pedantic and pernickety fellow in the University. It's – it's odd. No arrangements, none. Just this note left at the lodge. No apology for absence from the college meeting; nothing to the couple of students he'd arranged to see.'

'You've got the note?'

The Master took a folded sheet from his dove-grey jacket and handed it over:

Please keep any mail for me here. I shall be away for several days. Sudden irresistible offer – quite out of the blue. Tell my scout to look after my effects, i.e. to keep the rooms well dusted, put the laundry through and cancel all meals until further notice.

B-S

Morse felt a tingle in his veins as he read through the brief, typewritten message. But he said nothing.

'You see,' said the Master, 'I just don't think he wrote that.'

'No?'

'No, I don't.'

'When did the Lodge get this?'

'Monday morning – two days ago.'

'And when was he last seen here?'

'Last Friday. In the morning, it was. He left college at about quarter past eight, to catch the London train. One of the fellows here saw him on the station.'

'Did this note come through the post?'

'No. The porter says it was just left there.'

'Why are you so sure he didn't write it?'

'He just *couldn't* have written it. Look, Morse, I've known him for twenty-odd years, and there was never a man, apart from Housman, who was so contemptuous about any solecism in English usage. He was almost paranoiac about things like that. You see, he always used to draft the minutes of the college meetings, and even a comma out of place in the final version would bring down the wrath of the gods on the college secretary. He even used to type a draft before he'd put a bloody notice on the board!'

Morse looked at the letter again. 'You mean he'd have put commas after "sudden" – and "through"?'

'By Jove, yes! He'd *always* use commas there. But there's something else. Browne-Smith was the *only* man in England, I should think, who invariably argued for a comma after "i.e.".'

'Mm.'

'You don't sound very impressed.'

'Ah! But I am. I think you may be right.'

'Really?'

'You think he's got a bird somewhere?'

'He's never had a "bird", as you put it.'

'Is Jane Summers still in residence?'

The Master laughed aloud with genuine amusement. 'I saw her this morning, Morse, if you must know.'

'Did you tell her she'd got a First?' A smile was playing slowly around Morse's mouth, and the Master's shrewd eyes were again upon him.

'Not much point pretending with you, is there? But no! No, I *didn't* tell her that. But I did tell her that perhaps she had every reason to be – er, let's say, optimistic about her – ah, future. Anyway, it's time we went down for lunch. You ready to eat?'

'Can I keep this?' Morse held up the single sheet, and the Master nodded.

'Seriously, I'm just a fraction worried. And you just said, didn't you, that I might be right?'

'You *are* right. At least, you're almost certainly right in suggesting that he didn't *type* it. He could have dictated it, of course.'

'Why are you so sure?'

'Well,' said Morse, as the Master locked the door behind them, 'he was a literary pedant for a good many years before *you* met him. He was one of my "Mods" tutors, you see; and even then he'd bark away at the most trivial sort of spelling mistake as if it were a sin against the Holy Ghost. At the time, of course, it didn't seem to matter two farts in the universe; but in an odd sort of way I came to respect his views – and I still do. I'd never let a spelling mistake go through *my* secretary – not if I could help it.'

'Never?'

'*Never!*' said Morse, his grey-blue eyes sober and serious as the two men lingered on the landing outside the Master's rooms. 'And you can be absolutely sure of one thing, Master. Browne-Smith would have died sooner than misspell "irresistible".'

'You don't think – you don't think he *is* dead?'

' 'Course he's not!' said Morse, as the two old friends walked down the stairs.

Chapter Seven

Week beginning Wednesday, 16th July

In which those readers impatiently waiting to encounter the first corpse will not be disappointed, and in which interesting light is thrown on the character of the detective, Morse.

It had been 2.30 p.m. when Morse finally left Lonsdale; and after stocking himself up from a tobacconist's shop just along the High, he was back in his Kidlington office just before three o'clock, where nothing much appeared to have happened during his absence.

On leaving Lonsdale, he had promised the Master to 'keep an eye on things' (a quite meaningless phrase, as Morse saw it) should any aspect of Browne-Smith's sudden departure take on a slightly more sinister connotation.

To an observer, Morse's eyes would have appeared slightly 'set', as Shakespeare has it, and his mood was mellowly maudlin. And as he sat there, his freely-winged imagination glided easily back to the fateful days of his time at Oxford . . .

After eighteen months as a National Serviceman in the Royal Signals Regiment, Morse had come up to St John's College, where his first two years were the happiest and most purposeful of his life. He had worked hard at his texts, attended lectures regularly, been prompt with unseens and compositions; and it had been no surprise to his tutors when such an informed and intelligent young man had duly gained a First in Classical Moderations. With two years ahead of him – two years in which to study for Greats – the future seemed to loom as sure as the sun-bright day that would follow the rosy-fingered dawn – particularly so, since the slant of Morse's mind was ideally suited to the work ahead of him in History, Logic, and Philosophy. But in the middle of his third year he had met the girl who matched the joy of all his wildest dreams.

She was already a graduate of Leicester University, whence a series of glowing testimonials had proved sufficiently impressive for her application to take a D.Phil. at Oxford to be accepted by St Hilda's. For her first term, she had been allotted digs way out in the distances of Cowley Road. But amidst the horsehair sofas and the sombre, dark-brown furnishings, she had been unhappy and had jumped at the opportunity of a smaller flat in Number 22 St John Street (just off St Giles') at the start of the Hilary Term. It was so much brighter, so much nearer the heart of things, and only a short walk from the Bodleian Library, where she spent so much of her time. She felt happy in her new room. Life was good.

At this same time it was customary for the Dean of St John's to farm out most of his third-year undergraduates to some of the nearby College property and, from the start of the Michaelmas term, Morse had moved into St John Street: Number 24.

They first met one night in late February, during the interval of the OUDS's production of *Doctor Faustus* at the New Theatre, only some fifty yards or so away, in Beaumont Street. Morse had finally managed to order a pint of beer at the crowded bar when he felt a lightly-laid hand upon his shoulder – and turned round to find a pale face, the blonde hair high upswept, the hazel eyes looking into his with an air of pleading diffidence.

'Have you just ordered?'

'Yes – I'll soon be out of your way.'

'You wouldn't mind, would you, ordering a drink for me as well?'

'Pleasure!'

'Two gins-and-tonics, please.' She pushed a pound-note into his hand – and was gone.

She was seated in a far corner of the bar, next to a dark-haired dowdy-looking young woman; and Morse, after negotiating his way slowly through the throng, carefully placed the drinks on the table.

'You didn't mind, did you?'

It was the blonde who had spoken, looking up at him with widely innocent eyes; and Morse found himself looking at her keenly – noting her small and thinly-nostrilled nose, noting the tiny dimples in her cheeks, and the lips that parted (almost mischievously now) over the rather large but geometrically regular teeth.

' 'Course not! It's a bit of a squash in here, isn't it?'

'You enjoying the play?'

'Yes. Are you?'

'Oh yes! I'm a great Marlowe fan. So's Sheila, here. Er – I'm sorry. Perhaps you don't know each other?'

'I don't know *you*, either!' said Morse.

'There you are! What did I tell you?' It was the dark girl who had taken up the conversation. She smiled at Morse: 'Wendy here said she recognised *you*. She says you live next door to her.'

'Really?' Morse stood there, gaping ineffectually.

A bell sounded in the bar, signalling the start of the last act; and Morse, calling upon all his courage, asked the two girls if they might perhaps like to have a drink with him after the performance.

'Why not?' It was the saturnine Sheila who had answered. 'We'd love to, Wendy, wouldn't we!'

It was agreed that the trio should meet up again in the cocktail-bar of The Randolph, a stone's-throw away, just along the street.

For Morse, the last act seemed to drag its slow length interminably along, and he left the theatre well before the end. The name 'Wendy' was re-echoing through his mind as once the woods had welcomed 'Amaryllis'. With the bar virtually deserted, he sat and waited expectantly. Ten minutes. Fifteen minutes. The bar was filling up now, and twice, with some embarrassment, Morse had assured other customers that, yes, there *was* someone sitting in each of the empty seats at his table.

She came at last – Sheila, that is – looking around for him, coming across, and accepting his offer of a drink.

'What will – er – Wendy have?'

'She won't be coming, I'm afraid. She says she's sorry but she suddenly remembered . . .'

But Morse was no longer listening, for now the night seemed

drear and desolate. He bought the girl a second drink; then a third. She left at ten-thirty to catch her bus, and Morse watched with relief as she waved half-heartedly to him from the bar entrance.

It was trying to snow as Morse walked slowly back to St John Street, but he stopped where he knew he would stop. On the right of the door of Number 22, he saw four names, typed and slotted into folders, a plastic bell-push beside each one of them. The first name was 'Miss W. Spencer (Top Floor)', but no light shone at the highest window, and Morse was soon climbing the stairs to his cold bed-sitter.

For the next three days he spent much of the time hanging about in the vicinity of St John Street, missing lectures, missing meals, and missing, too, any sight of the woman he was aching to see once more. Had she been called away? Was she ill? The whole gamut of tragic forebodings presented itself to his mind as he frittered away his hours and his energies in fruitless and futile imaginings. On the fourth evening he walked over to The Randolph, drank two double-Scotches, walked back to St John Street, and with a thumping heart rang the bell at the top of the panel. And, when the door opened, she was standing there, a smile of gentle recognition in her eyes.

'You've been a long time,' she said.

'I didn't quite know—'

'You knew where to find me – I told you that.'

'I—'

'It wasn't *you* who made the first move, was it?'

'I—'

'Would you like to come in?'

Impetuously – even that first night – Morse told her that he loved her; and she, for her part, told him how very glad she was that they had met. After that, their days and weeks and months were spent in long, idyllic happiness: they walked together across the Oxfordshire countryside; went to theatres, cinemas, concerts, museums; spent much time in pubs and restaurants; and, after a while, much time in bed together, too. But, during those halcyon days, both were neglecting the academic work that was expected of them. At the end of the Trinity term, Morse was gently reminded by his tutor that he might be in danger of failing to satisfy the examiners the following year unless he decided to mount a forceful assault upon the works of Plato during the coming vacation. After a similar interview with her own supervisor, Wendy Spencer was firmly informed that unless her thesis began to show more obvious signs of progress, her grant – and therewith her doctorate – would be in serious jeopardy.

Surprisingly, perhaps, it was Morse who saw the more clearly the importance of some academic success – and who sought the more anxiously to promote it. But such success was not to be. Just before the Christmas vac a tearful Wendy announced that her doctorate was terminated; her grant, w.e.f. January 1st, withheld. Yet the two of them lived on very much as before: Wendy stayed on in her digs, and almost immediately got a job as a waitress in The Randolph; Morse tried hard to curb his beer consumption and occasionally read the odd chapter of Plato's *Republic*.

Ironically, it was one day before the anniversary of their first, wonderful evening together that Wendy received the telegram, informing her that her widowed mother had suffered a stroke, and that help was urgently required. So she had gone home – and stayed there. Scores of letters passed between the lovers during the dark months that followed; and twice Morse had made the journey to the West Country to see her. But he was very short of money now; and slowly he was learning to assimilate the truth that (for some reason) her mother was a more important figure in Wendy's life than he was. His performances for his tutors were now so pathetically poor that his college exhibition was rescinded, and he had the humiliating task of writing to beg his county authority to make up the deficit. Then, three weeks before Greats, he had received his last letter from her: she could not see him again; she had almost ruined his life already; she had a duty to stay with her mother, and had irrevocably decided to do so; she had loved him – she had loved him desperately – but now they had come to the end; she implored him not to reply to her letter; she urged him to do himself some semblance of justice in his imminent examination; *that* would always be important for her. Morse had immediately sent a telegram, begging her to meet him once more. But he received no reply – and had no money for a further journey. In his despair, he did nothing – absolutely nothing.

Two months later he learned that he had failed Greats; and, although the news was no surprise, he departed from Oxford a withdrawn and silent young man, bitterly belittled, yet not completely broken in spirit. It had been his sadly disappointed old father, a month or so before his death, who suggested that his only son might find a niche somewhere in the police force.

* * *

Morse's attractive young secretary came into the office and handed over his letters for signature.

'Do you want to dictate the others, sir?'

'A little later. I'll give you a ring.'

After she had gone, he continued his earlier train of thought – but not for long. In any case, there was nothing more to recall. Of Wendy Spencer he had never heard another word. She would still be alive, though, surely? Even at that minute – that very second – she'd be *somewhere*. He repeated to himself the line from 'Wessex Heights': 'But time cures hearts of tenderness – and now I can let her go.' It was a lie, of course. But so it had been for Hardy.

Nor had Morse ever met any of his Greats examiners since he had first come down from Oxford. Yet even now he could remember with dramatic clarity the six names that were subscribed to the class-list on that bleak day some thirty years ago:

> Wells (Chairman)
> Styler
> Stockton
> Sherwin-White
> Austin
> Browne-Smith

During the following week Morse did nothing about his tenuous promise to the Master. Well, virtually nothing. He *had* rung Lonsdale early on the Monday morning, but neither the Master, nor the Vice-Master, nor the Senior Fellow, nor the Bursar, was on the premises. Everyone had either gone or was about-to-be gone. With the heavy work over for another academic year, the corporate body of the University appeared to be taking a collective siesta, and the thought suddenly occurred to Morse that this would be a marvellous time to murder a few of the doddery old bachelor dons. No wives to worry about their whereabouts; no families to ring their fathers from railway stations; no landladies to whine about the unpaid rents. In fact, nobody would miss most of them *at all* – not, that is, until the middle of October.

It was on Wednesday, 23rd July, two days after his abortive phone-call to Lonsdale, that Morse himself, in mid-afternoon, received the news, recognising Sergeant Lewis's voice immediately.

'We've got a body, sir – or at least part—'

'Where are you?'

'Thrupp, sir. You know the—'

' 'Course I know it!'

'I think you'd better come.'

'I've got a lot of correspondence to get on with – *you* can handle things, can't you?'

'We fished it out of the canal.'

'Lots of people chuck 'emselves into—'

'I don't think this one drowned himself, sir,' said Lewis quietly.

So Morse got the Jaguar out of the yard, and drove the few miles out to Thrupp.

Chapter Eight

Wednesday, 23rd July

The necrophobic Morse reluctantly surveys a corpse, and converses with a cynical and ageing police-surgeon.

Two miles north of police headquarters in Kidlington, on the main A423 road to Banbury, an elbow turn to the right leads, after only three hundred yards or so, to the Boat Inn, which, together with about twenty cottages, a farm, and a depot of the Inland Waterways Executive, comprises the tiny hamlet of Thrupp. The inn itself, only some thirty yards from the waters of the Oxford Canal, has served generations of boatmen, past and present. But the working barges of earlier times, which brought down coal from the Midlands and shipped up beer from the Oxford breweries, have now yielded place to the privately-owned long-boats and pleasure-cruisers which ply their way placidly along the present waterway.

Chief Inspector Morse turned right at the inn, then left along the narrow road stretching between the canal and a row of small, grey-stoned, terraced cottages, their doors and multi-paned windows painted a clean and universal white. At almost any other time, Thrupp would have seemed a snugly secluded little spot; but already Morse could see the two white police cars pulled over on to the tow-path, beside a sturdy-looking drawbridge; and an ambulance, its blue light flashing, parked a little further ahead, where the road petered out into a track of grass-grown gravel. It is strange to relate (for a man in his profession) that in addition to incurable acrophobia, arachnophobia, myophobia, and ornithophobia, Morse also suffered from necrophobia; and had he known what awaited him now, it is doubtful whether he would have dared to view the horridly disfigured corpse at all.

A knot of thirty or so people, most of them from the gaudily-painted houseboats moored along the waterway, stood at a respectful distance from the centre of activities; and Morse, pushing his way somewhat officiously through, came face to face immediately with a grim-looking Lewis.

'Nasty business, sir!'

'Know who it is?'

'Not much chance.'

'What? You can *always* tell who they are – doesn't matter how long they've been in the water. You know that, surely? Teeth, hair, finger-nails, toe-nails—'

'You'd better come and look at him, sir.'

'Ha! Know it's a "him" do we? Well, that's something. Reduces the population by about fifty per cent at a stroke, that does.'

'You'd better come and look at him,' repeated Lewis quietly.

A uniformed police constable and two ambulance men moved aside as Morse walked towards the green tarpaulin sheet that covered a body recently fished from the murky-looking water. For a few moments, however, he was more than reluctant to pull back the tarpaulin. Instead, his dark eyebrows contracted to a frown as mentally he traced the odd configuration of the bulge beneath the winding-sheet. Surely the body had to be that of a child, for it appeared to be about three and a half feet long – no more; and Morse's up-curved nostrils betokened an even grislier revulsion. Adult suicide was bad enough. But the death of a child – agh! Accident? *Murder?*

Morse told the four men standing there to shield him from the silent onlookers as he pulled back the tarpaulin and – after only a few seconds – replaced it. His cheeks had grown ashen pale, and his eyes seemed stunned with horror. He managed only two hoarsely-spoken words: 'My God!'

He was still standing there, speechless and shaken, when a big, battered old Ford braked sharply beside the ambulance, from it emerging a mournful, hump-backed man who looked as though he should have taken late retirement ten years earlier. He greeted Morse with a voice that matched his lean, lugubrious mien.

'I thought I'd find you in the bar, Morse.'

'They're closed.'

'You don't sound very cheerful, old man?'

Morse pointed vaguely behind him, towards the sheet, and the police surgeon immediately knelt to his calling.

'Phew! *Very* interesting!'

Morse, his back still turned on the corpse, heard himself mutter something that vaguely concurred with such a finding, and thereafter left his sanguine colleague utterly in peace.

Slowly and carefully the surgeon examined the body, methodically entering notes into a black pocket-book. Much of what he wrote would be intelligible to one unversed in forensic medicine. Yet the first few lines were phrased with frightening simplicity:

First appearances: male (60–65?); Caucasian; torso well nourished (bit too well?); head (missing) severed from shoulders (amateurishly?) at roughly the fourth cervical vertebra; hands l. & r. missing, the wrists cut across the medial ligaments; legs l. & r. also missing, severed from torso about 5–6 inches below hip-joint (more professionally done?); skin – 'washerwoman' effect . . .

Finally, and with some difficulty, the surgeon rose to his feet and stood beside Morse, holding his lumbar regions with both hands as though in chronic agony.

'Know a cure for lumbago, Morse?'

'I thought *you* were the doctor.'

'Me? I'm just a poorly-paid pathologist.'

'You get lumbago in mid-*summer*?'

'Mid-*every*-bloody-season!'

'They say a drop of Scotch is good for most things.'

'I thought you said they're closed.'

'Emergency, isn't it?' Morse was beginning to feel slightly better.

One of the ambulance men came up to him. 'All right to take it away?'

'Might as well.'

'No!' It was the surgeon who spoke. 'Not for the moment. I want to have a few words with the chief inspector here first.'

The ambulance man moved away and the surgeon sounded unwontedly sombre. 'You've got a nasty case on your hands here, Morse, and – well, I reckon you ought to have a look at one or two things while we're *in situ*, as it were – you *were* a classicist once, I believe? Any clues going'll pretty certainly be gone by the time I start carving him up.'

'I don't think there's much point in that, Max. You just give him a good going-over – that'll be fine!'

In kindly fashion, Max put a hand on his old friend's shoulder. 'I know! Pretty dreadful sight, isn't it? But I've missed things in the past – you know that! And if—'

'All right. But I need a drink first, Max.'

'*After*. Don't worry – I know the landlord.'

'So do I,' said Morse.

'OK, then?'

'OK!'

But, as the surgeon drew back the tarpaulin once more, Morse found himself quite incapable of looking a second time at that crudely jagged neck. Instead he concentrated his narrowed eyes upon the only limbs that someone – *someone* (already the old instincts were quickened again) – had felt it safe to leave intact. The upper part of the man's body was dressed in a formal, dark-blue, pin-striped jacket, matching the material of the truncated trousers below; and, beneath the jacket, in a white shirt, adorned with a plain rust-red tie – rather awkwardly fastened. Morse shuddered as the surgeon peeled off the sodden jacket, and placed the squelching material by the side of the dismembered torso.

'You want the trousers too? – what's left of 'em?'

Morse shook his head. 'Anything in the pockets?'

The surgeon inserted his hands roughly into the left and right pockets; but his fingers showed through the bottom of each, and Morse felt as sick as some sensitively-palated patient in the dentist's chair having a wax impression taken of his upper jaw.

'Back pocket?' he suggested weakly.

'Ah!' The surgeon withdrew a sodden sheet of paper, folded over several times, and handed it to Morse. 'See what I mean? Good job we—'

'You'd have found it, anyway.'

'Think so? Who's the criminologist here, Morse? They pay *me* to look at the bodies – not a lump of pulp like that. I'd have sent the trousers to Oxfam, like as not – better still, the Boy Scouts, eh?'

Morse managed to raise a feeble grin, but he wanted the job over. 'Nothing else?'

Max shook his head; and as Morse (there being nothing less nauseating to contemplate) looked vaguely down along the out-stretched arms, the surgeon interrupted his thoughts.

'Not much good, arms, you know. Now if you've got teeth – which in our case we have not got – or—'

But Morse was no longer listening to his colleague's idle commentary. 'Will you pull his shirt-sleeves up for me, Max?'

'Might take a bit of skin with 'em. Depends how long—'

'Shut up!'

The surgeon carefully unfastened the cuff-links and pushed the sleeves slowly up the slender arms. 'Not exactly a weight-lifter, was he?'

'No.'

The surgeon looked at Morse curiously. 'You expecting to find a tattoo or something, with the fellow's name stuck next to his sweetheart's?'

'You never know your luck, Max. There might even be a name-tape on his suit somewhere.'

'Somehow I don't reckon you're going to have too much luck in this case,' said the surgeon.

'Perhaps not . . .' But Morse was hardly listening. He felt the sickness rising to the top of his gullet, but not before he'd noticed the slight contusion on the inner hollow between the left biceps and the fore-arm. Then he suddenly turned away from the body and retched up violently on the grass.

Sergeant Lewis looked on with a sad and vulnerable concern. Morse was his hero, and always would be. But even heroes had their momentary weaknesses, as Lewis had so often learned.

Chapter Nine

Wednesday, 23rd July

In which Morse's mind drifts elsewhere as the police-surgeon enunciates some of the scientific principles concerning immersion in fluids.

It was later that same afternoon that Morse, Lewis, and the police surgeon presented themselves at the Boat Inn, where the landlord, sensibly circumspect, informed the trio that it would of course be wholly improper for him to serve any alcoholic beverages at the bar; on the other hand the provision of three chairs in a back room and a bottle of personally-purchased Glenfiddich might not perhaps be deemed to contravene the nation's liquor laws.

'How long's he been dead?' was Morse's flatly-spoken, predictable gambit, and the surgeon poured himself a liberal tumbler before deigning to reply.

'Good question! I'll have a guess at it tomorrow.'

Morse poured himself an equally liberal portion, his sour expression reflecting a chronic distrust in the surgeon's calling.

'A week, perhaps?'

The surgeon merely shrugged his shoulders.

'Could be longer, you mean?'

'Or shorter.'

'Oh Christ! Come off it, Max!' Morse banged the bottle down on the table, and Lewis wondered if he himself might be offered a dram. He would have refused, of course, but the gesture would have been gratifying.

The surgeon savoured a few sips with the slow dedication of a man testing a dubious tooth with a mouthwash, before turning to Morse, his ugly face beatified: 'Nectar, old man!'

Morse, likewise, appeared temporarily more interested in the whisky than in any problems a headless, handless, legless corpse might pose to the Kidlington CID. 'They tell me the secret's in the water of those Scottish burns.'

'Nonsense! It's because they manage to get *rid* of the water.'

'Could be!' Morse nodded more happily now. 'But while we're talking of water, I just asked you—'

'You know nothing about water, Morse. Listen! If you find a body immersed in fresh water, you've got the helluva job finding out what happened. In fact, one of the trickiest problems in forensic medicine – about which you know bugger-all, of course – is to prove whether death *was* due to drowning.'

'But this fellow wasn't drowned. He had his head—'

'Shut up, Morse. You asked how long he'd been in the canal, right? You didn't ask me who sawed his head off!'

Morse nodded agreement.

'Well, *listen*, then! There are five questions I'm paid to ask myself when a body's found immersed in water, and in this particular case you wouldn't need a genius like me to answer most of them. First, was the person alive when entering the water? Answer: pretty certainly, no. Second, was death due to immersion? Answer: equally certainly, no. Third, was death rapid? Answer: the question doesn't apply, because death took place elsewhere. Fourth, did any other factors contribute to death? Answer: almost certainly, yes; the poor fellow was likely to have been clinically dead when somebody chopped him up and chucked him in the canal. Fifth, where did the body enter the water? Answer: God knows! Probably where it was found – as most of them are. But it could have drifted a fair way, in certain conditions. With a combination of bodily gases and other internal reactions, you'll often find a corpse floating up to the surface and then—'

But Morse interrupted him, turning to Lewis: 'How *did* we find him?'

'We had a call from a chap who was fishing there, sir. Said he'd seen something looking like a body half-floating under the water, just where we found him.'

'Did you get his name – this fisherman's?' Morse's question was sharp, and to Lewis his eyes seemed to glint with a frightening authority.

'I wasn't there myself, sir. I got the message from Constable Dickson.'

'He took down the name and address, of course?'

'Not quite, sir,' gulped Lewis. 'He got the name all right, but—'

'—the fellow rang off before giving his address!'

'You can't really blame—'

'Who's blaming *anybody*, Lewis? What *was* his name, by the way?'

'Rowbotham. Simon Rowbotham.'

'Christ! That's an unlikely sounding name.'

'But Dickson got it down all right, sir. He asked the fellow to spell it for him – he told me that.'

'I see I shall have to congratulate Constable Dickson the next time I have the misfortune to meet him.'

'We're only talking about a name, sir.' Lewis was feeling that incipient surge of frustrated anger he'd so often experienced with Morse.

'*Only?* What are you talking about? "*Simon*"? With a surname like "*Rowbotham*"? Lew-is! Now *George* Rowbotham – that's fine, that squares with your actual proletarian parentage. Or Simon *Carruthers*, or something – that's what you'd expect from some aristocrat from Saffron Walden. But *Simon Rowbotham*? Come off it, Lewis. The fellow who rang was making it up as he went along.'

The surgeon, who had remained sipping placidly during this oddly intemperate exchange, now decided it was time to rescue the hapless Lewis. 'You do talk a load of nonsense, Morse. I've never known your first name, and I don't give a sod what it is. For all I know, it's "Eric" or "Ernie" or something. But so bloody *what*?'

Morse, who had ever sought to surround his Christian name in the decent mists of anonymity, made no reply. Instead, he poured himself another measure of the pale yellow spirit, thereafter lapsing into silent thought.

It was Max who picked up the thread of the earlier discussion. 'At least you're not likely to get bogged down in any doubts about accident or suicide – unless you find some boat-propeller's sliced his head off – and his hands – and his legs.'

'No chance of that?'

'I haven't examined the body yet, have I?'

Morse grunted with frustration. 'I asked you, and I ask you again. How long's he been in the water?'

'I just told you. I haven't—'

'Can't you try a feeble bloody guess?'

'Not all that long – in the water, that is. But he may have been dead a few days before then.'

'Have a guess, for Christ's sake!'

'That's tricky.'

'It's always "tricky" for you, isn't it? You do actually think the fellow's *dead*, I suppose?'

The surgeon finished his whisky, and poured himself more, his lined face creasing into something approaching geniality. 'Time of death? That's always going to play a prominent part in your business, Morse. But it's never been my view that an experienced pathologist – such as myself – can ever really put too much faith in the accuracy of his observations. So many variables, you see—'

'Forget it!'

'Ah! But if someone actually *saw* this fellow being chucked in – well, we'd have a much better idea of things, um?'

Morse nodded slowly and turned his eyes to Lewis; and Lewis, in turn, nodded his own understanding.

'It shouldn't take long, sir. There's only a dozen or so houses along the towpath.'

He prepared to go. Before leaving, however, he asked one question of the surgeon. 'Have you got the slightest idea, sir, when the body might have been put in the canal?'

'Two, three days ago, Sergeant.'

'How the hell do you know that?' growled Morse after Lewis had gone.

'I *don't* really. But he's a polite fellow, your Lewis, isn't he? Deserves a bit of help, as I see it.'

'About two or three days, then . . .'

'Not much more – and probably been dead about a day longer. His skin's gone past the "washerwoman" effect, and that suggests he's certainly been in the water more than twenty-four hours. And I'd guess – *guess*, mind! – that we're past the "sodden" stage and almost up to the time when the skin gets blanched. Let's say about two, two-and-a-half days.'

'And nobody would be fool enough to dump him in during the hours of daylight, so—'

'Yep. Sunday night – that's about the time I'd *suggest*, Morse. But if I find a few live fleas on him, it'll mean I'm talking a load of balls; they'd usually be dead after twenty-four hours in the water.'

'He doesn't look much like a fellow who had fleas, does he?'

'Depends where he was before they pushed him in. For all we know, he could have been lying in the boot of a car next to a dead dog.' He looked across and saw the chief inspector looking less than happily into his glass.

'I can understand somebody chopping his head off, Max – even his hands. But why in the name of Sweeney Todd should anyone want to slice his *legs*?'

'Same thing. Identification.'

'You mean . . . there was something *below* his knees – couple
of wooden legs, or something?'
' "Artificial prostheses", that's what they call 'em now.'
'Or he might have had no toes?'
'Not many of that sort around . . .'
But Morse's mind was far away, the image of the gruesome
corpse producing a further spasm in some section of his gut.
'You're right, you know, Morse!' The surgeon happily poured
himself another drink. 'He probably wouldn't have *recognised* a
flea! Good cut of cloth, that suit. Pretty classy shirt, too. Sort of chap
who had a very-nice-job-thank-you: good salary, pleasant conditions
of work, carpet all round the office, decent pension . . .' Suddenly
the surgeon broke off, and seemed to arrive at one of his few firm
conclusions. 'You know what, Morse? I reckon he was probably a
bank manager!'
'Or an Oxford don,' added Morse quietly.

Chapter Ten

Wednesday, 23rd July

In spite of his toothache, Morse begins his investigations
with the reconstruction of a letter.

In spite of his unorthodox, intuitive, and seemingly lazy approach
to the solving of crime, Morse was an extremely competent admin-
istrator; and when he sat down again at his office desk that same
evening, all the procedures called for in a case of murder (and
this *was* murder) had been, or were about to be, put into effect.
Superintendent Strange, to whom Morse had reported on his return
to HQ, knew his chief inspector only too well.
'You'll want Lewis, of course?'
'Thank you, sir. Couple of frogmen, too.'
'How many extra men?'
'Well – er – none; not for the minute, anyway.'
'Why's that?'

'I wouldn't quite know what to ask them to do, sir,' had been Morse's simple and honest explanation.

And, indeed, as he looked at his wrist-watch (7.30 p.m. – 'Blast, missed *The Archers*!'), he was not at all sure what to ask himself, either. On his desk lay the soddenly promising letter found on the corpse; but his immediate preoccupation was a throbbing toothache which had been getting worse all day. He decided he would do something about it in the morning.

As he sat there, he was conscious that there was a deeper reason for his refusal of the Superintendent's offer of extra personnel. By temperament he was a loner, if only because, although never wholly content in the solitary state, he was almost invariably even more miserable in the company of others. There were a few exceptions, of course, and Lewis was one of them. Exactly why he enjoyed Lewis's company so much, Morse had never really stopped to analyse; but perhaps it was because Lewis was so totally unlike himself. Lewis was placid, good-natured, methodical, honest, unassuming, faithful, and (yes, he might as well come clean about it!) a bit *stolid*, too. Even that afternoon, the good Lewis had been insistently anxious to stay on until whatever hour, if by any chance Morse should consider his availability of any potential value. But Morse had not. As he had pointed out to his sergeant, they *might* pretty soon have a bit of luck and find out who the dead man was; the frogmen *might* just find a few oddments of identifiable limbs in the sludge of the canal waters by Aubrey's Bridge. But Morse doubted it. For, even at this very early stage of the case, he sensed that his major problem would not so much be who the murderer was, *but who exactly had been murdered*. It was Morse's job, though, to find the answer to both these questions; and so he started on his task, alternately stroking his slightly swollen left jaw and prodding down viciously on the offending double-fang. He took the letter lying on the desk in front of him, pressed it very carefully between sheets of blotting-paper, and then removed it. The paper was not so sopped and sodden as he had feared, and with a pair of tweezers he was soon able to unfold a strip about two inches wide and eight inches long. It was immediately apparent that this formed the left-hand side of a typewritten letter; and, furthermore, except for some minor blurring of letters at the torn edge, the message was gladdeningly legible:

Dear Sir,
This   is   a   most   unusua
realise.   But   please   re
because   what   I   am   pro
both   you   and   me.   My   wa   5
College   has   just   take
final   examinations   in   G
in   about   ten   or   twelve
an   old   man   and   I'm   de
how   she   has   got   on   ah   10
The   reason   for   my   r
ridiculously   impatient,
to   America   in   a   few
able   to   be   contacte
want   to   know   is   how   J   15
this.   I   have   spent   a
education,   and   she   is
I   realise   that   this
only   that   you   should   g
to   such   an   impropriet   20
publication   of   the   cl
July.
    If   you   can   possibly   se
I   shall   be   in   a   positi
unconventionally.   You   s   25
most   select   clubs,   sa
give   you   a   completely
delights   which   are   as
Please   do   give   me   a   r
may   be,   at   01-417 808   30
you   feel   able   to   do
result,   I   shall   give
able   to   enjoy,   at   no   c
the   most   discreet   er
ever imagined.   35
                    You

Morse sat back and studied the words with great joy. He'd been a life-long addict of puzzles and of cryptograms, and this was exactly the sort of work his mind could cope with confidently. First he enumerated the lines in 5s (as shown above); then he set his mind to work. It took him ten minutes, and another ten minutes to copy out his first draft. The general drift of the letter required no Aristotelian intellect to decipher – primarily because of the give-away clue in line 7. But it had been none too easy to concoct some continuum over a few of the individual word-breaks, especially 'wa–' in line 5; 'ah–' in line 10; 'cl–' in line 21; and 'sa–' in line 26.

This is the first draft that Morse wrote out:

Dear Sir,

This is a most unusua	l letter as I know you'll
realise. But please re	ad it with great care
because what I am pro	posing can benefit
both you and me. My wa	strel daughter at ——
College has just take	n (without much hope) her
final examinations in G	eography, and will get the result
in about ten or twelve	days' time. Now I am
an old man and I'm de	sperately anxious to know
how she has got on ah	ead of the official lists.
The reason for my r	equest is that I am
ridiculously impatient,	and in fact I am off
to America in a few	days' time where I may not be
able to be contacte	d for some while. All I
want to know is how J	—— got on, if you can tell me
this. I have spent a	great deal of money on her
education, and she is	the only child I have.
I realise that this	is an improper request. I ask
only that you should g	ive a thought to stooping
to such an impropriet	y. I think the official date for
publication of the cl	ass list is —— ——
July.	
If you can possibly se	e your way to this favour,
I shall be in a positi	on to pay you very well, if
unconventionally. You s	ee I manage some of the
most select clubs, sa	unas and parlours and I will
give you a completely	free access to the sexual
delights which are as	sociated with such places.
Please do give me a r	ing, whatever your decision
may be, at 01-417 808	——. If it so happens that
you feel able to do	what I ask about J——'s
result, I shall give	you details about how you'll be
able to enjoy, at no c	ost at all to yourself,
the most discreet er	otic thrills you can have
ever imagined.	

You   rs sincerely,

Morse was reasonably pleased with the draft. It lacked polish here and there, but it wasn't bad at all, really. Three specific problems, of course: the name of the college, the name of the girl, and the last bit of the telephone number. The college would be a bit more difficult now that almost all of them accepted women, but . . .

Suddenly Morse sat at his desk quite motionless, the blood tingling across his shoulders. Could it be? That 'G–'? It needn't be Geography or Geology or Geo-physics or whatever. And it wasn't. It was *Greats*! And that 'J–'? That wasn't Judith or Joanna or Jezebel. It was *Jane* – the girl the Master had indiscreetly mentioned to him! And that would solve the college automatically: it was *Lonsdale*!

Phew!

The telephone number wouldn't be much of a problem, either, since Lewis could soon sort that out. If it was a four-digit group, that would only mean ten possibilities; and if it was five-digits, that was only a hundred; and Lewis was a very patient man . . .

But the tooth was jabbing its pain along his jaw once more, and he made his way home, where doubling (as he invariably did) the dosage of all medical nostrums he took six Aspros, washed them down well with whisky, and went to bed. But at 2 a.m. we find him sitting up in bed, his hand caressing his jaw, the pain jumping in his gum like some demented dervish. And at 8 a.m. we find him standing outside a deserted dentist's premises in North Oxford, an inordinately long scarf wrapped round his jaw, waiting desperately for one of the receptionists to arrive.

Chapter Eleven

Thursday, 24th July

Wherein such diverse activities as dentistry, crossword-solving, and pike-angling make their appropriate contributions to Morse's view of things.

'You've not been looking after these too well, have you, Mr Morse?'

Since at this point, however, the dapperly-dressed dentist had his patient's mouth opened to its widest extremities, Morse was able only to produce a strained grunt from his swollen larynx.

'You ought to cut out the sugar,' continued the dentist, surveying so many signs of incipient decay, 'and some dental-floss wouldn't come amiss with all this . . . Ah! I reckon that's the little fellow that's been causing you—' He tapped one of the lower-left molars with a blunt instrument, and the recumbent Morse was almost levitated in agony. 'Ye-es, you've got a nasty little infection there . . . does *that* hurt?'

Again Morse's body jumped in agonising pain, before the chair was raised to a semi-vertical slant and he was ordered to 'rinse out'.

'You've got a nasty little infection there, as I say . . .'

Everything with the dentist appeared to warrant the epithet 'little', and Morse would have been more gratified had it been suggested to him that he was the victim of a massive great bloody infection stemming from an equally massive great bloody tooth that even now was throbbing mightily. He continued to sit in the chair, but the dentist himself was writing something across at his desk.

'Aren't you going to take it out?' asked Morse.

The dentist continued writing. 'We try to preserve as many teeth as we can these days, you know. And it's particularly important for *you* not to lose many more. You haven't got too many left, have you?'

'But it's giving me—'

'Here's a prescription for a little penicillin. Don't worry! It'll soon sort out the infection and get that little swelling down. Then if you come and see me again in – a week, shall we say?'

'A *week*?'

'I can't do anything till then. If I took it out now – well, let's say you'd have to be a brave man, Mr Morse.'

'Would I?' said Morse weakly. He finally rose from the chair, and his eyes wandered to the shelf of plaster-casts of teeth behind the dentist's desk, the upper jaws resting on the lower, a few canines missing here, a few molars there. It all seemed rather obscene to Morse, and reminded him of his junior-school history books, with their drawings of skulls labelled with such memorable names as *Eoanthropus dawsoni*, *Pithecanthropus erectus*, and the rest.

The dentist saw his interest and reached down a particularly ugly cast, snapping the jaws apart and together again like a ventriloquist at a dumb-show. 'Remarkable things teeth, you know. No two sets of teeth can ever be the same. Each set – well, it's unique, like finger-prints.' He looked at the squalid lump of plastering with infinite compassion, and it seemed quite obvious that teeth obsessed not only his working life but his private soul as well.

Morse stood beside him, waiting for the prescription; and when the dentist got to his feet Morse became surprisingly aware of how small a man the dentist was. Had it been the white coat that had given him the semblance of being taller? Had it been the fact that the last thing Morse had earlier been interested in was whether the kindly man who'd readily agreed to see one of his most irregular clients was a dwarf or a giant? Yet there was something else, wasn't there?

Morse's mind suddenly grasped it as he stood waiting at the Summertown chemist's. It had been when the dentist had been sitting at his desk – yes. Because the length of his back was that of a man of normal height; and so it must have been *the legs* . . .

'Are you a pensioner, sir?' asked the young assistant as she took his prescription. (My God! Could he really look as old as that?)

After an exhortation to stick religiously to the stated dosage, and also to be sure to complete the course, Morse was soon on his way to Kidlington, quite convinced now of the perfectly obvious fact that whoever had dismembered the corpse had been at desperate pains to conceal its identity.

Teeth? The murderer would have left a means of certain identification – 'unique', as his little torturer had said. Hands? If they had been deformed in any way, or one of them had? It was difficult for fellow humans to forget deformity. Legs? What if that exciting idea that had occurred to him at the chemist's . . .

But he was at HQ now, and the need for instant action was at hand. He swallowed twice the specified dosage of tablets, told himself that the marvellous stuff was already engaged in furious conflict with the 'little infection', and finally greeted Lewis at 9.30 a.m.

'You said you'd be here by eight, sir.'

'You're lucky to see me at all!' Morse snapped, as he unwrapped his scarf and bared his bulging jaw.

'Bad tooth, sir?'

'Not just *bad*, Lewis. It's the worst bloody tooth in England!'

'The missus always swears by—'

'Forget what your missus says! She's not a dentist, is she?'

So Lewis forgot it, and sat down silently.

Soon Morse was feeling better, and for an hour he discussed with Lewis both the letter and the curious thoughts that had been occurring to him.

'Someone certainly seems to be making it difficult for us,' said Lewis; and the sentence did little more than state in simple English the even simpler thought that had gradually dawned on Morse's mind. But for Lewis life was full of surprises, since he now heard Morse ask him to repeat exactly that same sentence. And as he did so, Lewis saw the familiar sight of his chief looking out over the concreted yard, or wherever it was those eyes, unblinking, stared with more than a hint of deeper understanding.

'Or it could be just the opposite,' Lewis heard him mumble enigmatically.

'Pardon, sir?'

'Do you reckon a cup of coffee would upset this tooth of mine?'

'Be all right, unless it's too hot.'

'Nip and get a couple of cups.'

After Lewis had gone, Morse unfolded *The Times* and looked at the crossword. 1 across: 'He lived perched up, mostly in sites around East, shivering (6,8).' Anagram, obviously: 'mostly in sites' round 'e'. Yes! He quickly wrote in 'Simon Stylites' – only to find himself one letter short. Of course! It was *Simeon* Stylites, and he was about to correct the letters, when he stopped.

It *couldn't* be, surely!

He wrote a circle of letters in the bottom margin of the newspaper, crossed off a few letters, then a few more – and stopped again. Not only could it be, it was! What an extraordinary—

'I told her to stick some extra cold milk in, sir.'

'Did you sugar it?'

'You do take sugar, don't you?'

'Bad for the teeth – surely you know that?'

'Shall I go and—'

'No – siddown. I've got something to show you. Oh God! This coffee's cold!'

'You haven't done much of the crossword.'

'Haven't I?' Morse was smiling serenely, and he thrust the paper across to Lewis who looked down uncomprehendingly at the almost illegible alterations in the top row of squares. But Lewis was happy. The chief was on to something – the chief was always on to something, and that was good. That's why he enjoyed working with Morse. Being on the receiving end of all the unpredictability, all the irascibility, all the unfairness – it was a cheap price to pay for working with him. And now he whistled softly to himself as Morse explained the riddle of the circle of letters he had printed.

'Do you want me to get on to it, sir?'

'No, I'd rather you got on with those telephone numbers.'

'Straightaway, you mean?'

Morse gestured gently towards the phone on his desk, a smile spreading lopsidedly across his swollen mouth. 'You said it was Dickson on the desk yesterday when we got the call from Thrupp?'

'Yes.'

'Well, you get on with things here, Lewis. I'm just going to have a little chat with Dickson.'

If Lewis's weakness in life was the smell of freshly-fried chips (and fast driving!), with Dickson it was the sight of amply-jammed doughnuts, and he sought to swallow his latest mouthful hastily as he saw Morse bearing down on him.

'Fingers a bit sticky this morning, Dickson?'

'Sorry, sir.'

'Sugar is bad for the teeth, didn't you know that?'

'Do you eat a lot yourself, sir?'

For the next few minutes Morse questioned Dickson patiently about the informant who had telephoned HQ about the corpse in the water by Aubrey's Bridge. The facts were clear. The man had not only given his name, he'd spelt it out; he hadn't been absolutely sure that what he had seen was a human body, but it most decidedly looked like one; the call had been made from a phone-box, and after the second lot of 'pip-pips' the line had gone dead.

'*Is* there a phone-box in Thrupp?'

'On the corner, by the pub, sir.'

Morse nodded, 'Did it not occur to you, my lad, that after getting this fellow's name you ought to have got his *address*? In the book of rules, isn't it?'

'Yes, sir, but—'

'Why didn't he want to keep talking, tell me that.'

'Probably ran out of 10ps.'

'He could have rung you again later.'

'Probably thought he'd – he'd already done his duty.'

'More than you did, eh?'

'Yes, sir.'

'Why didn't he stay there at Thrupp?'

'Not everybody likes seeing – sort of drowned people.'

Morse conceded the point, and moved on. 'What do they fish for there?'

'They say there's a few biggish pike up by the bridge.'

'Really? Who the hell's "they"?'

'Well, one of my lads, sir. He's been fishing for pike up there a few times.'

'Keen fisherman, is he?'

Dickson was feeling more at ease now. 'Yes, sir, he's joined the Oxford Pike Anglers' Association.'

'I see. Is the fellow who rang you up a member, too?'

Dickson swallowed hard. 'I don't know, sir.'

'Well, bloody well find out, will you!'

Morse walked away a few steps from the flustered Dickson; then he walked back. 'And I'll tell you something else, lad. If your man Rowbotham *is* a member of whatever it's called, I'll buy you every bloody doughnut in the canteen. And that's a promise!'

Morse walked over to the canteen, ordered another cup of coffee with plenty of milk, smoked a cigarette, assessed the virulence of his gnathic bacteria, noted the pile of approximately thirty-five doughnuts on the counter, and returned to his office.

It was Lewis who was beaming with pleasure now. 'Got it, I reckon, sir!' He showed Morse the list he made. 'Only four digits and so they're only the ten numbers. What do you think?'

Morse read the list:

8080 – J. Pettiford, Tobacconist, Piccadilly
8081 – Comprehensive Assurance Co., Shaftesbury Avenue
8082 – ditto
8083 – ditto
8084 – Douglas Schwartz, Reproductions, Old Compton Street
8085 – Ping Hong Restaurant, Brewer Street
8086 – Claude & Mathilde, Unisex Hairdressers, Lower Regent Street
8087 – Messrs. Levi & Goldstein, Antiquarian Books, Tottenham Court Road
8088 – The Flamenco Topless Bar, Soho Terrace

'There's one missing, Lewis.'

'You want me to—'

'I told you to try them all, I think.'

But whoever was renting number 8089 was clearly away from base, and Morse told Lewis to forget it.

'We are not, my friend, exactly driving through the trackless wastes of the Sahara with a broken axle, you agree? Now, if you can just make one more call and find out the price of a cheap-day second-class return to Paddington—'

'Are we going there?'

'Well, one of us'll have to, Lewis, and it's important for you to stay here, isn't it, because I've got one or two very interesting little things I want you to look into. So I'll – er – perhaps go myself.'

'It won't do your tooth much good.'

'Ah! That reminds me,' said Morse. 'I think it's about time I took another pill or two.'

Chapter Twelve

Thursday, 24th July

A brief interlude in which Sergeant Lewis takes his first steps
into the Examination Schools, the Moloch of Oxford's testing
apparatus.

It was late morning when, from its frontage on the High,
Sergeant Lewis entered the high-roofed, hammer-beamed lobby
of the Examination Schools. Never before had there been occasion
for him to visit this grove of Academe, and he felt self-conscious
as his heavy boots echoed over the mosaics of the marble floor,
patterned in green and blue and orange. At intervals, in front of
the oak-panelling that lined the walls, were stationed the white and
less-than-animated busts of former University Chancellors, former
loyal servants of the monarchy, and sundry other benefactors. And
along the walls themselves was a series of 'Faculty' headings:
Theology, Philosophy, Oriental Studies, Modern History, and
the rest; below which, behind glass, were pinned a line of
notices announcing the names of those candidates adjudged to
have satisfied, in varying degrees, the appropriate panels of the
Faculties' examiners.

On the *Literae Humaniores* ('Greats') board (as Morse had
assured him he would) Lewis duly found a long list of names,
categorised into Class I, Class II, Class III, and Pass Degree. He
noticed, too (as Morse had assured him he would), that a young
lady by the name of Summers (Jane) of Lonsdale College, had
secured a place in the first of these aforesaid categories. Then,
doing precisely as he had been told, Lewis looked to the bottom of
the list, where he saw the signatures of seven examiners. A few of
them were barely legible. But one of them was conspicuously clear:
the neatly penned signature of O. M. A. Browne-Smith. So Lewis
made a brief entry in his notebook, and wondered why Morse had
bothered to send him on this particular errand.

An attendant was seated in an office to the left of the lobby,
and Lewis was soon enlisting this man's ready assistance in learning
something of the processes involved in the evolution of the class-lists.
What happened, it seemed, was this. After candidates had finished
their written examinations, mark co-ordination meetings were held

by each of the examining panels, where 'classes' were provisionally allotted, and where borderline candidates at each class-boundary were considered for vivas, especially those candidates hovering between a First and a Second; finally, but then only the day before the definitive lists were due to be published, the chairman of the examiners (and no one else) was fully in possession of all the facts. At that point it was the duty of the chairman of examiners to summon his colleagues together in order to make a corporate, meticulous check of the final lists, and then to entrust the agreed document to one of the senior personnel of the Schools, whose task it now was to deliver the document for printing to the Oxford University Press. Immediately this was done, five copies of the lists were re-delivered to the waiting panel, who would usually be sitting around drinking tea and eating a few sandwiches during the hour or so's interval. There would follow the long and tedious checking of all results, the spellings of names, and the details of index-numbers and colleges, before the chairman would read aloud to his colleagues the final version, down to the last diaeresis and comma. Only then, if all were correct, would the chairman summon the Clerk of the Schools, in whose august presence each of the five copies would be signed in turn by each of the examiners. Then, at long last, the master-copy would be posted in the lobby of the Schools.

Lewis thanked the attendant, and clattered out across the entrance hall, where examinees, parents, and friends were still clustered eagerly round the notice-boards. For the first time in his life he felt a little envy for those white-tied, subfusc-suited students so happily perched upon the topmost boughs of the tree of knowledge. But such thoughts were futile. Anyway, he had his second assignment ahead of him – at the Churchill Hospital.

Morse was out when he returned, and so for a change it was Lewis who had some little time in which to ponder how the case was going. On the whole, he thought that Morse was probably right. Far from being stranded in the Sahara, they were following a fairly well-directed route, with signposts at almost all the early stages – quite certainly at the Examination Schools; but not (Lewis reminded himself) at the Churchill, where his enquiries had yielded nothing, and where Morse's confident predictions had clearly gone dramatically askew.

Chapter Thirteen

Thursday, 24th July

Quite fortuitously, Morse lights upon a set of college rooms
which he had no original intention of visiting.

Morse himself had decided to postpone for a day or two the
pleasures of a trip to Soho, and instead to make some more immediate enquiries in Oxford. Thus it is that just before midday he was
parking the Jaguar in one of the spaces at the back of Lonsdale
('Reserved for Senior Fellows'), walking through the front gate
('No Visitors'), and introducing himself at the Lodge. Here, a
bowler-hatted porter, very young but already equipped with the
requisite blend of servility and officiousness, was perfectly willing
to answer the questions Morse put to him: yes, most of the undergrads had now gone down for the long vac; yes, most of the dons
had also departed, amongst their number the Master, the Vice-
Master, the Investments Bursar, the Domestic Bursar, the Senior
Tutor, the Senior Fellow, the . . .
'Off to the Bahamas, all of them?'
'Continent mostly, sir – and Greece.'
'You think it's all those topless beaches, perhaps?'
For a few seconds the young porter leered as though he were
about to produce a dirty postcard from one of the innumerable
pigeon-holes, but he quickly resumed his dignity. 'I wouldn't know
about that, sir.'
'What about Dr Browne-Smith? Is he still away?'
'I've not seen him in college since we had a note from him . . .
and then we had a – just a minute.' He went over to his desk and
returned to the 'Enquiries' window with a sheaf of papers. In spite
of having to read them upside-down, Morse was able to read some of
the messages clearly: 'Professor M. Liebermann – back 6th August.
All post to Pension Heimstadt, Friederichstrasse 14, Zurich'; 'Mr G.
Westerby – off to Greece until end of August. Keep all mail at the
Lodge'; 'Dr Browne-Smith . . .'
'Here we are, sir.'
Morse took the handwritten sheet and read the few words:
'Away untill further notice no forwarding adress.' Mentally delet-
ing an 'l', inserting a 'd', and introducing a major stop into

mid-message, Morse handed the sheet back. 'Phone message, was it?'

'Yes, sir. Yesterday, I think it was – or Tuesday.'

'You took it yourself?'

The porter nodded.

'It was Dr Browne-Smith who rang?'

'I think so, yes.'

'You know him well?'

The young man shrugged. 'Pretty well.'

'You'd recognise his voice all right?'

'Well . . .'

'How long have you been here?'

'More than three months now.'

'Just let me have the key to his rooms, will you?' Morse pointed peremptorily to a bunch of keys hanging beside the pigeon-holes, and the porter did as he was told.

The book-lined room to which Morse admitted himself was shady and silent as the grave. Everywhere there were signs of the academic pursuits to which Browne-Smith had devoted his life: on the desk, a large stack of typescript of what appeared to be a forthcoming opus on Philip, father of Alexander the Great, and scores of photographs, slides, and postcards; on a bookcase beside the desk a marble bust of a sombre-featured Cicero; on the few square yards of the walls still free from books, many black-and-white photographs of temples, vases and statuary. But nothing untoward; nothing out of place.

Leading off this main room were two other rooms: one a bleakish-looking, rather dirty WC; the other a small bedroom, containing a single bed, hundreds more books, a white wash-basin and a large mahogany wardrobe. The door of the wardrobe creaked noisily as Morse opened it and looked vaguely along the line of suits and shirts. He told himself he should have brought a tape-measure, but he accepted the fact that usually such forward-planning was quite beyond him. Apart from patting a few pockets, his only other interest appeared to lie in a very large selection of socks, whence he abstracted a brand-new pair and stuffed them in his pocket.

Back in the main room, his eyes wandered along the shelves and into the alcoves (failing to observe the small cooking-ring); but again he seemed mildly satisfied. He picked up a virgin sheet of paper, flicked it into the portable typewriter which stood beside the typescript, and clumsily tapped his way through the leap of the lazy, brown fox over the something or other. Morse couldn't quite remember it all, but he knew he'd got most of the letters included.

As he closed the door behind him (forgetting to re-lock it), he felt a few more sudden jabs in his lower jaw; and, although that unsettled July had at last turned hot and sunny, he pulled his scarf round his throat once more as he stood on the wide, wooden landing. He looked around him, first up the stairs, then down them; then across to the room immediately opposite, where the name G. D. Westerby was printed above the door. Yes! He had seen that name ten minutes ago in the Porters' Lodge; and the owner of that name was, at that very moment, sunning himself on some Aegean island, surely. Yet the door stood slightly open, and Morse stepped silently across the landing and listened.

There was someone there. For a few seconds Morse felt a childlike shudder of fear, but only (he told himself) because of his recent prying in the quiet rooms behind him. Anyway, it would only be some staircase-scout doing a bit of tidying up, dusting . . . But suddenly the rustling noises ceased, succeeded by the more reassuring clean-cut metallic clacks of hammer upon nails; and Morse felt better. Pushing open the door he saw a room very similar to the one he had just left, except that tea-chests and packing crates (most of them with address labels already attached) were bestrewn over almost the whole of the carpet-area, in the midst of which a youth of no more than sixteen or seventeen, dressed in a khaki overall, was inexpertly fixing a lid to one of the wooden crates. As Morse came in, the youth looked up; but only it seemed from curiosity, for he promptly returned to his amateurish bangings.

'Excuse me, is Mr – er – Westerby in?'

'On holiday, I think,' said the spotty-faced youth.

'I'm – er – one of his colleagues. I was very much hoping to catch him before he went.' This explanation appeared unworthy of further comment, for the youth merely nodded and drove yet another nail askew into the wooden lath.

Almost exactly the same layout of rooms as opposite – even the similar positioning of the working desk, with a similar pile of typescript, and exactly the same model of portable typewriter. And Morse knew in a flash what he was about to do, although he had almost no idea of why he did it.

'I'll just leave a note for him, lad, if you'll let me through.'

From his pocket he took out the sheet he had just typed, and put the lazy, brown fox through his faltering paces once more.

'Your firm's moving the old boy, I see.'

'Yeah.'

'Lot of stuff – he always kept a lot of stuff.'

'Books!' (Clearly the youth had as yet no great respect for literature.)

The crate that was in the process of being lidded was doubtless packed with objects that were eminently breakable, since three-quarters of its contents appeared to be wrapped in crumpled newspaper. And there was another crate, alongside, presumably designated for a similar purpose, with a battalion of cut-glass objects, still unwrapped, surrounding it on the carpet. But other objects had already been deposited in this second crate – bulkier objects; and one in particular that lay snugly in the middle, swathed in past editions of *The Times*. It was about the shape of a medium-sized goldfish bowl, almost the size of a – yes! – almost the size of a head.

'I'm glad to see you're being careful with the old boy's valuables,' Morse heard himself saying as he knelt down beside this crate and, with a shaking hand, touched the packaged article, where his probing fingers soon felt the configurations of a human nose and a human mouth.

'What's this?' he managed to ask.

The youth looked across at him. 'Mr Gilbert told me to be very careful about that.'

'Who's Mr Gilbert?'

'*I'm* Mr Gilbert!'

Morse almost panicked as he turned to the door and saw a man of about sixty, perhaps – grey-flannelled and shirt-sleeved, with a pair of gold-rimmed, half-glasses on his nose, and a pair of no-nonsense eyes behind them. But there was something else about him – the first thing that anyone would notice: for, like Morse, he wore a scarf that draped his lower jaw.

'Hullo, Mr Gilbert. I'm – ah – one of Westerby's colleagues here. He asked me to look in from time to time to see, you know, that the stuff was being stowed away carefully.'

'We're looking after that all right, sir.'

'He's got some valuable things here—'

'Have no fears, sir! We're looking after everything beautifully.' With agility he picked his way across the room and stood above the still-kneeling Morse. 'You know we get more fusspots in this business, especially with the women—'

'But some of this stuff – well, you just couldn't replace it, could you?'

'No?' Mr Gilbert's tone sounded too knowledgeable for Morse

to demur. 'I'll tell you one thing, sir. Almost all my clients would prefer to collect their insurance money.'

'Perhaps so.' Morse rose to his feet, and as he did so Gilbert's shrewd eyes seemed to measure him for crating, like some melancholy undertaker surveying a corpse for coffining. 'It's just that he asked me—'

'Look around and check up, sir! We're only too anxious to give every satisfaction – aren't we, Charlie?'

The young assistant nodded. 'Yes, Mr Gilbert.'

Almost involuntarily Morse's eyes were drawn down once again to the head in the unlidded crate, and Gilbert's eyes were following.

'He's all right. Don't worry about him, sir. Took us a good ten minutes to put him to bed.'

'What is it?' asked Morse weakly.

'You want me to—' There was annoyance in Gilbert's face.

Morse nodded.

If it had taken ten minutes to put this particular valuable finally to rest, it took less than ten seconds to resurrect it. And it *was* a head, a marble head of Gerardus Mercator, the Flemish geographer – a head chopped off at the neck, like the head of the man who had been dragged from the canal out at Thrupp.

A somewhat foolish-looking Morse now hastened to take his leave, but before doing so he sought briefly to mitigate the awkward little episode. He addressed himself to Gilbert: 'You're a fellow sufferer, I see.'

For a second or two Gilbert's eyes looked puzzled – suspicious almost. 'Ah – the scarf – yes! Abscess. But the dentist won't touch it. What about you, sir?'

So Morse told him, and the two men chatted amiably enough for a couple of minutes. Then Morse departed.

From the window, Gilbert watched Morse as he walked towards the Lodge.

'How the hell did he get in?'

'I must have left the door open.'

'Well, you're going to have to learn to keep doors *shut* in this business – understand? One of the first rules of the trade, that is. Still, you've not been with us long, have you?'

'Month.' The youth looked surly, and Gilbert's tone was deliberately softer as he continued.

'Never mind – no harm done. You don't know who he is, do you?'

'No. But I saw him go into the room opposite, then I heard him come out again.'

'Opposite, eh?' Gilbert opened the door, and looked out. 'Mm. That must be Dr Browne-Smith, then.'

'He said he was a friend o' this fellah here.'

'Well, you believed him, didn't you?'

'Yeah – 'course.'

'As I say, though, we can't be too careful in this job, Charlie. Lots of valuables around. It's always the same.'

'He didn't take anything.'

'No, I'm sure he didn't. He – er – just sort of looked round, you say?'

'Yeah, looked around a bit – said he wanted to leave a message for this fellah, that's all.'

'Where's the message?' Gilbert's voice was suddenly sharp.

'I dunno. He just typed—'

'He *what*?'

The unhappy Charlie pointed vaguely to the portable. 'He just typed a little note on that thing, that's all.'

'Ah, I see. Well, if that's all . . .' Gilbert's face seemed to relax, and his tone was kindly again. 'But look, my lad. If you're going to make a success of this business, you've got to be a bit cagey, like me. When you're moving people, see, it's easy as wink for someone to nip in the property and pretend he's a relative or something. Then he nicks all the silver – and then where are we? Understand?'

'Yeah.'

'So. Let's start being cagey right away, OK? You be a good lad, and just nip down to the Lodge, and see if they know who that fellow was in here. It'll be a bit of good experience for you.'

Without enthusiasm, Charlie went out, and for a second time Gilbert walked over to the window, and waited until the young apprentice was out of sight. Then he put on a pair of working gloves, picked up the portable typewriter and crossed the landing. He knew that the door opposite was unlocked (since he had already tried it on his way up), and very swiftly he entered the room and exchanged the typewriter he carried for the one on Dr Browne-Smith's desk.

Gilbert was kneeling by one of the crates, carefully repacking the head of Gerardus Mercator, when a rather worried-looking Charlie returned.

'It was the *police*.'

'Really?' Gilbert kept his eyes on his work. 'Well, that's good news. Somebody must have seen you here and thought the college had a burglar or something. Yes – that explains it. You see, lad, there aren't many people in the colleges this time of year. They've nearly all gone, so it's a good time for burglars, understand?'

Charlie nodded, and was soon attaching an address label to the recently-lidded crate: G. D. Westerby, Esq., Flat 6, 29 Cambridge Way, London, WC1.

Chapter Fourteen

Thursday, 24th July

Preliminary investigations are now in full swing, and Morse appears unconcerned about the contradictory evidence that emerges.

It might perhaps appear to the reader that Morse had come off slightly the worse in the exchanges recorded in the previous chapter. But the truth is that after a late pub lunch Morse returned to his office exceedingly satisfied with his morning's work, since fresh ideas were breeding in profusion now.

He was still seated there, deep in thought, when three-quarters of an hour later the phone rang. It was the police-surgeon.

'Look, I'll cut out the technicalities. You can read 'em in my report – and anyway you wouldn't be able to follow 'em. Adult, male, Caucasian; sixtyish or slightly more; well nourished; no signs of any physical abnormality; pretty healthy except for the lungs, but there's no tumour there – in fact there's no tumour or neoplasm anywhere – we don't call it cancer these days, you know. By the way, you still smoking, Morse?'

'Get on with it!'

'Death before immersion—'

'You *do* surprise me.'

'—and probably curled up a bit after death.'

'He was carried there, you mean?'

'I said "probably".'

'In the boot of a car?'

'How the hell do I know!'

'Anything else?'

'Dismembered *after* death – pretty certain of that.'

'Brilliant,' mumbled Morse.

'And that's almost it, old man.'

Morse was secretly delighted with these findings, but for the moment he feigned a tone of disappointment. 'But aren't you going to tell me *how* he died? That's what they pay you for, isn't it?'

As ever, the surgeon sounded unperturbed. 'Tricky question, that. No obvious wounds – or unobvious ones for that matter. Somebody could have clobbered him about the head – a common enough cause of death, as well you know. But we haven't *got* a head, remember?'

'Not poisoned?' asked Morse quietly.

'Don't think so. It's never all that easy to tell when you've got your giblets soaked in water.'

'Didn't you bother to have a look at his guts?'

'Ah, yes. Drop of Scotch there, Morse. But, after all, there's a drop of Scotch in most – By the way, Morse, you still boozing?'

'I've not quite managed to cut it out.'

'And some kippers. You interested in kippers?'

'For breakfast?'

'He'd had some, yes. But whether he'd had 'em for breakfast—'

'You mean he might have had the Scotch for breakfast and the kippers for lunch?'

'We live in a strange world.'

'Nothing else?'

'As I said, that's almost the lot.'

With huge self-gratification, Morse now prepared to launch his Exocet. 'Well, thanks very much, Max. But if I may say so I reckon somebody at your end – I'm sure it isn't you! – deserves a hefty kick up the arse. As you know, I don't pretend to be a pathologist myself but—'

'I said it was "almost" the lot, Morse, and I know what you're going to say. I just thought I'd leave it to the end – you know, just to humour an old friend and all that.'

'It's that bloody *arm* I'm talking about!'

'Yes, yes! I know that. You just hold your horses a minute! I noticed you looking down at that arm, of course, almost as if you thought you'd made some wonderful discovery. Discovery? What? With that bloody great bruise there? You don't honestly think even a part-time hospital-porter could have missed that, do you?'

Morse growled his discomfiture down the phone, and the surgeon proceeded placidly.

'Funny thing, Morse. You just *happened* to be right in what you thought – not for the right reasons, though. That contusion on the left arm, it was nothing to do with giving blood. He must have just knocked himself somewhere – or somebody else knocked *him*. But you were right, he *was* a blood donor. Difficult to be certain, but I examined his arms very carefully and I reckon he'd probably had the needle about twenty to twenty-five times in his left arm; about twelve to fifteen in his right.'

'Mm.' For a few seconds Morse was silent. 'Send me the full report over, please, Max.'

'It won't help much.'

'*I'll* decide that, thank you very much.'

'What do I do with the corpse?'

'Put it in the bloody deep-freeze!'

A few minutes later, after slamming down the phone, Morse rang Lonsdale and asked for the college secretary.

'Can I help you?' She had a nice voice, but for once it didn't register with Morse.

'Yes! I want to know whether the college had kippers for breakfast on Friday 11th July.'

'I don't know. I could try to find out, I suppose.'

'Well, *find* out!' snapped Morse.

'Can I ring you back, sir?' She was obviously distressed, but Morse was crudely adamant.

'No! Do it now!'

Morse heard a hectic, whispered conversation at the other end of the line, and eventually a male voice, defensive but quite firm, took over.

'Andrews, here. Perhaps *I* could help you, Inspector.'

And, indeed, he could; for he happened to live with his family in Kidlington, and professed himself only too glad to call in at police HQ later that same afternoon.

Lewis, who had come in during this latter call, realised immediately that someone had seriously upset the chief, and he was not at all hopeful about how his own two items of information would be received – especially the second. But Morse appeared surprisingly amiable and listened attentively as Lewis recounted what he had learned at the Examination Schools.

'So you see, sir,' he concluded, 'no one, not even the chairman, could be absolutely certain of all the results until just before the final list goes up.'

Morse just nodded, and sat back almost happily.

But Lewis had barely begun his report on his second visit when Morse sat forward and exploded.

'You couldn't have looked carefully enough, Lewis! Of course he's bloody there!'

'But he's not, sir. I checked and re-checked everything – so did the girl.'

'Didn't it occur to you they'd probably put him under "Smith" or something?'

Lewis replied quietly: 'If you really want to know, I looked under "Brown", and "Browne" with an "e"; and "Smith", and "Smithe" with an "e"; and I looked through all the rest of the "B"s and the "S"s just in case his card was out of order. But you'd better face it, sir. Unless they've lost his records, *Dr Browne-Smith isn't a blood donor at all.*'

'Oh!' For some time Morse just sat there, and then he smiled. 'Why didn't you try under the "W"s?'

'Pardon?'

'Forget it! For the minute anyway. Now let me tell you a few interesting facts.'

So Morse, in turn, recounted his own morning's work, and finished up by handing over to Lewis the sheet of paper on which he had typed his two sentences.

'See that second one, Lewis?'

Lewis nodded as he looked down at the version beginning 'The laxy brown fox l3aped . . .'

'Well, that's the same typewriter as the one used for the letter we found on the body!'

Lewis whistled in genuine amazement. 'You're sure you're not mistaken, sir?'

'Lew-is!' (The eyes were almost frighteningly unblinking once more.) 'And there's something else.' He pushed across the desk the note that the Master of Lonsdale had given him earlier – the note supposedly left in the Porters' Lodge by Browne-Smith. '*That* was done on the same typewriter, too!'

'Whew!'

'So your next job—'

'Just a minute, sir. You're quite certain, are you, which typewriter it was?'

'Oh yes, Lewis. *It was Westerby's.*'

He was very happy now, and looked across at Lewis with the satisfaction of a man leaning over the parapet of infallibility.

So it was that Lewis was forthwith despatched to impound the two typewriters, whilst Morse took two more penicillin tablets and waited for the arrival of Mr Andrews, Ancient History Tutor of Lonsdale.

Chapter Fifteen

Thursday, 24th July

From two sources, Morse gains valuable insight into the workings of the human mind, and specifically into the mind of Dr Browne-Smith of Lonsdale.

Andrews ('a good young man', as Browne-Smith had earlier described him) turned out to be about Morse's age – a slim, bespectacled, shrewd-looking man of medium height who gave the immediate impression of not suffering fools at all gladly. For the time being he was (as he told Morse) the senior resident fellow at Lonsdale, in which capacity he was far from happy about the way the college secretary had been telephonically assaulted. But, yes: on Friday, 11th July, the college had breakfasted on kippers. That had been the question – and that was the answer.

So Morse began to like the man, and was soon telling him about the Master's mild anxiety over Browne-Smith, as well as about his own involvement in the matter.

'Let me come clean, Inspector. I know more about this than you think. Before he left, the Master told *me* he was worried about Browne-Smith.'

'If he's got any sense, he's *still* worried.'

'But we had a note from him.'

'Which he didn't write.'

'Can you prove that?' Andrews asked, as if prodding some semi-informed student into producing a piece of textual evidence.

'Browne-Smith's dead, I'm afraid, sir.'

For a few moments Andrews sat silently, his eyes betraying no sense of shock or surprise.

'Was he a blood donor?' asked Morse suddenly.

'I don't know. Not the sort of thing one broadcasts, would you say?'

'Some people have those "Give Blood" stickers on the car windows.'

'I don't remember seeing—'

'Did he have a car?'

'Big, black, thirsty Daimler.'

'Where's that now?'

'I've no idea.'

'What was his favourite tipple in the Common Room?'

'He liked a drop of Scotch, as most of us do, but he wasn't a big drinker. He was an Aristotelian, Inspector; with him it was always the half-way house between the too much and the too little – if you – er – follow what I'm saying.'

'Yes, I think I do.'

'You remember the Cambridge story that Trinity once saw Wordsworth drunk and once saw Porson sober? Well, I can tell you one thing: Lonsdale never once saw Browne-Smith drunk.'

'He was a bore, you mean?'

'I mean nothing of the sort. It's just that he couldn't abide woolly-mindedness, shoddiness, carelessness—'

'He wouldn't have made too many mistakes in English grammar?'

'Over his dead body!'

'Which is precisely where we stand, sir,' said Morse sombrely.

Andrews waited a moment or two. 'You really are quite sure of that?'

'He's dead,' repeated Morse flatly. 'His body was fished out of the canal up at Thrupp yesterday.'

Morse was conscious of the steady, scholarly eyes upon him as Andrews spoke: 'But I only read about that in the *Oxford Mail* this lunchtime. It said the body couldn't be identified.'

'Really?' Morse appeared genuinely surprised. 'Surely you don't believe everything you read in the newspapers, sir?'

'No, but I believe most of it,' replied Andrews simply and tellingly; and Morse abruptly switched his questioning.

'Dr Browne-Smith, sir. Was he a fit man – considering his age, I mean?'

For the first time Andrews appeared less than completely at ease. 'You know something about that?'

'Well, not officially, but . . .'

Andrews stared down at the threadbare carpet. 'Look, Inspector, the only reason the Master mentioned anything to me . . .'

'Go on!'

'. . . well, it's because I shall be taking over his duties in the College, you see.'

'After he retires?'

'Or before, I'm afraid. You – er – you knew, didn't you, that he'd only a few months to live?'

Morse nodded, quite convincingly.

'Tragic thing, Inspector – cancer of the brain.'

Morse shook his head. 'You're as bad as the Master, sir. "Cancer"? Forget the word! "Tumour", if you like – or "neoplasm". They're the generic terms we use these days for all those nasty things we used to call "cancer".' (He congratulated himself on remembering the gist of what the surgeon had told him earlier that afternoon.)

'I'm not a medical man myself, Inspector.'

'Nor me, really. But, you know, in this job you have to pick up a few things, sometimes. By the way, are you likely yourself to be much better off – financially, I mean – with Dr Browne-Smith out of the way?'

'What the hell's *that* supposed to mean?'

'It means we're dealing with murder, that's all,' said Morse, looking across the table with guileless eyes. 'And that's what they pay me for, sir – trying to find out who murdered people.'

'All right. If you must know, I shall be just over two thousand a year better off.'

'You're gradually shinning up the tree, sir.'

'Not so gradually, either!' Andrews' eyes glinted momentarily with the future prospects of further academic preferment, and momentarily Morse was taken aback by the honesty of his answer.

'But the Master's still got about ten years to go,' objected Morse.

'Eight actually.'

Strangely, this was neither an unpleasant nor an embarrassing moment, as though each man had perfectly understood and perfectly respected the other's thoughts.

'Head of House!' said Morse slowly. 'Great honour, isn't it?'

'For me it's always seemed the greatest honour.'

'Do most of the dons share your view?'

'Most of them – if they're honest.'

'Did Browne-Smith?'

'Oh, quite certainly, yes.'

'So he was a disappointed man?'

'Life's full of disappointments, Inspector.'

Morse nodded. 'Had Browne-Smith any physical abnormalities you can remember?'

'Don't think so – except for his finger, of course. He lost most of his right index-finger – accident in the war. But you probably knew all about that.'

Morse nodded, again quite convincingly. God, he'd forgotten all about that! And suddenly the hooked atoms were engaging and re-engaging themselves so rapidly in his mind that he was desperately anxious to rid himself of the worthy man seated opposite who had put the fire to so many fuses. So he stood up, expressed his thanks and showed the Lonsdale don to the door.

'There is just one thing,' said Andrews. 'I was meaning to mention it earlier, but you side-tracked me. Browne-Smith was never down to College breakfast in *my* time at Lonsdale – and that's fifteen years, now.'

'Well, that's very interesting, sir,' said Morse in a light tone that masked a heavy blow. 'You've been extremely helpful, sir, and thank you for coming along. There's just one more thing. Please, if you will, convey my apologies to the College secretary. I'm sorry I was rude to her – I'd like her to know that.'

'I'll certainly see that she does. She was upset, as I told you – and she's a lovely girl.'

'Is she?' said Morse.

As soon as Andrews had gone, Morse reached for the phone to put his query to the curator of the Medical Science Library at the Bodleian, and, a few minutes later, he was listening carefully to the answer.

'It's the definitive work, inspector – Dr J. P. F. Coole on *Carcinoma in the Brain*. This is what he's got to say – chapter six, by the way: "Tumours are broadly divided into malignant tumours, which invade and destroy surrounding tissues; and benign tumours, which do not. Most malignant tumours have the additional property of giving rise to metastases or secondary tumours in parts of the body remote from the primary growth. A minority of malignant tumours fall into the category of tumours of local malignancy which invade and destroy surrounding tissues, but never metastasise. There are several tumours of local malignancy that occur in or on the head." '

'Bit slower now,' interposed Morse.

' "Many brain tumours are local in their malignancy; for example, the *spongioblastoma multiforme* and the diffuse *astrocytoma*. All tumours inside the skull are potentially fatal, even if they are quite benign – as this term has already been defined in—" '

'Thanks. That's fine. From what you're saying, then, it's possible that a brain-tumour might not spread to somewhere else in the body?'

'That's what this fellow says.'

'Good. Now, one more thing. Would one of these brain-tumours perhaps result in some sort of irrationality? You know, doing things quite out of character?'

'Ah! That's in chapter seven. Just let me—'

'No, no. Just tell me vaguely, that'll be fine.'

'Well, judging from the case-histories, the answer's a pretty definite "yes". *Very* strange things, some of them did.'

'You see, I'm just wondering whether a man who'd got a brain-tumour, a man who'd been sober and meticulous all his life, might suddenly snap and—'

'By Jove, yes! Let me just quote that case of Olive Mainwearing from Manchester. Now, just let me—'

'No! Please don't bother. You've been wonderfully helpful, and I'm most grateful. The beer's on me next time we're together in the King's Arms.'

Morse sat back in his black leather chair, happily ignorant of the aforementioned Olive's extraordinary behaviour, and happily confident that at last he was beginning to see, through the mists, the outline of those further horizons.

Chapter Sixteen

Thursday, 24th July

Lewis again finds himself the unsuspecting catalyst as Morse considers the course of the case so far.

When Lewis came in half an hour later, he found Morse sitting motionless at his desk, staring down fixedly at his blotting-pad, the orange-and-brown-striped scarf still round his jaw, and the signature 'On-no-account-disturb-me' written overall.

Yet Lewis shattered the peace enthusiastically. 'It was Browne-Smith's typewriter, sir! Portable job, like you said. No doubt about it.'

Morse looked up slowly. 'It was Westerby's typewriter – I thought I told you that.'

'No, sir. It was *Browne-Smith's*. You must have made a mistake. Believe me – you can't get two identical typewriters.'

'I told you it was Westerby's,' repeated Morse calmly. 'Perhaps you didn't hear me properly.'

Lewis felt the anger rising within him: why couldn't Morse – just for once! – allow a fraction of credit for what, so conscientiously, he tried to do? 'I *did* hear what you said. You told me to find the typewriter—'

'I told you no such thing!' snapped Morse. 'I told you to get *Westerby's* typewriter. You *deaf*?'

Lewis breathed deeply, and very slowly shook his head.

'Well? *Did* you get Westerby's typewriter?'

'It wasn't there,' growled Lewis. 'The removal people must have taken it. And don't blame me for that! As I just said, sir, it would do me good just once in a while to get a bit of thanks for—'

'Lew-is!' beamed Morse. 'When – *when* will you begin to understand the value of virtually everything you do for me? Why do you misjudge me all the time? Listen! I remember perfectly well that the first sentence I typed out was done on Browne-Smith's typewriter, and the second on Westerby's. Now, just think! Since it was the *second*, as we know, that matched the letter we found in the dead man's pocket, it was on Westerby's typewriter that someone wrote our letter. Agreed? And now you come and tell me it was typed on Browne-Smith's? Well . . . you see what it all means, don't you?'

Over the years, Lewis had become skilled in situations such as this, knowing that Morse, like some inexperienced schoolmaster, was far more anxious to parade his own cleverness than to elicit any halting answer from his dimmer pupils. So it was that Lewis, with a knowing nod, sat back to listen.

'Of course you do! *Someone changed those typewriters.* And that, Lewis – does it not? – throws a completely new perspective on the whole case. And you know who's given me that new perspective? You!'

Sergeant Lewis sat back helplessly in his chair, feeling like a man just presented with the Wimbledon Challenge Cup after losing the last point of the tennis match. So he bowed towards the royal box, and waited. Not for long either, since Morse seemed excited.

'Tell me how you see this case, Lewis. You know – just in general.'

'Well, I reckon Browne-Smith gets a letter from somebody who's terribly anxious to know how someone's got on in this examination, and he says if you'll scratch my back I'll scratch yours: just tell me that little bit early and I'll see you get your little reward.'

'And then?'

'Well – like you, sir – this fellow Browne-Smith's a bachelor: he's quite tempted with the proposition put to him, and goes along with it.'

'So?'

'Well, then he finds out that the people who run these sex-places in Soho are pretty hard boys.'

'I wish you wouldn't start off every sentence with "Well".'

'You don't sound very convinced, sir?'

'Well, it all sounds a bit feeble, doesn't it? I mean, going to all that trouble just to get a girl's results a week or so early?'

'But you wouldn't understand these things. You've never had any children yourself, so you can't begin to imagine what it's like. I remember when my girls were expecting their eleven-plus results – then their O-levels – waiting for the letter-box to rattle and then being scared to open the envelope, just hoping and praying there'd be some good news inside. It sort of gets you, sir – all that waiting. It's always at the back of your mind, and sometimes you'd give anything just to *know*. You realise *somebody* knows – somebody typing out the results and putting them into envelopes and all the rest of it. And I tell you one thing, sir: I'd have given a few quid myself to save me all that waiting and all that worriting.'

Morse appeared temporarily touched by his sergeant's eloquence.
'Look, Lewis. If that's all there is to it, why don't we just ring up
this girl's father? You don't honestly think *he* wrote that letter, do
you?'

'Jane Summers's dad, you mean?' Lewis shook his head. 'Quite
impossible, sir.'

Morse sat upright in his chair. 'Why do you say that?'

'Both her parents were killed in a car-crash six years ago – I
rang up the college secretary. Very helpful, she was.'

'Oh, I see.' Morse unwound his scarf and looked a little
lost. 'Do you know, Lewis, I think you're a bit ahead of me in
this case.'

'No! I'm miles behind, sir – as well you know. But in my opinion
we shouldn't rule out the parent angle altogether. She could only
have been in her late teens when her parents died, and somebody
must have had legal responsibility for her – an uncle or a guardian
or something.'

Morse's eyes were suddenly shining; and taking the torn letter
from a drawer in his desk, he concentrated his brain upon it once
more, his perusal punctuated by 'Yes!', 'Of course!', and finally
'My son, you're a genius!'; whilst Lewis himself sank back in his
chair and dropped back a further furlong in the case.

'Very illuminating,' said Morse. 'You say that not even the
chairman would know the final results until a few hours before
the lists are put up?'

Lewis nodded: 'That's right.'

'But doesn't that cock up just about everything?'

'Unless, sir,' Lewis now felt happy with himself, 'she was way out
at the top of the list – the star of the whole show, sort of thing.'

'Mm. We could ring up the chairman?'

'Which I have done, sir.'

It was Morse himself who was happy now. The penicillin was
working its wonders, and he felt strangely content. 'And she *was*
the top of the list, of course?'

Lewis, too, knew that life was sometimes very good. 'She
was, sir. And if you want my opinion—'

'Of course, I do!'

'—if this girl's uncle or whatever turns out to own a sex-club
in Soho, we've probably found the key to the case, and the sooner
we get up there the better.'

'You've got a good point there, Lewis. On the other hand it's
vital for one of us to stay here.'

'Vital for *me*, I suppose?'

But Morse ignored the sarcasm, and adumbrated for the next half hour to his sergeant a few of the stranger thoughts that had criss-crossed his brain throughout the day.

It was getting late now; and, when Lewis left, Morse was free once more to indulge his own thoughts. At one time his mind would leap like a nimble-footed Himalayan goat; at another, it would stick for minutes on end like a leaden-footed diver in a sandbank. It was time to call it a day, that was obvious.

He was not quite finished, however, and before he left his office he did two things.

First, he amended his reconstruction of the fifth line of the torn letter so that it now read:

both you and me. My ward, Jane Summers of Lonsdale

Second, he took a sheet of paper and wrote the following short piece (reproduced below as it appeared in the *Oxford Mail* the following day):

CLUE TO MURDER

Customers of Marks and Spencers in the Oxford area are being asked to join in the hunt for the murderer of a 60-year-old man found in the canal at Thrupp. The bloodstained socks on the body (not yet identified) have been traced as one of just 2,500 pairs distributed around a handful of M & S stores in the Oxford region. The socks were of navy-blue cotton, with two light blue rings round the tops. Anyone who might have any information is asked to ring Kidlington 4343.

Only after dictating this absurd news-item (comma included) did Morse finally leave his office that day to return to his bachelor flat. There he played through the first act of *Die Walküre* and began to make significant inroads into the bottle just purchased from Augustus Barnett. When, at midnight, he looked around for his pyjamas, he couldn't quite remember why he had bothered the newspaper editor; yet he knew that when a man was utterly at a loss about what he should do, it was imperative that he should do *something* – like the motorist stuck in a snowdrift who decided to activate his blinkers alternately.

Chapter Seventeen

Friday, 25th July

Discussion of identity, and of death, leads the two detectives gradually nearer to the truth.

Lewis came in early the next morning (although not so early as Morse), and immediately got down to reading the medical report from the lab.

'Gruesome all this, isn't it, sir?'

'Not read it,' replied Morse.

'You know, chopping a chap's head off.'

'It's one way of killing someone. After all, the experiment has been tried on innumerable occasions and found to be invariably fatal.'

'But the head was cut off *after* he was dead – says so here.'

'I don't give two monkeys *how* he was killed. It's the *why* that we've got to sort out. *Why* did someone chop his head off – just tell me that, for a start.'

'Because we'd have identified him, surely. His teeth would have been there and—'

'Come off it! Helluva job that'd be, hawking some dental chart round a few million dentists—'

'Thousands, you mean.'

'—and perhaps he didn't *have* any teeth, like sometimes I wish I hadn't.'

'It says here that this chap might have been killed somewhere else and taken out to the canal later.'

'So?'

'What do people usually get carried around in?' asked Lewis.

'Cars?' (Morse hardly enjoyed being catechised himself.)

'Exactly! So if the body was too big to get into the boot of the car . . .'

'You cut him down to size.'

'That's it. It's like one of those ghost things, sir. You sort of tuck the head underneath the arm.'

'Where's the head now, then?'

'Somewhere in the canal.'

'The frogmen haven't found it.'

'Heads are pretty heavy, though. It's probably stuck way down in the mud.'

'What about the *hands*, Lewis? You reckon we're going to find them neatly folded next to the head? Or is some poor little beggar going to find them in his fishing-net?'

'You don't seem to think we're going to find them, sir.'

Morse was showing signs of semi-exasperation. 'You're missing the bloody point, Lewis! I'm not asking *where* they are. I'm asking *why* someone chopped them off.'

'Same as before. Must be because someone could have identified them. He may have had a tattoo on the back of his wrist or something.'

Morse sat quite still. He knew even then that Lewis had made a point of quite extraordinary significance, and his mind, like some downhill skier, had suddenly leaped into the air across a ridge and landed neatly upon a track of virgin snow . . .

Lewis's voice seemed to reach his ears as if through a wodge of tightly-packed cotton wool. 'And what about the legs, sir. Why do you think *they* were chopped off?'

'You mean *you* know?' Morse heard himself saying.

'Hardly that, sir. But it's child's play these days for the forensic boys to find a hundred-and-one things on clothes, isn't it? Hairs and threads and all that sort of thing—'

'Even if it's been in water for a few days?'

'Well, it might be more difficult then, I agree. But all I'm saying is that if we knew whose the body was—'

'We do, Lewis. You can be sure of that – surer than ever. It's Browne-Smith's.'

'All right. If it's Browne-Smith's body, then we shan't have much trouble in finding out if it's Browne-Smith's *suit*, shall we?'

Morse was frowning in genuine puzzlement. 'You're losing me, Lewis.'

'All I'm trying to say, sir, is that if someone carefully chopped off this fellow's head and his hands to stop us finding out who he was—'

'Yes?'

'—well, I don't reckon he would have left the fellow dressed in his own suit.'

'So someone dressed the corpse in someone else's suit, is that it?'

'Yes. You see, a lot of people could wear each other's jackets. I mean, I could wear yours – you're a bit fatter than I am round the middle, but it'd fit in a way. And with a jacket in the water a few days, it'd probably shrink a bit anyway, so no one's going to notice too much. *But*' – and here Lewis paused dramatically – 'if people start wearing each other's trousers, sir – well, you could find a few problems, couldn't you? They might be too long, or too short; and it wouldn't be difficult for anyone to see almost immediately that the suit was someone else's. Do you see what I mean? I think the dead man must have been several inches shorter, or several inches taller, than the fellow whose suit he was dressed in! And *that's* why the legs were chopped off. So as I see it, sir, if we can find out whose suit it is, we shall know one thing for certain: the owner of the suit isn't the corpse – he's probably the murderer!'

Morse sat where he was, looking duly impressed and appreciative. As a result of his visit to the dentist he had himself arrived at a very similar conclusion (although by a completely different route), but he felt it proper to congratulate his sergeant.

'You know, they say your eyes begin to deteriorate about the age of seven or eight, and that your brain follows suit about twenty years later. But your brain, Lewis? It seems to get sharper every day.'

Lewis leaned back happily. 'Must be working with you, sir.'

But Morse appeared not to hear him, staring out (as Lewis had so often seen him) across the concreted yard that lay outside his window. And thus he stared for many, many minutes; and Lewis had almost read the medical report through a second time before Morse spoke again.

'It's very sad about life, really, you know. There's only one thing certain about it, and that's death. We all die, sooner or later. Even old Max, with all his laudable caution, would probably accept that. "The boast of heraldry, the pomp of power . . .".'

'Pardon, sir?'

'We shall all die, Lewis – even you and me – just like that poor fellow we fished out of the pond. There are no exceptions.'

'Wasn't there just the *one*?' asked Lewis quietly.

'You believe that?'

'Yes.'

'Mm.'

'Why do you mention all this, sir – you know, about dying and so on?'

'I was just thinking about Browne-Smith, that's all. I was just thinking that a man we all thought was dead is probably alive again – that's all.'

That's all. For a little while Lewis had almost convinced himself that he might be a move or two ahead of Morse. Yet now, as he shook his head in customary bewilderment, he knew that Morse's mind was half a dozen moves ahead of all the world. So he sat where he was, like a disciple in the Scriptures at the feet of the Master, wondering why he ever bothered to think about anything himself at all.

Chapter Eighteen

Friday, 25th July

Morse decides to enjoy the hospitality of yet another member of Lonsdale's top brass, whilst Lewis devotes himself to the donkey work.

It was high time something was done, Morse knew that. There was the dead man's suit to start with, for surely Lewis had been right in maintaining that the minutest detritus of living would still be lingering somewhere in the most improbable crannies of pockets and sleeves. Then there was the mysterious man Gilbert, who had been given free (and official) access to the room in which the two letters had probably been typed: Gilbert the furniture-man, who might at that very minute be shifting the last of the crates and the crockery . . . Yes, it was high time the pair of them actually *did* something. *Necesse erat digitos extrahere.*

Morse was (as almost always when in a car) a morose and uncommunicative passenger as Lewis drove down to Lonsdale via St Giles' and the Cornmarket, then left at Carfax and into the High. At the Lodge, it was the same young porter on duty. But this time he refused to hand over the keys to any room before consulting higher authority; and Morse was still trying to get through to the Bursar when a man walked into the Lodge whom he had seen several times when he had dined at Lonsdale. It was the Vice-Master.

Ten minutes later, Lewis, with two keys in his hand, was climbing up the steps of Staircase T, whilst Morse was seating himself comfortably in a deep armchair in the Vice-Master's suite, and agreeing that although it was rather early in the day a glass of something might not be totally unwelcome.

'So you see, Inspector' (it was several minutes later) 'it's not a very happy story at all – not an unusual one, though. That pair could never have got on together, whatever happened; but there were no signs of open animosity – not, as I say, until five years ago.'

'Since when they've never even spoken to each other?'

'That's it.'

'And the reason for all this?'

'Oh, there's no great secret about that. I should think almost everyone in the college knows, apart from one or two of the younger fellows.'

'Tell me about it.'

It appeared that only two crucial ordinances had been decreed for election to the Mastership of Lonsdale College: first, that any nominand must be a layman; second, that such a person must be elected by the eight senior fellows of the college, with a minimum of six votes needed in favour, and with the election declared invalid if even a single vote was cast against. It had been common knowledge five years ago, in spite of the so-called 'secret' nature of the ballot, that when Dr Browne-Smith had been proposed and seconded, one solitary vote had thwarted his election hopes; equally common knowledge was the fact that when Mr Westerby's name, in turn, had been put forward, one single slip of paper was firmly printed with a 'No'. The third choice – the compromise candidate – had also been one of the college's senior fellows, and it had been a relief for everyone when the present Master had been voted into office, *nem. con.*

'Head of House!' said Morse slowly. 'Great honour, isn't it?' (He was suddenly conscious that he had repeated *verbatim* the question he had asked of Andrews.)

'Some people would give a lot for it, yes.'

'Would *you*?'

The Vice-Master smiled. 'No! You can leave me out of the running, Inspector. You see, I'm in holy orders, and so, as I said, I'm just not eligible.'

'I see,' said Morse. 'Now just getting back to Dr Browne-Smith for a minute. I'd be grateful, sir, if you could tell me something about his, well, his personal life.'

'Such as?' The Vice-Master's eyes were upon him, and Morse

found himself wondering how much, or how little, he could ever expect to know of the complex web of relationships within this tight community of Lonsdale.

'What about his health, for example?'

Again the shrewd look, as if the question had been fully expected. 'He was a very sick man, Inspector. But you knew that yesterday, didn't you? By the way, Andrews said you looked just a little surprised when he told you.'

'How long had *you* known?' countered Morse.

'Three weeks, I suppose. The Master called Andrews and me up to his room one evening after Hall. Strictly confidential, he said, and all that – but we had to know, of course, because of Browne-Smith's teaching commitments.'

'When did the Master think . . . ?'

'Certainly no longer than the end of the Hilary Term.'

'Mm.'

'And you're wondering whether his teaching days might not be over already. Am I right?'

'How much did Andrews tell you?' asked Morse.

'Everything. You didn't mind, I hope?'

Morse felt oddly uncomfortable with the man, and after asking a few more vague questions about Browne-Smith's lifestyle, he got up to go. 'You getting some holiday soon, sir?'

'Once the Master gets back. We usually alternate so that one of us is here for most of the vac. I know that some people haven't much time for all us lazy academic lay-abouts, but there's a lot to do in a college apart from looking after students. But you'd know that, of course.'

Morse nodded, and knew that he could very soon learn to dislike this unclerically-garbed parson intensely.

'We shall co-operate as much as we can,' continued the Vice-Master. 'You know that. But it would be nice to be kept in the picture – just a little, perhaps?'

'Nothing really to tell you, sir – not yet, anyway.'

'You don't even want to tell me why your sergeant took the key to Westerby's room as well?'

'Ah, that! Yes, I ought to have mentioned that, sir. You see, there's just a possibility that the corpse we found up in the canal wasn't Browne-Smith's after all.'

'Really?'

But Morse declined to elaborate further as he made his farewell and strode away across the quad, sensing those highly intelligent eyes upon him as he turned into the Porters' Lodge. From there he progressed, only some hundred yards, into the bar of the Mitre, where he had agreed to meet Lewis. He would be half an hour early, he realised that; but a thirty-minute wait in a pub was no great trial of patience to Morse.

Once inside Browne-Smith's room, Lewis had taken out of its plastic wrapper the dark-blue jacket found on the corpse and measured it carefully against the jackets in the bedroom wardrobe: it was the same length, the same measurement round the chest, of the same sartorial style, with a single slit at the back and slim lapels. There could be little doubt about it: the jacket had belonged to Browne-Smith. After rehanging the suits, Lewis methodically looked through the rest of the clothes, but learned only that each of the five pairs of shoes was size nine, and that four brand-new pairs of socks were all of navy-blue cotton with two light blue rings round the tops.

Westerby's rooms opposite were silent and empty now, only the faded-brown fitted carpet remaining, with oblong patches of pristine colour marking the erstwhile positions of the heavier furniture. Nothing else at all, except a plastic spoon and an empty jar of Nescafé on the draining-board in the kitchen.

Lewis's highly discreet enquiries in the college office produced (amongst other things) the information that Browne-Smith certainly wore a suit very similar to the one he now unwrapped once more; and the college secretary herself (whom even Lewis considered very beautiful) was firmest of all in such sad corroboration.

The young porter was still on duty when Lewis handed back the two keys, and was soon chatting freely enough when Lewis asked about 'Gilbert Removals'. As far as the porter could remember, Mr Gilbert himself had been down to T Staircase about four or five times; but he'd finished now, for Mr Westerby had at last been 'shifted'.

'Funny you should ask about Mr Gilbert, Sergeant. He's like your chief – both of 'em got the jaw-ache by the look of things.'

Lewis nodded and prepared to leave. 'Nuisance, teeth are, yes. Nothing much worse than an abscess on one of your front teeth, you know.'

The porter looked strangely at Lewis for a few seconds, for the words he had just heard were almost exactly (he could swear it) the words he had heard from the afflicted furniture-remover.

He told Lewis so . . . and Lewis told Morse, in the Mitre. Yet neither of them realised, at least for the present, that this brief and

seemingly insignificant little episode was to have a profound effect
upon the later stages of the case.

Chapter Nineteen

Friday, 25th July

Our two detectives have not yet quite finished with the
implications of severe dismemberment.

The case was working out well enough, thought Lewis, as he drove
Morse back through Summertown. The shops were in the same order
as they'd been two hours earlier when he had driven past them:
the RAC building, Budgens, Straw Hat Bakery, Allied Carpets,
Chicken Barbecue . . . yes, just the same. It was only a question
of seeing them in reverse order now, tracing them backwards, as it
were. Just like this case. Morse had traced things backwards fairly
well thus far, if somewhat haphazardly . . . And he wanted to ask
Morse two questions, though he knew better than to interrupt the
great man's thoughts in transit.

In Morse's mind, too, far more was surfacing from the murky
waters of a local canal than a bloated, mutilated corpse that had
been dragged in by a boat-hook as it threatened to drift down
again and out of reach. Other things had been surfacing all the
way along the towpath, as clue had followed clue. One thing at
least was fairly firmly established: the murderer – whoever that
might be – had either been quite extraordinarily subtle, or quite
inordinately stupid, in going to the lengths of dismembering a body,
and then leaving it in its own clothes. If it *was* in its own suit . . .
Lewis had done his job; and Lewis was sure that the suit was Browne-
Smith's. But what about the body? Oh yes, indeed – but what about
the body?

Back in Morse's office, Lewis launched into his questions: 'It's
pretty certainly Browne-Smith's body, don't you think, sir?'

'Don't know.'

'But surely—'

'I said I don't *bloody* know!'

So, Lewis, after a decent interval, asked his other question: 'Don't you think it's a bit of a coincidence that you and this Gilbert fellow should have a bad tooth at the same time?'

Morse appeared to find this an infinitely more interesting question, and he made no immediate reply. Then he shook his head decisively. 'No. Coincidences are far more commonplace than any of us are willing to accept. It's this whole business of *chance*, Lewis. We don't go in much for talking about chance and luck, and what a huge part they play in all our lives. But the Greeks did – *and* the Romans; they both used to worship the goddess of luck. And if you must go on about coincidences, you just go home tonight and find the forty-sixth word from the beginning of the forty-sixth psalm, and the forty-sixth word from the end of it – and see what you land up with! Authorised Version, by the way.'

'Say that again, sir?'

'Forget it, Lewis! Now, listen! Let's just get back to this case we're landed with and what we were talking about at lunchtime. If our murderer wants his victim to be identified, he does not – repeat *not* chop his head off. Quite apart from the facial features – features that could be recognised by some myopic moron from thirty yards away – you've got your balding head, your missing mandibles, and whatever – even the angle of your ears; and all of those things are going to lead to a certain identification. Somebody's going to know who he is, whether he's been floating in the Mississippi for a fortnight, or whether he's been up in Thrupp for three months. Agreed? And if our murderer is still anxious for his corpse to be identified, he does not – repeat *not* cut his hands off, either. Because that removes at one fell chop the one thing we know that gives him a unique and unquestionable individuality – his fingerprints!'

'What about the legs, sir?'

'Shut up a minute! And for Christ's sake try to follow what I'm telling you! It's hard enough for *me*!'

'I'm not finding much trouble, sir.'

'All I'm saying is that if the murderer wants the body to be recognised, he doesn't chop off his head and he doesn't chop off his hands – agreed?'

Lewis nodded: he agreed.

'And yet, Lewis, there are two other clues that lead quite clearly to a positive identification of the body; the suit – quite certainly now it seems it was Browne-Smith's suit; and then the letter – almost as certainly that was written to Browne-Smith. All right, it wasn't all *that* obvious; but you'd hardly need to be a Shylock—'

' "Sherlock", sir.'

'You see what I'm getting at, though?'

Lewis pondered the question, and finally answered, 'No.'

Morse, too, was beginning to wonder whether he himself was following the drift of his own logic, but he'd always had the greatest faith in the policy of mouthing the most improbable notions, in the sure certainty that by the law of averages some of them stood a more reasonable chance of being nearer to the truth than others. So he burbled on.

'Just suppose for a minute, Lewis, that the body *isn't* Browne-Smith's, but that somebody wanted it to *look* like his. All right? Now, if the murderer had left us the head, or the hands, or both, then we could have been quite sure that the body *wasn't* Browne-Smith's, couldn't we? As we know, Browne-Smith was suffering from an incurable brain-tumour, and with a skull stuck on the table in front of him even old Max might have been able to tell us there was something not all that healthy round the cerebral cortex – even if the facial features were badly disfigured. It's just the same with the hands – quite apart from fingerprints. Browne-Smith lost most of his right index-finger in the war, and not even your micro-surgeons can stick an artificial digit on your hand without even a delinquent like Dickson spotting it. So, if the hands, or at least the right hand, had been left attached to the body, and *if all the fingers were intact* – then again we'd have been quite sure that the body *wasn't* Browne-Smith's. You follow me? The two things that could have proved that the body wasn't his are both deliberately and callously removed.'

Lewis frowned, just about managing to follow the line of Morse's argument. 'But what about the suit? What about the letter?'

'All I'm saying, Lewis, is that perhaps someone's been trying mighty hard to convince us that it *was* Browne-Smith's body, that's all.'

'Aren't you making it all a bit too complicated?'

'Could be,' conceded Morse.

'I'm just a bit lost, you see, sir. We're usually looking for a murderer, aren't we? We've never had all this trouble with a body before.'

Morse nodded. 'But we're getting to know more about the murderer all the time! He's a very clever chap. He tries to lead us astray about the identity of the body, and he very nearly succeeds.'

'So?'

'So he's almost as clever as we are; and most of the clever people I know are – guess where, Lewis!'

'In the police force?'

Morse allowed himself a weak smile, but continued with his previous earnestness. 'In the University of Oxford! And what's more, I reckon I've got a jolly good idea about exactly *which* member of the University it is!'

'Uh?' Lewis looked across at his chief with surprise – and suspicion.

But Morse was off again. 'Let's just finish off this corpse. We're left with those legs, right? Now we've got some ideas about the head and the hands, but why chop the legs off?'

'Perhaps he lost a toe in a swimming accident off Bermuda or somewhere. Got his foot caught in the propeller of a boat or something.'

Morse was suddenly very still in his chair, for Lewis's flippant answer had lit another sputtering fuse. He reached for the phone, rang through on an internal extension to Superintendent Strange, and (to Lewis's complete surprise) asked for two more frogmen – if possible immediately – to search the bottom of the canal by Aubrey's Bridge.

'Now about those legs,' resumed Morse. 'At what point would you say they were chopped off?'

'Well, sort of here, sir.' Lewis vaguely put his hand on his femur. 'About halfway between—'

'Between pelvis and patella, that's right. Halfway, though, you say? But if we don't know how long his thighs were to start with, where exactly is that "halfway" of yours? It may have been meant to *look* halfway—'

'That's what I told you this morning, sir.'

'I know you did, yes! All I'm doing is to stick a bit more clarity into your thinking. You don't mind, I hope?'

'My mind's perfectly clear already, sir. He might have been a shorter man or a taller man, and, because Browne-Smith's about five-eleven, the odds are probably on him being shorter. It's the length of the femur, you see, that largely determines the height.'

'Oh!' said Morse. 'You don't happen to know how tall Westerby is – or was?'

'Five-five, sir – about that. I asked the college secretary – very nice girl.'

'Oh!'

'And I agree with all you've said, sir. Head, hands, legs – you've explained them all. If the murderer wanted us to think the body was Browne-Smith's, perhaps he couldn't have left any of them.'

The tables were turned now, and it was Morse's turn to look dubious. 'You don't think all this is getting a bit too complicated, do you, Lewis?'

'*Far* too complicated. We've got the suit and we've got the letter – both of them Browne-Smith's – and we know that he's gone missing somewhere. That would be quite enough for me, sir. But you seem to think that the man we're after is almost as clever as you are.'

Morse did not reply immediately, and Lewis noticed the look of curious exhilaration in the chief inspector's face. What, he wondered, had he suddenly thought of now?

Dickson called in a few minutes later to report that no one by the name of Simon Rowbotham was registered in the membership of the Pike Anglers' Association or in the membership of any other fishing-club in the vicinity of Oxford; and Lewis was disappointed with this news, for it gave a little more weight to the one freakish objection to his own firm view that the corpse they had found must be Browne-Smith's: the objection (as Morse had pointed out to him the previous morning) that *'Simon Rowbotham' was an exact anagram of 'O. M. A. Browne-Smith'*.

Chapter Twenty

Saturday, 26th July

An extremely brief envoi to the first part of the case.

At five minutes to four the next morning, Morse awoke and looked at his bedside clock. It seemed quite impossible that it should be so early, for he felt completely refreshed. He got out of bed and drew the curtains, standing for several minutes looking down on the utterly silent road, only a hundred yards from Banbury

Road roundabout . . . the road that led north out to Kidlington, and thence past the Thames Valley Police HQ up to the turn for Thrupp, where the waters would now be lapping and plopping gently against the houseboats as they lay at their overnight moorings.

Morse went into the bathroom, noticed that his jaw was almost normal again, swallowed the last of the penicillin tablets and returned to bed, where he lay on his back, his hands behind his head . . . There were still many pieces of flotsam that needed to be salvaged before the wreck of a man's life could wholly be reconstructed . . . salvaged from those canal waters which changed their colour from green to grey to yellow to black . . . to white . . . Morse almost dozed off again, momentarily imagining that he saw the outlines of a cunningly plotted murder, with himself – yes, Morse! – at the centre of a beautifully calculated deception. Of one thing he was now utterly sure: that, quite contrary to Lewis's happy convictions about the identity of the dead man, *the man they had found was quite certainly not Dr Browne-Smith of Lonsdale.*

Thereafter, Morse was impatient for the morning and for traffic noise and for the sight of people catching buses. Ovid, in the arms of his lover, had cried out to the midnight horses to gallop slow across the vault of heaven. But Morse was without a lover; and at a quarter to five he got up, made himself a cup of tea and looked out once again at the quiet street below, where he sensed a few vague flutterings and stirrings from the chrysalis of the night.

And Morse sensed rightly. For the next morning, like Browne-Smith before him, he received a long letter; a strange and extremely exciting letter.

THE END OF THE FIRST MILE

THE SECOND MILE

Chapter Twenty-one

Monday, 28th July

Morse, having been put on the right track by the wrong clues, now finds his judgement almost wholly vindicated.

Morse opened the door of his office a few minutes after eight to find Lewis reading the *Daily Mirror*.

'You seem very anxious to further our enquiries this morning, Lewis.'

Lewis folded up the newspaper. 'I'm afraid you've made a bad mistake, sir.'

'You mean you *are* busy on the case?'

'Not only that, sir. As I say, you've made a bad mistake.'

'Nonsense!'

'I was trying to do the coffee-break crossword and there was a clue there that just said "Carthorse (anagram)"—'

' "Orchestra",' interrupted Morse.

'I know that, sir. But "Simon Rowbotham" is *not* an anagram of "O. M. A. Browne-Smith"!'

'Of course it is!' Morse immediately wrote down the letters, and was checking them off one by one when suddenly he stopped. 'My God! You're right. There's an "o" instead of an "e", isn't there?'

'It was only by chance I checked it when I was—'

But Morse wasn't listening. Was he *wrong*, after all his mighty thoughts and bold deductions? Was Lewis *right* – with his simple-minded assertion that the case was becoming quite unnecessarily complicated? He shook his head in some dismay. Perhaps (he clutched at straws), perhaps if he himself had made a mistake over an anagram, so might Browne-Smith have done in concocting a completely bogus name? But he couldn't convince himself for a second, and the truth was that he felt lost.

At eight-thirty the phone rang, an excited voice announcing itself as Constable Dickson.

'I've just been reading last week's *Oxford Times*, sir.'

'Not on duty, I hope.'

'I'm off duty, sir. I'm at home.'

'Oh.'

'I've found him!'

'Found who?'

'Simon Rowbotham. I was reading the angling page – and his name's there. He came second in a fishing match out at King's Weir last Sunday.'

'Oh.'

'He lives in Botley, so it says.'

'I don't give a sod if he lives in Bootle.'

'Pardon, sir?'

'Thanks for letting me know, anyway.'

'Remember what you said about those doughnuts, sir?'

'No, I forget,' said Morse, and put the receiver down.

'Shall I go out and see him?' asked Lewis quietly.

'What the hell good would that do?' snapped Morse, thereafter lapsing into sullen silence.

Since it was marked 'Strictly Private and Confidential', the Registry had not opened the bulky white envelope, and it was lying there on Morse's blue blotting-pad when later the two men returned from coffee. Inside the envelope was a further sealed envelope (addressed, like the outer cover, to Chief Inspector E. Morse), and a covering letter from the Manager of the High Street branch of Barclays Bank, dated 26th July. It read as follows:

Dear Sir,

    We received the sealed envelope enclosed on Monday, 21st July, with instructions that it be posted to you personally on Saturday, 26th July. We trust you agree that we have discharged our obligation.

                                          Your faithfully . . .

Morse handed the note over to Lewis. 'What do you make of that?'

'Seems a lot of palaver to me, sir. Why not just post it straight to you?'

'I dunno,' said Morse. 'Let's hope it's full of fivers.'

'Aren't you going to open it?'

'Interesting,' said Morse, apparently unhearing. 'If this letter reached the bank on Monday, the 21st, it was probably written on Sunday, the 20th – and Max says that's the likeliest day that someone put the corpse in the canal.'

'But it's probably nothing to do with the case.'

'Well, we'll soon know.' Morse slit the envelope and began reading, and apart from a solitary 'My God!' (after the first few lines of the typewritten script) he read in utter silence, as totally engrossed, it seemed, as a dedicated pornophilist in a sex-shop.

When he had finished the long letter, he wore that look of almost sickening self-satisfaction frequently found on the face of any man whose judgement has been called into question, but thereafter proved correct.

Lewis took the letter now, immediately turning to the last page. 'There's no signature, sir.'

'Read it – just read it, Lewis,' said Morse blandly, as he reached for the phone and dialled the number of the bank.

'Manager, please.'

'He's rather tied up at the minute. Could you—'

'Chief Constable of Oxfordshire here, lad. Just tell him to get to the phone, please.' (Lewis had by now read the first page of the letter.)

'Can I help you?' asked the manager.

'I want to know whether Dr Browne-Smith – Dr O. M. A. Browne-Smith – of Lonsdale College is one of your clients.'

'Yes, he is.'

'We received a letter from you today, sir, and it's my duty to ask you if it was Dr Browne-Smith himself who asked you to forward it to us.'

'Ah, the letter, yes. I hoped the Post Office wouldn't keep you waiting too long.'

'You haven't answered my question, sir.'

'No, I haven't. And I can't, I'm afraid.'

'I think you can, sir, and I think you will – because we're caught up in a case of murder.'

'Murder? You're not – you're not saying Dr Browne-Smith's been murdered, surely?'

'No, I didn't say that.'

'Could you tell me exactly who it is that's been murdered?'

Morse hesitated – for too long. 'No, I can't, not just for the present. Enquiries are still at a very – er – delicate stage, and that's why we've got to expect the co-operation of everyone concerned – people like yourself, sir.'

The manager was also hesitant. 'It's very difficult for me. You see, it involves the whole question of the confidentiality of the bank.'

Morse sounded surprisingly mild and accommodating. 'I understand, sir. Let's leave it, shall we, for the present? But if it becomes an absolutely vital piece of information, we shall naturally have to come and question you.'

'Yes, I see that. But I shall have to take the matter up with the bank's legal advisers, of course.'

'Very sensible, sir. And thank you for your co-operation.'

Lewis, who had been half-reading the letter (with continued amazement) and also half-listening to this strange telephone conversation, now looked up to see Morse smiling serenely and waiting patiently for him to finish.

When he had done so, but before he had the chance to pass any comment, Morse asked him to give Barclays another ring, to tell them he was Chief Inspector Morse, and to find out whether they had a second client on their books: a Mr George Westerby, of Lonsdale.

The answer was quick and unequivocal: yes, they had.

Chapter Twenty-two

We have an exact transcript of the long letter, which was without salutation or subscription, studied by Chief Inspector Morse and by Sergeant Lewis, in the mid-morning of Monday, 28th July.

'Perhaps it is not too much to expect that you have made the necessary investigations? It would scarcely need an intellect as (potentially) powerful as your own accurately to have traced the sequence of events thus far. After all, you had my suit, did you not? That, most surely, should have led your assistants to my (agreed, rather limited) wardrobe at Lonsdale, where (I assume) the waist-band inches and the inside-leg measurements have already been minutely matched. But let us agree: the body was not mine. I did try, perhaps amateurishly, to make you think it was; yet I had little doubt that you would quickly piece together a reasonably coherent letter, the torn half of which I left in the back pocket of the trousers. You might therefore have had the reasonable suspicion that the corpse was me – but not for long, if I assess you right.

'But whichever way it is (either your thinking of me as one of the dead or as one of the non-dead), I see it my duty to inform you that I am alive, at least for a little while longer. (You will have discovered that, too?) Whose, then, is the body you found in the waters out at Thrupp? For it is not, most certainly not, my own. I repeat – whose is it? To find the answer to that question must be your next task, and it is a task in which I am prepared (even anxious) to offer some co-operation. As a child, did you ever play the game called "treasure-hunt", wherein a clue would lead from A to B? From, let us say, a little message hidden underneath a stone to a further message pinned behind a maple-tree? Well, let us go on a little, shall we? From B to C, as it were.

'I received the letter and immediately acted upon it. All very odd, was it not? I knew the girl mentioned, of course, for she was one of my own pupils; and, what is more, she was a girl acknowledged by all to be the outstanding classic of the year – if not of the decade. This was common knowledge, and it was totally predictable (why bother to ask me?) that her marks in the Greats papers would be higher than any of her contemporaries of either sex. Therefore the request to communicate (and that to some anonymous third party) this particular girl's result only a week or so before the publication of class-lists struck me as rather suspicious. (A poorly constructed sentence, but I have not time to recast it.) My reward, I was told, for divulging the result some days early would be a memorably pleasant one. You would agree, I think? Even an ageing (I always put the "e" in that word) bachelor like myself may be permitted his mildly erotic day-dreams. And, as I believe, I would hardly be committing the ultimate sin in informing the world of what the world already knew. But I am not telling you the whole truth, even now. Let me go back a little.

'I have a colleague living directly opposite me: a Mr G. Westerby. He and I have been fellow dons for far too many years, and it is an open secret that the relations between the two of us have been almost childishly hostile for a great deal of that time. This colleague (I prefer not to mention his name again) is now retiring; and, although I have never actively sought to learn of his immediate plans, I have naturally gleaned a few desultory facts about his purposes: he is now away on one of his customary cut-price holidays in the Greek islands; he is, on his return, to take up residence in some pretentiously fashionable flat in the Bloomsbury district; he has recently hired a firm of removal people to pack up the cheap collection of bric-à-brac his philistine tastes have considered valuable enough to accumulate during his overlong stay in the University. (Please forgive my cynical words.)

'Now – please pay careful attention! One day, only a few weeks ago, I saw a man walking up my own staircase; the man did not see me – not at that point anyway. He looked around him, first with the diffidence of a stranger, then with the confidence of an intimate; and he took the key he was holding and inserted it into Westerby's oak. For myself, I took little notice. If someone wished to burgle my colleague's valueless belongings, I felt little inclination to interfere. In fact, I was secretly interested – and amused. I learned that this stranger was the head of a London removals firm; that he had come to size up the task and to pack up the goods. A few days later, I saw this same individual again – although this time he wore a bright red scarf about his face, as if the wind blew uncommonly keenly, or as if the wretched fellow had recently returned from the dentist's chair. It was only a matter of days after this that I received a letter – istam epistolam; the letter you half-received yourself.

'Does all this sound rather mysterious and puzzling? No! Not to you, surely. For you have already guessed what I am about to say. Yes! I recognised the man; and the man brought back poignantly to me the one episode in my life of which I am bitterly – so bitterly! – ashamed. But again, I am getting ahead of myself – or behind. It depends upon which way you look at it.

'With assorted young assistants, this man reappeared three or four times, presumably to supervise the packaging-up of crates and boxes in my colleague's rooms. And on each of these subsequent occasions, the man wore the same gaudy scarf around the lower half of his face, as if (as I have said) a wayward tooth was inflicting upon him the acutest agony . . . or else as if he wished to keep his face concealed. Is one not, in such circumstances, quite justified in adding two and two together, and making of them twenty-two? Was he worried, perhaps, that I should recognise his face? Had he known it, however, his clumsy attempts at deception were futile. Why? Simply because <u>I had already recognised the man</u>. And because of this, I experienced little difficulty in linking the two contiguous events together: first, the arrival in Lonsdale of the one man in the world I had hoped and prayed I would never meet again; second, the arrival of the strangest letter I ever received in the whole of my time in the college. In sum, these two events appeared to me to add to more than twenty-two; yet not to more than I could cope with. Let us go on a bit.

'I followed up my invitation. Why not do so? I have never married. I have never, therefore, known the delights (if such they are) of the marriage-bed. Over-rated as I have frequently considered them, the illicit lure of sexual delights will almost always be a potential attraction to an old, unhonoured person like myself. (I don't <u>think</u> we have a hanging participle in the previous sentence.) And lascivious thoughts, albeit occasional ones, are not wholly alien even from such a dryasdustest man as me.

'Where are we then? Ah, yes. I went. I went through the doors that had been clearly labelled for my attention, and I knew where I was going; I knew exactly. It will be of little value to you to have a comprehensive account of subsequent events, although (to be fair to myself) they were not particularly sordid. The whole drama (I must admit it) was played with a carefully rehearsed verisimilitude, with myself acting a role that was equally carefully rehearsed. Yet at one stage (if I may continue the metaphor), I forgot my lines completely. And so, perhaps, would you have done. For a devastatingly lovely woman – a Siren fit to beguile the wily Ulysses himself – was almost, <u>almost</u> able to rob me of my robe of honour; and, perhaps more importantly, to rob me of my one defence – an army revolver which I had kept since my days in the desert, and which was even now still bulging reassuringly in my jacket-pocket.

'But again things are getting out of sequence, and we must go back. Who was the man I had seen on Staircase T at Lonsdale College? You will have to know. Yes, I am afraid you will have to know.

'I was a young officer in the desert during the battle of El Alamein. I was, I think, a good officer, in the sense that I tried to look after the men in my charge, left little to needless chance, enforced the orders I was given and faced the enemy with the conviction that this conflict – this one, surely – was as fully justified as any in the annals of Christendom. But I knew one thing that no one else could know. I knew that at heart I was a physical coward; and I always feared the thought that, if there were to come a time

when I should be called upon to show a personal, an individual –
as against a communal, corporate – act of courage, well, I knew
that I would fail. And that moment came. And I failed. It came –
I need not relate the shameful details – when a man pleaded with
me to risk my own life in trying to save the life of a man who was
trapped in a fiercely-burning tank. But enough of that. It hurts me
deeply, even now, to recall my cowardice.

'Let us now switch forward again. It was all phoney: I soon
began to realise that. There were those two bottles of everything,
for example: two of them – in whatever the client (in this case, me)
should happen to indulge. Why two? The one of them about two-
thirds empty (or is it one-third full?); the other completely intact,
with the plastic seal fixed round its top. Why go, then, to the new
bottle for the first, perfunctory drinks? I didn't know, but I soon
began to wonder. And then her accent! Oh dear! Had she been at
an audition, any director worth a tuppence of salt would have told
her to flush her Gallic vowels down the nearest ladies' lavatory.
And then at one point she opened her handbag – a handbag she
must have owned for twenty years. A professional whore with an
aged handbag? And not only that. She was introduced to me by an
unconvincing old hag as "Yvonne"; so why are the faded gilt initials
on the inside flap of her handbag clearly printed "W.S."? You see
where all this suspicion is leading? But I had my revolver. I was
going to be all right. I was all right. (How I hate underlining words
in typescript – but often it is necessary.) It was only when this lovely
girl (oh dear, she was lovely!) poured my final drink from the other
bottle (not the bottle I had drunk from before) that I knew exactly
what my situation was. I asked her to open the curtains a little, and
whilst she was doing this I poured the (doubtless doctored) contents
of my glass inside my trousers, in order that the impression should
be given that I had been incapable of controlling myself. (I know
you will understand the sense of what, so delicately, I have tried
to express.) You must understand that at this point she was quite
openly and wantonly naked, and I myself quite justifiably aroused.

'After that? If I may say so, I performed my part professionally.
Making vaguely somnolent noises, I now assumed the role of a man
(as the Americans have it) in a totally negative response situation.
Then the woman left me; and after hearing whispered communica-
tions on the other side of the door, I sensed that someone else was
in the room. Let us leave it there.

'I am getting tired with this lengthy typing, but it is important
that I should go on a little longer.

'You were a fool when you were an undergraduate – wasting, as you did, the precious talent of a clear, clean mind. It was me (or do you prefer "I"?) who marked some of your Greats papers, and even amidst the widespread evidence of your appalling ignorance there were moments of rare perception and sensitivity. But since that time you have made a distinguished reputation for yourself as a man of the Detective (as Dickens has it), and I was anxious that it should be a worthy brain that was to be pitted against my own. Why else should the body be discovered where it was? Who made sure that it should be found at Thrupp – a place almost in your own back-yard? You will, I suspect, have almost certainly discovered by now why I was not able to leave the head and the hands for your inspection? Yes, I think so. You would have been quite certain that it was not my body had I done so, and I wished to sharpen up your brain, for (believe me!) it will need to be as sharp as the sword of Achilles before your work is finished. Here then is a chance for you to show the sort of quality that was apparent in your early days at Oxford. Perhaps this case of yours will afford for you the opportunity to kill an ancient ghost, since I shall quite certainly (albeit posthumously) award you a "First" this time if you can grasp the inevitable (and basically so simple) logic of all these strange events.

'I shall make no further communication to you; and I advise you not to try to track me down, for you will not find me.

'Post Scriptum. I have just read this letter through and wish to apologise for the profusion of brackets. (I am not often over-influenced by the work of Bernard Levin.)'

Chapter Twenty-three

Monday, 28th July

Investigations proceed with a nominal line drawn down the middle of needful enquiries.

So many clues now, and as Morse and Lewis saw things there were four main areas of enquiry:

1. What were the real facts about that far-off day in the desert when Browne-Smith had faced his one real test of character – and (apparently) failed so lamentably?

2. Where exactly did Westerby (a name cropping up repeatedly now) fit into the increasingly complex pattern?

3. Who was the person whom Browne-Smith had met after his anti-climactic sexual encounter with the pseudonymous 'Yvonne'?

4. And (still, to Morse, the most vital question of all) whose was the body they had found?

Obviously the strands of these enquiries would interweave at many points; but it seemed sensible to the two detectives that each should make his own investigations for a day or two, with Lewis concentrating his attentions on the first two areas, and Morse on the second two.

Lewis spent most of the morning on the telephone, ringing, amongst other numbers, those of the War Office, the Ministry of Defence, the HQ of the Wiltshire Regiment, and the Territorial Unit at Devizes. It was a long, frustrating business; but by lunchtime he had a great deal of information, much of it useless, but some of it absolutely vital.

First, he discovered more about Browne-Smith: Captain, acting Major (Royal Wiltshires); served North Africa (1941–42); wounded El Alamein; Italy (1944–45); awarded the MC (1945).

Second, he learned something about Gilbert. There had been three Gilbert brothers, Albert, Alfred, and John. All had fought at El Alamein; the first two, both full corporals, had survived the campaign (although both of them had been wounded); the third, the youngest brother, had died in the same campaign. That was all.

But it couldn't be quite all, Lewis knew that. And it was from the Swindon branch of the British Legion that he learned the address of a man in the Wiltshires who must certainly have known the Gilbert brothers fairly well. Immediately after lunch, Lewis was driving out along the A420.

'Yes, I knew 'em, Sergeant – s'funny, I wur a sergeant, too, you know. Yes, there wur Alf 'n Bert – like as two peas in a pod, they wur. One of 'em, 'e got a bit o' the ol' shrapnel in the leg, and I 'ad a bit in the 'ead. We wur at base 'ospital for a while together, but I can't quite recolleck . . . Real lads, they wur – the pair of 'em!'

'Did you know the other one?' asked Lewis.

'Johnny! That wur 'is name. I didn't know 'im very well, though.'

'You don't know how he was killed?'

'No, I don't.'

'They were all tank-drivers, weren't they?'

'All of 'em – like me.'

'Was he killed in his tank?'

For the second time the old soldier looked rather vague and puzzled, and Lewis wondered whether the man's memory could be relied upon.

'There wur a bit of an accident as I recolleck. But 'e wurn't with us that morning, Sergeant – not when we all moved up 'long Kidney Ridge.'

'You don't remember what sort of accident?'

'No. It wur back at base, I seem to . . . But you get a lot of accidents in wartime, Sergeant. More'n they tell the folk back 'ome in Blighty.'

He was an engaging old boy; a sixty-nine-year-old widower for whom, it seemed, the war had been the only intermission of importance in a largely anonymous life, for there was no real sadness in him as he recalled those weeks and months of fighting in the desert – only an almost understandable nostalgia. So Lewis wrote down the facts, such as they were, in his painstakingly slow long-hand, and then took his leave.

Morse was away from the office when Lewis returned at 4.30 p.m. and of this fact he was strangely glad. All the way back from Swindon he had been wondering what that 'accident' might have been. He suspected that had Morse been there he would have guessed immediately; and it was a pleasant change to be able to tackle the problem at his own, rather slower, pace. He rang the War Office once again, was put through to the Archives section, and soon began to realise that he was on to something important.

'Yes, we might be able to help in some way. You're Thames Valley Police, you say?'

'That's right.'

'Why are you asking for information about this man?'

'It's in connection with a murder, sir.'

'I see. What's your number? Can't be too careful in these things – you'll know all about that.' He spoke with the monotone bark of a machine-gun.

So Lewis gave him his number, was rung back inside thirty seconds, and was given an extraordinary piece of information. Private John Gilbert of the Royal Wiltshires had not been killed in the El Alamein campaign. He had played no part in it. The night before the offensive, he had taken his army rifle, placed the muzzle inside his mouth, and shot himself through the brain. The incident had been hushed up on the highest orders; and that for obvious reasons. A few had known, of course – *had* to know. But 'officially' John Gilbert died on active service in the desert, and that is how his family and his friends had been informed.

'This is all in the strictest confidence, you understand that?'

'Of course, sir.'

'Never good for morale, that sort of thing, eh?'

Morse was having a far less fruitful day. He realised that with the first of his self-imposed assignments he could for the present make little headway, since that would necessitate some far from disagreeable investigations in Soho – a journey he had planned for the morrow. Which only left him with the same old tantalising problem that had monopolised his mind from the beginning: the identity of the corpse. From the embarrassment of clues contained in Browne-Smith's letter, the shortest odds must now be surely on the man whom Browne-Smith had finally encountered in London. But who was that man? Had it been *Gilbert*, as the letter so obviously suggested? Or was the body *Westerby's*? If Browne-Smith had killed anyone, then Westerby was surely the most likely of candidates. Or was the body that of someone who had not yet featured in the investigations? Some outsider? Someone as yet unknown who would make a dramatic entry only towards the finale of Act Five? A sort of *deus ex machina*? Morse doubted this last possibility – and amidst his doubts, quite suddenly the astonishing thought flashed through his mind that there might just be a *fourth* possibility. And the more Morse pondered the idea, the more he convinced himself that there was: the possibility that the puffed and sodden salt-white corpse was that of *Dr Browne-Smith*.

On the way home that evening, Lewis decided to risk his wife's wrath, to face the prospect of almost certainly reheated chips – and to call on Simon Rowbotham in Botley.

Simon Rowbotham invited him into the small terraced house

in which he lived with his mother. But Lewis declined, learning over the doorstep that Simon had been one of three anglers who had spotted the body, and that it was he, Simon, who had readily volunteered to dial the police in lieu of looking further upon the horror just emerging from the waters. He often fished out along the banks at Thrupp, a good place for specialists such as himself. As it happened, they were just about to form a new angling club there, for which he had volunteered his services as secretary. In fact (just as Lewis had called) he had been checking a proof of the new association's letter-head for the printer. They had managed to persuade a few well known people to support them; and clearly, for Simon Rowbotham, the world was entering an exciting phase.

Lewis waited until 8.30 p.m. before ringing Morse (who had been strangely absent somewhere since lunchtime). He found him at his flat and promptly reported his day's work.

When he had finished, Morse could hardly keep the excitement out of his voice. 'Just go over that bit about John Gilbert again, will you, Lewis?'

So Lewis repeated, as accurately as he could recall it, the news he had gleaned from the War Office archivist; and he felt very happy as he did so, for he knew that the news was pleasing to his master – a master, incidentally, who now had guessed the whole truth about the desert episode.

'You've done a marvellous day's work, old friend. Well done!'

'Did *you* find out anything new, sir?'

'Me? Well, yes and no, really. I've – I've been thinking about the case for most of the day. But nothing startling.'

'Anyway, have a good day in London tomorrow, sir!'

'What? Ah yes – tomorrow. I'll – er – give you a ring if I find out anything exciting.'

'Perhaps you'll do that, sir.'

'What? Ah yes – perhaps I will.'

A rather sad footnote to the events described in this chapter is that if Lewis had been slightly more interested in the formation of a new angling association and if he had asked to see the proof of the proposed letter-heading (but why should he?), he would have found that one of the two honorary vice-presidents listed at the top left-hand corner of the page was a man with a name which was now very familiar to him: Mr G. Westerby (Lonsdale College, Oxford).

Chapter Twenty-four

Tuesday, 29th July

Morse appears to have a powerful effect on two women,
one of whom he has never met.

For Lewis, a 10 a.m. visit to Lonsdale was pleasantly productive,
since the college secretary (she liked Lewis) had brought him a cup
of coffee, and been quite willing to talk openly about Westerby as
a person. So Lewis made his notes. Then he found out something
about *cars*, since – in spite of Morse's apparent indifference to the
problem – it seemed to him of great importance to discover exactly
how the corpse had been transported from London to Thrupp; and
he learned that Browne-Smith – doubtless on doctor's orders – had
sold his Daimler a month or so ago, whilst Westerby still ran a red
Metro, occasionally to be seen in the college forecourt.

'Why would Westerby want a car, though?' asked Lewis. 'He
lived in college.'

'I don't know. He's a bit secretive – doesn't tell anyone much
about what he does.'

'He must go *somewhere*?'

'I suppose so,' she nodded vaguely.

'Nice little car, the Metro. Economical!'

'Roomy in the back, too. You can take the seats out, you
know – get no end of stuff in there.'

'So they tell me, yes.'

'You've got a car, Sergeant?'

'I've got an old Mini, but I don't use it much. Usually go
to work on the bus and then use a police car.'

The college secretary looked down at her desk. 'Has Inspector
Morse got a car?'

Lewis found it an odd question. 'He's got a Jaguar. He's had a
Jaguar ever since I've known him.'

'You've known him long?'

'Long enough.'

'Is he a nice man?'

'Well, I wouldn't exactly call him "nice".'

'Do you like him?'

'I don't think you "like" Morse. He's not that sort of person, really.'

'But you get on well with him?'

'Usually. You see – well, he's the most remarkable man I've ever met, that's all.'

'He must think *you're* a remarkable man – if he works with you all the time, I mean.'

'No! I'm just, well . . .' Lewis didn't quite know how to finish, but he felt more than a little pride in the shadow of the compliment. 'Do you know him, then, Miss?'

She shook her pretty head. 'He spoke to me over the phone once, that's all.'

'Oh, he's terrible over the phone – always sounds so, I don't know, so cocky and nasty, somehow.'

'You mean . . . he's not *really* like that?'

'Not really,' said Lewis quietly. Then he noticed that the gentle eyes of the college secretary had suddenly drifted away from himself, and out towards a man she had never known or even seen. Momentarily he felt a twinge of jealousy.

Morse!

Down the dingy red-carpeted stairs, through the dingy red curtains, Morse, at 11 a.m., followed the same path that Browne-Smith had trodden eighteen days before him. He sat at a table in the Flamenco Topless Bar, and transacted his business with a milky-white maiden. It didn't take him long; and, after that, Browne-Smith's spunky antagonist behind the bar had proved no match for him, since for some reason she could not conceive of suggesting to *this* man, with the blue-grey eyes and the thinning, grey hair, that he could go across the way to the sauna if he wanted any further sexual gratification. He seemed to her coldly detached; and when he looked at her with eyes intensely still, she found herself answering his questions almost hypnotically. Thus it was that Morse, in a short space of time, had penetrated the door marked 'Private' at the rear of the drinking lounge.

At 1 p.m. he was riding in a taxi to an address he had known anyway – the address already pencilled firmly in his mind when that same morning he had left the Number One platform at Oxford on the 9.12 train. Perhaps he should have short-circuited the whole process; but on the whole he thought not, even though he had felt not the vaguest stir of virility as one of the girls had sat opposite him, sipping her exotic juice.

So far so good; and comparatively easy. The outlines of the pattern had been confirmed at every stage: Gilbert (one of twins, as Lewis had told him – interesting!) had quite fortuitously found a client in Oxford; and opposite his client's room he'd seen, in Gothic script, a name that for some reason was indelibly printed on his mind; with (doubtless) considerable ingenuity, he had lured this man to London – lured him to the address which Morse had just given to his taxi-driver, the same address that Morse had memorised from the wooden crates in the rooms of Westerby on Staircase T: 29 Cambridge Way, London, WC1. But what had happened after the suspicious and resourceful Browne-Smith had faced his *second* test of personal courage? What exactly had occurred when 'Yvonne' had left . . . and someone else had entered?

Such thoughts occupied Morse's mind as the taxi made its way (by an extremely circuitous route, it seemed to Morse) to Cambridge Way. Yet there were other thoughts, too: he could, of course, claim full expenses for his train fare (first-class, although he usually travelled second), tube fare, taxi fare, subsistence . . . Yes, he might *just* make enough on the day to settle down happily in the buffet car on his return and enjoy a couple of Scotches at someone else's expense. But would he be justified in sticking down on his claims-form such a ludicrous-looking item as 'Flamenco Revenge – £6'? On the whole, he thought, probably not.

He alighted, and stood alone in front of Number 29.

Chapter Twenty-five

Tuesday, 29th July

Lewis retraces some of his steps, and makes some startling new discoveries.

Lewis was back at Police HQ by 11.30 a.m., sensing that without further directions from on high he had gone as far as he was likely to go. But just for the moment he felt a little resentful about taking too many orders; and by noon he had taken the firm decision to revisit the scene of the crime. He didn't quite know why.

After drinking half a pint of bitter in the Boat Inn, he walked out along the road by the canal and up to Aubrey's Bridge. But there were no fishermen there this morning, and he turned his attention to his left as he walked slowly along, noting once more the authoritative notices posted regularly along the low, neat terrace: 'No mooring opposite these cottages.' The people here were obviously jealous of their acquired territories – doubtless rich enough, too, to own boats of their own and to regard it as some divine right that they should moor such craft immediately opposite their neatly-painted porches.

Then something stirred in Lewis's mind . . . If all these people were so anxious to preserve their rights and their privacy; if all those sharp eyes there were jealously watching the waterfront for the first signs of any territorial trespass – then, surely, in this quiet cul-de-sac that led to nowhere, where there was hardly room enough to execute a six-point turn in a car . . . yes! Surely, someone must have seen something? For the body must quite certainly have been pushed into the canal from the back of a car. How else? And yet Lewis, who had himself earlier questioned the tenants, had learned nothing of any strange car. Understandably, not every cottage had been inhabited at the time; the owners of some had been away – boating, or shopping in Oxford, or waiting in high places in large cities to motor down for a weekend of rural relaxation in their quiet country cottages.

Lewis had now reached the end of his walk, looking down as he did so at the water wherein the hideous body had been found. From this perusal he learned nothing. As he made his way back, however, he saw that the third cottage from the far end was 'For Sale', and he began to wonder whether such a property might not perhaps make a nice little investment for himself and the missus when he retired. Retired . . . And suddenly an exciting thought occurred to him. He knocked loudly on the door of the house for sale. No answer. Then he knocked at the house next door, which was opened by a freckle-faced lad of about twelve years of age.

'Is your mum in – or your dad?'

'No.'

'I was just trying to find out something about the house here.' Lewis pointed to the empty property.

'They want twenny thousand forrit – and it's got a leaky roof.'

'Lot of money,' said Lewis.

'Not worth it. It's been on the market a couple of months.'

Lewis nodded, sizing up this embryo property-evaluator. 'You live here?'

The boy nodded.

'Did you know the people next door – before it was for sale?'

'Not "people".'

'No?'

The young lad looked vaguely suspicious, but he blinked and agreed: 'No.'

'Look!' said Lewis. 'I'm a policeman and—'

'I know. I saw you when you was here before.'

'Shouldn't you have been at school?'

'I had the measles, didn't I? I was watching from the bedroom.'

'You didn't see anything sort of suspicious – before that, I mean?'

The boy shook his head.

'You say it wasn't "people" next door?'

'He's not in any trouble, is he?' The freckled face looked up at Lewis anxiously, as if it were a matter of deep concern to him that any trouble might have befallen the previous owner of the house next door.

'Not so far as I know.'

The boy looked down at the threshold and spoke quietly: 'He was good to me. Took me out in his Metro to King's Weir, once. Super fisherman he was – Mr Westerby.'

A Mercedes' horn blared imperiously as Lewis turned left on to the main road down to Kidlington, and he knew his mind was full of other things. He had just discovered a quite extraordinarily significant link between Westerby and the waterfront at Thrupp. And if someone had taken a body from London to Thrupp in a car (as someone must have done), there would have been no suspicions aroused by the familiar sight of a red Metro. No trouble at all. Not if that someone who had brought the body *had lived there himself*. What was more, this was the only car that had cropped up in the case so far, for Dr Browne-Smith had sold his large, black Daimler . . .

Lewis turned into HQ and sat down at Morse's desk, giving his bubbling thoughts the chance to simmer down. The green box-file containing the few documents on the case was lying open before him, and he riffled through the sheets – most of them his own reports. In fact (he told himself) there were only two *real* clues, anyway, whatever anyone might say: the suit, and the torn letter. Yes . . . and that torn letter was here, in his hands now – together with Morse's neatly-written reconstruction of the whole. He looked down at the torn half once more, and the final "G" in line 7 and the final "J" in line 15 suddenly shot out at him from the page. *Could* it be?

He parked the police car half on the pavement outside the Examination Schools and felt like a nervous punter in a betting-shop who can hardly bear to read the latest 1, 2, 3. The lists were still posted around the entrance hall, and quickly he found the board announcing the final honours list for Geography and read through the names. Whew! It not only could be – it *was*. 'Jennifer Bennet'. There she perched at the top of the list – that wonderful girl beginning with 'J' whom he had found on a board beginning with 'G'. And the college – Lonsdale. Lewis could hardly believe his eyes, or his luck. And there was more to come, for the bottom name of the examining sextet was none other than Westerby's!

It was an excited Lewis who drove back to Kidlington; but, even as he drove, the conflicting nature of his morning's findings was slowly becoming apparent to him. Most of what he had discovered was pointing with an insistent regularity in one direction – in the direction of George Westerby. And with Browne-Smith as the body and Westerby as the murderer, almost everything fitted the facts beautifully. Except . . . except that last bit. Because if the letter had been written to *Westerby*, and not to Browne-Smith . . . oh dear! Lewis was beginning to feel a little lost. He wondered if Morse had spent such a successful morning in London. He doubted it – doubted it genuinely. But how he longed to talk to Morse!

Back in the office, Lewis typed up his findings and although spelling had never been Lewis's strong suit, yet he felt rather pleased with his present reports, particularly with his little vignette of Westerby:

Londoner. Little dapper bumshious fellow – slightly deaf – pretty secretive. Tends to squint a bit, but this may be the usual cigarette at the corner of his mouth.

Chapter Twenty-six

Tuesday, 29th July

Unable to get any answer from the house in Cambridge Way,
Morse now reflects upon his meeting with the manager of the
Flamenco Topless Bar.

Like Browne-Smith before him, Morse walked slowly up the shallow
steps of Number 29 and rang the bell. But he, too, heard no sound
of ringing on the other side of the great black door. He rang again,
noticing as he did so the same board that Browne-Smith must have
seen, with its invitation to apply to 'Brooks & Gilbert (Sole Agents)'.
Almost imperceptibly he nodded; almost imperceptibly he smiled.
But there was still no sign of any movement in the house, and he
bent down to look through the highly polished brass letter-box. He
could make out the light-olive carpeting on the wide staircase that
faced him; but the place seemed ominously silent. He walked across
the street and looked up at the four-storied building, admiring the
clean-cut architecture, and the progressively foreshortened oblongs
of the window-frames, behind which – as far as he could see –
there was not the slightest tell-tale twitching of the curtainings.
So he walked away along the street, entered a small park, and sat
down on a bench, where he communed for many minutes with the
pigeons, and with his thoughts. On the taxi-journey he had sought
in his mind to minimise the risks he had already run that morning;
and yet, as he now began to realise, those risks had been decidedly
dangerous, especially after he had walked through the door marked
'Private' . . .

He'd started off in the quiet monotone of a man whose authority
was beyond that of other men: 'It matters to me not a single fart
in the cosmos, lad, whether you tell me about it here and now, or
in one of the cells of Her Majesty's nearest nick.'
  'I don't know who the bloody hell you think you are, talking
to me like that. Let me tell you—'
  'Before you tell me anything, just call in one of your tarts
out there, preferably the one with the biggest tits, and tell her to
bring me a large Scotch, preferably Bell's. On the house, I suggest
– because I'm here to *help* you, lad.'

'I was going to tell you that I've got friends here who'd gladly kick the guts out of the likes of you.'

' "Friends", you say?'

'Yeah – friends!'

'If you mean what you say, lad, I don't honestly think they're going to thank you very much if you bring *them* into this little business – and get 'em involved with *me*.'

'They're one helluva sight tougher than you, mate!'

'Oh no! You've got it all wrong, lad. And one little thing. You can curse and swear as much as you like with me, but you must never call me "mate" again! Is that understood? I've told you who I am, and I shan't be telling you again.'

The manager swallowed hard. 'I suppose you're going to tell me you've got a van full of squaddies outside. Is that it?'

Morse allowed a vague smile to form at the corners of his mouth. 'No, that's not it. I'm here completely on my own – and what's more no one else knows I'm here at all. Well, let's be honest, *almost* no one. And if we get along, you and me, I shan't even tell anyone that I've been here, either. No need really, is there?'

The manager was biting down hard on the nail of his left index finger, and Morse pressed home his obvious advantage.

'Let me give you a bit of advice. You're not a crook – you're not in the same league as most of the murderous morons I deal with every day. And, even if you were, I wouldn't need a posse of police to go around protecting *me*. You know why, lad?' Morse broke off for a few seconds, before focusing his eyes with almost manic ferocity upon the youngish man seated opposite him. Then he shook his head almost sorrowfully. 'No, you don't know why, do you? So let me tell you. It's because the archangels look after me, lad – always have done. And most especially when I'm pursuing my present calling as the protector of Law and eternal Justice!' Morse managed to give each of these mighty personages a capital letter; and pompous as he sounded, he also sounded very frightening.

Certainly, this was the impact upon the manager, for he appeared now to have little faith that he would be likely to emerge victorious from any conflict with the archangelic trio. He walked to the door, and sounded suddenly resigned as he asked 'Racquel' to fetch two double-Scotches; whilst, for a rather frightened Morse, the prospect of finding himself dead or dying in a Soho side-street was gradually receding.

The manager's story was brief.

The club was registered in the name of Soho Enterprises Limited, although he had never himself met anyone (or so he thought) directly from this syndicate. Business was transacted through a soberly-dressed intermediary – a Mr Schwenck – who periodically visited the bar to look around, and who collected takings and paid all salaries. About three weeks or so ago (he couldn't remember exactly), Mr Schwenck had announced that a certain Mr William would very soon be calling; that the said Mr William would make his requests known, and that no questions were to be asked. In fact, the bearded Mr William had requested very little, spurning equally the offers of hospitality from the bar and from the bra-less hostesses. He had taken away a projector and two reels of pornographic film, and announced that he would be back the following morning. And he had been, bringing with him a small blue card (given to the manager) and a cassette of some piano music (given to the girl behind the bar). Thereafter he had stood quietly at the bar, reading a paperback and drinking half a glass of lime-juice. Another man (so the manager had been informed) would probably be coming in that morning; and at some point this newcomer would be directed to the office where he was to be given the blue card, plus an address. That was all.

The young man appeared not overtly dishonest (albeit distinctly uncomfortable) as he told his little tale; and Morse found himself believing him.

'How much in it for you?' he asked.

'Nothing. I'm only—'

'Couple of hundred?'

'I told you—'

'Five hundred?'

'What? Just for—?'

'Forget it, lad! What was on the card?'

'Nothing really. It was just one of those cards that – that let you into places.'

'Which place?'

'I – I don't remember.'

'You didn't write it down?'

'No. I remembered it.'

'You've got a good memory?'

'Good enough.'

'But you just said you *can't* remember.'

'I can't. It was a good while ago now.'

'When exactly was it?'

'I can't—'

'Friday? Friday 11th July?'

'Could have been.'

'Did you get your projector and stuff back all right?'

' 'Course I did.'

'The next day?'

'Yes – er – I think it was the next day.'

For the first time Morse felt convinced that the man was lying. But why (Morse asked himself) should the man have lied to him on *that* particular point?

'About that address. Was it a number in Cambridge Way by any chance?'

Morse noted the dart of recognition in the manager's eyes, and was about to repeat his question when the telephone rang. The manager pounced on the receiver, clamping it closely to his right ear.

'Yes' (Morse could hear nothing of the caller's voice) 'Yes' (a quick, involuntary look across at Morse) 'Yes' (unease, quite certainly, in the manager's eyes) 'All right' (sudden relief in the manager's face?).

Morse's hand flashed across the table and snatched the receiver, but he heard only the dull, quiet purr of the dialling tone.

'Only the wife, Inspector. She wants me to take five pounds of potatoes home. Run out, she says. You know how these women are.'

Something had happened, Morse knew that. The young manager had got a shot of confidence from somewhere, and Morse began to wonder whether his patrons, Michael, Raphael and Gabriel, might not, after all, be called upon to fight his cause. He heard the door open quietly behind him – but not to admit the roundly bosomed Racquel with a further double-Scotch. In the doorway stood a diminutive Chinaman of about thirty years of age, his brown arms under the white, short-sleeved shirt as sleek and sinewy as the limbs of a Derby favourite in the Epsom paddock. It seemed to Morse a little humiliating to be cowed into instant submission by such a hominid; but Morse was. He rose to his feet, averted his gaze from the twin slits of horizontal hostility in the Chinaman's face, and thanked the manager civilly for his co-operation, rueing the fact that he was himself now far too decrepit even to enlist in the kung-fu classes advertised weekly in the *Oxford Times*. But the Chinaman guided him gently back to his chair; and it was more than half an hour (a period, however, of unmolested confinement) before Morse was allowed to leave the Topless Bar, whence he emerged into the upper world just after 1 p.m., deeply and gratefully inhaling the foul fumes of the cars that circled Piccadilly Circus, and crossing carefully to its west side, where he had a wait of only two minutes outside the Café Royal before a taxi pulled up in front of him.

'Where to, guv?'

Morse told him, infinitely preferring 'guv' to 'mate'.

Chapter Twenty-seven

Tuesday, 29th July, p.m.

In which Morse views a luxury block of flats in central London, catching an enigmatic glimpse of one of its tenants and looking longer upon our second corpse.

Morse had been sitting for over half an hour, pondering these and other things, when the extraordinary thought crossed his mind that he was in the middle of a park in the middle of opening hours with a pub only fifty yards away on the corner of the square. Yet somehow he sensed that events were gathering pace, and he walked past the Duke of Cambridge, went up the steps of Number 29, and rang the bell once more. This time he was in luck, for after a couple of minutes the great black door was opened.

'Yis, guv?'

He was a mournful-looking man in his mid-sixties, sweating slightly, wearing a beige-coloured working overall, carrying a caretaker's long-handled floor-mop, and fiddling with the controls of a stringed, National Health hearing-aid.

Morse explained who he was and, upon producing his identification, was reluctantly admitted across the threshold. The man (announcing himself as Hoskins – pronounced 'oskins) informed Morse that he had been the porter in the flats for just over a year now: 8.45 a.m. to 4.30 p.m., Tuesdays to Fridays, his job consisting mainly of keeping an eye on the properties and doing a bit of general cleaning during working hours. 'Nice little job, guv.'

'Still some flats for sale, I see?'

'No – not nah. Both of 'em sold. Should 'a' taken the notice darn, really – still, it's good for business, I s'pose.'

'*Both* of them sold?'

'Yis, guv. One of 'em's a gent from Oxford – bought it a coupla months back, 'e did.'

'And the other one?'

'Few days ago. Some foreign gent, I think it is.'

'The one from Oxford – that's Mr Westerby, isn't it?'

'You know 'im, then?'

'Is he in?'

'No. I 'aven't seen 'im since 'e came to look rarnd, like.' The man hesitated. 'Nuffin wrong, is there?'

'Everything's wrong, Mr Hoskins, I'm afraid. You'd better show me round his flat, if you will.'

Rather laboriously the man led the way up the stairs to the first floor, produced a key from his overall pocket, and opened the door across from the landing with the apprehension of a man who expects to cast his eye upon a carpet swimming with carnage. But the pale-grey carpeting in the small (and otherwise completely unfurnished) ante-room provided evidence only of a recent, immaculate hoovering.

'Main room's through there, guv.'

Inside this second room, half a dozen pieces of heavy, mahogany furniture stood at their temporary sites around the walls, whilst the floor space was more than half covered by oblong wooden crates, several piled on top of others – crates each labelled neatly with the name and new address of a G. O. Westerby, Esq., MA; crates which Morse had recognised immediately, especially the one, already opened, which had contained the head of Gerardus Mercator (now standing on the mantelpiece).

'Mr Westerby already been here?'

'Not seen 'im guv. But o' course, 'e might 'a' come later – after I was off. Looks like it, don't it?'

Morse nodded, looking aimlessly around the room, and then trying the two fitted wardrobes, both of which were unlocked, empty, dusty. And Morse frowned, knowing that somewhere something was wrong. He pointed back to the ante-room. 'Did you hoover the carpet in there?'

The man's face (Morse could have sworn it) had paled a few degrees. 'No – I just, as I said, look after the general cleaning, like – stairs and that sort o' thing.'

But Morse sensed that the man was lying, and found no difficulty in guessing why: a caretaker in a block of flats like this . . . half a dozen wealthy and undomesticated men . . . a few nice little backhanders now and again just to dust and to clean . . . Yes, Morse could imagine the picture all right; and it might well be that a caretaker in such a block of flats would know rather more about one or two things than he was prepared to admit. Yet Morse was singularly unsuccessful in eliciting even the slightest piece of information, and he changed the course of his questioning.

'Did *you* show Mr Westerby round here?'

'No, chap from the agents, it was – young fellow.'

'Always the same young fellow, is it?'

'Pardon, sir?'

'You say they've just sold the other flat?'

'Ah I see. No, I wasn't 'ere then.'

'It's not Mr Gilbert himself, is it – this young fellow you mention?'

'I wouldn't know – I never met 'im personally, like.'

'I see.' Again Morse sensed that the man was holding something back, and again he aimed blindly in the dark. 'You know when Mr Westerby called again . . . when was it, about a week, ten days ago?'

'I told you, sir. I only saw 'im the once – the day 'e looked rarnd the place.'

'I see.' But Morse saw nothing, apart from the fact that far from hitting any bull's eye he'd probably missed the target altogether. Without any clear purpose he proceeded to look into the small kitchen, and then into the bathroom; but the only thing that mildly registered in his mind was that the parquet flooring in each was sparklingly clean, and he felt quite convinced now that Hoskins (almost certainly in contravention of his contract) was working a very profitable little fiddle for himself with his mop and his cleansing-fluid.

So it was that slowly and disconsolately Morse followed what he now saw as the marginally devious little caretaker down the broad staircase towards the front door. And at that point, had it not been for one fortuitous occurrence, perhaps the simple yet quite astounding truth of the present case might never have beached upon the shores of light. For Morse had heard a lift descending, and now he saw a dark-skinned, grey-suited man emerge from the side of the entrance-hall.

'Arternoon, sir,' said Hoskins, touching some imaginary lock on his balding pate.

The affluent-looking Arab was walking in the opposite direction from the front door, and as he watched him Morse whispered to his companion: 'Where's *he* going?'

'There's a back entrance 'ere, guv . . .'

But Morse hardly heard, for the Arab himself had looked over his shoulder, and was in turn looking back towards Morse with a puzzled, vaguely worried frown.

'Who's he?' asked Morse very quietly.

' 'e lives on the—'

But again Morse was not listening, for his thoughts were travelling via the unsuspected lift towards the higher storeys. 'He finishes work early, doesn't he?'

' 'e can afford to, guv.'

'Yes. Like you can, sometimes, Hoskins! Take me up to the flat that's just been sold!'

The small but extraordinarily efficient lift brought them swiftly up to the top storey, where Hoskins nervously fingered a bouquet of silvery keys, finally finding the correct one, and pushing open the door for the policeman to enter.

Things were at last falling into place in Morse's mind, and as they stood by the opened door his aim was more deliberate.

'Did they give you the afternoon off, Hoskins?'

'What afternoon, guv?' the man protested. But not for long. It had been on the Friday, he confessed. He'd had a phone call, and been given a couple of fivers – huh! – just for staying away from the place.

Morse was nodding to himself as he entered the rooms. Yes . . . the Gilbert twins: one of them a housing agent; the other a removals man. Sell some property – and recommend a highly reputable and efficient removals firm; buy some property – and also recommend the same paragon of pantechniconic skills. Very convenient, and very profitable. Over the years the two brothers must have worked a neatly dovetailed little business . . .

Now, again, Morse looked around him at a potentially luxurious flat in central London: the small entrance hall, the living room, the bedroom, the kitchen, the bathroom – all newly decorated. No carpets yet, though; no curtains, either. But there was not a flick of cigarette ash, not even a forgotten tin-tack, on the light-oak boards, as spotless as those of an army barrack floor before the CO's inspection.

'You've been cleaning in here, too?' asked Morse.

The walls were professionally painted in lilac emulsion, the doors and fitted cupboards in brilliant-white gloss. And Morse, suddenly thinking back to his own bachelor flat with the heavy old walnut suite his mother had left him, began to envisage some lighter, brighter, modernistic furniture for himself as he opened one of the fitted wardrobes in the bedroom with its inbuilt racks and airy, deep recesses. And not just one of them!

But the second one was locked.

'You got the key for this, Hoskins?'

'No, sir. I only keep the keys for the doors. If people wants to lock things up . . .'

'Let's look in the kitchen!'

Beside the sink, Morse found a medium-sized screwdriver, the only object of any kind abandoned (it seemed) by the previous owner.

'Think this'll open it, Hoskins?'

'I – I don't want to get you in any trouble, sir – or me. I shouldn't really 'ave . . . I just don't think it's right to mess up the place and damage things, sir.'

(The 'sir's were coming thick and fast.)

It was time, Morse thought, for some reassurance. 'Look, Hoskins, this is my responsibility. I'm doing my duty as a police officer – you're doing your duty as a good citizen. You understand that?'

The miserable man appeared a modicum mollified and nodded silently. And indeed it was he, after a brief and ineffectual effort from Morse, who proved the more successful; for he managed to insert the screwdriver far enough into the gap between the side of the cupboard door and the surrounding architrave to gain sufficient leverage. Then, with a joint prising, the lock finally snapped, the wood splintered, and the door swung slowly open. Inside, slumped on the floor of the deep recess, was the body of a man, the head turned towards the wall; and almost exactly halfway between the shoulder-blades was a round hole in the dead man's sports-jacket, from which was oozing still a steady drip of bright-red blood, feeding a darker pool upon the floor. Almost squeamishly, Morse inserted his left hand under the lifeless, lolling head . . . and turned it towards him.

'My God!'

For a few moments the two men stood looking down on the face that stared back up at them with open, bulging eyes.

'Do you know who it is?' croaked Morse.

'I never seen him before, sir. I swear I 'aven't.' The man was shaking all over, and Morse noticed the ashen-grey pallor in his cheeks and the beads of sweat upon his forehead.

'Take it easy, old boy!' said Morse in a kindly, understanding voice. 'Just tell me where the nearest telephone is – then you'd better get off home for a while. We can always—'

Morse was about to lay a comforting hand upon the man's shoulder; but he was already too late, for now he found another body slumped about his feet.

Five minutes later, after dialling 999 from the telephone in the living-room, and after sending the old boy off home (having elicited a full name and home address from those gibbering lips), Morse stood once again looking down at the corpse in the cupboard recess. A tiny triangle of white card was showing above the top pocket of the jacket, and Morse bent down to extract it. There were a dozen or so similar cards there, but he took only one and read it – his face betraying only the grimmest confirmation. He'd known anyway, because he'd recognised the face immediately. It was the face of the man whom Morse had last (and first) seen in the rooms of George Westerby, Geography don at Lonsdale College, Oxford: the face of A. Gilbert, Esq., late proprietor of the firm Removals Anywhere.

Chapter Twenty-eight

Tuesday, 29th July

Morse meets a remarkable woman, and learns of another woman who might be more remarkable still.

On the left sat a very black gentleman in a very smart pin-striped suit, studying the pink pages of *The Financial Times*; on the right sat a long-haired young brunette, wearing enormous earrings, and reading *Ulysses*; in the middle sat Morse, impatiently fingering a small white oblong card; and all the while the tube-train clattered along the stations on the northbound Piccadilly line.

To Morse it seemed an inordinately long journey, and one during which he found it almost impossible to concentrate his mind. Perhaps it had been improper of him (as the plain-clothes sergeant had diffidently hinted) to have fled the scene of the recent crime so precipitately; quite certainly it had bordered upon the criminally negligent (as the plain-clothes sergeant had more forcefully asserted) that he had allowed the one and only other witness to have left the premises in Cambridge Way – whatever the state of shock that had paralysed the man's frame. But at least Morse had explained where he was going – had even given the address and the telephone number. And he could always do his best to explain, to apologise . . . later.

Arsenal. (Nearly there.)

The brunette's eyes flickered over Morse's face, but flashed back immediately to Bloom, as though the latter were a subject of considerably greater interest.

Finsbury Park. (Next stop.)

Suddenly Morse stiffened bolt upright in his seat, and this time it was the gentleman from the city whose bloodshot eyes turned suspiciously towards his travelling companion, as though he half expected to find a man in the initial throes of an epileptic fit.

That screwdriver . . . and that small, round hole in the middle of those sagging shoulder-blades . . . and he, Morse, a man who had lectured so often on proper procedure in cases of homicide, *he* had just left his own fine set of fingerprints around the bulbous handle of – the murder-weapon! Oh dear! Yes, there might well come, and fairly soon, the time for more than an apology, more than a little explanation.

For the moment, however, Morse was totally convinced that he was right (as indeed for once he was) in recognising the signs of a tide in the affairs of men that must be taken at the flood; and when he emerged from the underground into the litter-strewn streets of Manor House, he suspected that the gods were smiling happily upon him, for almost immediately he spotted Berrywood Court, a tall tenement block only some hundred yards away down Seven Sisters Road.

Mrs Emily Gilbert, an unlovely woman in her late fifties (her teeth darkly stained) capitulated quickly to Morse's urgent questioning. She'd known it was all silly; and she'd told her husband it might be dangerous as well. But it was just a joke, he'd said. Some joke!

She'd met another woman there in Cambridge Way – an attractive Scandinavian-looking woman who (so Mrs G. had thought) had been hired from one of the better-class clubs in Soho. They'd both been briefed by Albert (her husband) and – well, that was it really. This man had come to the place, and she (Mrs G.) had left the pair of them together in a first-floor flat (yes, Mr Westerby's flat). Then, after an hour or so, Albert had come up to tell her (she was waiting in an empty top-floor flat) that he was very pleased with the way things had gone, that she (Mrs G.) was a good old girl, and that the odd little episode could now be happily forgotten.

She had a strangely intense and rather pleasing voice, and Morse found himself gradually reassessing her. 'This other woman,' he asked, 'what was her name?'

'I was told to call her "Yvonne".'

'She didn't tell you where she lived? Where she worked?'

'No. But she was "class" – you know what I mean? She was sort of tasteful – beautifully made-up, lovely figure.'

'You don't know where she lives?'

'No. Albert'll probably be able to tell you, though.'

'Do you know where *he* is, Mrs Gilbert?'

She shook her head. 'In his sort of business you're off all the time. I know he's got a few jobs on in the Midlands – and one in Scotland – but he's always on the move. He just turns up here when he gets back.'

At this point, Morse felt a curious compassion for Emily Gilbert, for she seemed to him a brave sort of woman – yet one who would need to be even braver very soon. He knew, too, that time was running out; knew he had to find out more before he broke the cruel news.

'Just tell me anything you can, please, about this other woman – this "Yvonne". Anything you can remember.'

'I've told you – I don't—'

'Didn't you talk together?'

'Well, yes – but—'

'You don't have any idea where I can find her?'

'I think she lives south of the Thames somewhere.'

'No name of the road? No number of the house? Come on! Think, woman!'

But Morse had pushed things too far, for Mrs Gilbert now broke down and wept, and Morse was at a loss as to what to do, or what to say. So he did nothing; and such masterly inactivity proved to be the prudent course, for very soon she had wiped her wide and pleasing eyes and apologised sweetly for what she called her 'silliness'.

'Have you any children?' asked Morse.

She shook her head sadly.

It was hardly the most propitious moment, but Morse now rose from the sofa and placed his right hand firmly on her shoulder. 'Please be brave, Mrs Gilbert! I've got to tell you, I'm afraid, that your husband is dead.'

With a dramatic, convulsive jerk, her right hand snapped up to meet Morse's, and he felt the sinewy vigour of her fingers as they sought to clutch the comfort of his own. Then Morse told her, in a very quiet, gentle voice, as much (and as little) as he knew.

When he had finished, Mrs Gilbert asked him no questions, but got up from her chair, walked over to the window, lit a cigarette, and stared out over the long, bleak reservoir that lay below, where a swan glided effortlessly across the still waters. Then, finally, she turned towards him, and for the first time Morse realised that she must have been an adequately attractive woman . . . some few little summers ago. Her eyes, still glistening with tears, sought his.

'I lied to you, Inspector, and I shouldn't have done that. I *know* that other woman, you see. My husband occasionally gets – got involved in his brother's – well, let's say his brother's side of things, and he met her in one of the clubs a few weeks ago. I – I found out about it. You see – he wanted to leave me and go and – and go and live with her. But she—'

Mrs Gilbert broke off, and Morse nodded his understanding.

'But she didn't want him.'

'No, she didn't.'

'Did you tell him you'd found out?'

Mrs Gilbert smiled a wan sort of smile and she turned back to the window, her eyes drifting over and beyond the reservoir to where a DC10 droned in towards Heathrow. 'No! I wanted to keep him. Funny, isn't it? But he was the only thing I had.'

'It blew over?'

'Not really very much time for that, was there?'

Morse sat and looked once more at this very ordinary woman he had come to visit, and his mind drifted back to Molly Bloom in *Ulysses*, and he knew that Mrs Gilbert, too, was a woman who had offered, once, a presence and a bosom and a rose.

'Please tell me about this other woman.'

'I don't know her real name – they call her "Yvonne" at the

clubs. But I know her initials – W.S. – and I know where she lives
– 23A Colebourne Road, just south of Richmond Road. It's only
about five minutes' walk from the tube station . . .'

'You went to *see* her?'

'You don't know much about women, do you?'

'No, perhaps not,' agreed Morse. But he was impatient now. He
felt like a man with an enormously distended bladder who has been
kept talking on the phone for half an hour, and he walked across to
the door. 'Will you be all right, Mrs Gilbert?'

'Don't worry about me, Inspector. I'll give the GP a ring when
you've gone, and he'll give me a few tablets. They should take care
of me for a little while, shouldn't they?'

'Yes, I'm sure they will. I know how you must be feeling—'

'Of course you don't! You've not the faintest idea. It's not today
– it's not tonight. It's *tomorrow*. Can't you see that? You tell me
Albert's dead, and in an odd sort of way it doesn't register. It's a
shock, isn't it? And I'd be more than happy to live through one shock
after another, but . . .'

The tears were running freely again, and suddenly she moved
towards him and buried her head on his shoulder. And Morse
stood there by the door, awkward and inept; and (in his own
strange way) almost loving the woman who was weeping out her
heart against him.

It was several minutes before he was able to disengage himself
and finally to stand upon the threshold of the opened door.

'Please look after yourself, Mrs Gilbert.'

'I will. Don't worry about that.'

'If there's anything I can do to help . . .'

She almost smiled. 'Be gentle with the girl, Inspector. You see, I
know you're anxious to get away from here and see her, and I just
want you to know that she's the loveliest girl – woman – I've ever
met in all my life – that's all.'

Tears were spurting again now, and Morse leaned forward
and kissed her lightly on the forehead, in the sure knowledge that
this woman had somewhere touched his feelings deeply. And as he
walked slowly away up the road towards Manor House tube-station
he doubted whether Albert Gilbert had ever really known the
woman he had asked to marry him.

For all his conviction that the tide was running fully in his
favour, the open doors of the Manor Hotel proved irresistible, and
Morse wondered as he drained his pints and watched the pimps and

prostitutes walk by whether, in a life so full of strange coincidence, he might at last be facing the wildest and most wonderful coincidence of them all: 'W.S.'! Browne-Smith had mentioned those initials . . . and Emily Gilbert had just repeated them . . . and those were the selfsame glorious initials of a girl whom once he'd known, and loved too well.

Twenty minutes after Morse had left the seventh floor of Berrywood Court, a key was inserted into the outer door of the Gilberts' flat, and a man walked in and flung his jacket carelessly down upon the sofa.

Two minutes later, Albert Gilbert, of Removals Anywhere, was talking (somewhat incoherently) over the phone to his GP, explaining how, for no apparent reason, his wife had fainted quite away on his return, and desperately demanding some instructions, since even now she showed no signs of sense or sanity returning.

Chapter Twenty-nine

Tuesday, 29th July

All men, even those of a pessimistic nature, fall victim at certain points in their lives to the most extravagant of hopes.

As Mrs Gilbert had told him, Colebourne Road was no more than five minutes' walk from East Putney tube-station. But Morse appeared in no hurry, and when he reached the street-sign he stopped awhile and stood beneath it, deep in thought. Surely he couldn't be so utterly and stupidly sentimental as to harbour even the faintest hope that he was just about to see once more the woman whom he'd worshipped all those years ago. No, he told himself, he couldn't. And yet a wild, improbable hope lived on; and as if to nourish the hope, he entered the Richmond Arms on the corner of the street and ordered a double-Scotch. As he drank, his thoughts went back to the time when he'd visited his old mother in the Midlands, and gone off to an evening Methodist service to see if a girl, a very precious girl, was still in her place in

the choir-stalls, still raising her eyes to his at the end of each verse
of every hymn and smiling at him sweetly and seraphically. But she
hadn't been there – hadn't been there for thirty years, perhaps –
and he'd sat by a pillar alone that night. Morse walked to the bar
('Same again, please – Bell's'), and the name of Wendy Spencer
tripped trochaically across his brain . . . It couldn't be the same
woman, though. It *wasn't* the same woman. And yet, ye gods –
if gods ye be – please make it her!

Morse's heart was beating at an alarming rate and his throat
felt very dry as he rang the bell of Number 23. There was a light
downstairs, a light upstairs; and the odds were very strongly on her
being in.

'Yes?' The door was opened by a youngish, dark-complexioned
woman.

'I'm a police inspector, Miss—'

'Mrs – Mrs Price.'

'Ah yes – well, I'm looking for someone I think lives here.
I'm not quite sure of her name but—'

'I can't help you much then, can I?'

'I think she's sometimes called "Yvonne".'

'There's no one here by that name.'

The door had already closed an inch or two, but now there
was another voice. 'Anything *I* can do to help?'

A taller woman was standing behind Mrs Price, a woman
in a white bathrobe, a woman with freshly-showered and almost
shining skin, a woman awkwardly re-making the tumbled beauty
of her hair.

'He says he's a police inspector – says he's looking for someone
called "Yvonne",' explained an aggressive Mrs Price.

'Do you know her surname, Inspector?'

Morse looked at the white-clad woman who now had moved
towards the centre of the doorway, and a crushing wave of disappointment broke over him. 'Not yet, I'm afraid. But I know she lives
here – or she was shtaying – staying here until very recently.'

'Well you must have got it wrong—' began Mrs Price.

But the woman in white was interrupting her: 'Leave this to
me, Angela – it's all right. I think I may be able to help you,
Inspector. Won't you come in?'

Morse climbed the narrow stairs, noting the slim ankles of
the woman who preceded him.

'Would you like a drink?' she asked, as they sat opposite
each other in the small but beautifully furnished living-room.

314 THE SECOND INSPECTOR MORSE OMNIBUS

'Er – no. Perhaps not.'

'You've had enough already, you mean?'

'Does it show?'

She nodded – a faint smile upon lips that were thin and completely devoid of make-up. 'It's the "s"s that are always difficult, isn't it? When you've had too much drink, I mean – or when you begin wearing false teeth.'

Morse looked at her own, most beautifully healthy teeth. 'How would you know about that?'

'I sometimes drink too much.'

Morse let it go, for things were going very nicely – the conversation moving already on to a plane of easy familiarity. But it wasn't to last.

'What do you want, Inspector?' A hard, no-nonsense tone had come into her voice.

So Morse told her; and she listened in silence, occasionally crossing one naked leg over the other and then covering her knees with a sharp little tug at the robe, like some puritanical parson's wife at a vicarage tea-party. And almost from the start Morse felt the virtual certainty that 'Yvonne' had now been found – found sitting here in front of him, her head slightly to one side, sweeping up her blonde hair with her left hand and re-inserting a few of the multitudinous pins with her right.

When Morse had finished the first part of his tale, she reached for her handbag. 'Do you smoke, Inspector?'

Morse patted his jacket pocket, and suspected that he must have left his own recently-purchased packet in the pub.

'Here, have one of these.' Her bag was open now, the flap towards him; and seeing the faded gilt initials Morse knew that his silly hope was finally extinguished.

'You're very kind,' he heard himself say.

Had she seen something vulnerable in this strange inspector of police? In his mien? In his eyes? On his lips? Perhaps, indeed, she had, for her voice had been more gentle, and she now stood up and lit his cigarette, unconscious (or uncaring) that her robe was partly open at the top as she leaned towards him. Then she sat back in her chair again, and told him her own side of the story, still occasionally recrossing her lovely legs, but now no longer too concerned about concealing them.

She'd known Bert Gilbert for only a few weeks. He'd come into the sauna one morning – very much in control of himself – and asked her if she'd be willing to entertain a very special client of his;

yes, at the address Morse had mentioned; and, yes, with a sequel much as he'd described it. After that Gilbert had obviously taken a liking to her, spent a fair amount of money on her, and wanted to keep seeing her. *Had* kept seeing her. But he'd got jealous and morose, and was soon telling her that he wanted her to pack up her job and go to live with him. For her part, the whole thing had been the old familiar story of an ageing man behaving like an infatuated schoolboy – and she'd told him so.

That was all.

'What's your name?' asked Morse.

Her eyes were looking down at the thickly-piled carpet: 'Winifred – Winifred Stewart. Not much of a name, is it? Some people are christened with horrid names.'

'Mm.'

She looked up. 'What's your name?'

'They call me Morse: Inspector Morse.'

'But that's your *surname*.'

'Yes.'

'You don't want to tell me your Christian name?'

'No.'

'Like that, is it?' (She was smiling.)

Morse nodded.

'What about that drink? You've sobered up a bit, you know.'

But (quite amazingly) Morse had hardly heard her. 'Do you – do you go with lots of men?'

'Not lots, no. I'm a very expensive item.'

'You earn a lot of money?'

'More than you do.' Her voice had grown harsh again, and Morse felt sad and dejected.

'Do you get much pleasure from – er—'

'From having sex with clients? Not much, no. Occasionally though – if you want me to be honest.'

'I'm not sure I do,' said Morse.

She stood up and poured herself a glass of dry Vermouth, without renewing her offer to the chief inspector. 'You don't know much about life, do you?'

'Not much, no.' He seemed to her to look so lost and tired now, and she guessed he must have had a busy day. But had she known it, his mind was working at a furious rate. There was *something* (he knew it!) that he'd been missing all the way along; something he doubted he would learn from this disturbingly attractive woman; something that she probably couldn't tell him, anyway, even when she came (as he knew she would) to the second part of the tale she had to tell.

'When did you last see Gilbert?' he asked.

'I'm not sure—'

'You say you saw him quite a few times after you entertained his special client?'

It was puzzling to Morse how the tone of her voice could vary so vastly (and so suddenly) between the gentle and jarring. It was the latter again now.

'You mean did I go to bed with him?'

Morse nodded. And for the first time she was aware of the cold, almost merciless eyes that stared upon her, and she felt the sensation of a psychological and almost physical stripping as she answered him, her top lip quivering.

'Yes!'

'Was that after you'd met your *second* special client?'

Her startled eyes looked into his, and then down to the Wilton again. 'Yes,' she whispered.

'Please tell me all about that,' said Morse quietly.

For a few moments she said nothing; then she picked up her glass and quickly drained it.

'Before I do – would you like to come to bed with me?'

'No.'

'Are you sure?' She stood up and loosened her belt, allowing the sides of her bathrobe to fall apart before drawing them together again and retying the belt tightly around her waist.

'Quite sure,' lied Morse.

So Winifred Stewart (it was now past eight o'clock) told Morse about her second special client, a Mr Westerby, who also hailed from Oxford. And Morse listened very carefully, nodding at intervals and seemingly satisfied. But he *wasn't* satisfied. It was all interesting – of course it was; but it merely corroborated what he'd already known, or guessed.

'What about that drink?' he asked.

Mrs Angela Price looked knowingly at her husband when she finally heard the quiet voices on the doorstep. It was a quarter to midnight, and BBC 1 had already finished its transmission.

Lewis had finally gone to bed about ten minutes before Morse found a taxi on the Richmond Road. He'd hoped that Morse would have been back before now, and had tried repeatedly to get in touch with him, both at HQ and at his home. For he had received a remarkable piece of news that same afternoon from the young porter at Lonsdale, who had received a card by second post; a card from Greece; a card from Mr Westerby.

At 2 a.m., Winifred Stewart was still lying awake. The night was sultry and she wore no nightdress as she lay upon her bed, covered only by a lightweight sheet. She thought of Morse, and she felt inexpressibly glad that she had met him; longed, too, with one half of her mind, that he would come to visit her again. And yet she knew, quite certainly, that if he did her soul would be completely bared and she would tell him all she knew. Two-thirds of the tragic tale had now been told; and if ever he began to guess the final truth . . . Yet, with the other half of her mind she didn't want him back – ever – for she was now a very frightened woman.

At 3 a.m. she went to the bathroom to take some Disprin tablets.

At 4 a.m. she was still awake, and suddenly she felt the night had grown so very cold.

Chapter Thirty

Wednesday, 30th July

In which 'The Religion of the Second Mile' is fully explained, and Morse is peremptorily summoned to his superior.

As he sat back comfortably in a first-class compartment of the 10 a.m. '125' from Paddington, Morse felt the residual glow of a great elation. For now (as he knew) the veil of the temple had been rent in twain.

The previous night he had missed the last train to Oxford and only just managed to find, on the highest floor of a cheap hotel, a cramped and claustrophobic room in which the water-pipes had groaned and gurgled through the early hours. But it was in this selfsame mean and miserable room that Morse, as he lay on his back in the darkness with both hands behind his head, had finally seen the amazing light of truth. Half occupied with the lovely woman he had left so recently, half with the older problems that beset him still, his mind had steadfastly refused to rest. He sensed that he was *almost* there, and the facts of the case raced round and round his brain like an ever-accelerating whirligig. The old facts . . . and the new facts.

Not that he had learned much that was surprisingly new from Mrs Emily Gilbert. Nor, for that matter, from Miss Winifred Stewart – except for the confirmation that she had, indeed, agreed to entertain a second special guest from Oxford whose name was Mr Westerby. There had been a few other things, though. She'd told him, for example, that Emily had been simultaneously wooed by each of the Gilbert brothers; that, of the two, Alfred was considerably the more interesting and cultured – particularly because of his love of music; but that it was Albert who had won the prize with his livelier, albeit coarser, ways. The brothers were still very much alike (she'd told him) – extraordinarily so in appearance – but if they'd been holidaying together in Salzburg, Alfred would have gone to a Mozart concert and Albert to *The Sound of Music* . . . Yes, that was something new; but it hardly seemed to Morse of much importance. Far more important was what she *hadn't* told him, for he had sensed a deep unease within her when she'd told him of her time with Westerby: not the unease of a woman telling obvious untruths; the unease, rather, of a woman telling something less than all she knew . . .

It was at that very point in his whirling thoughts that Morse had jerked himself up in his bed, switched on the bedside lamp, and reached for the only object of comfort that the sombre room could offer him: the Gideon Bible that rested there beside the lamp. In two minutes his fumbling and excited fingers had found what he was seeking. There it was – St Matthew, Chapter Five, Verse Forty-One: 'And whosoever shall compel thee to go a mile, go with him twain.' He remembered vividly from his youth a sermon on that very text – from a wild, Welsh minister: 'The Religion of the Second Mile'. And it was with the forty-watt bulb shedding its feeble light over the Gideon Bible that Morse smiled to himself in unspeakable joy, like one who has travelled on a longer journey still – that third and final mile . . .

At last he knew the truth.

'In two minutes we shall be arriving at Oxford station,' came the voice over the microphone. 'Passengers for Banbury, Birmingham,

Charlbury . . .' Morse looked at his watch: 10.41 a.m. No need for
any great rush now – no need for any rush at all.

He walked from the station up to the bus-stop in Cornmarket;
and at 11.30 was back at Police HQ in Kidlington, where a
relieved-looking Lewis awaited him.

'Good time, sir?'

'Marvellous!' said Morse, seating himself in the black leather
chair and beaming benignly.

'We expected you back yesterday.'

' "We"? Who's that supposed to mean?'

'The super was after your blood last night, sir – *and* this morning.'

'Ah, I see.'

'I said you'd ring him as soon as you got in.'

Morse dialled Strange's number immediately. Engaged.

'How about you, Lewis? You have a good time?'

'I don't know, sir. There's *this*.'

He handed over the postcard he had picked up the previous evening from Lonsdale, and Morse looked down at a glossy photograph
of ancient stones. He turned the card over, and read that such
crumbling masonry was nothing less than the remains of the royal
palace of Philip II of Macedon (382–336 BC). Then he saw the large
Hellas stamp, featuring sea shells set against a blue-green background; then the message, neatly penned and very brief: 'Wonderful
weather. Any mail to Cambridge Way. Staying on a further week.
Regards to the Master – and to your good selves. G.W.'

'Lovely place, Greece, Lewis.'

'I wouldn't know, I'm afraid.'

'Perhaps Westerby doesn't know either,' said Morse slowly.

'Pardon, sir?'

'You'd better keep it, of course – but he's not in Greece. It's a
forgery – you can see that, surely!'

'But—'

'Look, Lewis! Look at that franking.'

Lewis looked closely but saw little more than a blackened circle,
with whatever lettering there may have been so smudged that it was
quite illegible. He could, though, just about decipher one or two of
the letters: there was an 'O' (certainly) and an 'N' (possibly) near
the beginning of one word, and the next word probably ended in
an 'E'. But he could make nothing of it, and looked up to find that
Morse was smiling still.

'I shouldn't take too much notice of it, Lewis. It's not too

difficult to get hold of a Greek postage-stamp, is it? And then
if you get a date-stamp and push it vaguely one way instead of
banging it straight down you'll get the same sort of blur as that.
You see, someone just brought the card into the Lodge and left
it handily upon a pile of mail. It's all a fake! And, if you like, I'll
tell you where the date-stamp comes from: it comes from *Lonsdale
College*.'

The phone rang before Lewis could make any answer, and a
harsh voice barked across the line: 'That you, Morse? Get over
here – and get over here quick!'

'I think you're in the dog-house,' said Lewis quietly.

But Morse appeared completely unconcerned as he rose to
his feet and put his jacket on.

'I'll tell you something else about that card, Lewis. We know a
man, don't we, who's been writing a book about our Mister Philip
Two of Macedon – remember?'

Yes, Lewis did remember. Just as Morse had done, he'd seen the
typescript on the desk in Browne-Smith's room, as well as the pile
of postcards that had lain beside it. And, as Morse walked across
to the door, he felt annoyed and disappointed with himself. There
was one thing Morse hadn't mentioned, though.

'Is the handwriting a fake as well, sir?'

'I haven't the faintest idea,' replied Morse. 'Why don't you go
and find out, if you can? No rush, though. I think the super and
I may well be in for rather a longish session.'

'Siddown, Morse!' growled Strange, his long gaunt face set grimly
and angrily. 'I heard last night – and again this morning – from
the Metropolitan Commissioner.' His eyes fixed Morse's as he
continued. 'It seems that a member of *my* force – *you*, Morse! –
was witness to a major crime in London yesterday; that you left the
scene of this crime without adequate explanation and in defiance of
normal police procedures; that you allowed the only other witness
of this crime to go off home – God! – a home incidentally which
doesn't exist; that you then went off to see a woman up in North
London to tell her that her husband had just been murdered; and if
all that's not enough,' the blood was rising in his face, 'you couldn't
even get the name of the bloody corpse right!'

Morse nodded agreement, but said nothing.

'You realise, don't you, that this is an extremely serious matter?'
Strange's voice was quieter now. 'It won't be in my hands, either.'

'No, I understand that. And you're right, of course – it's a very serious matter. The only thing is, sir, I don't think that even you quite understand how desperately serious it is.'

Strange had known Morse for many years and had marvelled many times at the exploits of this extraordinary and exasperating man. And there was something about the way in which Morse had just spoken that signalled a warning. It would be wise for him to listen, he knew that.

So he listened.

It was more than two hours later when Strange's middle-aged secretary saw the door open and the two men emerge. Earlier she had been informed that, short of a nuclear explosion, her boss was not to be disturbed; and she did know a little (how not?) of the reason for Morse's summons from on high. Yet now she saw that it was Strange's face which looked, of the two, the more drained and set; and she bent her head a little closer to the clattering keys, as if her presence there might cause embarrassment. The two men had said nothing more to each other, she was sure of that – except that Strange had murmured a muted 'Thank you' as Morse had walked across the room. Then, after Morse was gone, and just before her boss had closed his office door, she thought she heard him speak once more: 'My God!'

THE END OF THE SECOND MILE

THE THIRD MILE

Chapter Thirty-one

Friday, 1st August

Like some latter-day Pilgrim, one of the protagonists in this macabre case is determined to rid himself of his burden.

Two days after the events described in the previous chapter, a man looked about him with extreme circumspection before inserting one of his keys into the door at the rear entrance of the luxury flats in Cambridge Way. The coast was clear. Apart from the uniformed police constable standing outside the front entrance, he guessed (and guessed correctly) that at last he was alone. He moved silently up the carpeted staircase and let himself into the room that faced the first landing; there was just one thing he had to do. Once inside the flat he fixed his rather ancient hearing-aid into his right ear (exactly as he'd done three days before), flicked over the lock on the Yale (a precaution he'd earlier omitted to take), and took from his pocket a newly-purchased screwdriver – a larger, shinier, more effective instrument than the one which had bored its way through Gilbert's spine. He'd known the truth, of course, on that previous visit; known it immediately he'd entered the main sitting-room. For, although the crates seemed all (quite properly) still unopened, from the mantelpiece Mercator's head had stared at him accusingly . . .

After performing his grisly task – it took him only a few minutes – he retraced his steps to the rear entrance and let himself out into the bright afternoon sunlight, where he promptly hailed a taxi. He saw the driver's eyes flick to the mirror as his hearing-aid began to oscillate; so he turned off the volume and took it out. It had served its purpose well today, and he put it away and sought to relax as the taxi threaded its way through the heavy traffic. But

323

324 THE SECOND INSPECTOR MORSE OMNIBUS

his mind could give him little rest . . . If only on that terrifying
day . . . But no! Awaiting Gilbert had been an almost certain early
retribution. Money! That was all that Gilbert had demanded – then
more money. An odd compulsion (as it appeared to the man in the
taxi); certainly when compared with the motivations that dominated
his own life – the harbouring of inveterate hatreds, and the almost
manic ambition, sometimes so carefully concealed, for some degree
of worldly fame.

'Here we are, sir: Paddington.'

Why Paddington? Why not Euston, or Victoria, or Liverpool
Street? Why *any* railway station? Perhaps it was the anonymity
of such a place – a place at which he could deposit the burden of
his sin that lay so heavily in the supermarket carrier-bag he tightly
clutched as he walked through the swing doors of the Station Hotel
and turned right to the gentlemen's toilet. No one else was there,
and he closed the door behind him in the furthest of the cubicles
that faced the open pissoir. Here, he lifted the plastic ring of the
lavatory seat, climbed on to the circular fixture and lifted the covering of the porcelain cistern. But the water-filled cavity was far too
narrow – and suddenly he was jerked into a frozen stillness, for he
heard the door-catch click in a nearby cubicle. Something had to
be done quickly. He felt inside the carrier-bag and took out a flat
package wrapped round with a copy of *The Times* – a package which,
judging from its shape, might have held two sandwiches, and which
now plopped into the water and sank immediately to the bottom of
the cistern.

Still carrying the bulk of his burden, he walked out of the hotel
into the main-line station, where he drifted aimlessly about until he
saw the planks and scaffolding at the furthest end of Platform One.
He made his way slowly along this platform, intermittently turning
his eyes upwards to take in Brunel's magnificent wrought-iron roof
that arched above him. He had already seen the skip – half-full
of building rubble and general rubbish . . . Apart from a solitary
orange-coated workman a few yards up the line, he was alone.
Suddenly turning, he dropped his bag into the skip and sauntered
back towards the unmanned ticket-barrier. He would have enjoyed
a pot of searing hot tea and a buttered scone in the cool lounge of the
Station Hotel, but he dared not trust himself. He was shaking visibly
and the sweat was cold upon his forehead. It was time to return to
base, to lie down awhile, to tell himself that the task he'd so much
dreaded was now accomplished – if not accomplished well.

Crossing over Praed Street, he walked down to the bottom of

Spring Street and entered a small hotel just off to the left. No one was on duty at the reception-desk, and he lifted the hinged board, took his key (Number 16) off its wall-hook, and climbed the stairs. Although he had now been in the same hotel for many days, he still felt some hesitation about which way up the key went in; and again, now, he fiddled and scraped a bit before opening the door and admitting himself to the small but neatly-furnished room. He took off his jacket, placed it at the bottom of the single bed, wiped his forehead with a clean white handkerchief from the antique wardrobe – and experienced a vast relief at finding himself safely back in this temporary home. The Gideon Bible, in its plum-coloured boards, still lay on the table beside the pillow; the window, as he had left it, was still half-open, providing easy access (he was glad of it!) to the fire-escape that zigzagged down the narrow side of the hotel to the mean-looking courtyard below. Turning round, he saw that the door to the wash-room was open, too, and he promised himself (but in a little while) a cool and guilt-effacing shower.

For the moment he lay down on top of the coverlet, with that curious amalgam of elation that springs from defiance of danger and knowledge of accomplishment. As a boy, he'd known it when climbing Snowdon with a Scout troop: for all the other boys, the route alongside one precipitous face had seemed a commonplace occurrence – yet for himself a source of great and secret pride . . . It was strange that he should only have experienced that marvellous elation again so very late in life, and then so often in such a short period of time . . . He closed his eyes, and almost moved his mind towards some neutral gear, untroubled, disengaged . . .

But only a minute later his body was jarred into panic-stricken dread. Someone was standing over him; someone who said 'Good afternoon' – and nothing more.

'You! *You!*'

His eyeballs bulged in fear and incredulous surprise, and if either of these emotions could be said to have been in the ascendant, perhaps it was that of surprise. But even as he cowered upon the coverlet, the packing twine was cutting deep into his neck; and soon his frantic spluttering and croaking grew quieter and quieter – until it was completely stilled. So died George Westerby, late Scholar and Senior Fellow of Lonsdale College in the University of Oxford.

Chapter Thirty-two

Saturday, 2nd August

It is a characteristic of the British people that they complain about their railways. In this case, however, there appears little justification for such complaint.

It was 9.50 a.m. the following morning when the winsome receptionist looked up from her desk and took the room-key.

'Nice morning again, Mr Smith?'

He nodded and smiled – that distinctively lop-sided smile of his. Since he'd been there, she'd almost always been on duty in the mornings; often, too, in the evenings, when she'd taken his order for an early-morning pot of tea – and also for *The Times*.

'I've got to leave this morning; so if you'll make out my bill, please?'

He sat down in one of the armchairs just opposite the reception desk, and breathed in very deeply. He'd spent another deeply troubled night, fitfully falling into semi-slumber, then waking up to find his blue pyjamas soaked in chilling sweat. Throughout these hours his head had thumped away as though some alien fiend were hammering inside his skull; and it was only after early tea that finally he'd slept a little while. He woke just after 9 a.m., his head still aching, yet now with a dulled and tolerable pain. For a few minutes he had lain there almost happily, upon the creased and tumbled pillow. But soon the same old host of thoughts was streaming through the portals of his brain, his eyeballs rolling round beneath the shuttered lids. And one thought fought a leading way through all the crowd – and one decision was made.

'Mr Smith? Mr *Smith*?'

He heard her, and rose to pay the bill. Sometimes (as well he knew) his brain could play him false; but this particular contingency he had anticipated, and he paid his dues with ready cash, in notes of high denomination.

He left the Station Hotel (as Westerby had done before him) and walked to the ticket-office. Then, for many minutes, he stood in front of the high departures-board. But he could read nothing. His eyes no sooner focused on the times of trains for Oxford than the letters (white) upon their background (black) had leap-frogged astigmatically across his retina, leaving him in dizzied indecision.

He stepped to the nearest ticket-barrier.

'Can you tell me my best bet for Oxford, please?'

'Platform 9. Half-past ten. But you'll have to—'

'Thank you.'

The train was already in the platform and he pulled himself up into an empty first-class compartment, putting his ticket carefully into his wallet and leaning back against the head-rest . . .

Half an hour later he jerked forward as the train halted with something less than silken braking-power, and he looked out of the window: Reading. Still the solitary occupant of the compartment, he leant back again and closed his wearied eyes. Not long . . . and he'd be there!

Thirty-five minutes later he was jerked to a second awakening.

'Tickets, please!'

He was gratified that he could find his ticket so easily, but his head was throbbing wildly.

'This your ticket, sir?'

'Yes. Why?'

'I'm afraid you've missed your connection. We've just gone past Didcot. You're on your way to Swindon.'

'What? I don't understand—'

'You should have changed at Didcot for the Oxford train. You must have nodded off.'

'But I've got to get to Oxford. I've – I've just *got* to get there.'

'Nothing we can do, sir. You'll have to get the next train back from Swindon—'

'But it's urgent!'

'As I say, you'll just have to wait till we get to Swindon.' The collector punched the ticket and handed it back. 'We won't worry about any excess fare, sir. Genuine mistake, I'm sure.'

The next few minutes registered themselves in his mind as an aeon of frenzied agony. Sitting forward in his seat, he bit deep into the nails of his little fingers, fighting with all his powers to keep control of a brain that stood unsurely on a precipice.

Then the train stopped – more gently this time.

He was glad to find his legs steady as he got to his feet, and he felt much calmer now. He put the sweat-soaked handkerchief away inside his trouser-pocket, took his case from the luggage-rack, opened the left-hand door of the carriage – and stepped down into nothing. He fell on to the sharp stones of a slight embankment on the south side of the line, and lay there hurt and wholly puzzled. Yet, strangely, he felt profoundly comfortable there: it seemed so easy now to sleep. The sun was blazing down from the clear-blue sky, and his head – at last! – was free from pain.

'You all right, sir?'

The ticket-collector was crouching beside him, and he heard some faintly-sounding voices from afar.

'I'm sorry . . . I'm sorry . . .'

'Let me just help you up, sir. You'll be all right.'

'No! Please don't bother. I'm just sorry, that's all . . .'

He closed his eyes. But the sun was blazing still beneath his eyelids, glowing like some fiery orange, whirring and – ever larger – spinning down towards him.

But still there was no pain.

'I'll go and get some help, sir. Shan't be a minute.'

The ticket-collector vaulted nimbly up the shallow embankment, but already it was too late.

'Before you do that, please do one thing for me. I want to get a message to a Chief Inspector Morse – at the Thames Valley Police Headquarters. Please tell him I was – I was on my way to see him. Please tell him that *I* did it – do you understand me? Please tell him . . . that . . .'

But the man beside the track was speaking to himself; and even the curious heads that poked through nearby carriage-windows could make no sense of all the mumbled words.

Suddenly the sun exploded in a yellow flash and a jagged, agonising pain careered across his skull. With a supreme effort of will he opened his eyes once more; but all was dark now, and the sweat was pouring down his face and seeping inside his gaping mouth. He *had* a handkerchief, he knew: it was in his trouser-pocket. But he wanted a clean one. Yes, he had plenty of clean ones. Why, he'd only bought a box of Irish-linen ones so very recently . . . from the shop in the Turl . . . only a hundred yards away from Lonsdale College . . .

Another man now knelt beside the body – a young neuro-surgeon who was travelling up to Swindon General Hospital. But he could do nothing; and after a little while he looked up at the ticket-collector – then slowly shook his head.

Chapter Thirty-three

Saturday, 2nd August

Whose was the body found in the Thrupp canal? It becomes increasingly clear now that there are very few contenders remaining.

In recent years Lewis had seldom spent two nights away from Oxford, and he didn't care much for London. But it had been a busy and a fruitful time.

Late the previous Wednesday afternoon, Morse had insisted that it was to be he, Lewis, who should drive up the next morning. There was much to do (Morse had said): many loose ends to tie up; statements to be taken; and, not least, some needful explanations to be made. So Lewis had taken his instructions, had performed them more than adequately, and now (indulging his one real weakness in life) was driving far too fast along the M40 back to Oxford. It was mid-morning.

His London colleagues had been a friendly bunch, most of them speaking in a careless, aitchless Cockney – yet all of them shrewd and competent men. They could forgive Morse readily, of course, but none of them seemed to understand his actions very well. And Lewis, himself being only semi-enlightened, was unable to throw much further light. But certain things were now clear. The man found murdered in the top-storey flat in Cambridge Way was Alfred Gilbert, Esq., estate agent, and late bachelor of some parish or other in central London. The murder weapon (so plain for all to see!) had been the screwdriver so conveniently found at the scene of the crime, upon whose handle were some smudgy prints that might or (as Lewis hoped) might not be soon identifiable. For the present there were few other clues. Of 'Mr Hoskins' the police could find no trace, nor expected to do so, since the residents of Cambridge Way had always had a woman as their part-time concierge. But the police had been mildly mollified when Lewis had been able to produce Morse's description of the man – from his age to his height, from chest-measurement to weight, from the colour of his eyes to the size of his shoes.

After that, Lewis had done exactly as Morse had instructed. There had been three visits, three interviews, and three statements (slowly transcribed). First, the statement from the manager of the Flamenco Topless Bar; second, that from Miss Winifred Stewart, hostess at the Sauna Select; third, that from Mrs Emily Gilbert at her home in Berrywood Court. All three, in their various ways, had seemed to Lewis to be nervously defensive, and more than once he had found himself seriously doubting whether any of the trio was over-anxious to come completely clean. But Morse had blandly told him that any further investigations were not only futile but also quite unnecessary; and so he had ignored some obvious evasions, and merely written down what each had been prepared to tell him.

Then, without much difficulty, he'd been able to discover at least something about the Gilbert brothers. Albert and the late Alfred had been public partners in a property-cum-removals firm, and private partners in a company christened Soho Enterprises – the latter owning, in addition to the topless bar, two dubious book-shops and a small (and strictly members-only) pornographic cinema. The London police knew a good deal about these activities anyway and enquiries were still proceeding, but already it seemed perfectly clear that even sex was suffering from the general recession. Of which fact Lewis himself was glad, for he found the Soho area crude and sordid; and had the tempter looked along those streets, he could have entertained only the most desperate hope of pushing that broad and solid back through any of the doorways there. Finally, Lewis had been instructed to discover, if it were at all possible, the whereabouts of Albert Gilbert, Esq., although Morse had held out little prospect on that score – and Morse (as usual) had been right.

At the Headington roundabout Lewis was debating whether to call in for a few minutes and tell the missus he was safely home. But he didn't. He knew the chief would be waiting.

During the previous two days Morse had hardly over-exerted himself, fully recognising his own incompetence in such matters as mounting a man-hunt or supervising the search (yes – yet another one!) of the waters out at Thrupp. But he *had* done two things, in each case retracing the ground that Lewis had trodden before him. First, he had visited the Blood Transfusion Centre at the Churchill Hospital, where he asked to look through the current records; where after only a couple of minutes he nodded briefly; where he then asked to see the records for the previous five years, in this second instance spending rather longer before nodding again, pushing the drawers of the filing-cabinet to, thanking the clerk, and departing. Second, he'd driven down to the Examination Schools, where he spent more than an hour with the Curator, finally thanking him, too, and leaving with the contented look of a man who has found what he sought. Now, again, as he sat at his desk that Saturday morning, he looked contented – and with even better reason, for the call had come through at 9.30. He'd *known* there must be something in the waters of the Thrupp canal . . .

The sight of Lewis gladdened him even more. 'Get some egg and chips while you were away?'

Lewis grinned. 'Once or twice.'

'Well, let's hear from you. By the way, I hope you've noticed: hardly any swelling at all now, is there?'

Twenty minutes later the phone rang.

'Morse here. Can I help you?'

Lewis observed that the chief inspector's pale, ill-shaven face was tautening as he listened. Listened only; till finally he said, 'I'll be there as soon as I can,' and with a look of unwonted agitation slowly put the receiver down.

'What was all that about, sir?'

'That was London on the line – Westerby's just been found – he's been murdered – they found him this morning – in a bedroom near Paddington – strangled with packing-twine.'

It was Lewis's turn now to reflect with puzzlement on this troublous news. From what Morse had told him earlier, the case was almost over – with just a few arrests to come. So what on earth did *this* mean? But already Morse was on his feet and looking in his wallet.

'Look, Lewis! You just get those reports of yours sorted out and typed up – then get off home and see the missus. Nothing more for you today.'

'You sure there's nothing I can do?'

'Not got a couple of fivers to spare, have you?'

After Morse had left, Lewis rang his wife to say that he'd be in for a latish lunch. Then, beginning to get his documents in order, he reached for *Chambers Dictionary*: Morse was a fanatic about spelling.

The phone rang ten minutes later: it was the police-surgeon.

'Not there? Where the 'ell's he got to, then?'

'One or two complications in the case, I'm afraid.'

'Well, just tell the old bugger, will you, that the leg he's found would make the height about 5 foot 10 inches – 5 foot 11 inches. All right? Doesn't help all that much, perhaps, but it might cut out a few of the little 'uns.'

'*What* leg?' Lewis felt utterly confused.

'Didn't he tell you? Huh! Secretive sod, isn't he? He's had half a dozen divers out this last couple of days . . . Still, he was right, I suppose. Lucky, though! Just tell him anyway – if he comes back.'

'Perhaps he knew all the time,' said Lewis quietly.

The phone was going all the time now. A woman's voice was put through from the operator: but, no, she would speak to no one but Morse. Then Strange (himself, this time), who slammed down the receiver after learning that Morse had gone to London. Then another woman's voice – one Lewis thought he almost recognised: but she, too, refused to deal with any underling. Finally, a call came through from Dickson, on reception; a call that caused Lewis to jolt in amazement.

'You *sure*?'

'Yep. Swindon police, it was. Said he was dead when the ambulance got there.'

'But they're sure it's *him*?'

'That's what they said, Sarge – sure as eggs is eggs.' Lewis put down the phone. It would be impossible to contact Morse in transit: he never drove anything other than his privately-owned Jaguar. Would Morse be surprised? He'd certainly *looked* surprised about an hour ago on learning of the death of Westerby. So what about this? What about Dickson's latest information? That the body just recovered from a shallow embankment on the Didcot–Swindon railway-line was certainly that of Oliver Browne-Smith, late fellow of Lonsdale College, Oxford.

About the time that Lewis received his last call that morning, Morse was turning left at Hanger Lane on to the North Circular. He'd still (he knew) a further half-hour's driving in front of him, and with a fairly clear road he drove in a manner that verged occasionally upon the dangerous. But already he was too late. It had been a quarter of an hour earlier that the ambulance had taken away the broken body that lay directly beneath a seventh-storey window in Berrywood Court, just along the Seven Sisters Road.

* * *

Later the same afternoon, a business executive, immaculately dressed in a pin-striped suit, walked into the farthest cubicle of the gentlemen's toilet at the Station Hotel, Paddington. When he pulled the chain, the cistern seemed to be working perfectly, as though the presence of a pair of human hands as yet was causing little problem to the flushing mechanism.

Chapter Thirty-four

Monday, 4th August

In which Morse and Lewis retrace their journey as far as the terminus of the first milestone.

It was with growing impatience that Lewis waited from 8.15 a.m. onwards. Morse had arrived back in Oxford late the previous evening and had called in to see him, readily accepting Mrs Lewis's offer to cook him something, and thereafter settling down to watch television with the joyous dedication of a child. He had refused to answer Lewis's questions, affirming only that the sun would almost certainly rise on the morrow, and that he would be in the office – early.

At 9 a.m. there was still no sign of him, and for the umpteenth time Lewis found himself thinking about the astonishing fact that, of the four dubiously-associated and oddly-assorted men who had played their parts in the case, not *one* of them could now lay the slightest claim to be mistaken for the corpse that still lay in Max's deep-refrigeration unit: Browne-Smith had died of a brain haemorrhage beside a railway-track; Westerby had been strangled to death in a cheap hotel near Paddington; Alfred Gilbert had been found murdered in a room a couple of floors above Westerby's flat in Cambridge Way; and Albert Gilbert had thrown himself from a seventh-storey window in Berrywood Court. So the same old question still remained unanswered, and the simple truth was that they were running out of bodies.

But there *were* one or two items that Lewis had discovered

for himself, and at 9.30 a.m. he browsed through his neatly-typed reports once more. He'd learned, for example – from the manager of the topless bar – that Browne-Smith seemed to have been unaccountably slow in identifying himself by the agreed words: 'It's exactly twelve o'clock, I see.' Then (after applying a good deal of pressure) he'd learned from the same source that the ciné equipment had definitely not been returned to the bar the next day; in fact, it had been nearer a week before any of the bar-clients could indulge their voyeuristic fantasies again. There was a third fact, too: that neither the manager nor any of his hostesses had previously set eyes upon the man with the brownish beard who had sat beside the bar that fateful Friday when Browne-Smith had been tempted down from Oxford . . .

Morse finally arrived just before 9.45 a.m., his lower lip caked with blood.

'Sorry to be late. Just had her out. No trouble. Hardly felt a thing. "Decayed beyond redemption" – that's what the little fellow said.' He sat down expansively in his chair. 'Well, where do you want me to start?'

'At the beginning, perhaps?'

'No. Let's start before then, and get a bit of the background clear. While you were off gallivanting in London, Lewis, I called in to see your pal at the Examination Schools, and I asked him just one thing: I asked him what he thought were the potential areas for any crooked dealings in this whole business of the final lists. And he made some interesting suggestions. First, of course, there's the possibility of someone getting results ahead of the proper time. Now this isn't perhaps one of the major sins; but, as you told me yourself, all that waiting can become a matter of great anxiety: sometimes perhaps *enough* anxiety to make one or two people willing to pay – pay in *some* way – for learning results early. That's only the start of it, though. You see if there's some undergraduate who's *nearly* up to the first-class honours bracket, he's put forward for a viva-voce examination, but he's never told which particular part of his work he's going to be re-examined in. Now, if he *did* know, he'd be able to swot up on that side of things and get ready to catch all the hand-grenades they lobbed at him. Agreed? But let's go on a stage further. Our budding "First" would be an even shorter-odds favourite if he knew the *name* of the man who was going to viva him: he could soon find out this fellow's hobby-horses, read his books, and generally tune himself in to the right wavelength. Which leads on to the final consideration. If he did know exactly who it was who was going to settle his future, there'd always be the potential for a bit of *bribery* – the offer of money in return for that glowing recommendation for a "First". You see, Lewis? The whole process is full of loop-holes! I'm not saying anyone wriggles through 'em: I'm just telling you they're *there*. And, depending on what the rewards are, there might be a few susceptible dons who could feel tempted to go along with one or two suggestions, don't you think?'

Lewis nodded. 'Perhaps a few might, I suppose.'

'No "perhaps", Lewis – just a few *did*!'

Again Lewis nodded – rather sadly – and Morse continued.

'Then we found a corpse with a great big question-mark on the label round its neck.'

'It hadn't got a neck, sir.'

'That's true.'

'And there isn't a question-mark any longer?'

'Patience, Lewis!'

'But we had the letter to go on.'

'Even that, though. If we hadn't had a line on things to start with, the whole thing would have been a load of gobbledygook. Would *you* have made much of it without—'

'I wouldn't have made anything of it, anyway.'

'Don't underestimate yourself, Lewis – let me do it for you!'

'What about that blood-donor business?'

'Ah! Now if you've been a donor for a good many years you get a lot of little tiny marks—'

'As a matter of fact I got my gold badge last year – for fifty times, that is – in case you didn't know.'

'Oh!'

'So I don't really need you to tell me much about *that*.'

'But you *do*. Do you know when you have to pack up giving blood? What age, I mean?'

'No.'

'Well, you bloody should! Don't you read any of the literature? It's *sixty-five*.'

Lewis let the information sink in. 'You mean that Browne-Smith wouldn't have been on the current records . . .'

'Nor Westerby. They were both over sixty-five.'

'Ye-es. I should have looked in the old records.'

'It's all right. I've already checked. Browne-Smith *was* a donor until a couple of years ago. Westerby never: he'd had jaundice and that put him out of court, as I'm sure you'll know!'

'But the body *wasn't* Browne-Smith's.'

'No?' Morse smiled and wiped the blood gently from his mouth. 'Whose was it then?'

But Lewis shook his head. 'I'm just here to listen, sir.'

'All right. Let's start at the beginning. George Westerby is just finishing his stint at Lonsdale. He's looking for a place in London, and he finds one, and buys it. The estate agent tells him that all the removals from Oxford can easily be arranged, and that suits Westerby fine. He's got two places: his rooms in Lonsdale, and his little weekend cottage out at Thrupp. So Removals Anywhere come on to the scene – and the supremely important moment in the case arrives: Bert Gilbert notices the name opposite Westerby's rooms on T Staircase – the name of Dr O. M. A. Browne-Smith – the name of a man he'd always ranked among the legion of the damned – the man who'd been responsible for his younger brother's death.

'Now, very soon after this point – I'm sure of it! – we get a switch of brothers. Bert reports his extraordinary finding to his brother, and it's Alfred – by general consent the abler of the two – who now takes over. He finds out as much as he can about Browne-Smith, and devises a plan that makes it ridiculously easy for Browne-Smith to go along with things. He writes a letter on Westerby's typewriter – he's in Westerby's rooms whenever he likes now, remember – inviting Browne-Smith to do him a very small favour, and one that would entail no real compromise to Browne-Smith's academic integrity. This offer, as we know, was taken up, and off Browne-Smith goes to London. But we also know – because he told us – that Browne-Smith played his own cards with equal cunning. And in the end Gilbert's plan misfired – whatever that plan had been originally.

'Gilbert came into the room to find that Browne-Smith wasn't unconscious, as he'd expected. So they talked together straightaway; and it wasn't long before Gilbert discovered that the military records of young brother John were hardly a striking example of dedication to duty. In fact, far from being killed in action, he'd shot himself the night before El Alamein – and one of the few people who knew all this was Browne-Smith, John Gilbert's platoon officer. So when the whole story was out at last, there couldn't have been much wind left in the Gilberts' sails, because it was quite clear to them that Browne-Smith hadn't the slightest responsibility, direct or in-direct, for their brother's death! Now, at that point everything could have been over, Lewis. And if it had been, certainly four of the five people who've died in this case would still be alive. But . . .'

Yes, Lewis understood all this. It seemed simpler, though, now that Morse had put it into words. 'But then,' he said quietly, 'Browne-Smith saw the chance to duplicate—'

' "Replicate" – that's the word I'd use, Lewis.'

'—to replicate the process with Westerby.'

'That's it. That's the end of the first mile, and we're soon going to start on the second.'

'Off we go then, sir!'

'Do you fancy a cup of coffee?'

Lewis got to his feet. 'Any sugar?'

'Just a little, perhaps. You know it's a funny thing. There were no end of tins of coffee in Alfred Gilbert's flat, and not a single drop of alcohol!'

'Not everybody drinks, sir.'

' 'Course they do! He was just an oddball – that's for certain. And I'll tell you something else. When I was a lad I heard of a Methodist minister who was a bit embarrassed about being seen reading the Bible all the time – you know, on trains and buses. So he had a special cover made – a sort of cowboy cover with a gun-slinger on his horse; and he had this stuck round his Bible when he was reading Ezekiel or something. Well, I found a book in Gilbert's flat that was exactly the opposite. It had a cover on it called *Know Your Köchel Numbers*—'

'Pardon, sir?'

' "Köchel". He was the chap who put all Mozart's works into some sort of chronological order and gave 'em all numbers.'

'Oh.'

'I had a look in this book – and do you know what I found? It was a load of the lewdest pornography I've ever seen. I – er – I brought it with me, if you want to borrow it?'

'No, sir. You read it yourself. I—'

'I *have* read it.' The numbed lips were smiling almost guiltily: 'Read it twice, actually.'

'Did you find anything else in the flat?'

'Found a beard – a brownish beard. Sort of theatrical thing, stuck with Elastoplast.'

'That all?'

'Found a scarf, Lewis. Not quite so long as mine, but a nice scarf. Still, that was hardly a surprise, was it?'

'Just a little sugar, you say?'

'Well, perhaps a bit more than that.'

Lewis stood at the door. 'I wonder whether Gilbert had *his* tooth out.'

'Didn't need to, Lewis. He had false teeth – top and bottom.'

Chapter Thirty-five

Monday, 4th August

Gently we journey along the second mile, which appears to Morse to be adequately posted.

During the few minutes that Lewis was away, Morse was acutely conscious of the truth of the proposition that the wider the circle of knowledge the greater the circumference of ignorance. He was (he thought) like some tree-feller in the midst of the deepest forest who has effected a clearing large enough for his immediate purposes; but one, too, who sees around him the widening ring of undiscovered darkness wherein the wickedness of other men would never wholly be revealed. On his recent visit to London he had felled a few more trees; and doubtless he and Lewis (before the case was closed) would fell a few more still. But the men who might have directed his steps through the trackless forest were now all dead, leaving him with an odd collection of ugly, jagged stumps; ugly, jagged, awkward clues that could only tell a stark, truncated version of the truth. But that was all he had and – almost – it was enough, perhaps.

'Tell me more about the Gilberts,' said Lewis, handing across a paper cup of tepid coffee.

'Well, you know as much about their background as I do. Just remember one thing, though. We learned they were identical twins, so closely alike that even their friends got them muddled up occasionally. But when you get to your sixties, Lewis, you're bound to differ a bit: general signs of ageing, spots on the chin, gaps in the teeth, hair-style, scars, whether you're fatter or thinner, the way you dress – almost everything is going to mark some ever-widening difference as the years go by. Now, I never saw Bert Gilbert alive – and I didn't go and look at him when he was dead. You see, it was *Alfred* Gilbert I met in Westerby's rooms that day – with a scarf wrapped round the bottom half of his face and a phoney tale about an abscessed tooth.'

'He was frightened Browne-Smith would recognise him.'

'Not just that, though. As it happened, Browne-Smith had already recognised his brother – although Alfred Gilbert wasn't to know *that*. Like all visitors, Bert had already reported to the Porters' Lodge a couple of times, and Alfred was anxious that *no one* should know that he and his brother had switched roles. He carefully selected a young assistant who'd only just joined the firm and who wouldn't know and wouldn't care which brother did what anyway—'

'But why all the bother, sir? Seems so unnecessary.'

'Ah! But you're missing the point. The plan they'd concocted demanded far more shrewdness – and, yes, far more *knowledge* – than poor Bert could ever have coped with. Just think! It involved a close knowledge of Browne-Smith's position and duties in the college – and in the university. It involved an equally close knowledge of how final examinations work, and all the complicated procedures of results and so on. It's not *easy* to find all that stuff out. Not unless—'

'Unless *what*, sir?'

'When I went to London I found out quite a lot about Alfred Gilbert. He *wasn't* a bachelor. In fact, he was divorced about ten years ago, and his ex-wife—'

'I suppose you went to see her.'

'No. She's living in Salisbury – but I rang her up. They had one child, a son. Know what they christened him, Lewis?'

'John?'

Morse nodded. 'After the younger brother. He was a bright lad, it seems, won a place at Oxford to read Music, and got a very good "Second". In fact,' Morse continued with great deliberation, 'he had a viva for a "First".'

Lewis sat back in his chair. All the pieces seemed to be falling neatly into place – or almost all of them.

'Back to the main sequence of events, though. Browne-Smith went to London on Friday the 11th July, and that doesn't leave much time before most of the class-lists are due to be posted up. So if he decides – as he does – that he's going to repeat the broad outlines of the plan, he's got to get a move on. The Gilbert brothers had to be in on it, too, of course, and no doubt Browne-Smith agrees to pay them handsomely. There's no time for any chancy postal delay, so Browne-Smith drafts a careful letter to Westerby, and that letter, too, was probably written on Westerby's typewriter the next day, Saturday the 12th, when Alfred Gilbert went up to Oxford again, and when Westerby was out clearing up his odds and ends at Thrupp. The letter – "By Hand" it must have been – was left on Westerby's desk, I should think—'

'How do you know all this?'

'I don't really. But what I know for sure is that Westerby turned up at an address in London at 2 p.m. on Tuesday the 15th.'

'Not Cambridge Way, though, surely? That was his *own* address.'

'No – but Alfred Gilbert wasn't short of a few vacant properties, was he? And in fact it wasn't all that far from Westerby's flat, a little place—'

'Yes, all right, sir. Go on!'

'Now we come to the most fateful moment in the case. Westerby was given the same treatment as Browne-Smith: same pattern all through, same woman, same bottles of booze, with a few drops of chloral hydrate or something slipped in. But Westerby's not so canny as Browne-Smith was, and very soon he's lying there dead to the world on a creaking bed. *But what exactly happened then?* That's the key to the case, Lewis. Messrs. W and S are waiting outside—'

'*Who*, sir?'

'They're in your statement, Lewis – the men who made the arrangements at the topless bar. Haven't you heard of W. S. Gilbert?'

'Yes, but—'

'You know what "W. S." stands for, don't you? William Schwenck!'

'Oh.'

'You know, there's *something* to be said in the Gilberts' favour: at least they had a warped sense of humour. You remember the name Soho Enterprises is registered under?'

Lewis remembered: 'Sullivan!' He shook his head and then nodded. He knew he wasn't being very bright.

'Anyway,' continued Morse, 'Browne-Smith and Westerby are left alone. And when Westerby gradually comes round – with a splitting headache, I should think – he finds his age-long antagonist sitting on the bed beside him. And they talk – and no doubt soon they have a blazing row . . . and please remember that Browne-Smith's got his old army revolver with him! And yet . . . and yet, Lewis . . .'

'He doesn't use it,' added Lewis in a very quiet voice.

'No. Instead they stay there talking together for a long, long time; and finally they bring one of the Gilbert brothers in – and at that point the road is twisting again to take us forward on the third and final mile.'

Morse finished his coffee, and held out the plastic cup. 'I enjoyed that, Lewis. Little more sugar this time, perhaps?'

The phone rang whilst Lewis was gone. It was Max.

'Spending most of your time in Soho, I hear, Morse.'

'I'll let you into a secret, Max. My sexual appetite grows stronger year by year. What about yours?'

'About that leg. Lewis tell you about it?'

'He did.'

'Remember that piece you put in the paper? You got the colour of your socks wrong.'

'What do you expect. I hadn't got a leg to *go* on, had I?'

'They were purple!'

'Nice colour – purple.'

'With green-suede shoes?'

'You don't dress all that well yourself sometimes.'

'You said they were blue!'

'Just sticking the blinker out in the middle of a blizzard.'

'What? *What?*'

'I've not had your report yet.'

'Will it help?'

'Probably.'

'You know who it is?'

'Yes.'

'Want to tell me?'

So Morse told him; and for once the humpbacked man was lost for words.

THE SECOND INSPECTOR MORSE OMNIBUS

Chapter Thirty-six

Monday, 4th August

We near the end, with two miles and four furlongs of the long and winding road now completed.

'We found the body,' resumed Morse, 'on Wednesday the 23rd, and the odds are that it had been in the water about three days. So the man must have been murdered either the previous Saturday or Sunday.'

'He could have been murdered a few days before that, surely?'

'No chance. He was watching the telly on the Friday night!'

Lewis let it go. If Morse was determined to mystify him, so be it. He'd not interfere again unless he could help it. But one plea he did make. 'Why don't you simply tell me what you think happened – even if you're not quite sure about it here and there?'

'All right. A *third* man goes to London on Saturday the 19th, taking up an offer which nobody in this case seems able to refuse. This time, though, all the initial palaver is probably dispensed with, and there's no intermediary stop at the topless bar. This third man is murdered – by Browne-Smith. And if *both* the Gilberts were there, we've got four men on the scene with a body on their hands – a body they've got to get rid of. Of the four men, Westerby is wetting his pants with panic; and after a few tentative arrangements are made with him, he goes off – not, as we know, back to Oxford, but to a cheap hotel near Paddington. The other three – I think that Bert had probably kept out of the way while Westerby was still there – now confer about what can and what must be done. The body can't just be dumped anyhow and anywhere – for reasons that'll soon be clear, Lewis. It's going to be necessary, it's agreed, to sever the head, and to sever the hands. That gruesome task is performed, in London, by one of the Gilberts – I should think by Bert, the cruder of the pair – who promises Browne-Smith that the comparatively uncumbrous items he's just detached can be disposed of safely and without difficulty. Then two of the three, Browne-Smith and Bert Gilbert, drive off to Oxford in Westerby's Metro – and with Westerby's prior consent. It's probably the only car immediately available anyway; but it's got one incalculable asset, as you know, Lewis.

'Once in Oxford – this is late Sunday evening now – Browne-Smith lets himself into Lonsdale via the back door in the High and goes into his rooms and takes one item only – a suit. I'm pretty sure, by the way, that it must have been on a second trip to his rooms, later – after Westerby decided he'd little option but to cancel his Greek holiday – that he took the Lonsdale College stamp and one of his Macedonian postcards. Anyway, the two men drive out to Thrupp – the only likely stretch of water either of 'em can think of – where they stop, without any suspicion being roused, in Westerby's car, outside Westerby's cottage, to which Bert Gilbert has the key. Once inside with the body, Gilbert is willing (what he was paid for all this we shall never know!) to perform the final grisly task – of taking off the dead man's clothes and re-dressing him in Browne-Smith's suit. Then, long after the Boat Inn is closed, the two men carry the body the hundred yards or so along to the one point where no boats are moored or can be moored: the bend in the canal by Aubrey's Bridge. The job's done. It must have been in the early hours when the two of them get back to London, where the faithless Bert returns to his faithful Emily, and Browne-Smith to his room in the Station Hotel at Paddington. All right so far?'

'Are you making some of it up, sir?'

'Of course I bloody am! But it fits the clues, doesn't it? And what the hell *else* can I do? They're all *dead*, these johnnies. I'm just using what we *know* to fill in what we *don't* know. You don't object, do you? I'm just *trying*, Lewis, to match up the facts with the psychology of the four men involved. What do *you* think happened?'

Morse always got cross (as Lewis knew) when he wasn't sure of himself, especially when 'psychology' was involved – a subject Morse affected to despise; and Lewis regretted his interruption. But one thing worried him sorely: 'Do you really think Browne-Smith would have had the belly for all that business?'

'He wasn't a congenital murderer, if that's what you mean. But the one real mystery in this case is that one man – Browne-Smith – actually did so many inexplicable things. And there's more to come! What we've got to do, Lewis, is not to explain behaviour but to consider *facts*. And there's a very sad but also a very simple *factual* explanation of all this, as you know. I rang up a fellow in the Medical Library to learn something about brain-tumours, and he was telling me about the completely irrational behaviour that can sometimes result . . . Yes . . . I wonder just what Olive Mainwearing of Manchester actually *did* . . .'

'Pardon, sir?'

'You see, Lewis, we're not worried about his belly – we're worried about his *mind*. Because he acted with such a weird combination of envy, cunning, remorse, and just plain *ambivalence*, that I can't begin to fathom his motives.' Morse shook his head. 'I'll tell you one thing, Lewis. I'm just beginning to realise what a fine thing it is to have a mind like mine that's mainly motivated by thoughts of booze and sex – infinitely healthier! But let's go on. Just one more point about the body. Murderers aren't usually quite as subtle as people think; and you were absolutely right, as you know, when you mentioned that pleasure-cruiser off the Bahamas or somewhere. In Max's first report he said the legs were sheared off far more neatly than the other bits – and it's now clear that a boat-propeller hit the body and lopped the legs off. Well done!'

Lewis remained silent, deciding not to raise the subject of the corpse's socks.

'Back to Browne-Smith. His actions that next week are even stranger in some ways. *Abyssus humanae conscientiae!*'

Again, even more praiseworthily, Lewis remained silent.

'On the Monday his conscience was crucifying him, and he writes me – *me* – a long letter. I just don't know why we had the devious delivery through the bank . . . unless he thought he'd be giving himself a few days' grace in which he could cancel his confession. Because that's what it was. But it was something else, too. If you read the letter carefully, it contains a much more subtle message: in spite of vilifying Westerby throughout, it completely and deliberately exonerates him! And make no mistake; it was certainly Browne-Smith himself who wrote that letter. I *knew* him, and no one else could have caught that dry, exact, pernickety style. It's almost as though with one half of his fevered brain he *wanted* us – wanted *me*, one of his old pupils – to find out the whole truth; and yet at the same time the other half of his brain was trying to stop us all the time with those messages and cards . . . I dunno, Lewis.'

'I think the psychologists have a word for that sort of thing,' ventured Lewis.

'Well we won't bother about that, will we!'

The phone rang in the ensuing silence:

'That's good . . . Well done!' said Morse.

'Can you describe them a bit?' asked Morse.

'Yes, I thought so,' said Morse.

'No. Not the nicest job in the world, I agree. It'll be all right if I send my sergeant?' asked Morse.

'Fine. Tomorrow, then. And I'm grateful to you for ringing. It'll put a sort of finishing touch to things,' said Morse.

'Who was that, sir?'

'Do you know, there've been some thousands of occasions in my life when I've looked forward to a third pint of beer, but I can't ever recollect looking forward to a third cup of coffee before!'

He held out the plastic cup, and once more Lewis walked away.

Chapter Thirty-seven

Monday, 4th August

Morse almost completes his narrative of the main events – with a little help from his imaginative faculties.

Only recently had Morse encountered the use of the word 'faction' in the sense of a combination of fact and fiction. Yet such a combination was all he could claim in any convincing reconstruction of the final events of the present case. While Lewis was away, therefore, he reminded himself of the few awkward facts remaining that had to be fitted somehow into the puzzle: the fact that he had been forcibly (significantly?) detained for an extra half-hour after his interrogation of the manager of the topless bar; that the door of Number 29, Cambridge Way had (for what reason?) been finally opened to him; that the head of Gerardus Mercator had been prominently (accusingly?) displayed on the mantelpiece of Westerby's living-room; that an affluent Arab, doubtless a resident in the property, had looked round at him with such puzzlement (and suspicion?); and that somehow (via Browne-Smith?) Bert Gilbert had discovered Westerby's whereabouts in London, and (via the fire-escape?) managed to enter Westerby's room. Thus it was that when Lewis returned Morse was ready with his eschatology.

'The manager of the Flamenco, Lewis, has a wife, called "Racquel". When I got there, he tipped her the wink that something was seriously askew, and she made an urgent phone-call to "Mr Sullivan" – alias Alfred Gilbert – who in turn told her that whatever happened they'd got to keep me in the place for a while.

Why? Clearly because there was something that had to be done quickly, something that *could* be done quickly, before I turned up in Cambridge Way. The Gilberts, you see, were already collecting their pickings from Browne-Smith, but not as yet from Westerby. And so to remind Westerby that *he* was still up to his neck in hot water, too, they'd decided on a most appropriate niche for a corpse's head – that space in one of Westerby's crates where another head had originally nestled. It was imperative, therefore, that one of the Gilberts – Alfred, as it turned out – should go and clear away the damning evidence waiting in Westerby's flat. But late that same morning Westerby himself decided that it was reasonably safe now for him to return to his flat, and the first thing he saw there was the head of Mercator on the mantelpiece, and he suspected the grim truth immediately. Which is more than I did, Lewis! When Alfred Gilbert let himself in, Westerby was probably just opening the fateful crate; and somehow Westerby killed him—'

'Sir! That's not good enough. *How* did he do it? And why should he *need* to do it? They were both accomplices, surely?'

Morse nodded. 'Yes, they were. But just think a minute, Lewis, and try to picture things. Alfred Gilbert is in a frenetic rush to reach Cambridge Way. He doesn't know *why* the police have got on to Cambridge Way, but he does know what they'll find if they visit Westerby's flat. They'll find what he himself and his brother have left there, almost certainly with the intention of some future blackmail. And, as I say, that evidence has got to be removed with the utmost urgency. So he lets himself into the flat, never expecting to find Westerby there, and never, I suspect, actually seeing him anyway. Westerby's got his hearing-aid plugged in, although, as your own notes say, Lewis, he's only slightly deaf; and when he hears the scrape of the key in the lock, he beats a panic-stricken retreat into the bathroom, where he watches the intruder through the hinged gap of the partially open door.

'Now Westerby himself hasn't the faintest idea that the police are on their way, has he? What he *suspects* – what he's been strongly suspecting even before opening the crate – is that it's been Gilbert – who else? – who's misled him so wickedly. Instead of Gilbert getting rid of the murdered man's head, that same head is resting even now in one of his own crates! He's just found it! I think he sees in a flash how crude, how indescribably callous, his so-called accomplice has been. He sees something else, too, Lewis. He sees Gilbert walking straight over to the crate, and at that point he *knows* who it is who's been plotting to implicate him further – doubtless for even more money – in this tragic and increasingly hopeless mess. He feels in his soul a savage compulsion to rid himself of that fiend who's kneeling over the crate, and he creeps back into the room and with all the force he can muster he stabs his screwdriver between those shoulder-blades.

'Then? Well, I can only guess that Westerby must have dragged him into the bathroom straightaway: because while there were no blood-stains on the carpet, the bathroom floor had only just been cleaned. Yes, I saw that, Lewis!

'Next, using the bunch of keys he found in Gilbert's pocket, Westerby took the body up in the lift to the top-floor flat – a flat he knew was still vacant – a flat he'd probably looked over himself when he was deciding on his future home. He locked away the body in a cupboard there, then went down again, cleaned up his own flat in his apron, and heard – at last! – someone ringing the main door-bell – me! – and *answered* it. *Why*, Lewis? Surely that's utter folly for him! Unless – unless he'd previously arranged to *meet* someone in Cambridge Way. And the only man he'd have been anxious to meet at that point is the one man he's been avoiding like the plague for the last five years of his life – Browne-Smith! But instead – he finds *me*! And he now gives the performance of his life – impersonating a concierge called "Hoskins". You knew, Lewis, he was a Londoner? Yes. It's in your admirable notes on the man. I ought to have seen through the deception earlier, though; certainly I ought to have read the signs more intelligently when one of the tenants turned round and stared so curiously at me. But it *wasn't* just me: he was staring at *two* strangers!

'During that same lunchtime there were other things afoot. Alfred Gilbert had left a message for his brother, and now it was Bert Gilbert who got round to Cambridge Way as quickly as he could. There – I'm almost sure of it! – he met Browne-Smith; and Browne-Smith told Bert Gilbert that he'd seen *me* go in, admitted by Westerby. At that moment, Bert must have seen the emergency signals flashing at full beam. He had no key – Alfred had taken the bunch – either to the front door or the back; so the two of them agreed to split up, with Browne-Smith watching the front and Bert Gilbert the back. What happened then? Gilbert saw Westerby leave! So he went round to tell Browne-Smith; and both of them were very puzzled, and very frightened. *I* was still in there, and so was Alfred Gilbert! Probably it was at that point that Bert Gilbert got to know from Browne-Smith where Westerby was staying, because it's clear that later on he *did* know. For the moment, however, they

observed from a discreet distance – only to find that I didn't come
out before the police went *in*. So they knew something had gone
terribly wrong. Later, of course, they both learned of the murder
of Alfred Gilbert, and they both drew their own conclusion – the
same conclusion.

'In the days that followed Gilbert must have watched and
waited, because he knew that it would now be imperative for
Westerby to return to the flat to find out, one way or the
other, whether the police had discovered those objects hidden in
a relidded crate – objects, Lewis, which must have been a cause
of recurrent nightmares to him. When Westerby finally risked his
expedition, Gilbert made no attempt to abort the mission, because
it was just as valuable for himself as for Westerby. He followed his
quarry back from the flat to Paddington – for all I know he might
even have followed him into the gents where the London lads found
the corpse's hands. By the way, Lewis, you'd better tell the missus
you've got another trip tomorrow.

'But then Gilbert stopped tailing Westerby, and went along to
that nearby hotel, where he found an easy access to Westerby's room
– either by the fire-escape or by the seldom-tenanted reception desk.
But let's leave those details to our metropolitan colleagues, shall we?
They're going to find one or two people who saw something, surely?
It's not our job. After Westerby got back to his room? Well, I
dunno. But I'd like to bet that Westerby almost jumped out of
his wilting wits when he found himself confronted by the man he
thought he'd killed! You see, I doubt if at any stage Westerby was
aware that there *were* two Gilberts – even less that they were still
extraordinarily alike in physical appearance. Whatever the truth of
that may be, Westerby was strangled in his room, and the long and
tragic sequence of events has almost run its Aeschylean course.

'Not quite though. Browne-Smith had now decided that things
had gone far too far, and I vaguely suspect that he was on his way
to see *me* last Saturday. At least, we've got the evidence of the
ticket-collector that Browne-Smith had some very urgent business
here in Oxford. Pity . . . but perhaps it was for the best, Lewis.
Then, the same Saturday, Bert Gilbert went home and found –
as the police found – a note from his wife, Emily, saying that she
couldn't stand any more of it, and that she'd left him. And Bert
Gilbert – without any doubt the bravest of the three brothers – now
faced both the fear of discovery and the knowledge of failure. So he
opened his seventh-floor window – and he jumped . . . Poor sod!
Perhaps you think it's a bit out of character, Lewis, for Bert Gilbert

to do something as cowardly as that? But it was in the family, if you remember . . .'

During this account, Morse had forgotten his coffee, and he now looked down with distaste at the dark brown skin that had formed on its surface.

'Are the pubs open yet?' he asked.

'As always, sir, I think you know the answers to your own questions better than I do.'

'Well, they will be, I should think, by the time we get to Thrupp. Yes, we're going to have a quiet little drink together, my old friend, at the end of yet another case.'

'But you haven't told me yet—'

'You're quite right. There's one big central jigsaw-piece that's missing, isn't there?'

Chapter Thirty-eight

Monday, 4th August

The Third Milestone

In normal circumstances, thought Lewis, Morse would have looked a good deal happier as he mumbled 'Cheers' before burying his nose in the froth; but there was a sombre expression in the chief's face as he spoke quietly across a small table in the lounge-bar of the Boat Inn.

'If this case ever comes to court, Lewis, there'll be several crucial witnesses – but the most important of all of them will be the man who tries to tell the judge about the power of hatred that can spring from thwarted ambition; and there were two men in Lonsdale College who had exemplified that terrible hatred for many years.

'The particular reason for their hatred was an unusual one, perhaps – but also an extremely simple one. Each of them had failed to be elected to the Mastership of Lonsdale, the position they'd both craved. Now, as we found out, the college rules require a minimum of six of the eight votes available to be cast in favour of any candidate, and not a single vote against. So a man would be elected with six votes in his favour and two abstentions – but not with one abstention, *and one against*. Which, in Browne-Smith's case, is exactly what happened! Again, in Westerby's case, it's exactly what happened! So you hardly need to be a roaring genius to come up with the explanation that Westerby had probably voted against Browne-Smith, and Browne-Smith against Westerby. Hence the mutual, simmering hatred of those two senior fellows.

'But let me tell you a very strange thing, Lewis. In fact, you *do* need to be a genius to understand it! Not so much now, of course – but certainly at any earlier point in the case. Let's recap. The first man who went to London was confronted with a ghost from his past – the ghost of cowardice in war. But it was *the wrong ghost* that the Gilbert brothers conjured up that day, because Browne-Smith had nothing whatsoever to do with the death of their younger brother. Then a second man went to London, and you know what I'm going to say, don't you, Lewis? He, too was confronted with *the wrong ghost* from his own past. Westerby had *not* voted against Browne-Smith – he'd abstained. And, in turn, Westerby learned that Browne-Smith had *not* cast the solitary vote against his own election: he, too, had abstained. Yet *someone* had voted against each of them; and as they spoke together that night in London the blindingly obvious fact must have occurred to them – that it could well have been *the same man* in each case! And if it was, then they knew beyond any reasonable doubt exactly who that man must be!

'So we find a third man going to London to face his own particular ghost – this time *the right ghost*. And soon a man is found in the canal here: a man minus a very distinguished-looking head that was framed with a luxuriant crop of grey hair; a man minus the hands – particularly minus the little finger of his left hand on which he wore the large, onyx dress-ring that he never took off, and which his murderers couldn't remove from his fleshy finger; a man minus one of those flamboyant suits of his that were famed throughout the university; a man, Lewis, who had voted against two of his colleagues in the last election for the Mastership; a man – *the* man – who by his own machinations had finally been adopted as a compromise, third-choice candidate, and duly elected *nem. con.*; the man whose own ambition was even greater than that of his other colleagues, and his practical cunning infinitely more so; the same man who at the beginning of the case invited me to try to find out what had happened to Browne-Smith – not because he was worried, but because it was his *duty* – as Head of House! Yes, Lewis! The man we found in the water here was the *Master of Lonsdale.*'

Chapter Thirty-nine

A Premature Epilogue

At the end of the Michaelmas term that followed the events recorded in these chapters, it was no great surprise for Morse (or indeed for anyone) to hear that the man whom Dr Browne-Smith had once described as 'quite a good young man' had been elected to the Mastership of Lonsdale. More of a surprise for Morse was subsequently to receive an invitation to a buffet supper in Lonsdale to celebrate Andrews' election. And, without enthusiasm, he went.

Little was said that night about the tragic past, and Morse mingled amiably enough with the college members and their guests. The food was excellent, the wine plentiful; and Morse was just on his way out, feeling that after all it hadn't been so bad, when an extraordinarily attractive woman came up to him – a woman with vivacious eyes and blonde hair piled up on her head.

'You're Chief Inspector Morse, I think.'

He nodded, and she smiled.

'You don't know me, but we spoke on the phone once – only once! I, well, I just thought I'd like to say "hello", that's all. I'm the college secretary here.' Her left hand went up to her hair to re-align a straying strand – a hand that wore no ring.

'I'm awfully sorry about that! I sometimes get a bit cross, I'm afraid.'

'I did notice, yes.'

'You've forgiven me?'

'Of course! You're a bit of a genius, aren't you? Your sergeant thinks so, anyway. And some geniuses are a bit – well, sort of unusual, so they tell me.'

'I wish I'd spoken to you nicely.'

She smiled once again – a little sadly: 'I'm glad I've seen you.' Then, brightly: 'You enjoying yourself?'

'I am now.'

For a few seconds their eyes met, and Morse was reminded of some of the great lost days and a face that shone beyond all other faces.

'Would you like some coffee, Inspector?'

'Er, no. No thanks.'

A tall, gangling, bespectacled man in his mid-thirties had joined them.

'Ah, Anthony! Let me introduce you to Chief Inspector Morse!'

Morse shook the man's limp hand, and looked upon him briefly with distaste.

'Anthony's one of the Research Fellows here, and – and we're going to be married next term, aren't we, darling?'

Morse mumbled his congratulations, and after a few minutes announced that he must go. It was still only ten o'clock, and he could spend half an hour with himself in the Mitre. Red wine always made him a little sentimental – and more than a little thirsty.

Chapter Forty

The Final Discovery

The head of Gerardus Mercator (as indeed the whole of Westerby's estate) was bequeathed to the fellows of Lonsdale, and that fine head is still to be seen in an arched recess on the east side of High Table.

And what of that other fine head? It was finally found in the early March of the following year by two twelve-year-old boys playing on a Gravesend rubbish-tip. How the head ever reached such a distant and unlikely site remains a minor mystery; but it posed no other problems. The notes of the pathologist who first examined the skull recorded signs of a massive haemorrhage in the chambers of the upper brain, doubtless caused by the bullet still embedded there. Later forensic tests were to show that this bullet had been fired from a .38 Webley pistol – the make of pistol issued to officers of the Royal Wiltshire Regiment serving in the desert in 1942.

Last Seen Wearing

for J.C.F.P. and J.G.F.P.

Prelude

The Train Now Standing at Platform One

He felt quite pleased with himself. Difficult to tell for certain, of course; but yes, quite pleased with himself really. As accurately as it could his mind retraced the stages of the day's events: the questions of the interviewing committee – wise and foolish; and his own answers – carefully considered and, he knew, well-phrased. Two or three exchanges had been particularly satisfactory and, as he stood there waiting, a half-smile played across his firm, good-humoured lips. One he could recall almost verbatim.

'You don't think you may perhaps be a bit young for the job?'

'Well, yes. It will be a big job and I'm sure that there will be times – that is if you should appoint me – when I should need the experience and advice of older and wiser heads.' (Several of the older and wiser heads were nodding sagely.) 'But if my age is against me, there isn't much I can do about it, I'm afraid. I can only say that it's a fault I shall gradually grow out of.'

It wasn't even original. One of his former colleagues had recounted it to him and claimed it for his own. But it was a good story: and judging from the quietly-controlled mirth and the muted murmurs of appreciation, apparently none of the thirteen members of the selection committee had heard it before.

Mm.

Again the quiet smile played about his mouth. He looked at his watch. 7.30 p.m. Almost certainly he would be able to catch the 8.35 from Oxford, reaching London at 9.42; then over to Waterloo; and home by midnight perhaps. He'd be a bit lucky if he managed it, but who cared? It was probably those two double whiskies that were giving him such a glowing sense of elation, of expectancy, of being temporarily so much in tune with the music of the spheres. He would be offered the job, he felt – that was the long and the short of it.

February now. Six months' notice, and he counted off the months on his fingers: March, April, May, June, July, August. That would be all right: plenty of time.

His eyes swept leisurely along the rather superior detached houses that lined the opposite side of the road. Four bedrooms; biggish gardens. He would buy one of those prefabricated greenhouses, and grow tomatoes or cucumbers, like Diocletian . . . or was it Hercule Poirot?

He stepped back into the wooden shelter and out of the raw wind. It had begun to drizzle again. Cars swished intermittently by, and the surface of the road gleamed under the orange streetlights . . . Not quite so good, though, when they had asked him about his short time in the army.

'You didn't get a commission, did you?'

'No.'

'Why not, do you think?'

'I don't think that I was good enough. Not at the time. You need special qualities for that sort of thing.' (He was getting lost: waffle on, keep talking.) 'And I was er . . . well, I just hadn't got them. There were some extremely able men joining the army at that time – far more confident and competent than me.' Leave it there. Modest.

An ex-colonel and an ex-major nodded appreciatively. Two more votes, likely as not.

It was always the same at these interviews. One had to be as honest as possible, but in a dishonest kind of way. Most of his army friends had been ex-public-schoolboys, buoyed up with self-confidence, and with matching accents. Second lieutenants, lieutenants, captains. They had claimed their natural birthright and they had been duly honoured in their season. Envy had nagged at him vaguely over the years. He, too, had been a public-schoolboy . . .

Buses didn't seem very frequent, and he wondered if he would make the 8.35 after all. He looked out along the well-lit street, before retreating once more into the bus-shelter, its wooden walls predictably covered with scrawls and scorings of varying degrees of indecency. Kilroy, inevitably, had visited this shrine in the course of his infinite peregrinations, and several local tarts proclaimed to prospective clients their nymphomaniac inclinations. Enid loved Gary and Dave loved Monica. Variant readings concerning Oxford United betrayed the impassioned frustrations of the local football fans: eulogy and urination. All Fascists should go home immediately and freedom should be granted forthwith to Angola, Chile and Northern Ireland. A window had been smashed and slivers of glass sparkled sporadically amid the orange peel, crisp-packets and Cola tins. Litter! How it appalled him. He was far more angered

by obscene litter than by obscene literature. He would pass some
swingeing litter laws if they ever made him the supremo. Even in
this job he could do something about it. Well, if he got it . . .

Come on, bus. 7.45. Perhaps he should stay in Oxford for the
night? It wouldn't matter. If freedom should be granted to Angola
and the rest, why not to him? It had been a long time since he
had spent so long away from home. But he was losing nothing
– gaining in fact; for the expenses were extremely generous. The
whole thing must have cost the Local Authority a real packet. Six
of them short-listed – one from Inverness! Not that *he* would get the
job, surely. Quite a strange experience, though, meeting people like
that. One couldn't get too friendly. Like the contestants in a beauty
competition. Smile and scratch their eyes out.

Another memory glided slowly back across his mind. 'If you were
appointed, what do you think would be your biggest headache?'

'The caretaker, I shouldn't wonder.'

He had been amazed at the uproariously delighted reception given
to this innocent remark, and only afterwards had he discovered that
the current holder of the sinecure was an ogre of quite stupendous
obstinacy – an extraordinarily ill-dispositioned man, secretly and
profoundly feared by all.

Yes, he would get the job. And his first tactical triumph
would be the ceremonial firing of the wicked caretaker, with the
unanimous approbation of governors, staff and pupils alike. And
then the litter. And then . . .

'Waitin' for a bus?'

He hadn't seen her come in from the far side of the shelter.
Below her plastic hat tiny droplets of drizzle winked from the
carefully plucked eyebrows. He nodded. 'Don't seem very frequent,
do they?' She walked towards him. Nice-looking girl. Nice lips.
Difficult to say how old she was. Eighteen? Even younger, perhaps.

'There's one due about now.'

'That's good news.'

'Not a very nice night.'

'No.' It seemed a dismissive reply, and feeling a desire to keep
the conversation going, he wondered what to say. He might just
as well stand and talk as stand and be silent. His companion was
clearly thinking along similar lines and showed herself the slicker
practitioner.

'Goin' to Oxford?'

'Yes. I'm hoping to catch the 8.35 train to London.'

'You'll be all right.'

She unfastened her gleaming plastic mac and shook the raindrops to the floor. Her legs were thin, angular almost, but well proportioned; and the gentlest, mildest of erotic notions fluttered into his mind. It was the whisky.

'You live in London?'

'No, thank goodness. I live down in Surrey.'

'You goin' all that way tonight?'

Was he? 'It's not far really, once you've got across London.' She lapsed into silence. 'What about you? You going to Oxford?'

'Yeah. Nothing to do 'ere.'

She must be young, surely. Their eyes met and held momentarily. She had a lovely mouth. Just a brief encounter, though, in a bus-shelter, and pleasant – just a fraction more pleasant than it should have been. Yet that was all. He smiled at her, openly and guilelessly. 'I suppose there's plenty to do in the big wicked city of Oxford?'

She looked at him slyly. 'Depends what you want, don't it?' Before he could ascertain exactly what she wanted or what extra-mural delights the old university city could still provide, a red double-decker curved into the lay-by, its near front wheel splattering specks of dirty-brown water across his carefully polished black shoes. The automatic doors rattled noisily open, and he stepped aside for the girl to climb in first. She turned at the hand rail that led to the upper deck.

'Comin' upstairs?'

The bus was empty, and when she sat down on the back seat and blinked at him invitingly, he had little option or inclination to do otherwise than to sit beside her. 'Got any cigarettes?'

'No, I'm sorry. I don't smoke.'

Was she just a common slut? She almost acted like one. He must look a real city gent to her: immaculate dark suit, new white shirt, a Cambridge tie, well-cut heavy overcoat, and a leather brief-case. She would probably expect a few expensive drinks in a plush four-star lounge. Well, if she did, she was in for a big disappointment. Just a few miles on the top of a Number 2 bus. And yet he felt a subdued, magnetic attraction towards her. She took off her transparent plastic hat and shook out her long dark-brown hair. Soft, and newly washed.

A weary-footed conductor slowly mounted the circular staircase and stood before them.

'Two to Oxford, please.'

'Whereabouts?' The man sounded surly.

'Er, I'm going to the station . . .'

She said it for him. 'Two to the station, please.' The conductor wound the tickets mechanically, and disappeared dejectedly below.

It was completely unexpected, and he was taken by surprise. She put her arm through his, and squeezed his elbow gently against her soft body. 'I 'spect he thinks we're just off to the pictures.' She giggled happily. 'Anyway, thanks for buying the ticket.' She turned towards him and gently kissed his cheek with her soft, dry lips.

'You didn't tell me you were going to the station.'

'I'm not really.'

'Where are you going then?'

She moved a little closer. 'Dunno.'

For a frightening moment the thought flashed across his mind that she might be simple-minded. But no. He felt quite sure that for the present time at least she had an infinitely saner appreciation of what was going on than he. Yet he was almost glad when they reached the railway station. 8.17. Just over a quarter of an hour before the train was due.

They alighted and momentarily stood together in silence beneath the *Tickets: Buffet* sign. The drizzle persisted.

'Like a drink?' He said it lightly.

'Wouldn't mind a Coke.'

He felt surprised. If she was on the look-out for a man, it seemed an odd request. Most women of her type would surely go for gin or vodka or something with a bigger kick than Coke. Who was she? What did she want?

'You sure?'

'Yes, thanks. I don't go drinkin' much.'

They walked into the Buffet, where he ordered a double whisky for himself, and for her a Coke and a packet of twenty Benson & Hedges. 'Here we are.'

She seemed genuinely grateful. She quickly lit herself a cigarette and quietly sipped her drink. The time ticked on, the minute hand of the railway clock dropping inexorably to the half hour. 'Well, I'd better get on to the platform.' He hesitated a moment, and then reached beneath the seat for his brief-case. He turned towards her and once again their eyes met. 'I enjoyed meeting you. Perhaps we'll meet again one day.' He stood up, and looked down at her. She seemed more attractive to him each time he looked at her.

She said: 'I wish we could be naughty together, don't you?'

God, yes. Of course he did. He was breathing quickly and

suddenly the back of his mouth was very dry. The loudspeaker announced that the 8.35 shortly arriving at Platform One was for Reading and Paddington only; passengers for . . . But he wasn't listening. All he had to do was to admit how nice it would have been, smile a sweet smile and walk through the Buffet door, only some three or four yards away, and out on to Platform One. That was all. And again and again in later months and years he was bitterly to reproach himself for not having done precisely that.

'But where could we go?' He said it almost involuntarily. The pass at Thermopylae was abandoned and the Persian army was already streaming through.

Chapter One

> Beauty's ensign yet
> Is crimson in thy lips and in thy cheeks,
> And death's pale flag is not advanced there.
>
> Shakespeare, *Romeo and Juliet*, Act V

Three and a half years later two men were seated together in an office.

'You've got the files. Quite a lot of stuff to go on there.'

'But he didn't get very far, did he?' Morse sounded cynical about the whole proposition.

'Perhaps there wasn't very far to go.'

'You mean she just hopped it and – that was that.'

'Perhaps.'

'But what do you want me to do? Ainley couldn't find her, could he?'

Chief Superintendent Strange made no immediate answer. He looked past Morse to the neatly docketed rows of red and green box-files packed tightly along the shelves.

'No,' he said finally. 'No, he didn't find her.'

'And he was on the case right from the start.'

'Right from the start,' repeated Strange.

'And he got nowhere.' Strange said nothing. 'He wasn't a fool, was he?' persisted Morse. What the hell did it matter anyway? A girl leaves home and she's never seen again. So what? Hundreds of girls leave home. Most of them write back to their parents before long – at least as soon as the glamour rubs off and the money has trickled away. Some of them don't come home. Agreed. Some of them never do; and for the lonely waiters the nagging heartache returns with the coming of each new day. No. A few of them never come home . . . Never.

Strange interrupted his gloomy thoughts. 'You'll take it on?'

'Look, if Ainley . . .'

'No. *You* look!' snapped Strange. 'Ainley was a bloody sight better policeman than you'll ever be. In fact I'm asking you to take on this case precisely because you're *not* a very good policeman. You're too airy-fairy. You're too . . . I don't know.'

But Morse knew what he meant. In a way he ought to have been pleased. Perhaps he was pleased. But two years ago. Two whole years! 'The case is cold now, sir – you must know that. People forget. Some people need to forget. Two years is a long time.'

'Two years, three months and two days,' corrected Strange. Morse rested his chin on his left hand and rubbed the index finger slowly along the side of his nose. His blue eyes stared through the open window and on to the concrete surface of the enclosed yard. Small tufts of grass were sprouting here and there. Amazing. Grass growing through concrete. How on earth? Good place to hide a body – under concrete. All you'd need to do . . . 'She's dead,' said Morse abruptly.

Strange looked up at him. 'What on earth makes you say that?'

'I don't know. But if you don't find a girl after all that time – well, I should guess she's dead. It's hard enough hiding a dead body, but it's a hell of a sight harder hiding a living one. I mean, a living one gets up and walks around and meets other people, doesn't it? No. My guess is she's dead.'

'That's what Ainley thought.'

'And you agreed with him?'

Strange hesitated a moment, then nodded. 'Yes, I agreed with him.'

'He was really treating this as a murder inquiry, then?'

'Not officially, no. He was treating it for what it was – a missing person inquiry.'

'And unofficially?'

Again Strange hesitated. 'Ainley came to see me about this

case several times. He was, let's say, uneasy about it. There were certain aspects of it that made him very . . . very worried.'

Surreptitiously Morse looked at his watch. Ten past five. He had a ticket for the visiting English National Opera performance of *Die Walküre* starting at half-past six at the New Theatre.

'It's ten past five,' said Strange, and Morse felt like a young schoolboy caught yawning as the teacher was talking to him . . . School. Yes, Valerie Taylor had been a schoolgirl – he'd read about the case. Seventeen and a bit. Good looker, by all accounts. Eyes on the big city, like as not. Excitement, sex, drugs, prostitution, crime, and then the gutter. And finally remorse. We all felt remorse in the end. And then? For the first time since he had been sitting in Strange's office Morse felt his brain becoming engaged. What *had* happened to Valerie Taylor?

He heard Strange speaking again, as if in answer to his thoughts.

'At the end Ainley was beginning to get the feeling that she'd never left Kidlington at all.'

Morse looked up sharply. 'Now I wonder why he should think that?' He spoke the words slowly, and he felt his nerve-endings tingling. It was the old familiar sensation. For a while he even forgot *Die Walküre*.

'As I told you, Ainley was worried about the case.'

'You know why?'

'You've got the files.'

Murder? That was more up Morse's alley. When Strange had first introduced the matter he thought he was being invited to undertake one of those thankless, inconclusive, interminable, needle-in-a-haystack searches: panders, pimps and prostitutes, shady rackets and shady racketeers, grimy streets and one-night cheap hotels in London, Liverpool, Birmingham. Ugh! Procedure. Check. Re-check. Blank. Start again. *Ad infinitum*. But now he began to brighten visibly. And, anyway, Strange would have his way in the end, whatever happened. Just a minute, though. Why now? Why Friday, 12 September – two years, three months and two days (wasn't it?) after Valerie Taylor had left home to return to afternoon school? He frowned. 'Something's turned up, I suppose.'

Strange nodded. 'Yes.'

That was better news. Watch out you miserable sinner, whoever you are, who did poor Valerie in! He'd ask for Sergeant Lewis again. He liked Lewis.

'And I'm sure,' continued Strange, 'that you're the right man for the job.'

'Nice of you to say so.'

Strange stood up. 'You didn't seem all that pleased a few minutes ago.'

'To tell you the truth, sir, I thought you were going to give me one of those miserable missing-person cases.'

'And that's exactly what I am going to do.' Strange's voice had acquired a sudden hard authority. 'And I'm not *asking* you to do it – I'm *telling* you.'

'But you said . . .'

'*You* said. I didn't. Ainley was wrong. He was wrong because *Valerie Taylor is very much alive.*' He walked over to a filing cabinet, unlocked it, took out a small rectangular sheet of cheap writing paper, clipped to an equally cheap brown envelope, and handed both to Morse. 'You can touch it all right – no fingerprints. She's written home at last.'

Morse looked down miserably at the three short lines of drab, uncultured scrawl:

Dear Mum and Dad,
   Just to let you know I'm alright so don't worry. Sorry I've not written before, but I'm alright. Love Valerie.

There was no address on the letter.

Morse slipped the envelope from the clip. It was postmarked Tuesday, 2 September, London, EC4.

Chapter Two

We'll get excited with Ring seat (10)
Clue from a Ximenes crossword puzzle

On the left-hand side sat a man of vast proportions, who had come in with only a couple of minutes to spare. He had wheezed his way slowly along Row J like a very heavy vehicle negotiating a very narrow bridge, mumbling a series of breathless 'thank yous' as each of the seated patrons blocking his progress arose and pressed hard back against the tilted seats. When he had finally deposited his bulk in the seat next to Morse, the sweat stood out on his massive brow, and he panted awhile like a stranded whale.

On the other side sat a demure, bespectacled young lady in a long purple dress, holding a bulky opera score upon her knee. Morse had nodded a polite 'good evening' when he took his seat, but only momentarily had the lips creased before reassuming their wonted, thin frigidity. Mona Lisa with the guts-ache, thought Morse. He had been in more exhilarating company.

But there was the magnificent opera to relish once again. He thought of the supremely beautiful love-duet in Act 1, and he hoped that this evening's Siegmund would be able to cope adequately with that noble tenor passage – one of the most moving (and demanding) in all grand opera. The conductor strode along the orchestra pit, mounted the rostrum, and suavely received the plaudits of the audience. The lights were dimmed, and Morse settled back in his seat with delicious anticipation. The coughing gradually sputtered to a halt and the conductor raised his baton. *Die Walküre* was under way.

After only two minutes, Morse was conscious of some distracting movement on his right, and a quick glance revealed that the bespectacled Mona Lisa had extricated a torch from somewhere about her person and was playing the light laterally along the orchestrated score. The pages crinkled and crackled as she turned them, and for some reason the winking of the flashlight reminded Morse of a revolving lighthouse. Forget it. She would probably pack it up as soon as the curtain went up. Still, it was a little annoying. And it was hot in the New Theatre. He wondered if he should take his jacket off, and almost immediately became aware that one other member of the audience had already come to a firm decision on the same point. The mountain on his left began to quiver, and very soon Morse was a helpless observer as the fat man set about removing his jacket, which he effected with infinitely more difficulty than an ageing Houdini would have experienced in escaping from a strait-jacket. Amid mounting shushes and clicking of tongues the fat man finally brought his monumental toils to a successful climax and rose ponderously to remove the offending garment from beneath him. The seat twanged noisily against the back rest, was restored to its horizontal position, and groaned heavily as it sank once more beneath the mighty load. More shushes, more clickings – and finally a blissful suspension of hostilities in Row J, disturbed only for Morse's sensitive soul by the lighthouse flashings of the Lady with the Lamp. Wagnerites were a funny lot!

Morse closed his eyes and the well-known chords at last engulfed him. Exquisite . . .

For a second Morse thought that the dig in his left rib betokened a vital communication, but the gigantic frame beside him was merely fighting to free his handkerchief from the vast recesses of his trouser pocket. In the ensuing struggle the flap of Morse's own jacket managed to get itself entrapped, and his feeble efforts to free himself from the entanglement were greeted by a bleak and barren glare from Florence Nightingale.

By the end of Act 1, Morse's morale was at a low ebb. Siegmund was clearly developing a croaking throat, Sieglinde was sweating profusely, and a young philistine immediately behind him was regularly rustling a packet of sweets. During the first interval he retreated to the bar, ordered a whisky, and another. The bell sounded for the start of Act 2, and he ordered a third. And the young girl who had been seated behind Morse's shoulders during Act 1 had a gloriously unimpeded view of Act 2; and of Act 3, by which time her second bag of Maltesers had joined the first in a crumpled heap upon the floor.

The truth was that Morse could never have surrendered himself quite freely to unadulterated enjoyment that night, however propitious the circumstances might have been. At every other minute his mind was reverting to his earlier interview with Strange – and then to Ainley. Above all to Chief Inspector Ainley. He had not known him at all well, really. Quiet sort of fellow. Friendly enough, without ever being a friend. A loner. Not, as Morse remembered him, a particularly interesting man at all. Restrained, cautious, legalistic. Married, but no family. And now he would never have a family, for Ainley was dead. According to the eye-witness, it was largely his own fault – pulling out to overtake and failing to notice the fast-closing BMW looming in the outside lane of the M40 by High Wycombe. Miraculously no one else was badly hurt. Only Ainley, and Ainley had been killed. It wasn't like Ainley, that. He must have been thinking of something else . . . He had gone to London in his own car and in his own free time, just eleven days ago. It was frightening really – the way other people went on living. Great shock – oh yes – but there were no particular friends to mourn too bitterly. Except his wife . . . Morse had met her only once, at a police concert the previous year. Quite young, much younger than he was; pretty enough, but nothing to set the heart a-beating. Irene, or something like that? Eileen? Irene, he thought.

His whisky was finished and he looked around for the barmaid. No one. He was the only soul there, and the linen wiping-towels were draped across the beer pumps. There was little point in staying.

He walked down the stairs and out into the warm dusking street. A huge notice in red and black capitals covered the whole of the wall outside the theatre: ENGLISH NATIONAL OPERA, Mon. 1 Sept – Sat. 13 Sept. He felt a slight quiver of excitement along his spine. Monday the first of September. That was the day Dick Ainley had died. And the letter? Posted on Tuesday, the second of September. Could it be? He mustn't jump to conclusions though. But why the hell not? There was no eleventh commandment against jumping to conclusions, and so he jumped. Ainley had gone to London that Monday and something must have happened there. Had he perhaps found Valerie Taylor at last? It began to look a possibility. *The very next day* she had written home – after being away for more than two years. Yet there was something wrong. The Taylor case had been shelved, not closed, of course; but Ainley was working on something else, on that bomb business, in fact. So why? So why? Hold it a minute. Ainley had gone to London on his day off. Had he . . . ?

Morse walked back into the foyer, to be informed by a uniformed flunkey that the house was sold out and that the performance was half-way through anyway. Morse thanked him and stepped into the telephone kiosk by the door.

'I'm sorry, sir. That's for patrons only.' The flunkey was right behind him.

'I *am* a bloody patron,' said Morse. He took from his pocket the stub for Row J 26, stuck it under the flunkey's nose and ostentatiously and noisily closed the kiosk door behind him. A large telephone directory was stuck awkwardly in the metal pigeon-hole, and Morse opened it at the As. Adderley . . . Allen . . . back a bit . . . Ainley. Only one Ainley; and in next year's directory, even he would be gone. R. Ainley, 2 Wytham Close, Wolvercote.

Would she be in? It was already a quarter to nine. Irene or Eileen or whatever she was would probably be staying with friends. Mother or sister, most likely. Should he try? But what was he dithering about? He knew he would go anyway. He noted the address and walked briskly out past the flunkey.

'Goodnight, sir.'

As Morse walked to his car, parked in nearby St Giles', he regretted his childish sneer of dismissal to this friendly valediction.

The flunkey was only doing his job. Just as I am, said Morse to himself, as he drove without enthusiasm due north out of Oxford towards the village of Wolvercote.

Chapter Three

A man is little use when his wife's a widow.
Scottish proverb

At the Woodstock roundabout, on the northern ring-road perimeter of Oxford, Morse took the sharp left fork, and leaving the motel on his right drove over the railway bridge (where as a boy he had so often stood in wonder as the steam locomotives sped thunderously by) and down the hill into Wolvercote.

The small village consisted of little more than the square stone-built houses that lined its main street, and was familiar to Morse only because each of its two public houses boasted beer drawn straight from the wood. Without being too doctrinaire about what he was prepared to drink, Morse preferred a flat pint to the fizzy keg most breweries, misguidedly in his view, were now producing; and he seldom passed through the village without enjoying a jug of ale at the 'King Charles'. He parked the Jaguar in the yard, exchanged a few pleasantries with the landlady over his beer, and asked for Wytham Close.

He soon found it, a crescented cul-de-sac no more than a hundred yards back along the road on the right-hand side, containing ten three-storey terraced residences (pompously styled 'town houses'), set back from the adopted road, with steep concreted drives leading up to the built-in garages. Two street lamps threw a pale phosphorescence over the open-plan, well-tended grass, and a light shone from behind the orange curtains in the middle-storey window of No 2. The bell sounded harsh in the quiet of the darkened close.

A lower light was switched on in the entrance hall and a vaguely-lineated shadow loomed through the frosted glass of the front door.

'Yes?'

'I hope I'm not disturbing you,' began Morse.

'Oh. Hullo, Inspector.'

'I thought . . .'

'Won't you come in?'

Morse's decision to refuse the offer of a drink was made with such obvious reluctance that he was speedily prevailed upon to reverse it; and sitting behind a glass of gin and tonic he did his best to say all the right things. On the whole, he thought, he was succeeding.

Mrs Ainley was small, almost petite, with light-brown hair and delicate features. She looked well enough, although the darkness beneath her eyes bore witness to the recent tragedy.

'Will you stay on here?'

'Oh, I think so. I like it here.'

Indeed, Morse knew full well how attractive the situation was. He had almost bought a similar house here a year ago, and he remembered the view from the rear windows over the green expanse of Port Meadow across to the cluster of stately spires and the dignified dome of the Radcliffe Camera. Like an Ackerman print, only alive and real, just two or three miles away.

'Another drink?'

'I'd better not,' said Morse, looking appealingly towards his hostess.

'Sure?'

'Well, perhaps a small one.'

He took the plunge. 'Irene, isn't it?'

'Eileen.'

It was a bad moment. 'You're getting over it, Eileen?' He spoke the words in a kindly way.

'I think so.' She looked down sadly, and picked some non-existent object from the olive-green carpet. 'He was hardly marked, you know. You wouldn't really have thought . . .' Tears were brimming, and Morse let them brim. She was quickly over it. 'I don't even know why Richard went to London. Monday was his day off, you know.' She blew her nose noisily, and Morse felt more at ease.

'Did he often go away like that?'

'Quite often, yes. He always seemed to be busy.' She began to look vulnerable again and Morse trod his way carefully. It had to be done.

'Do you think when he went to London he was, er . . .'

'I don't know what he went for. He never told me much about his work. He always said he had enough of it at the office without talking about it again at home.'

'But he was worried about his work, wasn't he?' said Morse quietly.

'Yes. He always was a worrier, especially . . .'

'Especially?'

'I don't know.'

'You mean he was more worried – recently?'

She nodded. 'I think I know what was worrying him. It was that Taylor girl.'

'Why do you say that?'

'I heard him talking on the phone to the headmaster.' She made the admission guiltily as if she really had no business to know of it.

'When was that?'

'About a fortnight, three weeks ago.'

'But the school's on holiday, isn't it?'

'He went to the headmaster's house.'

Morse began to wonder what else she knew. 'Was that on one of his days off—?'

She nodded slowly and then looked up at Morse. 'You seem very interested.'

Morse sighed. 'I ought to have told you straight away. I'm taking over the Taylor case.'

'So Richard found something after all.' She sounded almost frightened.

'I don't know,' said Morse.

'And . . . and that's why you came, I suppose.' Morse said nothing. Eileen Ainley got up from her chair and walked briskly over to a bureau beside the window. 'Most of his things have gone, but you might as well take this. He had it in the car with him.' She handed to Morse a Letts desk diary, black, about six inches by four. 'And there's a letter for the accountant at the station. Perhaps you could take it for me?'

'Of course.' Morse felt very hurt. But he often felt hurt – it was nothing new.

Eileen left the room to fetch the envelope and Morse quickly opened the diary and found Monday 1 September. There was one entry, written in neatly-formed, minuscule letters: 42 Southampton Terrace. That was all. The blood tingled, and with a flash of utter certitude Morse knew that he hardly needed to look up the postal district of 42 Southampton Terrace. He *would* check it, naturally; he would look it up immediately he got home. But without the slightest shadow of doubt he knew it already. It would be EC4.

He was back in his North Oxford bachelor home by a quarter to eleven, and finally discovered the street map of London, tucked neatly away behind *The Collected Works of Swinburne* and *Extracts from Victorian Pornography*. (He must put that book somewhere less conspicuous.) Impatiently he consulted the alphabetical index and frowned as he found Southampton Terrace. His frown deepened as he traced the given co-ordinates and studied the grid square. Southampton Terrace was one of the many side-streets off the Upper Richmond Road, south of the river, beyond Putney Bridge. The postal district was SW12. He suddenly decided he had done enough for one day.

He left the map and the diary on top of the bookshelf, made himself a cup of instant coffee and selected from his precious Wagner shelf the Solti recording of *Die Walküre*. No fat man, no thin-lipped woman, no raucous tenor, no sweaty soprano distracted his mind as Siegmund and Sieglinde poured forth their souls in an ecstasy of recognition. The coffee remained untouched then gradually grew cold.

But even before the first side was played through, a fanciful notion was forming in his restless brain. There was surely a very simple reason for Ainley's visit to London. He should have thought of it before. Day off; busy, preoccupied, uncommunicative. He'd bet that was it! 42 Southampton Terrace. Well, well! *Old Ainley had been seeing another woman, perhaps.*

Chapter Four

As far as I could see there was no connection between them beyond the tenuous nexus of succession.

Peter Champkin

In different parts of the country on the Monday following Morse's interview with Strange, four fairly normal people were going about their disparate business. What each was doing was, in its own way, ordinary enough – in some cases ordinary to the point of tediousness. Each of them, with varied degrees of intimacy, knew the others, although one or two of them were hardly worthy of any intimate acquaintanceship. They shared one common bond, however, which in the ensuing weeks would inexorably draw each of them towards the centre of a criminal investigation. For each of them had known, again with varied degrees of intimacy, the girl called Valerie Taylor.

Mr Baines had been second master in Kidlington's Roger Bacon Comprehensive School since its opening three years previously. Before that time he had also been second master, in the very same buildings, although then they had housed a secondary modern school, now incorporated into the upper part of a three-tier comprehensive system – a system which in their wisdom or unwisdom (Baines wasn't sure) the Oxfordshire Education Committee had adopted as its answer to the problems besetting the educational world in general and the children of Kidlington in particular. The pupils would be returning the following day, Tuesday, 16 September, after a break of six and a half weeks, for much of which time, whilst some of his colleagues had motored off to Continental resorts, Baines had been wrestling with the overwhelmingly complex problems of the timetable. Such a task traditionally falls upon the second master, and in the past Baines had welcomed it. There was a certain intellectual challenge in dovetailing the myriad options and combinations of the curriculum to match the inclinations and capacities of the staff available; and, at the same time (for Baines), a vicarious sense of power. Sadly, Baines had begun to think of himself as a good loser, a best man but never the groom. He was now fifty-five, unmarried, a mathematician. He had applied for many headships over the years, and on two occasions had been the runner-up. His last application had been made three and a half years ago, for the headship of his present school, and he thought he'd had a fairly good chance; but even then, deep down, he knew that he was getting past it. Not that he had been much impressed by the man they appointed, Phillipson. Not at the time, anyway. Only thirty-four, full of new ideas. Keen on changing everything – as if change inevitably meant a change for the better. But over the last year or so he had learned to respect Phillipson a good deal more. Especially after that glorious showdown with the odious caretaker.

Baines was sitting in the small office which served as a joint HQ for himself and for Mrs Webb, the headmaster's secretary – a decent old soul who like himself had served in the old secondary modern school. It was mid-morning and he had just put the finishing touches to the staff dinner-duty roster. Everyone was neatly fitted in, except the headmaster, of course. And himself. He had to pick up his perks from somewhere. He walked across the cluttered office clutching the handwritten sheet.

'Three copies, my old sugar.'

'Immediately, I suppose,' said Mrs Webb good-naturedly, picking up another sealed envelope and looking at the addressee before deftly slitting it along the top with a paperknife.

'What about a cup of coffee?' suggested Baines.

'What about your roster?'

'OK. I'll make the coffee.'

'No you won't.' She got up from her seat, picked up the kettle, and walked out to the adjacent cloakroom. Baines looked ruefully at the pile of letters. The usual sort of thing, no doubt. Parents, builders, meetings, insurance, examinations. *He* would have been dealing with all that if . . . He poked haphazardly among the remaining letters, and suddenly a flicker of interest showed in his shrewd eyes. The letter was lying face down and on the sealed flap he read the legend 'Thames Valley Police'. He picked it up and turned it over. It was addressed to the headmaster with the words PRIVATE AND CONFIDENTIAL typed across the top in bold red capitals.

'What are you doing going through my mail?' Mrs Webb plugged in the kettle and with mock annoyance snatched the letter from him.

'See that?' asked Baines.

Mrs Webb looked down at the letter. 'None of our business, is it?'

'Do you think he's been fiddling his tax returns?' Baines chuckled deeply.

'Don't be silly.'

'Shall we open it?'

'We shall *not*,' said Mrs Webb.

Baines returned to his cramped desk and started on the prefects' roster. Phillipson would have to appoint half a dozen new prefects this term. Or, to be more precise, he would ask Baines to give him a list of possible names. In some ways the head wasn't such a bad chap.

Phillipson himself came in just after eleven. 'Morning, Baines. Morning, Mrs Webb.' He sounded far too cheerful. Had he forgotten that school was starting tomorrow?

'Morning, headmaster.' Baines always called him 'headmaster'; the rest of the staff called him 'sir'. It was only a little thing, but it was something.

Phillipson walked across to his study door and paused by his secretary's desk. 'Anything important, Mrs Webb?'

'I don't think so, sir. There's this, though.' She handed him the letter marked 'Private and Confidential', and Phillipson, with a slightly puzzled frown upon his face, entered his study and closed the door behind him.

In the newly-appointed county of Gwynedd, in a small semi-detached house on the outskirts of Caernarfon, another school-master was acutely conscious that school restarted on the morrow. They had returned home only the previous day from a travesty of a holiday in Scotland – rain, two punctures, a lost Barclaycard and more rain – and there was a host of things to be done. The lawn, for a start. Benefiting (where he had suffered) from a series of torrential downpours, it had sprouted to alarming proportions during their absence, and was in urgent need of an instant crop. At 9.30 a.m. he discovered that the extension for the electric mower was not functioning, and he sat himself down on the back-door step with a heavy heart and a small screwdriver.

Life seldom seemed to run particularly smoothly for David Acum, until two years ago assistant French master at the Roger Bacon Comprehensive School in Kidlington, and now, still an assistant French master, at the City of Caernarfon School.

He could find no fault with the fittings at either end of the extension wire, and finally went inside again. No sign of life. He walked to the bottom of the stairs and yelled, his voice betraying ill-temper and exasperation, 'Hey! Don't you think it's about time you got out of that bloody bed?'

He left it at that and, back in the kitchen, sat down cheerlessly at the table where half an hour earlier he had made his own breakfast, and dutifully taken a tray of tea and toast upstairs. Ineffectually he tinkered once more with one of the wretched plugs. She joined him ten minutes later, dressing-gowned and beslippered.

'What's eating you?'

'Christ! Can't you see? I suppose you buggered this up the last time you hoovered – not that I can remember when that was!'

She ignored the insult and took the extension from him. He watched her as she tossed her long blonde hair from her face and deftly unscrewed and examined the troublous plugs. Younger than he was – a good deal younger, it seemed – he found her enormously attractive still. He wondered, as he often wondered, whether he had made the right decision, and once more he told himself he had.

The fault was discovered and corrected, and David felt better.

'Cup of coffee, darling?' All sweetness and light.

'Not just yet. I've got to get cracking.' He looked out at the overgrown lawn and swore softly as faintly-dotted lines of slanting drizzle formed upon the window-pane.

A middle-aged woman, blowzy, unkempt, her hair in cylindrical curlers, materialised from a side door on the ground floor; her quarry was bounding clumsily down the stairs.

'I want to speak to yer.'

'Not now, sweetheart. Not now. I'm late.'

'If yer can't wait now yer needn't come back. Yer things'll be in the street.'

'Now just a minute, sweetheart.' He came close to her, leaned his head to one side and laid a hand on each of her shoulders. 'What's the trouble? You know I wouldn't do anything to upset you.' He smiled pleasantly enough and there was something approaching an engaging frankness in his dark eyes. But she knew him better.

'Yer've got a woman in yer room, 'aven't yer?'

'Now there's no need for you to get jealous, you know that.'

She found him repulsive now, and regretted those early days. 'Get 'er out and keep 'er out – there's to be no more women 'ere.' She slapped his hands from her shoulders.

'She'll be going, she'll be going – don't worry. She's only a young chick. Nowhere to kip down – you know how it is.'

'Now!'

'What do you mean, "now"?'

'Now!'

'Don't be daft. I'm late already, and I'll lose the job if I ain't careful. Be reasonable.'

'Yer'll lose yer bed an' all if yer don't do as I tell yer.'

The youth took a dirty five-pound note from his hip pocket. 'I suppose that'll satisfy you for a day or two, you old bitch.'

The woman took the money, but continued to watch him. 'It's got to stop.'

'Yeah. Yeah.'

'How long's she been 'ere?'

'A day or two.'

'Fortnight, nearer, yer bleedin' liar.'

The youth slammed the door after him, ran down to the bottom of the road, and turned right into the Upper Richmond Road.

Even by his own modest standards, Mr George Taylor had not made much of a success of his life. Five years previously, an unskilled manual worker, he had accepted 'voluntary redundancy' money after the shake-up that followed the reorganisation of the Cowley Steel plant, had then worked for almost a year driving a bulldozer on the M40 construction programme, and spent the next year doing little but casual jobs, and drinking rather too much and gambling rather too much. And then that terrible row and, as a result of it, his present employment. Each morning at 7.15 a.m. he drove his rusting, green Morris Oxford from his Kidlington council house into the city of Oxford, down past Aristotle Lane into Walton Street, and over the concreted track that led through the open fields, between the canal and the railway line, where lay the main city rubbish dump. Each morning of the working week for the past three years – including the day when Valerie had disappeared – he had made the same journey, with his lunch-time sandwiches and his working overalls beside him on the passenger seat.

Mr Taylor was an inarticulate man, utterly unable to rationalise into words his favourable attitude towards his present job. It would have been difficult for anyone. The foul detritus of the city was all around him, rotten food and potato peelings, old mattresses, piles of sheer filth, rats and always (from somewhere) the scavenger gulls. And yet he liked it.

At lunch-time on Monday the fifteenth, he was sitting with his permanent colleague on the site, a man with a miry face ingrained with dirt, in the wooden hut which formed the only semi-hygienic haven in this wilderness of waste. They were eating their sandwiches and swilling down the thick bread with a dirty-brown brew of ugly-looking tea. Whilst his companion mused over the racing columns of the *Sun*, George Taylor sat silent, a weary expression on his stolid face. The letter had brought the whole thing back to the forefront of his mind and he was thinking again of Valerie. Had he been right to persuade the wife to take it to the police? He didn't know. They would soon be round again; in fact he was surprised they hadn't been round already. It would upset the wife again – and she'd been nothing but a bag of nerves from the beginning. Funny that the letter had come just after Inspector Ainley was killed. Clever man, Ainley. He'd been round to see them only three weeks ago. Not official, like, but he was the sort of bloke who never let anything go. Like a dog with a bone.

Valerie . . . He'd thought a lot of Valerie.

A corporation vehicle lumbered to a halt outside the hut, and George Taylor poked his head through the door. 'On the top side, Jack. Shan't be a minute.' He pointed vaguely away to the far corner of the tip, swallowed the last few mouthfuls of his tea and prepared for the afternoon's work.

At the far edge of the tip the hydraulic piston whirred into life and the back of the lorry tilted slowly down and its contents were deposited upon the sea of stinking refuse.

For Morse, this same Monday was the first day of a frustrating week. Another series of incendiary devices had been set off over the weekend in clubs and cinemas, and the whole of the top brass, including himself, had been summoned into urgent conclave. It was imperative that all available police personnel should be mobilised. All known suspects from Irish republicans to international anarchists were to be visited and questioned. The Chief Constable wanted quick results.

On Friday morning a series of arrests were made in a dawn swoop, and later that day eight persons were charged with conspiracy to cause explosions in public places. Morse's own contribution to the successful outcome of the week's enquiries had been virtually nil.

Chapter Five

She turned away, but with the autumn weather
Compelled my imagination many days,
Many days and many hours.
                    T. S. Eliot, *La Figlia Che Piange*

As he lay abed on Sunday, 21 September, Morse was beset by the nagging feeling that there was so much to be done if only he could summon up the mental resolve to begin. It was like deferring a long-promised letter; the intention lay on the mind so heavily that the simple task seemed progressively to assume almost gigantic proportions. True, he had written to the headmaster of the Roger Bacon Comprehensive School – and had received an immediate and helpful reply. But that was all; and he felt reluctant to follow it up. Most of his fanciful notions about the Taylor girl had evaporated during the past week of sober, tedious routine, and he had begun to suspect that further investigation into Valerie's disappearance would involve little more than an unwelcome continuation of similar sober and tedious routine. But he was in charge now. It was up to him.

Half-past nine already. His head ached and he resolved on a day of total abstinence. He turned over, buried his head in the pillow, and tried to think of nothing. But for Morse such a blessed state of nihilism was utterly impossible. He finally arose at ten, washed and shaved and set off briskly down the road for a Sunday morning newspaper. It was no more than twenty minutes' walk and Morse enjoyed the stroll. His head felt clearer already and he swung along almost merrily, mentally debating whether to buy the *News of the World* or the *Sunday Times*. It was the regular hebdomadal debate which paralleled the struggle in Morse's character between the Coarse and the Cultured. Sometimes he bought one; sometimes he bought the other. Today he bought both.

At half-past eleven he switched on his portable to listen to Record Review on Radio Three, and sank back in his favourite armchair, a cup of hot, strong coffee at his elbow. Life was good sometimes. He picked up the *News of the World*, and for ten minutes wallowed in the Shocking Revelations and Startling Exposures which the researchers of that newspaper had somehow managed to rake together during the past seven days. There were several juicy articles and Morse started on the secret sex-life of a glamorous Hollywood pussycat. But it began to pall after the first few paragraphs. Ill-written and (more to the point) not even mildly titillating; it was always the same. Morse firmly believed that there was nothing so unsatisfactory as this kind of half-way-house pornography; he liked it hot or not at all. He wouldn't buy the wretched paper again. Yet he had made the same decision so many times before, and knew that next week again he would fall the same silly sucker for the same salacious front-page promises. But for this morning he'd had enough. So much so that he gave no more than a passing glance to a provocative photograph of a seductive starlet exposing one half of her million-dollar breasts.

After relegating (as always) the Business News Section to the waste-paper basket, he graduated to the *Sunday Times*. He winced to see that Oxford United had been comprehensively trounced, read the leading articles and most of the literary reviews, tried unsuccessfully to solve the bridge problem, and finally turned to the Letters. Pensions, Pollution, Private Medicine – same old topics; but a good deal of sound commonsense. And then his eye caught a letter which made him sit bolt upright. He read it and a puzzled look came to his face. August 24? He couldn't have bought the *Sunday Times* that week. He read the short letter again.

> To the Editor. Dear Sir,
> My wife and I wish to express our deep gratitude to your newspaper for the feature 'Girls who run away from Home' (Colour Suppt. August 24). As a direct result of reading the article, our only daughter, Christine, returned home last week after being away for over a year. We thank you most sincerely.
> Mr and Mrs J. Richardson (Kidderminster)

Morse got up and went to a large pile of newspapers neatly bundled in string, that lay in the hallway beside the front door. The Boy Scouts collected them once a month, and although Morse had never been a tenderfoot himself he gave the movement his qualified approval. Impatiently he tore at the string and delved into the pile. Thirty-first August. Fourteenth September. But no 24 August. It may have gone with the last pile. Blast. He looked through again, but it wasn't there. Now who might have a copy? He tried his next-door neighbour, but on reflection he might have saved himself the bother. What about Lewis? Unlikely, yet worth a try. He telephoned his number.

'Lewis? Morse here.'

'Ah. Morning, sir.'

'Lewis, do you take the *Sunday Times*?'

"Fraid not, sir. We have the *Sunday Mirror*.' He sounded somewhat apologetic about his Sabbath-day reading.

'Oh.'

'I could get you a copy, I suppose.'

'I've got today's. I want the copy for August the twenty-fourth.'

It was Sergeant Lewis's turn to say, 'Oh.'

'I can't really understand an intelligent man like you, Lewis, not taking a decent Sunday newspaper.'

'The sport's pretty good in the *Sunday Mirror*, sir.'

'Is it? You'd better bring it along with you in the morning, then.'

Lewis brightened. 'I won't forget.'

Morse thanked him and rang off. He had almost said he would swap it for his own copy of the *News of the World*, but considered it not improper to conceal from his subordinates certain aspects of his own depravity.

He could always get a back copy from the Reference Library. It could wait, he told himself. And yet it couldn't wait. Again he read the letter from the parents of the prodigal daughter. They would be extra pleased now, with a letter in the newspaper, to boot. Dad would probably cut it out and keep it in his wallet – now that the family unit was functioning once more. We were all so vain. Cuttings, clippings and that sort of thing. Morse still kept his batting averages somewhere . . .

And suddenly it hit him. It all fitted. Four or five weeks ago Ainley had resurrected the Taylor case of his own accord and pursued it in his own spare time. Some reporter had been along to Thames Valley Police and got Ainley to spill the beans on the Taylor girl. Ainley had given him the facts (no fancies with Ainley!) and somehow, as a result of seeing the facts again, he had spotted something that he had missed before. It was just like doing a crossword puzzle. Get stuck. Leave it for ten minutes. Try again – and eureka! It happened to everyone like that. And, he repeated to himself, *Ainley had seen something new.* That must be it.

As a corollary to this, it occurred to Morse that if Ainley had taken a hand in the article, not only would Valerie Taylor have been one of the missing girls featured, but Ainley himself would almost certainly have kept the printed article – just as surely as Mr J. Richardson would be sticking his own printed letter into his Kidderminster wallet.

He rang Mrs Ainley. 'Eileen?' (Right this time.) 'Morse here. Look, do you happen to have kept that bit of the *Sunday Times* – you know, that bit about missing girls?'

'You mean the one they saw Richard about?' He *had* been right. 'That's the one.'

'Yes. I kept it, of course. It mentioned Richard several times.'

'Can I, er, can I come round and have a look at it?'

'You can have it with pleasure. I don't want it any more.'

Some half an hour later, forgetful of his earlier pledge, Morse was seated with a pint of flat beer and a soggy steak-and-mushroom pie. He read the article through with a feeling of anti-climax. Six girls were featured – after the preliminary sociological blurb about the problems of adolescence – with a couple of columns on each of them. But the central slant was on the parents the girls had left behind them. 'The light in the hall has been left on every night since she went,' as one of the anguished mothers was reported. It was pathetic and it was distressing. There were pictures, too. First, pictures of the girls, although (of necessity) none of the photographs was of a very recent vintage, and two or three (including that of Valerie herself) were of less than definitive clarity. And thus it was for the first time that Chief Inspector Morse looked down upon the

face of Valerie Taylor. Of the six she would certainly be in the
running for the beauty crown – though run close by a honey of a
girl from Brighton. Attractive face, full mouth, come-hither eyes,
nice eyebrows (plucked, thought Morse) and long dark-brown hair.
Just the face – no figure to admire. And then, over the page, the
pictures of the parents. Mr and Mrs Taylor seemed an unremarkable
pair, seated unnaturally forward on the shabby sofa: Mr wearing a
cheap Woolworth tie, with his rolled-up sleeves revealing a large
purple tattoo on his broad right fore-arm; Mrs wearing a plain cotton
dress with a cameo brooch somewhat ostentatiously pinned to the
collar. And on a low table beside them, carefully brought into the
focus of the photograph, a cohort of congratulatory cards for their
eighteenth wedding anniversary. It was predictable and posed, and
Morse felt that a few tears might well have been nearer the truth.

He ordered another pint and sat down to read the commentary
on Valerie's disappearance.

Two years ago, the month of June enjoyed a long, unbroken spell of
sunny weather, and Tuesday 10 June was a particularly sweltering day
at the village of Kidlington in the county of Oxfordshire. At 12.30 p.m.
Valerie Taylor left the Roger Bacon Comprehensive School to walk to
her home in Hatfield Way on the council estate nearby, no more than six
or seven hundred yards from the school. Like many of her friends Valerie
disliked school dinners and for the previous year had returned home each
lunch-time. On the day of her daughter's disappearance Valerie's mother,
Mrs Grace Taylor, had prepared a ham salad, with blackcurrant tart and
custard for sweet, and together mother and daughter ate the meal at
the kitchen table. Afternoon lessons began again at 1.45, and Valerie
usually left the house at about 1.25. She did so on 10 June. Nothing
seemed amiss that cloudless Tuesday afternoon. Valerie walked down
the short front path, turned in the direction of the school, and waved
a cheery farewell to her mother. She has never been seen again.

Mr George Taylor, an employee of the Oxford City Corporation,
returned from work at 6.10 p.m. to find his wife in a state of considerable anxiety. It was quite unlike Valerie not to tell her mother if
she was likely to be late, yet at that point there seemed little cause for
immediate concern. The minutes ticked by; the quarters chimed on the
Taylors' grandfather clock, and then the hours. At 8.00 p.m. Mr Taylor
got into his car and drove to the school. Only the caretaker was still on
the premises and he could be of no help. Mr Taylor then called at the
homes of several of Valerie's friends, but they likewise could tell him
nothing. None of them could remember seeing Valerie that afternoon,
but it had been 'games' and it was nothing unusual for pupils to slip
away quietly from the sports field.

When Mr Taylor returned home it was 9.00 p.m. 'There must be some simple explanation,' he told his wife; but if there was, it was not forthcoming, and the time pressed slowly on. 10.00 p.m. 11.00 p.m. Still nothing. George Taylor suggested they should notify the police, but his wife was terrified of taking such a step.

When I interviewed them this week both Mr and Mrs Taylor were reluctant (and understandably so) to talk about the agonies they suffered that night. Throughout the long vigil it was Grace Taylor who feared the worst and suffered the most, for her husband felt sure that Valerie had gone off with some boyfriend and would be back the next morning. At 4.00 a.m. he managed to persuade his wife to take two sleeping tablets and he took her upstairs to bed.

She was sleeping when he left the house at 7.30 a.m., leaving a note saying that he would be back at lunch-time, and that if Valerie still had not returned they would have to call the police. In fact the police were notified earlier than that. Mrs Taylor had awoken at about nine and, in a distraught state, had rung them from a neighbour's telephone.

Detective Chief Inspector Ainley of the Thames Valley Police was put in charge of the case, and intensive enquiries were immediately begun. During the course of the next week the whole of the area in the vicinity of Valerie's home and the area of woodland behind the school were searched with painstaking care and patience; the river and the reservoir were dragged . . . But no trace was found of Valerie Taylor.

Inspector Ainley himself was frankly critical of the delay. At least twelve hours had been lost; fifteen, if the police had been notified as soon as the Taylors' anxiety had begun to deepen into genuine alarm.

Such delay is a common feature of the cases assembled here. Vital time lost; perhaps vital clues thrown to the wind – and all because parents think they will be wasting the time of the police and would seem to look foolish if the wayward offspring should suddenly turn up whilst the police were busy taking statements. It is a common human weakness, and it is only too easy to blame parents like the Taylors. But would we ourselves have acted all that differently? I knew exactly what Mrs Taylor meant when she said to me, 'I felt all the time that if we called the police something dreadful must have happened.' Illogical, you may say, but so very understandable.

Mr and Mrs Taylor still live on the council estate in Hatfield Way. For over two years now they have waited and prayed for their daughter to return. As in the five other cases discussed here, the police files remain open. 'No,' said Inspector Ainley, 'we shan't be closing them until we find her.'

Not bad reporting, thought Morse. There were several things in the article that puzzled him slightly, but he deliberately suppressed the fanciful notions that began to flood his mind. He had been right earlier. When Ainley had got the hard facts down on paper, he had spotted something that for over two years had lurked in the darkness and eluded his grasp. Some clue or other which had monopolised his attention and filled his spare time, and eventually, if indirectly, led to his death.

Just stick to the facts, Morse, stick to the facts! It would be difficult, but he would try. And tomorrow he and Lewis would start on the files wherein lay the facts as Ainley had gleaned them. Anyway, Christine was back in Kidderminster and, like as not, Valerie would be back in Kidlington before the end of the month. The naughty girls were all coming home and would soon be having the same sort of rows they'd had with mum and dad before they left. Life, alas, was like that.

Over his third pint of beer Morse could stem the flood of fancy no longer. He read the article through quickly once again. Yes, there was something wrong there. Only a small thing, but he wondered if it was the same small thing that had set Ainley on a new track . . . And the strangest notion began to formulate in the mind so recently dedicated to the pursuit of unembellished fact.

Chapter Six

He certainly has a great deal of fancy, and a very good memory; but, with a perverse ingenuity, he employs these qualities as no other person does.

Richard Brinsley Sheridan

As he knocked at the door of Morse's office Sergeant Lewis, who had thoroughly enjoyed the police routine of the previous week, wondered just what was in store for him now. He had worked with the unpredictable inspector before and got on fairly well with him; but he had his reservations.

Morse was seated in his black leather chair and before him on his untidy desk lay a green box-file.

'Ah. Come in, Lewis. I didn't want to start without you. Wouldn't be fair, would it?' He patted the box-file with a gesture of deep affection. 'It's all there, Lewis, my boy. All the facts. Ainley was

a fact man – no day-dreaming theorist was Ainley. And we shall
follow where the great man trod. What do you say?' And without
giving his sergeant the slightest opportunity to say anything, he
emptied the contents of the file face downwards upon the desk.
'Shall we start at the top or the bottom?'

'Might be a good idea to start at the beginning, don't you think,
sir?'

'I think we could make out a good case for starting at either
end – but we shall do as you say.' With some difficulty Morse
turned the bulky sheaf of papers the right way up.

'What exactly are we going to do?' asked Lewis blankly.

Morse proceeded to recount his interview with Strange, and then
passed across to Lewis the letter received from Valerie Taylor. 'And
we're taking over, Lewis – you happy about that?' Lewis nodded half-
heartedly. 'Did you remember the *Sunday Mirror*?'

Lewis dutifully took the paper from his coat pocket and handed
it to Morse, who took out his wallet, found his football coupon and
with high seriousness began to check his entry. Lewis watched him
as his eyes alternately lit up and switched off, before the coupon
was comprehensively shredded and hurled in the general direction
of the waste-paper basket.

'I shan't be spending next week in the Bahamas, Lewis. What
about you?'

'Nor me, sir.'

'Do you ever win anything?'

'Few quid last year, sir. But it's a million to one chance – getting
a big win.'

'Like this bloody business,' mumbled Morse, distastefully surveying the fruits of Ainley's labours.

For the next two and a half hours they sat over the Taylor
documents, occasionally conferring over an obscure or an interesting
point – but for the most part in silence. It would have been clear
to an independent witness of these proceedings that Morse read
approximately five times as quickly as his sergeant; but whether he
remembered five times as much of what he read would have been a
much more questionable inference. For Morse found it difficult to
concentrate his mind upon the documents before him. As he saw it,
the facts, the bare unadulterated facts, boiled down to little more
than he had read in the pub the previous day. The statements
before him, checked and signed, appeared merely to confirm the
bald, simple truth: after leaving home to return to school Valerie
Taylor had completely vanished. If Morse wanted a fact, well, he'd

got one. Parents, neighbours, teachers, classmates – all had been questioned at length. And amidst all their well-meaning verbosity they all had the same thing to say – nothing. Next, reports of Ainley's own interviews with Mr and Mrs Taylor, with the headmaster, with Valerie's form tutor, with her games mistress and with two of her boyfriends. (Ainley had clearly liked the headmaster, and equally clearly had disapproved of one of the boyfriends.) All nicely, neatly written in the small, rounded hand that Morse had already seen. But – nothing. Next, reports of general police enquiries and searches, and reports of the missing girl being spotted in Birmingham, Clacton, London, Reading, Southend, and a remote village in Morayshire. All wild-goose chases. All false alarms. Next, personal and medical reports on Valerie herself. She did not appear academically gifted in any way; or if she was, she had so far successfully concealed her scholastic potential from her teachers. School reports suggested a failure, except in practical subjects, to make the best of her limited abilities (familiar phrases!), but she seemed a personable enough young lady, well-liked (Morse drew his own conclusions) by her fellow pupils of either sex. On the day of her disappearance she was attested by school records to be seventeen years and five months old, and five feet six inches in height. In her previous academic year she had taken four CSE subjects, without signal success, and she was at that time sitting three GCE O-level subjects – English, French and Applied Science. From the medical report it appeared that Valerie was quite remarkably healthy. There were no entries on her National Health medical card for the last three years, and before that only measles and a bad cut on the index finger of her left hand. Next, a report over which Ainley had obviously (and properly) taken considerable pains, on the possibility of any trouble on the domestic front which may have caused friction between Valerie and her parents, and led to her running away from home. On this most important point Ainley had gone to the trouble of writing out two sheets of foolscap in his own fair hand; but the conclusions were negative. On the evidence of Valerie's form tutor (among whose manifold duties something designated 'pastoral care' appeared a high priority), on the evidence of the parents themselves, of the neighbours and of Valerie's own friends, there seemed little reason to assume anything but the perfectly normal ups-and-downs in the relationship between the members of the Taylor clan. Rows, of course. Valerie had been home very late once or twice from dances and discos, and Mrs Taylor could use a sharp tongue. (Who couldn't?) Ainley's own conclusion was that he could find no immediate cause within the family circle to

account for a minor squabble – let alone the inexplicable departure
of an only daughter. In short – nothing. Morse thought of the old
Latin proverb, *Ex nihilo nihil fit*. Out of nothing you'll get nothing.
Not that it helped in any way.

Apart from the typed and handwritten documents, there were
three maps: an ordnance-survey map of the Oxford district showing the areas covered by the search parties; a larger map of the
Oxfordshire region on which the major road and rail routes were
marked with cryptic symbols; and finally a sketch-map of the streets
between the Roger Bacon School and the Taylors' house, with
Valerie's route to and from her school carefully and neatly drawn
in in red Biro by the late chief inspector. Whilst Lewis was plodding
along, several miles behind his master, the master himself appeared
to be finding something of extraordinary interest in this last item:
his right hand shaded his forehead and he seemed to Lewis in the
throes of the deepest contemplation.

'Found something, sir?'

'Uh? What?' Morse's head jerked back and the idle daydream
was over.

'The sketch-map, sir.'

'Ah, yes. The map. Very interesting. Yes.' He looked at it
again, decided that he was unable to recapture whatever interest
may have previously lain therein and picked up the *Sunday Mirror*
once more. He read his horoscope: 'You're doing better than you
realise, so there could be a major breakthrough as far as romance
is concerned. This week will certainly blossom if you spend it with
someone witty and bright.'

He looked glumly across at Lewis, who for the moment at
least appeared neither very witty nor very bright.

'Well, Lewis. What do you think?'

'I've not quite finished yet, sir.'

'But you must have some ideas, surely.'

'Not yet.'

'Oh, come on. What do you think happened to her?'

Lewis thought hard, and finally gave expression to a conviction
which had grown steadily stronger the more he had read. 'I think
she got a lift and ended up in London. That's where they all end
up.'

'You think she's still alive, then?'

Lewis looked at his chief in some surprise. 'Don't you?'

'Let's go for a drink,' said Morse.

* * *

They walked out of the Thames Valley HQ and at the Belisha crossing negotiated the busy main road that linked Oxford with Banbury.

'Where are we going, sir?'

Morse took Ainley's hand-drawn map from his pocket. 'I thought we ought to take a gentle stroll over the ground, Lewis. You never know.'

The council estate was situated off the main road, to their left as they walked away from Oxford, and very soon they stood in Hatfield Way.

'We going to call?'

'Got to make a start somewhere, I suppose,' said Morse.

The house was a neat, well-built property, with a circular rose-bed cut into the centre of the well-tended front lawn. Morse rang the bell, and rang again. It seemed that Mrs Taylor was out. Inquisitively Morse peered through the front window, but could see little more than a large, red settee and a diagonal line of ducks winging their inevitable way towards the ceiling. The two men walked away, carefully closing the gate behind them.

'If I remember rightly, Lewis, there's a pub just around the corner.'

They ordered a cheese cob and a pint apiece and Morse handed to Lewis the Colour Supplement of 24 August.

'Have a quick look at that.'

Ten minutes later, with Morse's glass empty and Lewis's barely touched, it was clear that the quick look was becoming a rather long look, and Morse replenished his own glass with some impatience.

'Well? What's troubling you?'

'They haven't got it quite right, though, have they?'

Morse looked at him sharply. 'What's that supposed to mean?'

'Well. It says here that she was never seen again after leaving the house.'

'She wasn't.'

'What about the lollipop-man?'

'The *what*?'

'The lollipop-man. It was in the file.'

'Oh, was it?'

'You did seem a bit tired, I thought, sir.'

'Tired? Nonsense. You need another pint.' He drained what was left in his own glass, picked up Lewis's and walked across to the bar.

An elegantly dressed woman with a full figure and pleasingly slim legs had just bought a double whisky and was pouring a modicum of water into it, the heavy diamond rings on the fingers of her left hand sparkling wickedly and bright.

'Oh, and Bert, twenty Embassy, please.' The landlord reached behind him, handed over the cigarettes, squinted his eyes as he calculated the tariff, gave her the change, said, 'Ta, luv,' and turned his attention to Morse.

'Same again, sir?'

As the woman turned from the counter, Morse felt sure he had seen her somewhere before. He seldom forgot a face. Still, if she lived in Kidlington, he could have seen her anywhere. But he kept looking at her; so much so that Lewis began to suspect the inspector's intentions. She was all right – quite nice, in fact. Mid-thirties, perhaps, nice face. But the old boy must be hard up if . . .

Two dusty-looking builders came in, bought their ale and sat down to play dominoes. As they walked to the table one of them called over to the woman: 'Hallo, Grace. All right?' Morse showed little surprise. Hell of a sight better-looking than her photograph suggested, though.

At 1.20 Morse decided it was time to go. They walked back the way they had come, past the Taylors' house and down to the main road, busy at this time with a virtually continuous stream of traffic either way. Here they turned right and came up to the Belisha crossing.

'Do you think that's our lollipop-man?' asked Morse. In the middle of the road stood a white-coated attendant in a peak cap, wielding the sceptre of his authority like an arthritic bishop with a crook. Several pupils of the Roger Bacon School were crossing under the aegis of the standard-bearer, the girls in white blouses, grey skirts and red knee-length socks, the boys (it seemed to Morse) in assorted combinations of any old garments. When the attendant returned from mid-stream, Morse spoke to him in what he liked to think of as his intimate, avuncular manner.

'Been doing this long?'

'Just over a year.' He was a small, red-faced man with gnarled hands.

'Know the chap who did it before?'

'You mean old Joe? 'Course I did. 'E did it for – oh, five or six year.'

'Retired now, has he?'

'Ah. S'pose you could say so. Poor old Joe. Got knocked ovver

– feller on a motorbike. Mind you, old Joe were gettin' a bit slow. Seventy-two he were when he were knocked ovver. Broke 'is 'ip. Poor old Joe.'

'Not still in hospital, I hope?' Morse fervently prayed that poor old Joe was still limping along somewhere in the land of the living.

'No. Not 'im. Down at the old folkses place at Cowley.'

'Well, you be careful,' said Morse, as he and Lewis crossed over with another group of schoolchildren, and stood and watched them as they dawdled past the line of shops and the public lavatories, and reluctantly turned into the main drive leading to the school.

Back in the office, Morse read aloud the relevant part of the testimony of Mr Joseph Godberry, Oxford Road, Kidlington:

I almost always saw Valerie Taylor at dinner times, and I saw her on 10 June. She didn't cross by my Belisha because when I saw her she was on the other side of the road. She was running fairly quickly as if she was in a dickens of a hurry to meet somebody. But I remember she waved to me. I am quite sure it was Valerie. She would often stop and have a quick word with me. 'Joe' she called me, like most of them. She was a very nice girl and always cheery. I don't know what she did after I saw her. I thought she was going back to school.

Morse looked thoughtful. 'I wonder, now,' he said.

'Wonder what, sir?'

Morse was looking into the far distance, through the office window, and into the filmy blue beyond, excitement glowing in his eyes. 'I was just wondering if she was carrying a bag of some sort when old Joe Godberry saw her.'

Lewis looked as mystified as he felt, but received no further elucidation. 'You see,' said Morse, his eyes gradually refocusing on his sergeant, 'you see, if she *was*, I'm beginning to think that you're wrong.'

'Wrong, sir?'

'Yes, wrong. You said you thought Valerie Taylor was still alive, didn't you?'

'Well, yes. I think she is.'

'And I think, *think*, mind you, that you're wrong, Lewis. *I think that Valerie Taylor is almost certainly dead.*'

Chapter Seven

And French she spak ful faire and fetisly,
After the scole of Stratford atte Bowe,
For French of Paris was to hir unknowe.
                    Geoffrey Chaucer, *Canterbury Tales*

Donald Phillipson arrived in school at 8 a.m. on Tuesday morning. The Michaelmas term had been under way for one full week now and things were going well. The anti-litter campaign was proving moderately successful, the new caretaker seemed an amenable sort of fellow, and the Parent–Teacher Association had (somewhat surprisingly, he thought) backed him up to the hilt in his plea for a more rigid ruling on school uniforms. On the academic side, only four members of staff had left in the summer (one quarter the previous year's total), the GCE and CSE results had been markedly better than before, and the present term saw the first full intake of thirteen-plus pupils, among whom (if junior-school headmasters could be believed) were some real high-flyers. Perhaps in a few years' time there would be one or two Open Awards at Oxbridge . . . Yes, he felt more than a little pleased with himself and with life this Tuesday morning. The only thing that marred the immediate prospect was a cloud, rather larger than a man's hand, on the not-so-distant horizon. But he felt confident that he would be able to weather whatever storm might break from that quarter, although he must think things through rather more carefully than he had done hitherto.

At 8.20 the head boy and the head girl would be coming to his study, as they did each morning, and there were several matters requiring his prompt attention. He heard Mrs Webb come in at 8.15, and Baines at 8.30. Punctuality was sharper, too. He did a small amount of teaching with the sixth form (he was an historian), but he kept Tuesdays completely free. It had been his practice since he was appointed to take off Tuesday afternoons completely and he looked forward to a fairly gentle day.

The morning's activities went off well enough – even the singing of the hymns in assembly was improving – until 11.15 when Mrs Webb received the telephone call.

'Is the headmaster there?'

'Who shall I say is calling, please?'

'Morse. Inspector Morse.'

'Oh, just a minute, sir. I'll see if the headmaster's free.' She dialled the head's extension. 'Inspector Morse would like a word with you, sir. Shall I put him through?'

'Oh. Er. Yes, of course.'

Mrs Webb switched the outside call to the headmaster's study, hesitated a moment, and then quickly lifted the receiver to her ear again.

'. . . hear from you. Can I help?'

'I hope you can, sir. It's about the Taylor girl. There are one or two things I'd like to ask you about.'

'Look, Inspector. It's not really very convenient to talk at the minute – I'm interviewing some of the new pupils this morning. Don't you think it would be . . .' Mrs Webb put the phone down quickly and quietly, and when Phillipson came out her typewriter was chattering along merrily. 'Mrs Webb, Inspector Morse will be coming in this afternoon at three o'clock, so I shall have to be here. Can you arrange some tea and biscuits for us?'

'Of course.' She made a note in her shorthand book. 'Just the two of you?'

'No. Three. He's bringing a sergeant along – I forget his name.'

The anonymous sergeant himself was spending the same morning at the old people's home in Cowley, and finding Mr Joseph Godberry (in small doses) an interesting sort of fellow. He had fought at Mons in the '14–'18 War, had slept, by his own account, with all the tarts within a ten-mile radius of Rouen, and had been invalided out of the army in 1917 (probably from sexual fatigue, thought Lewis). He reminisced at considerable length as he sat by his bed in D ward, accepting his present confinement with a certain dignity and good humour. He explained that he could hardly walk now and recounted to Lewis in great detail the circumstances and consequences of his memorable accident. In fact the 'accident', together with Mons and Rouen, had become one of the major incidents of his life and times; and it was with some difficulty that Lewis managed to steer Joe's thoughts to the disappearance of Valerie Taylor. Oh, he remembered her, of course. Very nice girl, Valerie. In London, bet your bottom dollar. Very nice girl, Valerie.

But could Joe remember the day she disappeared? Lewis listened carefully as he rambled on, repeating with surprising coherence and accuracy most of what he had said in his statement to the police. In Lewis's opinion, he was a good witness, but he was becoming tired and Lewis felt the moment had come to put the one question which Morse had been so eager for him to ask.

'Do you remember by any chance if Valerie was carrying anything when you saw her that day – the day she disappeared?'

Joe moved uneasily in his chair and slowly turned his rheumy old eyes on Lewis. Something seemed to be stirring there and Lewis pressed home the point.

'You know what I mean, a carrier bag, or a case, or anything like that?'

'Funny you should say that,' he said at last. 'I never thought about it afore.' He looked as though he were about to haul out some hazy memory on to the shores of light, and Lewis held his breath and waited. 'I reckon as you're right, you know. She were carryin' something. That's it. She were carryin' a bag of some sort; carryin' it in 'er left hand, if me memory serves me correck.'

In Phillipson's study formalities were exchanged in friendly fashion. Morse asked polite questions about the school – quite at his best, thought Lewis. But the mood was to change swiftly.

Morse informed the headmaster that he had taken over the Taylor case from Chief Inspector Ainley, and the cease-fire was duly observed for a further few minutes, whilst the proper commiserations were expressed. It was only when he produced the letter from Valerie that Morse's manner appeared to Lewis to become strangely abrasive.

Phillipson read through the letter quickly.

'Well?' said Morse.

Lewis felt that the headmaster was more surprised by the sharp tone in the inspector's voice than by the arrival of a letter from his troublesome, long-lost ex-pupil.

'Well what?' Phillipson clearly was not a man easily bullied.

'Is it her writing?'

'I can't tell. Don't her parents know?'

Morse ignored the question. 'You can't tell me.' The statement was flat and final, with the tacit implication that he had expected something better.

'No.'

'Have you got some of her old exercise books we could look at?'

'I don't really know, Inspector.'

'Who would know?' Again the astringent impatience in his voice.

'Perhaps Baines would.'

'Ask him in, please,' snapped Morse.

'I'm sorry, Inspector, but Baines has this afternoon off. Tuesday is games afternoon and . . .'

'I know, yes. So Baines can't help us either. Who can?'

Phillipson got up and opened the study door. 'Mrs Webb? Will you come in here a minute, please?'

Was Lewis mistaken, or did she throw a rather frightened glance in Morse's direction?

'Mrs Webb, the inspector here wonders if any of Valerie Taylor's old exercise books may have been kept somewhere in the school. What do you think?'

'They may be in the store-room, I suppose, sir.'

'Would it be the usual practice for pupils themselves to keep them?' Morse addressed himself directly to the secretary.

'Yes, it would. But in this case I should think her desk would have been turned out at the end of term and the books would be . . .' She was getting lost and looked helplessly towards the headmaster.

'I'm sure Mrs Webb is right, Inspector. If the books are anywhere, they will be in the store-room.'

Mrs Webb nodded, swallowed hard and was given leave to withdraw.

'We'd better have a look in the store-room, then. You've no objections?'

'Of course not. But it's in a bit of a mess, I should think. You know how things are at the beginning of term.'

Morse smiled weakly and neither confirmed nor refuted his knowledge of such matters.

They walked along the corridor, down some steps, and turned off right through a classroom, wherein all the chairs were neatly placed upon the tops of the desks. The school was virtually deserted, but intermittent shrieks of joyous laughter from the direction of the sports field seemed to belie the view that games were too unpopular with the majority of pupils.

The headmaster unlocked the door to the large unwindowed, unventilated store-room, and when the three men entered Lewis found himself facing with some foreboding the piles of dusty textbooks, files and stationery.

'I'm afraid it may be a longish job,' said Phillipson, with some irritation in his voice. 'If you like, I could get some of the staff to go through all the old exercise books here.' He pointed vaguely to great piles of books stacked on wooden shelves along the far wall.

'That's very kind of you, headmaster, but we can deal with this all right. No problem. If we can call back to your office when we've finished here?' It was an unmistakable hint that the presence of the headmaster would not profit the present stage of the investigation, and Morse listened carefully as Phillipson retraced his steps to his study. 'He's a bit worried, wouldn't you say, Lewis?'

'I don't blame him, sir. You've been pretty sharp with him.'

'Serve him right,' said Morse.

'What's he done wrong?'

'I spoke to him on the phone this morning and he said he was interviewing some new pupils.'

'Perhaps he was,' suggested the honest Lewis.

'I had the feeling he didn't want to talk just then, and I was right.' Lewis looked at him quizzically. 'I heard a click on the line while we were talking. You can guess who was listening in.'

'Mrs Webb?'

'Mrs Webb. I rang again later and asked her why she'd been eavesdropping. She denied it, of course; but I told her I'd forget all about it if she told me the truth about who had been in the headmaster's study. She was scared – for her job, I suppose. Anyway, she said that nobody had been in with Phillipson when I rang.'

Lewis opened his mouth to say something but Morse was already pouncing on the piles of textbooks.

'Ah, Keats. Fine poet, Keats. You should read him, Lewis . . . Well, well, well. *Travels with a Donkey*.' He picked up a copy and began to read under the cobwebbed central light-bulb.

Lewis made for the far wall of the room, where whole stacks of exercise books, used and unused, mauve, green, blue and orange, were heaped upon the shelves, some bundled neatly, but the majority in loose disarray. Lewis, as always, tackled his task with systematic thoroughness, although he doubted whether he would find anything. Fortunately, it was a good deal easier going than he had thought.

Half an hour later he found them. A pile of loose books, eight of them, each with the name Valerie Taylor inscribed in capitals on the front cover. He blew the dust off the edges and savoured his brief moment of triumph.

'I've found them, sir.'

'Well done. Leave them where they are – don't touch them.'

'I already have, I'm afraid, sir.'

'Was there any dust on the top book?'

The sweet taste of success had already turned sour. 'I don't know.'

'Give 'em here.' Morse was clearly very cross and muttered angrily under his breath.

'Pardon, sir?'

'I said I think someone else may well have been looking at these books recently. That's what I said!'

'I don't think the top book *was* dusty, sir. Just the edges.'

'And where's the dust on the edges?'

'I blew it off.'

'You blew it off! Christ, man. We've got a murder on our hands here, and we're supposed to be investigating it – not blowing all the bloody clues away!'

He gradually calmed down, and with a silent Lewis returned to Phillipson's study. It was now 4.30 and apart from the headmaster and Mrs Webb the school was empty.

'I see you found the books.'

Morse nodded curtly, and the three men sat down once more. 'Bit of luck, really,' continued Phillipson. 'It's a wonder they weren't thrown away.'

'Where *do* you throw old books away?' It seemed an odd question.

'Funnily enough they get buried – down on the rubbish dump. It's a difficult job burning a whole lot of books, you know.'

'Unless you've got a fiery furnace,' said Morse slowly.

'Well, yes. But even—'

'You've got a furnace here?'

'Yes, we have. But—'

'And that would burn just about anything, would it?'

'Yes. But as I was going—' Again Morse cut him short.

'Would it burn a body all right?' His words hung in the air, and Lewis shivered involuntarily. Phillipson's eyes were steady as he looked directly at Morse.

'Yes. It would burn a body, and it wouldn't leave much trace, either.'

Morse appeared to accept the remark without the slightest surprise or interest. 'Let's get back to these books a minute, sir, if we may. Are there any missing?'

Phillipson hadn't the remotest idea and breathed an inner sigh of relief as Baines (answering an earlier urgent summons) knocked on the study door, was ushered in and introduced.

It was immediately clear that the second master was a mine of information on all curricular queries, and within ten minutes Morse had copies of the information he required: Valerie's timetable for the summer term in which she disappeared, her homework schedule for the same period, and a list of her subject teachers. No books, it seemed, were missing. He made some complimentary remarks on Baines's efficiency, and the second master's shrewd eyes blinked with gratification.

After they had all gone Phillipson sat behind his desk and groaned inwardly. In the space of one short afternoon the cloud on the horizon had grown to menacing proportions. What a bloody fool he had been!

As a husband and a father, Sergeant Lewis experienced the delights and despondencies, the difficulties and the duties of family life, and with Morse's blessing returned home at 5.45 p.m.

At the same time Morse himself, with no such responsibilities, returned to his office at police HQ. He was quite looking forward to his evening's work.

First he studied Valerie's timetable for each of her Tuesday mornings during that last summer term.

9.15–10.00   Environmental Studies
10.00–10.45   Applied Science
10.45–11.00   Break
11.00–11.45   Sociology
11.45–12.30   French

He contemplated with supercilious disdain the academic disciplines (sub-disciplines, he would call them) which were now monopolising the secondary school curricula. 'Environmental Studies', he doubted, was little more than a euphemism for occasional visits to the gasworks, the fire-station and the sewage installations; whilst for Sociology and Sociologists he had nothing but sour contempt, and could never discover either what was entailed in its subject-matter or how its practitioners deployed their dubious talents. With such a plethora of non-subjects crowding the timetable there was no room for the traditional disciplines taught in his own day . . . But French now. At least that had a bit of backbone, although he had always felt that a language which sanctioned the pronunciation of *donne*, *donnes* and *donnent* without the slightest differentiation could hardly deserve to be taken seriously. Anyway, she was studying French and it was French which won the day. He consulted the homework schedule and found that French was set on Friday evenings and (he guessed) it might be collected in and marked on the following Monday. He checked to see that French appeared on Monday's timetable. It did. And then handed back to the pupils on the Tuesday, perhaps? That is, if the teacher had remembered to set the homework and if the teacher had been conscientious enough to mark it straightaway. Who was the teacher, anyway? He looked at the list. Mr D. Acum. Well, a little inspection of Mr Acum's discharge of duty was called for, and Morse flicked through the orange exercise book until he came to the last entry. He found the date, Friday, 6th June, carefully filled in and neatly underlined. He then turned his attention to Valerie's efforts, which had entailed the translation from English into French of ten short sentences. Judging, however, from the enormous quantity of red ink the despairing D. Acum had seen fit to squander upon her versions, judging from the treble underlinings, and the pathetic 'Oh dear' written beside one particularly heinous blunder, Valerie's linguistic prowess seemed extraordinarily limited. But Morse's eye was not on the exercise itself. He had spotted it as soon as he turned to the page. Beneath the exercise Acum had written: 'See me immediately after the lesson.' Morse felt a shiver of excitement. 'After the lesson.' 12.30 p.m. Acum must have been one of the very last people to have seen Valerie before she . . . Before she what? He looked through his office window at the pale blue sky gradually edging into dusk – and he wondered. Had Ainley got on to Acum? Why had Acum wished to see Valerie Taylor that far-off Tuesday morning? The most likely answer, he supposed, was that Valerie would be ticked off good and proper for such disgusting work. But the simple fact remained: Acum had been one of the very last people to see Valerie alive.

Before leaving for home Morse looked once again at the short letter from Valerie and compared its handwriting with that of the exercise books. On the face of it, certainly, there seemed an undeniable similarity. But for a definitive opinion he would have to wait until the forensic experts had considered the specimens; and that would mean waiting until fairly late tomorrow evening, for he and Lewis had a trip to London in the morning. Would he believe them if their report stated categorically that the letter was written by Valerie Taylor? Yes. He would have no choice but to accept such a conclusion. But he thought he need have little worry on that score: for it was now his firm conviction that the letter had not been written by Valerie at all, but by someone who had carefully copied her writing – copied it rather *too* well, in fact. Further, Morse felt he knew who had copied it, although the reasons for the deception he could, at this stage, only dimly descry. Quite indubitably now, in his own mind, the case was one of wilful murder.

Chapter Eight

Gypsy Rose Lee, the strip-tease artist, has arrived in Hollywood with twelve empty trunks.
Harry P. Wade, American Columnist

Doubtless in its hey-day a fine example of neo-Georgian elegance,
the sturdily and attractively built house was now fallen on seedier
times, the stuccoed front dirty and chipped. Stuck to one of the
stout pillars which flanked the peeling front door was an outdated
poster announcing the arrival of Maharaj Ji, and on the other, in
black figures, the number 42.

The door was opened by a blowzy, middle-aged woman, a cigarette
drooping from her lips and a headscarf half hiding the hair-curlers –
like a caricature of the screen charlady. She seemed to eye them
shrewdly, but it may have been nothing more than the effect of
avoiding the smoke from her cigarette.

'Police. It's Mrs, er . . . ?'

'Gibbs. What can I do for yer?'

'Can we come in?'

She hesitated, then moved aside. The door was closed and the
two men stood awkwardly in the entrance hall, where they saw
neither seats nor chairs of any description, only a grandfather
clock showing the correct time (10.30), an overloaded coat-rack,
and an umbrella-stand incongruously housing a set of ancient golf
clubs. It became clear that they were not to be invited into the
cosiness of any inner sanctum.

'About three weeks ago, you had a call I think from one of
my colleagues – Inspector Ainley.' She considered the statement
guardedly, nodded, and said nothing. 'You may have read in the
papers that after he left here he was killed in a road accident.'

Mrs Gibbs hadn't, and the lady's latent humanity stirred to the
extent of a mumbled phrase of commiseration if not to the removal
of the cigarette from her lips, and Morse knew that he would have
to chance his arm a bit.

'He wrote, of course, a full report of his visit here and, er,
I think you will have a good idea why we've called again today.'

'Nothing to do with me, is it?'

Morse seized his opportunity. 'Oh, no, Mrs Gibbs. Nothing at
all. That was quite clear from the report. But naturally we need
your help, if you'll be kind enough . . .'

''E's not 'ere. 'E's at work – if yer can call it work. Not that 'e'll be 'ere much longer, anyway. Caused me quite enough trouble, 'e 'as.'

'Can we see his room?'

She hesitated. 'Yer got the authority?'

It was Morse's turn to hesitate, before suddenly producing an official-looking document from his breast pocket.

Mrs Gibbs fiddled in her apron pocket for her spectacles. 'That other policeman – 'e told me all about the legal position. Said as 'ow I shouldn't let anyone in 'ere as 'adn't got the proper authority.'

Trust Ainley, thought Morse. 'He was quite right of course.' Morse directed the now bespectacled lady's attention to an impressive-looking signature and beneath it, in printed capitals, CHIEF CONSTABLE (OXON). It was enough, and Morse quickly repocketed the cyclostyled letter about the retirement pensions of police officers at and above the rank of Chief Inspector.

They made their way up three flights of dusty stairs, where Mrs Gibbs produced a key from her multi-purpose apron pocket and opened a dingy, brown-painted door.

'I'll be downstairs when yer've finished.'

Morse contented himself with a mild 'phew' as the door closed, and the two men looked around them. 'So this was where Ainley came.' They stood in a bed-sitting room, containing a single (un-made) bed, the sheets dirty and creased, a threadbare settee, an armchair of more recent manufacture, a huge, ugly wardrobe, a black-and-white TV set and a small underpopulated bookcase. They passed through a door in the far wall, and found themselves in a small, squalid kitchen, with a greasy-looking gas cooker, a Formica-topped table and two kitchen stools.

'Hardly an opulent occupant?' suggested Morse. Lewis sniffed and sniffed again. 'Smell something?'

'Pot, I reckon, sir.'

'Really?' Morse beamed at his sergeant with delight, and Lewis felt pleased with himself.

'Think it's important, sir?'

'Doubt it,' said Morse. 'But let's have a closer look round. You stay here and sniff around – I'll take the other room.'

Morse walked straight to the bookcase. A copy of the *Goon Show Scripts* appeared to be the high-water mark of any civilised taste in the occupant's reading habits. For the rest there was little more than a stack of Dracula comics and half a dozen supremely pornographic magazines, imported from Denmark. The latter Morse decided to investigate forthwith, and seated in the armchair he was contentedly sampling their contents when Lewis called from the kitchen.

'I've found something, sir.'

'Shan't be a minute.' He thought guiltily of sticking one of the magazines in his pocket, but for once his police training got the better of him. And with the air of an Abraham prepared to sacrifice an Isaac upon the altar, he replaced the magazines in the bookcase and went through to his over-zealous sergeant.

'What about that, sir?' Morse nodded unenthusiastically at the unmistakable paraphernalia of the pot-smoker's paradise. 'Shall we pack this little lot up, sir?'

Morse thought for a while. 'No, we'll leave it, I think.' Lewis's eagerness wilted, but he knew better than to argue. 'All we need to find out now is who he is, Lewis.'

'I've got that, too, sir.' He handed the inspector an unopened letter from Granada TV Rental Service addressed to Mr J. Maguire.

Morse's eyes lit up. 'Well, well. We might have known it. One of the boyfriends, if I remember rightly. Well done, Lewis! You've done a good job.'

'You find anything, sir?'

'Me? Oh, no. Nothing, really.'

Mrs Gibbs, who was waiting for them as they reached the bottom of the stairs, expressed the hope that the visit was now satisfactorily terminated, and Morse said he hoped so, too.

'As I told yer, 'e won't be 'ere much longer, the trouble 'e's caused me.'

Sensing that she was becoming fractionally more communicative Morse kept the exchanges going. He had to, anyway.

'Great pity, you know, that Inspector Ainley was killed. You'd have finished with this business by now. It must be a bit of a nuisance . . .'

'Yes. He said as 'ow 'e 'oped he needn't come bothering me again.'

'Was, er, Mr Maguire here when he called?'

'No. 'E called about the same time as you gentlemen. 'Im' (pointing aloft) ' – 'e were off to work. Well, some people'd call it work, I s'pose.'

'Where does he work now?' Morse asked the question lightly enough, but the guarded look came back to her eyes.

'Same place.'

'I see. Well, we shall have to have a word with him, of course. What's the best way to get there from here?'

'Tube from Putney Bridge to Piccadilly Circus – least, that's the way 'e goes.'

'Could we park the car there?'

'In Brewer Street? Yer must be joking!'

Morse turned to Lewis. 'We'd better do as Mrs Gibbs says, Sergeant, and get the tube.'

On the steps outside Morse thanked the good lady profusely and, almost as an afterthought it seemed, turned to speak to her once more.

'Just one more thing, Mrs Gibbs. It may be lunch-time before we get up there. Have you any idea where Mr Maguire will be if he's not at work?'

'Like as not The Angel – I know 'e often 'as a drink in there.'

As they walked to the car Lewis decided to get it off his chest. 'Couldn't you just have asked her straight out where he worked?'

'I didn't want her to think I was fishing,' replied Morse. Lewis thought she must be educationally sub-normal if she hadn't realised that by now. But he let it go. They drove down to Putney Bridge, parked the car on a TAXIS ONLY plot, and caught the tube to Piccadilly Circus.

Somewhat to Lewis's surprise, Morse appeared to be fairly intimately conversant with the geography of Soho, and two minutes after emerging from the tube in Shaftesbury Avenue they found themselves standing in Brewer Street.

'There we are then,' said Morse, pointing to The Angel, Bass House, only thirty yards away to their left. 'Might as well combine business with a little pleasure, don't you think?'

'As you wish, sir.'

Over the beer, Morse asked the barman if the manager was around, and learned that the barman was the manager. Morse introduced himself, and said he was looking for a Mr J. Maguire.

'Not in any trouble, is he?' asked the barman.

'Nothing serious.'

'Johnny Maguire, you say. He works over the way at the strip club – The Penthouse. On the door, mostly.'

Morse thanked him, and he and Lewis walked over to the window and looked outside. The Penthouse was almost directly opposite.

'Ever been to a strip club, Lewis?'

'No. But I've read about 'em, of course.'

'Nothing like first-hand experience, you know. C'mon, drink up.'

Outside the club Morse surveyed the pictorial preview of the erotic delights to be savoured within. 18 GORGEOUS GIRLS. The sexiest show in London. 95p only. NO OTHER ADMISSION CHARGE.

'The real thing this is, gentlemen. Continuous performance. No G-strings.' The speaker was a ginger-haired youth, dressed in a dark green blazer and grey slacks, who sat in a small booth at the entrance lobby.

'Bit expensive, isn't it?' asked Morse.

'When you've seen the show, sir, you'll think it's cheap at the price.'

Morse looked at him carefully, and thought there was something approaching honesty in the dark eyes. Maguire – almost certainly; but he wouldn't run away. Morse handed over two pound-notes and took the tickets. To the young tout the policemen were just another couple of frustrated middle-aged voyeurs, and he had already spotted another potential customer studying the stills outside.

'The real thing this is, sir. Continuous performance. No G-strings.'

'You owe me 10p,' said Morse.

They walked through a gloomy passage-way and heard the music blaring from behind a screened partition, where sat a smallish, swarthy gentleman (Maltese, thought Morse) with a huge chest and bulging forearms.

He took the tickets and tore them across. 'Can I see membership cards, please?'

'What membership cards?'

'You must be members of the club, sir.' He reached for a small pad, and tore off two forms. 'Fill in, please.'

'Just a minute,' protested Morse. 'It says outside that there's no other admission charge and . . .'

'One pown each, please.'

'. . . We've paid our 95p and that's all we're paying.'

The small man looked mean and dangerous. He rose to his meagre height and moved a thick arm to Morse's jacket. 'Fill in, please. That will be one pown each.'

'Will it buggery!' said Morse.

The Maltese advanced slightly and his hands glided towards Morse's wallet-pocket.

Neither Morse nor Lewis were big men, and the last thing that Morse wanted at this juncture was a rough-house. He wasn't in very good condition anyway . . . But he knew the type well. Courage,

Morse! He brushed the man's hand forcibly from his jacket and stepped a menacing pace forward.

'Look, you miserable sod. You want a fight? That's fine. I wouldn't want to bruise my fist against your ugly chops, myself, but this pal of mine here will do it with the greatest pleasure. Just up his street. Army middle-weight champion till a year ago. Where shall we go, you dirty little squit?'

The little man sat back and sagged in his chair like a wilting balloon, and his voice was a punctured whine.

'You got to be members of the club. If you not I get prosecuted by police.'

'F— off,' said Morse, and with the ex-boxing champion behind him walked through the screen partition.

In the small auditorium beyond sat a sprinkling of males, dotted around on the three rows of seats facing the small, raised stage, on which a buxom blonde stripper had just, climactically, removed her G-string. At least one of the management's promises had been honoured. The curtains closed and there was a polite smatter of half-hearted applause.

'How did you know I was a boxing champion?' whispered Lewis.

'I didn't,' said Morse, with genuine surprise.

'You might get it right, though, sir. *Light* middle-weight.'

Morse grinned happily, and a disembodied voice from the wings announced the advent of The Fabulous Fiona. The curtains opened jerkily to reveal a fully-clothed Fiona; but it was immediately apparent that her fabulous body, whatever delights were soon to be unveiled, was signally bereft of any rhythmic suppleness as she struggled amateurishly to synchronise a few elementary dance-steps with the languorously suggestive music.

After The Sexy Susan and The Sensational Sandra even Morse was feeling a trifle blasé; but, as he explained to an unenthusiastic Lewis, there might be better things to come. And indeed The Voluptuous Vera and The Kinky Kate certainly did something to raise the general standard of the entertainment. There were gimmicks aplenty: fans, whips, bananas and rubber spiders; and Morse dug Lewis in the ribs as an extraordinarily shapely girl, dressed for a fancy-dress ball, titillatingly and tantalisingly divested herself of all but an incongruously ugly mask.

'Bit of class there, Lewis.'

But Lewis remained unimpressed; and when the turn came round for the reappearance of The Fabulous Fiona Morse reluctantly decided they had better go. The little gorilla was fleecing a thin, spotty-faced young man of his one pown membership fee as they walked out of the club into the dazzling sunshine of the London street. After a few breaths of comparatively clean air, Morse returned to the entrance and stood by the young man.

'What's your name, lad?'

'William Shakespeare. What's yours?' He looked at Morse with considerable surprise. Who the hell did he think he was? It was over two years since anyone had spoken to him in that tone of voice. At school, in Kidlington.

'Can we go and talk somewhere?'

'What *is* this?'

'John Maguire, if I'm not mistaken? I want to talk to you about Miss Valerie Taylor — I think you may have heard of her. Now we can do it quietly and sensibly, or you can come along with me and the sergeant here to the nearest police station. Up to you.'

Maguire was obviously worried. 'Look. Not here, please. I've got half an hour off at four o'clock. I'll meet you then. I'll be in there.' He pointed anxiously to a sleazy-looking snack-bar across the road next to The Angel.

Morse pondered what to do.

'Please,' urged Maguire. 'I'll be there. Honest, I will.'

It was a difficult decision, but Morse finally agreed. He thought it would be foolish to antagonise Maguire before he'd even started on him.

Morse gave quick instructions to Lewis as they walked away. He was to take a taxi back to Southampton Terrace and wait until Morse returned. If Maguire did decide to scuttle (it seemed unlikely, though) he would almost certainly go back there for some of his things.

At the end of the street Lewis found a cab almost immediately, and Morse guiltily strolled back to The Penthouse.

'You'd better give me another ticket,' demanded Morse brusquely. He walked once more down the murkily-lit passage, gave his ticket to a surprised and silent dwarf, and without further trouble re-entered the auditorium. He recognised The Voluptuous Vera without difficulty and decided that it would be no more than a minimal hardship thus to while away the next hour and a half. He just hoped the masked young lady was still on the bill . . .

At 4.00 p.m. they sat opposite each other in the snack bar.

'You knew Valerie Taylor then?'

'I was at school with her.'

'Her boyfriend, weren't you?'

'One of 'em.'

'Like that, was it?' Maguire was non-committal. 'Why did Inspector Ainley come to see you?'

'You know why.'

'Did you know he was killed in a road accident the day he saw you?'

'No, I didn't.'

'I asked you why he came to see you.'

'Same reason as you, I suppose.'

'He asked you about Valerie?'

Maguire nodded, and Morse had the feeling that the boy was suddenly feeling more relaxed. Had Morse missed the turning?

'What did you tell him?'

'What could I tell him? Nothing more to tell, is there? They got me to write out a statement when I was at school, and I told them the truth. Couldn't do much more than that, could I?'

'You told the truth?'

' 'Course I did. I couldn't have had anything to do with it. I was in school all day, remember?'

Morse did remember, although he cursed himself for not bringing the boy's statement with him. Maguire had stayed at school for dinner and had been playing cricket the whole afternoon. At the time he must have seemed a peripheral figure in the investigation. Still was, perhaps. But why, then, *why* had Ainley come to London just to see him again – after all that time? There must have been *something*, something big. Morse finished the last dregs of his cold coffee and felt a bit lost. His devious manoeuvrings of the day began to look unnecessarily theatrical. Why couldn't he be a straight police-man for once in his life? Still, he had a couple of trump cards, and one never knew. He prepared to play the first.

'I'll give you one more chance, Maguire, but this time I want the truth – all of it.'

'I've told you . . .'

'Let's get one thing straight,' said Morse. 'I'm interested in Valerie Taylor – that's all. I'm not worried about any of those other things . . .' He left the words in the air, and a flash of alarm glinted in the boy's eyes.

'What other things? I don't know what you're talking about.'

'We've been to your flat today, lad.'

'So?'

'Mrs Gibbs doesn't seem too happy, does she, about one or two things . . . ?'

'Old cow.'

'She didn't have to *tell* us anything, you know.'

'What am I supposed to have done? Come on – let's have it.'

'How long have you been on drugs, lad?'

It hit him solidly between the eyes, and his effort at recovery was short of convincing. 'What drugs?'

'I just told you, lad. We've been to your flat today.'

'And I suppose you found some pot. So what? Just about everybody smokes pot here.'

'I'm not talking about everybody.' Morse leaned forward and let him have it. 'I'm talking about you, lad. Smoking pot's illegal, you know that, and I could frogmarch you out of here and ship you to the nearest police station – remember that! But I've just told you, lad, I'm quite prepared to let it ride. Christ, why do you have to make it so hard for yourself? You can go back to your bloody flat and pump yourself with heroin for all I care. I'm just not bothered, lad – not if you co-operate with me. Can't you get that into your thick skull?'

Morse let it sink in a minute before continuing. 'I want to know just one thing – what you told Inspector Ainley, that's all. And if I can't get it out of you here, I'll take you in and I'll get it out of you somewhere else. Please yourself, lad.'

Morse picked up his overcoat from the seat beside him and draped it across his knees. Maguire stared dejectedly at the table-top and played nervously with a bottle of tomato ketchup. There was indecision in his eyes, and Morse timed what he hoped was his second trump card perfectly.

'How long had you known that Valerie was pregnant?' he asked quietly.

Bull's-eye. Morse replaced his coat on the seat beside him, and Maguire spoke more freely. 'About three weeks before.'

'Did she tell anyone else?'

Maguire shrugged his shoulders. 'She was a real sexy kid – everyone was after her.'

'How often did you go to bed with her?'

'Ten – dozen times, I suppose.'

'The truth, please, lad.'

'Well, three or four times, maybe. I don't know.'

'Where was this?'

'My place.'

'Your parents know?'

'No. They were out working.'

'And she said you were the father?'

'No. She wasn't like that. Said I could have been, of course.'

'Did you feel jealous?' Morse had a suspicion that he did, but Maguire made no answer. 'Was she very upset?'

'Just scared.'

'What of? Scandal?'

'More scared of her mum, I think.'

'Not her dad?'

'She didn't say so.'

'Did she talk about running away?'

'Not to me.'

'Who else might she have spoken to?' Maguire hesitated. 'She had another boyfriend, didn't she,' persisted Morse, 'apart from you?'

'Pete?' Maguire could relax again. 'He didn't even touch her.'

'But she might have spoken to him?' Maguire was amused, and Morse felt that his questioning had lost its impetus. 'What about her form tutor? She might have gone to her, perhaps?'

Maguire laughed openly. 'You don't understand.'

But suddenly Morse realised that he was beginning to understand, and as the dawn was slowly breaking in his mind, he leaned forward and fixed Maguire with blue eyes, hard and unblinking.

'She could have gone to the headmaster, though.' He spoke the words with quiet, taut emphasis, and the impact upon Maguire was dramatic. Morse saw the sudden flash of burning jealousy and knew that gradually, inch by inch, he was moving nearer to the truth about Valerie Taylor.

Morse took a taxi to Southampton Terrace where he found a patient Lewis awaiting him. The car was ready and they were soon heading out along the M40 towards Oxford. Morse's mind was simultaneously veering in every direction, and he lapsed into uncommunicative introversion. It wasn't until they left the three-lane motorway that he broke the long silence.

'Sorry you had such a long wait, Lewis.'

'That's all right, sir. You had a long wait, too.'

'Yes,' said Morse. He made no mention of his return to The Penthouse. He must have gone down a good deal already in his sergeant's estimation; he had certainly sunk quite low enough in his own.

It was five miles outside Oxford that Lewis exploded the minor bombshell.

'I was having a talk with Mrs Gibbs, sir, while you were with Mr Maguire.'

'Well?'

'I asked her why he'd been such a nuisance.'

'What did she say?'

'She told me that until recently he'd had a girl in the flat.'

'She *what*?'

'Yes, sir. Almost a month, she said.'

'But why the hell didn't you tell me before, man? You surely realise . . . ?' He glared at Lewis, incredulous and exasperated, and sank back in despair behind his safety-belt.

His stubborn conviction that Valerie was no longer alive would (one had thought) have been sorely tested when he looked back into his office at 8.00 p.m. Awaiting him was a report from the forensic laboratory, short and to the point.

'Sufficient similarities to warrant positive identification. Suggest that investigation proceed on firm assumption that letter was written by signatory, Miss Valerie Taylor. Please contact if detailed verification required.'

But Morse seemed far from impressed. In fact, he looked up from the report and smiled serenely. Reaching for the telephone directory, he looked up Phillipson, D. There was only one Phillipson: 'The Firs', Banbury Road, Oxford.

Chapter Nine

We hear, for instance, of a comprehensive school in Connecticut where teachers have three pads of coloured paper, pink, blue and green, which are handed out to pupils as authority to visit respectively the headmaster, the office or the lavatory.

Robin Davis, *The Grammar School*

Sheila Phillipson was absolutely delighted with her Oxford home, a four-bedroomed detached house, just below the Banbury Road roundabout. Three fully-grown fir trees screened the spacious front garden from the busy main road, and the back garden, with its two old apple trees and its goldfish pond, its beautifully conditioned lawn and its neatly tended borders, was an unfailing joy. With unimaginative predictability she had christened it 'The Firs'.

Donald would be late home from school; he had a staff meeting. But it was only a cold salad, and the children had already eaten. She could relax. At a quarter to six she was sitting in a deck-chair in the back garden, her eyes closed contentedly. The evening air was warm and still . . . She felt so proud of Donald; and of the children, Andrew and Alison, now contentedly watching the television. They were both doing so well at their primary school. And, of course, if they didn't really get the chances they deserved, they could always go to private schools; and Donald would probably send them there – in spite of what he'd told the parents at the last speech day. The Dragon, New College School, Oxford High, Headington – one heard such good reports. But that was all in the future. For the moment everything in the garden was lovely. She lifted her face to catch the last rays of the sloping sun and breathed in the scent of thyme and honeysuckle. Lovely. Almost too lovely, perhaps. At half-past six she heard the crunch of Donald's Rover on the drive.

Later in the evening Sheila did not recognise the man at the door, a slimly built man with a clean, sensitive mouth and wide light-blue eyes. He had a nice voice, she thought, for a police inspector.

In spite of Morse's protests that *Tom and Jerry* ranked as his very favourite TV programme, the children were immediately sent upstairs to bed. She was cross with herself for not having packed them off half an hour ago: toys littered the floor, and she fussily and apologetically gathered together the offending objects and took them out. On her return she found her visitor gazing with deep interest at a framed photograph of herself and her husband.

'Press photograph, isn't it?'

'Yes. We had a big party in Donald's, er, in my husband's first term here. All the staff, husbands and wives – you know the sort of thing. The *Oxford Mail* took that. Took a lot of photographs, in fact.'

'Have you got the other photographs?'

'Yes. I think so. Would you like to look at them? My husband won't be long. He's just finishing his bath.'

She rummaged about in a drawer of the bureau, and handed to Morse five glossy, black and white photographs. One of them, a group photograph, held his keen attention: the men in dinner-jackets and black bow-ties, the ladies in long dresses. Most of them looked happy enough.

'Do you know some of the staff?' she asked.

'Some of them.'

He looked again at the group. 'Beautifully clear photograph.'

'Very good, isn't it?'

'Is Acum here?'

'Acum? Oh yes, I think so. Mr Acum left two years ago. But I remember him quite well – and his wife.' She pointed them out on the photograph; a young man with a lively, intelligent face and a small goatee beard; and, her arm linked through his, a slim, boyish-figured girl, with shoulder-length blonde hair, not unattractive perhaps, but with a face (at least on this evidence) a little severe and more than a little spotty.

'You knew his wife, you say?' asked Morse.

Sheila heard the gurgling death-rattle of the bath upstairs, and for some inexplicable reason felt a cold shudder creeping along her spine. She felt just as she did as a young girl when she had once answered the phone for her father. She recalled the strange, almost frightening questions . . .

A shiningly fresh Phillipson came in. He apologised for keeping Morse waiting, and in turn Morse apologised for his own unheralded intrusion. Sheila breathed an inward sigh of relief, and asked if they'd prefer tea or coffee. With livelier brews apparently out of the question, Morse opted for coffee and, like a good host, the headmaster concurred.

'I've come to ask about Acum,' said Morse, with brisk honesty. 'What can you tell me about him?'

'Acum? Not much really. He left at the end of my first year here. Taught French. Well-qualified chap. Exeter – took a Second if I remember rightly.'

'What about his wife?'

'She had a degree in Modern Languages, too. They met at Exeter University, I think. In fact she taught with us for a term when one of the staff was ill. Not too successfully, I'm afraid.'

'Why was that?'

'Bit of a tough class – you know how it is. She wasn't really up to it.'

'They gave her a rough ride, you mean?'

'They nearly took her pants down, I'm afraid.'

'You're speaking metaphorically, I hope?'

'I hope so, too. I heard some hair-raising rumours, though. Still, it was my fault for taking her on. Too much of a blue-stocking for that sort of job.'

'What did you do?'

Phillipson shrugged. 'I had to get rid of her.'

'What about Acum himself? Where did he go?'

'One of the schools in Caernarfon.'

'He got promotion, did he?'

'Well no, not really. He'd only been teaching the one year, but they could promise him some sixth-form work. I couldn't.'

'Is he still there?'

'As far as I know.'

'He taught Valerie Taylor – you know that?'

'Inspector, wouldn't it be fairer if you told me why you're so interested in him? I might be able to help more if I knew what you were getting at.'

Morse pondered the question. 'Trouble is, I don't really know myself.'

Whether he believed him or not, Phillipson left it at that. 'Well, I know he taught Valerie, yes. Not one of his brightest pupils, I don't think.'

'Did he ever talk to you about her?'

'No. Never.'

'No rumours? No gossip?'

Phillipson took a deep breath, but managed to control his mounting irritation. 'No.'

Morse changed his tack. 'Have you got a good memory, sir?'

'Good enough, I suppose.'

'Good enough to remember what you were doing on Tuesday 2nd September this year?'

Phillipson cheated and consulted his diary. 'I was at a Head-masters' Conference in London.'

'Whereabouts in London?'

'It was at the Café Royal. And if you must know the conference started at . . .'

'All right. All right.' Morse held up his right hand like a priest pronouncing the benediction, as a flush of anger rose in the headmaster's cheeks.

'Why did you ask me that?'

Morse smiled benignly. 'That was the day Valerie wrote to her parents.'

'What the hell are you getting at, Inspector?'

'I shall be asking a lot of people the same question before I've finished, sir. And some of them will get terribly cross, I know that. But I'd rather hoped that you would understand.'

Phillipson calmed down. 'Yes, I see. You mean . . .'

'I don't mean anything, sir. All I know is that I have to ask a lot of awkward questions; it's what they pay me for. I suppose it's the same in your job.'

'I'm sorry. Go ahead and ask what you like. I shan't mind.'

'I shouldn't be too sure of that, sir.' Phillipson looked at him sharply. 'You see,' continued Morse, 'I want you to tell me, if you can, exactly what you were doing on the afternoon that Valerie Taylor disappeared.'

Mrs Phillipson brought in the coffee, and after she had retired once more to the kitchen the answer was neatly wrapped and tied.

'I had lunch at school that day, drove down into Oxford, and browsed around in Blackwell's. Then I came home.'

'Do you remember what time you got home?'

'About three.'

'You seem to remember that afternoon pretty well, sir.'

'It *was* rather an important afternoon, wasn't it, Inspector?'

'Did you buy any books?'

'I don't remember that much, I'm afraid.'

'Do you have an account with Blackwell's?'

Momentarily Phillipson hesitated. 'Yes. But . . . but if I'd just bought a paperback or something I would have paid in cash.'

'But you might have bought something more expensive?' Morse looked along the impressive rows of historical works that covered two walls of the lounge from floor to ceiling, and thought of Johnny Maguire's pathetic little collection.

'You could check up, I suppose,' said Phillipson curtly.

'Yes. I suppose we shall.' Morse felt suddenly very tired.

At half-past midnight Sheila Phillipson tiptoed quietly down the stairs and found the codeine bottle. It kept coming back to her mind and she couldn't seem to push it away from her – that terrible night when Donald had been making love to her, and called her Valerie. She'd never mentioned it, of course. She just couldn't.

Suddenly she jumped, a look of blind terror in her eyes, before subsiding with relief upon a kitchen stool.

'Oh, it's only you, Donald. You frightened me.'

'Couldn't you sleep either, darling?'

Chapter Ten

Not a line of her writing have I,
Not a thread of her hair.

Thomas Hardy, *Thoughts of Phena*

Morse seemed reluctant to begin any work when he arrived, late, in his office on Thursday morning. He handed Lewis the report on Valerie's letter and started on *The Times* crossword puzzle. He looked at his watch, marked the time exactly in the margin of the newspaper and was soon scribbling in letters at full speed. Ten minutes later he stopped. He allowed himself only ten minutes, and almost always completed it. But this morning one clue remained unsolved.

'What's this, Lewis? Six letters. Blank A – blank S – blank N. *Eyes had I – and saw not?*'

Lewis jotted down the letters and pretended to think. He just hadn't a crossword mind. 'Could it be "parson", sir?'

'Why on earth should it be "parson"?'

'Well, it fits.'

'So do a hundred and one other words.'

'Such as?' Morse struggled hard before producing 'damson'.

'I'd rather have my parson, sir.'

Morse put the paper aside. 'Well. What do you think?'

'Seems to be her writing, doesn't it?'

There was a knock on the door and a pretty young office girl deposited the morning post into the in-tray. Cursorily and distastefully Morse looked through the correspondence.

'Nothing urgent here, Lewis. Let's go along to the lab. I think Old Peters must be getting senile.'

Now in his early sixties, Peters had previously worked for twenty years as a Home Office pathologist, and somewhere along the line the juices of human fallibility had been squeezed from his cerebral processes. His manner was clinical and dry, and his words seemed to be dictated by a mini-computer installed somewhere inside his brain. His answers were slow, mechanical, definitive. He had never been known to argue with anyone. He just read the information-tapes.

'You think this is Valerie Taylor's writing, then?'

He paused and answered. 'Yes.'

'Can you ever be certain about things like handwriting, though?'

He paused and answered. 'No.'

'How certain are you?'

He paused and answered. 'Ninety per cent.'

'You'd be surprised then if it turned out that she didn't write it?'

He paused and the computer considered its reaction to the improbability. 'Yes. Surprised.'

'What makes you think she wrote it?'

He paused and lectured briefly and quietly on the evidence of loops and quirks and whorls. Morse battled on against the odds.

'You can forge a letter, though, can't you?'

He paused and answered. 'Of course.'

'But you don't think this was forged?'

He paused and answered. 'I think it was written by the girl.'

'But a person's handwriting changes over the years, doesn't it? I mean, the letter's written in almost exactly the same way as the exercise books.'

He paused and answered. 'There's a basic built-in style about all our handwriting. Slopes change, certainly, and other minor things. But whatever changes, there is still the distinctive style, carrying with it the essential features of our personal characteristics.' He paused again, and Lewis had the impression he was reading it all out of a book. 'In Greek, the word "character" means handwriting, they tell me.'

Lewis smiled. He was enjoying himself.

Morse put a penultimate problem to the computer. 'You wouldn't go into the witness box and say it definitely *was* her writing, would you?'

He paused and answered. 'I would tell a jury what I've told you – that the order of probability is somewhere in the region of ninety per cent.'

Morse turned as he reached the door. 'Could *you* forge her handwriting convincingly?'

The desiccated calculating-machine actually smiled and the hesitation this time was minimal. 'I've had a lot of experience in this field, you know.'

'You *could*, then?'

He paused and answered. '*I* could, yes.'

Back in his office Morse brought Lewis up to date with his visit the previous evening to the Phillipson residence.

'You don't like him much, do you, sir?'

Morse looked aggrieved. 'Oh, I don't dislike him. It's just that I don't think he's completely above-board with me, that's all.'

'We've all of us got things we'd like to hide, haven't we, sir?'

'Mm.' Morse was staring through the window. *Eyes had I – and saw not.* Six letters. It still eluded him. Like the answer to this case. A whole orchestra of instruments and some of them playing just slightly out of tune.

'Did you know that "orchestra" was an anagram of "carthorse", Lewis?'

Lewis didn't. He idly wrote down the letters and checked. 'So it is. Perhaps the clue you can't get is an anagram, sir.'

The light dawned in Morse's eyes. 'You're a genius. SAW NOT.' Sherlock Holmes picked up *The Times* again, wrote in the answer and beamed at his own Doctor Watson.

'Now let's consider the case so far.' Lewis sat back and listened. Morse was away.

'We can say, can we not, that the letter was either written by Valerie herself or by another person? Agreed?'

'With odds of nine to one on Valerie.'

'Yes, with strong odds on Valerie. Now if Valerie herself wrote the letter, we can reasonably assume that she is still alive, that she probably ran off to London, that she's still there, that she's quite happy where she is, doesn't want to come back to Kidlington – and that we're wasting our bloody time.'

'Not if we find her.'

'Of course we are. What do we do if we find her? Bring her back home to mummy and tell her what a naughty girl she's been? What's the point of that?'

'It would clear up the case, though.'

'If she wrote the letter, there *is* no case.'

Something had been troubling Lewis sorely since the previous evening and he got it off his conscience. 'Do you think what Mrs Gibbs told me was important, sir – you know, about the girl in Maguire's flat?'

'Doubt it,' said Morse.

'You don't think it could have been Valerie?'

'I keep telling you, Lewis. *She's dead* – whatever that pettifogging Peters says, *she couldn't have written that letter.*'

Lewis groaned inwardly. Once the chief got an idea stuck firmly in his brain, something cataclysmic was needed to dislodge it.

'Let's just assume for a minute that the letter was *not* written by Valerie. In that case it was written by someone who copied her writing, and copied it with enormous care and skill. Yes?'

'But why should anyone . . . ?'

'I'm coming to that. Why should anyone want to make us believe that Valerie was still alive *if in fact she was dead*? Well, as I see it, there is one simple and overwhelmingly convincing answer to that question. Someone wants us to believe Valerie is still alive because he or she sees a very real danger that further police investigation in the Taylor girl affair is likely to uncover the truth, Lewis – which is that Valerie is dead and that someone murdered her. I think that for some reason this someone began to get very scared, and wrote that letter to put us off the scent. Or more specifically, perhaps, to put Ainley off the scent.'

Lewis felt he could make no worthwhile contribution to such a weird hypothesis, and Morse continued.

'There is another possibility, though, and we mustn't discount it. The letter could have been written by someone for *precisely the opposite reason* – to put the police back on the scent. And if you think about it, that's precisely what has happened. Ainley was still working on the case – but unofficially. And when he was killed, if it hadn't been for the letter, the case would have been left where it was – unsolved and gradually forgotten. But once the letter arrived, what happened? Strange called me in and told me to take over, to reinvestigate the case officially. Precisely what we're doing now. Now let's follow this line of reasoning a bit further. Who would want the police to reopen the case? Not the murderer – that's for sure. Who then? It could be the parents, of course. They might think that the police weren't really doing much about things . . .'

Lewis looked stupefied. 'You don't honestly think the Taylors wrote the letter, do you?'

'Had the possibility not occurred to you?' asked Morse quietly.

'No.'

'Well it should have done. After all, they're as likely as anyone to make a good job of forging a letter in their daughter's handwriting. But there's a much more interesting possibility, I think. The letter could have been sent by someone who knew that Valerie had been murdered, who had a jolly good idea of who murdered her, and who wanted the murderer brought to justice.'

'But why . . . ?'

'Just a minute. Let's assume that such a person knew that Ainley was getting perilously close to the truth, had perhaps even helped Ainley towards the truth. What happens then? Tragedy. Ainley is killed and everything is back at square one. Look at it this way. Let's assume that Ainley went to London on the Monday and actually found Valerie Taylor alive. You with me? All right – the cat's out of the bag; she's been found. The next day she writes to her parents. There's no point in covering up any longer. If she doesn't tell them, Ainley will.'

'That seems to fit, sir.'

'Ah. But there's another interpretation, isn't there? Let's now assume that Ainley *didn't* find Valerie – and I don't think he did. Let's suppose he found something rather more sinister than Valerie Taylor alive and well. Because remember, Lewis, *something* took Ainley to London that day. We shall perhaps never know what, but he was getting nearer and nearer the truth all the time. And when he was killed someone, Lewis, *someone* desperately wanted his work to be followed up. And so the day after Ainley's death, a letter is written. It was written precisely because *Valerie Taylor was dead* – not alive, and it had exactly the effect it was intended to have. The case was reopened.'

The convolutions of Morse's theories were beginning to defeat Lewis's powers of logical analysis. 'I don't quite follow some of that, sir, but . . . you're still basing it all on the assumption that she didn't write the letter, aren't you? I mean if what Peters says is . . .'

The pretty office girl came in again and handed to Morse a buff-coloured file.

'Superintendent Strange stays you may be interested in this, sir. It's been tested for fingerprints – no good, he says.'

Morse opened the file. Inside was a cheap brown envelope, already opened, posted the previous day in central London, and addressed to the Thames Valley Police. The letter inside was written on ruled, white note-paper.

Dear Sir,
　　I hear you are trying to find me, but I don't want you to because I don't want to go back home.
　　Yours truly, Valerie Taylor.

He handed the letter to Lewis. 'Not the most voluminous of correspondents, our Valerie, is she?'

He picked up the phone and dialled the lab, and from the slight pause at the other end of the line he knew he must be speaking to the computer itself.

Chapter Eleven

All women become like their mothers. That is their tragedy.
                                                    Oscar Wilde

For the second time within twenty-four hours Morse found himself studying a photograph with more than usual interest. Lewis he had left in the office to make a variety of telephone calls, and he himself stood, arms akimbo, staring fixedly at the young girl who stared back at him, equally fixedly, from the wall of the lounge. Slim, with dark-brown hair and eyes that almost asked if you'd dare and a figure that clearly promised it would be wonderful if you found the daring. She was a very attractive girl and, like the elders in Troy who looked for the first time upon Helen, Morse felt no real surprise that she had been the cause of so much trouble.

'Lovely looking girl, your daughter.'

Mrs Taylor smiled diffidently at the photograph. 'It's not Valerie,' she said, 'it's me.'

Morse turned with undisguised astonishment in his eyes. 'Really? I didn't realise you were so much alike. I didn't mean to, er . . .'

'I used to be nice-looking, I suppose, in those days. I was seventeen when that was taken – over twenty years ago. It seems a long time.'

Morse watched her as she spoke. Her figure was a good deal thicker round the hips now, and her legs, though still slim, were faintly lined with varicose veins. But it was her face that had changed the most: a few wisps of greying hair trailed over the worn features, the teeth yellowing, the flesh around the throat no longer quite so firm. But she was still . . . Men were luckier, he thought; they seemed to age much less perceptibly than women. On a low cupboard against the right-hand wall behind her stood an elegant, delicately-proportioned porcelain vase. Somehow it seemed to Morse so incongruously tasteful and expensive in this drably-furnished room, and he found himself staring at it with a slightly puzzled frown.

They talked for half an hour or so, mostly about Valerie; but there was nothing she could add to what she had told so many people so many times before. She recalled the events of that far-off day like a nervous well-rehearsed pupil in a history examination. But that was no surprise to Morse. After all, as Phillipson had reminded him the previous evening, it *was* rather an important day. He asked her about herself and learned she had recently taken a job, just mornings, at the Cash and Carry stores – stocking up the shelves mostly; tiring, on her feet most of the time, but it was better than staying at home all day, and nice to have some money of her own. Morse refrained from asking how much she spent on drink and cigarettes, but there was something that he had to ask.

'You won't be upset, Mrs Taylor, if I ask you one or two rather personal questions, will you?'

'I shouldn't think so.'

She leaned back on the crimson settee and lit another cigarette, her hand shaking slightly. Morse felt he ought to have realised it before. He could see it in the way she sat, legs slightly parted, the eyes still throwing a distant, muted invitation. There was an overt if faded sensuality about the woman. It was almost tangible. He took a deep breath.

'Did you know that Valerie was pregnant when she disappeared?'

Her eyes grew almost dangerous. 'She wasn't pregnant. I'm her mother, remember? Whoever told you that was a bloody liar.' The voice was harsher now, and cheaper. The façade was beginning to crack, and Morse found himself wondering about her. Husband away; long, lonely days and daughter home only at lunch-times – and that only during Valerie's last year at school.

He hadn't meant to ask his next question. It was one of those things that wasn't really anyone else's business. It had struck him, of course, the first time he had glanced at the Colour Supplement: the cards for the eighteenth wedding anniversary, and Valerie at the time almost twenty – or would have been, had she still been alive. He took another deep breath.

'Was Valerie your husband's child, Mrs Taylor?'

The question struck home and she looked away. 'No. I had her before I knew George.'

'I see,' said Morse gently.

At the door she turned towards him. 'Are you going to see him?' Morse nodded. 'I don't mind what you ask him but . . . but please don't mention anything about . . . about what you just asked me. He was like a father to her always but he . . . he used to get teased a lot about Valerie when we were first married especially . . . especially since we didn't have any kids ourselves. You know what I mean. It hurt him, I know it did, and . . . and I don't want him hurt, Inspector. He's been a good man to me; he's always been a good man to me.'

She spoke with a surprising warmth of feeling and as she spoke
Morse could see the lineaments of an erstwhile beauty in her face.
He heard himself promise that he wouldn't. Yet he found himself
wondering who Valerie's real father had been, and if it might be
important for him to find out. If he *could* find out. If anyone knew
– including Valerie's mother.

As he walked slowly away he wondered something else, too.
There had been something, albeit hardly perceptible, something
slightly off-key about Mrs Taylor's nervousness; just a little more
than the natural nervousness of meeting a strange man – even a
strange policeman. It was more like the look he had several times
witnessed on his secretary's face when he had burst unexpectedly
into her office and found her hastily and guiltily covering up some
personal little thing that she hoped he hadn't seen. Had there been
someone else in the house during his interview with Mrs Taylor?
He thought so. In an instant he turned on his heel and spun round to
face the house he had just left – and he saw it. The right-hand curtain of an upstairs window twitched slightly and a vague silhouette
glided back against the wall. It was over in a flash. The curtain was
still; all sign of life was gone. A cabbage-white butterfly stitched its
way along the privet hedge – and then that, too, was gone.

Chapter Twelve

Even the dustbin lid is raised mechanically
   At the very last moment
You could dispose of a corpse like this
   Without giving the least offence.
                    D. J. Enright, *No Offence: Berlin*

It occurred to Morse as he drove down the Woodstock Road into
Oxford that although he had done most things in life he had never
before had occasion to visit a rubbish tip. In fact, as he turned into
Walton Street and slowed to negotiate the narrowing streets that led
down to Jericho, he could not quite account for the fact that he knew
exactly where to go. He passed Aristotle Lane and turned right into
Walton Well Road, over the humpbacked bridge that spanned the

canal, and stopped the Jaguar beside an open gate, where a notice informed him that unauthorised vehicles were not allowed to drive further and that offenders would be prosecuted by an official with (it seemed to Morse) the portentous title of Conservator and Sheriff of Port Meadow. He slipped the car into first gear and drove on, deciding that he would probably qualify in the 'authorised' category, and rather hoping that someone would stop him. But no one did. He made his way slowly along the concreted pathway, a thin belt of trees on his right and the open green expanse of Port Meadow on his left. Twice when corporation lorries came towards him he was forced off the track on to the grass, before coming finally to the edge of the site, where a high wooden gate over a deep cattle-grid effectively barred all further progress. He left the car and proceeded on foot, noting, as he passed another sign, that members of the public would be ill-advised to touch any materials deposited on the tip, treated as they were with harmful insecticides. He had gone more than 200 yards before he caught his first sight of genuine rubbish. The compacted surface over which he walked was flat and clear, scored by the caterpillar tracks of bulldozers and levellers, with only the occasional partially-submerged piece of sacking to betray the burial of the thousands of tons of rubbish beneath. Doubtless grass and shrubs would soon be burgeoning there, and the animals would return to their old territories and scurry once more in the hedgerows amid the bracken and the wild flowers. And people would come and scatter their picnic litter around and the whole process would begin again. Sometimes *homo sapiens* was a thoroughly disgusting species.

He made his way towards the only observable sign of life – a corrugated-iron shack, once painted green but ramshackle now and rusty, where an indescribably grimy labourer directed him deeper into the network of filth. Two magpies and an ominous-looking crow reluctantly took to flight as he walked by, and flapped their slow way across the blighted wilderness. At last Morse came to the main area of the tip: Pepsi and Coca-Cola tins, perished household gloves, lengths of rusting wire, empty cartons of washing-up liquid, and a disintegrating dart-board; biscuit tins, worn-out shoes, a hot-water bottle, ancient car seats and a comprehensive collection of cardboard boxes. Morse swatted away the ugly flies that circled his head, and was glad to find he had one last cigarette left. He threw the empty packet away; it didn't seem to matter much here.

George Taylor was standing beside a yellow bulldozer, shouting to its driver above the deep-throated growl of the engine, and pointing towards a great mound of earth and stones piled like a rampart along the side of the shallow tip. Morse idly conjured up the image of some archaeologist who, some thousand years hence, might seek to discover the life-style of twentieth-century man, and Morse commiserated with him on the dismal debris he would find.

George was a heavily-built, broad-shouldered man, not too intelligent, perhaps, but, as Morse saw him, honest and likeable enough. He sat down upon a ten-gallon paraffin tin, Morse himself having declined the offer of similar accommodation, supposing that by this time George's trousers were probably immune from the harmful effects of all insecticides. And so they talked, and Morse tried to picture the scene as it must have been each night in the Taylor household: George arriving home, dirty and tired, at 6.15 or thereabouts; Mrs Taylor cooking the evening meal and washing up the pots; and Valerie – but what did he know of Valerie? Occasionally condescending to do a modicum of homework? He didn't know. Three isolated personalities, under the same roof, somehow brought and kept together by that statistical unit beloved by the sociologists – the family. Morse asked about Valerie – her life at home, her life at school, her friends, her likes and her dislikes; but he learned little that was new.

'Have you ever thought that Valerie may have run away because she was expecting a baby?'

George slowly lit a Woodbine and contemplated the broken glass that littered the ground at his feet. 'You think of most things, don't you, when summat like that happens? I remembered when she were a young gal she were a bit late sometimes – and I used to think all sorts of things had happened.' Morse nodded. 'You got a family, Inspector?'

Morse shook his head and, like George, contemplated the ground about his feet.

' 'Sfunny, really. You think of the most terrible things. And then she'd come back and you'd feel all sort of happy and cross at the same time, if you know what I mean.'

Morse thought he knew; and for the first time in the case he saw something of the heartache and the sorrow of it all, and he began to hope that Valerie Taylor was still alive.

'Was she often late coming home?'

George hesitated. 'Not really. Well, not till she were about sixteen, anyway.'

'And then she was?'

'Well, not too late. Anyway, I allus used to wait up for her.'

Morse put it more bluntly. 'Did she ever stay out all night?'

'Never.' It was a firm and categorical answer, but Morse wondered if it were true.

'When was the latest she came in? After midnight?' George nodded rather sadly. 'Much after?'

'Sometimes.'

'Rows, were there?'

'The wife got cross, of course. Well, so did I, really.'

'She often stayed out late, then?'

'Well, no. Not often. Just once every few weeks, like, she'd say she was going to a party with her friends, or summat like that.' He rubbed his hand across his stubbled chin and shook his head. 'These days it's not like it was when we was boys. I don't know.'

They brooded silently and George kicked a flattened Coca-Cola tin a few yards further away.

'Did you give her much pocket money?' asked Morse.

'Quid a week – sometimes a bit more. And at weekends she used to work on the till down the supermarket. Used to spend it on clothes mostly – shoes, that sort of thing. She were never short of money.'

With a powerful snarl the bulldozer shovelled a few more cubic yards of earth across a stinking stretch of refuse, and then slowly retreated to manoeuvre diagonally into position behind the next heap, criss-crossing the ground with the patterned tracks that Morse had noticed earlier. And as the gleaming teeth of the scoop dug again into the crumbling soil, something stirred vaguely in the back of Morse's mind; but George was speaking again.

'That inspector what was killed, you know, he came to see me a few weeks back.'

Morse stood very still and held his breath, as if the slightest movement might be fatal. His question would appear, he hoped, to spring from casual curiosity.

'What did he want to see you about, Mr Taylor?'

' 'Sfunny really. He asked me the same as you. You know, about Valerie staying out at nights.'

Morse's blood ran slightly cold, and his blue eyes looked into the past and seemed to catch a glimpse of what had happened all that time ago . . . Another corporation lorry rumbled up the slight incline, ready to stock-pile the latest consignment of rubbish, and George stood up to direct proceedings.

'Not been much help, I'm afraid, Inspector.'

Morse shook George's dirty, calloused hand, and prepared to leave.

'Do you think she's alive, Inspector?'

Morse looked at him curiously. 'Do you?'

'Well, there's the letter, isn't there, Inspector?'

For some strange, intuitive reason Morse felt the question had somehow been wrong, and he frowned slightly as he watched George Taylor walk over to the lorry. Yes, there was the letter, and he hoped now that Valerie had written it, but . . .

He stood where he was and looked around him.

How would you like to be stuck in a filthy hole like this, Morse – probably for the rest of your life? And when anyone calls to see you, all you can offer is an old ten-gallon paraffin tin sprayed with harmful insecticide. You've got your own black leather chair and the white carpet and the desk of polished Scandinavian oak. Some people are luckier than others.

As he walked away the yellow bulldozer nudged its nose into another pile of earth; and soon the leveller would come and gradually smooth over the clay surface, like a passable cook with the chocolate icing on a cake.

Chapter Thirteen

Man kann den Wald nicht vor Baümen sehen.

German proverb

Lewis had gone home when Morse returned to his office at 5.30, and he felt it would probably be sensible for him to do the same. Many pieces of the jigsaw were now to hand, some of them big ugly pieces that looked as if they wouldn't fit anywhere; but they would – if only he had the time to think it all out. For the moment he was too much on top of things. Some of the trees were clear enough, but not the configuration of the forest. To stand back a bit and take a more synoptic view of things – that's what he needed.

He fetched a cup of coffee from the canteen, and sat at his desk. The notes that Lewis had made, and left conspicuously beneath a paperweight, he deliberately put to one side. There were other things in life than the Taylor case, although for the moment he couldn't quite remember what they were. He went through his in-tray and read through reports on the recent spate of incendiary bombings, the role of the police at pop festivals, and the vicious hooliganism after Oxford United's last home game. There were some interesting points. He crossed through his initials and stuck the reports in his out-tray. The next man on the list would do exactly the same; quickly glance through, cross through his initials, and stick them in his out-tray. There were too many reports, and the more there were the more self-defeating the whole exercise became. He would vote for a moratorium on all reports for the next five years.

He consulted his diary. The following morning he would be in the courts, and he'd better get home and iron a clean shirt. It was 6.25 and he felt hungry. Ah well. He'd call at the Chinese restaurant and take-away . . . He was pulling on his overcoat and debating between King Prawns and Chicken Chop Suey when the phone went.

'Personal call from a Mr Phillipson. Shall I put him through, sir?' The girl on the switchboard sounded weary too.

'You're working late tonight, Inspector.'

'I was just off,' said Morse with a yawn in his voice.

'You're lucky,' said Phillipson. 'We've got a Parents' Evening – shan't be home till ten myself.'

Morse was unimpressed and the headmaster got to the point.

'I thought I'd just ring up to say that I checked up at Blackwell's – you remember? – about buying a book.'

Morse looked at Lewis's notes and completed the sentence for him.

'. . . and you bought Momigliano's *Studies in Historiography* published by Weidenfeld and Nicolson at £2.50.'

'You checked, then?'

'Yep.'

'Oh well. I thought, er, I'd just let you know.'

'Thoughtful of you, sir. I appreciate it. Are you speaking from school?'

'From my study, yes.'

'I wonder if you've got a phone number for Mr Acum there?'

'Just a minute, Inspector.'

Morse kept the receiver to his ear and read through the rest of Lewis's notes. Nothing from Peters yet about that second letter; nothing much from anybody . . .

To anyone with less than extremely acute hearing it would have been quite imperceptible. But Morse heard it, and knew once again that someone had been eavesdropping on the headmaster's telephone conversations. Someone in the office outside the head's study; and Morse's brain slid easily along the shining grooves.

'Are you there, Inspector? We've got two numbers for Acum – one at school, one at home.'

'I'll take 'em both,' said Morse.

After cradling the receiver, he sat and thought for a moment. If Phillipson wanted to use the phone in his study, he would first dial 9, get an outside line automatically, and then ring the code and the number he wanted. Morse had noticed the set-up when he had visited the school. But if he, Morse, wanted to ring Phillipson, he wouldn't be able to get him unless someone was sitting by the switchboard in the outer office; and he doubted that the faithful Mrs Webb would be required that evening for the Parents' Evening.

He waited a couple of minutes and rang.

Brr. Brr. It was answered almost immediately.

'Roger Bacon School.'

'That the headmaster?' enquired Morse innocently.

'No. Baines here. Second master. Can I help you?'

'Ah, Mr Baines. Good evening, sir. As a matter of fact it was you I was hoping to get hold of. I, er, wonder if we might be able to meet again fairly soon. It's this Taylor girl business again. There are one or two points I think you could help me with.'

Baines would be free about a quarter to ten, and he could be in the White Horse soon after that. No time like the present.

Morse felt pleased with himself. He would have been even more pleased had he been able to see the deeply worried look on Baines's face as he shrugged into his gown and walked down into the Great Hall to meet the parents.

There was little point in going home now and he walked over to the canteen and found a copy of the *Telegraph*. He ordered sausages and mash, wrote the precise time in the right-hand margin of the back page and turned to 1 across. *Has been known to split under a grilling (7)*. He smiled to himself. It was too many letters for BAINES, so he wrote in SAUSAGE.

Back in the office he felt he was in good form. Crossword finished in only seven and a half minutes. Still, it was a bit easier than *The Times*. Perhaps this case would be easy if only he could look at it in the right way, and as Baines had said there was no time like the present. A long, quiet, cool, detached look at the case. But it never worked quite like that. He sat back and closed his eyes and for more than an hour his brain seethed in ceaseless turmoil. Ideas, ideas galore, but still the firm outline of the pattern eluded him. One or two of the pieces fitted firmly into place, but so many wouldn't fit at all. It was like doing the light-blue sky at the top of a jigsaw, with no clouds, not even a solitary sea-gull to break the boundless monochrome

By nine o'clock he had a headache. Leave it. Give it a rest and go back later. Like crosswords. It would come; it would come.

He consulted the STD codes and found that he would have to get Caernarfon through the operator. It was Acum who answered.

As succinctly as he could Morse explained the reason for his call, and Acum politely interjected the proper noises of understanding and approval. Yes, of course. Yes, of course he remembered Valerie and the day she had disappeared. Yes, he remembered it all well.

'Did you realise that you were one of the very last people to see Valerie before she, er, before she disappeared?'

'I must have been, yes.'

'In fact, you taught her the very last school lesson she ever had, I think?'

'Yes.'

'I mention this, sir, because I have reason to believe that you asked Valerie to see you after the lesson.'

'Ye-es. I think I did.'

'Remember why, sir?' Acum took his time and Morse wished that he could see the schoolmaster's face.

'If I remember rightly, Inspector, she was due to sit her O-level French the next week, and her work was, well, pretty dreadful, and I was going to have a word with her about it. Not that she had much chance in the exam, I'm afraid.'

'You said, sir, you were *going* to see her.'

'Yes, that's right. As it happened I didn't get a chance. She had to rush off, she said.'

'Did she say why?'

The answer was ready this time, and it took the wind out of Morse's sails. 'She said she'd got to see the head.'

'Oh, I see.' Another piece that didn't fit. 'Well, thank you, Mr Acum. You've been most helpful. I hope I've not interrupted anything important.'

'No. No. Just marking a few books, that's all.'

'Well, I'll leave you to it. Thanks very much.'

'Not at all. If I can help in any other way, don't hesitate
to ring me, will you?'

'Er, no. I won't. Thanks again.'

Morse sat still for many minutes and began to wonder if he
ought not to turn the jigsaw upside down and work the blue sky
in at the bottom. There was no doubt about it: he ought to have
gone home as he'd promised himself earlier. He was just walking
blindly in the forest bumping into one wretched tree after another.
But he couldn't go home yet; he had an appointment.

Baines was there already and got up to buy the inspector a drink.
The lounge was quiet and they sat alone in a corner and wished
each other good health.

Morse tried to size him up. Tweed jacket, grey slacks, balding
on top and rather flabby in the middle, but obviously nobody's
fool. His eyes were keen and Morse imagined the students would
never take too many liberties with Baines. He spoke with a slight
North Country accent and as he listened to Morse he picked away
at his nostrils with his index finger. Irritating.

What was the routine on Tuesday afternoons? Why was there no
register taken? Was there any likelihood that Valerie had, in fact,
returned to school that afternoon, and only later disappeared? How
did the pupils work the skiving that was obviously so widespread?
Was there any sort of skivers' den where the reluctant athletes could
safely hide themselves away? Have a smoke perhaps?

Baines seemed rather amused. He could give the boys and girls
a few tips about getting off games! By jove, he could. But it was
the staff's fault. The PE teachers were a bloody idle lot – worse
than the kids. Hardly bothered to get changed, some of them. And
anyway, there were so many activities: fencing, judo, table-tennis,
athletics, rounders, netball – all this self-expression nonsense. No
one really knew who was expected when and where. Bloody stupid.
Things had tightened up a bit with the new head, but – well. Baines
gave the impression that for all his possible virtues Phillipson had
a long way still to go. Where they went to? Plenty of places. He'd
found half a dozen smoking in the boiler-room one day, and the
school itself was virtually empty. Quite a few of them just sloped
off home though, and some didn't turn up at all. Anyway, like the
headmaster, he wasn't really involved on Tuesday afternoons. It
wasn't a bad idea, though, to get away from school occasionally
– have a free afternoon. The headmaster had tried to do it for
all the staff. Put all their free periods together and let them have

a morning or an afternoon off. Trouble was that it meant a hell of a lot of work for the chap who did the timetabling. Him!

As he talked on Morse wondered whether he still felt bitter towards Phillipson; whether he would be all that eager to throw out a lifeline to the drowning helmsman. He casually mentioned that he knew of Baines's ill luck in being pipped for the job; and bought more beer. Yes (Baines admitted), he'd been a bit unlucky perhaps, and more than once. He thought he could have run a school as well as most, and Morse felt he was probably right. Greedy and selfish (like most men), but shrewdly competent. Above all, thought Morse, he would have enjoyed power. And now that there no longer seemed much chance of power, perhaps a certain element of dark satisfaction in observing the inadequacies of others and quietly gloating over their misfortunes. There wasn't a word for it in English. The Germans called it *Schadenfreude*. Would Baines get the job if Phillipson left or if for some reason he *had* to leave? Morse thought he would be sure to. But how far would he go in actively promoting such a situation? Perhaps though, as usual, Morse was attributing too much cynical self-seeking to his fellow men, and he brought his attention back to the fairly ordinary man who sat opposite him, talking openly and amusingly about life in a comprehensive school.

'Did you ever teach Valerie yourself?' asked Morse.

Baines chuckled. 'In the first form – just for a year. She didn't know a trapezium from a trampoline.'

Morse grinned, too. 'Did you like her?'

It was a sobering question, and the shrewdness gleamed again in Baines's eyes.

'She was all right.' But it was an oddly unsatisfactory answer and Baines sensed it. He went on glibly about her academic prowess, or lack of it, and veered off into an anecdote about the time he'd found forty-two different spellings of 'isosceles' in a first-year examination.

'Do you know Mrs Taylor?'

'Oh, yes.' He stood up and suggested there was just time for another pint. Morse knew that the momentum had been broken, quite deliberately, and he felt very tempted to refuse. But he didn't. Anyway, he was going to ask Baines a rather delicate favour.

Morse slept fitfully that night. Broken images littered his mind, like the broken glass strewn about the rubbish tip. He tossed and turned; but the merry-go-round was out of control, and at 3.00 a.m.

he got up to make himself a cup of tea. Back in bed, with the light left on, he tried to concentrate his closed, swift-darting eyes on to a point about three inches in front of his nose, and gradually the spinning mechanism began to slow down, slower and slower, and then it stopped. He dreamed of a beautiful girl slowly unbuttoning her low-cut blouse and swaying her hips sensuously above him as she slid down the zip at the side of her skirt. And then she put her long slim fingers up to her face and moved the mask aside, and he saw the face of Valerie Taylor.

Chapter Fourteen

I am a man under authority.
St Matthew, Ch. 8, v. 9

It wasn't too bad working with Morse. Odd sort of chap, some-times, and should have got himself married long ago; everybody said that. But it wasn't too bad. He'd worked with him before, and enjoyed it most of the time. Sometimes he seemed a very ordinary sort of fellow. The real trouble was that he always had to find a complex solution to everything, and Lewis had enough experience of police work to know that most criminal activity owed its origins to simple, cheap, and sordid motives, and that few of the criminals themselves had sufficiently intelligent or tortuous minds to devise the cunning stratagems that Morse was wont to attribute to them. In Morse's mind the simple facts of any case seemed somewhere along the line to get fitted out with hooks and eyes which rendered the possibility of infinite associations and combinations. What the great man couldn't do, for all his gifts, was put a couple of simple facts together and come up with something obvious. The letters from Valerie were a case in point. The first one, Peters had said, was pretty certainly written by Valerie herself. Why then not work on the assumption that it *was*, and go on from there? But no. Morse had to believe the letter was forged, just because it would fit better with some fantastical notion that itself owed its abortive birth to some equally improbable hypothesis. And then there was the second letter. Morse hadn't said much about that; probably learned his lesson. But even if he had to accept that Valerie Taylor had written the letters, he would never be prepared to believe anything so simple as the fact that she'd got fed up with home and with school, and had just gone off, as hundreds of other girls did every year. Then why not Valerie? The truth was that Morse would find it all too easy; no fit challenge for that thoroughbred mind of his. Yes, that was it.

Lewis began to wish he could have a few days on his own in London; use his own initiative. He might find *something*. After all, Ainley probably had – well, according to Morse he had. But there again the chief was only guessing. There was no evidence for it. Wasn't it far more likely that Ainley hadn't found anything? If he was killed on the very day that he'd actually found some vital clue – after well over two years of finding nothing – it would be a huge coincidence. Too big. But no. Morse himself took such coincidences blithely in his stride.

He went to the canteen for a cup of tea and sat down by Constable Dickson.

'Solved the murder yet, Sarge?'

'What murder?'

Dickson grinned. 'Now don't tell me they've put old Morse on a missing persons case, 'cause I shan't believe you. Come on, Sarge, spill the beans.'

'No beans to spill,' said Lewis.

'Come off it! I was on the Taylor business, too, you know. Searched everywhere, we did – even dragged the reservoir.'

'Well, you didn't find the body. And if you don't have the body, Dickson boy, you don't have a murder, do you?'

'Ainley thought she was bumped off, though, didn't he?'

'Well, there's always the possibility, but . . . Look here, Dickson.' He swivelled round in his chair and faced the constable. 'You kill somebody, right? And you've got a body on your hands, right? How do you get rid of it? Come on, tell me.'

'Well, there's a hundred and one ways.'

'Such as?'

'Well, for a start, there's the reservoir.'

'But that was dragged, you say.'

Dickson looked mildly contemptuous. 'Yes, but I mean. A bloody great reservoir like that. You'd need a bit of luck, wouldn't you, Sarge?'

'What else?'

'There was that furnace in the school boiler-room. Christ, you wouldn't find much trace if they stuck you in there.'

'The boiler-room was kept locked.'

'Come off it! S'posed to have been, you mean. Anyway, *somebody's* got keys.'

'You're not much help, are you, Dickson?'

'Could have been buried easy enough, couldn't she? It's what usually happens to dead bodies, eh, Sarge?' He was inordinately amused by his own joke, and Lewis left him alone in his glory.

He returned to the office and sat down opposite the empty chair. Whatever he thought about Morse it wasn't much fun without him . . .

He thought about Ainley. *He* hadn't known about the letters. If he had . . . Lewis was puzzled. Why *hadn't* Morse worried more about the letters? Surely the two of them should be in London, not sitting on their backsides here in Kidlington. Morse was always saying they were a team, the two of them. But they didn't function as a team at all. Sometimes he got a pat on the back, but mostly he just did what the chief told him to. Quite right and proper, too. But he would dearly love to try the London angle. He could always suggest it, of course. Why not? Why indeed not? And if he found Valerie and proved Morse wrong? Not that he wanted to prove him wrong really, but Morse was such an obstinate blighter. In Lewis's garden, ambition was not a weed that sprouted freely.

He noted that Morse had obviously read the notes he had made, and felt mildly gratified. Morse must have come back to the office after seeing the Taylors; and Lewis wondered what wonderful edifice his superior officer had managed to erect on the basis of those two interviews.

The phone rang and he answered it. It was Peters.

'Tell Inspector Morse it's the same as before. Different pen, different paper, different envelope, different postmark. But the verdict's the same as before.'

'Valerie Taylor wrote it, you mean?'

Peters paused. 'I didn't say that, did I? I said the verdict's the same as before.'

'Same odds as before, then?'

He paused. 'The degree of probability is just about the same.'

Lewis thanked him and decided to communicate the information immediately. Morse had told him that if anything important came up, a message would always get through to him. Surely this was important enough? And while he was on the phone he would mention that idea of his. Sometimes it was easier on the phone.

He learned that Morse was in the witness box, but that he should be finished soon. Morse would ring back, and did so an hour later.

'What do you want, Lewis? Have you found the corpse?'

'No, sir. But Peters rang.'

'Did he now?' A note of sudden interest crept into Morse's voice. 'And what did the old twerp have to say this time?' Lewis told him and felt surprised at the mild reception given to this latest intelligence. 'Thanks for letting me know. Look, Lewis, I've finished here now and I'm thinking of taking the afternoon off. I had a bloody awful night's sleep and I think I'll go to bed. Look after my effects, won't you?'

To Lewis, he seemed to have lost interest completely. He'd tried his best to make a murder out of it; and now he'd learned he'd failed, he'd decided to go to bed! It was as good a time as any to mention that other little thing.

'I was just wondering, sir. Don't you think it might be a good idea if I went up to London? You know – make a few enquiries, have a look round— '

Morse interrupted him angrily from the other end of the line. 'What the hell are you talking about, man? If you're going to work with me on this case, for God's sake get one thing into that thick skull of yours, d'you hear? Valerie Taylor isn't living in London or anywhere else. You got that? She's dead.' The line was dead, too.

Lewis walked out of the office and slammed the door behind him. Dickson was in the canteen; Dickson was always in the canteen.

'Solved the murder yet, Sarge?'

'No I have not,' snarled Lewis. 'And nor has Inspector bloody Morse.'

He sat alone in the farthest corner and stirred his coffee with controlled fury.

Chapter Fifteen

'Tis a strange thing, Sam, that among us people can't
agree the whole week because they go different ways upon
Sundays.

George Farquhar

The brief Indian summer, radiant and beneficent, was almost
at an end. On Friday evening the forecast for the weekend was
unsettled, changeable weather with the possibility of high winds
and rain; and Saturday was already appreciably cooler, with dark
clouds from the west looming over North Oxfordshire. Gloomily the
late-night weatherman revealed to the nation a map of the British
Isles almost obliterated by a series of close, concentric millibars with
their epicentrum somewhere over Birmingham, and prophesied in
minatory tones of weak fronts and associated depressions. Sunday
broke gusty and raw, and although the threatened rain storm held
its hand, there was, at 9.00 a.m., a curiously deadened, almost
dream-like quality about the early morning streets, and the few
people there were seemed to move as in a silent film.

From Carfax (at the centre of Oxford), Queen Street leads
westwards, very soon changing its name to Park End Street; and off
Park End Street on the left-hand side and just opposite the railway
station, is Kempis Street, where stands a row of quietly-senescent
terraced houses. At five minutes past nine, the door of one of these
houses is opened, and a man walks to the end of the street, opens
the faded-green doors of his garage and backs out his car. It is a
dull black car, irresponsive, even in high summer, to any glancing
sunbeams, and the chrome on the front and rear bumpers is rusted
to a dirty brown. It is time he bought a new car, and indeed he
has more than enough money to do so. He drives to St Giles' and
up the Woodstock Road. It would be slightly quicker and certainly
more direct to head straight up the Banbury Road; but he wishes to
avoid the Banbury Road. At the top of the Woodstock Road he turns
right along the ring-road for some three or four hundred yards and
turns left at the Banbury Road roundabout. Here he increases his
speed to a modest 45 m.p.h. and passes out of Oxford and down the
long, gentle hill that leads to Kidlington. Here (inconspicuously, he
hopes) he leaves his car in a side street which is only a few minutes'
walk from the Roger Bacon Comprehensive School. It is a strange

decision. It is more than that; it is an incomprehensible decision. He walks fairly quickly, pulling his trilby hat further over his eyes and hunching deeper into his thick, dark overcoat. He walks up the slight incline, passing the prefabricated hut in which the Clerk of Works directs (and will direct) the perpetual and perennial alterations and extensions to the school; and as deviously as he can he penetrates the sprawling amalgam of outbuildings, permanent and temporary, wherein the pupils of secondary school age are initiated into the mysteries of the Sciences and the Humanities. Guardedly his eyes glance hither and thither, but there is no one to be seen. Thence over the black tarmac of the central play area and towards the two-storeyed, flat-roofed central administrative block, newly built in yellow brick. The main door is locked; but he has a key. He enters quietly and unlocks the door. Within, there is a deathly silence about the familiar surroundings; his footsteps echo on the parquet flooring, and the smell of the floor polish takes him back to times of long ago. Again he looks around him, then quickly mounts the stairs. The door to the secretary's office is locked; but he has a key, and enters and locks the door behind him. He walks over to the headmaster's study. The door is locked; but he has a key, and enters and feels a sudden fear. But there is no reason for the fear. He walks over to a large filing cabinet. It is locked; but he has a key, and opens it and takes out a file marked 'Staff Appointments'. He flicks through the thick file and replaces it; tries another; and another. At last he finds it. It is a sheet of paper he has never seen before; but it contains no surprises, for he has known its contents all along. In the office outside he turns on the electric switch of the copying machine. It takes only thirty seconds to make two copies (although he has been asked for only one). Carefully he replaces the original document in the filing cabinet, relocks the study door, unlocks and relocks the outer door, and makes his way down the stairs. Stealthily he looks outside. It is five minutes to ten. There is no one in sight as he lets himself out, relocks the main door and leaves the school premises. He is lucky. No one has seen him and he retraces his steps. A man is standing on the pavement by the car, but moves on, guiltily tugging a small white dog along the pavement and momentarily deferring the imminent defecation.

This same Sunday morning Sheila Phillipson is picking up the wind-falls under the apple trees. The grass needs cutting again, for in spite of the recent weeks of sunshine a few dark ridges of longish grass are sprouting in dark green patches; and with rain apparently imminent, she will mention it to Donald. Or will she? He has been touchy and withdrawn this last week – almost certainly because of that girl! It is unlike him, though. Hereto he has assumed the duties and responsibilities of the headship with a verve and a confidence that have slightly surprised her. No. It isn't like him to worry. There must be something more to it; something wrong somewhere.

She stands with the basket of apples on her arm and looks around: the tall fencing that keeps them so private, the bushes and shrubs and ground-cover that blend so wonderfully with their variegated greens. It is almost terrifyingly beautiful. And the more she treasures it all, the more frightened she is that she may lose it all. How she wants to keep everything just as it is! And as she stands beneath the apple-heavy boughs her face grows hard and determined. She *will* keep it all – for Donald, for the children, for herself. She will let nothing and no one take it from her!

Donald comes out to join her and says (praise be!) that it's high time he cut the grass again, and greets the promise of apple pie for dinner with a playfully loving kiss upon her cheek. Perhaps after all she is worrying herself over nothing.

At midday the beef and the pie are in the oven, and as she prepares the vegetables she watches him cutting the lawn. But the shaded patterns of the parallel swathes seem not so neat as usual – and suddenly she bangs her hands upon the window and shouts hysterically: 'Donald! For God's—' So nearly, so very nearly has he chewed up the electric flex of the lead with the blades of the mower. She has read of a young boy doing just that only a week ago: instantly and tragically fatal.

The Senior Tutor's secretary has had to come into Lonsdale College this Sunday morning. In common with many, she feels convinced there are far too many conferences, and wonders whether the Conference for the Reform of French Teaching in Secondary Schools will significantly affect the notorious inability of English children to learn the language of any other nation. So many conferences – especially before the start of the Michaelmas Term! She is efficient and has almost everything ready for the evening's business: lists of those attending, details of their schools, programmes for the following two days' activities, certifications of attendance and the menus for the evening's banquet. There remain only the name-tags, and using the red ribbon, and the upper case, she begins typing the name and provenance of each of the delegates. It is a fairly simple and quick operation. She then cuts up the names into neat rectangles and begins to fit them into the small celluloid holders: MR J. ABBOTT, The Royal Grammar School, Chelmsford; MISS P. ACKROYD, High Wycombe Technical College; MR D. ACUM, City of Caernarfon School . . . and so on, to the end of the list.

She is finished by midday and takes all her bits and pieces to the Conference Room, where at 6.30 p.m. she will sit behind the reception desk and greet the delegates as they arrive. To be truthful, she rather enjoys this sort of thing. Her hair will be most cunningly coiffured, and on her name-tag she has proudly printed 'Lonsdale College' as her own academic provenance.

With the new stretch of the M40 blasted through the heart of the Chilterns, the journey to and from London is now quicker than ever; and Morse feels reasonably satisfied with his day's work when he arrives back in Oxford just after 4.00 p.m. Lewis was quite right: there were one or two things that could only be checked in London, and Morse thinks that he has dealt with them. On his return he calls in at Police HQ and finds an envelope, heavily-sealed with Sellotape, and boldly marked for the attention of Chief Inspector Morse. The pieces are beginning to fall into place. He dials Acum's home number and waits.

'Hello?' It is a woman's voice.

'Mrs Acum?'

'Yes, speaking.'

'Could I have a word with your husband, please?'

'I'm afraid he's not here.'

'Will he be in later?'

'Well, no. He won't. He's away on a Teachers' Conference.'

'Oh, I see. When are you expecting him back, Mrs Acum?'

'He said he hoped to be back Tuesday evening – fairly late, though, I think.'

'I see.'

'Can I give him a message?'

'Er, no. Don't worry. It's not important. I'll try to ring him later in the week.'

'You sure?'

'Yes, that'll be fine. Thanks very much, anyway. Sorry to trouble you.'

'That's all right.'

Morse sits back and considers. As he's just said, it isn't really important.

* * *

Baines is not a man of regular habits, nor indeed of settled tastes. Sometimes he drinks beer, and sometimes he drinks Guinness. Occasionally, when a heavy burden weighs upon his mind, he drinks whisky. Sometimes he drinks in the lounge, and sometimes he drinks in the public bar; sometimes in the Station Hotel, and sometimes in the Royal Oxford, for both are near. Sometimes he doesn't drink at all.

Tonight he orders a whisky and soda in the lounge bar of the Station Hotel. It is a place with a very special and a very important memory. The bar is fairly small, and he finds he can easily follow long stretches of others' conversations; but tonight he is deaf to the chatter around him. It has been a worrying sort of day – though not worrying exactly; more a nervy, fluttery sort of day. Clever man, Morse!

Several of the customers are waiting for the London train: smartly dressed, apparently affluent. Later there will be a handful who have missed the train and who will book in for the night if there are vacancies; relaxed, worldly men with generous expense allowances and jaunty anecdotes. And just once in a while there is a man who deliberately misses his train, who rings his wife and tells his devious tale.

It had been a chance in a thousand, really – seeing Phillipson like that. Phillipson! One of the six on the short-list, a list that had included himself! A stroke of luck, too, that *she* had not seen him when, just after 8.30, they had entered arm-in-arm. And then they had actually appointed Phillipson! Well, well, well. And the little secret glittered and gleamed like a bright nugget of gold in a miser's hoard.

Phillipson, Baines, Acum; headmaster, second master, ex-Modern Languages master of the Roger Bacon School, and all thinking of Valerie Taylor as they lay awake that Sunday night listening as the wind howled and the rain beat down relentlessly. At last to each of them came sleep; but sleep uneasy and disturbed. Phillipson, Baines, Acum; and tomorrow night one of the three will be sleeping a sleep that is long and undisturbed; for tomorrow night at this same time one of the three will be dead.

Chapter Sixteen

They wish to know the family secrets and to be feared
accordingly.

Juvenal, Satire III, 113

Morse woke from a deep, untroubled sleep at 7.30 a.m. and
switched on Radio Oxford: trees uprooted, basements flooded,
outbuildings smashed to matchwood. But as he washed and shaved,
he felt happier than he had done since taking over the case. He saw
things more clearly now. There was a long way still to go but at least
he had made the first big breakthrough. He would have to apologise
to Lewis – that was only fit and proper; but Lewis would understand.
He backed out the Jaguar and got out to lock the garage doors. The
rain had ceased at last and everywhere looked washed and clean. He
breathed deeply – it was good to be alive.

He summoned Lewis to his office immediately, cleared his desk,
and cheated by having a quick preliminary look at 1 Across: *Code
name for a walrus (5)*. Ha! The clue was like a megaphone shouting
the answer at him. It was going to be his day!

Lewis greeted his chief defensively; he had not seen him since
the previous Thursday morning. Where Morse had been, he didn't
know, and what he'd been doing, he didn't really care.

'Look,' said Morse. 'I'm sorry I blasted your head off last
week. I know you don't worry about things like that, but I
do.'

It was a new angle, anyway, thought Lewis.

'And I feel I ought to apologise. It's not like me, is it,
to go off the deep end like that?'

It was hardly a question and Lewis made no reply.

'We're a team, Lewis, you and me – you must never forget
that . . .' He went on and on and Lewis felt better and better.
'You see, Lewis, the long and the short of it is that you were right
and I was wrong. I should have listened to you.' Lewis felt like a
candidate who learns that he has been awarded grade 1 although
he was absent for the examination.

'Yes,' continued Morse, 'I've had the chance to stand back and
see things a little more clearly, and I think we can now begin to see
what really happened.'

He was becoming rather pompous and self-satisfied, and Lewis tried to bring him down to earth. As far as he knew, Morse had been nowhere near the office since Thursday morning.

'There's that report from Peters on Valerie's second letter, sir. You remember, I rang you about it.'

Morse brushed the interruption aside. 'That's not important, Lewis. But I'm going to tell you something that *is* important.' He leaned back in the black leather chair and commenced an analysis of the case, an analysis which at several points had Sergeant Lewis staring at him in wide-eyed amazement, and despair.

'The one person who has worried me all along in this case has been Phillipson. Why? Because it's clear that the man is hiding something, and to keep things dark he's been forced to tell us lies.'

'He didn't lie about Blackwell's, sir.'

'No. But I'm not worried so much about what happened on the day when Valerie disappeared. That's where we've been making our mistake. We should have been concentrating much more on what happened *before* she disappeared. We should have been looking into the past for some incident, some relationship, *something*, that gives a coherent pattern to all the rest. Because, make no mistake, there *is* something buried away back there in the past, and if we can find it everything will suddenly click into place. It's the key, Lewis – a key that slips easily into the lock and when it turns it's smooth and silky and – hey presto! So, let's forget for a while who saw Valerie last and what colour knickers she was wearing. Let's go back long before that. For if I'm right, if I'm right . . .'

'You think you've found the key?'

Morse grew rather more serious. 'I think so, yes. I think that what we've got to reckon with in this case is *power*, the power that someone, by some means or other, can exercise over someone else.'

'Blackmail, you mean, sir?'

Morse paused before answering. 'It may have been; I'm not sure yet.'

'You think someone's blackmailing Phillipson, is that it?'

'Let's not rush, Lewis. Just suppose for a minute. Suppose you yourself did something shady, and no one found out. No one, that is, except for one other person. Let's say you bribed a witness, or planted false evidence or something like that. All right? If you got found out, you'd be kicked out of the force on your ear, and find yourself in jug, as likely as not. Your career would be ruined, and your family, too. You'd give a lot to keep things dark, and just let's suppose that I was the one who knew all about this, eh?'

'You'd have me by the . . .' Lewis thought better of it.

'I would, indeed. But not only that. I could also do some shady things myself, couldn't I? And get you to cover up for *me*. It would be dangerous, but it might be necessary. I could get you to compound the original crime you'd committed, by committing another, but committing it for *me*, not for yourself. From then on we'd sink or swim together, I know that; but we'd be fools to split on each other, wouldn't we?'

Lewis nodded. He was getting a bit bored.

'Just think, Lewis, of the ordinary people we come across every day. They do the same sort of things we do and have the same sort of hopes and fears as everybody else. And they're not really villains at all, but some of them occasionally do things they'd be frightened to death anyone else finding out about.'

'Pinching a bag of sugar from the supermarket – that sort of thing?'

Morse laughed. 'Your mind, as always, Lewis, leaps immediately to the limits of human iniquity! In the seventh circle of Dante's Hell we shall doubtless find the traitors, the mass murderers, the infant torturers, and the stealers of sugar from the supermarkets! But that's the sort of thing I mean, yes. Now just let that innocent mind of yours sink a little lower into the depths of human depravity, and tell me what you find.'

'You mean having another woman, sir?'

'How delicately you put things! Having another woman, yes. Jumping between the sheets with a luscious wench and thinking of nothing but that great lump of gristle hanging between your legs. And the little woman at home cooking a meal for you and probably pressing your pants or something. You make it all sound like having another pint of beer, Lewis; but perhaps you're right. It's not all that important in the long run. A quick blow-through, a bit of remorse and anxiety for a few days, and then it's all over. And you tell yourself you're a damned fool and you're not going to do it again. But what, Lewis, *what if someone finds out?*'

'Bit of hard luck.' He said it in such a way that Morse looked at him curiously.

'Have *you* ever had another woman?'

Lewis smiled. An old memory stirred and swam to the surface of his mind like a bubble in still water. 'I daren't tell you, sir. After all, I wouldn't want you to kick me out of the force, would I?'

The phone rang and Morse answered it. 'Good . . . Good . . .

That's good . . . Excellent.' Morse's half of the conversation seemed singularly unenlightening and Lewis asked him who it was. 'I'll come to that in a minute, Lewis. Now, where were we? Oh yes, I suspect – and, if I may say so, you tend to confirm my suspicion – that adultery is more widespread than even the League of Light would have us believe. And a few unlucky ones still get caught with their pants down, and a hell of a lot of others get away with it.'

'What are you getting at, sir?'

'Simply this.' He took a deep breath and hoped it wouldn't sound too melodramatic. 'I think that Phillipson had an affair with Valerie Taylor, that's all.'

Lewis whistled softly and slowly took it in. 'What makes you think that?'

'No one reason – just lots of little reasons. And above all, the fact that it's the only thing that makes sense of the whole wretched business.'

'I think you're wrong, sir. There's an old saying, isn't there – if you'll excuse the language – about not shitting on your own doorstep. Surely it would be far too risky? Her at the school and him headmaster? I don't believe it, sir. He's not such a fool as that, surely?'

'No, I don't think he is. But as I told you, I'm trying to look back further than that, to the time, let's say, before he became headmaster.'

'But he didn't know her then. He lived in Surrey.'

'Yes. But he came to Oxford at least once, didn't he?' said Morse slowly. 'He came up here when he was interviewed for the job. And in that sense, to use your own picturesque terminology, he wouldn't exactly be shitting on his own doorstep, would he?'

'But you just can't say things like that, sir. You've got to have some *evidence*.'

'Yes. We shall need some evidence, you're quite right. But just forgetting the evidence for a minute, what worries me is whether it's a *fact* or not; and I think that we've just got to assume that it *is* a fact. We *could* get the evidence – I'm sure of that. We could get it from Phillipson himself; and I think, Lewis, that there are one or two other persons who could tell us a good deal if they had a mind to.'

'You mean, sir, that you've not really got any evidence yet?'

'Oh, I wouldn't say that. One or two pointers, aren't there?'

'Such as?'

'Well, first of all there's Phillipson himself. *You* know he's hiding something as well as I do.' As was his wont, Morse blustered boldly through the weakest points in his argument. 'He doesn't talk about the girl in a natural way at all – not about the girl *herself*. It's almost as if he's frightened to remember her – as if he feels guilty about her in some way.' Lewis seemed stolidly unimpressed, and Morse left it. 'And then there's Maguire. By the way, I saw him again yesterday.'

Lewis raised his eyebrows. 'Did you? Where was that?'

'I, er, thought I ought to follow your advice after all. You were quite right, you know, about the London end. One or two loose ends to tie up, weren't there?'

Lewis opened his mouth, but got no further.

'When I first saw him,' continued Morse, 'it was obvious that he was jealous – plain miserably jealous. I think Valerie must have dropped the odd hint; nothing too specific, perhaps. And I tackled Maguire about it again yesterday, and – well, I'm sure there was a bit of gossip, at least among some of the pupils.'

Lewis continued to sit in glum silence.

'And then there was George Taylor. According to him it was just about that time – when Phillipson first came for the job, that is – that Valerie began staying out late. Again, I agree, nothing definite, but another suggestive indication, wouldn't you say?'

'To be truthful, sir, I wouldn't. I think you're making it all up as you're going along.'

'All right. I'll not argue. Just have a look at this.' He handed to Lewis the document that Baines had so carefully packaged for him. It was a photocopy of the expenses form that Phillipson had submitted to the Governors after the headship interviews. From the form it was immediately apparent that he had not reached home that evening; he had claimed for B and B at the Royal Oxford, and had arrived home at lunch-time on the following day.

'He probably missed his train,' protested Lewis.

'Don't think so,' said Morse. 'I've checked. The last of the interviews was over by a quarter to six, and there was a good train for Phillipson to catch at 8.35. And even if he'd missed that, there was another at 9.45. But he wouldn't miss it, would be? Two and three-quarter hours to get from Kidlington to Oxford? Come off it!'

'He probably felt tired – you know how it is.'

'Not too tired to cock his leg around Valerie Taylor.'

'It's just not fair to say that, sir.'

'Isn't it, now? Well, let me tell you something else, Lewis. I went to the Royal Oxford yesterday and found the old register. Do you know something? *There is no entry for any Phillipson that night.*'

'All right. He just tried to claim a few extra quid for nothing. He caught the train after all.'

'I bet he wouldn't like me to check up with his wife about that!' Morse was now regaining his momentum.

'You've not checked with her, then?'

'No. But I checked up on something else. I went round to the Station Hotel just opposite. Very interesting. They looked out their old register for me, and I'll give you one guess who the last entry on the list was.'

'He probably just got the names of the hotels muddled. They're pretty near each other.'

'Could be. But you see, Lewis, *there's no Phillipson there either*. Let me show you what there was, though.'

He passed over a photocopied sheet of paper and Lewis read what Morse had found:

'Mr E. Phillips, 41 Longmead Road, Farnborough.' He sat silently, and then looked again at the copy of the expenses form that Morse had given him earlier. It was certainly odd. Very, very odd.

'And,' continued Morse, 'I've checked on something else. There's no Mr Phillips who lives in Longmead Road, Farnborough, for the very simple reason there *is* no Longmead Road in Farnborough.'

Lewis considered the evidence. Initials? Move on one from D to E. Easy. Phillipson? Just leave off the last two letters. Could be. But something else was staring him in the face. The home address (as given on the expenses form) of Mr D. Phillipson was 14 Longmead Road, Epsom. Transpose the 1 and the 4, and move on one from E to F: Epsom to Farnborough.

'I should think Peters ought to be able to give us a line on the handwriting, sir.'

'We'll leave him out of it.' It sounded final.

'It's a bit suspicious, all right,' admitted Lewis. 'But where does Valerie Taylor fit in? Why her?'

'It's got to be her,' said Morse. 'It all adds up, don't you see?'

'No.'

'Well, let's just assume that what I suspect is the truth. Agreed? *Assume*, nothing more. Now, where are we? For some reason Phillipson meets Valerie, probably in Oxford, probably at the station buffet. He chats her up and – Bob's your uncle. Off they go to the Station Hotel – a bit of a roll round the bed, and she goes off home with a few quid in her pocket. I don't think she'd stay all night; probably a couple of hours or so – no more. It wouldn't be easy for her to leave the hotel after midnight, would it? Not without causing a bit of comment.'

'I still don't see why it should be Valerie, though. And even if you're right, sir, what's it all got to do with Valerie disappearing?'

Morse nodded. 'Tell me, Lewis. If *anyone* got to know about this little bit of philandering, who do you think it would be?'

'Phillipson could have told his wife, I suppose. You know, he would have felt guilty about it—'

'Mm.' It was Morse's turn to display a lack of enthusiasm and Lewis tried again.

'I suppose Valerie could have told someone?'

'Who?'

'Her mum?'

'She was a bit scared of her mum, wasn't she?'

'Her dad, then?'

'Could be.'

'I suppose someone could have seen them,' said Lewis slowly.

'I'm pretty sure someone did,' said Morse.

'And you think you know who it was?'

Again Morse nodded. 'So do you, I think.'

Did he? In such situations Lewis had learned to play it cleverly. 'You mean . . . ?' He tried to look as knowing as his utter lack of comprehension would permit, and mercifully Morse took up his cue.

'Yes. He's the only person connected with the case who lives anywhere near there. You don't make an excursion to the Station Hotel if you live in Kidlington, do you? Come to think of it, you don't make an excursion to the Station Hotel wherever you live. The beer there's bloody awful.'

Lewis understood now, but wondered how on earth they'd ever managed to get this far on such a flimsy series of hypotheses. 'He found out, you think?'

'Saw 'em, most probably.'

'You've not tackled him about it yet?'

'No, I want to get a few things straight first. But I shall be seeing him, have no fear.'

'I still don't see why you think it was Valerie.'

'Well, let's look at things from her point of view for a minute. She gets herself pregnant, right?'

'So you say, sir.'

'And so does Maguire.'

'We've got no real evidence.'

'No, not yet, I agree. But we may well have some fairly soon
– you'll see. For the minute let's just assume she's pregnant. I'm
pretty sure that Phillipson himself wouldn't have been the proud
daddy; in fact, I shouldn't think he ever dreamed of touching her
again. But if she were in trouble, daren't tell her parents, say –
who would she go to? As I see it, she may well have gone to someone who owed her a favour, someone who had some sort of moral
duty to help her, someone in fact who daren't *not* help her. In
short she'd probably go to Phillipson. And, as I see it, they cooked
up something between 'em. The Taylors – they'd almost certainly
have to be in on it – the Taylors, Phillipson and Valerie. I should
think that Phillipson arranged a place for her to go to in London,
paid the abortion clinic, and let the whole thing look like a runaway
schoolgirl lark. The Taylors are saved any local scandal and dis-
grace. Phillipson has paid his pound of flesh, and Valerie is let
off lightly for her sins. Yes, I think that's roughly what might
have happened; only roughly, mind you.'

'But how did she disappear?'

'Again I'm guessing. But I suspect that when she left home after
lunch she took a minimum of things with her – hence the bag or
basket, whatever it was; it had to look, you see, as if she was going
off to school in the normal way – the neighbours and so on might
see her. As it happens, they didn't – but that was pure chance. I
should think she went down the main road, probably nipped into
the ladies' lavatory by the shops and changed her school uniform
for something a bit trendier (don't forget the bag, Lewis!), and met
Phillipson who was waiting for her in his car further down the road
near the roundabout. They've probably got her case in the boot
already. He drove her down to the station in Oxford, gave her
full instructions, parked somewhere in town, bought a book at
Blackwell's and got home by three o'clock. Easy.' He stopped and
looked hopefully at Lewis. 'Well, something like that. What do you
think?'

'And I suppose she just gets rid of the baby like you say, finds
she likes London, gets in with a swinging set, and forgets all about
mum and dad and everything at home.'

'Something like that,' said Morse, without conviction.

'They put the police to a dickens of a lot of trouble for
nothing, then, didn't they?'

'Probably never thought we'd make so much fuss.'

'They'd have a good idea.'

Morse was looking increasingly uneasy. 'As I told you, Lewis, it's only a rough outline. Just remember that if Valerie had wanted to, she could have ruined Phillipson's career in a flash. Just think of the headlines! It'd be dynamite! And think of Valerie, too. She certainly wouldn't want to be carting a kid around at her age. And her parents . . .'

'A lot of parents don't seem to mind too much these days, sir.'

Morse was feeling cross and showed it. 'Well *they* did! They minded enough to go through with the whole bloody business; still *are* going through with it . . .'

Somewhere along the line the euphoria had turned to a saddened exasperation. He knew far better than Lewis could have told him that he hadn't really thought things through.

'You know, Lewis, something must have turned sour somewhere, mustn't it? Perhaps something went wrong . . .' He suddenly brightened. 'We shall have to find out, shan't we?'

'You think Valerie's still alive then, sir?'

Morse backed down with commendable grace. 'I suppose so, yes. After all she wrote home, didn't she? Or so you tell me.'

He had a cheek, this man Morse, and Lewis shook his head in dismay. Everything had pointed to a straightforward case of a girl running away from home. As everyone (including Morse) had said, it happens all the time. And what a dog's breakfast he'd made of it all!

But Lewis had to concede that there might be something worth salvaging from all that complicated nonsense. Valerie and Phillipson. *Could* be true, perhaps. But why did he have to invent all that fanciful stuff about changing in ladies' lavatories? Oh dear. But something else was worrying him.

'You said, sir, that you thought Baines might have found out about Phillipson and this girl – whoever she was.'

'I think he did. In fact, I think Baines knows a hell of a lot more about the whole caboodle than anybody.'

'More than you, sir?'

'God, yes. He's been watching and waiting, has Baines; and I suspect he'd be very happy for the truth – or most of it – to come out. Phillipson would be a dead duck then, and they'd have to appoint a new headmaster, wouldn't they? And they've got Baines –

a faithful servant who's been there all these years, runner-up at
the last appointment . . . why, I shouldn't think the Governors
would even advertise.'

'They'd have to, sir. It's the law.'

'Oh . . . Anyway, he'd get the job – sure as eggs are eggs.
And he'd love it. The thought of all that power, Lewis –
power over other people's lives. That's what Baines is hankering
after.'

'Don't you think,' said Lewis gently, 'that it would be a good
idea to get things on to a bit of a firmer footing, sir? I mean,
why not question Phillipson and Baines and the Taylors? You'd
probably get the truth out of one of them.'

'Perhaps.' Morse stood up and flexed his arms. 'But you're going
to be pleased with me, Lewis. At the beginning of this case I promised myself I'd stick to *facts*, and so far I've not done very well.
But you see a reformed character before you, my friend. First, I've
arranged to see Phillipson and Baines – together, mind you! –
tomorrow afternoon. Good touch, eh, Lewis? *Tuesday* afternoon.
Should be good, I reckon. No holds barred! And then – that phone
call you heard. Metropolitan Police, no less. They're going to help
us if they can; and they think they can. If Valerie did go up to
London for an abortion, she'd have to go to some sort of clinic,
wouldn't she? And we know exactly *when* she went. She might have
changed her name and address and God knows what. But those
boys in London are pretty sharp. If she *did* go to a clinic – even
a shady, back-street clinic – I reckon we've got her on toast. And
if they don't trace anything – well, we shall have to think again, I
suppose. But if we do find out where she went – and I think we
shall – well, we're there, aren't we? She had no money of her own,
that's for sure, and somebody, *somebody*, Lewis, had to fork out
pretty handsomely. And then? Then we take it from there.' Morse
sat down again. He was trying hard, but was convincing no one,
not even himself.

'You're not really very interested in finding her at all, are you,
sir?'

The sparkle had gone from Morse's eyes: Lewis was right, of
course. 'To tell you the truth, I shan't give two buggers if we never
find her. Perhaps we've found her, anyway. She may have been the
girl sharing Maguire's flat. I don't think so. But if she was –
so what? She may have been one of those strippers we saw; you
remember, the one with the mask and the bouncy tits. So what?

You know, Lewis, this whole case is beginning to get one almighty bore, and if all we're going to do is stir up a load of trouble and get poor old Phillipson the sack – I'd rather pack it up.'

'It's not like you to back out of anything, sir.'

Morse stared morosely at the blotting paper. 'It's just not my sort of case, Lewis. I know it's not a very nice thing to say, but I just get on better when we've got a body – a body that died from unnatural causes. That's all I ask. And we haven't got a body.'

'We've got a living body,' said Lewis quietly.

Morse nodded. 'I suppose you're right.' He walked across the room and stood by the door, but Lewis remained seated at the desk. 'What's the matter, Lewis?'

'I just can't help wondering where she is, sir. You know, at this very minute she must be somewhere, and if only we knew we could just go along there and find her. Funny, isn't it? But we can't find her, and I don't like giving up. I just wish we *could* find her, that's all.'

Morse walked back into the room and sat down again. 'Mm. I'd not thought of it quite like that before . . . I've been so cock-sure she was dead that I haven't really thought of her as being alive. And you're right. She's somewhere; at this very second she's sitting *somewhere*.' The blue eyes were beginning to glow once more and Lewis felt happier.

'Could be quite a challenge, couldn't it, sir?'

'Ye-es. Perhaps it's not such a bad job after all – chasing a young tart like Valerie Taylor.'

'You think we should try, then?'

'I'm beginning to think we should, yes.'

'Where do we start?'

'Where the hell do you think? She's almost certainly sitting somewhere in a luxury flat plucking her eyebrows.'

'But where, sir?'

'Where? Where do you think? London, of course. What was that postmark? EC4, wasn't it? She's within a few miles' radius of EC4. Sure to be!'

'That wasn't the postmark on the second letter she wrote.'

'Second letter? Oh yes. What was the postmark on that?'

Lewis frowned slightly. 'W1. Don't you remember?'

'W1, eh? But I wouldn't worry your head about that second letter, Lewis.'

'You wouldn't?'

'No, I wouldn't bother about it at all. You see, Lewis, I wrote that second letter myself.'

Chapter Seventeen

And all the woe that moved him so
That he gave that bitter cry,
And the wild regrets, and the bloody sweats,
None knew so well as I:
For he who lives more lives than one
More deaths than one must die.
                    Oscar Wilde, *The Ballad of Reading Gaol*

There were over one hundred and twenty of them, and it was too many. Why, if each of them were given leave to speak only for a minute, that would be two hours! But anyway, Acum didn't think he wanted to say anything. The great majority of the delegates were in their forties and fifties, senior men and women who, judging from their comments and their questions, sent forth an annual stream of gifted linguists to assume their natural Oxbridge birthrights.

He had felt tired after his five-and-a-half-hours' drive the previous day, and this morning's programme, conducted in a genteel atmosphere of rarefied intellectuality, had hardly succeeded in fostering any real *esprit de corps*. Speaking on 'Set Texts in the Sixth Form' the Senior Tutor had given voice softly and seriously to the delicate rhythms of Racine, and Acum began to wonder if the premier universities were not growing further and further out of touch with his own particular brand of comprehensive school. His main problem in the sixth was to recruit a handful of pupils who had just about reached the minimum requirement of a grade C in O-level French, and who, in the wake of their qualified triumphs, had promptly mislaid the substance of their erstwhile knowledge during two long months of carefree summer freedom. He wondered if other schools were different; if he himself, in some way, were to blame.

Fortunately the post-lunch discussion on the merits of the Nuffield French experiment was infinitely lighter and brighter, and Acum felt slightly more at home with his co-delegates. The Senior Tutor, the rhythms of Racine still rippling along through his mind, testified evangelically to the paramount need for a formal grammatical discipline in the teaching of all languages, including modern languages. And if Racine and Molière were not worth reading, reading with accuracy, and reading without the remotest possibility of misunderstanding arising from mistranslation – then we all might just as well forget literature and life. It sounded magnificent. And then that burly, cheerful fellow from Bradford had brought the academic argument down to earth with a magnificent thud: give him a lad or a lass with t'gumption to order t'pound of carrots at t'French greengrocer's shop, any dair! The conference exploded in glorious uproar. Slyly, a dignified old greybeard suggested that no Englishman, even one who had the good fortune to learn his native tongue in Yorkshire, had ever been confronted with an insuperable language-barrier in finding his way to a pissoir in Paris.

It was all good stuff now. The conference should have passed a vote of thanks to the burly Bradfordian and his pound of carrots. Even Acum nearly said something; and almost every other member of the silent majority nearly said something, too. There were just far too many there. Ridiculous, really. No one would notice if you were there or not. He was going out tonight, anyway. No one was going to miss him if he slipped away from the conference hall. He would be back long before the Porters' Lodge was shut at 11.00 p.m.

The school bell rang at 4.00 p.m., and the last lesson of the day was over. Streams of children emerged from classrooms and, like a nest of ants uncovered, bewilderingly crossed and recrossed to cloakrooms, to bicycle sheds, to societies, to games practices and to sundry other pursuits. More leisurely, the teachers threaded their way back through the milling throngs to the staff room; some to smoke, some to talk, some to mark. And very soon most of them, teachers and pupils alike, would be making their way home. Another day was done.

Baines returned from teaching a fourth-year mathematics set and dropped a pile of thirty exercise books on to his table. Twenty seconds each – no more; only ten minutes the lot. He might as well get them marked straightaway. Thank the Lord it wasn't like marking English or History, with all that reading to do. His practised eye had learned to pounce upon the pages in a flash. Yes, he would dash them off now.

'Mr Phillipson would like a word with you,' said Mrs Webb.

'Oh. Now?'

'As soon as you came in, he said.'

Baines knocked perfunctorily and entered the study.

'Have a seat a minute, Baines.'

Warily the second master took a seat. There was a serious edge to Phillipson's voice – like a doctor's about to inform you that you've only a few months more to live.

'Inspector Morse will be in again tomorrow afternoon. You know that, don't you?' Baines nodded. 'He wants to talk to us both – together.'

'He didn't mention that to me.'

'Well, that's what he's going to do.' Baines said nothing. 'You know what this probably means, don't you?'

'He's a clever man.'

'No doubt. But he won't be getting any further, will he?' The tone of Phillipson's voice was hard, almost the tone of a master to his pupil. 'You realise what I'm saying, don't you, Baines? Keep your mouth shut!'

'Yes, you'd like me to do that, wouldn't you?'

'I'm warning you!' The latent hatred suddenly blazed in Phillipson's eyes. No pretence now; only an ugly, naked hatred between them.

Baines got up, savouring supremely the moment of his power. 'Don't push me too far, Phillipson! And just remember who you're talking to.'

'Get out!' hissed Phillipson. The blood was pounding in his ears, and although a non-smoker he longed to light a cigarette. He sat motionless at his desk for many minutes and wondered how much longer the nightmare could go on. What a relief it would be to end it all – one way or another . . .

Gradually he grew calmer, and his mind wandered back again. How long ago was it now? Over three and a half years! And still the memory of that night came back to haunt him like a ghost unexorcised. That night . . . He could picture it all so vividly still . . .

He felt quite pleased with himself. Difficult to tell for certain, of course; but yes, quite pleased with himself really. As accurately as it could his mind retraced the stages of the day's events: the questions of

the interviewing committee – wise and foolish; and his own answers
– carefully considered . . .

Chapter Eighteen

In philological works . . . a dagger† signifies an obsolete word.
The same sign, placed before a person's name, signifies
deceased.

Rules for Compositors and Readers, OUP

This same Monday night or, to be accurate, Tuesday morning,
Morse was not in bed until 2.00 a.m., overtired and under-beered.
The euphoria of the earlier part of the day had now completely
passed, partly as a result of Lewis's sceptical disparagement, but
more significantly because of his own inability ever to fool himself
for very long. He still believed that some of the pieces had clicked
into place, but knew that many didn't fit at all; and a few didn't even
look like pieces of the same jigsaw. He recollected how in the army
he had been given a test for colour-blindness. A sheet of paper on
which a chaotically confused conglomeration of colour blocks were
printed had been magically metamorphosed when looked at through
differently coloured filter slides; a red filter, and there appeared an
elephant; a blue filter, and a lion leaped out at the eyes; a green
filter, and behold the donkey! Donkey . . . He'd been reading something about a donkey only a few days ago. Where had he read it?
Morse was not a systematic reader; he was a dipper-in. He looked
at the small pile of books on his bedside table underneath the alarm
clock. *The Road to Xanadu*, *A Selection of Kipling's Short Stories*,
The Life of Richard Wagner and *Selected Prose of A. E. Housman*.
It was in Housman, surely that bit about the donkey who couldn't
make up its asinine mind which bundle of hay to start on first.
Hadn't the stupid animal finally died of starvation? He soon found
the passage:

> An editor of no judgment, perpetually confronted with a couple of
> MSS to choose from, cannot but feel in every fibre of his being that
> he is a donkey between two bundles of hay.

Two MSS, and no judgment! That summed it up perfectly. One MS told him that Valerie Taylor was alive, and the other told him she was dead. And he still didn't know which MS a man of judgment should settle for. Oh Lord! Which of the wretched MSS had the correct reading? Had either?

He knew that at this rate he would never go to sleep, and he told himself to forget it all and think of something else. He picked up Kipling and began re-reading his favourite short story, *Love O' Women*. He firmly believed that Kipling knew more about women than Kinsey ever had, and he came back to a passage marked with vertical lines in the margin:

> . . . as you say, sorr, he was a man with an educashin, an' he used ut for his schames; an' the same educashin an' talkin' an' all that made him able to do fwhat he had a mind to wid a woman, that same wud turn back again in the long-run an' *tear him alive*.

Phew!

He thought back on what he'd learned about Valerie's sex-life. Nothing much, really. He thought of Maguire, and half-remembered something Maguire had said that didn't quite ring true. But he couldn't quite get hold of it and the memory slipped away again like a bar of soap in the bath.

Educashin. Most people were more interesting for a bit of education. More interesting to women . . . Some of these young girls must soon get tired of the drib-drab, wishy-washy drivel that sometimes passed for conversation. Some of them liked older men for just that reason; interesting men with some show of pretence for cultured pursuits, with a smattering of knowledge – with something more in mind than fiddling for their bra-straps after a couple of whiskies.

What *was* Valerie like? Had she gone for the older men? Phillipson? Baines? But surely not Baines. Some of her teachers, perhaps? Acum? He couldn't remember the other names. And then he suddenly caught the bar of soap. He'd asked Maguire how many times he'd been to bed with Valerie, and Maguire had said a dozen or so. And Morse had told him to come off it and tell him the truth, fully expecting a considerably increased count of casual copulations. But no. Maguire had come down, hadn't he? 'Well, three or four,' he'd said. Something like that. Probably hadn't slept with her at all! Morse sat up and considered. Why, ah why, hadn't he pressed this point with Maguire when he had seen him yesterday? Was she really pregnant after all? He had assumed so, and Maguire had seemingly confirmed his suspicions. But was she? It made sense if she was. But made sense of what? Of the preconceived pattern that Morse was building up, and into which, willy-nilly, the pieces were being forced into their places.

If only he knew what the problem *was*. Then he wouldn't be quite so restless, even if it proved beyond his powers. Problem! He remembered his old Latin master. Hm! Whenever *he* was confronted with an insoluble difficulty – a crux in the text, an absurdly complex chunk of syntax – he would turn to his class with a serious mien: 'Gentlemen, having looked this problem boldly in the face, we must now, I think, pass on.' Morse smiled at the recollection . . . It was getting very late. A crux in the Oxford Classical Text, marked by daggers . . . the daggered text . . . He was falling asleep. Texts, manuscripts, and a donkey in the middle braying and bellyaching, not knowing which way to turn . . . like Morse, like himself . . . His head fell to the right and his ear strained no more for the incomprehensible nocturnal clues. He fell asleep, the light still burning and Kipling's stories still held loosely in his hand.

Earlier the same evening Baines had opened his front door to find an unexpected visitor.

'Well, well! This *is* a surprise. Come in, won't you? Shall I take your coat?'

'No. I'll keep it on.'

'Well, at least you'll have a drop of something to cheer you up, eh? Can I offer you a glass of something? Nothing much in, though, I'm afraid.'

'If you like.'

His visitor following behind, Baines walked through to the small kitchen, opened the fridge, and looked inside. 'Beer? Lager?'

'Lager.'

Baines squatted on his haunches and reached inside. His left hand lay on the top of the fridge, the fingernails slightly dirty; his right hand reached far in as he bent forward. There were two bald patches on the top of his head, with a greying tuft of hair between them, temporarily thwarting the impending merger. He wore no tie, and the collar of his light-blue shirt was grubbily lined. He would have changed it the next day.

Chapter Nineteen

One morn I miss'd him on the custom'd hill.
Thomas Gray, *Elegy Written in a Country Churchyard*

Full morning assembly at the Roger Bacon Comprehensive School
began at 8.50. The staff stood at the back of the main hall, wearing
(at least those authorised to do so) the insignia of their respective
universities; it was something the head insisted on. Punctual to the
second, and flanked at some short distance in the rear by the second
master and the senior mistress, Phillipson, begowned and behooded,
walked from the back of the hall, and the pupils rose to their feet as
the procession made its way down the central gangway, climbed the
short flight of steps at the side and mounted on to the stage itself. The
routine seldom varied: a hymn sung, a prayer intoned, a passage read
from Holy Writ – and paid for one more day were the proper respects
to the Almighty. The last unsynchronised 'Amen' marked the end of
morning devotions, and gave the cue to the second master to recall
the attention of the assembled host to more terrestrial things. Each
morning he announced, in clear, unhurried tones, any changes in
the day's procedure necessitated by staff absences, house activities,
the times and places of society meetings, and the results of the
sports teams. And, always, reserved until the end, he read with
doomsday gravity a list of names; the names of pupils who would
report outside the staff room immediately after the assembly was
finished: the recalcitrants, the anarchists, the obstructionists, the
truants, the skivers, and the defectors in general from the rules
that governed the corporate life of the establishment.

As the procession walked up the central aisle on Tuesday morning, and as the school rose en bloc from their seats, several heads
turned towards each other and many whispered voices asked where
Baines could be; not even the oldest pupils could remember him
being away for a single day before. The senior mistress looked lop-
sided and lost: it was like the dissolution of the Trinity. Phillipson
himself read the notices, referring in no way to the absence of his
adjutant. The girls' hockey team had achieved a rare and decisive
victory, and the school greeted the news with unwonted enthusiasm.
The chess club would meet in the physics lab and 4C (for unspecified
criminality) would be staying in after school. The following pupils,
etc., etc. Phillipson turned away from the rostrum and walked out

through the wings. The school chattered noisily and prepared to go to their classrooms.

At lunch-time Phillipson spoke to his secretary.

'No word from Mr Baines yet?'

'Nothing. Do you think we should give him a ring?'

Phillipson considered for a moment. 'Perhaps we should. What do you think?'

'Not like him to be away, is it?'

'No, it isn't. Give him a ring now.'

Mrs Webb rang Baines's Oxford number and the distant burring seemed to echo in a vaulted, ominous silence.

'There's no answer,' she said.

At 2.15 p.m. a middle-aged woman took from her handbag the key to Baines's house; she cleaned for him three afternoons a week. Oddly, the door was unlocked and she pushed it open and walked in. The curtains were still drawn and the electric light was still turned on in the living-room, as well as in the kitchen, the door to which stood open wide. And even before she walked through to the kitchen she saw the slumped figure of Baines in front of the refrigerator, a long-handled household knife plunged deep into his back, the dried blood forming a horrid blotch upon the cotton shirt, like a deranged artist's study in claret and blue.

She screamed hysterically.

It was 4.30 p.m. before the fingerprint man and the photographer were finished, and before the humpbacked surgeon straightened his afflicted spine as far as nature would permit.

'Well?' asked Morse.

'Difficult to say. Anywhere from sixteen to twenty hours.'

'Can't you pin it down any closer?'

'No.'

Morse had been in the house just over an hour, for much of which time he had been sitting abstractedly in one of the armchairs in the living-room, waiting for the others to leave. He doubted they could tell him much, anyway. No signs of forcible entry, nothing stolen (or not apparently so), no fingerprints, no blood-stained footprints. Just a dead man, and a deep pool of blood and a fridge with an open door.

A police car jerked to a halt outside and Lewis came in. 'He wasn't at school this morning, sir.'

'Hardly surprising,' said Morse, without any conscious humour.

'Do we know when he was murdered?'

'Between eight o'clock and midnight, they say.'

'Pretty vague, sir.'

Morse nodded. 'Pretty vague.'

'Did you expect something like this to happen?'

Morse shook his head. 'Never dreamed of it.'

'Do you think it's all connected?'

'What do you think?'

'Somebody probably thought that Baines was going to tell us what he knew.' Morse grunted non-committally. 'Funny, isn't it, sir?' Lewis glanced at his watch. 'He'd have told us by now, wouldn't he? And I've been thinking, sir.' He looked earnestly at the inspector. 'There weren't many who knew you were going to see Baines this afternoon, were there? Only Phillipson really.'

'Each of them could have told somebody else.'

'Yes, but—'

'Oh, it's a good point. I see what you're getting at. How did Phillipson take the news, by the way?'

'Seemed pretty shattered, sir.'

'I wonder where he was between eight o'clock and midnight,' mumbled Morse, half to himself, as he eased himself out of the armchair. 'We'd better try to look like detectives, Lewis.'

The ambulance men asked if they could have the body, and Morse walked with them into the kitchen. Baines had been eased gently on to his right side, and Morse bent down and eased the knife slowly from the second master's back. What an ugly business murder was. It was a wooden-handled carving knife, 'Prestige, Made in England', some 35–36 centimetres long, the cutting blade honed along its entire edge to a razor-sharp ferocity. Globules of fresh pink blood oozed from the wicked-looking wound, and gradually seeped over the stiff clotted mess that once had been a blue shirt. They took Baines away in a white sheet.

'You know, Lewis, I think whoever killed him was bloody lucky. It's not too easy to stab a man in the back, you know. You've got to miss the spinal column and the ribs and the shoulder blades, and even then you've got to be lucky to kill someone straight off. Baines must have been leaning forward, slightly over to his right, and exposing about the one place that makes it comparatively easy. Just like going through a joint of beef.'

Lewis loathed the sight of death, and he felt his stomach turning over. He walked to the sink for a glass of water. The cutlery and the crockery from Baines's last meal were washed up

THE SECOND INSPECTOR MORSE OMNIBUS

and neatly stacked on the draining board, the dish cloth squeezed
out and draped over the bowl.

'Perhaps the post mortem'll tell us what time he had his supper,'
suggested Lewis hopefully.

Morse was unenthusiastic. He followed Lewis to the sink and
looked around half-heartedly. He opened the drawer at the right of
the sink unit. The usual collection: teaspoons, tablespoons, wooden
spoons, a fish slice, two corkscrews, kitchen scissors, a potato peeler,
various meat skewers, a steel – and a kitchen knife. Morse picked
up the knife and looked at it carefully. The handle was bone, and
the blade was worn away with constant sharpening into a narrowed
strip. 'He's had this a good while,' said Morse. He ran his finger
along the blade; it had almost the same cruel sharpness as the blade
that had lodged its head in Baines's heart.

'How many carving knives do you keep at home, Lewis?'

'Just the one.'

'You wouldn't think of buying another one?'

'No point, really, is there?'

'No,' said Morse. He placed the murder weapon on the kitchen
table and looked around. There seemed singularly little point in any
inspection, however intelligently directed, of the tins of processed
peas and preserved plums that lined the shelves of the narrow
larder.

'Let's move next door, Lewis. You take the desk; I'll have a
look at the books.'

Most of the bookshelves were taken up with works on mathematics, and Morse looked with some interest at a comprehensive
set of text books on the *School Mathematics Project*, lined up in
correct order from Book 1 to Book 10, and beside them the corre-
sponding Teachers' Guide for each volume. Morse delved diffidently
into Book 1.

'Know anything about modern maths, Lewis?'

'Modern maths? Ha! I'm an acknowledged expert. I do all
the kids' maths homework.'

'Oh.' Morse decided to puzzle his brain no more on how 23
in base 10 could be expressed in base 5, replaced the volume,
and inspected the rest of Baines's library. He'd been numerate
all right. But literate? Doubtful. On the whole Morse felt slightly
more sympathy with Maguire's uncompromising collection.

As he stood by the shelves the grim, brutal fact of Baines's
murder slowly sank into his mind. As yet it figured as an isolated
issue; he'd had no chance of thinking of it in any other context.

But he would be doing so soon, very soon. In fact some of the basic implications were already apparent. Or was he fooling himself again? No. It meant, for a start, that the donkey knew for certain which bundle of hay to go for, and that, at least, was one step forward. Baines must have known something. Correction. Baines must have known virtually everything. Was that the reason for his death, though? It seemed the likeliest explanation. But who had killed him? Who? From the look of things the murderer must have been known to Baines – known pretty well; must have walked into the kitchen and stood there as Baines reached inside the fridge for something. And the murderer had carried a knife – surely that was a reasonable inference? Had brought the knife into the house. But how the hell did anyone carry a knife as big as that around? Stuff it down your socks, perhaps? Unless . . .

From across the room a low-pitched whistle of staggering disbelief postponed any answers that might have been forthcoming to these and similar questions. Lewis's facial expression was one of thrilled excitement mingled with pained incredulity.

'You'd better come over here straightaway, sir.'

Morse himself looked down into the bottom right-hand drawer of the desk; and he felt the hairs at the nape of his neck grow stiff. A book lay in the drawer, an exercise book; an exercise book from the Roger Bacon Comprehensive School; and on the front of the exercise book a name, a most familiar name, was inscribed in capital letters: VALERIE TAYLOR: APPLIED SCIENCE. The two men looked at each other and said nothing. Finally Morse picked up the book gently, placing the top of each index finger along the spine; and as he did so, two loose sheets of paper fell out and fluttered to the floor. Morse picked them up and placed them on the desk. The sheets contained drafts of a short letter; a letter which began Dear Mum and Dad and ended Love Valerie. Several individual words were crossed out and the identical words, but with minor alterations to the lettering, written above them; and between the drafts were whole lines of individual letters, practised and slowly perfected: w's, r's, and t's. It was Lewis who broke the long silence.

'Looks as if you're not the only forger in the case, sir.' Morse made no reply. Somewhere at the back of his mind something clicked smoothly into place. So far in the case he had managed to catch a few of the half-whispers and from them half-divine the truth; but now it seemed the facts were shouting at him through a megaphone.

Baines, it was clear, had written the letter to Valerie's parents; and the evidence for Valerie being still alive was down to zero on the scale of probabilities. In one way Morse was glad; and in another he felt a deep and poignant sadness. For life was sweet, and we each of us had our own little hopes, and few of us exhibited overmuch anxiety to quit this vale of misery and tears. Valerie had a right to live. Like himself. Like Lewis. Like Baines, too, he supposed. But someone had decided that Baines had forfeited his right to live any longer and stuck a knife through him. And Morse stood silently at Baines's desk and knew that everyone expected him to discover who that someone was. And perhaps he would, too. At the rate he was going he would be able to know the truth before the day was out. Perhaps all he had to do was look through the rest of the drawers and find the whole solution neatly copied out and signed. But he hardly expected to find much else, and didn't. For the next hour he and Lewis carefully and patiently vetted the miscellaneous contents of each of the other drawers; but they found nothing more of any value or interest, except a recent photoprint of Phillipson's expenses form.

The phone stood on the top of the desk, a white phone, the same phone that had rung at lunch-time when Mrs Webb had called a man who then lay cold and dead beside the opened fridge. And then, suddenly, Morse noticed it. It had been under his nose all the time but he had ignored it because it was an item so naturally expected: a plastic, cream-coloured rectangular telephone index-system, whereby one pressed the alphabetical letter and the index opened automatically at the appropriate place. Half expecting to find his own illustrious self recorded, Morse pressed the 'M'; but there was nothing on the ruled card. Clearly none of Baines's more intimate acquaintances boasted a surname beginning with 'M'. So Morse pressed 'N'; and again he found no entry. And 'O'; and with the same result. Probably Baines had only recently acquired the index? It looked reasonably new and maybe he had not yet transcribed the numbers from an older list. But no such list had yet been found. Morse pressed 'P', and a slight shiver ran along his spine as he saw the one entry: Phillipson, with the headmaster's Oxford telephone number neatly appended thereto. Morse continued systematically through the remainder of the alphabet. Under 'R' was the number of the Oxford branch of the RAC, but nothing more. And under 'S', the number of a Sun Insurance agent. And then 'T'; and once again the slight, involuntary shiver down the spine. Taylor. And somewhere at the back of Morse's mind something else clicked smoothly into place. 'U', 'V' – nothing. 'W', Mr Wright, with an Oxford number: builder and decorator. On to 'X', 'Y', 'Z' –

nothing. 'A'. Morse looked carefully at the card and frowned, and whistled softly. Only one entry: Acum, the personal number (not the school's) written neatly in the appropriate column . . .

In all, there were fourteen entries only, most of which were as innocently explicable as the RAC and the interior decorator. And only three of the fourteen names appeared to have the slightest connection with the case: Acum, Phillipson, Taylor. Funny (wasn't it?) how the names seemed to crop up in trios. First, it had been Acum, Baines and Phillipson, and now Baines had got himself crossed off the list and another name had appeared almost magically in his place: the name of Taylor. Somewhere, yet again, in the farthest uncharted corners of Morse's mind, a little piece clicked smoothly into place.

Although the curtains had been drawn back as soon as the police arrived, the electric lights were still switched on, and Morse finally switched them off as he stood on the threshold. It was 5.30 p.m.

'What's next?' asked Lewis.

Morse pondered a while. 'Has the wife got the chips on, Lewis?'

'I 'spect so, sir. But I'm getting rather fond of dried-up chips.'

Chapter Twenty

Alibi (L. *alibi*, elsewhere, orig. locative – *alius*, other); the plea in a criminal charge of having been elsewhere at the material time.

Oxford English Dictionary

'He's not going to like it much.'

'Of course he's not going to like it much.'

'It's almost as good as saying we suspect him.'

'Well? We do, don't we?'

'Among others, you mean, sir?'

'Among others.'

'It's a pity they can't be just a bit more definite about the time.' Lewis sounded uneasy.

'Don't worry about that,' said Morse. 'Just get a complete schedule – from the time he left school to the time he went to bed.'

'As I say, sir, he's not going to like it very much.'

Morse got up and abruptly terminated the conversation. 'Well, he'll have to bloody well lump it, won't he?'

It was just after 6.30 p.m. when Morse pushed his way through the glass doors, left police HQ behind him and made his way slowly and thoughtfully towards the housing estate. He wasn't looking forward to it, either. As Lewis had said, it was almost as good as saying you suspected them.

The Taylors' green Morris Oxford was parked along the pavement, and it was the shirt-sleeved George himself who answered the door, hastily swallowing a mouthful of his evening meal.

'I'll call back,' began Morse.

'No. No need, Inspector. Nearly finished me supper. Come on in.' George had been sitting by himself in the kitchen finishing off a plate of stew and potatoes. 'Cup o' tea?'

Morse declined and sat opposite George at the rickety kitchen table.

'What can I do for you, Inspector Morse?' He filled an out-size cup with deep-brown tea and lit a Woodbine. Morse told him of Baines's murder. The news had broken just too late for the final edition of the *Oxford Mail*, a copy of which lay spread out on the table.

George's reaction was flat and unconcerned. He'd known Baines, of course – seen him at parents' evenings. But that was all. It seemed to Morse curious that George Taylor had so little to say or (apparently) to feel on learning of the death of a fellow human being he had known; yet neither was there a hint of machination or of malice in his eyes, and Morse felt now, as on the previous occasion they had met, that he rather liked the man. But sooner or later he had to ask him, in the hallowed phrases, to account for all his movements on the previous evening. For the moment he stood on the brink and postponed the evil moment; and mercifully George himself did a good deal of the work for him.

'The missus knew him better'n me. I'll tell her when she gets in. Mondays and Tuesdays she's allus off at Bingo down in Oxford.'

'Does she ever win?' The question seemed oddly irrelevant.

'Few quid now and then. In fact she won a bit last night, I reckon. But you know how it is – she spends about a quid a night anyway. Hooked on it, that's what she is.'

'How does she go? On the bus?'

'Usually. Last night, though, I was playing for the darts team down at the Jericho Arms, so I took her down with me, and she called in at the pub after she was finished, and then came home with me. It's on the bus, though, usually.'

Morse took a deep breath and jumped in. 'Look, Mr Taylor, it's just a formality and I know you'll understand, but, er, I've got to ask you exactly where you were last night.'

George seemed not in the least put out or perturbed. In fact – or was it a nothing, an imperceptibility, a fleeting flash of Morse's imagination? – there might have been the merest hint of relief in the friendly eyes.

Lewis was already waiting when Morse arrived back in his office at 7.30 p.m., and the two men exchanged notes. Neither of them, it appeared, had been in too much danger of flushing any desperado from his lair. The alibis were not perfect – far from it; but they were good enough. Phillipson (according to Phillipson) had arrived home from school about 5.15 p.m.; had eaten, and had left home, alone, at 6.35 p.m. to see the Playhouse production of *St Joan*. He had left his car in the Gloucester Green car park, and reached the theatre at 6.50 p.m. The play had lasted from 7.15 to 10.30 p.m., and apart from walking to the bar for a Guinness in the first interval he had not left his seat until just after 10.30 when he collected his car and drove back home. He remembered seeing the BBC 2 news bulletin at 11.00 p.m.

'How far's Gloucester Green from Baines's house?' asked Morse.

Lewis considered. 'Two, three hundred yards.'

Morse picked up the phone and rang the path lab. No. The humpbacked surgeon had not yet completed his scrutiny of various lengths of Baines's innards. No. He couldn't be more precise about the time of death. Eight to midnight. Well, if Morse were to twist his arm it might be 8.30 to 11.30 – even 11.00, perhaps. Morse cradled the phone, stared up at the ceiling for a while, and then nodded slowly to himself.

'You know, Lewis, the trouble with alibis is not that some people have 'em and some people don't. The real trouble is that virtually no one's likely to have a really water-tight alibi. Unless you've been sitting all night handcuffed to a couple of high court judges, or something.'

'You think Phillipson could have murdered Baines, then?'

'Of course he could.'

Lewis put his notebook away. 'How did you get on with the Taylors, sir?'

Morse recounted his own interview with George Taylor, and Lewis listened carefully.

'So *he* could have murdered Baines, too.'

Morse shrugged non-committally. 'How far's the Jericho Arms from Baines's place?'

'Quarter of a mile – no more.'

'The suspects are beginning to queue up, aren't they, Lewis?'

'Is Mrs Taylor a suspect?'

'Why not? As far as I can see, she'd have had no trouble at all. Left Bingo at 9 p.m. and called in at the Jericho Arms at 9.30 p.m. or so. On the way she walks within a couple of hundred yards of Baines's place, eh? And where does it all leave us? If Baines was murdered at about 9.30 last night – what have we got? Three of 'em – all with their telephone numbers on Baines's little list.'

'And there's Acum, too, sir. Don't forget him.'

Morse looked at his watch. It was 8 p.m. 'You know, Lewis, it would be a real turn-up for the books if Acum was playing darts in the Jericho Arms last night, eh? Or sitting at a Bingo board in the Town Hall.'

'He'd have a job, wouldn't he, sir? He's in Caernarfon.'

'I'll tell you one thing for sure, Lewis. Wherever Acum was last night he wasn't in Caernarfon.'

He picked up the phone and dialled a number. The call was answered almost immediately.

'Hello?' The line crackled fitfully, but Morse recognised the voice.

'Mrs Acum?'

'Yes. Who is it?'

'Morse. Inspector Morse. You remember, I rang you up—'

'Yes, of course I remember.'

'Is your husband in yet?'

'No. I think I mentioned to you, didn't I, that he wouldn't be back until late tonight?'

'How late will he be?'

'Not too late, I hope.'

'Before ten?'

'I hope so.'

'Has he got far to travel?'

'Quite a long way, yes.'

'Look, Mrs Acum. Can you please tell me where your husband has been?'

'I told you. He's been on a teachers' conference. Sixth-form French.'

'Yes. But where exactly was that?'

'Where? I'm not quite sure where he was staying.'

Morse was becoming impatient. 'Mrs Acum, you know what I mean. Where was the conference? In Birmingham?'

'Oh, I'm sorry. I see what you mean. It was in Oxford, actually.'

Morse turned to Lewis and his eyebrows jumped an inch. 'In Oxford, you say?'

'Yes. Lonsdale College.'

'I see. Well, I'll ring up again – about ten. Will that be all right?'

'Is it urgent, Inspector?'

'Well, let's say it's important, Mrs Acum.'

'All right, I'll tell him. And if he gets back before ten, I'll ask him to ring you.'

Morse gave her his number, rang off, and whistled softly. 'It gets curiouser and curiouser, does it not, Lewis? How far is Lonsdale College from Kempis Street?'

'Half a mile?'

'One more for the list, then. Though I suppose Acum's got just as good, or just as bad, an alibi as the rest of 'em.'

'Haven't you forgotten one possible suspect, sir?'

'Have I?' Morse looked at his sergeant in some surprise.

'Mrs Phillipson, sir. Two young children, soon in bed, soon asleep. Husband safely out of the way for three hours or so. She's got as good a motive as anybody, hasn't she?'

Morse nodded. 'Perhaps she's got a better motive than most.' He nodded again and looked sombrely at the carpet.

With a startling suddenness, a large spider darted across the floor with a brief, electric scurry – and, as suddenly, stopped – frozen into a static, frightening immobility. A fat-bodied, long-legged spider, the angular joints of the hairy limbs rising high above the dark squat body. Another scurry – and again the frozen immobility – more frightening in its stillness than in its motion. It reminded Morse of a game he used to play at children's parties called 'statues'; the music suddenly stopped and – still! Freeze! Don't move a muscle! Like the spider. It was almost at the skirting board now, and Morse seemed mesmerised. He was terrified of spiders.

'Did you see that whopper in Baines's bath?' asked Lewis.

'Shut up, Lewis. And put your foot on the bloody thing, quick!'

'Mustn't do that, sir. He's got a wife and kids waiting for him somewhere.' He bent down and slowly moved his hand towards the spider; and Morse shut his eyes.

Chapter Twenty-one

John and Mary are each given 20p
John gives 1p to Mary
How much more does Mary have than John?
                    Problem set in the 11+ examination

The urge to gamble is so universal, so deeply embedded in unregenerate human nature that from the earliest days the philosophers and moralists have assumed it to be evil. *Cupiditas*, the Romans called it – the longing for the things of this world, the naked, shameless greed for gain. It is the cause, perhaps, of all our troubles. Yet how easy it remains to understand the burning envy, felt by those possessing little, for those endowed with goods aplenty. And gambling? Why, gambling offers to the poor the shining chance of something got for nothing.

Crude analysis! For to some it is gambling itself, the very process and the very practice of gambling, that is so immensely pleasurable. So pleasurable indeed that gambling needs, for them, no spurious *raison d'être* whatsoever, no necessary prospect of the jackpots and the windfalls and the weekends in Bermuda; just the heady, heavy opiate of the gambling game itself with the promise of its thousand exhilarating griefs and dangerous joys. Win a million on the wicked spinning-wheel tonight, and where are you tomorrow night but back around the wicked spinning-wheel?

Every society has its games, and the games are just as revealing of the society as are its customs – for in a sense they are its customs: heads or tails, and *rouge ou noir*; and double or quits and clunk, clunk, clunk, in the pay-off tray as the triple oranges align themselves along the fruit machine; and odds of 10 to 1 as the rank outsider gallops past the post at Kempton Park; *and then came the first, saying, Lord, thy pound hath gained ten pounds. And he said unto him, Well done, thou good servant: because thou hast been faithful in a very little, have thou authority over ten cities.* And once a week, a hope a light-year distant, of half a million pounds for half a penny stake, where happiness is a line of Xs and a kiss from a buxom beauty queen. For some are lucky at the gambling game. And some are not, and lose more than they can properly afford and try to recoup their losses and succeed only in losing the little that is left; and finally, alas, all hope abandoned, sit them down alone in darkened garages and by the gas rings in the kitchens, or simply slit their throats – and die. And some smoke fifty cigarettes a day, and some drink gin or whisky; and some walk in and out of betting shops, and the wealthier reach for the phone.

But what wife can endure a gambling husband, unless he be a steady winner? And what husband will ever believe his wife has turned compulsive gambler, unless she be a poorer liar than Mrs Taylor is. And Mrs Taylor dreams she dwells in Bingo halls.

It had started some years back in the church hall at Kidlington. A dozen of them, no more, seated in rickety chairs with a clickety subfusc vicar calling the numbers with a dignified Anglican clarity. And then she had graduated to the Ritz in Oxford, where the acolytes sit comfortably in the curving tiers of the cinema seats and listen to the harsh metallic tones relayed by microphones across the giant auditorium. There is no show here of human compassion, little even of human intercourse. Only 'eyes down' in a mean-minded race to the first row, the first column, the first diagonal completed. Many of the players can cope with several cards simultaneously, a cold, pitiless purpose in their play, their mental antennae attuned only to the vagaries of the numerical combinations.

The game itself demands only an elementary level of numeracy, and not only does not require but cannot possibly tolerate the slightest degree of initiative or originality. Almost all the players almost win; the line is almost complete, and the card is almost full. Ye gods! Look down and smile once more! Come on, my little number, come! I'm *there*, if only, if only, if only . . . And there the women sit and hope and pray and bemoan the narrow miss and curse their desperate luck, and talk and think 'if only' . . .

Tonight Mrs Taylor caught the No. 2 bus outside the Ritz and reached Kidlington at 9.35 p.m.; she decided she would call in at the pub.

It was 9.35 p.m., too, when Acum rang, a little earlier than expected. He had been fortunate with the traffic (he said); on to the A5 at Towcester and a good clear run for a further five uncomplicated hours. He had left Oxford at 3.15, just before the conference had officially broken up. Jolly good conference, yes. The Monday night? Just a minute; let's think. In hall for dinner, and then there had been a fairly informal question-and-answer session afterwards. Very interesting. Bed about 10.30; a bit tired. No, as far as he remembered – no, he *did* remember; he hadn't gone out at all. Baines dead? What? Could Morse repeat that? Oh dear; very sorry to hear it. Yes, of course he'd known Baines – known him well. When did he die? Oh, Monday. Monday evening? Oh, yesterday evening, the one they'd just been speaking about. Oh, he saw now. Well, he'd told Morse what he could – sorry it was so little. Not been much help at all, had he?

Morse rang off. He decided that trying to interview by telephone was about as satisfactory as trying to sprint in diver's boots. There was no option; he would have to go up to Caernarfon himself, if . . . if what? Was it really likely that Acum had anything to do with Baines's death? If he had, he'd picked a pretty strange way of drawing almost inevitable attention to himself. And yet . . . And yet Acum's name had been floating unobtrusively along the main-stream of the case from the very beginning, and yesterday he had seen Acum's telephone number in the index file on Baines's desk. Mm. He would have to go and see him. He ought to have seen him before now; for whatever else he was or wasn't, Acum had been a central figure during that school summer when she'd disappeared. But . . . but you don't just come down to Oxford for a meeting and decide that while you're there you'll murder one of your ex-colleagues. Or do you? Who would suspect? After all, it was quite by accident that he himself had learned of Acum's visit to Oxford. Had Acum presumed . . . ? Augrrh! It was suddenly cold in the office and Morse felt tired. Forget it! He looked at his watch. 10 p.m. Just time for a couple of pints if he hurried.

He walked to the pub and pushed his way into the overcrowded public bar. The cigarette smoke hung in blue wreaths, head-high like undispersing morning mist, and the chatter along the bar and at the tables was raucous and interminable, the subtleties of conversational silence quite unknown. Cribbage, dominoes and darts and every available surface cluttered with glasses: glasses with handles and glasses without, glasses empty, glasses being emptied and glasses about to be emptied, and then refilled with the glorious, amber fluid. Morse found a momentary gap at the bar and pushed his way diffidently forward. As he waited his turn, he heard the fruit machine (to the right of the bar) clunking out an occasional desultory divi-dend, and he leaned across the bar to look more carefully. A woman was playing the machine, her back towards him. But he knew her well enough.

The landlord interrupted a new and improbable line of thought. 'Yes, mate?'

Morse ordered a pint of best bitter, edged his way a little further along the bar, and found himself standing only a few feet behind the woman playing the machine. She pushed her glass over the bar.

'Stick another double in there, Bert.'

She opened an inordinately large leather handbag and Morse saw the heavy roll of notes inside. Fifty pounds? More? Had she had a lucky night at Bingo?

She had not seen Morse – he was sure of that – and he observed her as closely as he could. She was drinking whisky and swapping mildly ribald comments with several of the pub's habitués. And then she laughed – a coarse, common cackle of a laugh, and curiously and quite unexpectedly Morse knew that he found her attractive, dammit! He looked at her again. Her figure was still good, and her clothes hung well upon her. Yes, all right, she was no longer a beauty, he knew that. He noticed the fingernails bitten down and broken; noticed the index finger of her right hand stained darkbrown with nicotine. But what the hell did it matter! Morse drained his glass and bought another pint. The germ of the new idea that had taken root in his mind would never grow this night. He knew why, of course. It was simple. He needed a woman. But he had no woman and he moved to the back of the room and found a seat. He thought, as he often thought, of the attractiveness of women. There had been women, of course; too many women, perhaps. And one or two who still could haunt his dreams and call to him across the years of a time when the day was fair. But now the leaves were falling round him: mid-forties; unmarried; alone. And here he sat in a cheap public bar where life was beer and fags and crisps and nuts and fruit machines and . . . The ashtray on the table in front of him was revoltingly full of stubs and ash. He pushed it away from him, gulped down the last of his beer and walked out into the night.

He was sitting in the bar of the Randolph Hotel with an architect, an older man, who talked of space and light and beauty, who always wore a bowler hat, who studied Greek and Latin verses, and who slept beneath a railway viaduct. They talked together of life and living, and as they talked a girl walked by with a graceful, gliding movement, and ordered her drink at the bar. And the architect nudged his young companion and gently shook his head in wistful admiration.

'My boy, how lovely, is she not? Extraordinarily, quite extraordinarily lovely.'

And Morse, too, had felt her beautiful and necessary, and yet had not a word to say.

Turning in profile as she left the bar the young girl flaunted the tantalising, tip-tilted outline of her breasts beneath her black sweater, and the faded architect, the lover of the classical poets, the sleeper beneath the viaduct, stood up and addressed her with grave politeness as she passed.

'My dear young lady. Please don't feel offended with me, or indeed with my dear, young friend here, but I wish you to know that we find you very beautiful.'

For a moment a look of incredulous pleasure glazed the painted eyes; and then she laughed – a coarse and common cackle of a laugh.

'Gee, boys, you ought to see me when I'm washed!' And she placed her right hand on the shoulder of the architect, the nails pared down to the quick and the index finger stained dark-brown with nicotine. And Morse woke up with a start in the early light of a cold and friendless dawn, as if some ghostly hand had touched him in his sleep.

Chapter Twenty-two

Life can only be understood backwards,
but it must be lived forwards.

Søren Kierkegaard

Morse was in his office by 7.30 a.m.

When he was a child, the zenith of terrestrial bliss had been a long, luxuriating lie in bed. But he was no longer a child, and the fitful bouts of sleep the night before had left him tired and edgy. His thoughts as he sat at his desk were becoming obsessive and his ability to concentrate had temporarily deserted him. The drive to the office had been mildly therapeutic, and at least he had *The Times* to read. The leaders of the superpowers had agreed to meet at Vladivostok, and the economy continued its downhill slide towards inevitable disaster. But Morse read neither article. He was becoming increasingly less well-informed about the state of the nation and the comings and goings of the mighty. It was a cowardly frame of mind, he knew that, but not entirely reprehensible. Certainly it wasn't very sensible to know too much about some things, and he seemed to be becoming peculiarly susceptible to auto-suggestion. Even a casual reminder that a nervous breakdown was no rarity in our society was enough to convince him that he would likely as not be wheeled off into a psychiatric ward tomorrow; and the last time he had braced himself to read an article on the causes of coronary thrombosis he had discovered that he exhibited every one of the major symptoms and had worked himself into a state of advanced panic. He could never understand why doctors could be anything but hyper-hypochondriacs, and supposed perhaps they were. He turned to the back page of *The Times* and took out his pen. He hoped it would be a real stinker this morning. But it wasn't. Nine and a half minutes.

He took a pad of paper and began writing, and was still writing when the phone rang an hour later. It was Mrs Lewis. Her husband was in bed with a soaring temperature. Flu, she thought. He'd been determined to go in to work, but her own wise counsels had prevailed and, much it appeared to her husband's displeasure, she had called the doctor. Morse, all sympathy, praised the good lady's course of action and warned her that the stubborn old so-and-so had better do as she told him. He would try to call round a bit later.

Morse smiled weakly to himself as he looked through the hurriedly written notes. It had all been for Lewis's benefit, and Lewis would have revelled in the routine. Phillipson: ticket office at the Playhouse; check row and number; occupants of seats on either side; check, trace, interview. The same with the Taylors and with Acum. The Ritz, the Jericho Arms and Lonsdale College. Ask people, talk to people, check and re-check, slowly and methodically probe and reconstruct. Yes, how Lewis would have enjoyed it. And, who knows? Something might have come of it. It would be irresponsible to neglect such obvious avenues of enquiry. Morse tore the sheets across the middle and consigned them to the waste-paper basket.

Perhaps he ought to concentrate his attention on the knife. Ah yes, the knife! But what the dickens was he supposed to do with the knife? If Sherlock were around he would doubtless deduce that the murderer was about five feet six inches tall, had tennis elbow and probably enjoyed roast beef every other Sunday. But what was *he* supposed to say about it? He walked to the cabinet and took it out; and summoning all his powers of logical analysis he stared at it with a concentrated intensity, and discovered that into his open and receptive mind came nothing whatsoever. He saw a knife – no more.

A household knife; and somewhere in the country, most probably somewhere in the Oxford area, there was a kitchen drawer without its carving knife. That didn't move forward the case one millimetre, did it? And could anyone really be sure whether a knife had been sharpened by a left- or a right-handed carver? Was it worth trying to find out? How fatuous the whole thing was becoming. But *how* the knife had been carried – now that was a much more interesting problem. Yes. Morse put the knife away. He sat back in the black leather chair, and once again he pondered many things.

The phone rang again at half-past ten, and Morse started abruptly and guiltily in his chair, and looked at the time in disbelief.

It was Mrs Lewis again. The doctor had called. Pharyngitis. At least three or four days in bed. But could Morse come round? The invalid was anxious to see him.

He certainly looked ill. The unshaven face was pale and the voice little more than a batrachian croak.

'I'm letting you down, Chief.'

'Nonsense. You get better, that's all. And be a good boy and do as the quack tells you.'

'Not much option with a missus like mine.' He smiled wanly, and supporting himself on one arm reached for his glass of weakly-pale orange juice. 'But I'm glad you've come, sir. You see, last night I had this terrible headache, and my eyes went all funny – sort of wiggly lines all the time. I couldn't recognise things very well.'

'You've got to expect summat to go wrong with you if you're ill,' said Morse.

'But I got to thinking about things. You remember the old boy on the Belisha crossing? Well, I didn't mention it at the time but it came back to me last night.'

'Go on,' said Morse quietly.

'It's just that I don't think he could see very well, sir. I reckon that's why he got knocked over and I just wondered if . . .'

Lewis looked at the inspector and knew instinctively that he had been right to ask him to come. Morse was nodding slowly and staring abstractedly through the bedroom window and on to the neatly kept strip of garden below, the beds trimmed and weeded, where a few late roses lingered languidly on.

* * *

Joe was still in the old people's home at Cowley, and lay in the same bed, half propped up on his pillows, his head lolling to the side, his thin mouth toothless and gaping. The sister who had accompanied Morse along the ward touched him gently.

'I've brought you a visitor.'

Joe blinked himself slowly awake and stared vaguely at them with unseeing eyes.

'It's a policeman, Mr Godberry. I think they must have caught up with you at last.' The sister turned to Morse and smiled attractively.

Joe grinned and his mouth moved in a senile chuckle. His hand groped feebly along the locker for his spectacle case, and finally he managed to hook an ancient pair of National Health spectacles behind his ears.

'Ah, I remember you, Sergeant. Nice to see you again. What can I do fo' you this time?'

Morse stayed with him for fifteen minutes, and realised how very sad it was to grow so old.

'You've been very helpful, Joe, and I'm very grateful to you.'

'Don't forget, Sergeant, to put the clock back. It's this month, you know. There's lots o' people forgits to put the clocks back. Huh. I remember once . . .'

Morse heard him out and finally got away. At the end of the ward he spoke again briefly to the sister.

'He's losing his memory a bit.'

'Most of them do, I'm afraid. Nice old boy, though. Did he tell you to put the clock back?'

Morse nodded. 'Does he tell everybody?'

'A lot of them seem to get a fixation about some little thing like that. Mind you, he's right, isn't he?' She laughed sweetly and Morse noticed she wore no wedding ring. *I hope you won't be offended, Sister, if I tell you that I find you very attractive.*

But the words wouldn't come, for he wasn't an architect who slept beneath the railway viaduct, and he could never say such things. Just as she couldn't. Morse wondered what she was thinking, and realised he would never know. He took out his wallet and gave her a pound note.

'Put it in the Christmas fund, Sister.'

Her eyes held his for a brief moment and he thought they were gentle and loving; and she thanked him nicely and walked briskly away. Fortunately The Cape of Good Hope was conveniently near.

Clocks! It reminded him. There was a good tale told in Oxford about the putting back of clocks. The church of St Benedict had a clock which ran by electricity, and for many years the complexities of putting back this clock had exercised the wit and wisdom of clergy and laity alike. The clock adorned the north face of the tower and its large hands were manoeuvred round the square, blue-painted dial by means of an elaborate lever device, situated behind the clock-face and reached via a narrow spiral staircase leading to the tower roof. The problem had been this. No one manipulating the lever immediately behind the clock-face could observe the effects of his manipulations, and so thick were the walls of the church tower that not even with a megaphone could an accomplice, standing outside the church, communicate to the manipulator the aforementioned effects. Each year, therefore, one of the churchwardens had taken upon himself to mount the spiral staircase, to manipulate the lever in roughly the right direction, to descend the staircase, to walk out of the church, to look upwards at the clock, to ascend the staircase once more, to give the lever a few more turns before descending again and repeating the process, until at last the clock was cajoled into a reluctant synchronisation. Such a lengthy and physically daunting procedure had been in operation for several years, until a mild-looking thurifer, rumoured to be one of the best incense-swingers in the business, had with becoming diffidence suggested to the minister that to remove the fuse from the fuse-box and to replace it after exactly sixty minutes might not only prove more accurate but also spare the rather elderly churchwarden the prospect of a coronary thrombosis. This idea, discussed at considerable length and finally accepted by the church committee, had proved wonderfully effective, and was now a firmly established practice.

Someone had told Morse the story in a pub, and he recalled it now. It pleased him. Lewis, but for his illness, would even now be running up and down the spiral staircase looking at his alibis. But that was out – at least for several days. It was up to Morse himself now to take the fuse away and set the clock aright. But not just for an hour – for much, much longer than that. In fact for two years, three months and more, to the day when Valerie Taylor had disappeared.

Chapter Twenty-three

For having considered God and himself
he will consider his neighbour.
Christopher Smart, *My Cat Jeoffrey*

Detective Constable Dickson soon realised he was on to something
and he felt as secretly excited as the poor woman was visibly nervous.
It was the sixth house he had visited, a house on the opposite side
of the street from Baines's and nearer the main road.

'You know, madam, that Mr Baines across the way was murdered
on Monday night?' Mrs Thomas nodded quickly. 'Er, did you know
Mr Baines?'

'Yes, I did. He's lived in the street nearly as long as I have.'

'I'm, er . . . we're, er, obviously anxious to find any witness who
might have seen someone going into Baines's house that night – or
coming out, of course.' Dickson left it at that and looked at her
hopefully.

In her late sixties now, scraggy-necked and flat-chested, Mrs
Thomas was a widow who measured her own life's joy by the
health and happiness of her white cat, which playfully and lovingly
gyrated in undulating spirals around her lower leg as she stood on the
threshold of her home. And as she stood there she was almost glad
that this young police officer had called, for she *had* seen something;
and several times the previous evening and again this Wednesday
morning she had decided she ought to report it to someone. It would
have been so easy in the first exciting hours when policemen had
been everywhere; later, too, when they had come and placed their
no-parking signs, like witches' hats, around the front of the house.
Yet it was all so hazy in her mind. More than once she wondered if
she could have imagined it, and she would die of shame if she were
to put the police to any trouble for no cause. It had always been like
that for Mrs Thomas; she had hidden herself unobtrusively away in
the corners of life and seldom ventured forth.

But, yes; she had seen something.

Her life was fairly orderly, if nothing else, and each evening
of the week, between 9.30 and 10.00 p.m., she put out the two
milk bottles and the two Co-op tokens on the front doorstep before
bolting the door securely, making herself a cup of cocoa, watching
News at Ten, and going to bed. And on Monday evening she

had seen something. If only at the time she had thought it might be important! Unusual, certainly, but only afterwards had she realised exactly how unusual it had been: for never had she seen a woman knocking at Baines's door before. Had the woman gone in? Mrs Thomas didn't think so, but she vaguely remembered that the light was burning in Baines's front room behind the faded yellow curtains. The truth was that it had all become so very frightening to her. Had the woman she had seen been the one who . . . ? Had she actually seen the . . . murderer? The very thought of it caused her to shiver throughout her narrow frame. Oh God, please not! Such a thing should never be allowed to happen to her – to her of all people. And as the panic rose within her, she again began to wonder if she'd dreamed it after all.

The whole thing was too frightening, especially since there was one thing that she knew might be very important. Very important indeed. 'You'd better come in, officer,' she said.

In the early afternoon she felt far less at ease than she had done with the constable. The man sitting opposite her in the black leather chair was pleasant enough, charming even; but his eyes were keen and hard, and there was a restless energy about his questions.

'Can you describe her, Mrs Thomas? Anything special about her – anything at all?'

'It was just the coat I noticed – nothing else. I told the constable . . .'

'Yes, I know you did; but tell me. Tell me, Mrs Thomas.'

'Well, that's all really – it was pink, just like I told the constable.'

'You're quite sure about that?'

She swallowed hard. Once more she was assailed by doubts from every quarter. She thought she was sure; she *was* sure, really, but could she just conceivably be wrong?

'I'm – I'm fairly sure.'

'What sort of pink?'

'Well, sort of . . .' The vision was fading rapidly now, had almost gone.

'Come on!' snapped Morse. 'You know what I mean. Fuchsia? Cyclamen? Er, lilac?' He was running out of shades of pink and received no help from Mrs Thomas. 'Light pink? Dark pink?'

'It was a fairly bright sort of . . .'

'Yes?'

It was no good, though; and Morse changed his tack and changed it again and again. Hair, height, dress, shoes, handbag

– on and on. He kept it up for more than twenty minutes. But try as she might Mrs Thomas was now quite incapable of raising any mental image whatsoever of Baines's late-night caller. Suddenly she knew that she was going to burst into tears, and she wanted desperately to go home. And just as suddenly it all changed.

'Tell me about your cat, Mrs Thomas.'

How he knew she had a cat, she hadn't the faintest idea, but the tension drained away from her like the pus from an abscess lanced by the dentist. She told him happily about her blue-eyed cat.

'You know,' said Morse, 'one of the most significant physical facts about the cat is so obvious that we often tend to forget it. A cat's face is flat between the eyes and so the eyes can work together. Stereoscopic vision they call it. Now, this is very rare among animals. You just think. The majority of animals have . . .' He went on for several minutes and Mrs Thomas was enthralled. But more than that; she was excited. It was all so clear again and she interrupted his discourse on the facial structure of the dog and told him all about it. Cerise pink coat – it might have been a herring-bone pattern, no hat, medium height, brownish hair. About ten minutes to ten. She was pretty certain about the time because . . .

She left soon afterwards, happy and relieved, and a nice policeman saw her safely back to her own cosy front-parlour, where the short-haired white cat lay indolently upon the sofa, momentarily opening the mysterious, stereoscopic eyes to greet his mistress's return.

Cerise. Morse got up and consulted the OED. 'A light, bright, clear red, like the colour of cherries.' Yes, that was it. For the next five minutes he stared vacantly through the window in the pose of Rodin's *Aristotle*; and at the end of that time he lifted his eyebrows slightly and nodded slowly to himself. It was time to get moving. He knew a coat like that, although he'd only seen it once – the colour of bright-pink cherries in the summer time.

Chapter Twenty-four

'Is there anybody there?' said the Traveller
Knocking on the moonlit door.

Walter de la Mare, *The Listeners*

Within the Phillipson family the financial arrangements were a matter of clear demarcation. Mrs Phillipson herself had a small private income accruing from interest received on her late mother's estate. This account she kept strictly separate from all other monies; and although her husband had known the value of the original capital inheritance, he had no more idea of his wife's annual income than she did of her husband's private means. For Phillipson himself also had a private account, in which he accumulated a not negligible annual sum from his examining duties with one of the national boards, from royalties on a moderately successful textbook, written five years previously, on Nineteenth-Century Britain, and from various incidental perks associated with his headship. In addition to these incomes there was, of course, Phillipson's monthly salary as a headmaster, and this was administered in a joint account on which both drew cash and wrote cheques for the normal items of household expenditure. The system worked admirably, and since by any standards the family was well-to-do, financial bickering had never blighted the Phillipsons' marriage; in fact financial matters had never caused the slightest concern to either party. Or had not done so until recently.

Phillipson kept his cheque book, his bank statements and all his financial correspondence in the top drawer of the bureau in the lounge, and he kept it locked. And in normal circumstances Mrs Phillipson would no more have dreamed of looking through this drawer than of opening the private and confidential letters which came through the letter-box week after week from the examination board. It was none of her business, and she was perfectly happy to keep it that way – in normal circumstances. But circumstances had been far from normal these last two weeks, and she had not lived with Donald for over twelve years without coming to know his moods and his anxieties. For she slept beside him every night and he was her husband, and she knew him. She knew with virtual certainty that whatever had lain so heavily upon his mind these last few days was neither the school, nor the inspector whose visit had been so strangely upsetting, nor even the ghost of Valerie Taylor that flitted perpetually across the twilit zone of his subconscious fears. It was a man. A man she had come to think of as wholly evil and wholly malignant. It was Baines.

No specific incident had led her to open her husband's drawer and to examine the papers within; it was more an aggregation of many minor incidents which had driven her lively imagination to the terminus – a terminus which the facts themselves may never have reached, but towards which (as she fearfully foresaw their implications) they seemed inevitably to be heading. Did he know that she had her own key to the drawer? Surely not. For otherwise, if there were something he was anxious to hide, he would have kept the guilty evidence at school and not at home. And she *had* looked – only last week, and many things were now so frighteningly clear. Assuredly she had heard the warning voices, and yet had looked and now could guess the truth: her husband was being blackmailed. And strangely enough she found that she could face the truth: it mattered less to her than she had dared to hope. But one thing was utterly certain. Never would she tell a living soul – never, never, never! She was his wife and she loved him, and would go on loving him. And if possible she would protect him; to the last ounce of her energy, to the last drop of her blood. She might even be able to do something. Yes, she might even be able to *do* something . . .

She seemed neither surprised nor dismayed to see him, for she had learned a great deal about herself the past few days. Not only was it better to face up to life's problems than to run away from them or desperately to pretend they didn't exist; it seemed far easier, too.

'Can we talk?' asked Morse.

She took his coat and hung it on the hall-stand behind the front door, beside an expensive-looking winter coat, the colour of ripening cherries.

They sat in the lounge, and Morse again noticed the photograph above the heavy mahogany bureau.

'Well, Inspector? How can I help you?'

'Don't you know?' replied Morse quietly.

'I'm afraid not.' She gave a little laugh and the hint of a smile played at the corners of her mouth. She spoke carefully, almost like a self-conscious teacher of elocution, the 'd' and the 't' articulated separately and distinctly.

'I think you do, Mrs Phillipson, and it's going to be easier for both of us if you're honest with me from the start because believe me, my love, you're going to be honest with me before we've finished.'

The niceties were gone already, the words direct and challenging, the easy familiarity almost frightening. As if she were looking in on herself from the outside, she wondered what her chances were against him. It depended, of course, on what he knew. But surely there was nothing he *could* know?

'What am I supposed to be honest about?'

'Can't we keep this between ourselves, Mrs Phillipson? That's why I've called now, you see, while your husband's still at school.'

He noted the first glint of anxiety in the light-brown eyes; but she remained silent, and he continued. 'If you're in the clear, Mrs Phillipson—' He had repeated her name with almost every question, and she felt uncomfortable. It was like the repeated blows of a battering ram against a beleaguered city.

'*In the clear?* What *are* you talking about?'

'I think you called at Mr Baines's house on Monday night, Mrs Phillipson.' The tone of his voice was ominously calm, but she only shook her head in semi-humorous disbelief.

'You can't really be serious, can you, Inspector?'

'I'm always serious when I'm investigating murder.'

'You don't think – you can't think that I had anything to do with *that*? On Monday night? Why, I hardly knew the man.'

'I'm not interested in how well you knew him.' It seemed an odd remark and her eyebrows contracted to a frown.

'What *are* you interested in?'

'I've told you, Mrs Phillipson.'

'Look, Inspector. I think it's about time you told me exactly why you're here. If you've got something you want to say to me, please say it. If you haven't . . .'

Morse, in a muted way, admired her spirited performance. But he had just reminded Mrs Phillipson, and now he reminded himself: he was investigating murder.

When he spoke again his words were casual, intimate almost. 'Did you like Mr Baines?'

Her mouth opened as if to speak and, as suddenly, closed again; and whatever doubts had begun to creep into Morse's mind were now completely removed.

'I didn't know him very well. I just told you that.' It was the best answer she could find, and it wasn't very good.

'Where were you on Monday evening, Mrs Phillipson?'

'I was here of course. I'm almost always here.'

'What time did you go out?'

'Inspector! I just told—'

'Did you leave the children on their own?'

'Of course I didn't – I meant I wouldn't. I could never—'

'What time did you get back?'

'Back? Back from where?'

'Before your husband?'

'My husband was out – that's what I'm telling you. He went to the theatre, The Playhouse—'

'He sat in row M seat 14.'

'If you say so, all right. But he wasn't home until about eleven.'

'Ten to, according to him.'

'All right, ten to eleven. What does—'

'You haven't answered my question, Mrs Phillipson.'

'What question?'

'I asked you what time *you* got home, not your husband.' His questions were flung at her now with breakneck rapidity.

'You don't think I would go out and leave—'

'Go out? Where to, Mrs Phillipson? Did you go on the bus?'

'I didn't go anywhere. Can't you understand that? How could I possibly go out and leave—'

Morse interrupted her again. She was beginning to crack, he knew that; her voice was high-pitched now amidst the elocutionary wreckage.

'All right – you didn't leave your children alone – I believe you – you love your children – of course you do – it would be illegal to leave them on their own – how old are they?'

Again she opened her mouth to speak, but he pushed relentlessly, remorselessly on.

'Have you heard of a baby-sitter, Mrs Phillipson? – somebody who comes in and looks after your children while you go out – do you hear me? – while you go out – do you want me to find out who it was? – or do you want to tell me? – I could soon find out, of course – friends, neighbours – do you want me to find out, Mrs Phillipson? – do you want me to go and knock next door? – and the door next to that? – of course, you don't, do you? You know, you're not being very sensible about this, are you, Mrs Phillipson?' (He was speaking more slowly and calmly now.) 'You see, I *know* what happened on Monday night. Someone saw you, Mrs Phillipson; someone saw you in Kempis Street. And if you'd like to tell me why you were there and what you did, it would save a lot of time and trouble. But if you won't tell me, then I shall have to—'

Of a sudden she almost shrieked as the incessant flow of words began to overwhelm her. 'I told you! I don't know what you're talking about! You don't seem to understand that, do you? *I just don't know what you're talking about!*'

Morse sat back in the armchair, relaxed and unconcerned. He looked about him, and once more fastened his gaze on the photograph of the headmaster and his wife above the large bureau. And then he looked at his wristwatch.

'What time do the children get home?' His tone was suddenly friendly and quiet, and Mrs Phillipson felt the panic welling up within her. She looked at her own wristwatch and her voice was shaking as she answered him.

'They'll be home at four o'clock.'

'That gives us an hour, doesn't it, Mrs Phillipson? I think that's long enough – my car's outside. You'd better put your coat on – the pink one, if you will.'

He rose from the armchair, and fastened the front buttons of his jacket. 'I'll see that your husband knows if . . .' He took a few steps towards the door, but she laid her hand upon him as he moved past her.

'Sit down, please, Inspector,' she said quietly.

She had gone (she said). That was all, really. It was like suddenly deciding to write a letter or to ring the dentist or to buy some restorer for the paint brushes encrusted stiff with last year's gloss. She asked Mrs Cooper next door to baby-sit, said she'd be no longer than an hour at the very latest, and caught the 9.20 p.m. bus from the stop immediately outside the house. She got off at Cornmarket, walked quickly through Gloucester Green and reached Kempis Street by about a quarter to ten. The light was shining in Baines's front window – she had never been there before – and she summoned up all her courage and knocked on the front door. There was no reply. Again she knocked – and again there was no reply. She then walked along to the lighted window and tapped upon it hesitantly and quietly with the back of her hand; but she could hear no sound and could make out no movement behind the cheap yellow curtains. She hurried back to the front door, feeling as guilty as a young schoolgirl caught out of her place in the classroom by the headmistress. But still nothing happened. She had so nearly called the whole thing off there and then; but her resolution had been wrought-up to such a pitch that she made one last move. She tried the door – and found it unlocked. She opened it slightly, no more than a foot or so, and called his name.

'Mr Baines?' And then slightly louder, '*Mr Baines?*' But she received no reply. The house seemed strangely still and the sound of her own voice echoed eerily in the high entrance hall. A cold shiver of fear ran down her spine, and for a few seconds she felt sure that he was there, very near to her, watching and waiting . . . And suddenly a panic-stricken terror had seized her and she had rushed back to the lighted, friendly road, crossed over by the railway station and, with her heart pounding in her ribs, tried to get a grip on herself. In St Giles' she caught a taxi and arrived home just after ten.

That was her story, anyway. She told it in a flat, dejected voice, and she told it well and clearly. To Morse it sounded in no way like the tangled, mazy machinations of a murderer. Indeed a good deal of it he could check fairly easily: the baby-sitter, the bus conductor, the taxi-driver. And Morse felt sure that all would verify the outline of her story, and confirm the approximate times she'd given. But there was no chance of checking those fateful moments when she stood outside the door of Baines's house . . . Had she gone in? And if she had, what terrible things had then occurred? The pros and cons were counter-poised in Morse's mind, with the balance tilting slightly in Mrs Phillipson's favour.

'Why did you want to see him?'

'I wanted to talk to him, that's all.'

'Yes. Go on.'

'It's difficult to explain. I don't think I knew myself what I was going to say. He was – oh, I don't know – he was everything that's *bad* in life. He was mean, he was vindictive, he was – sort of calculating. He just delighted in seeing other people squirm. I'm not thinking of anything in particular, and I don't really know all that much about him. But since Donald has been headmaster he's – how shall I put it? – he's waited, hoping for things to go wrong. He was a cruel man, Inspector.'

'You hated him?'

She nodded hopelessly. 'Yes, I suppose I did.'

'It's as good a motive as any,' said Morse sombrely.

'It might seem so, yes.' But she sounded unperturbed.

'Did your husband hate Baines, too?' He watched her carefully and saw the light flash dangerously in her eyes.

'Don't be silly, Inspector. You can't possibly think that Donald had anything to do with all this. I know I've been a fool, but you can't . . . It's impossible. He was at the theatre all night. You know that.'

'Your husband would have thought it was impossible for *you* to be knocking at Baines's door that night, wouldn't he? You were here, at home, with the children, surely?' He leaned forward and spoke more curtly again now. 'Make no mistake, Mrs Phillipson, it would have been a hell of a sight easier for him to leave the theatre than it was for you to leave here. And don't try to tell me otherwise!'

He sat back impassively in the chair. He sensed an evasion somewhere in her story, a half-truth, a curtain not yet fully drawn back; and at the same time he knew that he was almost there, and all he had to do was sit and wait. And so he sat and waited; and the world of the woman seated opposite him was slowly beginning to fall apart, and suddenly, dramatically, she buried her head in her hands and wept uncontrollably.

Morse fished around in his pockets and finally found a crumpled apology for a paper handkerchief, and pushed it gently into her right hand.

'Don't cry,' he said softly. 'It won't do either of us any good.'

After a few minutes the tears dried up, and soon the snivelling subsided. 'What *can* do us any good, Inspector?'

'It's very easy, really,' said Morse in a brisk tone. 'You tell me the truth, Mrs Phillipson. You'll find I probably know it anyway.'

But Morse was wrong – he was terribly wrong. Mrs Phillipson could do little more than reiterate her strange little story. This time, however, with a startling addition – an addition which caught Morse, as he sat there nodding sceptically, like an uppercut to the jaw. She hadn't wanted to mention it because . . . because, well, it seemed so much like trying to get herself out of a mess by pushing someone else into it. But she could only tell the truth, and if that's what Morse was after she thought she'd better tell it. As she had said, she ran along to the main street after leaving Baines's house and crossed over towards the Royal Oxford Hotel; and just before she reached the hotel she saw someone she knew – knew very well – come out of the lounge door and walk across the road to Kempis Street. She hesitated and her tearful eyes looked pleadingly and pathetically at Morse.

'Do you know who it was, Inspector? It was David Acum.'

Chapter Twenty-five

For oily or spotty skin, first cleanse face and throat, then
pat with a hot towel. Smooth on an even layer of luxurious
'Ladypak', avoiding the area immediately around the eyes.
                              Directions for applying a beauty mask

At 6.20 a.m. the following morning Morse was on the road: it
would take about five hours. He would have enjoyed the drive
more with someone to talk to, especially Lewis, and he switched
on the Jaguar's radio for the 7 a.m. news. The world seemed
strangely blighted: abroad there were rumours of war and famine,
and at home more bankruptcies and unemployment – and a missing
lord who had been dredged up from a lake in east Essex. But the
morning was fresh and bright, the sky serene and cloudless, and
Morse drove fast. He had left Evesham behind him and was well
on the way to Kidderminster before he met any appreciable volume
of traffic. The 8 a.m. news came and went, with no perceptible
amelioration of the cosmic plight, and Morse switched over to Radio
Three and listened lovingly to the Brandenburg Concerto No. 5 in
D. The journey was going well, and he was through Bridgnorth and
driving rather too quickly round the Shrewsbury ring road by 9 a.m.
when he decided that a Schönberg string quartet might be a little
above his head, and switched off. He found himself vaguely pondering the lake in east Essex, and remembering the reservoir behind
the Taylors' home, before switching that off, too, and concentrating with appropriate care and attention upon the perils of the busy
A5. At Nesscliffe, some twelve miles north of Shrewsbury, he turned
off left along the B4396 towards Bala. Wales now, and the pale-
green hills rose ever more steeply. He was making excellent time
and he praised the gods that his journey was not being made on
a dry Welsh Sunday. He was feeling thirsty already. But he was
through Bala and swinging in the long left-handed loop around
Llyn Tegid (reservoir again!) long before the pubs were open; and
through the crowded streets of Portmadoc, festooned still with the
multi-coloured bunting of high summer, and past the Lloyd George
Museum in Llanystumdwy, and still the hands on the fascia clock
were some few minutes short of eleven. He might just as well drive
on. At Four Crosses he turned right on to the Pwllheli–Caernarfon
road, and drove on into the Lleyn Peninsula, past the triple peaks of

the Rivals and on to the coastal road, with the waters of Caernarfon
Bay laughing and glittering in the sunshine to his left. He would stop
at the next likely-looking hostelry. He had passed one in the last
village, but the present tract of road afforded little for the thirsty
traveller; and he was only two or three miles south of Caernarfon
itself when he spotted the sign: BONT-NEWYDD. Surely the village
where the Acums lived? He pulled in to the side of the road, and
consulted the file in his brief-case. Yes, it was. 16 St Beuno's Road.
He enquired of an ageing passer-by and learned that he was only a
few 'undred yaards from St Beuno's Road, and that The Prince of
Wales was just around the corner. It was five minutes past eleven.

As he sampled the local brew, he debated whether he should
call at the Acums' home. Did the modern languages master come
home for lunch? Morse's original plan had been to go direct to
the City of Caernarfon School, preferably about lunch-time. But
perhaps it would do no harm to have a little chat with Mrs Acum
first? Temporarily he shelved the decision, bought another pint, and
considered the forthcoming interview. Acum had lied, of course,
about not leaving the conference; for Mrs Phillipson could not
have had the faintest notion that Acum would be in Oxford on
that Monday night. How could she? Unless . . . but he dropped
the fanciful line of thought. The beer was good, and at noon he
was happily discussing with his host the sorry Sunday situation in
the thirsty counties and the defacement of the Welsh road signs by
the Nationalists. And ten minutes later, legs astraddle, he stood and
contemplated the defacement of the landlord's lavatory walls by a
person or persons unknown. Several of the graffiti were unintelli-
gible to the non-Welsh-speaker; but one that was scrawled in his
native tongue caught Morse's eye, and he smiled in approbation as
his bladder achingly emptied itself:

The penis mightier than the sword

It was now 12.15 p.m., and if Acum were coming home to lunch,
there was an obvious danger of his passing Morse in the opposite
direction. Well, there was one pretty certain way of finding out.
He left the Jaguar at The Prince of Wales and walked.

St Beuno's Road led off right from the main road. The houses
were small here, built of square, grey, granite blocks, and tiled
with the purplish-blue Ffestiniog slate. The grass in the tiny front
gardens was of a green two or three shades paler than the English

variety, and the soil looked tired and undernourished. The front door was painted a Cambridge blue, with the black number 16 dextrously worked in the florid style of a Victorian theatre-bill. Morse knocked firmly, and after a brief interval the door opened; but opened only slightly, and then to reveal a strangely incongruous sight. A woman stood before him, her face little more than a white mask, with slits left open for the eyes and mouth, a blood-red towel swathed around the top of her head where (as, alas, with most of the blondes) the tell-tale roots of the hair betrayed its darker origins. It was curious to witness the lengths to which the ladies were prepared to go in order to improve upon the natural gifts their maker had endowed them with; and in the depths of Morse's mind there stirred the dim remembrance of the fair-haired woman with the spotty face in the staff photograph of the Roger Bacon Comprehensive School. He knew that this must be Mrs Acum. Yet it was not the beauty pack, smeared though it doubtless was with a practised skill, that chiefly held the inspector's rapt attention. She was holding a meagre white towel to the top of her shoulders, and as she stood half hidden by the door, it was immediately apparent that behind the towel the woman was completely naked. Morse felt as lecherous as a billy-goat. A Welsh billy-goat, perhaps. It must have been the beer.

'I've called to see your husband. Er, it is Mrs Acum, isn't it?'

The head nodded, and a hair-line fracture of the carefully assembled mask appeared at the corners of the white mouth. Was she laughing at him?

'Will he be back home for lunch?'

The head shook, and the top of the towel drooped tantalisingly to reveal the beautifully-moulded outline of her breasts.

'He's at school, I suppose?'

The head nodded, and the eyes stared blandly through the slits.

'Well, I'm sorry to have bothered you, Mrs Acum, especially at, er, such, er . . . We've spoken to each other before, you know – over the phone, if you remember. I'm Morse. Chief Inspector Morse from Oxford.'

The red towel bobbed on her head, the mask almost breaking through into a smile. They shook hands through the door, and Morse was conscious of the heady perfume on her skin. He held her hand for longer than he need have done, and the white towel dropped from her right shoulder; and for a brief and beautiful moment he stared with shameless fascination at her nakedness. The nipple was fully erect and he felt an almost irresistible urge to hold it there and then between his fingers. Was she inviting him in? He looked again at the passive mask. The towel was now in place again, and she stood back a little from the door; it was fifty-fifty. But he had hesitated too long, and the chance, if chance it was, was gone already. He lacked, as always, the bogus courage of his own depravity, and he turned away from her and walked back slowly towards The Prince of Wales. At the end of the road he stopped, and looked back; but the light-blue door was closed upon him and he cursed the conscience that invariably thus doth make such spineless cowards of us all. It was perhaps something to do with status. People just didn't expect such base behaviour from a chief inspector, as if such eminent persons were somehow different from the common run of lewd humanity. How wrong they were! How wrong! Why, even the mighty had their little weaknesses. Good gracious, yes. Just think of old Lloyd George. The things they said about Lloyd George! And he was a prime minister . . .

He climbed into the Jaguar. Oh God, such beautiful breasts! He sat motionless at the wheel for a short while, and then he smiled to himself. He reckoned that Constable Dickson could almost have hung his helmet there! It was an irreverent thought, but it made him feel a good deal better. He pulled carefully out of the car park and headed north on the final few miles of his journey.

Chapter Twenty-six

Merely corroborative detail, to add artistic verisimilitude to an otherwise bald and unconvincing narrative.

W. S. Gilbert, *The Mikado*

A small group of boys was kicking a football around at the side of a large block of classrooms which abutted on to the wide sports fields, where sets of rugby and hockey posts demarked the area of grass into neatly white-lined rectangles. The rest of the school was having lunch. The two men walked three times around the playing fields, hands in pockets, heads slightly forward, eyes downcast. They were about the same build, neither man above medium height; and to the football players they seemed unworthy of note, anonymous almost. Yet one of the two men pacing slowly over the grass was a chief inspector of police, and the other, one of their very own teachers, was a suspect in a murder case.

Morse questioned Acum about himself and his teaching career; about Valerie Taylor and Baines and Phillipson; about the conference in Oxford, times and places and people. And he learned nothing that seemed of particular interest or importance. The schoolmaster appeared pleasant enough – in a nondescript sort of way; he answered the inspector's questions with freedom and with what seemed a fair degree of guarded honesty. And so Morse told him, told him quietly yet quite categorically, that he was a liar; told him that he had indeed left the conference that Monday evening, at about 9.30 p.m., told him that he had walked to Kempis Street to see his former colleague, Mr Baines, and that he had been seen there; told him that, if he persisted in denying such a plain, incontrovertible statement of the truth, he, Morse, had little option but to take him back to Oxford where he would be held for questioning in connection with the murder of Mr Reginald Baines. It was as simple as that! And, in fact, it proved a good deal simpler than even Morse had dared to hope; for Acum no longer denied the plain, incontrovertible statement of the truth which the inspector had presented to him. They were on their third and final circuit of the playing fields, far away from the main school buildings, by the side of some neglected allotments, where the ramshackle sheds rusted away sadly in despairing disrepair. Here Acum stopped and nodded slowly.

'Just tell me what you did, sir, that's all.'

'I'd been sitting at the back of the hall – deliberately – and I left early. As you say, it was about half-past nine, or probably a bit earlier.'

'You went to see Baines?' Acum nodded. 'Why did you go to see him?'

'I don't know, really. I was getting a bit bored with the conference, and Baines lived fairly near. I thought I'd go and see if he was in and ask him out for a drink. It's always interesting to talk about old times, you know the sort of thing – what was going on at school, which members of staff were still there, which ones had left, what they were doing. You know what I mean.'

He spoke naturally and easily, and if he were a liar he seemed to Morse a fairly fluent one.

'Well,' continued Acum, 'I walked along there. I was in a bit of a hurry because I knew the pubs would be closed by half-past ten and time was getting on. I had a drink on the way and it must have been

getting on for ten by the time I got there. I'd been there before, and
thought he must be in because the light was on in the front room.'

'Were the curtains drawn?' For the first time since they had
been talking together, Morse's voice grew sharper.

Acum thought for a moment. 'Yes, I'm almost certain they were.'

'Go on.'

'Well, I thought, as I say, that he must be in. So I knocked
pretty loudly two or three times on the door. But he didn't answer,
or at least he didn't seem to hear me. I thought he might be in the
front room perhaps with the TV on, so I went to the window and
knocked on it.'

'Could you hear the TV? Or see it?'

Acum shook his head; and to Morse it was all beginning to
sound like a record stuck in its groove. He knew for certain what
was coming next.

'It's a funny thing, Inspector, but I began to feel just a bit
frightened – as if I were sort of trespassing and shouldn't really
be there at all; as if he knew that I was there but didn't want to
see me . . . Anyway, I went back to the door and knocked again,
and then I put my head round the door and shouted his name.'

Morse stood quite still, and considered his next question with
care. If he was to get his piece of information, he wanted it to
come from Acum himself without too much prompting.

'You put your head round the door, you say?'

'Yes. I just felt sure he was there.'

'Why did you feel that?'

'Well, there was a light in the front room and . . .' He hesitated
for a moment, and seemed to be fumbling around in his mind for
some fleeting, half-forgotten impression that had given him this
feeling.

'Think back carefully, sir,' said Morse. 'Just picture yourself
there again, standing at the door. Take your time. Just put yourself
back there. You're standing there in Kempis Street. Last Monday
night . . .'

Acum shook his head slowly and frowned. He said nothing for
a minute or two.

'You see, Inspector, I just had this idea that he was somewhere
about. I almost *knew* he was. I thought he might just have slipped
out somewhere for a few seconds because . . .' It came back to
him then, and he went on quickly. 'Yes, that's it. I remember now.
I remember why I thought he must be there. It wasn't just the light
in the front window. There was a light on in the hall because the

front door was open. Not wide open, but standing ajar as if he'd just slipped out and would be back again any second.'

'And then?'

'I left. He wasn't there. I just left, that's all.'

'Why didn't you tell me all this when I rang you, sir?'

'I was frightened, Inspector. I'd been there, hadn't I? And he was probably lying there all the time – murdered. I was frightened, I really was. Wouldn't you have been?'

Morse drove into the centre of Caernarfon, and parked his car alongside the jetty under the great walls of the first Edward's finest castle. He found a Chinese restaurant nearby, and greedily gulped down the oriental fare that was set before him. It was his first meal for twenty-four hours, and he temporarily dismissed all else from his mind. Only over his coffee did he allow his restless brain to come to grips with the case once more; and by the time he had finished his second cup of coffee he had reached the firm conclusion that, whatever improbabilities remained to be explained away, especially the reasons given for calling on Baines, both Mrs Phillipson and David Acum had told him the truth, or something approximating to the truth, at least as far as their evidence concerned itself with the visits made to the house in Kempis Street. Their accounts of what had taken place there were so clear, so mutually complementary, that he felt he should and would believe them. That bit about the door being slightly open, for example – exactly as Mrs Phillipson had left it before panicking and racing down to the lighted street. No. Acum could not have made that up. Surely not. Unless . . . It was the second time that he had qualified his conclusions with that sinister word 'unless'; and it troubled him. Acum and Mrs Phillipson. Was there any link at all between that improbable pair? If link there was, it had to have been forged at some point in the past, at some point more than two years ago, at the Roger Bacon Comprehensive School. Could there have been something? It was an idea, anyway. Yet as he drove out of the castle car park, he decided on balance that it was a lousy idea. In front of the castle he passed the statue erected to commemorate the honourable member for Caernarfon (Lloyd George, no less) and as he drove out along the road to Capel Curig, his brain was as jumbled and cluttered as a magpie's nest.

He stopped briefly in the pass of Llanberis, and watched the tiny figures of the climbers, conspicuous only by their bright orange anoraks, perched at dizzying heights on the sheer mountain faces that towered massively above the road on either side. He felt profoundly thankful that whatever the difficulties of his own job he was spared the risk, at every second, and every precarious hand- and foot-hold, of a vertical plunge to a certain death upon the rocks far, far below. Yet, in his own way, Morse knew that he too was scaling a peak and knew full well the blithe exhilaration of reaching to the summit. So often there was only one way forward, only one. And when one route seemed utterly impossible, one had to look for the nearly impossible alternative, to edge along the face of the cliff, to avoid the impasse, and to lever oneself painstakingly up to the next ledge, and look up again and follow the only route. On the death of Baines, Morse had considered only a small group of likely suspects. The murderer could, of course, have been someone completely unconnected with the Valerie Taylor affair; but he doubted it. There had been five of them, and he now felt that the odds against Mrs Phillipson and David Acum had lengthened considerably. That left the Taylors, the pair of them, and Phillipson himself. It was time he tried to put together the facts, many of them very odd facts, that he had gleaned about these three. It must be one of them, surely; for he felt convinced now that Baines had been murdered before the visits of Mrs Phillipson and David Acum. Yes, that was the only way it could have been. He grasped the firm fact with both hands and swung himself on to a higher ledge, and discovered that from this vantage point the view seemed altogether different.

He drove to Capel Curig and there turned right on to the A5 towards Llangollen. And even as he drove he began to see the pattern. He ought to have seen it before; but with the testimony of Mrs Phillipson and Acum behind him, it became almost childishly easy now to fit the pieces into quite a different pattern. One by one they clicked into place with a simple inevitability, as on and on he drove at high speed, passing Shrewsbury and, keeping to the A5, rattling along the old Watling Street and almost missing the turning off for Daventry and Banbury. It was now nearly 8 p.m. and Morse was feeling the effects of his long day. He found his mind wandering off to that news item he had heard about the unfortunate lord in the Essex reservoir; and as he was leaving the outskirts of Banbury an oncoming car flashed its lights at him. He realised that he had been drifting dangerously over the centre of the road, and jerked himself into a startled wakefulness. He resolved not to allow his concentration to waver one centimetre, opened the side window and breathing deeply upon the cool night air, sang in a mournful baritone, over and over again, the first and only verse he could remember of 'Lead, Kindly Light'.

He drove straight home and locked up the garage. It had been a long day; he hoped he would sleep well.

Chapter Twenty-seven

All happy families are alike, but each unhappy family is unhappy in its own way.

Leo Tolstoy

Lewis was getting better. He got up for a couple of hours just after Morse had arrived back in Oxford, with the aid of the banister made his careful way downstairs, and joined his surprised wife on the sofa in front of the television set. His temperature was normal now, and though he felt weak on his legs and sapped of his usual energy, he knew he would soon be back in harness. Many of the hours in bed he had spent in thinking, thinking about the Taylor case; and that morning he had been suddenly struck by an idea so novel and so exciting that he had persuaded his wife to ring the station immediately. But Morse was out: off to Wales, they said. It puzzled Lewis: the Principality in no way figured in his own new-minted version of events, and he guessed that Morse had followed one of his wayward fancies about Acum, wasted a good many gallons of police petrol, and advanced the investigation not one whit. But that wasn't quite fair. In the hands of the chief inspector things seldom stood still; they might go sideways, or even backwards, and often (Lewis agreed) they went forwards. But they seldom stood still. Yes, Lewis had been deeply disappointed not to catch him. Everything – well, almost everything – fitted so perfectly. It had been that item on his bedside radio at eight o'clock that had started the chain reaction; that item about some big noise being washed up in a reservoir. He knew they had dredged the reservoir behind the Taylors' home; but you could never be sure in such a wide stretch of water as that; and anyway it didn't really matter much whether it was in the reservoir or somewhere else. That was just the starting point. And then there was that old boy at the Belisha crossing, and the basket, and – oh, lots of other things. How he wished he'd caught the chief at the station! The

really surprising thing was that Morse hadn't thought of it himself.
He usually thought of everything – and more! But later, as the day
wore on, he began to think that Morse probably *had* thought of it.
After all, it was Morse himself who had suggested, right out of the
blue, that she was carrying a basket.

Laboriously, during the afternoon, Lewis wrote it all down, and
when he had finished the initial thrill was already waning, and he
was left only with the quiet certainty that it had indeed been, for him,
a remarkable brainwave, and that there was a very strong possibility
that he might be right. At 9.15 p.m. he rang the station himself, but
Morse had still not shown up.

'Probably gone straight home – or to a pub,' said the desk sergeant.
Lewis left a message, and prayed that for the morrow the chief had
planned no trip to the Western Isles.

Donald Phillipson and his wife sat silently watching the nine o'clock
news on BBC television. They had said little all evening, and now
that the children were snugly tucked up in bed, the little had dried up
to nothing. Once or twice each of them had almost asked a question
of the other, and it would have been the same question: is there
anything you want to tell me? Or words to that effect. But neither of
them had braved it, and at a quarter-past ten Mrs Phillipson brought
in the coffee and announced that she was off to bed.

'You've had your fill tonight, haven't you?'
He mumbled something inaudible, and lumbered along unsteadily,
trying with limited success to avoid bumping into her as they walked
side by side along the narrow pavement. It was 10.45 p.m. and their
home was only two short streets away from the pub.

'Have you ever tried to work out how much you spend a week on
beer and fags?'
It hurt him, and it wasn't fair. Christ, it wasn't fair.
'If you want to talk about money, my gal, what about your Bingo?
Every bloody night nearly.'
'You just leave my Bingo out of it. It's about the one pleasure I've
got in life, and don't you forget it. And some people *win* at Bingo;
you know that, don't you? Don't tell me you're so ignorant you don't
know that.'
'Have you won recently?' His tone was softer and he hoped very
much that she had.
'I've told you. You keep your nose out of it. I spend my own
money, thank you, not yours; and if I win that's my business, isn't it?'

'You were lashing out a bit with your money tonight, weren't you? Bit free with your favours all round, if you ask me.'

'What's that supposed to mean?' Her voice was very nasty.

'Well, you—'

'Look, if I want to treat some of my friends to a drink, that's my look-out, isn't it? It's my money, too!'

'I only meant—'

They were at the front gate now and she turned on him, her eyes flashing. 'And don't you ever dare to say anything again about my favours! Christ! You're a one to talk, aren't you – you – *bastard*!'

Their holiday together, the first for seven years, was due to begin at the weekend. The omens seemed hardly favourable.

It was half-past eleven when Morse finally laid his head upon the pillows. He shouldn't have had so much beer really, but he felt he'd deserved it. It would mean shuffling along for a pee or two before the night was out. But what the hell! He felt at peace with himself and with the world in general. Beer was probably the cheapest drug on the market, and he only wished that his GP would prescribe it for him on the National Health. Ah, this was good! He turned into the pillows. Old Lewis would be in bed, too. He would see Lewis first thing in the morning; and he was quite sure that however groggy his faithful sergeant was feeling he would sit up in his sick bed and blink with a pained, incredulous surprise. For tomorrow morning he would be able to reveal the identity of the murderer of Valerie Taylor and that of the murderer of Reginald Baines, to boot. Or, to be slightly more accurate, just the one identity; for it had been the same hand which had murdered them both, and Morse now knew whose hand it was.

Chapter Twenty-eight

An ill-favoured thing, sir, but mine own.
Shakespeare, *As You Like It*

'How're you doing then, my old friend?'

'Much better, thanks. Should be fit again any day now.'

'Now you're not to rush things, remember that. There's nothing spoiling.'

'Isn't there, sir?' The tone of the voice caught the inspector slightly unawares, and he looked at Lewis curiously.

'What's on your mind?'

'I tried to get hold of you yesterday, sir.' He sat up in bed and reached to the bedside table. 'I thought I had a bright idea. I may be wrong, but . . . Well, here it is anyway, for what it's worth.' He handed over several sheets of notepaper, and Morse shelved his own pronouncements and sat down beside the bed. His head ached and he stared reluctantly at his sergeant's carefully written notes.

'You want me to read all this?'

'I just hope it's worth reading, that's all.'

And Morse read; and as he read a wan smile crept across his mouth, and here and there he nodded with rigorous approbation, and Lewis sank back into his pillows with the air of a pupil whose essay is receiving the alpha accolade. When he had finished, Morse took out his pen.

'Don't mind if I make one or two slight alterations, do you?' For the next ten minutes he went methodically through the draft, correcting the more heinous spelling errors, inserting an assortment of full-stops and commas, and shuffling several of the sentences into a more comprehensible sequence. 'That's better,' said Morse finally, handing back to a rueful-looking Lewis his amended masterpiece. It was an improvement, though. Anyone could see that.

To begin with, the evidence seemed to point to the fact that Valerie Taylor was alive. After all, her parents received a letter from her. But we then discovered that the letter was almost certainly not written by Valerie at all. So. Instead of assuming that she's alive, we must face the probability that she's dead, and we must ask ourselves the old question: who was the last person to see her alive? The answer is Joe Godberry, a short-sighted old fellow who ought never to have been in charge of a Belisha crossing in the first place. Could he have been wrong? He could, and in my view he was wrong: that is, he didn't see Valerie Taylor at all on the afternoon she disappeared. He says quite firmly that he did see her, but might he not have been mistaken? Might he just have seen someone who looked like Valerie? Well? Who looked like Valerie? Chief Inspector Morse himself thought that a photograph of Mrs Taylor was one of her daughter Valerie, and this raises an interesting possibility. Could the person seen by Godberry have been not Valerie but Valerie's mother? [Lewis had underlined the words thickly, and it was at this point on his first reading that Morse had nodded his approval.] If it was Valerie's mother there are two important implications. First, that the last person to see Valerie alive was none other than her own mother at lunch-time that same day. Second, that this person – Valerie's mother – had gone to a great deal of trouble to establish the fact that her daughter had left the house and returned to afternoon school. On this second point we know that mother and daughter were very similar in build and figure generally, and Mrs Taylor is still fairly slim and attractive. [It was at this point that Morse nodded again.] What was the best way of convincing anyone who might notice, the neighbours, say, or the Belisha man or the shop assistants, that Valerie had left home after lunch that day? The answer is fairly obvious. The uniform of the school which Valerie attended was quite distinctive, especially the red socks and the white blouse. Mrs Taylor could dress up in the uniform herself, run quickly down the road, keep on the far side of the crossing, and with a bit of luck there would be no trouble in persuading anyone, even the police, that her daughter had left home. We learned that on the particular Tuesday afternoon in question, Valerie would be most unlikely to be missed anyway. Games afternoon – and a real shambles. So. Let us assume that Mrs Taylor dresses up as her daughter and makes her way towards school. Chief Inspector Morse suggested early on that the person seen by Godberry was perhaps carrying a basket or some such receptacle. [Lewis had made a sorry mess of the spelling.] Now, if she had been carrying <u>clothes</u> [heavily scored by Lewis] the situation is becoming very interesting. Once Mrs Taylor has created the impression that Valerie has left for school, it is equally important that she should not create the further impression that Valerie has returned home some five or ten minutes later. Because if someone sees Valerie, or someone who looks like Valerie, returning to the Taylors' house, the careful plan is ruined. When Valerie is reported missing, the enquiries will naturally centre on the house, not on the area around the school. But she can deal with this without too much trouble. In the basket <u>Mrs Taylor has put her own clothes</u>. She goes into the ladies', just past the shopping area, and changes back into them, and then walks back, as unobtrusively as she can, probably by a roundabout route, to her own house. The real question now is this. Why all this palaver? Why should Mrs Taylor have to go to all this trouble and risk? There can only be one answer. To create the firm impression that Valerie is alive <u>when in fact she is dead</u>. If Valerie had arrived home for lunch, and if Valerie did not leave the house again, we must assume that she was killed at some time during the lunch hour in her own home. And there was, it seems, only one other person in the Taylor household during that time: Valerie's own mother. It is difficult to believe, but the facts seem to point to the appalling probability that <u>Valerie was murdered by her own mother</u>. Why? We can only guess. There is some evidence that Valerie was pregnant. Perhaps her mother flew at her in a wild rage and struck her much harder than she intended to. We may learn the truth from Mrs Taylor herself. The next thing is – what to do? And here we have the recorded evidence of the police files. The fact is that the police were not called in until the next morning.

Why so much delay? Again an answer readily presents itself. [Morse had admired his sergeant's style at this point, and the nod had signified a recognition of a literary nicety rather than any necessary concurrence with the argument.] Mrs Taylor had to get rid of the body. She waited, I think, obviously in great distress, until her husband arrived home about six; and then she told him what had happened. He has little option. He can't leave his poor wife to face the consequences of the terrible mess she's got herself into, and the two of them plan what to do. Somehow they get rid of the body, and I suspect the reservoir behind the house is the first place that occurs to them. I know that this was dragged at the time, but it's terribly easy to miss anything in so large a stretch of water. I can only suggest that it is thoroughly dragged again.

Lewis put the document back on the bedside table and Morse tapped him in congratulatory fashion upon the shoulder.

'I think it's time they made you up to inspector, my old friend.'

'You think I may be right then, sir?'

'Yes,' said Morse slowly, 'I do.'

Chapter Twenty-nine

Incest is only relatively boring.
Inscription on the lavatory wall of an Oxford pub

Lewis leaned back into his pillows, and felt content. He would never make an inspector, he knew that, didn't even want to try. But to beat old Morse at his own game – my goodness, that was something!

'Got a drop of booze in the house?' asked Morse.

Ten minutes later he was sipping a liberal helping of whisky as Lewis dunked a chunk of bread into his Bovril.

'There are one or two things you could add to your admirable statement, you know, Lewis.' A slightly pained expression appeared on Lewis's face, but Morse quickly reassured him. 'Oh, that's pretty certainly how it happened, I'm sure of that. But there are just one or two points where we can be even more specific, I think, and one or two where we shall need a clearer picture not so much of what happened as of why it happened. Let's just go over a few of the things you say. Mrs Taylor dresses up as Valerie. I agree. You mention the school uniform and you rightly stress how distinctive this uniform is. But there's surely another small point. Mrs Taylor would not only wish in a positive way to be mistaken for her daughter, but in a negative sort of way not to be recognised facially as who she was – Valerie's mother. After all, it's the face that most of us look at – not the clothes. And here I think her hair would be all-important. Their hair was the same colour, and Mrs Taylor is still too young to have more than a few odd streaks of grey. When we saw her she wore her hair on the top of her head, but I'd like to bet that when she lets it down it gives her much the same sort of look that Valerie had; and with long shoulder-length hair, doubtless brushed forward over her face, I think the disguise would be more than adequate.'

Lewis nodded; but as the inspector said, it was only a small point.

'Now,' continued Morse, 'we surely come to the central point, and one that you gloss over rather too lightly, if I may say so.' Lewis looked stolidly at the counterpane, but made no interruption. 'It's this. What could possibly have been the motive that led Mrs Taylor to murder Valerie? Valerie! Her only daughter! You say that Valerie was pregnant, and although it isn't firmly established, I think the overwhelming probability is that she *was* pregnant; perhaps she had told her mother about it. But there's another possibility, and one that makes the whole situation far more sinister and disturbing. It isn't easy, I should imagine, for a daughter to hide a pregnancy from her mother for too long, and I think on balance it may well have been Mrs Taylor who accused Valerie of being pregnant – rather than Valerie who told her mother. But whichever way round it was, it surely can't add up to a sufficient motive for murdering the girl. It would be bad enough, I agree. The neighbours would gossip and everyone at school would have to know, and then there'd be the uncles and aunts and all the rest of 'em. But it's hardly a rare thing these days to have an unmarried mother in the family, is it? It could have happened as you say it did, but I get the feeling that Valerie's pregnancy had been known to Mrs Taylor for several weeks before the day she was murdered. And I think that on that Tuesday lunch-time Mrs Taylor tackled her daughter – she may have tackled her several times before – on a question which was infinitely more important to her than whether her daughter was pregnant or not. A question which was beginning to send her out of her mind; for she had her own dark and terrifying suspicions which would give her no rest, which poisoned her mind day and night, and which she had to settle one way or the other. And that question was this:

who was the father of Valerie's baby? To begin with I automatically assumed that Valerie was a girl of pretty loose morals who would jump into bed at the slightest provocation with some of her randy boyfriends. But I think I was wrong. I ought to have seen through Maguire's sexual boastings straightaway. He may have put his dirty fingers up her skirt once or twice, but I doubt that he or any of the other boys did much more. No. I should think that Valerie got an itch in her knickers as often – more often perhaps – than most young girls. But the indications all along the line were that her own particular weakness was *for older men*. Men about your age, Lewis.'

'And yours,' said Lewis. But the mood in the quiet bedroom was sombre, and neither man seemed much amused. Morse drained his whisky and smacked his lips.

'Well, Lewis? What do you think?'

'You mean Phillipson, I suppose, sir?'

'Could have been, but I doubt it. I think he'd learned his lesson.'

Lewis thought for a moment and frowned deeply. Was it possible? Would it tie in with the other business? 'Surely you don't mean Baines, do you, sir? She must have been willing to go to bed with *anyone* if she let Baines . . .' He broke off. How sickening it all was!

Morse brooded a while, and stared through the bedroom window. 'I thought of it, of course. But I think you're right. At least I don't think she would have gone to bed *willingly* with Baines. And yet, you know, Lewis, it would explain a great many things if it *was* Baines.'

'I thought you had the idea that he was seeing Mrs Taylor – not Valerie.'

'I think he was,' said Morse. 'But, as I say, I don't think it was Baines.' He was speaking more slowly now, almost as if he were working through some new equation which had suddenly flashed across his mind; some new problem that challenged to some extent the validity of the case he was presenting. But reluctantly he put it aside, and resumed the main thread of his argument. 'Try again, Lewis.'

It was like backing horses. Lewis had backed the favourite, Phillipson, and lost; he'd then chosen an outsider, an outsider at least with a bit of form behind him, and lost again. There weren't many other horses in the race. 'You've got the advantage over me, sir. You went to see Acum yesterday. Don't you think you ought to tell me about it?'

'Leave Acum out of it for the minute,' said Morse flatly.

So Lewis reviewed the field again. There was only one other possibility, and he was surely a non-starter. Surely. Morse couldn't seriously . . . 'You don't mean . . . you can't mean you think it was . . . George Taylor?'

'I'm afraid I do, Lewis, and we'd both better get used to the grisly idea as quickly as we can. It's not pleasant, I know; but it's not so bad as it might be. After all, he's not her natural father, as far as we know, and so we're not fishing around in the murky waters of genuine incest or anything like that. Valerie would have known perfectly well that George wasn't her real father. They all lived together, and became as intimate as any other family. But intimate with one vital difference. Valerie grew into a young girl, and her looks and her figure developed, and *she was not his daughter*. I don't know what happened. What I do know is that we can begin to see one overwhelming motive for Mrs Taylor murdering her own daughter: the suspicion, gradually edging into a terrible certainty, that her only daughter was expecting a baby and that the father of that baby was her own husband. I think that on that Tuesday Mrs Taylor accused her daughter of precisely that.'

'It's a terrible thing,' said Lewis slowly, 'but perhaps we shouldn't be too hard on her.'

'I don't feel hard on anybody,' rejoined Morse. 'In fact, I feel some sympathy for the wretched woman. Who wouldn't? But if all this is true, you can see what the likely train of events is. When George Taylor arrives home he's caught up in it all. Like a fly in a spider's web. His wife *knows*. It's no good him trying to wash his hands of the whole affair: he's the *cause* of it all. So, he goes along with her. What else can he do? What's more, he's in a position, the remarkably fortunate position, of being able to dispose, without suspicion and without too much trouble, of virtually anything, including a body. And I don't mean in the reservoir. George works at a place where vast volumes of rubbish and waste are piled high every day, and the same day buried without trace below the ground. And don't forget that Taylor was a man who had worked on road construction – *driving a bulldozer*. If he arrives at work half an hour early, what's to stop him using the bulldozer that's standing all ready, with the keys invitingly hung up for him on a nail in the shack? Nothing. Who would know? Who would care? No, Lewis, I don't think they put her into the reservoir. I think she lies buried out there on the rubbish dump.' Morse stopped for a second or two, and visualised the course of events anew.

'I think that Valerie must have been put into a sack or some sort of rubbish bag, and consigned for the long night to the boot of Taylor's old Morris. And in the morning he drove off early, and dumped her there, amid all the other mouldering rubbish; and he started up the bulldozer and buried her under the mounds of soil that stood ready at the sides of the tip. That's about it, Lewis. I'm very much afraid that's just about what happened. I should have been suspicious before, especially about the police not being called in until the next morning.'

'Do you think they'll find her body after all this time?'

'I should think so. It'll be a horribly messy business – but I should think so. The surveyor's department will know roughly which parts of the tip were levelled when and where, and I think we shall find her. Poor kid!'

'They put the police to a hell of a lot of trouble, didn't they?'

Morse nodded. 'It must have taken some guts to carry it through the way they did, I agree. But when you've committed a murder and got rid of the body, it might not have been so difficult as you think.'

A stray thought had been worrying Lewis as Morse had expounded his views of the way things must have happened.

'Do you think Ainley was getting near the truth?'

'I don't know,' said Morse. 'He might have had all sorts of strange ideas before he'd finished. But whether he got a scent of the truth or not doesn't really matter. What matters is that other people thought he was getting near the truth.'

'Where do you think the letter fits in, sir?'

Morse looked away. 'Yes, the letter. Remember the letter was probably posted before whoever sent it knew that Ainley was dead. I thought at the time that the whole point of it was to concentrate police attention away from the scene of the crime and on to London; and it seemed a possibility that the Taylors had cooked it up themselves because they thought Ainley was coming a bit too close for comfort.'

'But you don't think so now?'

'No. Like you, I think we've got to accept the evidence that it was almost certainly written by Baines.'

'Any idea why he wrote it?'

'I think I have, although—'

The front doorbell rang in mid-sentence, and almost immediately Mrs Lewis appeared with the doctor. Morse shook hands with him and got up to go.

'There's no need for you to go. Shan't be with him long.'

'No, I'll be off,' said Morse. 'I'll call back this afternoon, Lewis.'

He let himself out and drove back to the police HQ at Kidlington. He sat in his black leather chair and looked mournfully at his in-tray. He would have to catch up with his correspondence very soon. But not today. Perhaps he had been glad of the interruption in Lewis's bedroom, for there were several small points in his reconstruction of the case which needed further cerebration. The truth was that Morse felt a little worried.

Chapter Thirty

Money often costs too much.
Ralph Waldo Emerson

For the next hour he sat, without interruption, without a single telephone call, and thought it all through, beginning with the question that Lewis had put to him: why had Baines written the letter to the Taylors? At twelve noon, he rose from his chair, walked along the corridor and knocked at the office of Superintendent Strange.

Half an hour later, the door reopened and the two men exchanged a few final words.

'You'll have to produce one,' said Strange. 'There's no two ways about it, Morse. You can hold them for questioning, if you like, but sooner or later we want a body. In fact, we've got to have a body.'

'I suppose you're right, sir,' said Morse. 'It's a bit fanciful without a body, as you say.'

'It's a bit fanciful *with* a body,' said Strange.

Morse walked to the canteen, where the inevitable Dickson was ordering a vast plate of meat and vegetables.

'How's Sergeant Lewis, sir? Have you heard?'

'Much better. I saw him this morning. He'll be back any day.'

He thought of Lewis as he ordered his own lunch, and knew that he had not finally resolved the question that his sergeant had put to him. Why had Baines written that letter? He had thought of all the possible reasons that anyone ever had for writing a letter, but was still not convinced that he had a satisfactory answer. It would come, though. There was still a good deal about Baines he didn't know, but he had set enquiries in progress several days ago, and even bank managers and income-tax inspectors didn't take all that long, surely.

He ought to have had a closer look through his in-tray; and he would. For the moment, however, he thought that a breath of fresh air would do him good, and he walked out into the main road, turned right and found himself walking towards the pub. He didn't wish to see Mrs Taylor, and he was relieved to find that she wasn't there. He ordered a pint, left immediately he had finished it, and walked down towards the main road. Two shops he had never paid any attention to before lay off a narrow service road at the top of Hatfield Way, one a general provisions store, the other a fresh fruiterer, and Morse bought a small bunch of black grapes for the invalid. It seemed a kind thought. As he walked out, he noticed a small derelict area between the side of the provisions store and the next row of council houses. It was no more than ten square yards in extent, with two or three bicycle racks, the bric-à-brac of builders' carts from years ago – half bricks, a flattened heap of sand; and strewing the area the inevitable empty cigarette cartons and crisps packets. Two cars stood in the small area, unobtrusive and unmolested. Morse stopped and took his bearings and realised that he was only some forty or fifty yards from the Taylors' house, a little further down towards the main road on the left. He stood quite still and gripped the bag of grapes more firmly. Mrs Taylor was in the front garden. He could see her quite clearly, her hair piled rather untidily on top of her head, her back towards him, her slim legs more those of a schoolgirl than a mother. In her right hand she held a pair of secateurs, and she was bending over the rose trees and clipping off the faded blooms. He found himself wondering if he would have been able to recognise her if she suddenly rushed out of the gate in a bright school uniform with her hair flowing down to her shoulders; and it made him uneasy, for he felt that he *would* have been able to tell at once that she was a woman and not a girl. You couldn't really disguise some things, however hard you tried; and perhaps it was very fortunate for Mrs Taylor that none of the neighbours *had* seen her that Tuesday lunch-time, and that old Joe Godberry's eyes had grown so tired and dim. And all of a sudden he saw it all plainly, and the blood tingled in his arms. He glanced around again at the small piece of waste land, shielded from the Taylors' home by the wall of the council house, looked again at the Taylors' front garden, where the wilted petals were now piled neatly at the edge of the narrow lawn, turned on his heel and walked back the long way round to police HQ.

He had been right about his in-tray. There were detailed statements about Baines's financial position, and Morse raised his eyebrows in some surprise as he studied them, for Baines was better off than he had thought. Apart from insurance policies, Baines had over £5,000 in the Oxford Building Society, £6,000 tied up in a high-interest long-term loan with Manchester Corporation, £4,500 in his deposit account with Lloyds, as well as £150 in his current account with the same bank. It all added up to a tidy sum, and schoolmasters, even experienced second masters, weren't all that highly recompensed. The pay cheques for the previous year had all been paid directly into the deposit account, and Morse noticed with some surprise that the withdrawals on the current account had seldom amounted to more than thirty pounds per month over that period. It seemed clear from the previous year's tax returns that Baines had no supplementary monies accruing to him from examination fees or private tuition, and although he may have risked not declaring any such further income, Morse thought that on the whole it was unlikely. The house, too, belonged to Baines: the final payment had been made some six years previously. Of course, he may well have been left a good deal of money by his parents and other relatives; but the fact remained that Baines somehow had managed to live on about seven or eight pounds a week for the last twelve months. Either he was a miser or, what seemed more likely, he was receiving a supply of ready cash fairly regularly from some quarter or quarters. And it hardly needed a mind as imaginative as Morse's to make one or two intelligent deductions on that score. There must have been several people who had shed no tears when Baines had died; indeed there had been one person who had been unable to stand it any longer and who had stuck him through with a carving knife.

Chapter Thirty-one

To you, Lord Governor,
Remains the censure of this hellish villain –
The time, the place, the torture. O enforce it!
Shakespeare, *Othello*, Act V

Lewis was sitting up in his dressing-gown in the front room when Morse returned at a quarter to three.

'Start next Monday, sir – Sunday if you want me – and I can't tell you how glad I am.'

'It'll all be over then with a bit of luck,' said Morse. 'Still, we may have another homicidal lunatic roaming the streets before then, eh?'

'You really think this is nearly finished, sir?'

'I saw Strange this morning. We're going ahead tomorrow. Bring in both the Taylors and then start digging up all the rubbish dump – if we have to; though I think George will co-operate, even if his wife doesn't.'

'And you think it all links up with Baines's murder?'

Morse nodded. 'You were asking this morning about Baines writing that letter, and the truth is I don't quite know yet. It could have been to put the police off the scent, or to put them on – take your pick. But I feel fairly sure that one way or another it would keep his little pot boiling.'

'I don't quite follow you, sir.'

Morse told him of Baines's financial position, and Lewis whistled softly. 'He really was a blackmailer, then?'

'He was certainly getting money from somewhere, probably from more than one source.'

'Phillipson, for sure, I should think.'

'Yes. I think Phillipson had to fork out a regular monthly payment; not all that much perhaps, certainly not a ruinous sum for a man in Phillipson's position. Let's say twenty, thirty pounds a month. I don't know. But I shall know soon. There can be little doubt that Baines saw him the night he was going back home after his interview; saw him with a bit of stuff – more than likely Valerie Taylor. He could have ruined Phillipson's position straightaway, of course, but that doesn't seem to have been the way that Baines's warped and devious mind would usually work. It gave him power to keep the intelligence to himself – to himself, that is, and to Phillipson.'

'He had as good a reason as anybody for killing Baines, didn't he?'

'He had, indeed. But he didn't kill Baines.'

'You sound pretty sure of yourself, sir.'

'Yes, I am sure,' said Morse quietly. 'Let's just go on a bit. I think there was another member of staff Baines had been blackmailing.'

'You mean Acum?'

'Yes, Acum. It seemed odd to me from the start that he should leave a fairly promising situation in the modern languages department here at the Roger Bacon, and take up a very similar position in a very similar school right up in the wilds of North

Wales – away from his friends and family and the agreeable life of
a university town like Oxford. I think that there must have been a
little flurry of a minor scandal earlier in the year that Acum left. I
asked him about it when I saw him yesterday, but he wouldn't have
any of it. It doesn't matter much, though, and Phillipson will have
to come clean anyway.'

'What do you think happened?'

'Oh, the usual thing. Somebody caught him with one of the
girls with his trousers down.'

Lewis leaned his head to one side and smiled rather wearily.
'I suppose you think it may have been Valerie Taylor, sir?'

'Why not?' said Morse. 'She seems to have made most of the
men put their hands on their cocks at some time, doesn't she? I
should think that Phillipson got to know and Baines, too – oh yes,
I'm sure Baines got to know – and they got together and agreed
to hush things up if Acum would agree to leave as soon as it was
practicable to do so. And I shouldn't think that Acum had any
option. He'd be asked to leave whatever happened, and his wife
would probably find out and – well, it would have seemed like the
end of the world to a young fellow like Acum.'

'And you think Baines had the bite on Acum?'

'Pretty certain of it. I should think that Acum' (Morse chose his
words carefully) '– judging from the little I've seen of his wife –
would have been a bloody fool to have ruined his career just for
the sake of a brief infatuation with one of his pupils. And he didn't.
He played the game and cleared out.'

'And paid up.'

'Yes. He paid up, though I shouldn't think Baines was stupid
enough to expect too much from a former colleague who was
probably fairly hard up anyway. Just enough, though. Just enough
for Baines to relish another little show of power over one of his
fellow human beings.'

'I suppose you're going to tell me next that Baines had the
bite on the Taylors as well.'

'No. Just the opposite, in fact. I reckon that Baines was
paying money to Mrs Taylor.'

Lewis sat up. Had he heard aright? 'You mean Mrs Taylor
was blackmailing *Baines*?'

'I didn't say that, did I? Let's go back a bit. We've agreed
that Baines got to know about Phillipson's little peccadillo at the
Station Hotel. Now I can't imagine that Baines would merely be
content with the Phillipson angle. I think that he began to grub

around on the Taylor side of the fence. Now, Lewis. What did he find? You remember that George Taylor was out of work at the time, and that far from being a potential source of blackmail the Taylors were in dire need of money themselves. And especially Mrs Taylor. Baines had met them several times at parents' evenings, and I should guess that he arranged to see Mrs Taylor privately, and that he pretty soon read the temperature of the water correctly.'

'But Baines wasn't the type of man who went around doing favours.'

'Oh no. The whole thing suited Baines splendidly.'

'But he gave her money, you think?'

'Yes.'

'But she wouldn't take his money just like that, would she? I mean . . . she wouldn't expect . . .'

'Wouldn't expect to get the money for nothing? Oh no. She had something to give him in return.'

'What was that?'

'What the hell do you think it was? You weren't born yesterday, were you?'

Lewis felt abashed. 'Oh, I see,' he said quietly.

'Once a week in term time, if you want me to keep guessing. Tuesdays, likely as not, when he had the afternoon off. *Tuesday afternoons*, Lewis. Do you see what that means?'

'You mean,' stammered Lewis, 'that Baines probably . . . probably . . .'

'Probably knew more about the fate of Valerie Taylor than we thought, yes. I should think that Baines would park somewhere near the Taylors' house – not too near – and wait until Valerie had gone off back to school. Then he'd go in, get his pound of flesh, pay his stamp duty—'

'Bit dangerous, wasn't it?'

'If you're a bachelor like Baines and you're dying to spill your oats – well . . . After all, no one would *know* what was going on. Lock the door and—'

Lewis interrupted him. 'But if they'd arranged to meet the day that Valerie disappeared it would have been crazy for Mrs Taylor to have murdered her daughter.'

'It was crazy anyway. I don't think she would have worried too much if the police force was out the front and the fire brigade was out the back. Listen. What I think may have happened on that Tuesday is this. Baines parked pretty near the house, probably in

a bit of waste land near the shops, just above the Taylors' place.
He waited until afternoon school had started, and then he saw something very odd. He saw Valerie, or who he thought was Valerie,
leave by the front door and run down the road. Then he went up
to the house and knocked – we didn't find a key, did we? – and
he got no answer. It's all a bit odd. Has his reluctant mistress –
well, let's hope she was reluctant – has she slipped out for a
minute? He can almost swear she hasn't, but he can't be absolutely
sure. He walks back, frustrated and disappointed, and scratches
his balls in the car; and something tells him to wait. And about
ten minutes later he sees Mrs Taylor walking – probably walking
in a great hurry – out of one of the side streets and going into the
house. Has she been out over the lunch-time? Unusual, to say the
least. But there's something odder still – far odder. Something that
makes him sit up with a vengeance. Valerie – he would remember
now – had left with a basket; and here is Valerie's mother returning *with the very same basket*. Does he guess the truth? I don't
know. Does he go to the house again and knock? Probably so.
And I would guess she told him she couldn't possibly see him that
afternoon. So Baines walks away, and drives home, and wonders
. . . Wonders even harder the next day when he hears of Valerie's
disappearance.'

'He guessed what had happened, you think?'

'Pretty sure he did.'

Lewis thought for a minute. 'Perhaps Mrs Taylor just couldn't
face things any longer, sir, and told him that everything was
finished; and he in turn might have threatened to go to the
police.'

'Could be, but I should be very surprised if Baines was killed
to stop him spilling the beans – or even some of them. No, Lewis.
I just think that he was killed because he was detested so viciously
that killing him was an act of superb and joyous revenge.'

'You think that Mrs Taylor murdered him, then?'

Morse nodded. 'You remember the first time we saw Mrs
Taylor in the pub? Remember that large American-style handbag
she had? It was a bit of a puzzle at first to know how anyone
could ever cart such a big knife around. But the obvious way
to do it is precisely the way Mrs Taylor chose. Stick it in a
handbag. She got to Kempis Street at about a quarter-past nine,
I should think, knocked on the door, told a surprised Baines some
cock-and-bull story, followed him into the kitchen, agreed to his
offer of a glass of something, and as he bends down to get the

beer out of the fridge, she takes her knife out and – well, we know the rest.'

Lewis sat back and considered what Morse had said. It all hung loosely together, perhaps, but he was feeling hot and tired.

'Go and have a lie down,' said Morse, as if reading his thoughts. 'You've had about enough for one day.'

'I think I will, sir. I shall be much better tomorrow.'

'Don't worry about tomorrow. I shan't do anything until the afternoon.'

'It's the inquest in the morning, though, isn't it?'

'Formality. Pure formality,' said Morse. 'I shan't say much. Just get him identified and tell the coroner we've got the bloodhounds out. "Murder by person or persons unknown." I don't know why we're wasting public money on having an inquest at all.'

'It's the law, sir.'

'Mm.'

'And tomorrow afternoon, sir?'

'I'm bringing the Taylors in.'

Lewis stood up. 'I feel a bit sorry for him, sir.'

'Don't you feel a bit sorry for *her*?' There was a sharp edge on Morse's voice; and after he had gone Lewis wondered why he'd suddenly turned so sour.

At four o'clock that same afternoon, as Morse and Lewis were talking together and trying to unravel the twisted skein of the Valerie Taylor case, a tall military-looking man was dictating a letter to one of the girls from the typing pool. He had some previous experience of the young lady in question, and decided it would be sensible to make the letter even briefer than he had intended; for although it would contain no earth-shattering news, he was anxious for it to go in the evening post. He had tried to phone earlier but had declined to leave a message when he learned that the only man who could have any possible interest in the matter was out – whereabouts temporarily unknown. At four-fifteen the letter was signed and in the evening postbag.

The bombshell burst on Morse's desk at 8.45 a.m. the following morning.

Chapter Thirty-two

When you have eliminated the impossible, whatever remains,
however improbable, must be the truth.
A. Conan Doyle, *The Sign of the Four*

'It's a mistake, I tell you. It's some clown of a sergeant who's
ballsed the whole thing up.' His voice was strident, exasperated.
He was prepared to forgive a certain degree of inadequacy, but
never incompetence of this order. The voice at the other end of
the line sounded firm and assured, like a kindly parent seeking to
assuage a petulant child.

'There's no mistake, I'm afraid. I've checked it myself. And for
heaven's sake calm down a bit, Morse, my old friend. You asked
me to do something for you, and I've done it. If it comes as a bit
of a shock—'

'*A bit of a shock!* Christ Almighty, it's not just a bit of a shock,
believe me; it's sheer bloody lunacy!'

There was a short delay at the other end. 'Look, old boy, I
think you'd better come up and see for yourself, don't you? If
you still think it's a mistake – well, that's up to you.'

'Don't keep saying "if" it's a mistake. It *is* a mistake – you can
put your shirt and your underpants on that, believe me!' He calmed
himself down as far as he could and resumed the conversation in a
tone more befitting his station. 'Trouble is I've got a damned inquest
today.'

'Shouldn't let that worry you. Anybody can do that for you.
Unless you've arrested somebody, of course.'

'No, no,' muttered Morse, 'nothing like that. It would have been
adjourned anyway.'

'You sound a bit fed up one way or another.'

'I bloody *am* fed up,' snapped Morse, 'and who wouldn't be?
I've got the case all ready for bed and you send me a scratty little
note that's blown the top off the whole f— thing! How would *you*
feel?'

'You didn't expect us to find anything – is that it?'

'No,' said Morse, 'I didn't. Not a load of cock like that,
anyway.'

'Well, as I say, you'll be able to see for yourself. I suppose it
could have been somebody else with the same name, but it's a

whacking big coincidence if that's the case. Same name, same dates. No, I don't think so. You'd be pushing your luck, I reckon.'

'And I'm going on pushing it,' rejoined Morse, 'pushing it like hell, have no fear. Coincidences do happen, don't they?' It sounded more like a plea to the gods than a statement of empirical truth.

'Perhaps they do, sometimes. It's my fault, though. I should have got hold of you yesterday. I did try a couple of times in the afternoon, but . . .'

'You weren't to know. As far as you were concerned it was just one more routine enquiry.'

'And it wasn't?' said the voice softly.

'And it wasn't,' echoed Morse. 'Anyway, I'll get there as soon as I can.'

'Good. I'll get the stuff ready for you.'

Chief Inspector Rogers of New Scotland Yard put down the phone and wondered why the letter he had dictated and signed the previous afternoon had blown up with such obvious devastation in Morse's face. The carbon copy, he noticed, was still lying in his out-tray, and he picked it up and read it through again. It still seemed pretty harmless.

CONFIDENTIAL

For the attention of Det. Chief Inspector Morse,
Thames Valley Police HQ,
Kidlington, Oxon.

Dear Morse,

You asked for a check on the abortion clinics for the missing person, Valerie Taylor. Sorry to have taken so long about it, but it proved difficult. The trouble is all these semi-registered places where abortions still get done unofficially – no doubt for a whacking private fee. Anyway, we've traced her. She was at the East Chelsea Nursing Home on the dates you gave us. Arrived 4.15 p.m. Tuesday, under her own name, and left some time Friday a.m. by taxi. About three months pregnant. No complications. Description fits all along the line, but we could check further. She had a room-mate who might not be too difficult to trace. We await your further instructions.

Yours sincerely,

P.S. Don't forget to call when you're this way again. The beer at the Westminster is drinkable – just!

Chief Inspector Rogers shrugged his shoulders and put the carbon back in the out-tray. Morse! He always had been a funny old bird.

Morse himself sat back in his black leather chair and felt like a man who had just been authoritatively informed that the moon really was made of green cheese after all. Scotland Yard! They must have buggered it all up – must have done! But whatever they'd done, it was little use pretending he could go ahead with his intended schedule. What was the good of bringing two people in for questioning about the murder of a young girl if on the very day she was supposed to be lying dead in the boot of a car she had walked as large as life into some shabby nursing home in East Chelsea – of all places? For a few seconds Morse almost considered the possibility of taking the new information seriously. But he couldn't quite manage it. It just *couldn't* be right, and there was a fairly easy way of proving that it wasn't right. Central London lay no more than sixty miles away.

He went in to see Strange, and the superintendent, reluctantly, agreed to stand in for him at the inquest.

He rang Lewis, and told him he had to go off to London – he mentioned nothing more – and learned that Lewis would be reporting for duty again the next morning. That is, if he was needed. And Morse said, in a rather weak voice, that he thought he probably would be.

Chapter Thirty-three

She'll be wearing silk pyjamas when she comes.
                                        Popular song

By any reckoning Yvonne Baker was a honey. She lived alone – or to be accurate she rented a single flat – in a high-rise tenement block in Bethune Road, Stoke Newington. She would have preferred a slightly more central spot and a slightly more luxurious apartment. But from Manor House tube station in Seven Sisters Road, just ten minutes' walk away, she could be in Central London in a further twenty minutes; and anyone looking around the tasteful and expensive décor of her flat would have guessed (correctly) that, whether from money honourably earned in the cosmetic department of an exclusive store in Oxford Street, or from other unspecified sources of income, Miss Baker was a young woman of not unsubstantial means.

At half-past six she lay languorously relaxed upon her costly counterpane, idly painting her long, beautifully-manicured nails with a particularly revolting shade of sickly-green varnish. She wore a peach-coloured satin dressing-gown, her legs, invitingly long and slender, drawn up to her waist, her thoughts centred on the evening ahead of her. The real trouble with pyjama parties was that some of the guests hadn't quite the courage to conform to the code, and wore enough under their nightshirts or pyjamas to defeat the whole object of the simple exercise. At least *she* would show them. Some of the girls would wear a bra and panties, but she wasn't going to. Oh no. She experienced a tingle of excitement at the thought of dancing with the men, and of knowing only too clearly the effect that she would have upon them. It was a gorgeous feeling anyway, wearing so little. So sensuous, so abandoned!

She finished her left hand, held it up before her like a policeman stopping the traffic, and flexed her fingers. She then poured some removing fluid on to a wad of cottonwool and proceeded to rub off all the varnish. Her hands looked better without any nail polish, she decided. She stood up, unfastened and took off her dressing-gown, and carefully lifted out of one of the wardrobe drawers a pair of palish-green pyjamas. She had a beautiful body, and like so many of her admirers she was inordinately conscious of it. She admired herself in the long wall-mirror, fastened all but the top button of her pyjama top and began to brush her long, luxuriant, honey-coloured hair. She would be collected by car at half-past seven, a she glanced again at the alarm clock on her bedside table. Three-quarters of an hour. She walked into the living room, put a record on the turntable, and lit a cigarette of quite improbable length.

The doorbell rang at ten minutes to seven, and her first thought was that the alarm clock must be slow again. Well, if it was, so much the better. She walked gaily to the door and opened it with a beaming smile upon her soft, full lips, a smile which slowly contracted and finally faded away as she stared at a man she had never seen before, who stood rather woodenly upon the threshold. Middle-aged and rather sour.

'Hello,' she managed.

'Miss Baker?' Miss Baker nodded. 'I'm Chief Inspector Morse. I'd like to come in and have a word with you, if I may.'

'Of course.' A slightly worried frown puckered the meticulously plucked eyebrows as she stood aside and closed the door behind him.

As he explained the reason for his visit, she felt that he was the only man within living memory upon whom she appeared to have no visibly erotic effect. In her pyjamas, too! He was brisk and business-like. Two years the previous June she had shared, had she not, a room in the East Chelsea Nursing Home with a girl named Valerie Taylor? He wanted to know about this girl. Everything she could conceivably remember – every single little thing.

The doorbell rang again at twenty-five past seven and Morse told her in an unexpectedly peremptory tone to get rid of him, whoever he was.

'I hope you realise I'm going out to a party tonight, Inspector.' She sounded vexed, but in reality was not so vexed as she appeared. In an odd sort of way he was beginning to interest her.

'So I see,' said Morse, eyeing the pyjamas. 'Just tell him you'll be another half hour with me – at least.' She decided she liked his voice. 'And tell him I'll take you myself if he can't wait.' She decided she'd rather like that.

Morse had already learned enough; and he knew – had known earlier, really – that what Rogers had written was true. There was now no doubt whatsoever that Valerie Taylor had somehow found her way into a London abortion clinic on the very same day on which she had disappeared. The doctor who ran the nursing home had been pleasantly co-operative, but had categorically refused to break what he termed the code of professional confidentiality by revealing the identity of the person or persons who had negotiated Miss Taylor's visit. It had amazed Morse that the affluent abortionist should have heard of, let alone practised, any code of professional confidentiality; but short of a forcible entry into his filing cabinets, the ambivalent doctor made it abundantly clear that further information was not forthcoming.

After explaining the situation to her pyjama-bottomed beau, Miss Baker retired briefly to the bedroom, examined herself once more in the mirror, and wrapped her dressing-gown – not too tightly – around her. She was beginning to feel chilly.

'There was no need to worry too much about me,' said Morse. 'I'm pretty harmless with women, they say.' For the first time she smiled at him, fully and freely, and immediately Morse wished she hadn't.

'I'll take it off again if you'll turn the fire on, Inspector.' She purred the words at him, and the danger bells were ringing in his head.

'I shan't keep you much longer, Miss Baker.'

'Most people call me Yvonne.' She smiled again and lay back in the armchair. No one ever called Morse by his Christian name.

'I'll turn on the fire if you're not careful,' he said. But he didn't.

'You tell me she said she was from Oxford – not from Kidlington?'

'From where?'

'Kidlington. It's just outside Oxford.'

'Oh, is it? No. She said Oxford, I'm sure of that.'

Perhaps she would anyway, thought Morse. It did sound a bit more imposing. He had nearly finished. 'Just one last thing, and I want you to think very hard, Miss – er, Yvonne. Did Miss Taylor mention to you at any stage who the father was? Or who she thought the father was?'

She laughed openly. 'You're so beautifully delicate, Inspector. But as a matter of fact she did, yes. She was quite a lass really, you know.'

'Who was it?'

'She said something about one of her teachers. I remember that because I was a bit surprised to learn she was still a schoolgirl. She looked much older than that. She seemed much more . . . much more *knowing* somehow. She was nobody's fool, I can tell you that.'

'This teacher,' said Morse. 'Did she say anything else about him?'

'She didn't mention his name, I don't think. But she said he'd got a little beard and it tickled her every time he . . . every time . . . you know.'

Morse took his eyes from her and stared sadly down at the thick-piled, dark green carpet. It had been a crazy sort of day.

'She didn't say what he taught? What subject?'

She thought a moment. 'Do you know, I . . . I rather think she did. I think she said he was a French teacher or something.'

He drove her into the West End, tried to forget that she was off to an open-ended orgy dressed only in the pyjamas he had eyed so lovingly in her flat, and decided that life had passed him by.

He dropped her in Mayfair, where she thanked him, a little sadly, and turned towards him and kissed him fully on the lips with her soft, open mouth. And when she was gone, he looked after her, the flared pale-green bottoms of her pyjamas showing below the sleek fur coat. There had been many bad moments that day, but as he sat there in the Jaguar, slowly wiping the gooey, deep-orange lipstick from his mouth, he decided that this was just about the worst.

Morse drove back to Soho and parked his car on the double yellow lines immediately in front of the Penthouse Club. It was 9 p.m. At a glance he could see that the man seated at the receipt of custom was not Maguire, as he hoped it would be. But he was almost past caring as he walked into the foyer.

''Fraid you can't leave your car there, mate.'

'Perhaps you don't know who I am,' said Morse, with the arrogant authority of a Julius Caesar or an Alexander walking among the troops.

'I don't care who you are, mate,' said the young man, rising to his feet, 'you just can't . . .'

'I'll tell you who I am, sonny. My name's Morse. M-O-R-S-E. Got that? And if anyone comes along and asks you whose car it is, tell 'em it's mine. And if they don't believe you, just refer 'em to me, sonny boy – sharpish!' He walked past the desk and through the latticed doorway.

'But . . .' Morse heard no more. The Maltese dwarf sat dutifully at his post, and in a perverse sort of way Morse was glad to see him.

'You remember me?'

It was clear that the little man did. 'No need for ticket, sir. You go in. Ticket on me.' He smiled weakly, but Morse ignored the offer.

'I want to talk to you. My car's outside.' There was no argument, and they sat side by side in the front.

'Where's Maguire?'

'He gone. He just gone. I do' know where.'

'When did he leave?'

'Two day, three day.'

'Did he have a girlfriend here?'

'Lots of girls. Some of the girls here, some of the girls there. Who know?'

'There was a girl here recently – she wore a mask. I think her name was Valerie, perhaps.'

The little man thought he saw the light and visibly relaxed. 'Valerie? No. You mean Vera. Oh yeah. Boys oh boys!' He was beginning to feel more confident now and his dirty hands expressively traced the undulating contours of her beautiful body.

'Is she here tonight?'

'She gone, too.'

'I might have known it,' muttered Morse. 'She's buggered off with Maguire, I suppose.'

The little man smiled, revealed a mouthful of large, brilliantly white teeth, and shrugged his oversized shoulders. Morse repressed his strong desire to smash his fist into the leering face, and asked one further question.

'Did *you* ever take her out, you filthy little bastard?'

'Sometimes. Who know?' He shrugged his shoulders again and spread out his hands, palms uppermost, in a typically Mediterranean gesture.

'Get out.'

'You want to come in, mister policeman? See pretty girls, no?'

'Get out,' snarled Morse.

For a while Morse sat on silently in his car and pondered many things. Life was down to its dregs, and he had seldom felt so desolate and defeated. He recalled his first interview with Strange at the very beginning of the case, and the distaste he had felt then at the prospect of trying to find a young girl in the midst of this corrupt and corrupting city. And now, again, he had to presume that she was alive. For all his wayward unpredictability, there was at the centre of his being an inner furnace of passion for truth, for logical analysis; and inexorably now the facts, almost all the facts, were pointing to the same conclusion – that he had been wrong, wrong from the start.

A constable, young, tall, confident, tapped sharply on the car window. 'Is this your car, sir?'

Morse wound the window down and wearily identified himself.

'Sorry, sir. I just thought . . .'

'Of course you did.'

'Can I be of any assistance, sir?'

'Doubt it,' replied Morse. 'I'm looking for a young girl.'

'She live round here, sir?'

'I don't know,' said Morse. 'I don't even know if she lives in London. Not much hope for me, is there?'

'But you mean she's been seen round here recently?'

'No,' said Morse quietly. 'She's not been seen anywhere for over two years.'

'Oh, I see, sir,' said the young man, seeing nothing. 'Well, perhaps I can't help much, then. Good night, sir.' He touched his helmet, and walked off, uncomprehending, past the gaudy strip clubs and the pornographic bookshops.

'No,' said Morse to himself, 'I don't think you can.'

He started the engine and drove via Shepherd's Bush and the White City towards the M40. He was back in his office just before midnight.

It did not even occur to him to go straight home. He was fully aware, even if he could give no explanation for it, of the curious fact that his mind was never more resilient, never sharper, than when apparently it was beaten. On such occasions his brain would roam restlessly around his skull like a wild and vicious tiger immured within the confines of a narrow cage, ceaselessly circumambulating, snarling savagely – and lethal. During the whole of the drive back to Oxford he had been like a chess player, defeated only after a monumental struggle, who critically reviews and analyses the moves and the motives for the moves that have led to his defeat. And already a new and strange idea was spawning in the fertile depths of his mind, and he was impatient to get back.

At three minutes to midnight he was poring over the dossiers on the Taylor case with the frenetic concentration of a hastily-summoned understudy who had only a few minutes in which to memorise a lengthy speech.

At 2.30 a.m. the night sergeant, carrying a steaming cup of coffee on a tray, tapped lightly and opened the door. He saw Morse, his hands over his ears, his desk strewn with documents, and an expression of such profound intensity upon his face that he quickly and gently put down the tray, reclosed the door, and walked quickly away.

He called again at 4.30 a.m. and carefully put down a second cup of coffee beside the first, which stood where he had left it, cold, ugly-brown, untouched. Morse was fast asleep now, his head leaning back against the top of the black leather chair, the neck of his white shirt unfastened, and an expression on his face as of a young child for whom the vivid terrors of the night were past . . .

It had been Lewis who had found her. She lay supine upon the bed, fully-clothed, her left arm placed across the body, the wrist slashed cruelly deep. The white coverlet was a pool of scarlet, and blood had dripped its way through the mattress. Clutched in her right hand was a knife, a wooden-handled carving knife, 'Prestige, Made in England', some 35–36 centimetres long, the cutting blade honed along its entire edge to a razor-sharp ferocity.

Chapter Thirty-four

Things are not always what they seem;
the first appearance deceives many.

Phaedrus

Lewis reported back for duty at eight o'clock and found a freshly-shaven Morse seated at his desk. He could scarcely hide his disappointment as Morse began to recount the previous day's events, and found himself quite unable to account for the inspector's sprightly tone. His spirits picked up, however, when Morse mentioned the crucial evidence given by Miss Baker, and after hearing the whole story, he evinced little surprise at the string of instructions that Morse proceeded to give him. There were several phone calls to make and he thought he began to understand the general tenor of the inspector's purpose.

At 9.30 he had finished, and reported back to Morse.

'Feel up to the drive then?'

'I don't mind driving one way, sir, but—'

'Settled then. I'll drive there, you drive back. Agreed?'

'When were you thinking of going, sir?'

'Now,' said Morse. 'Give the missus a ring and tell her we should be back about, er . . .'

'Do you mind me mentioning something, sir?'

'What's worrying you?'

'If Valerie was in that nursing home—'

'She was,' interrupted Morse.

'—well, someone had to take her and fetch her and pay for her and everything.'

'The quack won't tell us. Not yet, anyway.'

'Isn't it fairly easy to guess, though?'

'Is it?' said Morse, with apparent interest.

'It's only a guess, sir. But if they were all in it together – you know, to cover things up . . .'

'All?'

'Phillipson, the Taylors and Acum. When you come to think of it, it would kill a lot of birds with one stone, wouldn't it?'

'How do you mean?'

'Well, if you're right about Phillipson and Valerie, he'd have a bit of a guilt complex about her and feel morally bound to help out, wouldn't he? And then there's the Taylors. It would save them any scandal and stop Valerie mucking up her life completely. And then there's Acum. It would get him out of a dickens of a mess at the school and save his marriage into the bargain. They've all got a stake in it.'

Morse nodded and Lewis felt encouraged to continue. 'They could have cooked it all up between them: fixed up the clinic, arranged the transport, paid the bill, and found a job for Valerie to go to afterwards. They probably hadn't the faintest idea that her going off like that would create such a fuss, and once they started on it, well, they just had to go through with it. So they all stuck together. And told the same story.'

'You may well be right.'

'If I am, sir, don't you think it would be a good idea to fetch Phillipson and the Taylors in? I mean, it would save us a lot of trouble.'

'Save us going all the way to Caernarfon, you mean?'

'Yes. If they spill the beans, we can get Acum brought down here.'

'What if they all stick to their story?'

'Then we'll have to go and get him.'

'I'm afraid it's not quite so easy as that,' said Morse.

'Why not?'

'I tried to get Phillipson first thing this morning. He went off to Brighton yesterday afternoon – to a Headmasters' Conference.'

'Oh.'

'And the Taylors left by car for Luton airport at 6.30 yesterday morning. They're spending a week on a package tour in the Channel Islands. So the neighbours say.'

'Oh.'

'And,' continued Morse, 'we're still trying to find out who killed Baines, remember?'

'That's why you've asked the Caernarfon police to pick him up?'

'Yep. And we'd better not keep him waiting too long. It's about four and a half hours – non-stop. So we'll allow five. We might want to give the car a little rest on the way.'

Outside a pub, thought Lewis, as he pulled on his overcoat. But Lewis thought wrong.

The traffic this Sunday morning was light and the police car made its way quickly up through Brackley and thence to Towcester where it turned left on to the A5. Neither man seemed particularly anxious to sustain much conversation, and a tacit silence soon prevailed between them, as if they waited tensely for the final wicket to fall in a test match. The traffic decelerated to a paralytic crawl at road works in Wellington, and suddenly Morse switched on full headlights and the blue roof-flasher, and wailing like a dalek in distress the car swept past the stationary column of cars and soon was speeding merrily along once more out on the open road. Morse turned to Lewis and winked almost happily.

Along the Shrewsbury ring-road, Lewis ventured a conversational gambit. 'Bit of luck about this Miss Baker, wasn't it?'

'Ye-es.' Lewis looked at the inspector curiously. 'Nice bit of stuff, sir?'

'She's a prick-teaser.'

'Oh.'

They drove on through Betws-y-coed: Caernarfon 25 miles.

'The real trouble,' said Morse suddenly, 'was that I thought she was dead.'

'And now you think she's still alive?'

'I very much hope so,' said Morse, with unwonted earnestness in his voice. 'I very much hope so.'

At five minutes to three they came to the outskirts of Caernarfon, where ignoring the sign directing traffic to the city centre Morse turned left on to the main Pwllheli Road.

'You know your way around here then, sir?'

'Not too well. But we're going to pay a brief visit before we meet Acum.' He drove south to the village of Bont-Newydd, turned left off the main road, and stopped outside a house with the front door painted Cambridge blue.

'Wait here a minute.'

Lewis watched him as he walked up the narrow front path and knocked on the door; and knocked again. Clearly there was no one at home. But then of course David Acum *wouldn't* be there; he was three miles away, detained for questioning on the instructions of the Thames Valley Police. Morse came back to the car and got in. His face seemed inexplicably grave.

'No one in, sir?'

Morse appeared not to hear. He kept looking around him, occasionally glancing up into the driving mirror. But the quiet street lay preternaturally still in the sunny autumn afternoon.

'Shan't we be a bit late for Acum, sir?'

'Acum?' The inspector suddenly woke from his waking dreams. 'Don't worry about Acum. He'll be all right.'

'How long do you plan to wait here?'

'How the hell do I know!' snapped Morse.

'Well, if we're going to wait, I think I'll just—' He opened the near-side door and began to unfasten his safety-belt.

'Stay where you are.' There was a note of harsh authority in the voice, and Lewis shrugged his shoulders and closed the door again.

'If we're waiting for Mrs Acum, don't you think she may have gone with him?'

Morse shook his head. 'I don't think so.'

The time ticked on inexorably, and it was Morse who finally broke the silence. 'Go and knock again, Lewis.'

But Lewis was no more successful than Morse had been; and he returned to the car and slammed the door with some impatience. It was already half-past three.

'We'll give her another quarter of an hour,' said Morse.

'But why are we waiting for *her*, sir? What's she got to do with it all? We hardly know anything about her, do we?'

Morse turned his light-blue eyes upon his sergeant and spoke with an almost fierce simplicity. 'That's where you're wrong, Lewis. We know more about her – far more about her – than about anyone else in the whole case. You see, the woman living here with David Acum is not his real wife at all – she's the person we've been looking for from the very beginning.' He paused and let his words sink in. 'Yes, Lewis. The woman who's been living here for the past two years as Acum's wife is not his wife at all – *she's Valerie Taylor.*'

Chapter Thirty-five

'Now listen, you young limb,' whispered Sikes. 'Go softly up the steps straight afore you, and along the little hall, to the street door: unfasten it, and let us in.'

Charles Dickens, *Oliver Twist*

Lewis's mouth gaped in flabbergasted disbelief as this astonishing intelligence partially percolated through his consciousness. 'You can't mean . . .'

'But I *do* mean. I mean exactly what I say. And that's why we're sitting here waiting, Lewis. We're waiting for Valerie Taylor to come home at last.'

For the moment Lewis was quite incapable of any more intelligent comment than a half-formed whistle. 'Phew!'

'Worth waiting another few minutes for, isn't she? After all this time?'

Gradually the implications of what the inspector had just told him began to register more significantly in Lewis's mind. It meant . . . it meant . . . But his mental processes seemed now to be anaesthetised, and he gave up the unequal struggle. 'Don't you think you ought to put me in the picture, sir?'

'Where do you want me to start?' asked Morse, in a slightly brisker tone.

'Well, first of all you'd better tell me what's happened to the *real* Mrs Acum.'

'Listen, Lewis. In this case you've been right more often than I have. I've made some pretty stupid blunders – as you know. But at last we're getting near the truth, I think. You ask me what's happened to the real Mrs Acum. Well, I don't know for certain. But let me tell you what I think may have happened. I've hardly got a shred of evidence for it, but as I see things it must have happened something like this.

'What do we know about Mrs Acum? A bit prim and proper, perhaps. She's got a slim, boyish-looking figure, and long shoulder-length blonde hair. Not unattractive, maybe, in an unusual sort of way, but no doubt very self-conscious about the blotch of ugly spots all over her face. Then think about Valerie. She's a real honey, by all accounts. A nubile young wench, with a sort of animal sexuality about her that proves fatally attractive to the opposite sex – the men and the boys alike. Now just put yourself in Acum's place. He finds Valerie in his French class, and he begins to fancy her. He thinks she may have a bit of ability, but neither the incentive nor the inclination to make anything of it. Well, from whatever motives, he talks to her privately and suggests some extra tuition. Now let's try to imagine what might have happened. Let's say Mrs Acum has joined a Wednesday sewing-class at Headington Tech. – I know, Lewis, but don't interrupt: it doesn't matter about the details. Where was I? Yes. Acum's free then on Wednesday evenings, and we'll say that he invites Valerie round to his house. But one night in March the evening-class is cancelled – let's say the teacher's got flu – and Mrs Acum arrives home unexpectedly early, about a quarter to eight, and she finds them both in bed together. It's a dreadful humiliation for her, and she decides that their marriage is finished. Not that she necessarily wants to ruin Acum's career. She may feel she's to blame in some way: perhaps she doesn't enjoy sex; perhaps she can't have any children – I don't know. Anyway, as I say, it's finished between them. They continue to live together, but they sleep in different rooms and hardly speak to each other. And however hard she tries, she just can't bring herself to forgive him. So they agree to separate when the summer term is over, and Acum knows it will be better for both of them if he gets a new post. Whether he told Phillipson the truth or not doesn't really matter. Perhaps he didn't tell him anything when he first handed in his resignation; but he may well have had to say something when Valerie tells him that she's expecting a baby and that he's almost certainly the father. So, as you yourself said this morning, Lewis, they all decide to put their heads together. Valerie, Acum, Phillipson and Mrs Taylor – I don't know about George. They arrange the clinic in London and fix up the house in North Wales here, where Valerie comes immediately after the abortion, and where Acum will join her just as soon as the school term ends. And Valerie arrives and acts the dutiful little wife, decorating the place and getting things straight and tidy; *and she's still here.* Where the real Mrs Acum is, I don't know; but we should be able to find out easily enough. If you want me to make a guess, I'd say she's living with her mother, in a little village somewhere near Exeter.'

For several minutes Lewis sat motionless within the quiet car until, aroused at length by the very silence, he took a yellow duster from the glove compartment and wiped the steamy windows. Morse's imaginative reconstruction of events seemed curiously convincing, and several times during the course of it Lewis's head had nodded an almost involuntary agreement.

Morse himself suddenly looked once more at his wristwatch. 'Come on, Lewis,' he said. 'We've waited long enough.'

The side gate was locked, and Lewis clambered awkwardly over. The small top window of the back kitchen was open slightly, and by climbing on to the rainwater tub he was able to get his arm through the narrow gap and open the latch of the main window. He eased himself through on to the draining board, jumped down inside, and breathing heavily walked to the front door to let the inspector in. The house was eerily silent.

'No one here, sir. What do we do?'

'We'll have a quick look round,' said Morse. 'I'll stay down here. You try upstairs.'

The steps on the narrow flight of stairs creaked loudly as Lewis mounted aloft, and Morse stood below and watched him, his heart pounding against his ribs.

There were only two bedrooms, each of them opening almost directly off the tiny landing: one to the right, the other immediately in front. First Lewis tried the one to his right, and peered round the door. The junk room, obviously. A single bed, unmade, stood against the far wall; and the bed itself and the rest of the limited space available were strewn with the necessary and the unnecessary oddments that had yet to find for themselves a permanent place in the disposition of the Acum household: several bell-jars of home-made wine, bubbling intermittently; a vacuum cleaner, with its box of varied fitments; dusty lampshades; old curtain rails; the mounted head of an old, moth-eaten deer; and a large assortment of other semi-treasured bric-à-brac that cluttered up the little room. But nothing else. Nothing.

Lewis left the room and tried the other door. It would be the bedroom, he knew that. Tentatively he pushed open the door slightly further and became aware of something scarlet lying there upon the bed, bright scarlet – the colour of new-spilt blood. He opened the door fully now and went inside. And there, draped across the pure white coverlet, the arms neatly folded across the bodice, the waist tight-belted and slim, lay a long, red-velvet evening dress.

Chapter Thirty-six

No one does anything from a single motive.
S. T. Coleridge, *Biographia Literaria*

They sat downstairs in the small kitchen.

'It looks as if our little bird has flown.'

'Mm.' Morse leaned his head upon his left elbow and stared blankly through the window.

'When did you first suspect all this, sir?'

'Sometime last night, it must have been. About half-past three, I should think.'

'This morning, then.'

Morse seemed mildly surprised. It seemed a long, long time ago. 'What put you on to it, though?'

Morse sat up and leaned his back against the rickety kitchen chair. 'Once we learned that Valerie was probably still alive, it altered everything, didn't it? You see, from the start I'd assumed she was dead.'

'You must have had *some* reason.'

'I suppose it was the photograph more than anything,' replied Morse. 'The one of the genuine Mrs Acum that Mrs Phillipson showed me. It was a clear-cut, glossy photograph – not like the indistinct and out-of-date ones we've got of Valerie. Come to think of it, I doubt if either of us will recognise Valerie when we *do* see her. Anyway, I met who I *thought* was Mrs Acum when I first came up here to Caernarfon, and although she had a towel round her head I couldn't help noticing that she wasn't a natural blonde at all. The roots of her hair were dark, and for some reason' (he left it at that) 'the detail, well, just stuck with me. She'd dyed her hair, anyone could see that.'

'But we don't know that the real Mrs Acum is a natural blonde.'

'No, that's true,' admitted Morse.

'Not much to go on then, is it?'

'There was something else, Lewis.'

'What was that?'

Morse paused before replying. 'In the photograph I saw of Mrs Acum, she had a sort of, er, sort of a boyish figure, if you know what I mean.'

'Bit flat-chested you mean, sir?'

'Yes.'

'So?'

'The woman I saw here – well, she wasn't flat-chested, that's all.'

'She could have been wearing a padded bra. You just can't tell for certain, can you?'

'Can't you?' A gentle, wistful smile played momentarily about the inspector's mouth, and he enlightened the innocent Lewis no further. 'I ought to have guessed much earlier. Of course I should. They just don't have anything in common at all: Mrs Acum – and Valerie Taylor. Huh! I don't think you'd ever find anyone less like a bluestocking than Valerie. And I've spoken to her *twice* over the phone, Lewis! More than that, I've actually *seen* her!' He shook his head in self-reproach. 'Yes. I really should have guessed the truth a long, long time ago.'

'From what you said, though, sir, you didn't see much of her, did you? You said she had this beauty-pack—'

'No, not much of her, Lewis. Not much . . .' His thoughts were very far away.

'What's all this got to do with the car-hire firms you're trying to check?' asked Lewis suddenly.

'Well, I've got to try to get *some* hard evidence against her, haven't I? I thought, funnily enough, of letting her give me the evidence herself, but . . .'

Lewis was completely lost. 'I don't quite follow you.'

'Well, I thought of ringing her up this morning first thing and tricking her into giving herself away. It would have been very easy, really.'

'It would?'

'Yes. All I had to do was to speak to her in French. You see, the real Mrs Acum is a graduate from Exeter, remember? But from what we know about poor Valerie's French, I doubt she can get very much further than *bonjour*.'

'But *you* can't speak French either, can you, sir?'

'I have many hidden talents of which as yet you are quite unaware,' said Morse a trifle pompously.

'Oh.' But Lewis had a strong suspicion that Morse knew about as much (or as little) French as he did. And what's more, he'd had no answer to his question. 'Aren't you going to tell me why you'll be checking on the car-hire firms?'

'You've had enough shocks for one day.'

'I don't think one more'll make much difference,' replied Lewis.

'All right, I'll tell you. You see, we've not only found Valerie; *we've also found the murderer of Baines.*' Lewis opened and closed his mouth like a stranded goldfish, but no identifiable vocable emerged.

'You'll understand soon enough,' continued Morse. 'It's fairly obvious if you think about it. She has to get from Caernarfon to Oxford, right? Her husband's got the car. So, what does she do? Train? Bus? There aren't any services. And anyway, she's got to get there quickly, and there's only one thing she can do and that's to hire a car.'

'But we don't know yet that she *did* hire a car,' protested Lewis. 'We don't even know she can drive.'

'We shall know soon enough.'

The 'ifs' were forgotten now, and Morse spoke like a minor prophet enunciating necessary truths. And with gradually diminishing reluctance, Lewis was beginning to sense the inevitability of the course of events that Morse was sketching out for him, and the inexorable logic working through the enquiry they'd begun together. A young schoolgirl missing, and more than two years later a middle-aged schoolmaster murdered; and no satisfactory solution to either mystery. Just two insoluble problems. And suddenly, in the twinkling of an eye, there were no longer two problems – no longer even one problem; for somehow each had magically solved the other.

'You think she drove from here that day?'

'And back,' said Morse.

'And it was Valerie who . . . who killed Baines?'

'Yes. She must have got there about nine o'clock, as near as dammit.'

Lewis's mind ranged back to the night when Baines was murdered. 'So she could have been in Baines's house when Mrs Phillipson and Acum called,' he said slowly.

Morse nodded. 'Could have been, yes.'

He stood up and walked along the narrow hallway. From the window in the front room he could see two small boys, standing at a respectful distance from the police car and trying with cautious curiosity to peer inside. But for the rest, nothing. No one left and no one came along the quiet street.

'Are you worried, sir?' asked Lewis quietly, when Morse sat down again.

'We'll give her a few more minutes,' replied Morse, looking at his watch for the twentieth time.

'I've been thinking, sir. She must be a brave girl.'

'Mm.'

'And he was a nasty piece of work, wasn't he?'

'He was a shithouse,' said Morse with savage conviction. 'But I don't think that Valerie would ever have killed Baines just for her own sake.'

'What *was* her motive then?'

It was a simple question and it deserved a simple answer, but Morse began with the guarded evasiveness of a senior partner in the Circumlocution Office.

'I'm a bit sceptical about the word "motive", you know, Lewis. It makes it sound as if there's just got to be one – one big, beautiful motive. But sometimes it doesn't work like that. You get a mother slapping her child across its face because it won't stop crying. Why does she do it? You can say she just wants to stop the kid from bawling its head off, but it's not really true, is it? The motive lies much deeper than that. It's all bound up with lots of other things:

she's tired, she's got a headache, she's fed up, she's just plain disillusioned with the duties of motherhood. Anything you like. When once you ask yourself what lies in the murky depths below what Aristotle called the immediate cause . . . You know anything about Aristotle, Lewis?'

'I've heard of him, sir. But you still haven't answered my question.'

'Ah, no. Well, let's just consider for a minute the position that Valerie found herself in that day. For the first time for over two years, I should think, she finds herself completely on her own. Since Acum came to join her, he's no doubt been pretty protective towards her, and for the first part of their time together here he's probably been anxious for Valerie not to be caught up in too much of a social whirl. She stays in. *And she'd bleached her hair* – probably right at the beginning. Surprising, isn't it, Lewis, how so many of us go to the trouble of making a gesture – however weak and meaningless? A sop to Cerberus, no doubt. As you know, Acum's real wife had long, blonde hair – that's the first thing anyone would notice about her; it's the first thing I noticed about her when I saw her photograph. Perhaps Acum asked her to do it; may have helped his conscience. Anyway, he must have been glad she *did* dye her hair. You remember the photograph of Valerie in the Colour Supplement? If he saw it, he must have been a very worried man. It wasn't a particularly clear photograph, I know. It had been taken over three years previously, and a young girl changes a good deal – especially between leaving school and becoming to all intents and purposes a married woman. But it still remained a photograph of Valerie and, as I say, I should think Acum was jolly glad about her hair. As far as we know, no one *did* spot the likeness.'

'Perhaps they don't read the *Sunday Times* in Caernarfon.'

For all his anti-Welsh prejudices, Morse let it go. 'She's on her own at last, then. She can do what she likes. She probably feels a wonderful sense of freedom, freedom to do something for herself – something that now, for the first time, *can* in fact be done.'

'I can see all that, sir. But *why*? That's what I want to know.'

'Lewis! Put yourself in the position Valerie and her mother and Acum and Phillipson and God knows who else must have found themselves. They've all got their individual and their collective secrets – big and little – and somebody else knows all about them. Baines knows. Somehow – well, we've got a jolly good idea how – he got to know things. Sitting all those years in that little office of his, with the telephone there and all the correspondence, he's been at the nerve-centre of a small community – the Roger Bacon School. He's second master there, and it's perfectly proper that he *should* know what's going on. All the time his ears are tuned in to the slightest rumours and suspicions. He's like a bug in the Watergate Hotel: he picks it all up and he puts it all together. And it gives to his sinister cast of character just the nourishment it craves for – the power over other people's lives. Think of Phillipson for a minute. Baines can put him out of a job any day he chooses – but he doesn't. You see, I don't think he gloried so much in the actual exercise of his power as—'

'He did actually blackmail Phillipson, though, didn't he?'

'I think so, yes. But even blackmail wouldn't be as sweet for a louse like Baines as the thought that he *could* blackmail – whenever he wanted to.'

'I see,' said the blind man.

'And Mrs Taylor. Think what he knows about her: about the arrangements for her daughter's abortion, about her elaborate lies to the police, about her heavy drinking, about her money troubles, about her anxiety that George Taylor – the only man who's ever treated her with any decency – should be kept in the dark about some of her wilder excesses.'

'But surely everybody must have known she went to Bingo most nights and had a drop of drink now and then?'

'Do you know how much she spent on Bingo and fruit machines? Even according to George it was a pound a night, and she's hardly likely to tell him the truth, is she? And she drinks like a fish – you know she does. Lunch-times as well.'

'So do you, sir.'

'Yes, but . . . well, I only drink in moderation, you know that. Anyway, that's only the half of it. You've seen the way she dresses. Expensive clothes, shoes, accessories – the lot. And jewellery. You noticed the diamonds on her fingers? God knows what they're worth. And do you know what her husband is? He's a dustman! No, Lewis. She's been living way, way beyond her means – you must have realised that.'

'All right, sir. Perhaps that's a good enough motive for Mrs Taylor, but—'

'I know. Where does Valerie fit in? Well, I should think Mrs Taylor probably kept in touch with her daughter by phone – letters would be far too dangerous – and Valerie must have had a pretty good idea of what was going on: that her mother was getting hopelessly mixed up with Baines – that she was getting like a drug-addict, loathing the whole thing in her saner moments but just not being able to do without it. Valerie must have realised that one way or another her mother's life was becoming one long misery, and she probably guessed how it was all likely to end. Perhaps her mother had hinted that she was coming to the end of her tether and couldn't face up to things much longer. I don't know.

'And then just think of Valerie herself. Baines knows all about her, too: her promiscuous background, her night with Phillipson, her affair with Acum – and all its consequences. He knows the lot. And at any time he can ruin *everything*. Above all he can ruin David Acum, because once it gets widely known that he's likely to start fiddling around with some of the girls he's supposed to be teaching, he'll have one hell of a job getting a post in *any* school, even in these permissive days. And I suspect, Lewis, that in a strange sort of way Valerie has gradually grown to love Acum more than anyone or anything she's ever wanted. I think they're happy together – or as happy as anyone could hope to be under the circumstances. Do you see what I mean, then? Not only was her mother's happiness threatened at every turn by that bastard Baines, but equally the happiness of David Acum. And one day she suddenly found herself with the opportunity of doing something about it all: at one swift, uncomplicated swoop to solve *all* the problems, and she could do that by getting rid of Baines.'

Lewis pondered awhile. 'Didn't she ever think that Acum might be suspected, though? He was in Oxford, too – she knew that.'

'No, I don't suppose she gave it a thought. I mean, the chance that Acum himself would go along to Baines's place at the very same time as she did – well, it's a thousand to one against, isn't it?'

'Odd coincidence, though.'

'It's an odd coincidence, Lewis, that the 46th word from the beginning and the 46th word from the end of the 46th Psalm in the Authorised Version should spell "Shakespear".'

Aristotle, Shakespeare and the Book of Psalms. It was all a bit too much for Lewis, and he sat in silence deciding that he'd missed out somewhere along the educational line. He'd asked his questions and he'd got his answers. They hadn't been the best answers in the world, perhaps, but they just about added up. It was, one could say, satisfactory.

Morse stood up and went over to the kitchen window. The view was magnificent, and for some time he stared across at the massive peaks of the Snowdon range. 'We can't stay here for ever, I suppose,' he said at last. His hands were on the edge of the sink, and almost involuntarily he pulled open the right-hand drawer. Inside he saw a wooden-handled carving knife, new, 'Prestige, Made in England', and he was on the point of picking it up when he heard the rattle of a Yale key in the front-door lock. Swiftly he held up a finger to his mouth and drew Lewis back with him against the wall behind the kitchen door. He could see her quite clearly now, the long, blonde hair tumbling over her shoulders, as she fiddled momentarily with the inner catch, withdrew the key, and closed the door behind her.

Thinly-veiled anger yet little more than mild surprise showed on her face as Morse stepped into the hallway. 'That's your car outside, I suppose.' She said it in a bleak almost contemptuous voice. 'I'd just like to know what right you think you've got to burst into my house like this!'

'You've every right to feel angry,' said Morse defencelessly, lifting up his left hand in a feeble gesture of pacification. 'I'll explain everything in a minute. I promise I will. But can I just ask you one question first? That's all I ask. Just one question. It's very important.'

She looked at him curiously, as if he were slightly mad.

'You speak French, don't you?'

'Yes.' Frowning, she put down her shopping basket by the door, and stood there quite still, maintaining the distance between them. 'Yes, I do speak French. What's that—?'

Morse took the desperate plunge. '*Avez-vous appris français à l'école?*'

For a brief moment only she stared at him with blank, uncomprehending eyes, before the devastating reply slid smoothly and idiomatically from her tutored lips. '*Oui. Je l'ai étudié d'abord à l'école et après pendant trois ans à l'Université. Alors je devrais parler la langue assez bien, n'est-ce pas?*'

'*Et avez-vous rencontré votre mari à Exeter?*'

'*Oui. Nous étions étudiants là-bas tous les deux. Naturellement, il parle français mieux que moi. Mais il est assez évident que vous parlez français comme un Anglais typique, et votre accent est abominable.*'

Morse walked back into the kitchen with the air of an educationally subnormal zombie, sat down at the table, and held his head between his hands. Why had he bothered anyway? He had known already. He had known as soon as she had closed the front door and turned her face towards him – a face still blotched with ugly spots.

'Would you both like a cup of tea?' asked Mrs Acum, as the embarrassed Lewis stepped forward sheepishly from behind the kitchen door.

Chapter Thirty-seven

The gaudy, blabbing and remorseful day
Is crept into the bosom of the sea.

Henry IV, Part II

As he slumped back in the passenger seat, Morse presented a picture of stupefied perplexity. They had left Caernarfon just after 9 p.m., and it would be well into the early hours before they arrived in Oxford. Each left the other to his private thoughts, thoughts that criss-crossed ceaselessly the no man's land of failure and futility.

The interview with Acum had been a very strange affair. Morse seemed entirely to have lost the thread of the inquiry, and his early questions had been almost embarrassingly apologetic. It had been left to Lewis to press home some of the points that Morse had earlier made, and after an initial evasiveness Acum had seemed almost glad to get it all off his chest at last. And as he did so, Lewis was left wondering where the inspector's train of thought had jumped the rails and landed in such a heap of crumpled wreckage by the track; for many of Morse's assumptions had been correct, it seemed. Almost uncannily correct.

Acum (on his own admission now) had indeed been attracted to Valerie Taylor and several times had intercourse with her; including a night in early April (not March) when his wife had returned home early one Tuesday (not Wednesday) evening from night school in Oxpens (not Headington) where she was attending art (not sewing) classes. Her teacher was down with shingles (not with flu), and the class was cancelled. It was just after eight o'clock (not a quarter to) when Mrs Acum had returned and found them lying together across the settee (not in bed), and the upshot had been veritably volcanic, with Valerie, it seemed, by far the least confounded of that troubled trio. There followed, for Acum and his wife, a succession of bleak and barren days. It was all over between them –

she insisted firmly upon that; but she agreed to stay with him until their separation could be effected with a minimum of social scandal. He himself decided he must move in any case, and applied for a job in Caernarfon; and although he had been questioned by Phillipson at some length about his motives for a seemingly meaningless move to a not particularly promising post, he had told him nothing of the truth. Literally nothing. He could only pray that Valerie would keep her mouth shut, too.

Not until about three weeks before her disappearance had he spoken personally to Valerie again, when she told him that she was expecting a baby, a baby that was probably his. She appeared (or so it seemed to Acum) completely confident and unconcerned and told him everything would be all right. She begged of him one thing only: that if she were to run away he would say nothing and know nothing – that was all; and although he had pressed her about her intentions, she would only repeat that she would be all right. Did she need any money? She told him she would let him know, but, smiling slyly as she told him, she said that she was going to be all right. Everything was 'all right'. Everything was always 'all right' with Valerie. (It was at this point in Lewis's interrogation, and only at this point, that Morse had suddenly pricked up his ears and asked a few inconsequential questions.) It appeared, however, that the money side of things was not completely 'all right', for only a week or so before the day she disappeared Valerie had approached Acum and told him she would be very grateful for some money if he could manage it. She hadn't pressed her claim on him in any way, but he had been only too glad to help; and from the little enough they had managed to save – and with his wife's full knowledge – he had raised one hundred pounds. And then she had gone; and like everyone else he hadn't the faintest idea where she had gone to, and he had kept his silence ever since, as Valerie had asked him to.

Meanwhile in the Acum household the weeping wounds were at last beginning to heal; and with Valerie gone they had tried, for the first time since that dreadful night, to discuss their sorry situation with some degree of rationality and mutual understanding. He told her that he loved her, that he realised now how very much she meant to him, and how desperately he hoped that they would stay together. She had wept then, and said she knew how disappointed he must be that she could have no children of her own . . . And as the summer term drew towards its close they had decided – almost happily decided – that they would stay together, and try to patch their marriage up. In any case there had never been the slightest question of divorce: for his wife was a Roman Catholic.

So, continued Acum, they had moved together to North Wales, and life was happy enough now – or had been so until the whole thing had once more exploded in their faces with the murder of Reggie Baines, of which (he swore on his solemn honour) he was himself completely innocent. Blackmail? The whole idea was laughable. The only person who had any hold on him was Valerie Taylor, and of Valerie Taylor he had seen or heard nothing whatsoever since the day of her disappearance. Whether she were alive or whether she were dead, he had no idea – no idea at all.

There the interview had finished. Or almost finished. For it was Morse himself who had administered the *coup de grâce* which finally put his tortured and tortuous theory out of all its pain.

'Does your wife drive a car?'

Acum looked at him with mild surprise. 'No. She's never driven a yard in her life. Why?'

Lewis relived the interview as he drove on steadily through the night. And as he recalled the facts that Acum had recounted, he felt a deepening sympathy with the sour, dejected, silent figure slumped beside him, smoking (unusually) cigarette after cigarette, and feeling (if the truth be told) unconscionably angry with himself . . .

Why had he gone wrong? *Where* had he gone wrong? The questions re-echoed in Morse's mind as if repeated by some interminable interlocutor installed inside his brain. He thought back to his first analysis of the case – the one in which he had cast Mrs Taylor as the murderer not only of Reginald Baines but also of her daughter Valerie. How easy now to see why *that* was wrong! His reasoning had run aground upon the Rock Improbable and the Rock Impossible: the glaring improbability that Mrs Taylor had murdered her only daughter (mothers just didn't do that sort of thing very often, did they?); and the plain impossibility that *anyone* had murdered Valerie on the day she disappeared, since three days later, alive and well, she had climbed into the back of a taxi outside a London abortion clinic. Yes, the first analysis had been brutally smashed to pieces by the facts, and now lay sunk without a trace beneath the sea. It was as simple as that.

And what of the second analysis? *That* had seemed on the face of it to answer all the facts, or nearly all of them. What had gone wrong with that? Again his logic had foundered upon the Reef of

Unreason: the glaring improbability that Valerie Taylor had either
sufficient motive or adequate opportunity to murder a man who
seemed to pose little more than a peripheral threat to her future
happiness; and the plain impossibility that the woman living with
David Acum was Valerie Taylor. She wasn't. She was Mrs Acum.
And Analysis One lay side by side with Analysis Two – irrecoverable
wrecks upon the ocean floor.

Almost frenetically Morse tried to wrench his thoughts away from
it all. He tried to conjure up a dream of fair women; and, failing
this, he essayed to project upon his mind a raw, uncensored film
of rank eroticism; he tried so very hard . . . But still the wretched
earth-bound realities of the Taylor case crowded his brain, forbade
those flights of half-forbidden fancies, and jolted him back to his
inescapable mood of gloom-ridden despondency. Facts, facts, facts!
Facts that one by one he once again reviewed as they marched and
counter-marched across his mind. If only he'd stuck to the facts!
Ainley was dead – that was a fact. Somebody had written a letter
the very day after he died – that was a fact. Valerie had been alive
on the days immediately following her disappearance – that was a
fact. Baines was dead – that was a fact. Mrs Acum was Mrs Acum
– that was a fact. But where did he go from there? He began to
realise how few the facts had been; how very, very few. A lot of
possible facts; a fair helping of probable facts; but few that ranked as
positive facts. And once again the facts remarshalled themselves and
marched across the parade ground . . . He shook his head sharply
and felt he must be going mad.

Lewis, he could see, was concentrating hard upon the road.
Lewis! Huh! It had been Lewis who had asked him the one question,
the only question, that had completely floored him: *Why had Baines
written the letter?* Why? He had never grappled satisfactorily with
that question, and now it worried away at his brain again. Why?
Why? Why?

It was as they swept along the old Watling Street, past Wellington,
that Morse in a flash conceived a possible answer to this importunate
question; an answer of astonishing and devastating simplicity. And
he nursed his new little discovery like a frightened mother sheltering
her only child amid the ruin of an earthquake-stricken city . . . The
merry-go-round was slowing now . . . the pubs were long shut and
the chips were long cold . . . his mind was getting back to normal
now . . . This was better! Methodically he began to undress Miss
Yvonne Baker.

* * *

Lewis had the road virtually to himself now. It was past 1.00 a.m. and the two men had not exchanged a single word. Strangely, the silence had seemed progressively to reinforce itself, and conversation now would seem as sacrilegious as a breaking of the silence before the cenotaph.

As he drove the last part of the journey his mind roved back beyond the oddly-unreal events of the last few hours, and dwelt again on the early days of the Valerie Taylor case. She'd just hopped it, of course – he'd said so right at the beginning: fed up with home and school, she'd yearned for the brighter lights, the excitement and the glamour of the big city. Got shot of the unwanted baby, and finished up in a groovy, swinging set. Contented enough; even happy, perhaps. The last thing she wanted was to go back home to her moody mother and her stolid step-father. We all felt like that occasionally. We'd all like a fresh start in a new life. Like being born again . . . He'd felt like running away from home when he was her age . . . Concentrate, Lewis! Oxford 30 miles. He glanced at the inspector and smiled quietly to himself. The old boy was fast asleep.

They were within ten miles of Oxford when Lewis became vaguely conscious of Morse's mumbled words, muddled and indistinct; just words without coherent meaning. Yet gradually the words assumed a patterned sequence that Lewis almost understood: 'Bloody photographs – wouldn't recognise her – huh! – bloody things – huh!'

'We're here, sir.' It was the first time he had spoken for more than five hours and his voice sounded unnaturally loud.

Morse shrugged himself awake and blinked around him. 'I must have dozed off, Lewis. Not like me, is it?'

'Would you like to drop in at my place for a cup of coffee and a bite to eat?'

'No. But thanks all the same.' He eased himself out of the car like a chronic arthritic, yawned mightily, and stretched his arms. 'We'll take tomorrow off, Lewis. Agreed? We've just about deserved it, I reckon.'

Lewis said he reckoned, too. He parked the police car, backed out his own and waved a weary farewell.

Morse entered Police HQ and made his way along the dimly-lit corridor to his office, where he opened his filing cabinet and riffled through the early documents in the Valerie Taylor case. He found it almost immediately, and as he looked down at the so familiar letter, once more his mind was sliding easily along the shining grooves. It must be. It must be!

He wondered if Lewis would ever forgive him.

Chapter Thirty-eight

And then there were two.

Ten Little Nigger Boys

'. . . *not generally appreciated. We all normally assume that the sex instinct is so obviously overriding, so primitively predominant that it must . . .*' Morse, newly-woken and surprisingly refreshed, switched over to Radio Three; and thence to Radio Oxford. But none of the channels seemed anxious to inform him of the time of day, and he turned back to Radio Four. '. . . *and above all, of course, by Freud. Let us assume, for example, that we have been marooned on a desert island for three days without food, and ask ourselves which of the bodily instincts most craves its instant gratification.*' With sudden interest Morse turned up the volume: the voice was donnish, slightly effeminate. '*Let us imagine that a beautiful blonde appears with a plate of succulent steak and chips . . .*' Leaning over to turn the volume higher still, Morse inadvertently nudged the tuning knob, and by the time he had re-centred the station it was clear that the beautiful blonde had lost on points. '. . . *as we tuck into the steak and . . .*' Morse switched off. 'Shert erp, you poncy twit!' he said aloud, got out of bed, pulled on his clothes, walked downstairs and dialled the speaking clock. 'At the first stroke it will be eleven – twenty-eight – and forty seconds.' She sounded nice, and Morse wondered if she were a blonde. It was over twenty-four hours since he had eaten, but for the moment steak and chips was registering a poor third on the instinct index.

Without bothering to shave he walked round to the Fletchers' Arms where he surveyed with suspicion a pile of 'freshly-cut' ham sandwiches beneath their plastic cover and ordered a glass of bitter. By 12.45 p.m. he had consumed four pints, and felt a pleasing lassitude pervade his limbs. He walked slowly home and fell fully-clothed into his bed. This was the life.

He felt lousy when he woke again at 5.20 p.m., and wondered if he were in the old age of youth or the youth of old age.

By 6 p.m. he was seated in his office, clearing up the litter from his desk. There were several messages lying there, and one by one he relegated them to an in-tray which never had been clear and never would be clear. There was one further message, on the telephone pad: 'Ring 01-787 24392'. Morse flicked through the telephone book and found that 787 was the STD code for Stoke Newington. He rang the number.

'Hello?' The voice was heavy with sex.

'Ah. Morse here. I got your message. Er, can I help?'

'Oh, Inspector,' purred the voice. 'It was yesterday I tried to get you, but never mind. I'm so glad you rang.' The words were slow and evenly spaced. 'I just wondered if you wanted to see me again – you know, to make a statement or something? I wondered if you'd be coming down again . . . perhaps?'

'That's very kind of you, Miss – er, Yvonne. But I think Chief Inspector Rogers will be along to see you. We shall need a statement, though – you're quite right about that.'

'Is he as nice as you are, Inspector?'

'Nowhere near,' said Morse.

'All right, whatever you say. But it would be so nice to see you again.'

'It would, indeed,' said Morse with some conviction in his voice.

'Well, I'd better say goodbye then. You didn't mind me ringing, did you?'

'No, er, no, of course I didn't. It's lovely to hear your voice again.'

'Well, don't forget if you're ever this way you must call in to see me.'

'Yes, I will,' lied Morse.

'I really would love to see you again.'

'Same here.'

'You've got my address, haven't you?'

'Yes, I've got it.'

'And you'll make a note of the phone number?'

'Er, yes. Yes, I'll do that.'

'Goodbye, then, till we see each other again.' From the tone of her voice Morse guessed she must be lying there, her hands sensuously sliding along those beautiful limbs; and all he had to do was to say, yes, he'd be there! London wasn't very far away, and the night was still so young. He pictured her as she had been on the night that he had met her, the top button of the pyjama jacket already undone; and in his mind's eye his fingers gently unfastened the other buttons, one by one, and slowly drew the sides apart.

'Goodbye,' he said sadly.

He walked to the canteen and ordered black coffee.

'I thought you were taking the day off,' said a voice behind him.

'You must love this bloody place, Lewis!'

'I rang up. They said you were here.'

'Couldn't you stick it at home?'

'No. The missus says I get under her feet.'

They sat down together, and it was Lewis who put their thoughts into words. 'Where do we go from here, sir?'

Morse shook his head dubiously. 'I don't know.'

'Will you tell me one thing?'

'If I can.'

'Have you *any* idea at all about who killed Baines?'

Idly Morse stirred the strong black coffee. 'Have you?'

'The real trouble is we seem to be eliminating all the suspects. Not many left, are there?'

'We're not beaten yet,' said Morse with a sudden and unexpected lift of spirits. 'We got a bit lost in the winding mazes, and we still can't see the end of the road, but . . .' He broke off and stared through the window. In a sudden gust of wind a shower of leaves rained down from the thinning trees.

'But what, sir?'

'Somebody once said that the end is the beginning, Lewis.'

'Not a particularly helpful thing to say, was it?'

'Ah, but I think it was. You see, we know what the beginning was.'

'Do we?'

'Oh yes. We know that Phillipson met Valerie Taylor one night, and we know that when he was appointed headmaster he discovered that she was one of his own pupils. That was where it all began, and that's where we've got to look now. There's nowhere else to look.'

'You mean . . . Phillipson?'

'Or Mrs Phillipson.'

'You don't think—'

'I don't think it matters much which of them you go for. They had the same motive; they had the same opportunity.'

'How do we set about it?'

'How do *you* set about it, you mean. I'm leaving it to you, Lewis.'

'Oh.'

'Want a bit of advice?' Morse smiled weakly. 'Bit of a cheek, isn't it, me giving you advice?'

'Of course I want your advice,' said Lewis quietly. 'We both know that.'

'All right. Here's a riddle for you. You look for a leaf in the forest, and you look for a corpse on the battlefield. Right? Where do you look for a knife?'

'An ironmonger's shop?'

'No, not a *new* knife. A knife that's been used – used continuously; used so much that the blade is wearing away.'

'A butcher's shop?'

'Warmer. But we haven't got a butcher in the case, have we?'

'A kitchen?'

'Ah! Which kitchen?'

'Phillipson's kitchen?'

'They'd only have one knife. It would be missed, wouldn't it?'

'Perhaps it *was* missed.'

'I don't think so, somehow, though you'll have to check. No, we need to find a place where knives are in daily use; a lot of knives; a place where no one would notice the loss of a single knife; a place at the very heart of the case. Come on, Lewis! Lots of people cutting up spuds and carrots and meat and everything . . .'

'The canteen at the Roger Bacon School,' said Lewis slowly.

Morse nodded. 'It's an idea, isn't it?'

'Ye-es.' Lewis pondered for a while and nodded his agreement. 'But you say you want *me* to look into all this? What about you?'

'I'm going to look into the only other angle we've got left.'

'What's that?'

'I've told you. The secret of this case is locked away in the beginning: Phillipson and Valerie Taylor. You've got one half; I've got the other.'

'You mean . . . ?' Lewis had no idea what he meant.

Morse stood up. 'Yep. You have a go at the Phillipsons. I shall have to find Valerie.' He looked down at Lewis and grinned disarmingly. 'Where do you suggest I ought to start looking?'

Lewis stood up, too. 'I've always thought she was in London, sir. You know that. I think she just . . .'

But Morse was no longer listening. He felt the icy fingers running along his spine, and there was a sudden wild elation in the pale blue eyes. 'Why not, Lewis? Why not?'

He walked back to his office, and dialled the number immediately. After all, she *had* invited him, hadn't she?

Chapter Thirty-nine

The only way of catching a train I ever discovered is to
miss the one before.

G. K. Chesterton

'Mummy?' Alison managed a very important frown upon her
pretty little face as her mother tucked her early into bed at
8 p.m.

'Yes, darling?'

'Will the policemen be coming to see Daddy again when he
gets back?'

'I don't think so, darling. Don't start worrying your little
head about that.'

'He's not gone away to prison or anything like that, has he?'

'Of course he hasn't, you silly little thing! He'll be back tonight,
you know that, and I'll tell him to come in and give you a big kiss
– I promise.'

Alison was silent for a few moments. 'Mummy, he's not done
anything wrong, has he?'

'No, you silly little thing. Of course he hasn't.'

Alison frowned again as she looked up into her mother's
eyes. 'Even if he *did* do something wrong, he'd still be my Daddy,
wouldn't he?'

'Yes. He'd still be your Daddy, whatever happened.'

'And we'd forgive him, wouldn't we?'

'Yes, my darling . . . And you'd forgive Mummy, too, wouldn't
you, if she did something wrong? Especially if . . .'

'Don't worry, Mummy. God forgives everybody, doesn't he? And
my teacher says that we must all try to be like him.'

Mrs Phillipson walked slowly down the stairs, and her eyes were
glazed with tears.

Morse left the Jaguar at home and walked down from North Oxford
to the railway station. It took him almost an hour and he wasn't at
all sure why he'd decided to do it; but his head felt clear now and the
unaccustomed exercise had done him good. At twenty-past eight he
stood outside the station buffet and looked around him. It was dark,
but just across the way the street lights shone on the first few houses
in Kempis Street. So close! He hadn't quite realised just how close

to the railway station it was. A hundred yards? No more, certainly. Get off the train on Platform 2, cross over by the subway, hand your ticket in . . . For a second or two he stood stock still and felt the old familiar thrill that coursed along his nerves. He was catching the 8.35 train – the same train that Phillipson could have caught that fateful night so long ago . . . Paddington about 9.40. Taxi. Let's see . . . Yes, with a bit of luck he'd be there about 10.15.

He bought a first-class ticket and walked past the barrier on to Platform No. 1, and almost immediately the loudspeaker intoned from somewhere in the station roof: 'The train now arriving at Platform 1 is for Reading and Paddington only. Passengers for . . .' But Morse wasn't listening.

He sat back comfortably and closed his eyes. Idiot! Idiot! It was all so simple really. Lewis had found the pile of books in the store-room and had sworn there'd been no dust upon the top one; and all Morse had done had been to shout his faithful sergeant's head off. Of course there had been no dust on the top book! Someone had taken a book from the top of the self-same pile – a book that was doubtless thick with dust by then. Taken it recently, too. So very recently in fact that the book at the top of the remaining pile was virtually free from dust when Lewis had picked it up. Someone. Yes, a someone called Baines who had taken it home and studied it very hard. *But not because he'd wished to forge a letter in Valerie Taylor's hand.* That had been one of Morse's biggest mistakes. There was, as he had guessed the night before, a blindingly obvious answer to the question of why Baines had written the letter to Valerie's parents. *The answer was that he hadn't.* Mr and Mrs Taylor had received the letter on the Wednesday morning and had been in two minds about taking it to the police – George Taylor himself had told Morse exactly that. Why? Obviously because they couldn't decide whether it had come from Valerie or not: it might just have been a hoax. It must surely have been Mrs Taylor who had taken it to Baines; and Baines had very sensibly taken an exercise book from the store-room and written out his own parallel version of the brief message, copying as accurately as he could the style and shape of Valerie's own lettering as he found it in the Applied Science book. And then he'd compared the letter from Valerie with his own painstaking effort, and pronounced to Mrs Taylor that at least in his opinion the letter seemed completely genuine. That was how things must have happened. And there was something else, too. The logical corollary of all this was that Mr and Mrs Taylor had no idea at all about where Valerie was. For more than two years they had heard nothing whatsoever from her. And if both of them were genuinely puzzled about the letter, there seemed one further inescapable conclusion: *the Taylors were completely in the clear.* Go on, Morse! Keep going! With a smooth inevitability the pieces were falling into place. Keep going!

Well, if this hypothesis were correct, the overwhelming probability was that Valerie was alive and that she had written the letter herself. It was just as Peters said it was; just as Lewis said it was; just as Morse himself had said it *wasn't.* Moreover, as he had learned the previous evening, there was a very interesting and suggestive piece of corroborative evidence. Acum had given it to him: Valerie was always using the expression 'all right', he'd said. And on his return Morse had checked the letter once again:

Just to let you know I'm alright so don't worry. Sorry I've not written before but I'm alright.

And Ainley (poor old Ainley!) had not only known that she was still alive; he'd actually found her – Morse felt sure of that now. Or, at the very least, he'd discovered where she could be found. Stolid, painstaking old Ainley! A bloody sight better cop than he himself would ever be. (Hadn't Strange said the same thing – right at the beginning?) Valerie could never have guessed the full extent of the hullabaloo that her disappearance had caused. After all, hundreds of young girls went missing every year. Hundreds. But had she suddenly learned of it, so long after the event? Had Ainley actually met her and told her? It seemed entirely probable now, since the very next day she had sat down and written to her parents for the very first time. That was all. Just a brief scratty little letter! And that prize clown Morse had been called in. Big stuff. Christ! What a mess, what a terribly unholy mess he'd made of everything!

They were well into the outskirts of London now, and Morse walked out to the corridor and lit a cigarette. Only one thing worried him now: the thought that had flashed across his mind as he stood outside the station buffet and looked across at Kempis Street. But he'd know soon enough now; so very soon he'd know it all.

Chapter Forty

For she and I were long acquainted
And I knew all her ways.
                                    A. E. Housman, *Last Poems*

It was just after ten-thirty when he paid and tipped the taxi-driver:
it cost him more than the return first-class fare to London. At
the bottom of the building he found, as before, the lift for the
even-numbered floors on his left and that for the odd on his right.
He remembered the floor. Of course he did.

She was radiant. That was the best epithet for her, although
there were many others. She wore a thin black sweater in which
her full and bra-less breasts bobbed irresistibly; and a long black
skirt, slit high along her leg and leaving a sublime uncertainty of
what she wore below. Her mouth, just as he had seen it last, was
stickily seductive, the lips moist and slightly parted, the teeth so
gleaming white. O Lord, have mercy on our souls!

'What would you like to drink, Inspector? Whisky? Gin?'

'Whisky, please. Lovely.'

She disappeared into the kitchen, and Morse moved quickly over
to a small shelf of books beside the deeply-leathered divan. Rapidly
he flicked open the front cover of the books there, and as rapidly
replaced them. Only one of them held his attention, and that only
for a few seconds, when the blue eyes momentarily flashed with a
glint of satisfaction, if not surprise.

He was seated on the divan when she returned with a large whisky
in a cut-glass tumbler and sat down beside him.

'Aren't *you* drinking?'

Her eyes met his and held them. 'In a minute,' she whispered,
linking her arm through his, the tips of her fingers gently tracing
slow designs along his wrist.

Softly he took her hand in his, and for a short sweet second the
thrill was that of a sharp electric shock that shot along his veins,
and a zig-zag current that sparked across his temples. He looked
down at her delicately-fingered left hand, and saw across the bottom
of the index finger the faint white line of an old scar – like the
scar that was mentioned in the medical report on Valerie Taylor,
when she had cut herself with a carving knife – in Kidlington, when
she was a pupil at the Roger Bacon School.

'What shall I call you?' she asked suddenly. 'I can't go on calling you "Inspector" all night, can I?'

'It's a funny thing,' said Morse, 'but no one ever calls me by my Christian name.'

Lightly she touched his cheek with her lips, and her hand moved slowly along his leg. 'Never mind. If you don't like your name, you can always change it, you know. There's no law against that.'

'No, there isn't. I could always change it if I wanted to, I suppose. Just like you changed yours.'

Her body stiffened and she took her hand away. 'And what on earth is *that* supposed to mean?'

'You told me your name was Yvonne the last time I saw you. But that isn't your real name, is it? Is it, Valerie?'

'*Valerie?* You can't possibly . . .' But she was unable to articulate her thoughts beyond that point, and a look of profound perplexity appeared to cross her beautiful face. She stood up. 'Look, Inspector, or whatever your name is, my name's Yvonne Baker – you'd better get that straight before we go any further. If you don't believe me you can ring the couple on the floor below. I was at school in Seven Sisters Road with Joyce—'

'Go ahead,' said Morse blandly. 'Ring up your old school pal if you want to. Why not tell her to come up to see us?'

A look of anger flashed across her face and momentarily made it less than beautiful. She hesitated; then walked over the phone and dialled a number.

Morse leaned back and sipped his whisky contentedly. Even from across the room he could hear the muted, metallic purrs with perfect clarity; he found himself mentally counting them . . . Finally she put down the phone and came back to sit beside him once more. He reached to the book-shelf, abstracted a small hard-bound copy of *Jane Eyre*, and opened the front cover. Inside was the label of the Roger Bacon Comprehensive School, on which Valerie's own name appeared, appended to those of her literary predecessors:

> Angela Lowe   5C
> Mary Ann Baldwin 5B
> Valerie Taylor   5C

He passed it across to her. 'Well?'

She shook her head in exasperation. 'Well what?'

'Is it yours?'

'Of course it isn't mine. It's Valerie's – you can see that. She gave it me to read in the clinic. It was one of her O-level set books, and she thought I'd enjoy reading it. But I never got round to it and I . . . I just forgot to give it her back, that's all.'

'And that's your story?'

'It isn't a *story*. It's the *truth*. I don't know—'

'What went wrong at home, Valerie? Did you—'

'Oh *God*! What the hell are you on about? I'm not *Valerie*. It's . . . I . . . I . . . I just don't know where to start. Look, my parents live in Uxbridge – can you understand that? I can ring them. *You* can ring them. I—'

'I know your parents, Valerie. You got so fed up with them that you left them. Left them without a word of explanation – at least until Ainley found you. And then at long last you *did* write home— '

'What are you *talking* about? Ainley? Who's he? I've . . . Oh, what's the good!' Her voice had grown shrill and harsh, but suddenly she subsided almost helplessly against the back of the divan. 'All right, Inspector! Have it your way. You tell *me* what happened.'

'You wrote home then,' continued Morse. 'You hadn't realised what a terrible fuss you'd caused until Inspector Ainley saw you. But Ainley was killed. He was killed in a road accident on his way back to Oxford on the very same day he saw you.'

'I'm sorry to interrupt, Inspector. But I thought I was Yvonne Baker. When did I suddenly change to Valerie Taylor?' Her voice was quite calm now.

'You met Yvonne in the abortion clinic. You were fed up with home, fed up with school; and Yvonne . . . well, probably, she put the idea into your head. For argument's sake, let's say she was a girl with lots of money, rich parents – probably going off to Switzerland or somewhere for a year's holiday after it was all over. Why not take her name? Start a new life? You've nothing to lose, have you? You'd decided not to go back home, whatever happened. You hardly saw your mother anyway, except at lunch-times, and her only real interests in life were booze and Bingo – and men, of course. And then there's your step-father: not very bright, perhaps, but likeable enough, in an odd sort of way. That is until he started getting a bit too fond of his beautiful step-daughter. And your mother got to know about that, I think, and when you got yourself pregnant, she suspected a terrible thing. She suspected that he might well be the father, didn't she? And she flew into an almighty rage about it, and for you this was the last straw. You just had to go; and you *did* go. But fortunately you had someone to help you; your headmaster.

There's no need to go into all that –but *you* know all about it as well as I do. You could count on him – always. He fixed up the clinic, and he gave you some money. You'd probably packed a case the night before and arranged to meet him somewhere to stow it away safely in the boot of the car. And then on the Tuesday he picked you up just after school had started for the afternoon and took you to the railway station. You only had a bag with you – no doubt with your clothes in it – and you changed on the train and arrived at the clinic. Shall I go on?'

'Yes, please. It's quite fascinating!'

'You just interrupt me if I go wrong, that's all.'

'But . . .' She gave it up and sat there silently shaking her head.

'I'm guessing now,' continued Morse, 'but I should think Yvonne put you on to a job – let's say a job in a West End store. The school-leavers hadn't crowded the market yet, and it was fairly easy for you. You'd need a testimonial or a reference, I realise that. But you rang Phillipson and told him the position, and he took care of that. It was your first job. No bother. No employment cards, or stamps or anything. So that was that.'

Morse turned and looked again at the chic, sophisticated creature beside him. They wouldn't recognise her back in Kidlington now, would they? They'd remember only the young schoolgirl in her red socks and her white blouse. They would always attract the men, these two – mother and daughter alike. Somehow they shared the same intangible yet pervasive sensuality, and the Lord had fashioned them so very fair.

'Is that the finish?' she asked quietly.

Morse's reply was brusque. 'No, it's not. Where were you last Monday night?'

'Last Monday night? What's that got to do with you?'

'What train did you catch the night that Baines was killed?'

She looked at him in utter astonishment now. 'What train are you talking about? I haven't—'

'Didn't you go there that night?'

'Go *where*?'

'You know where. You probably caught the 8.15 from Paddington and arrived in Oxford at about 9.30.'

'You must be *mad*! I was in Hammersmith last Monday night.'

'Were you?'

'Yes, I *was*. I always go to Hammersmith on Monday nights.'

'Go on.'

'You really want to know?' Her eyes grew softer again, and she

shook her head sadly. 'If you must know there's a sort of . . . sort
of party we have there every Monday.'

'What time?'

'Starts about nine.'

'And you were there last Monday?'

She nodded, almost fiercely.

'You go every Monday, you say?'

'Yes.'

'Why aren't you there tonight?'

'I . . . well, I just thought . . . when you rang . . .' She looked
at him with doleful eyes. 'I didn't think it was going to be like
this.'

'What time do these parties finish?'

'They don't.'

'You stay all night, you mean.'

She nodded.

'Sex parties?'

'In a way.'

'What the hell's that supposed to mean?'

'You know. The usual sort of thing: films to start with . . .'

'Blue films?'

Again she nodded.

'And then?'

'Oh God! Come off it. Are you trying to torture yourself, or
something?'

She was far too near the truth, and Morse felt miserably embarrassed. He got to his feet and looked round fecklessly for his
coat. 'You'll have to give me the address, you realise that.'

'But I can't. I'd—'

'Don't worry,' said Morse wearily. 'I shan't pry any more than
I have to.'

He looked once more around the expensive flat. She must earn
a lot of money, somehow; and he wondered if it was all much compensation for the heartache and the jealousy that she must know
as well as he. Or perhaps we weren't all the same. Perhaps it wasn't
possible to live as she had done and keep alive the finer, tenderer
compassions.

He looked across at her as she sat at a small bureau, writing
something down: doubtless the address of the bawdy house in
Hammersmith. He had to have that, whatever happened. But did
it matter all that much? He knew instinctively that she was there
that night, among the wealthy, lecherous old men who gloated

over pornographic films, and pawed and fondled the figures of
the high-class prostitutes who sat upon their knees unfastening their
flies. So what? He was a lecherous old man, too, wasn't he? Very
nearly, anyway. Just a sediment of sensitivity still. Just a little. Just
a little.

She came over to him, and for a moment she was very
beautiful again. 'I've been very patient with you, Inspector, don't
you think?'

'I suppose so, yes. Patient, if not particularly co-operative.'

'Can I ask *you* a question?'

'Of course.'

'Do you want to sleep with me tonight?'

The back of Morse's throat felt suddenly very dry. 'No.'

'You really mean that?'

'Yes.'

'All right.' Her voice was brisker now. 'Let me be "co-operative"
then, as you call it.' She handed him a sheet of notepaper on which
she had written two telephone numbers.

'The first one's my father's. You may have to drag him out of
bed, but he's almost certainly home by now. The other one's the
Wilsons, downstairs. As I told you, I was at school with Joyce. I'd
like you to ring them both, please.'

Morse took the paper and said nothing.

'Then there's this.' She handed him a passport. 'I know it's
out of date, but I've only been abroad once. To Switzerland, three
years ago last June.'

With a puzzled frown Morse opened the passport and the unmistakable face of Miss Yvonne Baker smiled up at him in gentle
mockery from a Woolworth Polyfoto. Three years last June . . .
whilst Valerie Taylor was still at school in Kidlington. Well before
she . . . before . . .

Morse took off his coat and sat down once again on the divan.
'Will you ring your friends below, Yvonne? And if you're feeling
very kind, can I please ask you to pour me another whisky? A
stiff one.'

At Paddington he was informed that the last train to Oxford
had departed half an hour earlier. He walked into the cheerless
waiting room, put his feet up on the bench, and soon fell fast
asleep.

At 3.30 a.m. a firm hand shook him by the shoulder, and he
looked up into the face of a bearded constable.

'You can't sleep here, sir. I shall have to ask you to move on, I'm afraid.'

'You surely don't begrudge a man a bit of kip, do you, Officer?'

'I'm afraid I shall have to ask you to move on, sir.'

Morse almost told him who he was. But simultaneously the other sleepers were being roused and he wondered why he should be treated any differently from his fellow men.

'All right, Officer.' Huh! 'All right': that's what Valerie would have said. But he put the thought aside and walked wearily out of the station. Perhaps he'd have more luck at Marylebone. He needed a bit of luck somewhere.

Chapter Forty-one

Pilate saith unto him, What is truth?
St John, ch. 18

Donald Phillipson was a very worried man. The sergeant had been very proper, of course, and very polite: 'routine enquiries', that was all. But the police were getting uncomfortably close. A knife that might be missing from the school canteen – that was perfectly understandable: but from his own kitchen! And it was no great surprise that he himself should be suspected of murder: but Sheila! He couldn't talk to Sheila, and he wouldn't let her talk to him: the subject of Valerie Taylor and, later, the murder of Baines lay between them like a no man's land, isolated and defined, upon which neither dared to venture. How much did Sheila know? Had she learned that Baines was blackmailing him? Had she learned or half-guessed the shameful reason? Baines himself may have hinted at the truth to her. Baines! God rot his soul! But whatever Sheila had done or intended to do on the night that Baines was killed was utterly unimportant, and he wished to know nothing of it. Whichever way you looked at it, it was he, Donald Phillipson, who was guilty of murdering Baines.

The walls of the small study seemed gradually to be closing in around him. The cumulative pressures of the last three years had now become too strong, and the tangled web of falsehood and deceit had enmeshed his very soul. If he were to retain his sanity he had to do *something*; something to bring a period of peace to a conscience tortured to its breaking-point; something to atone for all the folly and the sin. Again he thought of Sheila and the children and he knew that he could hardly face them for much longer. And interminably his thoughts went dancing round and round his head and always settled to the same conclusion. Whichever way you looked at it, it was he and only he who was guilty of murdering Baines.

Morning school was almost over, and Mrs Webb was tidying up her desk as he walked through.

'I shan't be in this afternoon, Mrs Webb.'

'No. I realise that, sir. You never are on Tuesdays.'

'Er, no. Tuesday afternoon, of course. I'd, er . . . I'd forgotten for the minute.'

It was like hearing the phone in a television play: he knew there was no need to answer it himself. He still felt wretchedly tired and he buried his head again in the pillows. Having found no more peace at Marylebone than at Paddington, he had finally arrived back in Oxford at 8.05 a.m., and had taken a taxi home. One way or another it had been an expensive débâcle.

An hour later the phone rang again. Shrill, peremptory, now, registering at a higher level of his consciousness; and shaking his head awake, he reached for the receiver on the bedside table. He yawned an almighty 'Yeah?' into the mouthpiece and levered himself up to a semi-vertical position.

'Lewis? What the hell do you want?'

'I've been trying to get you since two o'clock, sir. It's—'

'What? What time is it now?'

'Nearly three o'clock, sir. I'm sorry to disturb you but I've got a bit of a surprise for you.'

'Huh, I doubt it.'

'I think you ought to come, though. We're at the station.'

'Who do you mean by "we"?'

'If I told you that, sir, it wouldn't be a surprise, would it?'

'Give me half an hour,' said Morse.

He sat down at the table in Interview Room One. In front of him lay a document, neatly typed but as yet unsigned, and he picked it up and read it:

I have come forward voluntarily to the police to make this statement, and I trust that to some extent this may weigh in my favour. I wish to plead guilty to the murder of Mr Reginald Baines, late second master of the Roger Bacon Comprehensive School, Kidlington, Oxon. The reasons I had for killing him are not, in my view, strictly relevant to the criminal procedings that will be brought against me, and there are certain things which everyone should have the right to hold sacrosanct. About the details of the crime, too, I wish for the present to say nothing. I am aware that the question of deliberate malice and premeditation may be of great importance, and for this reason I wish to notify my lawyer and to take the benefit of his advice.

I hereby certify that this statement was made by me in the presence of Sergeant Lewis, CID, Thames Valley Police, on the day and at the time subscribed. Your obedient servant,

Morse looked up from the sheet of typing and turned his light-blue eyes across the table.

'You can't spell "proceedings",' he said.

'Your typist, Inspector. Not me.' Morse reached for his cigarettes and offered them across. 'No, thank you, I don't smoke.'

Without dropping his eyes, Morse lit a cigarette and drew upon it deeply. His expression was a mixture of vague distaste and tacit scepticism. He pointed to the statement. 'You want this to go forward?'

'Yes.'

'As you wish.'

They sat silently, as if neither had anything further to say to the other. Morse looked across to the window, and outside on to the concrete yard. He'd made so many stupid blunders in the case; and no one was likely to thank him overmuch for making yet another. It was the only sensible solution, perhaps. Or *almost* the only sensible solution. Did it matter? Perhaps not. But still upon his face remained the look of dark displeasure.

'You don't like me much, do you, Inspector?'

'I wouldn't say that,' replied Morse defensively. 'It's just . . . it's just that you've never got into the habit of telling me the truth, have you?'

'I've made up for it now, I hope.'

'*Have you?*' Morse's eyes were hard and piercing, but to his question there was no reply.

'Shall I sign it now?'

Morse remained silent for a while. 'You think it's better this way?' he asked very quietly. But again there was no reply, and

Morse passed across the statement and stood up. 'You've got a pen?'

Sheila Phillipson nodded, and opened her long, expensive leather handbag.

'Do you believe her, sir?'

'No,' said Morse simply.

'What do we do, then?'

'Ah, let her cool her heels in a cell for a night. I dare say she's got a good idea what happened, but I just don't think she killed Baines, that's all.'

'She's covering up for Phillipson, you think?'

'Could be. I don't know.' Morse stood up. 'And I'll tell you something else, Lewis: I don't bloody well care! I think whoever killed Baines deserves a life peerage – not a life sentence.'

'But it's still our job to find out who did, sir.'

'Not for much longer, it isn't. I've had a bellyful of this lot – and I've failed. I'm going to see Strange in the morning and ask him to take me off the case.'

'He won't be very happy about that.'

'He's never very happy about anything.'

'It doesn't sound like you, though, sir.'

Morse grinned almost boyishly. 'I've disappointed you, haven't I, Lewis?'

'Well, yes, in a way – if you're going to pack it all in now.'

'Well, I am.'

'I see.'

'Life's full of disappointments, Lewis. I should have thought you'd learned that by now.'

Alone Morse walked back to his office. If the truth could be told he felt more than a little hurt by what Lewis had just said. Lewis was right, of course, and had spoken with such quiet integrity: *but it's still our job to find out who did it.* Yes, he knew that; but he'd tried and tried and *hadn't* found out who did it. Come to think of it, he hadn't even found out if Valerie Taylor were alive or dead . . . Just now he'd tried to believe Sheila Phillipson; but the plain fact was that he couldn't. Anyway, if what she said were true, it was much better for someone else to finish off the formalities. Much better. And if she were just shielding her husband . . . He let it go. He had sent Lewis round to see Phillipson, but the headmaster was neither at home nor at school, and for the time being the neighbours were looking after the children.

Whatever happened, this Tuesday afternoon was now the end, and he thought back to that first Tuesday afternoon in Phillipson's study . . . What, if anything, had he missed in the case? What small, apparently insignificant detail that might have set him on the proper tracks? He sat for half an hour and thought and thought, and thought himself nowhere. It was no good: his mind was stale and the wells of imagination and inspiration were dry as the Sahara sands. Yes, he *would* see Strange in the morning and hand it all over. He could still make a decision when he wanted to, whatever Lewis might think.

He walked over to the filing-cabinet and for the last time took out the mass of documents on the case. They now filled two bulging box-files, and pulling back the spring clips Morse tipped the contents of each haphazardly on to his desk. At least he ought to put the stuff into some sort of order. It wouldn't take all that long, and his mind positively welcomed the prospect of an hour or two of fourth-grade clerical work. Neatly and methodically he began stapling odd notes and sheets to their respective documents, and ordering the documents themselves into a chronological sequence. He remembered the last time he had tipped the contents (not so bulky then) on to his desk, when Lewis had noticed that odd business about the lollipop-man. A red herring, that, as it turned out. Yet it *could* have been a vitally important point, and he himself had missed it. Had he missed anything else, amidst this formidable bumf? Ah, forget it! It was too late now, and he continued with his task. Valerie's reports next. They'd better go into some sort of order, too, and he shuffled them into their sequence. Three reports a year: Autumn term; Spring term; Summer term. No reports at all for the first year in the school, but all the others were there – except one: the report for the Summer term of the fourth year. Why was that? He hadn't noticed that before . . . The brain was whirring into life once more – but no! Morse snapped off the current impatiently. It was nothing. The report was just lost; lots of things got lost. Nothing at all sinister about that . . . Yet in spite of himself he stopped what he was doing and sat back again in the black leather chair, his fingertips together on his lower lip, his eyes resting casually on the school reports that lay before him. He'd read them all before, of course, and knew their contents well. Valerie had been one of those many could-do-better-if-she-tried pupils. Like all of us . . . In fact, the staff at the Roger Bacon School could quite easily have dispensed with terminal reports in Valerie's case: they were all very much the same, and one would have done quite as well as another. Any one. The last one, for example – the report on her Spring term's progress (or rather lack of it) in the year in which she'd disappeared. Idly Morse looked down at it again. Acum's signature was there beside the French: 'Could do so well if only she tried. Her accent is surprisingly good, but her vocabulary and grammar are still very weak.' Same old comment. In fact there was only one subject in which Valerie had apparently not hidden her light beneath the bushel of her casual indifference; and oddly enough that was Applied Science and Technology. Funny, really, girls tackling subjects like that. But the curriculum had undergone mysterious developments since his own school days. He picked up the earlier reports and read some of the comments of the science staff: 'Good with her hands'; 'A good term's work'; 'Has good mechanical sense'. He got up from his chair and went over to the shelf where earlier he'd stacked Valerie's old exercise books. It was there: Applied Science and Technology. Morse flicked through the pages. Yes, the work was good, he could see that – surprisingly good . . . *Hold it a minute!* He looked through the book again, more carefully now, and read the headings of the syllabus: Work; Energy; Power; Velocity Ratio; Efficiency of Machines; Simple Machines; Levers; Pulleys; Simple Power-transmission Systems; Car Engines; Clutches . . .

He walked back to his desk slowly, like a man in a dreamlike daze, and read the last Spring term report once more: French, and Applied Science and Technology . . .

Suddenly the hair on his flesh stood erect. He felt a curious constriction in his throat, and a long shiver passed icily down his spine. He reached for the phone and his hand shook as he dialled the number.

Chapter Forty-two

I came fairly to kill him honestly.
Beaumont and Fletcher, *The Little French Lawyer*

Valerie Taylor unscrewed the latest tube of skin-lotion – her sixth prescription. The last time she'd been to the doctor he'd asked rather pointedly if she were worried about anything; and perhaps she was. But not to *that* extent. She'd never worried overmuch about anything, really: just wanted to live in the present and enjoy herself . . . Carefully she smeared some of the white cream over the ugly spots. How she prayed they would go! Over a month now – and still they persisted, horribly. She'd tried almost everything, including those face-mask things: in fact she had been wearing one of them when Chief Inspector Morse had called. Mm. She thought of Morse. Bit old, perhaps, but then she'd always felt attracted to the older men. Not that David was old. Quite young, really, and he'd been awfully nice to her, but . . .

Morse's face, when she'd answered him in French! She smiled at the recollection. Phew! What a bit of luck that had been! Just as well she'd been with David on those two trips to France with his sixth-formers, although she'd probably have been all right anyway. It had taken a fair bit of cajoling on David's part, but as it turned out she'd really enjoyed her two years in the French Conversation Class at Caernarfon Tech. At the very least it was a chance to get out once a week, and it got so boring being on her own in the house all day. Nothing to do; nothing much to do if she *did* get out more. Not that she blamed David, but . . .

Bloody spots! She wiped off the lotion and applied a new layer. It might be better to leave them alone – let the sun get at them. But the sky this Tuesday evening was a sullen grey, and the weather would soon be getting cold again; far colder than it would be in the south. Like last winter. Brrh! She didn't intend to face another winter like that . . . The washing-up was done and David sat downstairs in the living-room marking exercise books. He was always marking exercise books. He would be awfully upset, of course, but . . .

She stepped over to the wardrobe and took out the long red velvet dress she'd taken to the cleaners last week. Inclining her head slightly, she held it against her body and stood before the mirror. Dinner-plates, parties, dancing . . . It had been such a long time since she'd been out – been out *properly*, that is . . . The dark roots of her hair had now grown almost half an inch into the pseudo-blonde, and it all began to look so *obvious*. She would buy another bottle of 'Poly-bleach' tomorrow. Or would she bother? After all, she'd got to Oxford and back pretty easily . . . Not that she would hire a car again. Couldn't afford it, for a start. Much easier to get a bus into Bangor, and then hitch-hike down the A5. A lot of men still drove the roads and hoped that every mile they'd see a lone, attractive girl. Yes, that would be much easier, and the A5 went all the way to London . . .

It was a good job she'd mentioned the car to David. That really *had* worried her – whether they'd check up on the car-hire firms. She'd not told David the truth, of course; just said she'd gone to see her mother. Yes, she'd admitted how silly and dangerous it was, and had promised David never to think of doing it again. But it had been a very sensible precaution that – warning him to tell them that she couldn't drive. If they ever asked, that was. And Morse had asked, it seemed. Clever man, Morse . . . She'd been a fraction naughty – hadn't she? – the first time he had called. Yes. And the second time – phew! That had perhaps been the very worst moment of all, when she'd opened the door and found him looking through her kitchen drawer. She'd bought a new one, naturally, but it had been *exactly* the same sort of knife, brand new . . . Funny, really; he hadn't even mentioned it . . .

Valerie looked at herself once more in the mirror. The spots looked better now, and she closed the bedroom door behind her . . . Morse! She smiled to herself as she walked down the creaking stairs. His face! *Oui. Je l'ai étudié d'abord à l'école et après . . .*

The phone rang in Caernarfon Police HQ and the switchboard put the call through to the duty inspector.

'All right. Put him on.' He clamped his hand firmly over the mouthpiece and mumbled a few hurried words *sotto voce* to the sergeant sitting opposite. 'It's Morse again.'

'Morse, sir?'

'Yes, you remember. That fellow from Oxford who buggered us all about at the weekend. I wonder what . . . Hello. Can I help you?'

Epilogue

There are tears of things and mortal matters touch the heart.

Virgil, *Aeneid I*

It was not until Saturday morning that a somewhat disgruntled Lewis was at last summoned into Morse's office to hear something of the final developments.

The Caernarfon police had felt (with some justification, admitted

Morse) that they had insufficient evidence on which to hold Valerie
Taylor – even if they accepted Morse's vehement protestations that
the woman living as Mrs Acum *was* Valerie Taylor. And when Morse
himself had arrived on Wednesday morning, it had been too late:
the driver of the 9.50 a.m. bus from Bont-Newydd to Bangor had
remembered her clearly; and a petrol-pump attendant had noticed
her ('So would you have done, Officer!') as she stood beside the
forecourt waiting to thumb a lift down the A5.

Lewis had listened carefully, but one or two things still puzzled
him. 'So it must have been Baines who wrote the letter?'

'Oh yes. It couldn't have been Valerie.'

'I wouldn't be *too* sure, sir. She's a pretty clever girl.'

And I'm a clown, thought Morse. The car, the French, and
the spots: a combination of circumstance and coincidence which
had proved too much even for *him* to accept; a triple-oxer over
which he would normally have leaped with the blithest assurance,
but at which, in this instance, he had so strangely refused. After
all, it would have been very odd if a mechanically-minded girl like
Valerie hadn't even bothered to take a driving-test; and she wasn't
too bad at *spoken* French – even at school. Those reports! If only—

'Big coincidence, wasn't it – about the spots, I mean?'

'No, not really, Lewis. Don't forget that both of them were sleeping with Acum; and Acum's got a beard.'

It was something else that Lewis hadn't considered, and he let
it go. 'She's gone to London, I suppose, sir?'

Morse nodded wearily, a wry smile upon his lips. 'Back to square
one, aren't we?'

'You think we'll find her?'

'I don't know. I suppose so – in the end.'

On Saturday afternoon the Phillipson family motored to the
White Horse Hill at Uffington. For Andrew and Alison it was
a rare treat, and Mrs Phillipson watched them lovingly as they
gambolled with gay abandon about the Downs. So much had
passed between her and Donald these last few days. On Tuesday
evening their very lives together had seemed to be hanging by the
slenderest of threads. But now, this bright and chilly afternoon,
the future stretched out before them, open and free as the broad
landscape around them. She would write, she decided, a long,
long letter to Morse, and try to thank him from the bottom of
her heart. For on that terrible evening it had been Morse who
had found Donald and brought him to her; it had been Morse

who had seemed to know and to understand all things about them both . . .

On Saturday evening Mrs Grace Taylor sat staring blankly through the window on to the darkened street. They had returned from their holiday in mid-afternoon, and things seemed very much the same as she had left them. At a quarter-past eight, by the light of the street lamp, she saw Morse walking slowly, head down, towards the pub. She gave him no second thought.

Earlier in the evening she had gone out into the front garden and clipped off the heads of a few last fading roses. But there had been one late scarlet bloom that was still in perfect flower. She had cut that off too, and it now stood on the mantelshelf, in a cheap glass vase that Valerie had won on a shooting stall at St Giles' Fair, beneath the ducks that winged their way towards the ceiling in the empty room behind her.

Some of them never did come home . . . never.